Praise for

SEVEN STONES TO STAND OR FALL

"A must-own collection for lovers of [Diana] Gabaldon's mega-popular, riveting *Outlander* books." —*B&N Reads*

"Rejoice! . . . As always with Gabaldon's work, expect passionate characters woven into real, deeply researched historical events with the perfect tartan pattern." —*British Heritage Travel Magazine*

"Fans of the series won't be disappointed." —*PopSugar*

"*Seven Stones to Stand or Fall* is the collection Gabaldon fans have long awaited." —*Hypable*

Praise for the Outlander novels

AN ECHO IN THE BONE

"Adventure, history, romance, fantasy and sex, all you've come to expect from Gabaldon." —*The Arizona Republic*

"Diana Gabaldon gives her legion of fans excellent value in *An Echo in the Bone.* . . . Pages fly by and leave readers hungering to know what comes next for a set of engagingly colorful characters who by now feel like old friends." —*BookLoons.com*

"*An Echo in the Bone* is a wonderful, adventure-filled, emotion-packed reunion with the Frasers. . . . Meticulous research of historical events, facts, and people, flora and fauna, geography, food, clothing, and weaponry brings the eighteenth century to vivid life. . . . Don't miss the long-awaited continuation of this fabulous series. It will keep you up late for a few nights!" —*Romance Reviews Today*

A BREATH OF SNOW AND ASHES

"Time travelers revolutionize colonial America with . . . cliff-hangers galore, in Gabaldon's sixth Outlander epic." —*Kirkus Reviews*

"This compulsively readable mix of authentically set historical fiction and completely satisfying romance maps both violent loss and strong family ties. . . . The large scope of the novel allows Gabaldon to do what she does best, paint in exquisite detail the lives of her characters." —*Booklist*

"Essential for every fiction collection." —*Library Journal*

THE FIERY CROSS

"Each and every one of its 979 pages abounds with Ms. Gabaldon's sexy combination of humor, wild adventure and, underlying it all, the redemptive power of true love." —*The Dallas Morning News*

"Fans of the series will be delighted with this novel and there are threads left dangling for another mega epic from the great author."
—*Midwest Book Review*

"It is a grand adventure written on a canvas that probes the heart, weighs the soul and measures the human spirit across ten generations." —CNN

DRUMS OF AUTUMN

"Unforgettable characters . . . richly embroidered with historical detail . . . I just can't put it down." —*The Cincinnati Post*

"Wonderful . . . This is escapist historical fiction at its best."
—*San Antonio Express-News*

VOYAGER

"Triumphant . . . Her use of historical detail and a truly adult love story confirm Gabaldon as a superior writer." —*Publishers Weekly*

"An amazing read." —*Arizona Tribune*

"Memorable storytelling." —*The Seattle Times*

DRAGONFLY IN AMBER

"A triumph! A powerful tale layered in history and myth. I loved every page." —Nora Roberts

"Compulsively readable." —*Publishers Weekly*

"Diana Gabaldon is a born storyteller. . . . The pages practically turn themselves." —*The Arizona Republic*

OUTLANDER

"Marvelously entertaining . . . a page-turner of the highest order and a good read from start to finish." —*Chattanooga Times*

"Absorbing and heartwarming . . . lavishly evokes the land and lore of Scotland." —*Publishers Weekly*

"History comes deliciously alive on the page." —New York *Daily News*

Praise for Diana Gabaldon's novels featuring Lord John Grey

"Call it what you will—historical adventure, conspiracy thriller—it's an engrossing story, masterfully paced, with exciting plot twists, swift reversals, and robust characterizations."
 —*The Globe and Mail*, on *The Scottish Prisoner*

"[Diana Gabaldon's] writing is always vivid and often lyrical."
 —*The Washington Post*, on *Lord John and the Brotherhood of the Blade*

"[A] thoroughly entertaining and wonderfully witty historical mystery set in the richly detailed, occasionally bawdy world of Georgian England." —*Booklist*, on *Lord John and the Private Matter*

SEVEN STONES TO STAND OR FALL

By Diana Gabaldon

The Outlander Series
OUTLANDER
DRAGONFLY IN AMBER
VOYAGER
DRUMS OF AUTUMN
THE FIERY CROSS
A BREATH OF SNOW AND ASHES
AN ECHO IN THE BONE
WRITTEN IN MY OWN HEART'S BLOOD

The Lord John Series
LORD JOHN AND THE PRIVATE MATTER
LORD JOHN AND THE BROTHERHOOD OF THE BLADE
THE CUSTOM OF THE ARMY *(novella)*
LORD JOHN AND THE HAND OF DEVILS *(collected novellas)*
THE SCOTTISH PRISONER
A PLAGUE OF ZOMBIES *(novella)*

Salmagundi*
THE OUTLANDISH COMPANION *(nonfiction)*
THE EXILE *(graphic novel)*
THE OUTLANDISH COMPANION VOLUME TWO *(nonfiction)*
A LEAF ON THE WIND OF ALL HALLOWS *(novella)*
THE SPACE BETWEEN *(novella)*
VIRGINS *(novella)*
"I GIVE YOU MY BODY . . ." *(nonfiction)*
SEVEN STONES TO STAND OR FALL *(collected novellas)*

---

* *a collection of disparate elements*

SEVEN STONES TO STAND OR FALL

A Collection of Outlander Fiction

DIANA GABALDON

BANTAM BOOKS
NEW YORK

2018 Bantam Books Trade Paperback Edition

Copyright © 2017 by Diana Gabaldon
"The Custom of the Army" copyright © 2010 by Diana Gabaldon
"The Space Between" copyright © 2013 by Diana Gabaldon
"A Plague of Zombies" copyright © 2011 by Diana Gabaldon
"A Leaf on the Wind of All Hallows" copyright © 2010 by Diana Gabaldon
"Virgins" copyright © 2013 by Diana Gabaldon

Published in the United States by Bantam Books, an imprint of Random House, a division of Penguin Random House LLC, New York.

BANTAM BOOKS and the HOUSE colophon are registered trademarks of Penguin Random House LLC.

Originally published in hardcover in the United States by Delacorte Press, an imprint of Random House, a division of Penguin Random House LLC, in 2017.

"The Custom of the Army" was originally published in *Warriors,* edited by George R. R. Martin and Gardner Dozois, published by Tor books, a division of Macmillan, in 2010. "The Space Between" was originally published in *The Mad Scientist's Guide to World Domination: Original Short Fiction for the Modern Evil Genius,* edited by John Joseph Adams, published by Tor Books, a division of Macmillan, in 2013. "A Plague of Zombies" was originally published as "Lord John and the Plague of Zombies" in *Down These Strange Streets: All-New Stories of Urban Fantasy,* edited by George R. R. Martin and Gardner Dozois, published by Ace Books, a division of Penguin, in 2011. "A Leaf on the Wind of All Hallows" was originally published in *Songs of Love and Death: All Original Tales of Star-Crossed Love,* edited by George R. R. Martin, published by Gallery Books, a division of Simon & Schuster, in 2010. "Virgins" was originally published in *Dangerous Women,* edited by George R. R. Martin and Gardner Dozois, published by Tor Books, a division of Macmillan, in 2013.

ISBN 978-0-399-59343-7
Ebook ISBN 978-0-399-59344-4

Printed in the United States of America on acid-free paper

randomhousebooks.com

8 9

Book design by Virginia Norey

This book is dedicated with the greatest respect and gratitude to Karen Henry, Rita Meistrell, Vicki Pack, Sandy Parker, and Mandy Tidwell (collectively known as "the Cadre of Eyeball-Numbing Nitpickery") for their invaluable help in spotting errors, inconsistencies, and assorted rubbish.

(Any errors remaining in the text are purely the responsibility of the author, who not only blithely ignores inconsistencies on occasion, but has been known to deliberately perpetrate others.)

CONTENTS

INTRODUCTION

A Chronology of the *Outlander* Series

If you picked this book up under the misapprehension that it's the ninth novel in the main *Outlander* series, it's not. I apologize.

So, if it's not the ninth novel, what is it? Well, it's a collection of seven . . . er . . . things, of varying length and content, but all having to do with the *Outlander* universe. As for the title . . . basically, it's the result of my editor not liking my original title choice, *Salmagundi.** Not that I couldn't see her point . . . Anyway, there was a polite request via my agent for something more in line with the "resonant, poetic" nature of the main titles.

Without going too much into the mental process that led to this (words like "sausage-making" and "rock-polishing" come to mind), I wanted a title that at least suggested that there were a number of elements in this book (hence the *Seven*), and *Seven Stones* just came naturally, and that was nice ("stone" is always a weighty word) and suitably alliterative but not a complete poetic thought (or rhythm). So, a bit more thinkering (no, that's not a typo), and I came up with *to Stand or Fall,* which sounded suitably portentous.

It took a bit of *ex post facto* thought to figure out what the heck that *meant,* but things usually do mean something if you think long enough. In this instance, the "stand or fall" has to do with people's response to grief and adversity: to wit, if you aren't killed outright by whatever happened, you have a choice in how the rest of your life is lived—you keep standing, though battered and worn by time and elements, still a buttress and a signpost—or you fall and return quietly to the earth from which you sprang, your elements giving succor to those who come after you.

---

* *Salmagundi: 1) A collection of disparate elements, or 2) a dish composed of meats, fruits, vegetables, and/or any other items the cook has on hand, often provided as an* ad hoc *accompaniment to an insufficient meal.*

SO. THIS IS (as the front cover suggests) a collection of seven novellas (fiction shorter than a novel but longer than a short story), though all of them are indeed part of the *Outlander* universe and do intersect with the main novels.

Five of the novellas included in this book were originally written for various anthologies over the last few years; two are brand-new and have never been published before: "A Fugitive Green" and "Besieged."

Owing to differences among publishers in different countries, some of the previously published novellas may subsequently have been published in print form as a four-story collection (in the UK and Germany) or as separate ebooks (in the United States). *Seven Stones* provides a complete print collection for those readers who like tactile books and includes the two new stories.

Since the novellas fit into the main series at different points (and involve a number of different characters), below is an overall chronology of the *Outlander* series, to explain Who, What, and When.

THE *OUTLANDER* SERIES includes three kinds of stories:

The Big, Enormous Books of the main series, which have no discernible genre (or all of them);

The Shorter, Less Indescribable Novels, which are more or less historical mysteries (though dealing also with battles, eels, and assorted sexual practices);

And

The Bulges,—these being short(er) pieces that fit somewhere inside the story lines of the novels, much in the nature of squirming prey swallowed by a large snake. These deal frequently—but not exclusively—with secondary characters, are prequels or sequels, and/or fill some lacuna left in the original story lines.

The Big Books of the main series deal with the lives and times of Claire and Jamie Fraser. The shorter novels focus on the adventures of Lord John Grey but intersect with the larger books (*The Scottish Prisoner*, for example, features both Lord John and Jamie Fraser in a shared story). The novellas all feature people from the main series, including Jamie and/or Claire on occasion. The description below explains which characters appear in which stories.

Most of the shorter Lord John novels and novellas (so far) fit within a large lacuna left in the middle of *Voyager,* in the years between 1756 and 1761. Some of the Bulges also fall in this period; others don't.

So, for the reader's convenience, the detailed listing here shows the sequence of the various elements in terms of the story line. *However, it should be noted that the shorter novels and novellas are all designed in such a way that they may be read alone,* without reference either to one another or to the Big, Enormous Books—should you be in the mood for a light literary snack instead of the nine-course meal with wine pairings and dessert trolley.

(For your added convenience, the description of each story includes the dates covered in it, and,—if it has been published before, the original anthology title and year of publication are also given. This information will be mostly useful to collectors and hardcore bibliophiles, but we aim to please as many people as possible.)

"Virgins" (novella)—Set in 1740 in France. In which Jamie Fraser (aged nineteen) and his friend Ian Murray (aged twenty) become young mercenaries. [Originally published in the anthology *Dangerous Women,* eds. George R. R. Martin and Gardner Dozois, 2012.]

Outlander (novel)—If you've never read any of the series, I'd suggest starting here. If you're unsure about it, open the book anywhere and read three pages; if you can put it down again, I'll give you a dollar. (1946/1743)

Dragonfly in Amber (novel)—It doesn't start where you think it's going to. And it doesn't end how you think it's going to, either. Just keep reading; it'll be fine. (1968/1744–46)

"A Fugitive Green" (novella)—Set in 1744–45 in Paris, London, and Amsterdam, this is the story of Lord John's elder brother, Hal (Harold, Earl Melton and Duke of Pardloe), and his (eventual) wife, Minnie—at the time of this story a seventeen-year-old dealer in rare books with a sideline in forgery, blackmail, and burglary. Jamie Fraser also appears in this one.

Voyager (novel)—This won an award from *EW* magazine for "Best Opening Line." (To save you having to find a copy just to read the opening, it was: *He was dead. However, his nose throbbed painfully, which he thought odd in the circumstances.*) If you're reading the series in order rather than piecemeal, you do want to read this book before tackling the novellas. (1968/1746–67)

Lord John and the Hand of Devils, "Lord John and the Hellfire Club" (short story)—Just to add an extra layer of confusion, *The Hand of Devils* is a collection that includes three novellas. The first one, "Lord John and the Hellfire Club," is set in London in 1756 and deals with a red-haired man who approaches Lord John Grey with an urgent plea for help, just before dying in front of him. [Originally published in the anthology *Past Poisons,* ed. Maxim Jakubowski, 1998.]

Lord John and the Private Matter (novel)—Set in London in 1757, this is a historical mystery steeped in blood and even less-savory substances, in which Lord John meets (in short order) a valet, a traitor, an apothecary with a sure cure for syphilis, a bumptious German, and an unscrupulous merchant prince.

Lord John and the Hand of Devils, "Lord John and the Succubus" (novella)—The second novella in the *Hand of Devils* collection finds Lord John in Germany in 1757, having unsettling dreams about Jamie Fraser, unsettling encounters with Saxon princesses, night hags, and a really disturbing encounter with a big blond Hanoverian graf. [Originally published in the anthology *Legends II,* ed. Robert Silverberg, 2003.]

Lord John and the Brotherhood of the Blade (novel)—The second full-length novel focused on Lord John (though Jamie Fraser also appears) is set in 1758, deals with a twenty-year-old family scandal, and sees Lord John engaged at close range with exploding cannon and even more dangerously explosive emotions.

Lord John and the Hand of Devils, "Lord John and the Haunted Soldier" (novella)—The third novella in this collection is set in 1758, in London and the Woolwich Arsenal. In which Lord John faces a court of inquiry into the explosion of a cannon and learns that there are more-dangerous things in the world than gunpowder.

"The Custom of the Army" (novella)—Set in 1759. In which his lordship attends an electric-eel party in London and consequently ends up at the Battle of Quebec. He's just the sort of person things like that happen to. [Originally published in *Warriors,* eds. George R. R. Martin and Gardner Dozois, 2010.]

The Scottish Prisoner (novel)—This one's set in 1760, in the Lake District, London, and Ireland. A sort of hybrid novel, it's divided evenly between Jamie Fraser and Lord John Grey, who are recounting their different perspectives in a tale of politics, corruption, murder, opium dreams, horses, and illegitimate sons.

"A Plague of Zombies" (novella)—Set in 1761 in Jamaica, when Lord John is sent in command of a battalion to put down a slave rebellion and discovers a hitherto unsuspected affinity for snakes, cockroaches, and zombies. [Originally published in *Down These Strange Streets,* eds. George R. R. Martin and Gardner Dozois, 2011.]

Drums of Autumn (novel)—The fourth novel of the main series, this one begins in 1767, in the New World, where Jamie and Claire find a foothold in the mountains of North Carolina, and their daughter, Brianna, finds a whole lot of things she didn't expect, when a sinister newspaper clipping sends her in search of her parents. (1969–1970/1767–70)

The Fiery Cross (novel)—The historical background to this, the fifth novel of the main series, is the War of the Regulation in North Carolina (1767–1771), which was more or less a dress rehearsal for the oncoming Revolution. In which Jamie Fraser becomes a reluctant Rebel, his wife, Claire, becomes a conjure-woman, and their grandson, Jeremiah, gets drunk on cherry bounce. Something Much Worse happens to Brianna's husband, Roger, but I'm not telling you what. This won several awards for "Best Last Line," but I'm not telling you that, either. (1770–1772)

A Breath of Snow and Ashes (novel)—Sixth novel of the main series, this book won the 2006 Corine International Prize for Fiction and a Quill Award (this book beat novels by both George R. R. Martin *and* Stephen King, which I thought was pretty entertaining; I mean, how often does *that* happen?). All the books have an internal "shape" that I see while I'm writing them. This one looks like the Hokusai print titled "The Great Wave Off Kanagawa." Think *tsunami*—two of them. (1773–1776/1980)

An Echo in the Bone (novel)—Set in America, London, Canada, and Scotland, this is the seventh novel of the main series. The book's cover image reflects the internal shape of the novel: a caltrop. That's an ancient military weapon that looks like a child's jack with sharp points; the Romans used them to deter elephants, and the highway patrol still uses them to stop fleeing perps in cars. This book has four major story lines: Jamie and Claire; Roger and Brianna (and family); Lord John and William; and Young Ian, all intersecting in the nexus of the American Revolution—and all the stories have sharp points. (1776–1778/1980)

Written in My Own Heart's Blood (novel)—The eighth book of the main series, *Blood* begins where *An Echo in the Bone* leaves off, in the summer of 1778 (and the autumn of 1980). The American Revolution is in full roar, and a lot of fairly horrifying things are happening in Scotland in the 1980s, too.

"A Leaf on the Wind of All Hallows" (short story [no, really, it is])—Set (mostly) in 1941–43, this is the story of What Really Happened to Roger MacKenzie's parents. [Originally published in the anthology *Songs of Love and Death*, eds. George R. R. Martin and Gardner Dozois, 2010.]

"The Space Between" (novella)—Set in 1778, mostly in Paris, this novella deals with Michael Murray (Young Ian's elder brother), Joan MacKimmie (Marsali's younger sister), the Comte St. Germain (who is Not Dead After All), Mother Hildegarde, and a few other persons of interest. The space between *what?* It depends who you're talking to. [Originally published in the anthology *The Mad Scientist's Guide to World Domination*, ed. John Joseph Adams, 2013]

"Besieged" (novella)—Set in 1762 in Jamaica and Havana. Lord John, about to leave his post as temporary military governor of Jamaica, learns that his mother is in Havana, Cuba. Which would be fine, save that the British Navy is on its way to lay siege to the city. Attended by his valet, Tom Byrd, an ex-zombie named Rodrigo, and Rodrigo's homicidally inclined wife, Azeel, Lord John sets out to rescue the erstwhile Dowager Duchess of Pardloe before the warships arrive.

NOW, REMEMBER . . .

You can read the short novels and novellas by themselves, or in any order you like. I would recommend reading the Big, Enormous Books of the main series in order, though. Hope you enjoy them all!

SEVEN STONES TO STAND OR FALL

THE CUSTOM OF THE ARMY

INTRODUCTION

ONE OF THE PLEASURES OF WRITING HISTORICAL fiction is that the best parts aren't made up. This particular story came about as the result of my having read Wendy Moore's excellent biography of Dr. John Hunter, *The Knife Man*—and my having read at the same time a brief facsimile book printed by the National Park Service, detailing regulations of the British Army during the American Revolution.

I wasn't *looking* for anything in particular in either of these books; just reading for background, general information on the period, and the always alluring chance of stumbling across something fascinating, like electric eel parties in London (these, along with Dr. Hunter himself—who appears briefly in this story—are a matter of historical record).

As for British Army regulations, a little of that stuff goes a long way; as a novelist, you want to resist the temptation to tell people things just because you happen to know them. Still, that book too had its little nuggets, such as the information that the word "bomb" was common in the eighteenth century, and that (in addition to merely meaning "an explosive device") it referred also to a wrapped and tarred parcel of shrapnel shot from a cannon (though we must be careful not to use the word "shrapnel," as it's derived from Lt. Henry Shrapnel of the Royal Artillery, who took the original "bomb" concept and developed the "shrapnel shell," a debris-filled bomb filled also with gunpowder and designed to explode in mid-air after being fired from a cannon; unfortunately, he did this in 1784, which was inconvenient, as "shrapnel" is a pretty good word to have when writing about warfare).

Among the other bits of interesting trivia, though, I was struck by a brief description of the procedure for courts-martial: *The custom of the army is that a court-martial be presided over by a senior officer and such a number of other officers as he shall think fit to serve as council, these being generally four in number, but can be more but not generally less than three. . . . The person accused shall have the right to call witnesses in his support, and the council shall question these, as well as any other persons whom they may wish, and shall thus determine the circumstances, and if conviction ensue, the sentence to be imposed.*

And that was it. No elaborate procedures for the introduction of evidence, no standards for conviction, no sentencing guidelines, no requirements for who could or should serve as "council" to a court-martial—just "the custom of the army." The phrase—rather obviously—stuck in my head.

This story is for Karen Henry, Aedile Curule,
and Chief Bumblebee-Herder

ALL THINGS CONSIDERED, it was probably the fault of the electric eel. John Grey could—and for a time, did—blame the Honorable Caroline Woodford, as well. And the surgeon. And certainly that blasted poet. Still . . . no, it was the eel's fault.

The party had been at Lucinda Joffrey's house. Sir Richard was absent; a diplomat of his stature could not have countenanced something so frivolous. Electric-eel parties were a mania in London just now, but owing to the scarcity of the creatures, a private party was a rare occasion. Most such parties were held at public theaters, with the fortunate few selected for encounter with the eel summoned onstage, there to be shocked and sent reeling like ninepins for the entertainment of the audience.

"The record is forty-two at once!" Caroline had told him, her eyes wide and shining as she looked up from the creature in its tank.

"Really?" It was one of the most peculiar things he'd seen, though not very striking. Nearly three feet long, it had a heavy, squarish body with a blunt head, which looked to have been inexpertly molded out of sculptor's clay, and tiny eyes like dull glass beads. It had little in common with the lashing, lithesome eels of the fish market—and certainly did not seem capable of felling forty-two people at once.

The thing had no grace at all, save for a small thin ruffle of a fin that ran the length of its lower body, undulating as a gauze curtain does in the wind. Lord John expressed this observation to the Honorable Caroline and was accused in consequence of being poetic.

"Poetic?" said an amused voice behind him. "Is there no end to our gallant major's talents?"

Lord John turned, with an inward grimace and an outward smile, and bowed to Edwin Nicholls.

"I should not think of trespassing upon your province, Mr. Nicholls," he said politely. Nicholls wrote execrable verse, mostly upon the subject of love, and was much admired by young women of a certain turn of mind. The Honorable Caroline wasn't one of them; she'd written a very clever parody of his style, though Grey thought Nicholls had not heard about it. He hoped not.

"Oh, don't you?" Nicholls raised one honey-colored brow at him and glanced briefly but meaningfully at Miss Woodford. His tone was jocular, but his look was not, and Grey wondered just how much Mr. Nicholls had had to drink. Nicholls was flushed of cheek and glittering of eye, but that might be only the heat of the room, which was considerable, and the excitement of the party.

"Do you think of composing an ode to our friend?" Grey asked, ignoring Nicholls's allusion and gesturing toward the large tank that contained the eel.

Nicholls laughed, too loudly—yes, quite a bit the worse for drink—and waved a dismissive hand.

"No, no, Major. How could I think of expending my energies upon such a gross and insignificant creature, when there are angels of delight such as this to inspire me?" He leered—Grey did not wish to impugn the fellow, but he undeniably leered—at Miss Woodford, who smiled, with compressed lips, and tapped him rebukingly with her fan.

Where was Caroline's uncle? Grey wondered. Simon Woodford shared his niece's interest in natural history and would certainly have escorted her. . . . Oh, there. Simon Woodford was deep in discussion with Dr. Hunter, the famous surgeon—what had possessed Lucinda to invite *him*? Then he caught sight of Lucinda, viewing Dr. Hunter over her fan with narrowed eyes, and realized that she *hadn't* invited him.

John Hunter was a famous surgeon—and an infamous anatomist. Rumor had it that he would stop at nothing to bag a particularly desirable body—whether human or not. He did move in society, but not in the Joffreys' circles.

Lucinda Joffrey had most expressive eyes. Her one claim to beauty, they were almond-shaped, clear gray in color, and capable of sending remarkably minatory messages across a crowded room.

Come here! they said. Grey smiled and lifted his glass in salute to her but made no move to obey. The eyes narrowed further, gleaming dangerously, then cut abruptly toward the surgeon, who was edging toward the tank, his face alight with curiosity and acquisitiveness.

The eyes whipped back to Grey.

Get rid of him! they said.

Grey glanced at Miss Woodford. Mr. Nicholls had seized her hand in his and appeared to be declaiming something; she looked as though she wanted the hand back. Grey looked back at Lucinda and shrugged, with a small gesture toward Mr. Nicholls's ochre-velvet back, expressing regret that social responsibility prevented his carrying out her order.

"Not only the face of an angel," Nicholls was saying, squeezing Caroline's fingers so hard that she squeaked, "but the skin, as well." He stroked her hand, the leer intensifying. "What do angels smell like in the morning, I wonder?"

Grey measured him up thoughtfully. One more remark of that sort, and he might be obliged to invite Mr. Nicholls to step outside. Nicholls was tall and heavily built, outweighed Grey by a couple of stone, and had a reputation for bellicosity. *Best try to break his nose first,* Grey thought, shifting his weight, *then run him headfirst into a hedge. He won't come back in if I make a mess of him.*

"What are you looking at?" Nicholls inquired unpleasantly, catching Grey's gaze upon him.

Grey was saved from reply by a loud clapping of hands—the eel's proprietor calling the party to order. Miss Woodford took advantage of the distraction to snatch her hand away, cheeks flaming with mortification. Grey moved at once to her side and put a hand beneath her elbow, fixing Nicholls with an icy stare.

"Come with me, Miss Woodford," he said. "Let us find a good place from which to watch the proceedings."

"Watch?" said a voice beside him. "Why, surely you don't mean to *watch,* do you, sir? Are you not curious to try the phenomenon yourself?"

It was Hunter himself, bushy hair tied carelessly back, though decently dressed in a damson-red suit, and grinning up at Grey; the surgeon was broad-shouldered and muscular but quite short—barely five foot two, to Grey's five-six. Evidently he had noted Grey's wordless exchange with Lucinda.

"Oh, I think—" Grey began, but Hunter had his arm and was tugging him toward the crowd gathering round the tank. Caroline, with an alarmed glance at the glowering Nicholls, hastily followed him.

"I shall be most interested to hear your account of the sensation," Hunter was saying chattily. "Some people report a remarkable euphoria, a momentary disorientation . . . shortness of breath or dizziness—sometimes pain in the chest. You have not a weak heart, I hope, Major? Or you, Miss Woodford?"

"Me?" Caroline looked surprised.

Hunter bowed to her.

"I should be particularly interested to see your own response, ma'am," he said respectfully. "So few women have the courage to undertake such an adventure."

"She doesn't want to," Grey said hurriedly.

"Well, perhaps I *do,*" she said, and gave him a little frown, before glancing at the tank and the long gray form inside it. She gave a brief shiver—but Grey recognized it, from long acquaintance with the lady, as a shiver of anticipation rather than revulsion.

Dr. Hunter recognized it, too. He grinned more broadly and bowed again, extending his arm to Miss Woodford.

"Allow me to secure you a place, ma'am."

Grey and Nicholls both moved purposefully to prevent him, collided, and were left scowling at each other as Dr. Hunter escorted Caroline to the tank and introduced her to the eel's owner, a small dark-looking creature named Horace Suddfield.

Grey nudged Nicholls aside and plunged into the crowd, elbowing his way ruthlessly to the front. Hunter spotted him and beamed.

"Have you any metal remaining in your chest, Major?"

"Have I—what?"

"Metal," Hunter repeated. "Arthur Longstreet described to me the operation in which he removed thirty-seven pieces of metal from your chest—most impressive. If any bits remain, though, I must advise you against trying the eel. Metal conducts electricity, you see, and the chance of burns—"

Nicholls had made his way through the throng, as well, and gave an unpleasant laugh, hearing this.

"A good excuse, Major," he said, a noticeable jeer in his voice. He was very drunk indeed, Grey thought. Still—

"No, I haven't," he said abruptly.

"Excellent," Suddfield said politely. "A soldier, I understand you are, sir? A bold gentleman, I perceive—who better to take first place?"

And before Grey could protest, he found himself next to the tank, Caroline Woodford's hand clutching his, her other held by Nicholls, who was glaring malevolently.

"Are we all arranged, ladies and gentlemen?" Suddfield cried. "How many, Dobbs?"

"Forty-five!" came a call from his assistant in the next room, through which the line of participants snaked, joined hand-to-hand and twitching with excitement, the rest of the party standing well back, agog.

"All touching, all touching?" Suddfield cried. "Take a firm grip of your friends, please, a very firm grip!" He turned to Grey, his small face alight. "Go ahead, sir! Grip it tightly, please—just there, just there before the tail!"

Disregarding his better judgment and the consequences to his lace cuff, Grey set his jaw and plunged his hand into the water.

In the split second when he grasped the slimy thing, he expected something like the snap one got from touching a Leyden jar and making it spark. Then he was flung violently backward, every muscle in his body contorted, and he found himself on the floor, thrashing like a landed fish, gasping in a vain attempt to recall how to breathe.

The surgeon, Mr. Hunter, squatted next to him, observing him with bright-eyed interest.

"How do you feel?" he inquired. "Dizzy at all?"

Grey shook his head, mouth opening and closing like a goldfish's, and with some effort thumped his chest. Thus invited, Mr. Hunter leaned down at once, unbuttoned Grey's waistcoat, and pressed an ear to his shirtfront. Whatever he heard—or didn't—seemed to alarm him, for he jerked up, clenched both fists together, and brought them down on Grey's chest with a thud that reverberated to his backbone.

This blow had the salutary effect of forcing breath out of his lungs; they filled again by reflex, and suddenly he remembered how to breathe. His heart also seemed to have been recalled to a sense of its duty, and began beating again. He sat up, fending off another blow from Mr. Hunter, and sat blinking at the carnage round him.

The floor was filled with bodies. Some still writhing, some lying still, limbs outflung in abandonment; some already recovered and being helped to their feet by friends. Excited exclamations filled the air, and Suddfield stood by his eel, beaming with pride and accepting congratulations. The eel itself seemed annoyed; it was swimming round in circles, angrily switching its heavy body.

Edwin Nicholls was on hands and knees, Grey saw, rising slowly to his feet. He reached down to grasp Caroline Woodford's arms and help her to rise. This she did, but so awkwardly that she lost her balance and fell face-first into Mr. Nicholls. He in turn lost his own balance and sat down hard, the Honorable Caroline atop him. Whether from shock, excitement, drink, or simple boorishness, he seized the moment—and Caroline—and planted a hearty kiss upon her astonished lips.

Matters thereafter were somewhat confused. He had a vague impression that he *had* broken Nicholls's nose—and there was a set of burst and swollen knuckles on his right hand to give weight to the supposition. There was a lot of noise, though, and he had the disconcerting feeling of not being altogether firmly confined within his own body. Parts of him seemed to be constantly drifting off, escaping the outlines of his flesh.

What *did* remain inside was distinctly jangled. His hearing—still somewhat impaired from the cannon explosion a few months before—had given up entirely under the strain of electric shock. That is, he could hear, but what he heard made no sense. Random words reached him through a fog of buzzing and ringing, but he could not connect them sensibly to the moving mouths around him. He wasn't at all sure that his own voice was saying what he meant it to, for that matter.

He was surrounded by voices, faces—a sea of feverish sound and movement. People touched him, pulled him, pushed him. He flung out an arm, trying as much to discover where it was as to strike anyone, but felt the impact of flesh. More noise. Here and there a face he recognized: Lucinda, shocked and furious; Caroline, distraught, her red hair disheveled and coming down, all its powder lost.

The net result of everything was that he was not positive whether he had called Nicholls out or the reverse. Surely Nicholls must have challenged him? He had a vivid recollection of Nicholls, gore-soaked handkerchief held to his nose and a homicidal light in his narrowed eyes. But then he'd found himself outside, in his shirtsleeves, standing in the little park that fronted the Joffreys' house, with a pistol in his hand. He wouldn't have chosen to fight with a strange pistol, would he?

Maybe Nicholls had insulted him, and he had called Nicholls out without quite realizing it?

It had rained earlier, was chilly now; wind was whipping his shirt round his body. His sense of smell was remarkably acute; it seemed to be the only thing working properly. He smelled smoke from the chimneys, the damp green of the plants, and his own sweat, oddly metallic. And something faintly foul—something redolent of mud and slime. By reflex, he rubbed the hand that had touched the eel against his breeches.

Someone was saying something to him. With difficulty, he fixed his attention on Mr. Hunter, standing by his side, still with that look of penetrating interest. *Well, of course. They'd need a surgeon,* he thought dimly. *Have to have a surgeon at a duel.*

"Yes," he said, seeing Hunter's eyebrows raised in inquiry of some sort. Then, seized by a belated fear that he had just promised his body to the surgeon were he killed, seized Hunter's coat with his free hand.

"You . . . don't . . . touch me," he said. "No . . . knives. Ghoul," he added for good measure, finally locating the word. Hunter nodded, seeming unoffended.

The sky was overcast, the only light shed by the distant torches at the house's entrance. Nicholls was a whitish blur, coming closer.

Someone grabbed Grey, turned him forcibly about, and he found himself back-to-back with Nicholls, the bigger man's heat startling, so near.

Shit, he thought suddenly. *Is he any kind of a shot?*

Someone spoke and he began to walk—he thought he was walking—until an outthrust arm stopped him, and he turned in answer to someone pointing urgently behind him.

Oh, hell, he thought wearily, seeing Nicholls's arm come down. *I don't care.*

He blinked at the muzzle flash—the report was lost in the shocked gasp from the crowd—and stood for a moment, wondering whether he'd been hit. Nothing seemed amiss, though, and someone nearby was urging him to fire.

Frigging poet, he thought. *I'll delope and have done. I want to go home.* He raised his arm, aiming straight up into the air, but his arm lost contact with his brain for an instant, and his wrist sagged. He jerked, correcting it, and his hand tensed on the trigger. He had barely time to jerk the barrel aside, firing wildly.

To his surprise, Nicholls staggered a bit, then sank down onto the grass. He sat propped on one hand, the other clutched dramatically to his shoulder, head thrown back.

It had begun to rain, quite hard. Grey blinked water off his lashes and shook his head. The air tasted sharp, like cut metal, and for an instant he had the impression that it smelled . . . purple.

"That can't be right," he said aloud, and found that his ability to speak seemed to have come back. He turned to speak to Hunter, but the surgeon had, of course, darted across to Nicholls, was peering down the neck of the poet's shirt. There was blood on it, Grey saw, but Nicholls was refusing to lie down, gesturing vigorously with his free hand. Blood was running down his face from his nose; perhaps that was it.

"Come away, sir," said a quiet voice at his side. "It'll be bad for Lady Joffrey else."

"What?" He looked, surprised, to find Richard Tarleton, who had been his ensign in Germany, now in the uniform of a Lancers lieutenant. "Oh. Yes, it will." Dueling was illegal in London; for the police to arrest Lucinda's guests in the park before her house would be a scandal—not something that would please her husband, Sir Richard, at all.

The crowd had already melted away, as though the rain had rendered them soluble. The torches by the door had been extinguished. Nicholls was being helped off by Hunter and someone else, lurching away through the increasing rain. Grey shivered. God knew where his coat or cloak was.

"Let's go, then," he said.

GREY OPENED HIS eyes.

"Did you say something, Tom?"

Tom Byrd, his valet, had produced a cough like a chimney sweep's, at a distance of approximately one foot from Grey's ear. Seeing that he had obtained his employer's attention, he presented the chamber pot at port arms.

"His Grace is downstairs, me lord. With her ladyship."

Grey blinked at the window behind Tom, where the open drapes showed a dim square of rainy light.

"Her ladyship? What, the duchess?" What could have happened? It couldn't be past nine o'clock. His sister-in-law never paid calls before afternoon, and he had never known her to go anywhere with his brother during the day.

"No, me lord. The little 'un."

"The little—oh. My goddaughter?" He sat up, feeling well but strange, and took the utensil from Tom.

"Yes, me lord. His Grace said as he wants to speak to you about 'the events of last night.'" Tom had crossed to the window and was looking censoriously at the remnants of Grey's shirt and breeches, these stained with grass, mud, blood, and powder stains, and flung carelessly over the back of the chair. He turned a reproachful eye on Grey, who closed his own, trying to recall exactly what the events of last night had been.

He felt somewhat odd. Not drunk, he hadn't been drunk; he had no headache, no uneasiness of digestion. . . .

"Last night," he repeated, uncertain. Last night had been confused, but he did remember it. The eel party. Lucinda Joffrey, Caroline . . . Why on earth ought Hal to be concerned with . . . what, the duel? Why should his brother care about such a silly affair—and even if he did, why appear at Grey's door at the crack of dawn with his six-month-old daughter?

It was more the time of day than the child's presence that was unusual; his brother often did take his daughter out, with the feeble excuse that the child needed air. His wife accused him of wanting to show the baby off— she was beautiful—but Grey thought the cause somewhat more straight-forward. His ferocious, autocratic, dictatorial brother—Colonel of his own regiment, terror of both his own troops and his enemies—had fallen in love with his daughter. The regiment would leave for its new posting within a month's time. Hal simply couldn't bear to have her out of his sight.

Thus he found the Duke of Pardloe seated in the morning room, Lady Dorothea Jacqueline Benedicta Grey cradled in his arm and gnawing on a rusk her father held for her. Her wet silk bonnet, her tiny rabbit-fur bunting, and two letters, one open, one still sealed, lay upon the table at the duke's elbow.

Hal glanced up at him.

"I've ordered your breakfast. Say hallo to Uncle John, Dottie." He turned the baby gently round. She didn't remove her attention from the rusk but made a small chirping noise.

"Hallo, sweetheart." John leaned over and kissed the top of her head, covered with a soft blond down and slightly damp. "Having a nice outing with Daddy in the pouring rain?"

"We brought you something." Hal picked up the opened letter and, raising an eyebrow at his brother, handed it to him.

Grey raised an eyebrow back and began to read.

"What?!" He looked up from the sheet, mouth open.

"Yes, that's what I said," Hal agreed cordially, "when it was delivered to my door, just before dawn." He reached for the sealed letter, carefully balancing the baby. "Here, this one's yours. It came just after dawn."

Grey dropped the first letter as though it were on fire and seized the second, ripping it open.

Oh, John, it read without preamble, *forgive me, I couldn't stop him, I really couldn't, I'm SO sorry. I told him, but he wouldn't listen. I'd run away, but I don't know where to go. Please, please do something!* It wasn't signed but didn't need to be. He'd recognized the Honorable Caroline Woodford's writing, scribbled and frantic as it was. The paper was blotched and puckered—with tearstains?

He shook his head violently, as though to clear it, then picked up the first letter again. It was just as he'd read it the first time—a formal demand from Alfred, Lord Enderby, to His Grace the Duke of Pardloe, for satisfaction regarding the injury to the honor of his sister, the Honorable Caroline Woodford, by the agency of His Grace's brother, Lord John Grey.

Grey glanced from one document to the other, several times, then looked at his brother.

"What the devil?"

"I gather you had an eventful evening," Hal said, grunting slightly as he bent to retrieve the rusk Dottie had dropped on the carpet. "No, darling, you don't want that anymore."

Dottie disagreed violently with this assertion and was distracted only by Uncle John picking her up and blowing in her ear.

"Eventful," he repeated. "Yes, it was, rather. But I didn't do anything to Caroline Woodford save hold her hand whilst being shocked by an electric eel, I swear it. Gleeglgleeglgleegl-pppppsssshhhhh," he added to Dottie, who shrieked and giggled in response. He glanced up to find Hal staring at him.

"Lucinda Joffrey's party," he amplified. "Surely you and Minnie were invited?"

Hal grunted. "Oh. Yes, we were, but I had a prior engagement. Minnie didn't mention the eel. What's this I hear about you fighting a duel over the girl, though?"

"What? It wasn't—" He stopped, trying to think. "Well, perhaps it was, come to think. Nicholls—you know, that swine who wrote the ode to Minnie's feet?—he kissed Miss Woodford, and she didn't want him to, so I punched him. Who told you about the duel?"

"Richard Tarleton. He came into White's cardroom late last night and said he'd just seen you home."

"Well, then, you likely know as much about it as I do. Oh, you want

Daddy back now, do you?" He handed Dottie to his brother and brushed at a damp patch of saliva on the shoulder of his coat.

"I suppose that's what Enderby's getting at." Hal nodded at the earl's letter. "That you made the poor girl publicly conspicuous and compromised her virtue by fighting a scandalous duel over her. I suppose he's got a point."

Dottie was now gumming her father's knuckle, making little growling noises. Hal dug in his pocket and came out with a silver teething ring, which he offered her in lieu of his finger, meanwhile giving Grey a sidelong look.

"You don't want to marry Caroline Woodford, do you? That's what Enderby's demand amounts to."

"God, no." Caroline was a good friend—bright, pretty, and given to mad escapades—but marriage? Him?

Hal nodded.

"Lovely girl, but you'd end in Newgate or Bedlam within a month."

"Or dead," Grey said, gingerly picking at the bandage Tom had insisted on wrapping round his knuckles. "How's Nicholls this morning, do you know?"

"Ah." Hal rocked back a little, drawing a deep breath. "Well . . . dead, actually. I had rather a nasty letter from his father, accusing you of murder. That one came over breakfast; didn't think to bring it. Did you mean to kill him?"

Grey sat down quite suddenly, all the blood having left his head.

"No," he whispered. His lips felt stiff and his hands had gone numb. "Oh, Jesus. No."

Hal swiftly pulled his snuffbox from his pocket, one-handed, dumped out the vial of smelling salts he kept in it, and handed it to his brother. Grey was grateful; he hadn't been going to faint, but the assault of ammoniac fumes gave him excuse for watering eyes and congested breathing.

"Jesus," he repeated, and sneezed explosively several times in a row. "I didn't aim to kill—I swear it, Hal. I deloped. Or tried to," he added honestly.

Lord Enderby's letter now made more sense, as did Hal's presence. What had been a silly affair that should have disappeared with the morning dew had become—or would, directly the gossip had time to spread—not merely a scandal but quite possibly something worse. It was not unthinkable that he *might* be arrested for murder. Quite without warning, the figured carpet yawned at his feet, an abyss into which his life might vanish.

Hal nodded and gave him his own handkerchief.

"I know," he said quietly. "Things . . . happen sometimes. That you don't intend—that you'd give your life to have back."

Grey wiped his face, glancing at his brother under cover of the gesture.

Hal looked suddenly older than his years, his face drawn by more than worry over Grey.

"Nathaniel Twelvetrees, you mean?" Normally he wouldn't have mentioned that matter, but both men's guards were down.

Hal gave him a sharp look, then glanced away.

"No, not Twelvetrees. I hadn't any choice about that. And I did mean to kill him. I meant . . . what led to that duel." He grimaced. "Marry in haste, repent at leisure." He looked at the note on the table and shook his head. His hand passed gently over Dottie's head. "I won't have you repeat my mistakes, John," he said quietly.

Grey nodded, wordless. Hal's first wife had been seduced by Nathaniel Twelvetrees. Hal's mistakes notwithstanding, Grey had never intended marriage with anyone and didn't now.

Hal frowned, tapping the folded letter on the table in thought. He darted a glance at John and sighed, then set the letter down, reached into his coat, and withdrew two further documents, one clearly official, from its seal.

"Your new commission," he said, handing it over. "For Crefeld," he said, raising an eyebrow at his brother's look of blank incomprehension. "You were brevetted lieutenant-colonel. You didn't remember?"

"I—well . . . not exactly." He had a vague feeling that someone—probably Hal—had told him about it, soon after Crefeld, but he'd been badly wounded then and in no frame of mind to think about the army, let alone to care about battlefield promotion. Later—

"Wasn't there some confusion over it?" Grey took the commission and opened it, frowning. "I thought they'd changed their minds."

"Oh, you do remember, then," Hal said, eyebrow still cocked. "General Wiedman gave it to you after the battle. The confirmation was held up, though, because of the inquiry into the cannon explosion, and then the . . . ah . . . kerfuffle over Adams."

"Oh." Grey was still shaken by the news of Nicholls's death, but mention of Adams started his brain functioning again. "Adams. Oh. You mean Twelvetrees held up the commission?" Colonel Reginald Twelvetrees, of the Royal Artillery: brother to Nathaniel and cousin to Bernard Adams, the traitor awaiting trial in the Tower as a result of Grey's efforts the preceding autumn.

"Yes. Bastard," Hal added dispassionately. "I'll have him for breakfast, one of these days."

"Not on my account, I hope," Grey said dryly.

"Oh, no," Hal assured him, jiggling his daughter gently to prevent her fussing. "It will be a purely personal pleasure."

Grey smiled at that, despite his disquiet, and put down the commission. "Right," he said, with a glance at the fourth document, which still lay folded on the table. It was an official-looking letter and had been opened; the seal was broken. "A proposal of marriage, a denunciation for murder, and a new commission—what the devil's that one? A bill from my tailor?"

"Ah, that. I didn't mean to show it to you," Hal said, leaning carefully to hand it over without dropping Dottie. "But under the circumstances . . ."

Hal waited, noncommittal, as Grey opened the letter and read it. It was a request—or an order, depending how you looked at it—for the attendance of Major Lord John Grey at the court-martial of one Captain Charles Carruthers, to serve as witness of character for the same. In . . .

"In Canada?" John's exclamation startled Dottie, who crumpled up her face and threatened to cry.

"Hush, sweetheart." Hal jiggled faster, hastily patting her back. "It's all right; only Uncle John being an ass."

Grey ignored this, waving the letter at his brother.

"What the devil is Charlie Carruthers being court-martialed for? And why on earth am I being summoned as a character witness?"

"Failure to suppress a mutiny," Hal said. "As to why you—he asked for you, apparently. An officer under charges is allowed to call his own witnesses, for whatever purpose. Didn't you know that?"

Grey supposed that he had, in an academic sort of way. But he had never attended a court-martial himself; it wasn't a common proceeding, and he had no real idea of the shape of the proceedings. He glanced sideways at Hal.

"You say you didn't mean to show it to me?"

Hal shrugged and blew softly over the top of his daughter's head, making the short blond hairs furrow and rise like wheat in the wind.

"No point. I meant to write back and say that as your commanding officer I required you here; why should you be dragged off to the wilds of Canada? But given your talent for awkward situations . . . What did it feel like?" he inquired curiously.

"What did—oh, the eel." Grey was accustomed to his brother's lightning shifts of conversation and made the adjustment easily. "Well, it was rather a shock."

He laughed—if tremulously—at Hal's glower, and Dottie squirmed round in her father's arms, reaching out her own plump little arms appealingly to her uncle.

"Flirt," he told her, taking her from Hal. "No, really, it was remarkable. You know how it feels when you break a bone? That sort of jolt that goes right through you before you feel the pain, and you go blind for a moment and feel as if someone's driven a nail through your belly? It was like that, only much stronger, and it went on for longer. Stopped my breath," he admitted. "Quite literally. And my heart, too, I think. Dr. Hunter—

you know, the anatomist?—was there and pounded on my chest to get it started again."

Hal was listening with close attention and asked several questions, which Grey answered automatically, his mind occupied with this latest surprising communiqué.

Charlie Carruthers. They'd been young officers together, though from different regiments. Fought beside each other in Scotland, gone round London together for a bit on their next leave. They'd had—well, you couldn't call it an affair. Three or four brief encounters—sweating, breathless quarters of an hour in dark corners that could be conveniently forgotten in daylight or shrugged off as the result of drunkenness, not spoken of by either party.

That had been in the Bad Time, as he thought of it: those years after Hector's death, when he'd sought oblivion wherever he could find it—and found it often—before slowly recovering himself.

Likely he wouldn't have recalled Carruthers at all, save for the one thing.

Carruthers had been born with an interesting deformity—he had a double hand. While Carruthers's right hand was normal in appearance and worked quite as usual, there was another, dwarf hand that sprang from his wrist and nestled neatly against its larger partner. Dr. Hunter would probably pay hundreds for that hand, Grey thought, with a mild lurch of the stomach.

The dwarf hand had only two short fingers and a stubby thumb—but Carruthers could open and close it, though not without also opening and closing the larger one. The shock when Carruthers had closed both of them simultaneously on Grey's prick had been nearly as extraordinary as had the electric eel's.

"Nicholls hasn't been buried yet, has he?" he asked abruptly, the thought of the eel party and Dr. Hunter causing him to interrupt some remark of Hal's.

Hal looked surprised.

"Surely not. Why?" He narrowed his eyes at Grey. "You don't mean to attend the funeral, do you?"

"No, no," Grey said hastily. "I was only thinking of Dr. Hunter. He, um, has a certain reputation, and Nicholls did go off with him. After the duel."

"A reputation as what, for God's sake?" Hal demanded impatiently.

"As a body snatcher," Grey blurted.

There was a sudden silence, awareness dawning in Hal's face. He'd gone pale.

"You don't think—no! How could he?"

"A . . . um . . . hundredweight or so of stones substituted just prior to the coffin's being nailed shut is the usual method—or so I've heard," Grey said, as well as he could with Dottie's fist poked up his nose.

Hal swallowed. Grey could see the hairs rise on his wrist.

"I'll ask Harry," Hal said, after a short silence. "The funeral can't have been arranged yet, and if . . ."

Both brothers shuddered reflexively, imagining all too exactly the scene as an agitated family member insisted upon raising the coffin lid, to find . . .

"Maybe better not," Grey said, swallowing. Dottie had left off trying to remove his nose and was patting her tiny hand over his lips as he talked. The feel of it on his skin . . .

He peeled her gently off and gave her back to Hal.

"I don't know what use Charles Carruthers thinks I might be to him—but, all right, I'll go." He glanced at Lord Enderby's note, Caroline's crumpled missive. "After all, I suppose there are worse things than being scalped by red Indians."

Hal nodded, sober.

"I've arranged your sailing. You leave tomorrow." He stood and lifted Dottie. "Here, sweetheart. Kiss your Uncle John goodbye."

A MONTH LATER, Grey found himself, Tom Byrd at his side, climbing off the *Harwood* and into one of the small boats that would land them and the battalion of Louisbourg grenadiers with whom they had been traveling on a large island near the mouth of the St. Lawrence River.

He had never seen anything like it. The river itself was larger than any he had ever seen, nearly half a mile across, running wide and deep, a dark blue-black under the sun. Great cliffs and undulating hills rose on either side of the river, so thickly forested that the underlying stone was nearly invisible. It was hot, and the sky arched brilliant overhead, much brighter and much wider than any sky he had seen before. A loud hum echoed from the lush growth—insects, he supposed, birds, and the rush of the water, though it felt as if the wilderness were singing to itself, in a voice heard only in his blood. Beside him, Tom was fairly vibrating with excitement, his eyes out on stalks, not to miss anything.

"Cor, is that a red Indian?" he whispered, leaning close to Grey in the boat.

"I don't suppose he can be anything else," Grey replied, as the gentleman loitering by the landing was naked save for a breechclout, a striped blanket slung over one shoulder, and a coating of what—from the shimmer of his limbs—appeared to be grease of some kind.

"I thought they'd be redder," Tom said, echoing Grey's own thought. The Indian's skin was considerably darker than Grey's own, to be sure, but a rather pleasant soft brown in color, something like dried oak leaves. The Indian appeared to find them nearly as interesting as they had found him; he was eyeing Grey in particular with intent consideration.

"It's your hair, me lord," Tom hissed in Grey's ear. "I told you you ought to have worn a wig."

"Nonsense, Tom." At the same time, Grey experienced an odd frisson up the back of the neck, constricting his scalp. Vain of his hair, which was blond and thick, he didn't commonly wear a wig, choosing instead to bind and powder his own for formal occasions. The present occasion wasn't formal in the least. With the advent of freshwater aboard, Tom had insisted upon washing Grey's hair that morning, and it was still spread loose upon his shoulders, though it had long since dried.

The boat crunched on the shingle, and the Indian flung aside his blanket and came to help the men run it up the shore. Grey found himself next to the man, close enough to smell him. He smelled quite unlike anyone Grey had ever encountered: gamy, certainly—he wondered, with a small thrill, whether the grease the man wore might be bear fat—but with the tang of herbs and a sweat like fresh-sheared copper.

Straightening up from the gunwale, the Indian caught Grey's eye and smiled.

"You be careful, Englishman," he said, in a voice with a noticeable French accent, and, reaching out, ran his fingers quite casually through Grey's loose hair. "Your scalp would look good on a Huron's belt."

This made the soldiers from the boat all laugh, and the Indian, still smiling, turned to them.

"They are not so particular, the Abenaki who work for the French. A scalp is a scalp—and the French pay well for one, no matter what color." He nodded genially to the grenadiers, who had stopped laughing. "You come with me."

THERE WAS A small camp on the island already, a detachment of infantry under a Captain Woodford—whose name gave Grey a slight wariness but who turned out to be no relation, thank God, to Lord Enderby's family.

"We're fairly safe on this side of the island," he told Grey, offering him a flask of brandy outside his own tent after supper. "But the Indians raid the other side regularly—I lost four men last week, three killed and one carried off."

"You have your own scouts, though?" Grey asked, slapping at the mosquitoes that had begun to swarm in the dusk. He had not seen the Indian who had brought them to the camp again, but there were several more in camp. Most clustered together around their own fire, but one or two squatted, bright-eyed and watchful, among the Louisbourg grenadiers who had crossed with Grey on the *Harwood*.

"Yes, and trustworthy for the most part," Woodford said, answering Grey's unasked question. He laughed, though not with any humor. "At least we hope so."

Woodford gave him supper, and they had a hand of cards, Grey exchanging news of home for gossip of the current campaign.

General Wolfe had spent no little time at Montmorency, below the town of Quebec, but had nothing but disappointment from his attempts there, and so had abandoned that post, regathering the main body of his troops some miles upstream from the Citadel of Quebec. The so-far impregnable fortress, perched on sheer cliffs above the river, commanded both the river and the plains to the west with her cannon, obliging English warships to steal past under cover of night—and not always successfully.

"Wolfe'll be champing at the bit, now his grenadiers are come," Woodford predicted. "He puts great store by those fellows; fought with 'em at Louisbourg. Here, Colonel, you're being eaten alive—try a bit of this on your hands and face." He dug about in his campaign chest and came up with a tin of strong-smelling grease, which he pushed across the table.

"Bear grease and mint," he explained. "The Indians use it—that, or cover themselves with mud."

Grey helped himself liberally; the scent wasn't quite the same as what he had smelled earlier on the scout, but it was very similar, and he felt an odd sense of disturbance in its application. Though it did discourage the biting insects.

He had made no secret of the reason for his presence and now asked openly about Carruthers.

"Where is he held, do you know?"

Woodford frowned and poured more brandy.

"He's not. He's paroled; has a billet in the town at Gareon, where Wolfe's headquarters are."

"Ah?" Grey was mildly surprised—but, then, Carruthers was not charged with mutiny but rather with failure to suppress one—a rare charge. "Do you know the particulars of the case?"

Woodford opened his mouth, as though to speak, but then drew a deep breath, shook his head, and drank brandy. From which Grey deduced that probably everyone knew the particulars but that there was something fishy about the affair. Well, time enough. He'd hear about the matter directly from Carruthers.

Conversation became general, and after a time Grey said good night. The grenadiers had been busy; a new little city of canvas tents had sprung up at the edge of the existing camp, and the appetizing smells of fresh meat roasting and tea brewing were rising on the air.

Tom had doubtless managed to raise his own tent, somewhere in the mass. Grey was in no hurry to find it, though; he was enjoying the novel sensations of firm footing and solitude, after weeks of crowded shipboard life. He cut outside the orderly rows of new tents, walking just beyond the glow of the firelight, feeling pleasantly invisible, though still close enough for safety—or at least he hoped so. The forest stood only a few yards away, the outlines of trees and bushes still visible, the dark not quite complete.

A drifting spark of green drew his eye, and he felt delight well up in him. There was another . . . another . . . ten, a dozen, and the air was suddenly full of fireflies, soft green sparks that winked on and off, glowing like tiny distant candles among the dark foliage. He'd seen fireflies once or twice before, in Germany, but never in such abundance. They were simple magic, pure as moonlight.

He could not have said how long he watched them, wandering slowly along the edge of the encampment, but at last he sighed and turned toward the center, full-fed, pleasantly tired, and with no immediate responsibility to do anything. He had no troops under his command, no reports to write . . . nothing, really, to do until he reached Gareon and Charlie Carruthers.

With a sigh of peace, he closed the flap of his tent and shucked his outer clothing.

He was roused abruptly from the edge of sleep by screams and shouts, and sat bolt upright. Tom, who had been asleep on his bed sack at Grey's feet, sprang up like a frog onto hands and knees, scrabbling madly for pistol and shot in the chest.

Not waiting, Grey seized the dagger he had hung on the tent peg before retiring and, flinging back the flap, peered out. Men were rushing to and fro, colliding with tents, shouting orders, yelling for help. There was a glow in the sky, a reddening of the low-hanging clouds.

"Fireships!" someone shouted. Grey shoved his feet into his shoes and joined the throng of men now rushing toward the water.

Out in the center of the broad dark river stood the bulk of the *Harwood*, at anchor. And coming slowly down upon her were one, two, and then three blazing vessels. A raft, stacked with flammable waste, doused with oil and set afire. A small boat, its mast and sail flaming bright against the night. Something else—an Indian canoe, with a heap of burning grass and leaves? Too far to see, but it was coming closer.

He glanced at the ship and saw movement on deck—too far to make out individual men, but things were happening. The ship couldn't raise anchor and sail away, not in time—but she was lowering her boats, sailors setting out to try to deflect the fireships, keep them away from the *Harwood*.

Absorbed in the sight, he had not noticed the shrieks and shouts still coming from the other side of the camp. But now, as the men on the shore fell silent, watching the fireships, they began to stir, realizing belatedly that something else was afoot.

"Indians," the man beside Grey said suddenly, as a particularly high, ululating screech split the air. "Indians!"

This cry became general, and everyone began to rush in the other direction.

"Stop! Halt!" Grey flung out an arm, catching a man across the throat and knocking him flat. He raised his voice in the vain hope of stopping the rush. "You! You and you—seize your neighbor, come with me!" The man he had knocked down bounced up again, white-eyed in the starlight.

"It may be a trap!" Grey shouted. "Stay here! Stand to your arms!"

"Stand! Stand!" A short gentleman in his nightshirt took up the cry in a cast-iron bellow, adding to its effect by seizing a dead branch from the ground and laying about himself, turning back those trying to get past him to the encampment.

Another spark grew upstream, and another beyond it: more fireships. The boats were in the water now, mere dots in the darkness. If they could fend off the fireships, the *Harwood* might be saved from immediate destruction; Grey's fear was that whatever was going on in the rear of the encampment was a ruse designed to pull men away from the shore, leaving the ship protected only by her marines. The French could then send down a barge loaded with explosives, or a boarding craft, hoping to elude detection while everyone was dazzled or occupied by the blazing fireships and the raid.

The first of the fireships had drifted harmlessly onto the far shore and was burning itself out on the sand, brilliant and beautiful against the night. The short gentleman with the remarkable voice—clearly he was a sergeant, Grey thought—had succeeded in rallying a small group of soldiers, whom he now presented to Grey with a brisk salute.

"Will they go and fetch their muskets, all orderly, sir?"

"They will," Grey said. "And hurry. Go with them, Sergeant—it is Sergeant?"

"Sergeant Aloysius Cutter, sir," the short gentleman replied with a nod, "and pleased to know an officer what has a brain in his head."

"Thank you, Sergeant. And fetch back as many more men as fall conveniently to hand, if you please. With arms. A rifleman or two, if you can find them."

Matters thus momentarily attended to, he turned his attention once more to the river, where two of the *Harwood*'s small boats were herding one of the fireships away from the transport, circling it and pushing water with their oars; he caught the splash of their efforts and the shouts of the sailors.

"Me lord?"

The voice at his elbow nearly made him swallow his tongue. He turned with an attempt at calmness, ready to reproach Tom for venturing out into the chaos, but before he could summon words, his young valet stooped at his feet, holding something.

"I've brought your breeches, me lord," Tom said, voice trembling. "Thought you might need 'em, if there was fighting."

"Very thoughtful of you, Tom," he assured his valet, fighting an urge to laugh. He stepped into the breeches and pulled them up, tucking in his shirt. "What's been happening in the camp, do you know?"

He could hear Tom swallow hard.

"Indians, me lord," Tom said. "They came screaming through the tents, set one or two afire. They killed one man I saw, and . . . and scalped him." His voice was thick, as though he might be about to vomit. "It was nasty."

"I daresay." The night was warm, but Grey felt the hairs rise on arms and neck. The chilling screams had stopped, and while he could still hear considerable hubbub in the camp, it was of a different tone now: no random shouting, just the calls of officers, sergeants, and corporals ordering the men, beginning the process of assembly, of counting noses and reckoning damage.

Tom, bless him, had brought Grey's pistol, shot bag, and powder, as well as his coat and stockings. Aware of the dark forest and the long, narrow trail between the shore and the camp, Grey didn't send Tom back but merely told him to keep out of the way as Sergeant Cutter—who, with good military instinct, had also taken time to put his breeches on—came up with his armed recruits.

"All present, sir," Cutter said, saluting. "'Oom 'ave I the honor of h'addressing, sir?"

"I am Lieutenant-Colonel Grey. Set your men to watch the ship, please, Sergeant, with particular attention to dark craft coming downstream, and then come back to report what you know of matters in camp."

Cutter saluted and promptly vanished with a shout of "Come on, you shower o' shit! Look lively, look lively!"

Tom gave a brief, strangled scream, and Grey whirled, drawing his dagger by reflex, to find a dark shape directly behind him.

"Don't kill me, Englishman," said the Indian who had led them to the camp earlier. He sounded mildly amused. "*Le capitaine* sent me to find you."

"Why?" Grey asked shortly. His heart was still pounding from the shock. He disliked being taken at a disadvantage, and disliked even more the thought that the man could easily have killed him before Grey knew he was there.

"The Abenaki set your tent on fire; he supposed they might have dragged you and your servant into the forest."

Tom uttered an extremely coarse expletive and made as though to dive directly into the trees, but Grey stopped him with a hand on his arm.

"Stay, Tom. It doesn't matter."

"The bloody hell you say," Tom replied heatedly, agitation depriving him of his normal manners. "I daresay I can find you more smallclothes, not as that will be easy, but what about your cousin's painting of her and the little 'un she sent for Captain Stubbs? What about your good hat with the gold lace?!?"

Grey had a brief moment of alarm—his young cousin Olivia had sent a miniature of herself and her newborn son, charging Grey to deliver this to her husband, Captain Malcolm Stubbs, presently with Wolfe's troops. He clapped a hand to his side, though, and felt with relief the oval shape of the miniature in its wrappings, safe in his pocket.

"That's all right, Tom; I've got it. As to the hat . . . we'll worry about that later, I think. Here—what is your name, sir?" he inquired of the Indian, unwilling to address him simply as "you."

"Manoke," said the Indian, still sounding amused.

"Quite. Will you take my servant back to the camp?" He saw the small, determined figure of Sergeant Cutter appear at the mouth of the trail and, firmly overriding Tom's protests, shooed him off in care of the Indian.

IN THE EVENT, all five fireships either drifted or were steered away from the *Harwood*. Something that might—or might not—have been a boarding craft did appear upstream but was frightened off by Grey's impromptu troops on the shore, firing volleys—though the range was woefully short; there was no possibility of hitting anything.

Still, the *Harwood* was secure, and the camp had settled into a state of uneasy watchfulness. Grey had seen Woodford briefly upon his return, near dawn, and learned that the raid had resulted in the deaths of two men and the capture of three more, dragged off into the forest. Three of the Indian raiders had been killed, another wounded—Woodford intended to interview this man before he died but doubted that any useful information would result.

"They never talk," he'd said, rubbing at his smoke-reddened eyes. His face was pouchy and gray with fatigue. "They just close their eyes and start singing their damned death songs. Not a blind bit of difference what you do to 'em—they just keep on singing."

Grey had heard it, or thought he had, as he crawled wearily into his borrowed shelter toward daybreak. A faint, high-pitched chant that rose and fell like the rush of the wind in the trees overhead. It kept up for a bit, then stopped abruptly, only to resume again, faint and interrupted, as he teetered on the edge of sleep.

What was the man saying? he wondered. Did it matter that none of the men hearing him knew what he said? Perhaps the scout—Manoke, that was his name—was there; perhaps he would know.

Tom had found Grey a small tent at the end of a row. Probably he had ejected some subaltern, but Grey wasn't inclined to object. It was barely big enough for the canvas bed sack that lay on the ground and a box that served as table, on which stood an empty candlestick, but it was shelter. It had begun to rain lightly as he walked up the trail to camp, and the rain was now pattering busily on the canvas overhead, raising a sweet, musty scent. If the death song continued, it was no longer audible over the sound of the rain.

Grey turned over once, the grass stuffing of the bed sack rustling softly beneath him, and fell at once into sleep.

HE WOKE ABRUPTLY, face-to-face with an Indian. His reflexive flurry of movement was met with a low chuckle and a slight withdrawal, rather than a knife across the throat, though, and he broke through the fog of sleep in time to avoid doing serious damage to the scout Manoke.

"What?" he muttered, and rubbed the heel of his hand across his eyes. "What is it?" *And why the devil are you lying on my bed?*

In answer to this, the Indian put a hand behind his head, drew him close, and kissed him. The man's tongue ran lightly across his lower lip, darted like a lizard's into his mouth, and then was gone.

So was the Indian.

He rolled over onto his back, blinking. A dream. It was still raining, harder now. He breathed in deeply; he could smell bear grease, of course, on his own skin, and mint—was there any hint of metal? The light was stronger—it must be day; he heard the drummer passing through the aisles of tents to rouse the men, the rattle of his sticks blending with the rattle of the rain, the shouts of corporals and sergeants—but still faint and gray. He could not have been asleep for more than half an hour, he thought.

"Christ," he muttered, and, turning himself stiffly over, pulled his coat over his head and sought sleep once again.

THE *HARWOOD* TACKED slowly upriver, with a sharp eye out for French marauders. There were a few alarms, including another raid by hostile Indians while camped on shore. This one ended more happily, with four marauders killed and only one cook wounded, not seriously. They were obliged to loiter for a time, waiting for a cloudy night, in order to steal past the fortress of Quebec, menacing on its cliffs. They were spotted, in fact, and one or two cannon fired in their direction, but to no effect. And at last came into port at Gareon, the site of General Wolfe's headquarters.

The town itself had been nearly engulfed by the growing military encampment that surrounded it, acres of tents spreading upward from the settlement on the riverbank, the whole presided over by a small French Catholic mission, whose tiny cross was just visible at the top of the hill that lay behind the town. The French inhabitants, with the political indifference of merchants everywhere, had given a Gallic shrug and set about happily overcharging the occupying forces.

The general himself was elsewhere, Grey was informed, fighting inland, but would doubtless return within the month. A lieutenant-colonel without brief or regimental affiliation was simply a nuisance; he was provided with suitable quarters and politely shooed away. With no immediate duties to fulfill, he gave a shrug of his own and set out to discover the whereabouts of Captain Carruthers.

It wasn't difficult to find him. The *patron* of the first tavern Grey visited directed him at once to the habitat of *le capitaine,* a room in the house of a widow named Lambert, near the mission church. Grey wondered whether he would have received the information as readily from any other tavern-keeper in the village. Charlie had liked to drink when Grey knew him, and evidently he still did, judging from the genial attitude of the *patron* when Carruthers's name was mentioned. Not that Grey could blame him, under the circumstances.

The widow—young, chestnut-haired, and quite attractive—viewed the English officer at her door with a deep suspicion, but when he followed his request for Captain Carruthers by mentioning that he was an old friend of the captain's, her face relaxed.

"Bon," she said, swinging the door open abruptly. "He needs friends."

He ascended two flights of narrow stairs to Carruthers's attic, feeling the air about him grow warmer. It was pleasant at this time of day but must grow stifling by mid-afternoon. He knocked and felt a small shock of pleased recognition at hearing Carruthers's voice bid him enter.

Carruthers was seated at a rickety table in shirt and breeches, writing, an inkwell made from a gourd at one elbow, a pot of beer at the other. He looked at Grey blankly for an instant, then joy washed across his features, and he rose, nearly upsetting both.

"John!"

Before Grey could offer his hand, he found himself embraced—and returned the embrace wholeheartedly, a wash of memory flooding through him as he smelled Carruthers's hair, felt the scrape of his unshaven cheek against Grey's own. Even in the midst of this sensation, though, he felt the slightness of Carruthers's body, the bones that pressed through his clothes.

"I never thought you'd come," Carruthers was repeating, for perhaps the fourth time. He let go and stepped away smiling as he dashed the back of his hand across his eyes, which were unabashedly wet.

"Well, you have an electric eel to thank for my presence," Grey told him, smiling himself.

"A what?" Carruthers stared at him blankly.

"Long story—tell you later. For the moment, though—what the devil have you been doing, Charlie?"

The happiness faded somewhat from Carruthers's lean face but didn't disappear altogether.

"Ah. Well. That's a long story, too. Let me send Martine for more beer." He waved Grey toward the room's only stool and went out before Grey could protest. He sat, gingerly, lest the stool collapse, but it held his weight. Besides the stool and table, the attic was very plainly furnished; a narrow cot, a chamber pot, and an ancient washstand with an earthenware basin and ewer completed the ensemble. It was very clean, but there was a faint smell of something in the air—something sweet and sickly, which he traced at once to a corked bottle standing at the back of the washstand.

Not that he had needed the smell of laudanum; one look at Carruthers's gaunt face told him enough. He glanced at the papers Carruthers had been working on. They appeared to be notes in preparation for the court-martial; the one on top was an account of an expedition undertaken by troops under Carruthers's command, on the orders of a Major Gerald Siverly.

Our orders instructed us to march to a village called Beaulieu, there to ransack and fire the houses, driving off such animals as we encountered. This we did. Some men of the village offered us resistance, armed with scythes and other implements. Two of these were shot, the others fled. We returned with two wagons filled with flour, cheeses, and small household goods, three cows, and two good mules.

Grey got no further before the door opened. Carruthers came in and sat on the bed, nodding toward the papers.

"I thought I'd best write everything down. Just in case I don't live long enough for the court-martial." He spoke matter-of-factly and, seeing the look on Grey's face, smiled faintly. "Don't be troubled, John. I've always known I'd not make old bones. This"—he turned his right hand upward, letting the drooping cuff of his shirt fall back—"isn't all of it." He tapped his chest gently with his left hand.

"More than one doctor's told me I have some gross defect of the heart. Don't know, quite, if I have two of those, too"—he grinned, the sudden, charming smile Grey remembered so well—"or only half of one, or what. Used to be I just went faint now and then, but it's getting worse. Sometimes I feel it stop beating and just flutter in my chest, and everything begins to go all black and breathless. So far, it's always started beating again—but one of these days it isn't going to."

Grey's eyes were fixed on Charlie's hand, the small dwarf hand curled against its larger fellow, looking as though Charlie held a strange flower cupped in his palm. As Grey watched, both hands opened slowly, the fingers moving in strangely beautiful synchrony.

"All right," he said quietly. "Tell me."

Failure to suppress a mutiny was a rare charge—difficult to prove and thus unlikely to be brought, unless other factors were involved. Which, in the present instance, they undoubtedly were.

"Know Siverly, do you?" Carruthers asked, taking the papers onto his knee.

"Not at all. I gather he's a bastard." Grey gestured at the papers. "What kind of bastard, though?"

"A corrupt one." Carruthers tapped the pages square, carefully evening the edges, eyes fixed on them. "That—what you read—it wasn't Siverly. It's General Wolfe's directive. I'm not sure whether the point is to deprive the fortress of provisions, in hopes of starving them out eventually, or to put pressure on Montcalm to send out troops to defend the countryside, where Wolfe could get at them—possibly both. But he means deliberately to terrorize the settlements on both sides of the river. No, we did this under the general's orders." His face twisted a little, and he looked up suddenly at Grey. "You remember the Highlands, John?"

"You know that I do." No one involved in Cumberland's cleansing of the Highlands would ever forget. He had seen many Scottish villages like Beaulieu.

Carruthers took a deep breath.

"Yes. Well. The trouble was that Siverly took to appropriating the plunder we took from the countryside—under the pretext of selling it in order to make an equitable distribution among the troops."

"What?" This was contrary to the normal custom of the army, whereby any soldier was entitled to what plunder he seized. "Who does he think he is, an admiral?" The navy did divide shares of prize money among the crew, according to formula—but the navy was the navy; crews acted much more as single entities than did army companies, and there were Admiralty courts set up to deal with the sale of captured prize ships.

Carruthers laughed at the question.

"His brother's a commodore. Perhaps that's where he got the notion. At any rate," he added, sobering, "he never did distribute the funds. Worse—he began withholding the soldiers' pay. Paying later and later, stopping pay for petty offenses, claiming that the pay chest hadn't been delivered—when several men had seen it unloaded from the coach with their own eyes.

"Bad enough—but the soldiers were still being fed and clothed adequately. But then he went too far."

Siverly began to steal from the commissary, diverting quantities of supplies and selling them privately.

"I had my suspicions," Carruthers explained, "but no proof. I'd begun to watch him, though—and he knew I was watching him, so he trod carefully for a bit. But he couldn't resist the rifles."

A shipment of a dozen new rifles, vastly superior to the ordinary Brown Bess musket, and very rare in the army.

"I think it must have been a clerical oversight that sent them to us in the first place. We hadn't any riflemen, and there was no real need for them. That's probably what made Siverly think he could get away with it."

But he hadn't. Two private soldiers had unloaded the box and, curious at the weight, had opened it. Excited word had spread—and excitement had turned to disgruntled surprise when, instead of new rifles, muskets showing considerable wear were later distributed. The talk—already angry—had escalated.

"Egged on by a hogshead of rum we confiscated from a tavern in Levi," Carruthers said with a sigh. "They drank all night—it was January; the nights are damned long in January here—and made up their minds to go and find the rifles. Which they did—under the floor in Siverly's quarters."

"And where was Siverly?"

"In his quarters. He was rather badly used, I'm afraid." A muscle by Carruthers's mouth twitched. "Escaped through a window, though, and made his way through the snow to the next garrison. It was twenty miles. Lost a couple of toes to frostbite but survived."

"Too bad."

"Yes, it was." The muscle twitched again.

"What happened to the mutineers?"

Carruthers blew out his cheeks, shaking his head.

"Deserted, most of them. Two were caught and hanged pretty promptly; three more rounded up later; they're in prison here."

"And you—"

"And I." Carruthers nodded. "I was Siverly's company adjutant. I didn't know about the mutiny—one of the ensigns ran to fetch me when the men started to move toward Siverly's quarters—but I did arrive before they'd finished."

"Not a great deal you could do under those circumstances, was there?"

"I didn't try," Carruthers said bluntly.

"I see," Grey said.

"Do you?" Carruthers gave him a crooked smile.

"Certainly. I take it Siverly is still in the army and still holds a command? Yes, of course. He might have been furious enough to prefer the original charge against you, but you know as well as I do that, under normal circumstances, the matter would likely have been dropped as soon as the general facts were known. You insisted on a court-martial, didn't you? So that you can make what you know public." Given Carruthers's state of health, the knowledge that he risked a long imprisonment if convicted apparently didn't trouble him.

The smile straightened and became genuine.

"I knew I chose the right man," Carruthers said.

"I am exceedingly flattered," Grey said dryly. "Why me, though?"

Carruthers had laid aside his papers and now rocked back a little on the cot, hands linked around one knee.

"Why you, John?" The smile had vanished, and Carruthers's gray eyes were level on his. "You know what we do. Our business is chaos, death, destruction. But you know why we do it, too."

"Oh? Perhaps you'd have the goodness to tell me, then. I've always wondered."

Humor lighted Charlie's eyes, but he spoke seriously.

"Someone has to keep order, John. Soldiers fight for all kinds of reasons, most of them ignoble. You and your brother, though—" He broke off, shaking his head. Grey saw that his hair was streaked with gray, though he knew Carruthers was no older than himself.

"The world is chaos and death and destruction. But people like you— you don't stand for that. If there is any order in the world, any peace—it's because of you, John, and those very few like you."

Grey felt he should say something but was at a loss as to what that might be. Carruthers rose and came to Grey, putting a hand—the left—on his shoulder, the other gently against his face.

"What is it the Bible says?" Carruthers said quietly. "Blessed are they who hunger and thirst for justice, for they shall be satisfied? I hunger, John," he whispered. "And you thirst. You won't fail me." The fingers of Charlie's secret moved on his skin, a plea, a caress.

The custom of the army is that a court-martial be presided over by a senior officer and such a number of other officers as he shall think fit to serve as council, these being generally four in number, but can be more but not generally less than three. The person accused shall have the right to call witnesses in his support, and the council shall question these, as well as any other persons whom they may wish, and shall thus determine the circumstances and, if conviction ensue, the sentence to be imposed.

THAT RATHER VAGUE statement was evidently all that existed in terms of written definition and directive regarding the operations of courts-martial—or was all that Hal had turned up for him in the brief period prior to his departure. There were no formal laws governing such courts, nor did the law of the land apply to them. In short, the army was—as always, Grey thought—a law unto itself.

That being so, he might have considerable leeway in accomplishing what Charlie Carruthers wanted—or not, depending upon the personalities and professional alliances of the officers who composed the court. It would behoove him to discover these men as soon as possible.

In the meantime, he had another small duty to discharge.

"Tom," he called, rummaging in his trunk, "have you discovered Captain Stubbs's billet?"

"Yes, me lord. And if you'll give over ruining your shirts there, I'll tell you." With a censorious look at his master, Tom nudged him deftly aside. "What you a-looking for in there, anyway?"

"The miniature of my cousin and her child." Grey stood back, permitting Tom to bend over the open chest, tenderly patting the abused shirts back into their tidy folds. The chest itself was rather scorched, but the soldiers had succeeded in rescuing it—and Grey's wardrobe, to Tom's relief.

"Here, me lord." Tom withdrew the packet and handed it gently to Grey. "Give me best to Captain Stubbs. Reckon he'll be glad to get that. The little 'un's got quite the look of him, don't he?"

It took some time, even with Tom's direction, to discover Malcolm Stubbs's billet. The address—insofar as it could be called one—lay in the poorer section of the town, somewhere down a muddy lane that ended abruptly at the river. Grey was surprised at this; Stubbs was a most sociable sort, and a conscientious officer. Why was he not billeted at an inn, or a good private house, near his troops?

By the time Grey found the lane, he had an uneasy feeling; this grew markedly as he poked his way through the ramshackle sheds and the knots of filthy, polyglot children that broke from their play, brightening at the novel sight. They followed him, hissing unintelligible speculations to one another but staring blankly at him, mouths open, when he asked after Captain Stubbs, pointing at his own uniform by way of illustration, with a questioning wave at their surroundings.

He had made his way all the way down the lane, and his boots were caked with mud, dung, and a thick plastering of the leaves that drifted lazily from the giant trees, before he discovered someone willing to answer him. This was an ancient Indian sitting peacefully on a rock at the river's edge, wrapped in a striped British trade blanket, fishing. The man spoke a mixture of three or four languages, only two of which Grey understood, but this basis of understanding was adequate.

"*Un, deux, trois,* in back," the ancient told him, pointing a thumb up the lane, then jerking this appendage sideways. Something in an aboriginal tongue followed, in which Grey thought he detected a reference to a woman—doubtless the owner of the house where Stubbs was billeted. A concluding reference to *"le bon capitaine"* seemed to reinforce this impression, and, thanking the gentleman in both French and English, Grey retraced his steps to the third house up the lane, still trailing a line of curious urchins like the ragged tail of a kite.

No one answered his knock, but he went round the house—followed by the children—and discovered a small hut behind it, smoke coming from its gray stone chimney.

The day was beautiful, with a sky the color of sapphires, and the air was suffused with the ripeness of late summer. The door of the hut was ajar, to admit the fresh air, but he did not push it open. Instead, he drew his dagger from his belt and knocked with the hilt—to admiring gasps from his audience at the appearance of the knife. He repressed the urge to turn round and bow to them.

He heard no footsteps from within, but the door opened suddenly, revealing a young Indian woman, whose face blazed with joy at beholding him.

He blinked, startled, and in that blink of an eye, the joy disappeared and the young woman clutched at the doorjamb for support, her other hand fisted into her chest.

"*Batinse!?*" she gasped, clearly terrified. "*Qu'est-ce qui s'passe?*"

"*Rien,*" he replied, equally startled. "*Ne vous inquietez pas, madame. Est-ce que Capitaine Stubbs habite ici?*" Don't perturb yourself, madame. Does Captain Stubbs live here?

Her eyes, already huge, rolled back in her head, and he seized her arm, fearing lest she faint at his feet. The largest of the urchins following him rushed forward and pushed the door open, and he put an arm round the woman's waist and half-dragged, half-carried her into the house.

Taking this as invitation, the rest of the children crowded in behind him, murmuring in what appeared to be sympathy, as he lugged the young woman to the bed and deposited her thereon. A small girl, wearing little more than a pair of drawers snugged round her insubstantial waist with a piece of string, pressed in beside him and said something to the young woman. Not receiving an answer, the girl behaved as though she had, turning and racing out of the door.

Grey hesitated, not sure what to do. The woman was breathing, though pale, and her eyelids fluttered.

"Voulez-vous un petit eau?" he inquired, turning about in search of water. He spotted a bucket of water near the hearth, but his attention was distracted by an object propped beside it: a cradleboard, with a swaddled infant bound to it, blinking large, curious eyes in his direction.

He knew already, of course, but knelt down before the infant and waggled a tentative forefinger at it. The baby's eyes were big and dark, like its mother's, and the skin a paler shade of her own. The hair, though, was not straight, thick, and black. It was the color of cinnamon and exploded from the child's skull in a nimbus of the same curls that Malcolm Stubbs kept rigorously clipped to his scalp and hidden beneath his wig.

"Wha' happen with *le capitaine*?" a peremptory voice demanded behind him. He turned on his heels and, finding a rather large woman looming over him, rose to his feet and bowed.

"Nothing whatever, madame," he assured her. *Not yet, it hasn't.* "I was merely seeking Captain Stubbs to give him a message."

"Oh." The woman—French, but plainly the younger woman's mother or aunt—left off glowering at him and seemed to deflate somewhat, settling back into a less threatening shape. "Well, then. *D'un urgence,* this message?" She eyed him; clearly, other British officers were not in the habit of visiting Stubbs at home. Most likely Stubbs had an official billet elsewhere, where he conducted his regimental business. No wonder they thought he'd come to say that Stubbs was dead or injured. *Not yet,* he added grimly to himself.

"No," he said, feeling the weight of the miniature in his pocket. "Important, but not urgent." He left then. None of the children followed him.

NORMALLY, IT WAS not difficult to discover the whereabouts of a particular soldier, but Malcolm Stubbs seemed to have disappeared into thin air. Over the course of the next week, Grey combed headquarters, the military encampment, and the village, but no trace of his disgraceful cousin-by-marriage could be found. Still odder, no one appeared to have missed the captain. The men of Stubbs's immediate company merely shrugged in confusion, and his superior officer had evidently gone off upriver to inspect the state of various postings. Frustrated, Grey retired to the riverbank to think.

Two logical possibilities presented themselves—no, three. One, Stubbs had heard about Grey's arrival, supposed that Grey would discover exactly what he had discovered, and had in consequence panicked and deserted. Two, he'd fallen afoul of someone in a tavern or back alley, been killed, and was presently decomposing quietly under a layer of leaves in the woods. Or, three—he'd been sent somewhere to do something, quietly.

Grey doubted the first exceedingly; Stubbs wasn't prone to panic, and if he had heard of Grey's arrival, Malcolm's first act would have been to come and find him, thus preventing his poking about in the village and finding what he'd found. He dismissed that possibility accordingly.

He dismissed the second still more promptly. Had Stubbs been killed, either deliberately or by accident, the alarm would have been raised. The army did generally know where its soldiers were, and if they weren't where they were meant to be, steps were taken. The same held true for desertion.

Right, then. If Stubbs was gone and no one was looking for him, it naturally followed that the army had sent him to wherever he'd gone. Since no one seemed to know where that was, his mission was presumably secret. And given Wolfe's current position and present obsession, that almost certainly meant that Malcolm Stubbs had gone downriver, searching for some way to attack Quebec. Grey sighed, satisfied with his deductions. Which in turn meant that—barring his being caught by the French, scalped or abducted by hostile Indians, or eaten by a bear—Stubbs would be back eventually. There was nothing to do but wait.

He leaned against a tree, watching a couple of fishing canoes make their way slowly downstream, hugging the bank. The sky was overcast and the air light on his skin, a pleasant change from the day's earlier heat. Cloudy skies were good for fishing; his father's gamekeeper had told him that. He wondered why—were the fish dazzled by sun, and thus sought murky hiding places in the depths, but rose toward the surface in dimmer light?

He thought suddenly of the electric eel, which Suddfield had told him lived in the silt-choked waters of the Amazon. The thing did have remarkably small eyes, and its proprietor had opined that it was able to use its electrical abilities in some way to discern, as well as to electrocute, its prey.

He couldn't have said what made him raise his head at that precise moment, but he looked up to find one of the canoes hovering in the shallow water a few feet from him. The Indian paddling the canoe gave him a brilliant smile.

"Englishman!" he called. "You want to fish with me?"

A small jolt of electricity ran through him and he straightened up. Manoke's eyes were fixed on his, and he felt in memory the touch of lips and tongue and the scent of fresh-sheared copper. His heart was racing—go off in company with an Indian he barely knew? It might easily be a trap. He could end up scalped or worse. But electric eels were not the only ones to discern things by means of a sixth sense, he thought.

"Yes!" he called. "Meet you at the landing!"

TWO WEEKS LATER, he stepped out of Manoke's canoe onto the landing, thin, sunburned, cheerful, and still in possession of his hair. Tom Byrd would be beside himself, he reflected; he'd left word as to what he was doing but naturally had been able to give no estimate of his return. Doubtless poor Tom would be thinking he'd been captured and dragged off into slavery or scalped, his hair sold to the French.

In fact, they had drifted slowly downriver, pausing to fish wherever the mood took them, camping on sandbars and small islands, grilling their catch and eating their supper in smoke-scented peace, beneath the leaves of oak and alder. They had seen other craft now and then—not only canoes but many French packet boats and brigs, as well as two English warships, tacking slowly up the river, sails bellying, the distant shouts of the sailors as foreign to him just then as the tongues of the Iroquois.

And in the late summer dusk of the first day, Manoke had wiped his fingers after eating, stood up, casually untied his breechclout, and let it fall. Then waited, grinning, while Grey fought his way out of shirt and breeches.

They'd swum in the river to refresh themselves before eating; the Indian was clean, his skin no longer greasy. And yet he seemed to taste of wild game, the rich, uneasy tang of venison. Grey had wondered whether it was the man's race that was responsible or only his diet?

"What do I taste like?" he'd asked, out of curiosity.

Manoke, absorbed in his business, had said something that might have been "cock" but might equally have been some expression of mild disgust, so Grey thought better of pursuing this line of inquiry. Besides, if he *did* taste of beef and biscuit or Yorkshire pudding, would the Indian recognize that? For that matter, did he really want to know, if he did? He did not, he decided, and they enjoyed the rest of the evening without benefit of conversation.

He scratched the small of his back where his breeches rubbed, uncomfortable with mosquito bites and the peel of fading sunburn. He'd tried the native style of dress, seeing its convenience, but had scorched his bum by lying too long in the sun one afternoon and thereafter resorted to breeches, not wishing to hear any further jocular remarks regarding the whiteness of his arse.

Thinking such pleasant but disjointed thoughts, he'd made his way halfway through the town before noticing that there were many more soldiers in evidence than there had been when he'd left. Drums were pattering up and down the sloping, muddy streets, calling men from their billets, the rhythm of the military day making itself felt. His own steps fell naturally into the beat of the drums; he straightened and felt the army reach out suddenly, seizing him, shaking him out of his sunburned bliss.

He glanced involuntarily up the hill and saw the flags fluttering above the large inn that served as field headquarters. Wolfe had returned.

GREY FOUND HIS own quarters, reassured Tom as to his well-being, submitted to having his hair forcibly untangled, combed, perfumed, and tightly bound up in a formal queue, and, with his clean uniform chafing his sunburned skin, went to present himself to the general, as courtesy demanded. He knew James Wolfe by sight—Wolfe was about his own age, had fought at Culloden, been a junior officer under Cumberland during the Highland campaign—but did not know him personally. He'd heard a great deal about him, though.

"Grey, is it? Pardloe's brother, are you?" Wolfe lifted his long nose in Grey's direction, as though sniffing at him, in the manner of one dog inspecting another's backside. Grey trusted he would not be required to reciprocate and instead bowed politely.

"My brother's compliments, sir."

Actually, what his brother had had to say was far from complimentary.

"Melodramatic ass" was what Hal had said, hastily briefing him before his departure. "Showy, bad judgment, terrible strategist. Has the devil's own luck, though, I'll give him that. *Don't* follow him into anything stupid."

Wolfe nodded amiably enough.

"And you've come as a witness for who is it—Captain Carruthers?"

"Yes, sir. Has a date been set for the court-martial?"

"Dunno. Has it?" Wolfe asked his adjutant, a tall, spindly creature with a beady eye.

"No, sir. Now that his lordship is here, though, we can proceed. I'll tell Brigadier Lethbridge-Stewart; he's to chair the proceeding."

Wolfe waved a hand.

"No, wait a bit. The brigadier will have other things on his mind. 'Til after . . ."

The adjutant nodded and made a note.

"Yes, sir."

Wolfe was eyeing Grey, in the manner of a small boy bursting to share some secret.

"D'you understand Highlanders, Colonel?"

Grey blinked, surprised.

"Insofar as such a thing is possible, sir," he replied politely, and Wolfe brayed with laughter.

"Good man." The general turned his head to one side and appraised Grey. "I've got a hundred or so of the creatures; been thinking what use they might be. I think I've found one—a small adventure."

The adjutant smiled despite himself, then quickly erased the smile.

"Indeed, sir?" Grey said cautiously.

"Somewhat dangerous," Wolfe went on carelessly. "But, then, it's the Highlanders—no great mischief should they fall. Would you care to join us?"

"*Don't follow him into anything stupid.*" Right, Hal, he thought. Any suggestions on how to decline an offer like that from one's titular commander?

"I should be pleased, sir," he said, feeling a brief ripple of unease down his spine. "When?"

"In two weeks—at the dark of the moon." Wolfe was all but wagging his tail in enthusiasm.

"Am I permitted to know the nature of the . . . er . . . expedition?"

Wolfe exchanged a look of anticipation with his adjutant, then turned eyes shiny with excitement on Grey.

"We're going to take Quebec, Colonel."

SO WOLFE THOUGHT he had found his *point d'appui*. Or, rather, his trusted scout, Malcolm Stubbs, had found it for him. Grey returned briefly to his quarters, put the miniature of Olivia and little Cromwell in his pocket, and went to find Stubbs.

He didn't bother thinking what to say to Malcolm. It was as well, he thought, that he hadn't found Stubbs immediately after his discovery of the Indian mistress and her child; he might simply have knocked Stubbs down, without the bother of explanation. But time had elapsed, and his blood was cooler now. He was detached.

Or so he thought, until he entered a prosperous tavern—Malcolm had elevated tastes in wine—and found his cousin-by-marriage at a table, relaxed and jovial among his friends. Stubbs was aptly named, being approximately five foot four in both dimensions, a fair-haired fellow with an inclination to become red in the face when deeply entertained or deep in drink.

At the moment, he appeared to be experiencing both conditions, laughing at something one of his companions had said, waving his empty glass in the barmaid's direction. He turned back, spotted Grey coming across the floor, and lit up like a beacon. He'd been spending a good deal of time out of doors, Grey saw; he was nearly as sunburned as Grey himself.

"Grey!" he cried. "Why, here's a sight for sore eyes! What the devil brings you to the wilderness?" Then he noticed Grey's expression, and his joviality faded slightly, a puzzled frown growing between his thick brows.

It hadn't time to grow far. Grey lunged across the table, scattering glasses, and seized Stubbs by the shirtfront.

"You come with me, you bloody swine," he whispered, face shoved up against the younger man's, "or I'll kill you right here, I swear it."

He let go then and stood, blood hammering in his temples. Stubbs rubbed at his chest, affronted, startled—and afraid. Grey could see it in the wide blue eyes. Slowly, Stubbs got up, motioning to his companions to stay.

"No bother, chaps," he said, making a good attempt at casualness. "My cousin—family emergency, what?"

Grey saw two of the men exchange knowing glances, then look at Grey, wary. They knew, all right.

Stiffly, he gestured for Stubbs to precede him, and they passed out of the door in a pretense of dignity. Once outside, though, he grabbed Stubbs by the arm and dragged him round the corner into a small alleyway. He pushed Stubbs hard, so that he lost his balance and fell against the wall; Grey kicked his legs out from under him, then knelt on his thigh, digging his knee viciously into the thick muscle. Stubbs uttered a strangled noise, not quite a scream.

Grey dug in his pocket, hand trembling with fury, and brought out the miniature, which he showed briefly to Stubbs before grinding it into the man's cheek. Stubbs yelped, grabbed at it, and Grey let him have it, rising unsteadily off the man.

"How dare you?" he said, low-voiced and vicious. "How dare you dishonor your wife, your son?"

Malcolm was breathing hard, one hand clutching his abused thigh, but was regaining his composure.

'It's nothing," he said. "Nothing to do with Olivia at all." He swallowed, wiped a hand across his mouth, and took a cautious glance at the miniature in his hand. "That the sprat, is it? Good . . . good-looking lad. Looks like me, don't he?"

Grey kicked him brutally in the stomach.

"Yes, and so does your *other* son," he hissed. "How could you do such a thing?"

Malcolm's mouth opened, but nothing came out. He struggled for breath like a landed fish. Grey watched without pity. He'd have the man split and grilled over charcoal before he was done. He bent and took the miniature from Stubbs's unresisting hand, tucking it back in his pocket.

After a long moment, Stubbs achieved a whining gasp, and the color of his face, which had gone puce, subsided back toward its normal brick color. Saliva had collected at the corners of his mouth; he licked his lips, spat, then sat up, breathing heavily, and looked at Grey.

"Going to hit me again?"

"Not just yet."

"Good." He stretched out a hand, and Grey took it, grunting as he helped Stubbs to his feet. Malcolm leaned against the wall, still panting, and eyed him.

"So, who made you God, Grey? Who are you to sit in judgment of me, eh?"

Grey nearly hit him again but desisted.

"Who am *I*?" he echoed. "Olivia's fucking cousin, that's who! The nearest male relative she's got on this continent! And you, need I remind you—and evidently I do—are her fucking husband. Judgment? What the devil d'you mean by that, you filthy lecher?"

Malcolm coughed and spat again.

"Yes. Well. As I said, it's nothing to do with Olivia—and so it's nothing to do with you." He spoke with apparent calmness, but Grey could see the pulse hammering in his throat, the nervous shiftiness of his eyes. "It's nothing out of the ordinary—it's the bloody custom, for God's sake. Everybody—"

He kneed Stubbs in the balls.

"Try again," he advised Stubbs, who had fallen down and was curled into a fetal position, moaning. "Take your time; I'm not busy."

Aware of eyes upon him, Grey turned to see several soldiers gathered at the mouth of the alley, hesitating. He was still wearing his dress uniform, though—somewhat the worse for wear but clearly displaying his rank—and when he gave them an evil look, they hastily dispersed.

"I should kill you here and now, you know," he said to Stubbs after a few moments. The rage that had propelled him was draining away, though, as he watched the man retch and heave at his feet, and he spoke wearily. "Better for Olivia to have a dead husband, and whatever property you leave, than a live scoundrel, who will betray her with her friends—likely with her own maid."

Stubbs muttered something indistinguishable, and Grey bent, grasping him by the hair, and pulled his head up.

"What was that?"

"Wasn't . . . like that." Groaning and clutching himself, Malcolm maneuvered gingerly into a sitting position, knees drawn up. He gasped for a bit, head on his knees, before being able to go on.

"You don't know, do you?" He spoke low-voiced, not raising his head. "You haven't seen the things I've seen. Not . . . done what I've had to do."

"What do you mean?"

"The . . . the killing. Not . . . battle. Not an honorable thing. Farmers. Women . . ." Grey saw Stubbs's heavy throat move, swallowing. "I—we— for months now. Looting the countryside, burning farms, villages." He sighed, broad shoulders slumping. "The men, they don't mind. Half of them are brutes to begin with." He breathed. "Think . . . nothing of shooting a man on his doorstep and taking his wife next to his body." He swallowed. "'Tisn't only Montcalm who pays for scalps," he said in a low voice. Grey couldn't avoid hearing the rawness in his voice, a pain that wasn't physical.

"Every soldier's seen such things, Malcolm," he said after a short silence, almost gently. "You're an officer. It's your job to keep them in check." *And you know damned well it isn't always possible,* he thought.

"I know," Malcolm said, and began to cry. "I couldn't."

Grey waited while he sobbed, feeling increasingly foolish and uncomfortable. At last, the broad shoulders heaved and subsided. After a moment, Malcolm said, in a voice that quivered only a little, "Everybody finds a way, don't they? And there're not that many ways. Drink, cards, or women." He raised his head and shifted a bit, grimacing as he eased into a more comfortable position. "But you don't go in much for women, do you?" he added, looking up.

Grey felt the bottom of his stomach drop but realized in time that Malcolm had spoken matter-of-factly, with no tone of accusation.

"No," he said, and drew a deep breath. "Drink, mostly."

Malcolm nodded, wiping his nose on his sleeve.

"Drink doesn't help me," he said. "I fall asleep, but I don't forget. I just dream about . . . things. And whores—I—well, I didn't want to get poxed and maybe . . . well, Olivia," he muttered, looking down. "No good at cards," he said, clearing his throat. "But sleeping in a woman's arms—I can sleep then."

Grey leaned against the wall, feeling nearly as battered as Malcolm Stubbs. Pale green aspen leaves drifted through the air, whirling round them, settling in the mud.

"All right," he said eventually. "What do you mean to do?"

"Dunno," Stubbs said, in a tone of flat resignation. "Think of something, I suppose."

Grey reached down and offered a hand; Stubbs got carefully to his feet and, nodding to Grey, shuffled toward the alley's mouth, bent over and holding himself as though his insides might fall out. Halfway there, though, he stopped and looked back over his shoulder. There was an anxious look on his face, half embarrassed.

"Can I . . . The miniature? They are still mine, Olivia and the—my son."

Grey heaved a sigh that went to the marrow of his bones; he felt a thousand years old.

"Yes, they are," he said, and, digging the miniature out of his pocket, tucked it carefully into Stubbs's coat. "Remember it, will you?"

TWO DAYS LATER, a convoy of troop ships arrived, under the command of Admiral Holmes. The town was flooded afresh with men hungry for unsalted meat, fresh baked bread, liquor, and women. And a messenger arrived at Grey's quarters, bearing a parcel for him from his brother, with Admiral Holmes's compliments.

It was small but packaged with care, wrapped in oilcloth and tied about with twine, the knot sealed with his brother's crest. That was unlike Hal, whose usual communiqués consisted of hastily dashed-off notes, generally employing slightly fewer than the minimum number of words necessary to convey his message. They were seldom signed, let alone sealed.

Tom Byrd appeared to think the package slightly ominous, too; he had set it by itself, apart from the other mail, and weighted it down with a large bottle of brandy, apparently to prevent it escaping. That, or he suspected Grey might require the brandy to sustain him in the arduous effort of reading a letter consisting of more than one page.

"Very thoughtful of you, Tom," he murmured, smiling to himself and reaching for his penknife.

In fact, the letter within occupied less than a page, bore neither salutation nor signature, and was completely Hal-like.

> *Minnie wishes to know whether you are starving, though I don't know what she proposes to do about it, should the answer be yes.*
> *The boys wish to know whether you have taken any scalps—they are confident that no red Indian would succeed in taking yours; I share this opinion. You had better bring three tommyhawks when you come home.*
> *Here is your paperweight; the jeweler was most impressed by the quality of the stone. The other thing is a copy of Adams's confession. They hanged him yesterday.*

The other contents of the parcel consisted of a small washleather pouch and an official-looking document on several sheets of good parchment, this folded and sealed—this time with the insignia of George II. Grey left it lying on the table, fetched one of the pewter cups from his campaign chest, and filled it to the brim with brandy, wondering anew at his valet's perspicacity.

Thus fortified, he sat down and took up the little pouch, from which he decanted into his hand a small, heavy gold paperweight, made in the shape of a half-moon set among ocean waves. It was set with a faceted—and very large—sapphire, which glowed like the evening star in its setting. Where had James Fraser acquired such a thing?

He turned it in his hand, admiring the workmanship, but then set it aside. He sipped his brandy for a bit, watching the official document as though it might explode. He was reasonably sure it would.

He weighed the document in his hand and felt the breeze from his window lift the pages a little, like the flap of a sail just before it fills and bellies with a snap.

Waiting wouldn't help. And Hal plainly knew what it said, anyway; he'd tell Grey eventually, whether he wanted to know or not. Sighing, he put by his brandy and broke the seal.

I, Bernard Donald Adams, do make this confession of my own free will . . .

Was it? he wondered. He did not know Adams's handwriting, could not tell whether the document had been written or dictated—no, wait. He flipped over the sheets and examined the signature. Same hand. All right, he had written it himself.

He squinted at the writing. It seemed firm. Probably not extracted under torture, then. Perhaps it was the truth.

"Idiot," he said under his breath. "Read the goddamned thing and have done with it!"

He drank the rest of his brandy at a gulp, flattened the pages upon the stone of the parapet, and read, at last, the story of his father's death.

THE DUKE HAD suspected the existence of a Jacobite ring for some time and had identified three men whom he thought involved in it. Still, he made no move to expose them until the warrant was issued for his own arrest, upon the charge of treason. Hearing of this, he had sent at once to Adams, summoning him to the duke's country home at Earlingden.

Adams did not know how much the duke knew of his own involvement but did not dare to stay away, lest the duke, under arrest, denounce him. So he armed himself with a pistol and rode by night to Earlingden, arriving just before dawn.

He had come to the conservatory's outside doors and been admitted by the duke. Whereupon "some conversation" had ensued.

> *I had learned that day of the issuance of a warrant for arrest upon the charge of treason, to be served upon the body of the Duke of Pardloe. I was uneasy at this, for the duke had questioned both myself and some colleagues previously, in a manner that suggested to me that he suspected the existence of a secret movement to restore the Stuart throne.*
>
> *I argued against the duke's arrest, as I did not know the extent of his knowledge or suspicion, and feared that, if placed in exigent danger himself, he might be able to point a finger at myself or my principal colleagues, these being Victor Arbuthnot, Lord Creemore, and Sir Edwin Bellman. Sir Edwin was urgent upon the point, though, saying that it would do no harm; any accusations made by Pardloe could be dismissed as simple attempts to save himself, with no grounding in fact—while the fact of his arrest would naturally cause a widespread assumption of guilt and would distract any attentions that might at present be directed toward us.*
>
> *The duke, hearing of the warrant, sent to my lodgings that evening and summoned me to call upon him at his country home immediately. I dared not spurn this summons, not knowing what evidence he might possess, and therefore rode by night to his estate, arriving soon before dawn.*

Adams had met the duke there, in the conservatory. Whatever the form of this conversation, its result had been drastic.

> *I had brought with me a pistol, which I had loaded outside the house. I meant this only for protection, as I did not know what the duke's demeanor might be.*

Dangerous, evidently. Gerard Grey, Duke of Pardloe, had also come armed to the meeting. According to Adams, the duke had withdrawn his pistol from the recesses of his jacket—whether to attack or merely threaten was not clear—whereupon Adams had drawn his own pistol in panic. Both men fired; Adams thought the duke's pistol had misfired, since the duke could not have missed at the distance.

Adams's shot did not misfire, nor did it miss its target, and seeing the blood upon the duke's bosom, Adams had panicked and run. Looking back, he had seen the duke, mortally stricken but still upright, seize the branch of the peach tree beside him for support, whereupon the duke had used the last of his strength to hurl his own useless weapon at Adams before collapsing.

John Grey sat still, slowly rubbing the parchment sheets between his fingers. He wasn't seeing the neat strokes in which Adams had set down his bloodless account. He saw the blood. A dark red, beautiful as a jewel where the sun through the glass of the roof struck it suddenly. His father's hair, tousled as it might be after hunting. And the peach, fallen to those same tiles, its perfection spoiled and ruined.

He set the papers down on the table; the wind stirred them, and, by reflex, he reached for his new paperweight to hold them down.

What was it Carruthers had called him? Someone who keeps order. *"You and your brother,"* he'd said. *"You don't stand for that. If there is any order in the world, any peace—it's because of you, John, and those very few like you."*

Perhaps. He wondered if Carruthers knew the cost of peace and order—but then recalled Charlie's haggard face, its youthful beauty gone, nothing left in it now save the bones and the dogged determination that kept him breathing.

Yes, he knew.

NEARLY TWO WEEKS later, just after full dark, they boarded the ships. The convoy included Admiral Holmes's flagship, the *Lowestoff;* three men of war: the *Squirrel, Sea Horse,* and *Hunter;* a number of armed sloops; others loaded with ordnance, powder, and ammunition; and a number of transports for the troops—1,800 men in all. The *Sutherland* had been left below, anchored just out of firing range of the fortress, to keep an eye on the enemy's motions; the river there was littered with floating batteries and prowling small French craft.

Grey traveled with Wolfe and the Highlanders aboard *Sea Horse* and spent the journey on deck, too keyed up to bear being below.

His brother's warning kept recurring in the back of his mind—"Don't *follow him into anything stupid"*—but it was much too late to think of that, and, to block it out, he challenged one of the other officers to a whistling contest. Each party was to whistle the entirety of "The Roast Beef of Old England," the loser the man who laughed first. He lost, but did not think of his brother again.

Just after midnight, the big ships quietly furled their sails, dropped anchor, and lay like slumbering gulls on the dark river. Anse au Foulon, the landing spot that Malcolm Stubbs and his scouts had recommended to General Wolfe, lay seven miles downriver, at the foot of sheer and crumbling slate cliffs that led upward to the Plains of Abraham.

"Is it named for the biblical Abraham, do you think?" Grey had asked curiously, hearing the name, but had been informed that, in fact, the cliff top comprised a farmstead belonging to an ex-pilot named Abraham Martin.

On the whole, he thought this prosaic origin just as well. There was likely to be drama enough enacted on that ground, without thought of ancient prophets, conversations with God, nor any calculation of how many just men might be contained within the fortress of Quebec.

With a minimum of fuss, the Highlanders and their officers, Wolfe and his chosen troops—Grey among them—debarked into the small *bateaux* that would carry them silently down to the landing point.

The sounds of oars were mostly drowned by the river's rushing, and there was little conversation in the boats. Wolfe sat in the prow of the lead boat, facing his troops, looking now and then over his shoulder at the shore. Quite without warning, he began to speak. He didn't raise his voice, but the night was so still that those in the boat had little trouble in hearing him. To Grey's astonishment, he was reciting "Elegy Written in a Country Churchyard."

Melodramatic ass, Grey thought—and yet could not deny that the recitation was oddly moving. Wolfe made no show of it. It was as though he was simply talking to himself, and a shiver went over Grey as Wolfe intoned:

> *The boast of heraldry, the pomp of power,*
> *And all that beauty, all that wealth e'er gave,*
> *Awaits alike the inevitable hour.*

"The paths of glory lead but to the grave," Wolfe ended, so low-voiced that only the three or four men closest heard him. Grey was near enough to hear him clear his throat, with a small "hem" noise, and saw his shoulders lift.

"Gentlemen," Wolfe said, lifting his voice, as well, "I should rather have written those lines than have taken Quebec."

There was a faint stir and a breath of laughter among the men.

So would I, Grey thought. *The poet who wrote them is likely sitting by his cozy fire in Cambridge, eating buttered crumpets, not preparing to fall from a great height or get his arse shot off.*

He didn't know whether this was simply more of Wolfe's characteristic drama. Possibly—possibly not, he thought. He'd met Colonel Walsing by the latrines that morning, and Walsing had mentioned that Wolfe had given him a pendant the night before, with instructions to deliver it to Miss Landringham, to whom Wolfe was engaged.

But, then, it was nothing out of the ordinary for men to put their personal valuables into the care of a friend before a hot battle. Were you killed or badly injured, your body might be looted before your comrades managed to retrieve you, and not everyone had a trustworthy servant with whom to leave such items. Grey himself had often carried snuffboxes, pocket watches, or rings into battle for friends—he'd had a reputation for luck, prior to Crefeld. No one had asked him to carry anything tonight.

He shifted his weight by instinct, feeling the current change, and Simon Fraser, next to him, swayed in the opposite direction, bumping him.

"Pardon," Fraser murmured. Wolfe had made them all recite poetry in French round the dinner table the night before, and it was agreed that Fraser had the most authentic accent, he having fought with the French in Holland some years prior. Should they be hailed by a sentry, it would be his job to reply. Doubtless, Grey thought, Fraser was now thinking frantically in French, trying to saturate his mind with the language, lest any stray bit of English escape in panic.

"De rien," Grey murmured back, and Fraser chuckled, deep in his throat.

It was cloudy, the sky streaked with the shredded remnants of retreating rain clouds. That was good; the surface of the river was broken, patched with faint light, fractured by stones and drifting tree branches. Even so, a decent sentry could scarcely fail to spot a train of boats.

Cold numbed his face, but his palms were sweating. He touched the dagger at his belt again; he was aware that he touched it every few minutes, as if needing to verify its presence, but couldn't help it and didn't worry about it. He was straining his eyes, looking for anything—the glow of a careless fire, the shifting of a rock that was not a rock . . . Nothing.

How far? he wondered. Two miles, three? He'd not yet seen the cliffs himself, was not sure how far below Gareon they lay.

The rush of water and the easy movement of the boat began to make him sleepy, tension notwithstanding, and he shook his head, yawning exaggeratedly to throw it off.

"Quel est ce bateau?" What boat is that? The shout from the shore seemed anticlimactic when it came, barely more remarkable than a night bird's call. But the next instant Simon Fraser's hand crushed his, grinding the bones together, as Fraser gulped air and shouted, *"Celui de la Reine!!"*

Grey clenched his teeth, not to let any blasphemous response escape. If the sentry demanded a password, he'd likely be crippled for life, he thought. An instant later, though, the sentry shouted, *"Passez!"* and Fraser's death grip relaxed. Simon was breathing like a bellows but nudged him and whispered, *"Pardon,"* again.

"De fucking *rien,"* he muttered, rubbing his hand and tenderly flexing the fingers.

They were getting close. Men were shifting to and fro in anticipation, even more than Grey—checking their weapons, straightening coats, coughing, spitting over the side, readying themselves. Still, it was a nerve-wracking quarter-hour more before they began to swing toward shore— and another sentry called from the dark.

Grey's heart squeezed like a fist, and he nearly gasped with the twinge of pain from his old wounds.

"Qui etes-vous? Que sont ces bateaux?" a French voice demanded suspiciously. *Who are you? What boats are those?*

This time, he was ready and seized Fraser's hand himself. Simon held on and, leaning out toward the shore, called hoarsely, *"Des bateaux de provisions! Tasiez-vous—les anglais sont proches!"* *Provision boats! Be quiet—the British are nearby!* Grey felt an insane urge to laugh but didn't. In fact, the *Sutherland was* nearby, lurking out of cannon shot downstream, and doubtless the frogs knew it. In any case, the guard called, more quietly, *"Passez!"* and the train of boats slid smoothly past and round the final bend.

The bottom of the boat grated on sand, and half the men were over at once, tugging it farther up. Wolfe half-leapt, half-fell over the side in eagerness, all trace of somberness gone. They'd come aground on a small sandbar just offshore, and the other boats were beaching now, a swarm of black figures gathering like ants.

Twenty-four of the Highlanders were meant to try the ascent first, finding—and, insofar as possible, clearing, for the cliff was defended not only by its steepness but by abatis, nests of sharpened logs—a trail for the rest. Simon's bulky form faded into the dark, his French accent changing at once into the sibilant Gaelic as he hissed the men into position. Grey rather missed his presence.

He was not sure whether Wolfe had chosen the Highlanders for their skill at climbing or because he preferred to risk them rather than his other troops. The latter, he thought. Wolfe regarded the Highlanders with distrust and a certain contempt, as did most English officers. Those officers, at least, who'd never fought with them—or against them.

From his spot at the foot of the cliff, Grey couldn't see them, but he could hear them: the scuffle of feet, now and then a wild scrabble and a clatter of falling small stones, loud grunts of effort, and what he recognized as Gaelic invocations of God, his mother, and assorted saints. One man near him pulled a string of beads from the neck of his shirt, kissed the tiny cross attached to it, and tucked it back; then, seizing a small sapling that grew out of the rock face, he leapt upward, kilt swinging, broadsword swaying from his belt in brief silhouette, before the darkness took him. Grey touched his dagger's hilt again, his own talisman against evil.

It was a long wait in the darkness; to some extent he envied the Highlanders, who, whatever else they might be encountering—and the scrabbling noises and half-strangled whoops as a foot slipped and a comrade grabbed a hand or arm suggested that the climb was just as impossible as it seemed—were not dealing with boredom.

A sudden rumble and crashing came from above, and the shore party scattered in panic as several sharpened logs plunged out of the dark, dislodged from an abatis. One of them had struck point-down no more than six feet from Grey and stood quivering in the sand. With no discussion, the shore party retreated to the sandbar.

The scrabblings and gruntings grew fainter and abruptly ceased. Wolfe, who had been sitting on a boulder, stood up, straining his eyes upward.

"They've made it," he whispered, and his fists curled in an excitement that Grey shared. "God, they've made it!"

Well enough, and the men at the foot of the cliff held their breaths; there was a guard post at the top of the cliff. Silence, bar the everlasting noise of tree and river. And then a shot.

Just one. The men below shifted, touching their weapons, ready, not knowing for what.

Were there sounds above? Grey could not tell and, out of sheer nervousness, turned aside to urinate against the side of the cliff. He was fastening his flies when he heard Simon Fraser's voice above.

"Got 'em, by God!" he said. "Come on, lads—the night's not long enough!"

The next few hours passed in a blur of the most arduous endeavor Grey had seen since he'd crossed the Scottish Highlands with his brother's regiment, bringing cannon to General Cope. No, actually, he thought, as he stood in darkness, one leg wedged between a tree and the rock face, thirty feet of invisible space below him and rope burning through his palms with an unseen deadweight of two hundred pounds or so on the end, this was worse.

The Highlanders had surprised the guard, shot their fleeing captain in the heel, and made all of them prisoner. That was the easy part. The next thing was for the rest of the landing party to ascend to the cliff top, now that the trail—if there was such a thing—had been cleared. There they would make preparations to raise not only the rest of the troops now coming down the river aboard the transports but also seventeen battering cannon, twelve howitzers, three mortars, and all of the necessary encumbrances in terms of shell, powder, planks, and limbers necessary to make this artillery effective. At least, Grey reflected, by the time they were done, the vertical trail up the cliffside would likely have been trampled into a simple cow path.

As the sky lightened, Grey looked up for a moment from his spot at the top of the cliff, where he was now overseeing the last of the artillery as it was heaved over the edge, and saw the *bateaux* coming down again like a flock of swallows, they having crossed the river to collect an additional 1,200 troops that Wolfe had directed to march to Levi on the opposite shore, there to lie hidden in the woods until the Highlanders' expedient should have been proved.

A head, cursing freely, surged up over the edge of the cliff. Its attendant body lunged into view, tripped, and sprawled at Grey's feet.

"Sergeant Cutter!" Grey said, grinning as he bent to yank the little sergeant to his feet. "Come to join the party, have you?"

"Jesus fuck," replied the sergeant, belligerently brushing dirt from his coat. "We'd best win, that's all I can say." And, without waiting for reply, he turned round to bellow down the cliff, "Come ON, you bloody rascals! 'Ave you all eaten lead for breakfast, then? Shit it out and step lively! CLIMB, God damn your eyes!"

The net result of this monstrous effort being that, as dawn spread its golden glow across the Plains of Abraham, the French sentries on the walls of the Citadel of Quebec gaped in disbelief at the sight of more than four thousand British troops drawn up in battle array before them.

Through his telescope, Grey could see the sentries. The distance was too great to make out their facial expressions, but their attitudes of alarm and consternation were easy to read, and he grinned, seeing one French officer clutch his head briefly, then wave his arms like one dispelling a flock of chickens, sending his subordinates rushing off in all directions.

Wolfe was standing on a small hillock, long nose lifted as though to sniff the morning air. Grey thought he probably considered his pose noble and commanding; he reminded Grey of a dachshund scenting a badger; the air of alert eagerness was the same.

Wolfe wasn't the only one. Despite the ardors of the night, skinned hands, battered shins, twisted knees and ankles, and a lack of food and sleep, a gleeful excitement ran through the troops like wine. Grey thought they were all giddy with fatigue.

The sound of drums came faintly to him on the wind: the French, beating hastily to quarters. Within minutes, he saw horsemen streaking away from the fortress, and he smiled grimly. They were going to rally whatever troops Montcalm had within summoning distance, and Grey felt a tightening of the belly at the sight.

The matter hadn't really been in doubt; it was September, and winter was coming on. The town and fortress had been unable to provision themselves for a long siege, owing to Wolfe's scorched-earth policies. The French were there, the English before them—and the simple fact, apparent to both sides, was that the French would starve long before the English did. Montcalm would fight; he had no choice.

Many of the men had brought canteens of water, some a little food. They were allowed to relax sufficiently to eat, to ease their muscles— though none of them ever took their attention from the French gathering before the fortress. Employing his telescope further, Grey could see that, while the mass of milling men was growing, they were by no means all trained troops; Montcalm had called his militias from the countryside— farmers, fishermen, and *coureurs du bois,* by the look of them—and his Indians. Grey eyed the painted faces and oiled topknots warily, but his acquaintance with Manoke had deprived the Indians of much of their terrifying aspect—and they would not be nearly so effective on open ground, against cannon, as they were sneaking through the forest.

It took surprisingly little time for Montcalm to ready his troops, impromptu as they might be. The sun was no more than halfway up the sky when the French lines began their advance.

"HOLD your fucking fire, you villains! Fire before you're ordered, and I'll give your fuckin' heads to the artillery to use for cannonballs!" He heard the unmistakable voice of Sergeant Aloysius Cutter, some distance back but clearly audible. The same order was being echoed, if less picturesquely, through the British lines, and if every officer on the field had one eye firmly on the French, the other was fixed on General Wolfe, standing on his hillock, aflame with anticipation.

Grey felt his blood twitch and moved restlessly from foot to foot, trying to ease a cramp in one leg. The advancing French line stopped, knelt, and fired a volley. Another from the line standing behind them. Too far, much too far to have any effect. A deep rumble came from the British troops— something visceral and hungry.

Grey's hand had been on his dagger for so long that the wire-wrapped hilt had left its imprint on his fingers. His other hand was clenched upon a saber. He had no command here, but the urge to raise his sword, gather the eyes of his men, hold them, focus them, was overwhelming. He shook his shoulders to loosen them and glanced at Wolfe.

Another volley, close enough this time that several British soldiers in the front lines fell, knocked down by musket fire.

"Hold, hold!" The order rattled down the lines like gunfire. The brimstone smell of slow match was thick, pungent above the scent of powder smoke; the artillerymen held their fire, as well.

French cannon fired, and balls bounced murderously across the field, but they seemed puny, ineffectual, despite the damage they did. How many French? he wondered. Perhaps twice as many, but it didn't matter. It wouldn't matter.

Sweat ran down his face, and he rubbed a sleeve across to clear his eyes. "Hold!"

Closer, closer. Many of the Indians were on horseback; he could see them in a knot on the left, milling. Those would bear watching. . . .

"Hold!"

Wolfe's arm rose slowly, sword in hand, and the army breathed deep. His beloved grenadiers were next to him, solid in their companies, wrapped in sulfurous smoke from the match tubes at their belts.

"Come on, you buggers," the man next to Grey was muttering. "Come on, come on!"

Smoke was drifting over the field, low white clouds. Forty paces. Effective range.

"Don't fire, don't fire, don't fire . . ." someone was chanting to himself, struggling against panic.

Through the British lines, sun glinted on the rising swords, the officers echoing Wolfe's order.

"Hold . . . hold . . ."

The swords fell as one.

"FIRE!" and the ground shook.

A shout rose in Grey's throat, part of the roar of the army, and he was charging with the men near him, swinging his saber with all his might, finding flesh.

The volley had been devastating; bodies littered the ground. He leapt over a fallen Frenchman, brought his saber down upon another, caught halfway in the act of loading, took him in the cleft between neck and shoulder, yanked his saber free of the falling man, and went on.

The British artillery was firing as fast as the guns could be served. Each boom shook his flesh. He gritted his teeth, squirmed aside from the point of a half-seen bayonet, and found himself panting, eyes watering from the smoke, standing alone.

Chest heaving, he turned round in a circle, disoriented. There was so much smoke around him that he could not for a moment tell where he was. It didn't matter.

An enormous blur of something passed him, shrieking, and he dodged by instinct and fell to the ground as the horse's feet churned by. Grey heard as an echo the Indian's grunt, the rush of the tomahawk blow that had missed his head.

"Shit," he muttered, and scrambled to his feet.

The grenadiers were hard at work nearby; he heard their officers' shouts, the bang and pop of their explosions as they worked their way stolidly through the French like the small mobile batteries they were.

A grenade struck the ground a few feet away, and he felt a sharp pain in his thigh; a metal fragment had sliced through his breeches, drawing blood.

"Christ," he said, belatedly aware that being in the vicinity of a company of grenadiers was not a good idea. He shook his head to clear it and made his way away from them.

He heard a familiar sound that made him recoil for an instant from the force of memory—wild Highland screams, filled with rage and berserk glee. The Highlanders were hard at work with their broadswords—he saw two of them appear from the smoke, bare legs churning beneath their kilts, pursuing a pack of fleeing Frenchman, and felt laughter bubble up through his heaving chest.

He didn't see the man in the smoke. His foot struck something heavy and he fell, sprawling across the body. The man screamed, and Grey scrambled hastily off him.

"Sorry. Are you—Christ, Malcolm!"

He was on his knees, bending low to avoid the smoke. Stubbs was gasping, grasping desperately at Grey's coat.

"Jesus." Malcolm's right leg was gone below the knee, flesh shredded and the white bone splintered, butcher-stained with spurting blood. Or . . . no. It wasn't gone. It—the foot, at least—was lying a little way beyond, still clad in shoe and tattered stocking.

Grey turned his head and threw up.

Bile stinging the back of his nose, he choked and spat, turned back, and grappled with his belt, wrenching it free.

"Don't—" Stubbs gasped, putting out a hand as Grey began wrapping the belt round his thigh. His face was whiter than the bone of his leg. "Don't. Better—better if I die."

"The devil you will," Grey replied briefly.

His hands were shaking, slippery with blood. It took three tries to get the end of the belt through the buckle, but it went at last, and he jerked it tight, eliciting a yell from Stubbs.

"Here," said an unfamiliar voice by his ear. "Let's get him off. I'll— shit!" He looked up, startled, to see a tall British officer lunge upward, blocking the musket butt that would have brained Grey. Without thinking, he drew his dagger and stabbed the Frenchman in the leg. The man screamed, his leg buckling, and the strange officer pushed him over, kicked him in the face, and stamped on his throat, crushing it.

"I'll help," the man said calmly, bending to take hold of Malcolm's arm, pulling him up. "Take the other side; we'll get him to the back."

They got Malcolm up, his arms round their shoulders, and dragged him, paying no heed to the Frenchman thrashing and gurgling on the ground behind them.

Malcolm lived, long enough to make it to the rear of the lines, where the army surgeons were already at work. By the time Grey and the other officer had turned him over to the surgeons, the battle was over.

Grey turned to see the French scattered and demoralized, fleeing toward the fortress. British troops were flooding across the trampled field, cheering, overrunning the abandoned French cannon.

The entire battle had lasted less than a quarter of an hour.

He found himself sitting on the ground, his mind quite blank, with no notion how long he had been there, though he supposed it couldn't have been much time at all.

He noticed an officer standing near him and thought vaguely that the man seemed familiar. Who . . . Oh, yes. Wolfe's adjutant. He'd never learned the man's name.

He stood up slowly, stiff as a nine-day pudding.

The adjutant was simply standing there. His eyes were turned in the direction of the fortress and the fleeing French, but Grey could tell that he wasn't really seeing either. Grey glanced over his shoulder, toward the hillock where Wolfe had stood earlier, but the general was nowhere in sight.

"General Wolfe?" he said.

"The general . . ." the adjutant said, and swallowed thickly. "He was struck."

Of course he was, silly ass, Grey thought uncharitably. *Standing up there like a bloody target, what could he expect?* But then he saw the tears standing in the adjutant's eyes and understood.

"Dead, then?" he asked, stupidly, and the adjutant—why had he never thought to ask the man's name?—nodded, rubbing a smoke-stained sleeve across a smoke-stained countenance.

"He . . . In the wrist first. Then in the body. He fell and crawled—then he fell again. I turned him over . . . told him the battle was won, the French were scattered."

"He understood?"

The adjutant nodded and took a deep breath that rattled in his throat. "He said—" He stopped and coughed, then went on more firmly. "He said that in knowing he had conquered, he was content to die."

"Did he?" Grey said blankly. He'd seen men die, often, and imagined it much more likely that if James Wolfe had managed anything beyond an inarticulate groan, his final word had likely been either "shit," or "oh, God," depending upon the general's religious leanings, of which Grey had no notion.

"Yes, good," he said meaninglessly, and turned toward the fortress. Ant trails of men were streaming toward it, and in the midst of one such stream he saw Montcalm's colors, fluttering in the wind. Below the colors, small in the distance, a man in general's uniform rode his horse, hatless, hunched and swaying in the saddle, his officers bunched close on either side, anxious lest he fall.

The British lines were reorganizing, though it was clear no further fighting would be required. Not today. Nearby, he saw the tall officer who had saved his life and helped him to drag Malcolm Stubbs to safety, limping back toward his troops.

"The major over there," he said, nudging the adjutant and nodding. "Do you know his name?"

The adjutant blinked, then firmed his shoulders.

"Yes, of course. That's Major Siverly."

"Oh. Well, it would be, wouldn't it?"

ADMIRAL HOLMES, third in command after Wolfe, accepted the surrender of Quebec five days later, Wolfe and his second, Brigadier Monckton, having perished in battle. Montcalm was dead, too; had died the morning following the battle. There was no way out for the French save surrender; winter was coming on, and the fortress and its city would starve long before its besiegers.

Two weeks after the battle, John Grey returned to Gareon and found that smallpox had swept through the village like an autumn wind. The mother of Malcolm Stubbs's son was dead; her mother offered to sell him the child. He asked her politely to wait.

Charlie Carruthers had perished, too, the smallpox not waiting for the weakness of his body to overcome him. Grey had the body burned, not wishing Carruthers's hand to be stolen, for both the Indians and the local *habitants* regarded such things superstitiously. He took a canoe by himself and, on a deserted island in the St. Lawrence, scattered his friend's ashes to the wind.

He returned from this expedition to discover a letter, forwarded by Hal, from Dr. John Hunter, surgeon and anatomist. He checked the level of brandy in the decanter and opened it with a sigh.

My dear Lord John,

I have heard some recent conversation regarding the unfortunate death of Mr. Nicholls, including comments indicating a public perception that you were responsible for his death. In case you shared

*this perception, I thought it might ease your mind to know that in
fact you were not.*

Grey sank slowly onto a stool, eyes glued to the sheet.

*It is true that your ball did strike Mr. Nicholls, but this accident
contributed little or nothing to his demise. I saw you fire upward
into the air—I said as much to those present at the time, though most
of them did not appear to take much notice. The ball apparently
went up at a slight angle and then fell upon Mr. Nicholls from above.
At this point, its power was quite spent, and, the missile itself being
negligible in size and weight, it barely penetrated the skin above
his collarbone, where it lodged against the bone, doing no further
damage.*

*The true cause of his collapse and death was an aortic aneurysm,
a weakness in the wall of one of the great vessels emergent from
the heart; such weaknesses are often congenital. The stress of the
electric shock and the emotion of the duello that followed apparently
caused this aneurysm to rupture. Such an occurrence is untreatable
and invariably fatal, I am afraid. There is nothing that could
have saved him.*

*Your servant,
John Hunter, Surgeon*

Grey was conscious of a most extraordinary array of sensations. Relief—
yes, there was a sense of profound relief, as of waking from a nightmare.
There was also a sense of injustice, colored by the beginnings of indignation; by God, he had nearly been married! He might, of course, also have
been maimed or killed as a result of the imbroglio, but that seemed relatively inconsequent; he was a soldier, after all—such things happened.

His hand trembled slightly as he set the note down. Beneath relief,
gratitude, and indignation was a growing sense of horror.

I thought it might ease your mind . . . He could see Hunter's face saying
this; sympathetic, intelligent, and cheerful. It was a straightforward remark but one fully cognizant of its own irony.

Yes, he was pleased to know he had not caused Edwin Nicholls's death.
But the means of that knowledge . . . Gooseflesh rose on his arms and he
shuddered involuntarily, imagining—

"Oh, God," he said. He'd been once to Hunter's house—to a poetry
reading, held under the auspices of Mrs. Hunter, whose salons were famous. Dr. Hunter did not attend these but sometimes would come down
from his part of the house to greet guests. On this occasion, he had done
so and, falling into conversation with Grey and a couple of other scientifi-

cally minded gentlemen, had invited them up to see some of the more interesting items of his famous collection: the rooster with a transplanted human tooth growing in its comb, the child with two heads, the fetus with a foot protruding from its stomach.

Hunter had made no mention of the walls of jars, these filled with eyeballs, fingers, sections of livers . . . or of the two or three complete human skeletons that hung from the ceiling, fully articulated and fixed by a bolt through the tops of their skulls. It had not occurred to Grey at the time to wonder where—or how—Hunter had acquired these.

Nicholls had had an eyetooth missing, the front tooth beside the empty space badly chipped. If he ever visited Hunter's house again, might he come face-to-face with a skull with a missing tooth?

He seized the brandy decanter, uncorked it, and drank directly from it, swallowing slowly and repeatedly, until the vision disappeared.

His small table was littered with papers. Among them, under his sapphire paperweight, was the tidy packet that the widow Lambert had handed him, her face blotched with weeping. He put a hand on it, feeling Charlie's doubled touch, gentle on his face, soft around his heart.

"You won't fail me."

"No," he said softly. "No, Charlie, I won't."

WITH MANOKE'S HELP as translator, Grey bought the child, after prolonged negotiation, for two golden guineas, a brightly colored blanket, a pound of sugar, and a small keg of rum. The grandmother's face was sunken, not with grief, he thought, but with dissatisfaction and weariness. With her daughter dead of the smallpox, her life would be harder. The English, she conveyed to Grey through Manoke, were cheap bastards; the French were much more generous. He resisted the impulse to give her another guinea.

It was full autumn now, and the leaves had all fallen. The bare branches of the trees spread black ironwork flat against a pale-blue sky as he made his way upward through the town, to the French mission. There were several small buildings surrounding the tiny church, with children playing outside; some of them paused to look at him, but most of them ignored him—British soldiers were nothing new.

Father LeCarré took the bundle gently from him, turning back the blanket to look at the child's face. The boy was awake; he pawed at the air, and the priest put out a finger for him to grasp.

"Ah," he said, seeing the clear signs of mixed blood, and Grey knew the priest thought the child was his. He started to explain, but, after all, what did it matter?

"We will baptize him as a Catholic, of course," Father LeCarré said, looking up at Grey. The priest was a young man, rather plump, dark, and clean-shaven, but with a gentle face. "You do not mind that?"

"No." Grey drew out a purse. "For his maintenance. I will send an additional five pounds each year, if you will advise me once a year of his continued welfare. Here—the address to which to write." A sudden inspiration struck him—not that he did not trust the good father, he assured himself, only . . . "Send me a lock of his hair," he said. "Every year."

He was turning to go when the priest called him back, smiling.

"Has the infant a name, sir?"

"A—" He stopped dead. The boy's mother had surely called him something, but Malcolm Stubbs hadn't thought to tell Grey what it was before being shipped back to England. What should he call the child? Malcolm, for the father who had abandoned him? Hardly.

Charles, maybe, in memory of Carruthers . . .

". . . one of these days, it isn't going to."

"His name is John," he said abruptly, and cleared his throat. "John Cinnamon."

"Mais oui," the priest said, nodding. *"Bon voyage, Monsieur—et voyez avec le Bon Dieu."*

"Thank you," he said politely, and went away, not looking back, down to the riverbank where Manoke waited to bid him farewell.

AUTHOR'S NOTES

THE BATTLE OF QUEBEC IS JUSTLY FAMOUS AS ONE of the great military triumphs of the eighteenth-century British Army. If you go today to the battlefield at the Plains of Abraham (in spite of this poetic name, it really was just named for the farmer who owned the land, one Abraham Martin; I suppose "The Plains of Martin" just didn't have the same ring to it), you'll see a plaque at the foot of the cliff there, commemorating the heroic achievement of the Highland troops who climbed this sheer cliff from the river below, clearing the way for the entire army—*and* their cannon, mortars, howitzers, and accompanying impedimenta—to make a harrowing overnight ascent and confront General Montcalm with a jaw-dropping spectacle by the dawn's early light.

If you go up onto the field itself, you'll find another plaque, this one put up by the French, explaining (in French) what a dirty, unsportsmanlike trick this was for those sneaky British to have played on the noble troops defending the Citadel. Ah, perspective.

General James Wolfe, along with Montcalm, was of course a real historical character, as was Brigadier Simon Fraser (whom you will have met—or will meet later—in *An Echo in the Bone*). My own rule of thumb when dealing with historical persons in the context of fiction is to try not to portray them as having done anything worse than what I *know* they did, according to the historical record.

In General Wolfe's case, Hal's opinion of his character and abilities is one commonly held and recorded by a number of contemporary military commentators. And there is documentary proof of his attitude toward the Highlanders, whom he used for this endeavor, in the form of the letter quoted in the story: ". . . no great mischief if they fall." (Allow me to recommend a wonderful novel by Alistair MacLeod, titled *No Great Mischief*. It isn't about Wolfe; it's a novelized history of a family of Scots who settle in Nova Scotia, beginning in the eighteenth century and carrying on through the decades, but it is from Wolfe's letter that the book takes its title, and he's mentioned.)

Wolfe's policy with regard to the *habitant* villages surrounding the Citadel (looting, burning, general terrorizing of the populace) is a matter of record. It wasn't (and isn't) an unusual thing for an invading army to do.

General Wolfe's dying words are also a matter of historical record, but like Lord John, I take leave to doubt that that's really what he said. He *is* reported by several sources to have recited Gray's "Elegy Written in a Country Churchyard" in the boat on the way to battle— and I think that's a sufficiently odd thing to have done, that the reports are probably true.

As for Simon Fraser, he's widely reported to have been the British officer who fooled the French lookouts by calling out to them in French as the boats went by in the darkness—and he undoubtedly spoke excellent French, having campaigned in France years before. As for the details of exactly what he said—accounts vary, and that's not really an important detail, so I rolled my own.

Now, speaking of French . . . Brigadier Fraser spoke excellent French. I don't. I can read that language, but I can't speak or write it, possess absolutely no grammar, and have a really low tolerance for diacritical marks. So for the purposes of this story I did as I always do in such cases; I solicit the opinions of several native speakers of French for those bits of dialogue that occur in that language. What you see in this story is due to the assistance of these kind and helpful speakers. I fully expect—because it happens every time I include French in a story—to receive indignant email from assorted French speakers denouncing the French dialogue. If the French was provided to me by a Parisian, someone from Montreal will tell me *that's* not right; if the original source was *Quebecois,* outraged screams emanate from the mother country. And if it came from a textbook or (*quelle horreur*) an academic source . . . well, *bonne chance* with that. There's also the consideration that it's very difficult to spot typographical errors in a language you can't speak. But we do our best. My apologies for anything egregious.

Now, you may notice that John Hunter is referred to in various places either as "Mr. Hunter," or as "Dr. Hunter." By long-standing tradition, English surgeons are (and were) addressed as "Mr." rather than "Dr."—presumably a nod to their origins as barbers with a sanguinary sideline. However, John Hunter, with his brother William, was also a formally trained physician, as well as an eminent scientist and anatomist—hence entitled also to the honorific "Dr."

THE SPACE BETWEEN

INTRODUCTION

The Comte St. Germain

THERE WAS AN HISTORICAL PERSON (QUITE POSSI-bly more than one) who went by this name. There are also numerous reports (mostly unverified) of a person by this name who appears in various parts of Europe over parts of two centuries. These observations have led some to speculate that the Comte (or *a* Comte of that name) was a practitioner of the occult, a mystic, or even a time traveler.

Let's put it this way: The Comte St. Germain in this story is not intended to portray the documented historical person of that name.

HE STILL DIDN'T KNOW why the frog hadn't killed him. Paul Rakoczy, Comte St. Germain, picked up the vial, pulled the cork, and sniffed cautiously, for the third time, but then recorked it, still dissatisfied. Maybe. Maybe not. The scent of the dark-gray powder in the vial held the ghost of something familiar—but it had been thirty years.

He sat for a moment, frowning at the array of jars, bottles, flasks, and pelicans on his workbench. It was late afternoon, and the early spring sun of Paris was like honey, warm and sticky on his face, but glowing in the rounded globes of glass, throwing pools of red and brown and green on the wood from the liquids contained therein. The only discordant note in this peaceful symphony of light was the body of a large rat, lying on its back in the middle of the workbench, a pocket watch open beside it.

The comte put two fingers delicately on the rat's chest and waited patiently. It didn't take so long this time; he was used to the coldness as his mind felt its way into the body. Nothing. No hint of light in his mind's eye, no warm red of a pulsing heart. He glanced at the watch: half an hour.

He took his fingers away, shaking his head.

"Mélisande, you evil bitch," he murmured, not without affection. "You didn't think I'd try anything *you* sent me on myself, did you?"

Still . . . he himself had stayed dead a great while longer than half an hour when the frog had given him the dragon's blood. It had been early evening when he went into Louis's Star Chamber thirty years before, heart beating with excitement at the coming confrontation—a duel of wizards, with a king's favor as the stakes—and one he'd thought he'd win. He remembered the purity of the sky, the beauty of the stars just visible, Venus bright on the horizon, and the joy of it in his blood. Everything always had a greater intensity when you knew life could cease within the next few minutes.

And an hour later he thought his life *had* ceased, the cup falling from his numbed hand, the coldness rushing through his limbs with amazing speed, freezing the words "I've lost," an icy core of disbelief in the center of his mind. He hadn't been looking at the frog; the last thing he had seen through darkening eyes was the woman—La Dame Blanche—her face over the cup she'd given him appalled and white as bone. But what he recalled, and recalled again now, with the same sense of astonishment and avidity, was the great flare of blue, intense as the color of the evening sky beyond Venus, that had burst from her head and shoulders as he died.

He didn't recall any feeling of regret or fear, just astonishment. This was nothing, however, to the astonishment he'd felt when he regained his senses, naked on a stone slab in a revolting subterranean chamber next to a drowned corpse. Luckily, there had been no one alive in that disgusting grotto, and he had made his way—reeling and half blind, clothed in the drowned man's wet and stinking shirt—out into a dawn more beautiful than any twilight could ever be. So—ten to twelve hours from the moment of apparent death to revival.

He glanced at the rat, then put out a finger and lifted one of the small, neat paws. Nearly twelve hours. Limp; the rigor had already passed. It was warm up here at the top of the house. Then he turned to the counter that ran along the far wall of the laboratory, where a line of rats lay, possibly insensible, probably dead. He walked slowly along the line, prodding each body. Limp, limp, stiff. Stiff. Stiff. All dead, without doubt. Each had had a smaller dose than the last, but all had died—though he couldn't yet be positive about the latest. Wait a bit more, then, to be sure.

He needed to know. Because the Court of Miracles was talking. And they said the frog was back.

The English Channel

THEY DID SAY that red hair was a sign of the devil. Joan eyed her escort's fiery locks consideringly. The wind on deck was fierce enough to make her eyes water, and it jerked bits of Michael Murray's hair out of its binding so they did dance round his head like flames, a bit. You might expect his face to be ugly as sin if he was one of the devil's, though, and it wasn't.

Lucky for him, he looked like his mother in the face, she thought critically. His younger brother, Ian, wasn't so fortunate, and that without the heathen tattoos. Michael's was a fairly pleasant face, for all it was blotched with windburn and the lingering marks of sorrow, and no wonder, him having just lost his father, and his wife dead in France no more than a month before that.

But she wasn't braving this gale in order to watch Michael Murray, even if he might burst into tears or turn into Auld Horny on the spot. She touched her crucifix for reassurance, just in case. It had been blessed by the priest, and her mother'd carried it all the way to St. Ninian's Spring and dipped it in the water there, to ask the saint's protection. And it was her mother she wanted to see, as long as ever she could.

She pulled her kerchief off and waved it, keeping a tight grip lest the wind make off with it. Her mother was growing smaller on the quay, waving madly, too, Joey behind her with his arm round her waist to keep her from falling into the water.

Joan snorted a bit at sight of her new stepfather but then thought better and touched the crucifix again, muttering a quick Act of Contrition in penance. After all, it was she herself who'd made that marriage happen, and a good thing, too. If not, she'd still be stuck to home at Balriggan, not on her way at last to be a Bride of Christ in France.

A nudge at her elbow made her glance aside, to see Michael offering her a handkerchief. Well, so. If her eyes were streaming—aye, *and* her nose—it was no wonder, the wind so fierce as it was. She took the scrap of cloth with a curt nod of thanks, scrubbed briefly at her cheeks, and waved her kerchief harder.

None of his family had come to see Michael off, not even his twin sister, Janet. But they were taken up with all there was to do in the wake of Old Ian Murray's death, and no wonder. No need to see Michael to the ship, either—Michael Murray was a wine merchant in Paris, and a wonderfully well-traveled gentleman. She took some comfort from the knowledge that he knew what to do and where to go and had said he would see her safely delivered to the Convent of Angels, because the thought of making her way through Paris alone and the streets full of people all speaking French— though she knew French quite well, of course. She'd been studying it all the winter, and Michael's mother helping her—though perhaps she had better not tell the reverend mother about the sorts of French novels Jenny Murray had in her bookshelf, because . . .

"Voulez-vous descendre, mademoiselle?"

"Eh?" She glanced at him, to see him gesturing toward the hatchway that led downstairs. She turned back, blinking—but the quay had vanished, and her mother with it.

"No," she said. "Not yet. I'll just . . ." She wanted to see the land so long as she could. It would be her last sight of Scotland, ever, and the thought made her wame curl into a small, tight ball. She waved a vague hand toward the hatchway. "You go, though. I'm all right by myself."

He didn't go but came to stand beside her, gripping the rail. She turned away from him a little, so he wouldn't see her weep, but on the whole she wasn't sorry he'd stayed.

Neither of them spoke, and the land sank slowly, as though the sea swallowed it, and there was nothing round them now but the open sea, glassy gray and rippling under a scud of clouds. The prospect made her dizzy, and she closed her eyes, swallowing.

Dear Lord Jesus, don't let me be sick!

A small shuffling noise beside her made her open her eyes, to find Michael Murray regarding her with some concern.

"Are ye all right, Miss Joan?" He smiled a little. "Or should I call ye Sister?"

"No," she said, taking a grip on her nerve and her stomach and drawing herself up. "I'm no a nun yet, am I?"

He looked her up and down, in the frank way Hieland men did, and smiled more broadly.

"Have ye ever *seen* a nun?" he asked.

"I have not," she said, as starchily as she could. "I havena seen God or the Blessed Virgin, either, but I believe in them, too."

Much to her annoyance, he burst out laughing. Seeing the annoyance, though, he stopped at once, though she could see the urge still trembling there behind his assumed gravity.

"I do beg your pardon, Miss MacKimmie," he said. "I wasna questioning the existence of nuns. I've seen quite a number of the creatures with my own eyes." His lips were twitching, and she glared at him.

"Creatures, is it?"

"A figure of speech, nay more, I swear it! Forgive me, Sister—I ken not what I do!" He held up a hand, cowering in mock terror. The urge to laugh made her that much more cross, but she contented herself with a simple "mmphm" of disapproval.

Curiosity got the better of her, though, and after a few moments spent inspecting the foaming wake of the ship, she asked, not looking at him, "When ye saw the nuns, then—what were they doing?"

He'd got control of himself by now and answered her seriously.

"Well, I see the Sisters of Notre Dame, who work among the poor all the time in the streets. They always go out by twos, ken, and both nuns will be carrying great huge baskets, filled with food, I suppose—maybe medicines? They're covered, though—the baskets—so I canna say for sure what's in them. Perhaps they're smuggling brandy and lace down to the docks—" He dodged aside from her upraised hand, laughing.

"Oh, ye'll be a rare nun, Sister Joan! *Terror daemonum, solatium miserorum . . .*"

She pressed her lips tight together, not to laugh. Terror of demons—the cheek of him!

"Not Sister Joan," she said. "They'll give me a new name, likely, at the convent."

"Oh, aye?" He wiped hair out of his eyes, interested. "D'ye get to choose the name yourself?"

"I don't know," she admitted.

"Well, though—what name would ye pick, if ye had the choosing?"

"Er . . . well . . ." She hadn't told anyone, but, after all, what harm could it do? She wouldn't see Michael Murray again once they reached Paris. "Sister Gregory," she blurted.

Rather to her relief, he didn't laugh.

"Oh, that's a good name," he said. "After St. Gregory the Great, is it?"

"Well . . . aye. Ye don't think it's presumptuous?" she asked, a little anxious.

"Oh, no!" he said, surprised. "I mean, how many nuns are named Mary? If it's not presumptuous to be named after the mother o' God, how can it be highfalutin to call yourself after a mere pope?" He smiled at that, so merrily that she smiled back.

"How many nuns *are* named Mary?" she asked, out of curiosity. "It's common, is it?"

"Oh, aye, ye said ye'd not seen a nun." He'd stopped making fun of her, though, and answered seriously. "About half the nuns I've met seem to be called Sister Mary Something—ye ken, Sister Mary Polycarp, Sister Mary Joseph . . . like that."

"And ye meet a great many nuns in the course o' your business, do ye?" Michael Murray was a wine merchant, the junior partner of Fraser *et Cie*— and, judging from the cut of his clothes, did well enough at it.

His mouth twitched, but he answered seriously.

"Well, I do, really. Not every day, I mean, but the sisters come round to my office quite often—or I go to them. Fraser *et Cie* supplies wine to most o' the monasteries and convents in Paris, and some will send a pair of nuns to place an order or to take away something special—otherwise, we deliver it, of course. And even the orders who dinna take wine themselves—and most of the Parisian houses do, they bein' French, aye?—need sacramental wine for their chapels. And the begging orders come round like clockwork to ask alms."

"Really." She was fascinated: sufficiently so as to put aside her reluctance to look ignorant. "I didna ken . . . I mean . . . so the different orders do quite different things, is that what ye're saying? What other kinds are there?"

He shot her a brief glance but then turned back, narrowing his eyes against the wind as he thought.

"Well . . . there's the sort of nun that prays all the time—contemplative, I think they're called. I see them in the cathedral all hours of the day and night. There's more than one order of that sort, though; one kind wears gray habits and prays in the chapel of St. Joseph, and another wears black;

ye see them mostly in the chapel of Our Lady of the Sea." He glanced at her, curious. "Will it be that sort of nun that you'll be?"

She shook her head, glad that the wind-chafing hid her blushes.

"No," she said, with some regret. "That's maybe the holiest sort of nun, but I've spent a good bit o' my life being contemplative on the moors, and I didna like it much. I think I havena got the right sort of soul to do it verra well, even in a chapel."

"Aye," he said, and wiped back flying strands of hair from his face. "I ken the moors. The wind gets into your head after a bit." He hesitated for a moment. "When my uncle Jamie—your da, I mean—ye ken he hid in a cave after Culloden?"

"For seven years," she said, a little impatient. "Aye, everyone kens that story. Why?"

He shrugged.

"Only thinking. I was no but a wee bairn at the time, but I went now and then wi' my mam, to take him food there. He'd be glad to see us, but he wouldna talk much. And it scared me to see his eyes."

Joan felt a small shiver pass down her back, nothing to do with the stiff breeze. She saw—suddenly *saw*, in her head—a thin, dirty man, the bones starting in his face, crouched in the dank, frozen shadows of the cave.

"Da?" she scoffed, to hide the shiver that crawled up her arms. "How could anyone be scairt of him? He's a dear, kind man."

Michael's wide mouth twitched at the corners.

"I suppose it would depend whether ye'd ever seen him in a fight. But—"

"Have you?" she interrupted, curious. "Seen him in a fight?"

"I have, aye. BUT—" he said, not willing to be distracted, "I didna mean *he* scared me. It was that I thought he was haunted. By the voices in the wind."

That dried up the spit in her mouth, and she worked her tongue a little, hoping it didn't show. She needn't have worried; he wasn't looking at her.

"My own da said it was because Jamie spent so much time alone, that the voices got into his head and he couldna stop hearing them. When he'd feel safe enough to come to the house, it would take hours sometimes before he could start to hear *us* again—Mam wouldna let us talk to him until he'd had something to eat and was warmed through." He smiled, a little ruefully. "She said he wasna human 'til then—and, looking back, I dinna think she meant that as a figure of speech."

"Well," she said, but stopped, not knowing how to go on. She wished fervently that she'd known this earlier. Her da and his sister were coming on to France later, but she might not see him. She could maybe have talked to Da, asked him just what the voices in his head were like—what they said. Whether they were anything like the ones she heard.

NEARLY TWILIGHT, and the rats were still dead. The comte heard the bells of Notre Dame calling *sept* and glanced at his pocket watch. The bells were two minutes before their time, and he frowned. He didn't like sloppiness. He stood up and stretched himself, groaning as his spine cracked like the ragged volley of a firing squad. No doubt about it, he *was* aging, and the thought sent a chill through him.

If. If he could find the way forward, then perhaps . . . but you never knew, that was the devil of it. For a little while, he'd thought—hoped— that traveling back in time stopped the process of aging. That initially seemed logical, like rewinding a clock. But, then again, it *wasn't* logical, because he'd always gone back farther than his own lifetime. Only once he'd tried to go back just a few years, to his early twenties. *That* was a mistake, and he still shivered at the memory.

He went to the tall gabled window that looked out over the Seine.

That particular view of the river had changed barely at all in the last two hundred years; he'd seen it at several different times. He hadn't always owned this house, but it had stood in this street since 1620, and he always managed to get in briefly, if only to reestablish his own sense of reality after a passage.

Only the trees changed in his view of the river, and sometimes a strange-looking boat would be there. But the rest was always the same and no doubt always would be: the old fishermen, catching their supper off the landing in stubborn silence, each guarding his space with outthrust elbows, the younger ones, barefoot and slump-shouldered with exhaustion, laying out their nets to dry, naked little boys diving off the quay. It gave him a soothing sense of eternity, watching the river. Perhaps it didn't matter so much if he must one day die?

"The devil it doesn't," he murmured to himself, and glanced up at the sky. Venus shone bright. He should go.

Pausing conscientiously to place his fingers on each rat's body and ensure that no spark of life remained, he passed down the line, then swept them all into a burlap bag. If he was going to the Court of Miracles, at least he wouldn't arrive empty-handed.

JOAN WAS STILL reluctant to go below, but the light was fading, the wind getting up regardless, and a particularly spiteful gust that blew her petticoats right up round her waist and grabbed her arse with a chilly hand made her yelp in a very undignified way. She smoothed her skirts hastily and made for the hatchway, followed by Michael Murray.

Seeing him cough and chafe his hands at the bottom of the ladder made her sorry; here she'd kept him freezing on deck, too polite to go below and leave her to her own devices, and her too selfish to see he was cold, the poor man. She made a hasty knot in her handkerchief, to remind her to say an extra decade of the rosary for penance, when she got to it.

He saw her to a bench and said a few words to the woman sitting next to her, in French. Obviously he was introducing her, she understood that much—but when the woman nodded and said something in reply, she could only sit there openmouthed. She didn't understand a word. Not a word!

Michael evidently grasped the situation, for he said something to the woman's husband, which drew her attention away from Joan, and engaged them in a conversation that let Joan sink quietly back against the wooden wall of the ship, sweating with embarrassment.

Well, she'd get into the way of it, she reassured herself. Bound to. She settled herself with determination to listen, picking out the odd word here and there in the conversation. It was easier to understand Michael; he spoke slower and didn't swallow the back half of each word.

She was trying to puzzle out the probable spelling of a word that *sounded* like "pwufgweemiarniere" but surely couldn't be, when her eye caught a slight movement from the bench opposite, and the gurgling vowels caught in her throat.

A man sat there, maybe close to her own age, which was twenty-five. He was good-looking, if a bit thin in the face, decently dressed—and he was going to die.

There was a gray shroud over him, the same as if he were wrapped in mist, so his face showed through it. She'd seen that same thing—the grayness lying on someone's face like fog—seen it twice before and knew it at once for death's shadow. Once it had been on an elderly man, and that might have been only what anybody could see, because Angus MacWheen *was* ill, but then again, and only a few weeks after, she'd seen it on the second of Vhairi Fraser's little boys, and him a rosy-faced wee bairn with dear chubby legs.

She hadn't wanted to believe it. Either that she saw it or what it meant. But four days later, the wean was crushed in the lane by an ox that was maddened by a hornet's sting. She'd vomited when they told her, and couldn't eat for days after, for sheer grief and terror. Because could she have stopped it if she'd said? And what—dear Lord, *what*—if it happened again?

Now it had, and her wame twisted. She leapt to her feet and blundered toward the companionway, cutting short some slowly worded speech from the Frenchman.

Not again, not again! she thought in agony. *Why show me such things? What can I do?*

She pawed frantically at the ladder, climbing as fast as she could, gasping for air, needing to be away from the dying man. How long might it be, dear Lord, until she reached the convent, and safety?

THE MOON WAS rising over the Île de la Cité, glowing through the haze of cloud. He glanced at it, estimating the time; no point in arriving at Madame Fabienne's house before the girls had taken their hair out of curling papers and rolled on their red stockings. There were other places to go first, though: the obscure drinking places where the professionals of the court fortified themselves for the night ahead. One of those was where he had first heard the rumors—he'd see how far they had spread and would judge the safety of asking openly about Maître Raymond.

That was one advantage to hiding in the past, rather than going to Hungary or Sweden—life at this court tended to be short, and there were not so many who knew either his face or his history, though there would still be stories. Paris held on to its *histoires.* He found the iron gate—rustier than it had been; it left red stains on his palm—and pushed it open with a creak that would alert whatever now lived at the end of the alley.

He had to *see* the frog. Not meet him, perhaps—he made a brief sign against evil—but see him. Above all else, he needed to know: had the man—if he was a man—aged?

"Certainly he's a man," he muttered to himself, impatient. "What else could he be, for heaven's sake?"

He could be something like you, was the answering thought, and a shiver ran up his spine. *Fear?* He wondered. *Anticipation of an intriguing philosophical mystery? Or possibly . . . hope?*

"WHAT A WASTE of a wonderful arse," Monsieur Brechin remarked in French, watching Joan's ascent from the far side of the cabin. "And, *mon Dieu,* those legs! Imagine those wrapped around your back, eh? Would you have her keep the striped stockings on? I would."

It hadn't occurred to Michael to imagine that, but he was now having a hard time dismissing the image. He coughed into his handkerchief to hide the reddening of his face.

Madame Brechin gave her husband a sharp elbow in the ribs. He grunted but seemed undisturbed by what was evidently a normal form of marital communication.

"Beast," she said, with no apparent heat. "Speaking so of a Bride of Christ. You will be lucky if God himself doesn't strike you dead with a lightning bolt."

"Well, she isn't his bride yet," Monsieur protested. "And who created that arse in the first place? Surely God would be flattered to hear a little sincere appreciation of his handiwork. From one who is, after all, a connoisseur in such matters." He leered affectionately at Madame, who snorted.

A faint snigger from the young man across the cabin indicated that Monsieur was not alone in his appreciation, and Madame turned a reproving glare on the young man. Michael wiped his nose carefully, trying not to catch Monsieur's eye. His insides were quivering, and not entirely from either amusement or the shock of inadvertent lust. He felt very queer.

Monsieur sighed as Joan's striped stockings disappeared through the hatchway.

"Christ will not warm her bed," he said, shaking his head.

"Christ will not fart in her bed, either," said Madame, taking out her knitting.

"*Pardonnez-moi . . .*" Michael said in a strangled voice, and, clapping his handkerchief to his mouth, made hastily for the ladder, as though seasickness might be catching.

It wasn't *mal de mer* that was surging up from his belly, though. He caught sight of Joan, dim in the evening light at the rail, and turned quickly, going to the other side, where he gripped the rail as though it were a life raft and let the overwhelming waves of grief wash through him. It was the only way he'd been able to manage these last few weeks. Hold on as long as he could, keeping a cheerful face, until some small unexpected thing, some bit of emotional debris, struck him through the heart like a hunter's arrow, and then hurry to find a place to hide, curling up in mindless pain until he could get a grip on himself.

This time, it was Madame's remark that had come out of the blue, and he grimaced painfully, laughing in spite of the tears that poured down his face, remembering Lillie. She'd eaten eels in garlic sauce for dinner—those always made her fart with a silent deadliness like poison swamp gas. As the ghastly miasma had risen up round him, he'd sat bolt upright in bed, only to find her staring at him, a look of indignant horror on her face.

"How *dare* you?" she'd said, in a voice of offended majesty. "*Really,* Michel."

"You *know* it wasn't me!"

Her mouth had dropped open, outrage added to horror and distaste.

"Oh!" she gasped, gathering her pug-dog to her bosom. "You not only fart like a rotting whale, you attempt to blame it on my poor puppy! *Cochon!*" Whereupon she had begun to shake the bedsheets delicately, using her free hand to waft the noxious odors in his direction, addressing censorious remarks to Plonplon, who gave Michael a sanctimonious look before turning to lick his mistress's face with great enthusiasm.

"Oh, Jesus," he whispered, and, sinking down, pressed his face against the rail. "Oh, God, lass, I love you!"

He shook silently, head buried in his arms, aware of sailors passing now and then behind him, but none of them took notice of him in the dark. At last the agony eased a little, and he drew breath.

All right, then. He'd be all right now, for a time. And he thanked God, belatedly, that he had Joan—or Sister Gregory, if she liked—to look after for a bit. He didn't know how he'd manage to walk through the streets of Paris to his house, alone. Go in, greet the servants—would Jared be there?—face the sorrow of the household, accept their sympathy for his father's death, order a meal, sit down . . . and all the time wanting just to throw himself on the floor of their empty bedroom and howl like a lost soul. He'd have to face it, sooner or later—but not just yet. And right now he'd take the grace of any respite that was offered.

He blew his nose with resolution, tucked away his mangled handkerchief, and went downstairs to fetch the basket his mother had sent. He couldn't swallow a thing himself, but feeding Joan would maybe keep his mind off things for that one minute more.

"That's how ye do it," his brother Ian had told him, as they leant together on the rail of their mother's sheep pen, the winter's wind cold on their faces, waiting for their da to find his way through dying. "Ye find a way to live for that one more minute. And then another. And another." Ian had lost a wife, too, and knew.

He'd wiped his face—he could weep before Ian, while he couldn't with his elder brother or the girls, certainly not in front of his mother—and asked, "And it gets better after a time, is that what ye're telling me?"

His brother had looked at him straight on, the quiet in his eyes showing through the outlandish Mohawk tattoos.

"No," he'd said softly. "But after a time, ye find ye're in a different place than ye were. A different person than ye were. And then ye look about and see what's there with ye. Ye'll maybe find a use for yourself. *That* helps."

"Aye, fine," he said, under his breath, and squared his shoulders. "We'll see, then."

TO RAKOCZY'S SURPRISE, there was a familiar face behind the rough bar. If Maximilian the Great was surprised to see him, the Spanish dwarf gave no indication of it. The other drinkers—a pair of jugglers, each missing an arm (but the opposing arm), a toothless hag who smacked and muttered over her mug of arrack, and something that looked like a ten-year-old girl but almost certainly wasn't—turned to stare at him but, seeing nothing remarkable in his shabby clothing and burlap bag, turned back to the business of getting sufficiently drunk as to do what needed to be done tonight.

He nodded to Max and pulled up one of the splintering kegs to sit on.

"What's your pleasure, *señor*?"

Rakoczy narrowed his eyes; Max had never served anything but arrack. But times had changed; there was a stone bottle of something that might be beer and a dark glass bottle with a chalk scrawl on it, standing next to the keg of rough brandy.

"Arrack, please, Max," he said—better the devil you know—and was surprised to see the dwarf's eyes narrow in return.

"You knew my honored father, I see, *señor*," the dwarf said, putting the cup on the board. "It's some time since you've been in Paris?"

"*Pardonnez*," Rakoczy said, accepting it and tossing it back. If you could afford more than one cup, you didn't let it linger on the tongue. "Your honored . . . late father? Max?"

"Maximiliano el Maximo," the dwarf corrected him firmly.

"To be sure." Rakoczy gestured for another drink. "And whom have I the honor to address?"

The Spaniard—though perhaps his accent wasn't as strong as Max's had been—drew himself up proudly. "Maxim Le Grand, *a su servicio*!"

Rakoczy saluted him gravely and threw back the second cup, motioning for a third and, with a gesture, inviting Maxim to join him.

"It has been some time since I was last here," he said. No lie there. "I wonder if another old acquaintance might be still alive—*Maître* Raymond, otherwise called the frog?"

There was a tiny quiver in the air, a barely perceptible flicker of attention, gone almost as soon as he'd sensed it—somewhere behind him?

"A frog," Maxim said, meditatively pouring himself a drink. "I don't know any frogs myself, but should I hear of one, who shall I say is asking for him?"

Should he give his name? No, not yet.

"It doesn't matter," he said. "But word can be left with Madame Fabienne. You know the place? In the Rue Antoine?"

The dwarf's sketchy brows rose, and his mouth turned up at one corner.

"I know it."

Doubtless he did, Rakoczy thought. "El Maximo" hadn't referred to Max's stature, and probably "Le Grand" didn't, either. God had a sense of justice, as well as a sense of humor.

"Bon." He wiped his lips on his sleeve and put down a coin that would have bought the whole keg. *"Merci."*

He stood up, the hot taste of the brandy bubbling at the back of his throat, and belched. Two more places to visit, maybe, before he went to Fabienne's. He couldn't visit more than that and stay upright; he *was* getting old.

"Good night." He bowed to the company and gingerly pushed open the cracked wooden door; it was hanging by one leather hinge, and that looked ready to give way at any moment.

"Ribbit," someone said very softly, just before the door closed behind him.

MADELEINE'S FACE LIGHTED when she saw him, and his heart warmed. She wasn't very bright, poor creature, but she was pretty and amiable and had been a whore long enough to be grateful for small kindnesses.

"Monsieur Rakoczy!" She flung her arms about his neck, nuzzling affectionately.

"Madeleine, my dear." He cupped her chin and kissed her gently on the lips, drawing her close so that her belly pressed against his. He held her long enough, kissing her eyelids, her forehead, her ears—so that she made high squeaks of pleasure—that he could feel his way inside her, hold the weight of her womb in his mind, evaluate her ripening.

It felt warm, the color in the heart of a dark crimson rose, the kind called *sang de dragon*. A week before, it had felt solid, compact as a folded fist; now it had begun to soften, to hollow slightly as she readied. Three more days? he wondered. Four?

He let her go, and when she pouted prettily at him, he laughed and raised her hand to his lips, feeling the same small thrill he had felt when he first found her, as the faint blue glow rose between her fingers in response to his touch. She couldn't see it—he'd raised their linked hands to her face before and she had merely looked puzzled—but it was there.

"Go and fetch some wine, *ma belle*," he said, squeezing her hand gently. "I need to talk to Madame."

Madame Fabienne was not a dwarf, but she was small, brown, and mottled as a toadstool—and as watchful as a toad, round yellow eyes seldom blinking, never closed.

"Monsieur le Comte," she said graciously, nodding him to a damask chair in her *salon*. The air was scented with candle wax and flesh—flesh of a far better quality than that on offer in the court. Even so, Madame had come from that court and kept her connections there alive; she made no bones about that. She didn't blink at his clothes, but her nostrils flared at him, as though she picked up the scent of the dives and alleys he had come from.

"Good evening, Madame," he said, smiling at her, and lifted the burlap bag. "I brought a small present for Leopold. If he's awake?"

"Awake and cranky," she said, eyeing the bag with interest. "He's just shed his skin—you don't want to make any sudden moves."

Leopold was a remarkably handsome—and remarkably large—python; an albino, quite rare. Opinion of his origins was divided; half of Madame Fabienne's clientele held that she had been given the snake by a noble client—some said the late King himself—whom she had cured of impotence. Others said the snake had once *been* a noble client, who had refused to pay her for services rendered. Rakoczy had his own opinions on that one, but he liked Leopold, who was ordinarily tame as a cat and would sometimes come when called—as long as you had something he regarded as food in your hand when you called.

"Leopold! Monsieur le Comte has brought you a treat!" Fabienne reached across to an enormous wicker cage and flicked the door open, withdrawing her hand with sufficient speed as to indicate just what she meant by "cranky."

Almost at once, a huge yellow head poked out into the light. Snakes had transparent eyelids, but Rakoczy could swear the python blinked irritably, swaying up a coil of its monstrous body for a moment before plunging out of the cage and swarming across the floor with amazing rapidity for such a big creature, tongue flicking in and out like a seamstress's needle.

He made straight for Rakoczy, jaws yawning as he came, and Rakoczy snatched up the bag just before Leopold tried to engulf it—or Rakoczy—whole. He jerked aside, hastily seized a rat, and threw it. Leopold flung a coil of his body on top of the rat with a thud that rattled Madame's spoon in her teabowl, and before the company could blink, he had whipped the rat into a half-hitch knot of coil.

"Hungry as well as ill-tempered, I see," Rakoczy remarked, trying for nonchalance. In fact, the hairs were prickling over his neck and arms. Normally, Leopold took his time about feeding, and the violence of the python's appetite at such close quarters had shaken him.

Fabienne was laughing, almost silently, her tiny sloping shoulders quivering beneath the green Chinese silk tunic she wore.

"I thought for an instant he'd have you," she remarked at last, wiping her eyes. "If he had, I shouldn't have had to feed him for a month!"

Rakoczy bared his teeth in an expression that might have been taken for a smile.

"We cannot let Leopold go hungry," he said. "I wish to make a special arrangement for Madeleine—it should keep the worm up to his yellow arse in rats for some time."

Fabienne put down her handkerchief and regarded him with interest.

"Leopold has two cocks, but I can't say I've ever noticed an arse. Twenty *écus* a day. Plus two extra if she needs clothes."

He waved an easy hand, dismissing this.

"I had in mind something longer." He explained what he had in mind and had the satisfaction of seeing Fabienne's face go quite blank with stupefaction. It didn't stay that way more than a few moments; by the time he had finished, she was already laying out her initial demands.

When they finally came to agreement, they had drunk half a bottle of decent wine, and Leopold had swallowed the rat. It made a small bulge in the muscular tube of the snake's body but hadn't slowed him appreciably; the coils slithered restlessly over the painted canvas floorcloth, glowing like gold, and Rakoczy saw the patterns of his skin like trapped clouds beneath the scales.

"He *is* beautiful, no?" Fabienne saw his admiration and basked a little in it. "Did I ever tell you where I got him?"

"Yes, more than once. And more than one story, too." She looked startled, and he compressed his lips. He'd been patronizing her establishment for no more than a few weeks, this time. He'd known her fifteen years before—though only a couple of months, that time. He hadn't given his name then, and a madam saw so many men that there was little chance of her recalling him. On the other hand, he also thought it unlikely that she troubled to recall to whom she'd told which story, and this seemed to be the case, for she lifted one shoulder in a surprisingly graceful shrug and laughed.

"Yes, but this one is true."

"Oh, well, then." He smiled and, reaching into the bag, tossed Leopold another rat. The snake moved more slowly this time and didn't bother to constrict its motionless prey, merely unhinging its jaw and engulfing it in a single-minded way.

"He is an old friend, Leopold," she said, gazing affectionately at the snake. "I brought him with me from the West Indies, many years ago. He is a *Mystère,* you know."

"I didn't, no." Rakoczy drank more wine; he had sat long enough that he was beginning to feel almost sober again. "And what is that?" He was interested—not so much in the snake but in Fabienne's mention of the West Indies. He'd forgotten that she claimed to have come from there, many years ago, long before he'd known her the first time.

The *afile* powder had been waiting in his laboratory when he'd come back; no telling how many years it had sat there—the servants couldn't recall. Mélisande's brief note—*Try this. It may be what the frog used*—had not been dated, but there was a brief scrawl at the top of the sheet, saying, *Rose Hall, Jamaica*. If Fabienne retained any connections in the West Indies, perhaps . . .

"Some call them *loa*"—her wrinkled lips pursed as she kissed the word—"but those are the Africans. A *Mystère* is a spirit, one who is an intermediary between the Bondye and us. Bondye is *le bon Dieu,* of course," she explained to him. "The African slaves speak very bad French. Give him another rat; he's still hungry, and it scares the girls if I let him hunt in the house."

Another two rats and the snake was beginning to look like a fat string of pearls. He was showing an inclination to lie still, digesting. The tongue still flickered, tasting the air, but lazily now.

Rakoczy picked up the bag again, weighing the risks—but, after all, if news came from the Court of Miracles, his name would soon be known in any case.

"I wonder, Madame, as you know everyone in Paris"—he gave her a small bow, which she graciously returned—"are you acquainted with a certain man known as *Maître* Raymond? Some call him the frog," he added.

She blinked, then looked amused.

"You're looking for the frog?"

"Yes. Is that funny?" He reached into the sack, fishing for a rat.

"Somewhat. I should perhaps not tell you, but since you are so accommodating"—she glanced complacently at the purse he had put beside her teabowl, a generous deposit on account—"*Maître Grenouille* is looking for *you.*"

He stopped dead, hand clutching a furry body.

"What? You've seen him?"

She shook her head and, sniffing distastefully at her cold tea, rang the bell for her maid.

"No, but I've heard the same from two people."

"Asking for me by name?" Rakoczy's heart beat faster.

"Monsieur le Comte St. Germain. That *is* you?" She asked with no more than mild interest; false names were common in her business.

He nodded, mouth suddenly too dry to speak, and pulled the rat from the sack. It squirmed suddenly in his hand, and a piercing pain in his thumb made him hurl the rodent away.

"*Sacrebleu!* It bit me!"

The rat, dazed by impact, staggered drunkenly across the floor toward Leopold, whose tongue began to flicker faster. Fabienne, though, uttered a sound of disgust and threw a silver-backed hairbrush at the rat. Startled by the clatter, the rat leapt convulsively into the air, landed on and raced directly over the snake's astonished head, disappearing through the door into the foyer, where—by the resultant scream—it evidently encountered the maid before making its ultimate escape into the street.

"*Jésus Marie,*" Madame Fabienne said, piously crossing herself. "A miraculous resurrection. Two weeks before Easter, too."

IT WAS A SMOOTH passage; the shore of France came into sight just after dawn the next day. Joan saw it, a low smudge of dark green on the horizon, and felt a little thrill at the sight, in spite of her tiredness.

She hadn't slept, though she'd reluctantly gone below after nightfall, there to wrap herself in her cloak and shawl, trying not to look at the young man with the shadow on his face. She'd lain all night, listening to the snores and groans of her fellow passengers, praying doggedly and wondering in despair whether prayer was all she could do.

She often wondered whether it was because of her name. She'd been proud of her name when she was small; it was a heroic name, a saint's name, but also a warrior's name. Her mother'd told her that, often and often. She didn't think her mother had considered that the name might also be haunted.

Surely it didn't happen to everyone named Joan, though, did it? She wished she knew another Joan to ask. Because if it *did* happen to them all, the others would be keeping it quiet, just as she did.

You didn't go round telling people that you heard voices that weren't there. Still less that you saw things that weren't there, either. You just *didn't*.

She'd heard of a seer, of course; everyone in the Highlands had. And nearly everyone she knew at least claimed to have seen the odd fetch or had a premonition that Angus MacWheen was dead when he didn't come home that time last winter. The fact that Angus MacWheen was a filthy auld drunkard and so yellow and crazed that it was heads or tails whether he'd die on any particular day, let alone when it got cold enough that the loch froze, didn't come into it.

But she'd never *met* a seer—there was the rub. How did you get into the way of it? Did you just tell folk, *"Here's a thing . . . I'm a seer,"* and they'd nod and say, *"Oh, aye, of course; what's like to happen to me next Tuesday?"* More important, though, how the devil—

"Ow!" She'd bitten her tongue fiercely as penance for the inadvertent blasphemy, and clapped a hand to her mouth.

"What is it?" said a concerned voice behind her. "Are ye hurt, Miss MacKimmie? Er . . . Sister Gregory, I mean?"

"Mm! No. No, I jutht . . . bit my tongue." She turned to Michael Murray, gingerly touching the injured tongue to the roof of her mouth.

"Well, that happens when ye talk to yourself." He took the cork from a bottle he was carrying and held the bottle out to her. "Here, wash your mouth wi' that; it'll help."

She took a large mouthful and swirled it round; it burned the bitten place, but not badly, and she swallowed, as slowly as possible, to make it last.

"Jesus, Mary, and Bride," she breathed. "Is that *wine?*" The taste in her mouth bore some faint kinship with the liquid she knew as wine—just as apples bore some resemblance to horse turds.

"Aye, it *is* pretty good," he said modestly. "German. Umm . . . have a wee nip more?"

She didn't argue and sipped happily, barely listening to his talk, telling about the wine, what it was called, how they made it in Germany, where he got it . . . on and on. Finally she came to herself enough to remember her manners, though, and reluctantly handed back the bottle, now half empty.

"I thank ye, sir," she said primly. "'Twas kind of ye. Ye needna waste your time in bearing me company, though; I shall be well enough alone."

"Aye, well . . . it's no really for your sake," he said, and took a reasonable swallow himself. "It's for mine."

She blinked against the wind. He was flushed, but not from drink or wind, she thought.

She managed a faint interrogative "Ah . . . ?"

"Well, what I want to ask," he blurted, and looked away, cheekbones burning red. "Will ye pray for me? Sister? And my—my wife. The repose of—of—"

"Oh!" she said, mortified that she'd been so taken up with her own worries as not to have seen his distress. *Think you're a seer, dear Lord, ye dinna see what's under your neb; you're no but a fool, and a selfish fool at that.* She put her hand over his where it lay on the rail and squeezed tight, trying to channel some sense of God's goodness into his flesh. "To be sure I will!" she said. "I'll remember ye at every Mass, I swear it!" She wondered briefly whether it was proper to swear to something like that, but after all . . . "And your poor wife's soul, of course I will! What . . . er . . . what was her name? So as I'll know what to say when I pray for her," she explained hurriedly, seeing his eyes narrow with pain.

"Lilliane," he said, so softly that she barely heard him over the wind. "I called her Lillie."

"Lilliane," she repeated carefully, trying to form the syllables like he did. It was a soft, lovely name, she thought, slipping like water over the rocks at the top of a burn. *You'll never see a burn again,* she thought with a pang, but dismissed this, turning her face toward the growing shore of France. "I'll remember."

He nodded in mute thanks, and they stood for some little while, until she realized that her hand was still resting on his and drew it back with a jerk. He looked startled, and she blurted—because it was the thing on the top of her mind—"What was she like? Your wife?"

The most extraordinary mix of emotions flooded over his face. She couldn't have said what was uppermost—grief, laughter, or sheer bewilderment—and she realized suddenly just how little of his true mind she'd seen before.

"She was . . ." He shrugged and swallowed. "She was my wife," he said, very softly. "She was my life."

She should know something comforting to say to him, but she didn't.

She's with God? That was the truth, she hoped, and yet clearly to this young man, the only thing that mattered was that his wife was not with *him*.

"What happened to her?" she asked instead, baldly, only because it seemed necessary to say something.

He took a deep breath and appeared to sway a little; he'd finished the rest of the wine, she saw, and she took the empty bottle from his hand, tossing it overboard.

"The influenza. They said it was quick. Didn't feel quick to me—and yet, it was, I suppose it was. It took two days, and God kens well that I recall every second of those days—yet it seems that I lost her between one heartbeat and the next. And I—I keep lookin' for her there, in that space between."

He swallowed. "She—she was . . ." The words "with child" came so quietly that she barely heard them.

"Oh," Joan said softly, very moved. "Oh, *a chuisle*." "Heart's blood," it meant, and what *she* meant was that his wife had been that to him—dear Lord, she hoped he hadn't thought she meant—no, he hadn't, and the tight-wound spring in her backbone relaxed a little, seeing the look of gratitude on his face. He did know what she'd meant and seemed glad that she'd understood.

Blinking, she looked away—and caught sight of the young man with the shadow on him, leaning against the railing a little way down. The breath caught in her throat at sight of him.

The shadow was darker in the morning light. The sun was beginning to warm the deck, frail white clouds swam in the blue of clear French skies, and yet the mist now swirled and thickened, obscuring the young man's face, wrapping round his shoulders like a shawl.

Dear Lord, tell me what to do! Her body jerked, wanting to go to the young man, speak to him. But to say what? *"You're in danger, be careful"*?

He'd think she was mad. And if the danger was a thing he couldn't help, like with wee Ronnie and the ox, what difference might her speaking make?

She was dimly aware of Michael staring at her, curious. He said something to her, but she wasn't listening, listening hard instead inside her head. Where were the damned voices when you bloody *needed* one?

But the voices were stubbornly silent, and she turned to Michael, the muscles of her arm jumping, she'd held so tight to the ship's rigging.

"I'm sorry," she said. "I wasna listening properly. I just—thought of something."

"If it's a thing I can help ye with, Sister, ye've only to ask," he said, smiling faintly. "Oh! And speak of that, I meant to say—I said to your mam, if she liked to write to you in care of Fraser *et Cie*, I'd see to it that ye got the letters." He shrugged, one-shouldered. "I dinna ken what the rules are at the convent, aye? About getting letters from outside."

Joan didn't know that, either, and had worried about it. She was so relieved to hear this that a huge smile split her face.

"Oh, it's that kind of ye!" she said. "And if I could—maybe write back . . . ?"

His smile grew wider, the marks of grief easing in his pleasure at doing her a service.

"Anytime," he assured her. "I'll see to it. Perhaps I could—"

A ragged shriek cut through the air, and Joan glanced up, startled, thinking it one of the seabirds that had come out from shore to wheel round the ship, but it wasn't. The young man was standing on the rail, one hand on the rigging, and before she could so much as draw breath, he let go and was gone.

MICHAEL WAS WORRIED for Joan; she sat slumped in the coach, not bothering to look out of the window, until a faint waft of the cool breeze touched her face. The smell was so astonishing that it drew her out of the shell of shocked misery in which she had traveled from the docks.

"Mother o' God!" she said, clapping a hand to her nose. "What *is* that?"

Michael dug in his pocket and pulled out the grubby rag of his handkerchief, looking dubiously at it.

"It's the public cemeteries. I'm sorry, I didna think—"

"Moran taing." She seized the damp cloth from him and held it over her face, not caring. "Do the French not *bury* folk in their cemeteries?" Because, judging from the smell, a thousand corpses had been thrown out on wet ground and left to rot, and the sight of darting, squabbling flocks of black corbies in the distance did nothing to correct this impression.

"They do." Michael felt exhausted—it had been a terrible morning—but struggled to pull himself together. "It's all marshland over there, though; even coffins buried deep—and most of them aren't—work their way through the ground in a few months. When there's a flood—and there's a flood whenever it rains—what's left of the coffins falls apart, and . . ." He swallowed, just as pleased that he'd not eaten any breakfast.

"There's talk of maybe moving the bones at least, putting them in an ossuary, they call it. There are mine workings, old ones, outside the city— over there"—he pointed with his chin—"and perhaps . . . but they havena done anything about it yet," he added in a rush, pinching his nose fast to get a breath in through his mouth. It didn't matter whether you breathed through your nose or your mouth, though; the air was thick enough to taste.

She looked as ill as he felt, or maybe worse, her face the color of spoilt custard. She'd vomited when the crew had finally pulled the suicide aboard, pouring gray water and slimed with the seaweed that had wrapped round his legs and drowned him. There were still traces of sick down her front, and her dark hair was lank and damp, straggling out from under her cap. She hadn't slept at all, of course—neither had he.

He couldn't take her to the convent in this condition. The nuns maybe wouldn't mind, but she would. He stretched up and rapped on the ceiling of the carriage.

"Monsieur?"

"Au château, vite!"

He'd take her to his house first. It wasn't much out of the way, and the convent wasn't expecting her at any particular day or hour. She could wash, have something to eat, and put herself to rights. And if it saved him from walking into his house alone, well, they did say a kind deed carried its own reward.

BY THE TIME they'd reached the Rue Trémoulins, Joan had forgotten—partly—her various reasons for distress, in the sheer excitement of being in Paris. She had never seen so many people in one place at the same time—and that was only the folk coming out of Mass at a parish church! Round the corner, a pavement of fitted stones stretched wider than the whole River Ness, and those stones covered from one side to the other in barrows and wagons and stalls, rioting with fruit and vegetables and flowers and fish and meat . . . She'd given Michael back his filthy handkerchief and was panting like a dog, turning her face to and fro, trying to draw all the wonderful smells into herself at once.

"Ye look a bit better," Michael said, smiling at her. He was still pale himself, but he, too, seemed happier. "Are ye hungry yet?"

"I'm famished!" She cast a starved look at the edge of the market. "Could we stop, maybe, and buy an apple? I've a bit of money. . . ." She fumbled for the coins in her stocking top, but he stopped her.

"Nay, there'll be food a-plenty at the house. They were expecting me this week, so everything will be ready."

She stared longingly at the market for a brief moment, then turned obligingly in the direction he pointed, craning out the carriage window to see his house as they approached.

"That's the biggest house I've ever seen!" she exclaimed.

"Och, no," he said, laughing. "Lallybroch's bigger than that."

"Well . . . this one's *taller*," she replied. And it was—a good four stories, and a huge roof of lead slates and green-coppered seams, with what must be more than a score of glass windows set in, and . . .

She was still trying to count the windows when Michael helped her down from the carriage and offered her his arm to walk up to the door. She was goggling at the big yew trees set in brass pots and wondering how much trouble it must be to keep those polished, when she felt his arm go suddenly rigid as wood.

She glanced at Michael, startled, then looked where he was looking—toward the door of his house. The door had swung open, and three people were coming down the marble steps, smiling and waving, calling out.

"Who's that?" Joan whispered, leaning close to Michael. The one short fellow in the striped apron must be a butler; she'd read about butlers. But the other man was a gentleman, limber as a willow tree and wearing a coat and waistcoat striped in lemon and pink—with a hat decorated with . . . well, she supposed it must be a feather, but she'd pay money to see the bird it came off. By comparison, she had hardly noticed the woman, who was dressed in black. But now she saw that Michael had eyes only for the woman.

"Lé—" he began, and choked it back. "Lé—Léonie. Léonie is her name. My wife's sister."

Joan looked sharp then, because from the look of Michael Murray, he'd just seen his wife's ghost. But Léonie seemed flesh and blood, slender and pretty, though her own face bore the same marks of sorrow as did Michael's, and her face was pale under a small, neat black tricorne with a tiny curled blue feather.

"Michel," she said. "Oh, Michel!" And with tears brimming from eyes shaped like almonds, she threw herself into his arms.

Feeling extremely superfluous, Joan stood back a little and glanced at the gentleman in the lemon-striped waistcoat—the butler had tactfully withdrawn into the house.

"Charles Pépin, mademoiselle," he said, sweeping off his hat. Taking her hand, he bowed low over it, and now she saw the band of black mourning he wore around his bright sleeve. *"A votre service."*

"Oh," she said, a little flustered. "Um. Joan MacKimmie. *Je suis* . . . er . . . um . . ."

"Tell him not to do it," said a sudden small, calm voice inside her head, and she jerked her own hand away as though he'd bitten her.

"Pleased to meet you," she gasped. "Excuse me." And, turning, threw up into one of the bronze yew pots.

JOAN HAD BEEN afraid it would be awkward, coming to Michael's bereaved and empty house, but had steeled herself to offer comfort and support, as became a distant kinswoman and a daughter of God. She might have been miffed, therefore, to find herself entirely supplanted in the department of comfort and support—quite relegated to the negligible position of guest, in fact, served politely and asked periodically if she wished more wine, a slice of ham, some gherkins . . . but otherwise ignored, while Michael's servants, sister-in-law, and . . . she wasn't quite sure of the position of M. Pépin, though he seemed to have something personal to do with Léonie—perhaps someone had said he was her cousin?—all swirled round Michael like perfumed bathwater, warm and buoyant, touching him, kissing him—well, all right, she'd heard of men kissing one another in France, but she couldn't help staring when M. Pépin gave Michael a big wet one on both cheeks—and generally making a fuss over him.

She was more than relieved, though, not to have to make conversation in French, beyond a simple *merci* or *s'il vous plaît* from time to time. It gave her a chance to settle her nerves—and her stomach, and she would say the wine was a wonder for that—and to keep a close eye on Monsieur Charles Pépin.

"Tell him not to do it." And just what d'ye mean by that? she demanded of the voice. She didn't get an answer, which didn't surprise her. The voices weren't much for details.

She couldn't tell whether the voices were male or female; they didn't seem either one, and she wondered whether they might maybe be angels— angels didn't have a sex, and doubtless that saved them a lot of trouble. Joan of Arc's voices had had the decency to introduce themselves, but not hers, oh, no. On the other hand, if they *were* angels and told her their names, she wouldn't recognize them anyway, so perhaps that's why they didn't bother.

Well, so. Did this particular voice mean that Charles Pépin was a villain? She squinted closely at him. He didn't look it. He had a strong, good-looking face, and Michael seemed to like him—after all, Michael must be a fair judge of character, she thought, and him in the wine business.

What was it Monsieur Charles Pépin oughtn't to do, though? Did he have some wicked crime in mind? Or might he be bent on doing away with himself, like that poor wee gomerel on the boat? There was still a trace of slime on her hand, from the seaweed.

She rubbed her hand inconspicuously against the skirt of her dress, frustrated. She hoped the voices would stop once she was in the convent. That was her nightly prayer. But if they didn't, at least she might be able to tell someone there about them without fear of being packed off to a madhouse or stoned in the street. She'd have a confessor, she knew that much. Maybe he could help her discover what God had meant, landing her with a gift like this, and no explanation what she was to do with it.

In the meantime, Monsieur Pépin would bear watching; she should maybe say something to Michael before she left. *Aye, what?* she thought, helpless.

Still, she was glad to see that Michael grew less pale as they all carried on, vying to feed him tidbits, refill his glass, tell him bits of gossip. She was also pleased to find that she mostly understood what they were saying, as she relaxed. Jared—that would be Jared Fraser, Michael's elderly cousin, who'd founded the wine company, and whose house this was—was still in Germany, they said, but was expected at any moment. He had sent a letter for Michael, too; where was it? No matter, it would turn up . . . and Madame Nesle de La Tourelle had had a fit, a veritable *fit*, at court last Wednesday, when she came face-to-face with Mademoiselle de Perpignan wearing a confection in the particular shade of pea green that was de La Tourelle's alone, and God alone knew why, because she always looked like a cheese in it, and had slapped her own maid so hard for pointing this out that the poor girl flew across the rushes and cracked her head on one of the mirrored walls—and cracked the mirror, too, very bad luck that, but no one could agree whether the bad luck was de La Tourelle's, the maid's, or de Perpignan's.

Birds, Joan thought dreamily, sipping her wine. *They sound just like cheerful wee birds in a tree, all chattering away together.*

"The bad luck belongs to the seamstress who made the dress for de Perpignan," Michael said, a faint smile touching his mouth. "Once de La Tourelle finds out who it is." His eye lighted on Joan then, sitting there with a fork—an actual fork, and silver, too!—in her hand, her mouth half open in the effort of concentration required to follow the conversation.

"Sister Joan—Sister Gregory, I mean—I'm that sorry, I was forgetting. If ye've had enough to eat, will ye have a bit of a wash, maybe, before I deliver ye to the convent?"

He was already rising, reaching for a bell, and before she knew where she was, a maidservant had whisked her off upstairs, deftly undressed her, and, wrinkling her nose at the smell of the discarded garments, wrapped Joan in a robe of the most amazing green silk, light as air, and ushered her into a small stone room with a copper bath in it, then disappeared, saying something in which Joan caught the word *"eau."*

She sat on the wooden stool provided, clutching the robe about her nakedness, head spinning with more than wine. She closed her eyes and took deep breaths, trying to put herself in the way of praying. God was everywhere, she assured herself, embarrassing as it was to contemplate him being with her in a bathroom in Paris. She shut her eyes harder and firmly began the rosary, starting with the Joyful Mysteries.

She'd got through the Visitation before she began to feel steady again. This wasn't quite how she'd expected her first day in Paris to be. Still, she'd have something to write home to Mam about, that was for sure. If they let her write letters in the convent.

The maid came in with two enormous cans of steaming water and up-ended these into the bath with a tremendous splash. Another came in on her heels, similarly equipped, and between them they had Joan up, stripped, and stepping into the tub before she'd so much as said the first word of the Lord's Prayer for the third decade.

They said French things to her, which she didn't understand, and held out peculiar-looking instruments to her in invitation. She recognized the small pot of soap and pointed at it, and one of them at once poured water on her head and began to wash her hair!

She had for months been bidding farewell to her hair whenever she combed it, quite resigned to its loss, for whether she must sacrifice it im-mediately, as a postulant, or later, as a novice, plainly it must go. The shock of knowing fingers rubbing her scalp, the sheer sensual delight of warm water coursing through her hair, the soft wet weight of it lying in ropes down over her breasts—was this God's way of asking if she'd truly thought it through? Did she know what she was giving up?

Well, she did, then. And she *had* thought about it. On the other hand . . . she couldn't make them stop, really; it wouldn't be mannerly. The warmth of the water was making the wine she'd drunk course faster through her blood, and she felt as though she were being kneaded like toffee, stretched and pulled, all glossy and falling into languid loops. She closed her eyes and gave up trying to remember how many Hail Marys she had yet to go in the third decade.

It wasn't until the maids had hauled her, pink and steaming, out of the bath and wrapped her in a most remarkable huge fuzzy kind of towel that she emerged abruptly from her sensual trance. The cold air coalesced in her stomach, reminding her that all this luxury was indeed a lure of the devil—for lost in gluttony and sinful bathing, she'd forgot entirely about the young man on the ship, the poor despairing sinner who had thrown himself into the sea.

The maids had gone for the moment. She dropped at once to her knees on the stone floor and threw off the coddling towels, exposing her bare skin to the full chill of the air in penance.

"*Mea culpa, mea culpa, mea maxima culpa,*" she breathed, knocking a fist against her bosom in a paroxysm of sorrow and regret. The sight of the drowned young man was in her mind, soft brown hair fanned across his cheek, eyes half closed, seeing nothing—and what terrible thing was it that he'd seen, or thought of, before he jumped, that he'd screamed so?

She thought briefly of Michael, the look on his face when he spoke of his poor wife—perhaps the young brown-haired man had lost someone dear and couldn't face his life alone?

She should have spoken to him. That was the undeniable, terrible truth. It didn't matter that she didn't know what to say. She should have trusted God to give her words, as he had when she'd spoken to Michael.

"Forgive me, Father!" she said urgently, out loud. "Please—forgive me, give me strength!"

She'd betrayed that poor young man. And herself. *And* God, who'd given her the terrible gift of sight for a reason. And the voices . . .

"Why did ye not tell me?" she cried. "Have ye nothing to say for yourselves?" Here she'd thought the voices those of angels, and they weren't—just drifting bits of bog mist, getting into her head, pointless, useless . . . useless as she was, oh, Lord Jesus . . .

She didn't know how long she knelt there, naked, half drunk, and in tears. She heard the muffled squeaks of dismay from the French maids, who poked their heads in and just as quickly withdrew them, but paid no attention. She didn't know if it was right even to pray for the poor young man—for suicide was a mortal sin, and surely he'd gone straight to hell. But she couldn't give him up; she couldn't. She felt somehow that he'd been her charge, that she'd carelessly let him fall, and surely God would not hold the young man entirely responsible when it was she who should have been watching out for him.

And so she prayed, with all the energy of body and mind and spirit, asking mercy. Mercy for the young man, for wee Ronnie and wretched auld Angus—mercy for poor Michael, and for the soul of Lillie, his dear wife, and their babe unborn. And mercy for herself, this unworthy vessel of God's service.

"I'll do better!" she promised, sniffing and wiping her nose on the fluffy towel. "Truly, I will. I'll be braver. I will."

MICHAEL TOOK THE candlestick from the footman, said good night, and shut the door. He hoped Sister almost-Gregory was comfortable; he'd told the staff to put her in the main guest room. He was fairly sure she'd sleep well. He smiled wryly to himself; unaccustomed to wine, and obviously nervous in company, she'd sipped her way through most of a decanter of Jerez sherry before he noticed, and was sitting in the corner with unfocused eyes and a small inward smile that reminded him of a painting he had seen at Versailles, a thing the steward had called *La Gioconda*.

He couldn't very well deliver her to the convent in such a condition and had gently escorted her upstairs and given her into the hands of the chambermaids, both of whom regarded her with some wariness, as though a tipsy nun were a particularly dangerous commodity.

He'd drunk a fair amount himself in the course of the afternoon and more at dinner. He and Charles had sat up late, talking and drinking rum punch. Not talking of anything in particular; he had just wanted not to be alone. Charles had invited him to go to the gaming rooms—Charles was an inveterate gambler—but was kind enough to accept his refusal and simply bear him company.

The candle flame blurred briefly at thought of Charles's kindness. He blinked and shook his head, which proved a mistake; the contents shifted abruptly, and his stomach rose in protest at the sudden movement. He barely made it to the chamber pot in time and, once evacuated, lay numbly on the floor, cheek pressed to the cold boards.

It wasn't that he couldn't get up and go to bed. It was that he couldn't face the thought of the cold white sheets, the pillows round and smooth, as though Lillie's head had never dented them, the bed never known the heat of her body.

Tears ran sideways over the bridge of his nose and dripped on the floor. There was a snuffling noise, and Plonplon came squirming out from under the bed and licked his face, whining anxiously. After a little while, he sat up and, leaning against the side of the bed with the dog in one arm, reached for the decanter of port that the butler had left—by instruction—on the table beside it.

THE SMELL WAS appalling. Rakoczy had wrapped a woolen comforter about his lower face, but the odor seeped in, putrid and cloying, clinging to the back of the throat, so that even breathing through the mouth didn't preserve you from the stench. He breathed as shallowly as he could, though, picking his way carefully past the edge of the cemetery by the narrow beam of a dark lantern. The mine lay well beyond it, but the stench carried amazingly when the wind blew from the east.

The chalk mine had been abandoned for years; it was rumored to be haunted. It was. Rakoczy knew what haunted it. Never religious—he was a philosopher and a natural scientist, a rationalist—he still crossed himself by reflex at the head of the ladder that led down the shaft into those spectral depths.

At least the rumors of ghosts and earth demons and the walking dead would keep anyone from coming to investigate strange light glowing from the subterranean tunnels of the workings, if it was noticed at all. Though just in case . . . he opened the burlap bag, still redolent of rats, and fished out a bundle of pitchblende torches and the oiled-silk packet that held several lengths of cloth saturated with *salpêtre,* salts of potash, blue vitriol, verdigris, butter of antimony, and a few other interesting compounds from his laboratory.

He found the blue vitriol by smell and wrapped the cloth tightly around the head of one torch, then—whistling under his breath—made three more torches, each impregnated with different salts. He loved this part. It was so simple, and so astonishingly beautiful.

He paused for a minute to listen, but it was well past dark and the only sounds were those of the night itself—frogs chirping and bellowing in the distant marshes by the cemetery, wind stirring the leaves of spring. A few hovels sat a half mile away, only one with firelight glowing dully from a smoke hole in the roof. *Almost a pity there's no one but me to see this.* He took the little clay firepot from its wrappings and touched a coal to the cloth-wrapped torch. A tiny green flame flickered like a serpent's tongue, then burst into life in a brilliant globe of ghostly color.

He grinned at the sight, but there was no time to lose; the torches wouldn't last forever, and there was work to be done. He tied the bag to his belt and, with the green fire crackling softly in one hand, climbed down into darkness.

He paused at the bottom, breathing deep. The air was clear, the dust long settled. No one had been down here recently. The dull white walls glowed soft, eerie under the green light, and the passage yawned before him, black as a murderer's soul. Even knowing the place as well as he did, and with light in his hand, it gave him a qualm to walk into it.

Is that what death is like? he wondered. A black void that you walked into with no more than a feeble glimmer of faith in your hand? His lips compressed. Well, he'd done *that* before, if less permanently. But he disliked the way that the notion of death seemed always to be lurking in the back of his mind these days.

The main tunnel was large, big enough for two men to walk side by side, and the roof was high enough above him that the roughly excavated chalk lay in shadow, barely touched by his torch. The side tunnels were smaller, though. He counted the ones on the left and, despite himself, hurried his step a little as he passed the fourth. That was where *it* lay, down the side tunnel, a turn to the left, another to the left—was it "widdershins" the English called it, turning against the direction of the sun? He thought that was what Mélisande had called it when she'd brought him here. . . .

The sixth. His torch had begun to gutter already, and he pulled another from the bag and lit it from the remains of the first, which he dropped on the floor at the entrance to the side tunnel, leaving it to flare and smolder behind him, the smoke catching at his throat. He knew his way, but even so, it was as well to leave landmarks, here in the realm of everlasting night. The mine had deep rooms, one far back that showed strange paintings on the wall, of animals that didn't exist but had an astonishing vividness, as though they would leap from the wall and stampede down the passages. Sometimes—rarely—he went all the way down into the bowels of the earth, just to look at them.

The fresh torch burned with the warm light of natural fire, and the white walls took on a rosy glow. So did the painting at the end of the corridor, this one different: a crude but effective rendering of the Annunciation. He didn't know who had made the paintings that appeared unexpectedly here and there in the mines—most were of religious subjects, a few most emphatically *not*—but they were useful. There was an iron ring in the wall by the Annunciation, and he set his torch into it.

Turn back at the Annunciation, then three paces . . . He stamped his foot, listening for the faint echo, and found it. He'd brought a trowel in his bag, and it was the work of a few moments to uncover the sheet of tin that covered his cache.

The cache itself was three feet deep and three feet square—he found satisfaction in the knowledge of its perfect cubicity whenever he saw it; any alchemist was by profession a numerologist, as well. It was half full, the contents wrapped in burlap or canvas, not things he wanted to carry openly through the streets. It took some prodding and unwrapping to find the pieces he wanted. Madame Fabienne had driven a hard bargain but a fair one: two hundred *écus* a month times four months for the guaranteed exclusive use of Madeleine's services.

Four months would surely be enough, he thought, feeling a rounded shape through its wrappings. In fact, he thought one night would be enough, but his man's pride was restrained by a scientist's prudence. And even if . . . there was always some chance of early miscarriage; he wanted to be sure of the child before he undertook any more personal experiments with the space between times. If he knew that something of himself—someone with his peculiar abilities—might be left, just in case *this* time . . .

He could feel *it* there, somewhere in the smothered dark behind him. He knew he couldn't hear it now; it was silent, save on the days of solstice and equinox or when you actually walked into it . . . but he felt the sound of it in his bones, and it made his hands tremble on the wrappings.

The gleam of silver, of gold. He chose two gold snuffboxes, a filigreed necklace, and—with some hesitation—a small silver salver. Why did the void not affect metal? he wondered for the thousandth time. In fact, carrying gold or silver eased the passage—or at least he thought so. Mélisande had told him it did. But jewels were always destroyed by the passage, though they gave the most control and protection.

That made some sense; everyone knew that gemstones had a specific vibration that corresponded to the heavenly spheres, and the spheres themselves of course affected the earth: *As above, so below.* He still had no idea exactly *how* the vibrations should affect the space, the portal . . . *it.* But thinking about it gave him a need to touch them, to reassure himself, and he moved wrapped bundles out of the way, digging down to the left-hand corner of the wood-lined cache, where pressing on a particular nail-head caused one of the boards to loosen and turn sideways, rotating smoothly on spindles. He reached into the dark space thus revealed and found the small washleather bag, feeling his sense of unease dissipate at once when he touched it.

He opened it and poured the contents into his palm, glittering and sparking in the dark hollow of his hand. Reds and blues and greens, the brilliant white of diamonds, the lavender and violet of amethyst, and the golden glow of topaz and citrine. Enough?

Enough to travel back, certainly. Enough to steer himself with some accuracy, to choose how far he went. But enough to go forward?

He weighed the glittering handful for a moment, then poured them carefully back. Not yet. But he had time to find more; he wasn't going anywhere for at least four months. Not until he was sure that Madeleine was well and truly with child.

"JOAN." MICHAEL PUT his hand on her arm, keeping her from leaping out of the carriage. "Ye're *sure,* now? I mean, if ye didna feel quite ready, ye're welcome to stay at my house until—"

"I'm ready." She didn't look at him, and her face was pale as a slab of lard. "Let me go, please."

He reluctantly let go of her arm but insisted upon getting down with her and ringing the bell at the gate, stating their business to the portress. All the time, though, he could feel her shaking, quivering like a blancmange. Was it fear, though, or just understandable nerves? He'd feel a bit cattywampus himself, he thought with sympathy, were he making such a shift, beginning a new life so different from what had gone before.

The portress went away to fetch the mistress of postulants, leaving them in the little enclosure by the gatehouse. From here, he could see across a sunny courtyard with a cloister walk on the far side and what looked like extensive kitchen gardens to the right. To the left was the looming bulk of the hospital run by the order and, beyond that, the other buildings that belonged to the convent. It was a beautiful place, he thought—and hoped the sight of it would settle her fears.

She made an inarticulate noise, and he glanced at her, alarmed to see what looked like tears slicking her cheeks.

"Joan," he said more quietly, and handed her his fresh handkerchief.

"Dinna be afraid. If ye need me, send for me, anytime; I'll come. And I meant it about the letters."

He would have said more, but just then the portress reappeared with Sister Eustacia, the postulant mistress, who greeted Joan with a kind motherliness that seemed to comfort her, for the girl sniffed and straightened herself and, reaching into her pocket, pulled out a little folded square, obviously kept with care through her travels.

"J'ai une lettre," she said in halting French. *"Pour Madame le . . . pour . . .* Reverend Mother?" she said in a small voice. "Mother Hildegarde?"

"Oui?" Sister Eustacia took the note with the same care with which it was proffered.

"It's from . . . her," Joan said to Michael, having plainly run out of French. She still wouldn't look at him. "Da's . . . er . . . wife. You know. Claire."

"Jesus Christ!" Michael blurted, making both the portress and the postulant mistress stare reprovingly at him.

"She said she was a friend of Mother Hildegarde. And if she was still alive . . ." She stole a look at Sister Eustacia, who appeared to have followed this.

"Oh, Mother Hildegarde is certainly alive," she assured Joan, in English. "And I'm sure she will be most interested to speak with you." She tucked the note into her own capacious pocket and held out a hand. "Now, my dear child, if you are quite ready . . ."

"Je suis prêt," Joan said, shaky but dignified. And so Joan MacKimmie of Balriggan passed through the gates of the Convent of Angels, still clutching Michael Murray's clean handkerchief and smelling strongly of his dead wife's scented soap.

MICHAEL HAD DISMISSED his carriage and wandered restlessly about the city after leaving Joan at the convent, not wanting to go home. He hoped they would be good to her, hoped that she'd made the right decision.

Of course, he comforted himself, she wouldn't actually be a nun for some time. He didn't know quite how long it took, from entering as a postulant to becoming a novice to taking the final vows of poverty, chastity, and obedience, but at least a few years. There would be time for her to be sure. And at least she was in a place of safety; the look of terror and distress on her face as she'd shot through the gates of the convent still haunted him. He strolled toward the river, where the evening light glowed on the water like a bronze mirror. The deckhands were tired and the day's shouting had died away. In this light, the reflections of the boats gliding homeward seemed more substantial than the boats themselves.

He'd been surprised at the letter and wondered whether that had anything to do with Joan's distress. He'd had no notion that his uncle's wife had anything to do with le Couvent des Anges—though now he cast his mind back, he did recall Jared mentioning that Uncle Jamie had worked in Paris in the wine business for a short time, back before the Rising. He supposed Claire might have met Mother Hildegarde then . . . but it was all before he was born.

He felt an odd warmth at the thought of Claire; he couldn't really think of her as his auntie, though she was. He'd not spent much time with her alone at Lallybroch—but he couldn't forget the moment when she'd met him, alone at the door. Greeted him briefly and embraced him on impulse. And he'd felt an instant sense of relief, as though she'd taken a heavy burden from his heart. Or maybe lanced a boil on his spirit, as she might one on his bum.

That thought made him smile. He didn't know what she was—the talk near Lallybroch painted her as everything from a witch to an angel, with most of the opinion hovering cautiously around "faerie," for the Auld Ones were dangerous, and you didn't talk too much about them—but he liked her. So did Da and Young Ian, and that counted for a lot. And Uncle Jamie, of course—though everyone said, very matter-of-fact, that Uncle Jamie was bewitched. He smiled wryly at that. Aye, if being mad in love with your wife was bewitchment.

If anyone outside the family kent what she'd told them—he cut that thought short. It wasn't something he'd forget, but it wasn't something he wanted to think about just yet, either. The gutters of Paris running with blood . . . He glanced down involuntarily, but the gutters were full of the usual assortment of animal and human sewage, dead rats, and bits of rubbish too far gone to be salvaged for food even by the street beggars.

He walked, making his way slowly through the crowded streets, past La Chapelle and the Tuileries. If he walked enough, sometimes he could fall asleep without too much wine.

He sighed, elbowing his way through a group of buskers outside a tavern, turning back toward the Rue Trémoulins. Some days, his head was like a bramble patch: thorns catching at him no matter which way he turned, and no path leading out of the tangle.

Paris wasn't a large city, but it was a complicated one; there was always somewhere else to walk. He crossed the Place de la Corcorde, thinking of what Claire had told them, seeing there in his mind the tall shadow of a terrible machine.

JOAN HAD HAD her dinner with Mother Hildegarde, a lady so ancient and holy that Joan had feared to breathe too heavily, lest Mother
Hildegarde fragment like a stale croissant and go straight off to heaven in
front of her. Mother Hildegarde had been delighted with the letter Joan
had delivered, though; it brought a faint flush to her face.

"From my . . . er . . ." Martha, Mary, and Lazarus, what was the French
word for "stepmother"? "Ahh . . . the wife of my . . ." Fittens, she didn't
know the word for "stepfather," either! "The wife of my father," she
ended weakly.

"You are the daughter of my good friend Claire!" Mother had exclaimed. "And how is she?"

"Bonny, er . . . *bon,* I mean, last I saw her," said Joan, and then tried to
explain, but there was a lot of French being spoken very fast, and she gave
up and accepted the glass of wine that Mother Hildegarde offered her. She
was going to be a sot long before she took her vows, she thought, trying
to hide her flushed face by bending down to pat Mother's wee dog, a
fluffy, friendly creature the color of burnt sugar, named Bouton.

Whether it was the wine or Mother's kindness, her wobbly spirit steadied. Mother had welcomed her to the community and kissed her forehead
at the end of the meal, before sending her off in the charge of Sister Eustacia to see the convent.

Now she lay on her narrow cot in the dormitory, listening to the breathing of a dozen other postulants. It sounded like a byre full of cows and had
much the same warm, humid scent—bar the manure. Her eyes filled with
tears, the vision of the homely stone byre at Balriggan sudden and vivid in
her mind. She swallowed them back, though, pinching her lips together.
A few of the girls sobbed quietly, missing home and family, but she
wouldn't be one of them. She was older than most—a few were nay more
than fourteen—and she'd promised God to be brave.

It hadn't been bad during the afternoon. Sister Eustacia had been very
kind, taking her and a couple of other new postulants round the walled
estate, showing them the big gardens where the convent grew medicinal
herbs and fruit and vegetables for the table, the chapel where devotions
were held six times a day, plus Mass in the mornings, the stables and kitchens, where they would take turns working—and the great Hôpital des
Anges, the order's main work. They had seen the *hôpital* only from the
outside, though; they would see the inside tomorrow, when Sister Marie-
Amadeus would explain their duties.

It was strange, of course—she still understood only half what people
said to her and was sure from the looks on their faces that they understood

much less of what she tried to say to *them*—but wonderful. She loved the spiritual discipline, the hours of devotion, with the sense of peace and unity that came upon the sisters as they chanted and prayed together. Loved the simple beauty of the chapel, amazing in its clean elegance, the solid lines of granite and the grace of carved wood, a faint smell of incense in the air, like the breath of angels.

The postulants prayed with the others but did not yet sing. They would be trained in music—such excitement! Mother Hildegarde had been a famous musician in her youth, it was rumored, and considered it one of the most important forms of devotion.

The thought of the new things she'd seen, and the new things to come, distracted her mind—a little—from thoughts of her mother's voice, the wind off the moors, the . . . She shoved these hastily away and reached for her new rosary, this a substantial thing with smooth wooden beads, lovely and comforting in the fingers.

Above all, there was peace. She hadn't heard a word from the voices, hadn't seen anything peculiar or alarming. She wasn't foolish enough to think she'd escaped her dangerous gift, but at least there might be help at hand if—when—it came back.

And at least she already knew enough Latin to say her rosary properly; Da had taught her. *"Ave, Maria,"* she whispered, *"gratia plena, Dominus tecum,"* and closed her eyes, the sobs of the homesick fading in her ears as the beads moved slow and silent through her fingers.

Next day

MICHAEL MURRAY STOOD in the aisle of the aging shed, feeling puny and unreal. He'd waked with a terrible headache, the result of having drunk a great deal of mixed spirits on an empty stomach, and while the headache had receded to a dull throb at the back of his skull, it had left him feeling trampled and left for dead. His cousin Jared, owner of Fraser *et Cie,* looked at him with the cold eye of long experience, shook his head and sighed deeply, but said nothing, merely taking the list from his nerveless fingers and beginning the count on his own.

He wished Jared had rebuked him. Everyone still tiptoed round him, careful of him. And like a wet dressing on a wound, their care kept the wound of Lillie's loss open and weeping. The sight of Léonie didn't help, either—so much like Lillie to look at, so different in character. She said they must help and comfort each other and, to that end, came to visit every other day, or so it seemed. He really wished she would . . . just go away, though the thought shamed him.

"How's the wee nun, then?" Jared's voice, dry and matter-of-fact as always, drew him out of his bruised and soggy thoughts. "Give her a good send-off to the convent?"

"Aye. Well—aye. More or less." Michael mustered up a feeble smile. He didn't really want to think about Sister Gregory this morning, either.

"What did ye give her?" Jared handed the checklist to Humberto, the Italian shed-master, and looked Michael over appraisingly. "I hope it wasna the new Rioja that did that to ye."

"Ah . . . no." Michael struggled to focus his attention. The heady atmosphere of the shed, thick with the fruity exhalations of the resting casks, was making him dizzy. "It was Moselle. Mostly. And a bit of rum punch."

"Oh, I see." Jared's ancient mouth quirked up on one side. "Did I never tell ye not to mix wine wi' rum?"

"Not above two hundred times, no." Jared was moving, and Michael followed him perforce down the narrow aisle, the casks in their serried ranks rising high above on either side.

"Rum's a demon. But whisky's a virtuous dram," Jared said, pausing by a rack of small blackened casks. "So long as it's a good make, it'll never turn on ye. Speakin' of which"—he tapped the end of one cask, which gave off the resonant deep *thunk* of a full barrel—"what's this? It came up from the docks this morning."

"Oh, aye." Michael stifled a belch and smiled painfully. "That, cousin, is the Ian Alastair Robert MacLeod Murray memorial *uisge baugh*. My da and Uncle Jamie made it during the winter. They thought ye might like a wee cask for your personal use."

Jared's brows rose and he gave Michael a swift sideways glance. Then he turned back to examine the cask, bending close to sniff at the seam between the lid and staves.

"I've tasted it," Michael assured him. "I dinna think it will poison ye. But ye should maybe let it age a few years."

Jared made a rude noise in his throat, and his hand curved gently over the swell of the staves. He stood thus for a moment as though in benediction, then turned suddenly and took Michael into his arms. His own breathing was hoarse, congested with sorrow. He was years older than Da and Uncle Jamie but had known the two of them all their lives.

"I'm sorry for your faither, lad," he said after a moment, and let go, patting Michael on the shoulder. He looked at the cask and sniffed deeply. "I can tell it will be fine." He paused, breathing slowly, then nodded once, as though making up his mind to something.

"I've a thing in mind, *a charaid*. I'd been thinking, since ye went to Scotland—and now that we've a kinswoman in the church, so to speak . . . Come back to the office with me, and I'll tell ye."

IT WAS CHILLY in the street, but the goldsmith's back room was cozy as a womb, with a porcelain stove throbbing with heat and woven wool hangings on the walls. Rakoczy hastily unwound the comforter about his neck. It didn't do to sweat indoors; the sweat chilled the instant one went out again, and next thing you knew, it would be *la grippe* at the best, pleurisy or pneumonia at the worst.

Rosenwald himself was comfortable in shirt and waistcoat, without even a wig, only a plum-colored turban to keep his polled scalp warm. The goldsmith's stubby fingers traced the curves of the octofoil salver, turned it over—and stopped dead. Rakoczy felt the tingle of warning at the base of his spine and deliberately relaxed himself, affecting a nonchalant self-confidence.

"Where did you get this, monsieur, if I may ask?" Rosenwald looked up at him, but there was no accusation in the goldsmith's aged face—only a wary excitement.

"It was an inheritance," Rakoczy said, glowing with earnest innocence. "An elderly aunt left it—and a few other pieces—to me. Is it worth anything more than the value of the silver?"

The goldsmith opened his mouth, then shut it, glancing at Rakoczy. Was he honest? Rakoczy wondered with interest. *He's already told me it's something special. Will he tell me why, in hopes of getting other pieces? Or lie, to get this one cheap?* Rosenwald had a good reputation, but he was a Jew.

"Paul de Lamerie," Rosenwald said reverently, his index finger tracing the hallmark. "This was made by Paul de Lamerie."

A shock ran up Rakoczy's backbone. *Merde!* He'd brought the wrong one!

"Really?" he said, striving for simple curiosity. "Does that mean something?"

It means I'm a fool, he thought, and wondered whether to snatch the thing back and leave instantly. The goldsmith had carried it away, though, to look at it more closely under the lamp.

"De Lamerie was one of the very best goldsmiths ever to work in London—perhaps in the world," Rosenwald said, half to himself.

"Indeed," Rakoczy said politely. He was sweating freely. *Nom d'une pipe!* Wait, though—Rosenwald had said "was." De Lamerie was dead, then, thank God. Perhaps the Duke of Sandringham, from whom he'd stolen the salver, was dead, too? He began to breathe more easily.

He never sold anything identifiable within a hundred years of his acquisition of it; that was his principle. He'd taken the other salver from a rich merchant in a game of cards in the Low Countries in 1630; he'd stolen this one in 1745—much too close for comfort. Still . . .

His thoughts were interrupted by the chime of the silver bell over the door, and he turned to see a young man come in, removing his hat to reveal a startling head of dark-red hair. He was dressed *à la mode* and addressed the goldsmith in perfect Parisian French, but he didn't look French. A long-nosed face with faintly slanted eyes. There was a slight sense of familiarity about that face, yet Rakoczy was sure he'd never seen this man before.

"Please, sir, go on with your business," the young man said with a courteous bow. "I meant no interruption."

"No, no," Rakoczy said, stepping forward. He motioned the young man toward the counter. "Please, go ahead. Monsieur Rosenwald and I are merely discussing the value of this object. It will take some thought." He snaked out an arm and seized the salver, feeling a little better with it clasped to his bosom. He wasn't sure; if he decided it was too risky to sell, he could slink out quietly while Rosenwald was busy with the redheaded young man.

The Jew looked surprised but, after a moment's hesitation, nodded and turned to the young man, who introduced himself as one Michael Murray, partner in Fraser *et Cie*, the wine merchants.

"I believe you are acquainted with my cousin Jared Fraser?"

Rosenwald's round face lighted at once. "Oh, to be sure, sir! A man of the most exquisite taste and discrimination. I made him a wine cistern with a motif of sunflowers, not a year past!"

"I know." The young man smiled, a smile that creased his cheeks and narrowed his eyes, and that small bell of recognition rang again. But the name held no familiarity to Rakoczy—only the face, and that only vaguely.

"My uncle has another commission for you, if it's agreeable?"

"I never say no to honest work, monsieur." From the pleasure apparent on the goldsmith's rubicund face, honest work that paid very well was even more welcome.

"Well, then—if I may?" The young man pulled a folded paper from his pocket but half-turned toward Rakoczy, eyebrow cocked in inquiry. Rakoczy motioned him to go on and turned himself to examine a music box that stood on the counter—an enormous thing the size of a cow's head, crowned with a nearly naked nymph festooned with the airiest of gold draperies and dancing on mushrooms and flowers, in company with a large frog.

"A chalice," Murray was saying, the paper laid flat on the counter. From the corner of his eye, Rakoczy could see that it held a list of names. "It's a presentation to the chapel at le Couvent des Anges, to be given in memory of my late father. A young cousin of mine has just entered the convent there as a postulant," he explained. "So Monsieur Fraser thought that the best place."

"An excellent choice." Rosenwald picked up the list. "And you wish all of these names inscribed?"

"Yes, if you can."

"Monsieur!" Rosenwald waved a hand, professionally insulted. "These are your father's children?"

"Yes, these at the bottom." Murray bent over the counter, his finger tracing the lines, speaking the outlandish names carefully. "At the top, these are my parents' names: Ian Alastair Robert MacLeod Murray, and Janet Flora Arabella Fraser Murray. Now, also, I—we, I mean—we want these two names, as well: James Alexander Malcolm MacKenzie Fraser, and Claire Elizabeth Beauchamp Fraser. Those are my uncle and aunt; my uncle was very close to my father," he explained. "Almost a brother."

He went on saying something else, but Rakoczy wasn't listening. He grasped the edge of the counter, vision flickering so that the nymph seemed to leer at him.

Claire Fraser. That had been the woman's name, and her husband, James, a Highland lord from Scotland. That was who the young man resembled, though he was not so imposing as . . . But La Dame Blanche! It was her, it had to be.

And in the next instant, the goldsmith confirmed this, straightening up from the list with an abrupt air of wariness, as though one of the names might spring off the paper and bite him.

"That name—your aunt, she'd be? Did she and your uncle live in Paris at one time?"

"Yes," Murray said, looking mildly surprised. "Maybe thirty years ago—only for a short time, though. Did you know her?"

"Ah. Not to say I was personally acquainted," Rosenwald said, with a crooked smile. "But she was . . . known. People called her La Dame Blanche."

Murray blinked, clearly surprised to hear this.

"Really?" He looked rather appalled.

"Yes, but it was all a long time ago," Rosenwald said hastily, clearly thinking he'd said too much. He waved a hand toward his back room. "If you'll give me a moment, monsieur, I have a chalice actually here, if you would care to see it—and a paten, too; we might make some accommodation of price, if you take both. They were made for a patron who died suddenly, before the chalice was finished, so there is almost no decoration—plenty of room for the names to be applied, and perhaps we might put the, um, aunt and uncle on the paten?"

Murray nodded, interested, and, at Rosenwald's gesture, went round the counter and followed the old man into his back room. Rakoczy put the octofoil salver under his arm and left, as quietly as possible, head buzzing with questions.

JARED EYED MICHAEL over the dinner table, shook his head, and bent to his plate.

"I'm not drunk!" Michael blurted, then bent his own head, face flaming. He could feel Jared's eyes boring into the top of his head.

"Not now, ye're not." Jared's voice wasn't accusing. In fact, it was quiet, almost kindly. "But ye have been. Ye've not touched your dinner, and ye're the color of rotten wax."

"I—" The words caught in his throat, just as the food had. Eels in garlic sauce. The smell wafted up from the dish, and he stood up suddenly, lest he either vomit or burst into tears.

"I've nay appetite, cousin," he managed to say, before turning away. "Excuse me."

He would have left, but he hesitated that moment too long, not wanting to go up to the room where Lillie no longer was but not wanting to look petulant by rushing out into the street. Jared rose and came round to him with a decided step.

"I'm nay verra hungry myself, *a charaid*," Jared said, taking him by the arm. "Come sit wi' me for a bit and take a dram. It'll settle your wame."

He didn't much want to, but there was nothing else he could think of doing, and within a few moments he found himself in front of a fragrant applewood fire, with a glass of his father's whisky in hand, the warmth of both easing the tightness of chest and throat. It wouldn't cure his grief, he knew, but it made it possible to breathe.

"Good stuff," Jared said, sniffing cautiously but approvingly. "Even raw as it is. It'll be wonderful aged a few years."

"Aye. Uncle Jamie kens what he's about; he said he'd made whisky a good many times in America."

Jared chuckled.

"Your uncle Jamie usually kens what he's about," he said. "Not that knowing it keeps him out o' trouble." He shifted, making himself more comfortable in his worn leather chair. "Had it not been for the Rising, he'd likely have stayed here wi' me. Aye, well . . ." The old man sighed with regret and lifted his glass, examining the spirit. It was still nearly as pale as water—it hadn't been casked above a few months—but had the slightly viscous look of a fine strong spirit, as if it might climb out of the glass if you took your eye off it.

"And if he had, I suppose I'd not be here myself," Michael said dryly.

Jared glanced at him, surprised.

"Och! I didna mean to say ye were but a poor substitute for Jamie, lad." He smiled crookedly, and his hooded eyes grew moist. "Not at all. Ye've been the best thing ever to come to me. You and dear wee Lillie, and . . ." He cleared his throat. "I . . . well, I canna say anything that will help, I ken that. But . . . it won't always be like this."

"Won't it?" Michael said bleakly. "Aye, I'll take your word for it." A silence fell between them, broken only by the hissing and snap of the fire. The mention of Lillie was like an awl digging into his breastbone, and he took a deeper sip of the whisky to quell the ache. Maybe Jared was right to mention the drink to him. It helped, but not enough. And the help didn't last. He was tired of waking to grief and headache both.

Shying away from thoughts of Lillie, his mind fastened on Uncle Jamie instead. He'd lost his wife, too, and from what Michael had seen of the aftermath, it had torn his soul in two. Then she'd come back to him, and he was a man transformed. But in between . . . he'd managed. He'd found a way to be.

Thinking of Auntie Claire gave him a slight feeling of comfort: as long as he didn't think too much about what she'd told the family, who—or what—she was, and where she'd been while she was gone those twenty years. The brothers and sisters had talked among themselves about it afterward; Young Jamie and Kitty didn't believe a word of it, Maggie and Janet weren't sure—but Young Ian believed it, and that counted for a lot with Michael. And she'd looked at him—right at him—when she said what was going to happen in Paris. He felt the same small thrill of horror now, remembering. *The Terror. That's what it will be called, and that's what it will be. People will be arrested for no cause and beheaded in the Place de la Concorde. The streets will run with blood, and no one—no one— will be safe.*

He looked at his cousin; Jared was an old man, though still hale enough. Michael knew there was no way he could persuade Jared to leave Paris and his wine business. But it would be some time yet—if Auntie Claire was right. No need to think about it now. But she'd seemed so sure, like a seer, talking from a vantage point after everything had happened, from a safer time.

And yet she'd come back from that safe time, to be with Uncle Jamie again.

For a moment, he entertained the wild fantasy that Lillie wasn't dead but only swept away into a distant time. He couldn't see or touch her, but the knowledge that she was doing things, was alive . . . maybe it was knowing that, thinking that, that had kept Uncle Jamie whole. He swallowed, hard.

"Jared," he said, clearing his own throat. "What did ye think of Auntie Claire? When she lived here?"

Jared looked surprised but lowered his glass to his knee, pursing his lips in thought.

"She was a bonny lass, I'll tell ye that," he said. "Verra bonny. A tongue like the rough side of a rasp, if she took against something, though—and decided opinions." He nodded, twice, as though recalling a few, and grinned suddenly. "Verra decided indeed!"

"Aye? The goldsmith—Rosenwald, ye ken?—mentioned her when I went to commission the chalice and he saw her name on the list. He called her La Dame Blanche." This last was not phrased as a question, but he gave it a slight rising inflection, and Jared nodded, his smile widening into a grin.

"Oh, aye, I mind that! 'Twas Jamie's notion. She'd find herself now and then in dangerous places without him—ken how some folk are just the sort as things happen to—so he put it about that she was La Dame Blanche. Ken what a White Lady is, do ye?"

Michael crossed himself, and Jared followed suit, nodding.

"Aye, just so. Make any wicked sod with villainy in mind think twice. A White Lady can strike ye blind or shrivel a man's balls, and likely a few more things than that, should she take the notion. And I'd be the last to say that Claire Fraser couldn't, if she'd a mind to." Jared raised the glass absently to his lips, took a bigger sip of the raw spirit than he'd meant to, and coughed, spraying droplets of memorial whisky halfway across the room.

Rather to his own shock, Michael laughed.

Jared wiped his mouth, still coughing, but then sat up straight and lifted his glass, which still held a few drops.

"To your da. *Slàinte mhath!*"

"*Slàinte!*" Michael echoed, and drained what remained in his own glass. He set it down with finality and rose. He'd drink nay more tonight.

"*Oidhche mhath, mo bhràthair-athar no mathar.*"

"Good night, lad," said Jared. The fire was burning low but still cast a warm ruddy glow on the old man's face. "Fare ye well."

Next night

MICHAEL DROPPED HIS key several times before finally managing to turn it in the old-fashioned lock. It wasn't drink; he'd not had a drop since the wine at supper. Instead, he'd walked the length of the city and back, accompanied only by his thoughts; his whole body quivered and he felt mindless with exhaustion, but he was sure he would sleep. Jean-Baptiste had left the door unbarred, according to his orders, but one of the footmen was sprawled on a settle in the entryway, snoring. He smiled a little, though it was an effort to raise the corners of his mouth.

"Bolt the door and go to bed, Alphonse," he whispered, bending and shaking the man gently by the shoulder. The footman stirred and snorted, but Michael didn't wait to see whether he woke entirely. There was a tiny oil lamp burning on the landing of the stairs, a little round glass globe in the gaudy colors of Murano. It had been there since the first day he came from Scotland to stay with Jared, years before, and the sight of it soothed him and drew his aching body up the wide, dark stair.

The house creaked and talked to itself at night; all old houses did. To-night, though, it was silent, the big copper-seamed roof gone cold and its massive timbers settled into somnolence.

He flung off his clothes and crawled naked into bed, head spinning. Tired as he was, his flesh quivered and twitched, his legs jerking like a spit-ted frog's, before he finally relaxed enough to fall headfirst into the seeth-ing cauldron of dreams that awaited him.

She was there, of course. Laughing at him, playing with her ridiculous pug. Running a hand filled with desire across his face, down his neck, eas-ing her body close, and closer. Then they were somehow in bed, with the wind blowing cool through gauzy curtains, too cool, he felt cold, but then her warmth came close, pressed against him. He felt a terrible desire but at the same time feared her. She felt utterly familiar, utterly strange—and the mixture thrilled him.

He reached for her and realized that he couldn't raise his arms, couldn't move. And yet she was against him, writhing in a slow squirm of need, greedy and tantalizing. In the way of dreams, he was at the same time in front of her, behind her, touching, and seeing from a distance. Candle glow on naked breasts, the shadowed weight of solid buttocks, falling drapes of parting white, one round, firm leg protruding, a pointed toe rooting gently between his legs. Urgency.

She was curled behind him then, kissing the back of his neck, and he reached back, groping, but his hands were heavy, drifting; they slid help-less over her. Hers on him were firm, more than firm—she had him by the cock, was working him. Working him hard, fast and hard. He bucked and heaved, suddenly released from the dream swamp of immobility. She loosed her grip, tried to pull away, but he folded his hand round hers and rubbed their folded hands hard up and down with joyous ferocity, spilling himself convulsively, hot wet spurts against his belly, running thick over their clenched knuckles.

She made a sound of horrified disgust, and his eyes flew open. Staring into them were a pair of huge, bugging eyes, over a gargoyle's mouth full of tiny, sharp teeth. He shrieked.

Plonplon leaped off the bed and ran to and fro, barking hysterically. There was a body behind him. Michael flung himself off the bed, tangled in a winding sheet of damp, sticky bedclothes, then fell and rolled in panic.

"Jesus, Jesus, Jesus!"

On his knees, he gaped, rubbed his hands hard over his face, shook his head. Could *not* make sense of it, couldn't.

"Lillie," he gasped. "Lillie!"

But the woman in his bed, tears running down her face, wasn't Lillie; he realized it with a wrench that made him groan, doubling up in the desolation of fresh loss.

"Oh, Jesus!"

"Michel, Michel, please, please forgive me!"

"You . . . what . . . for God's *sake* . . . !"

Léonie was weeping frantically, reaching out toward him.

"I couldn't help it. I'm so lonely, I wanted you so much!"

Plonplon had ceased barking and now came up behind Michael, nosing his bare backside with a blast of hot, moist breath.

"Va-t'en!"

The pug backed up and started barking again, eyes bulging with offense.

Unable to find any words suitable to the situation, he grabbed the dog and muffled it with a handful of sheet. He got unsteadily to his feet, still holding the squirming pug.

"I—" he began. "You—I mean . . . oh, Jesus Christ!" He leaned over and put the dog carefully on the bed. Plonplon instantly wriggled free of the sheet and rushed to Léonie, licking her solicitously. Michael had thought of giving her the dog after Lillie's death, but for some reason this had seemed a betrayal of the pug's former mistress and brought Michael near to weeping.

"I can't," he said simply. "I just can't. You go to sleep now, lass. We'll talk about it later, aye?"

He went out, walking carefully, as though very drunk, and closed the door gently behind him. He got halfway down the main stair before realizing he was naked. He stood there, his mind blank, watching the colors of the Murano lamp fade as the daylight grew outside, until Paul saw him and ran up to wrap him in a cloak and lead him off to a bed in one of the guest rooms.

RAKOCZY'S FAVORITE gaming club was the Golden Cockerel, and the wall in the main salon was covered by a tapestry featuring one of these creatures, worked in gold thread, wings spread, and throat swollen as it crowed in triumph at the winning hand of cards laid out before it. It was a cheerful place, catering to a mix of wealthy merchants and lesser nobility, and the air was spicy with the scents of candle wax, powder, perfume, and money.

He'd thought of going to the offices of Fraser *et Cie,* making some excuse to speak to Michael Murray, and maneuvering his way into an inquiry about the whereabouts of the young man's aunt. Upon consideration, though, he thought such a move might make Murray wary—and possibly lead to word getting back to the woman, if she was somewhere in Paris. That was the last thing he wanted to happen.

Better, perhaps, to instigate his inquiries from a more discreet distance. He'd learned that Murray occasionally came to the Cockerel, though he himself had never seen him there. But if he was known . . .

It took several evenings of play, wine, and conversation before he found Charles Pépin. Pépin was a popinjay, a reckless gambler, and a man who liked to talk. And to drink. He was also a good friend of the young wine merchant's.

"Oh, the nun!" he said, when Rakoczy had—after the second bottle—mentioned having heard that Murray had a young relative who had recently entered the convent. Pépin laughed, his handsome face flushed.

"A less likely nun I've never seen—an arse that would make the archbishop of Paris forget his vows, and he's eighty-six if he's a day. Doesn't speak any sort of French, poor thing—the girl, not the archbishop. Not that I for one would be wanting to carry on a lot of conversation if I had her to myself, you understand. . . . She's Scotch; terrible accent . . ."

"Scotch, you say." Rakoczy held a card consideringly, then put it down. "She is Murray's cousin—would she perhaps be the daughter of his uncle James?"

Pépin looked blank for a moment.

"I don't really—oh, yes, I do know!" He laughed heartily, and laid down his own losing hand. "Dear me. Yes, she did say her father's name was Jay-mee, the way the Scotches do; that must be James."

Rakoczy felt a ripple of anticipation go up his spine. *Yes!* This sense of triumph was instantly succeeded by a breathless realization. The girl was the daughter of La Dame Blanche.

"I see," he said casually. "And which convent did you say the girl has gone to?"

To his surprise, Pépin gave him a suddenly sharp look.

"Why do you want to know?"

Rakoczy shrugged, thinking fast.

"A wager," he said, with a grin. "If she is as luscious as you say . . . I'll bet you five hundred *louis* that I can get her into bed before she takes her first vows."

Pépin scoffed.

"Oh, never! She's tasty, but she doesn't know it. And she's virtuous, I'd swear it. And if you think you can seduce her inside the convent . . . !"

Rakoczy lounged back in his chair and motioned for another bottle.

"In that case . . . what do you have to lose?"

Next day

SHE COULD SMELL the *hôpital* long before the small group of new postulants reached the door. They walked two by two, practicing custody of the eyes, but she couldn't help a quick glance upward at the building, a three-story chateau, originally a noble house that had—rumor said—been given to Mother Hildegarde by her father, as part of her dowry when she joined the church. It had become a convent house and then gradually had been given over more and more to the care of the sick, the nuns moving to the new chateau built in the park.

It was a lovely old house—on the outside. The odor of sickness, of urine and shit and vomit, hung about it like a cloying veil, though, and she hoped she wouldn't vomit, too. The little postulant next to her, Sister Miséricorde de Dieu (known to all simply as Mercy), was as white as her veil, eyes fixed on the ground but obviously not seeing it: she stepped smack on a slug and gave a small cry of horror as it squished under her sandal.

Joan looked hastily away; she would never master custody of the eyes, she was sure. Nor yet custody of thought.

It wasn't the notion of sick people that troubled her. She'd seen sick people before, and they wouldn't be expecting her to do more than wash and feed them; she could manage that easily. It was fear of seeing those who were about to die—for surely there would be a great many of those in a hospital. And what might the voices tell her about *them*?

As it was, the voices had nothing to say. Not a word, and after a little she began to lose her nervousness. She *could* do this and in fact, to her surprise, quite enjoyed the sense of competence, the gratification of being able to ease someone's pain, give them at least a little attention—and if her French made them laugh (and it did), that at least took their minds off pain and fear for a moment.

There were those who lay under the veil of death. Only a few, though, and it seemed somehow much less shocking here than when she had seen it on Vhairi's lad or the young man on the ship. Maybe it was resignation, perhaps the influence of the angels for whom the *hôpital* was named . . . Joan didn't know, but she found that she wasn't afraid to speak to or touch the ones she knew were going to die. For that matter, she observed that the other sisters, even the orderlies, behaved gently toward these people, and it occurred to her that no particular sight was needed to know that the man with the wasting sickness, whose bones poked through his skin, was not long for this world.

Touch him, said a soft voice inside her head. *Comfort him.*

All right, she said, taking a deep breath. She had no idea how to comfort anyone, but she bathed him, as gently as she could, and coaxed him to take a few spoonsful of porridge. Then she settled him in his bed, straightening his nightshirt and the thin blanket over him.

"Thank you, Sister," he said, and, taking her hand, kissed it. "Thank you for your sweet touch."

She went back to the postulants' dormitory that evening feeling thoughtful, but with a strange sense of being on the verge of discovering something important.

That night

RAKOCZY LAY WITH his head on Madeleine's bosom, eyes closed, breathing the scent of her body, feeling the whole of her between his palms, a slowly pulsing entity of light. She was a gentle gold, traced with veins of incandescent blue, her heart deep as lapis beneath his ear, a living stone. And, deep inside, her red womb, open, soft. Refuge and succor. Promise.

Mélisande had shown him the rudiments of sexual magic, and he'd read about it with great interest in some of the older alchemical texts. He'd never tried it with a whore, though—and, in fact, hadn't been trying to do it this time. And yet it had happened. Was happening. He could see the miracle unfolding slowly before him, under his hands.

How odd, he thought dreamily, watching the tiny traces of green energy spread upward through her womb, slowly but inexorably. He'd thought it happened instantly, that a man's seed found its root in the woman and there you were. But that wasn't what was happening at all. There were *two* types of seed, he now saw. She had one; he felt it plainly, a brilliant speck of light, glowing like a fierce, tiny sun. His own—the tiny green animalcula—were being drawn toward it, bent on immolation.

"Happy, *chéri?*" she whispered, stroking his hair. "Did you have a good time?"

"Most happy, sweetheart." He wished she wouldn't talk, but an unexpected sense of tenderness toward her made him sit up and smile at her. She also began to sit up, reaching for the clean rag and douching syringe, and he put a hand on her shoulder, urging her to lie back down.

"Don't douche this time, *ma belle,*" he said. "A favor to me."

"But—" She was confused; usually he was insistent upon cleanliness.

"Do you *want* me to get with child?" For he had stopped her using the wine-soaked sponge beforehand, too.

"Yes, of course," he said, surprised. "Did Madame Fabienne not tell you?"

Her mouth dropped open.

"She did *not*. What—why, for God's sake?" In agitation, she squirmed free of his restraining hand and swung her legs out of bed, reaching for her wrapper. "You aren't—what do you mean to do with it?"

"Do with it?" he said, blinking. "What do you mean, do with it?"

She had the wrapper on, pulled crookedly round her shoulders, and had backed up against the wall, hands plastered against her stomach, regarding him with open fear.

"You're a *magicien;* everyone knows that. You take newborn children and use their blood in your spells!"

"What?" he said, rather stupidly. He reached for his breeches but changed his mind. He got up and went to her instead, putting his hands on her shoulders.

"No," he said, bending down to look her in the eye. "No, I do no such thing. Never." He used all the force of sincerity he could summon, pushing it into her, and felt her waver a little, still fearful but less certain. He smiled at her.

"Who told you I was a *magicien,* for heaven's sake? I am a *philosophe, chérie*—an inquirer into the mysteries of nature, no more. And I can swear to you, by my hope of heaven"—this being more or less nonexistent, but why quibble?—"that I have never, not once, used anything more than the water of a man-child in any of my investigations."

"What, little boys' piss?" she said, diverted. He let his hands relax but kept them on her shoulders.

"Certainly. It's the purest water one can find. Collecting it is something of a chore, mind you"—she smiled at that; good—"but the process does not the slightest harm to the infant, who will eject the water whether anyone has a use for it or not."

"Oh." She was beginning to relax a little, but her hands were still pressed protectively over her belly, as though she felt the imminent child already. *Not yet,* he thought, pulling her against him and feeling his way gently into her body. *But soon!* He wondered if he should remain with her until it happened; the idea of feeling it as it happened inside her—to be an intimate witness to the creation of life itself! But there was no telling how long it might take. From the progress of his animalcula, it could be a day, even two.

Magic, indeed.

Why do men never think of that? he wondered. Most men—himself included—regarded the engendering of babies as necessity, in the case of inheritance, or nuisance, but *this* . . . But then, most men would never know what he now knew or see what he had seen.

Madeleine had begun to relax against him, her hands at last leaving her belly. He kissed her, with a real feeling of affection.

"It will be beautiful," he whispered to her. "And once you are well and truly with child, I will buy your contract from Fabienne and take you away. I will buy you a house."

"A *house?*" Her eyes went round. They were green, a deep, clear emerald, and he smiled at her again, stepping back.

"Of course. Now, go and sleep, my dear. I shall come again tomorrow."

She flung her arms around him, and he had some difficulty in extracting himself, laughing, from her embraces. Normally he left a whore's bed with no feeling save physical relief. But what he had done had made a connection with Madeleine that he had not experienced with any woman save Mélisande.

Mélisande. A sudden thought ran through him like the spark from a Leyden jar. *Mélisande.*

He looked hard at Madeleine, now crawling happily naked and white-rumped into bed, her wrapper thrown aside. That bottom . . . the eyes, the soft blond hair, the gold-white of fresh cream.

"Chérie," he said, as casually as he might, pulling on his breeches, "how old are you?"

"Eighteen," she said, without hesitation. "Why, monsieur?"

"Ah. A wonderful age to become a mother." He pulled the shirt over his head and kissed his hand to her, relieved. He had known Mélisande Robicheaux in 1744. He had not, in fact, just committed incest with his own daughter.

It was only as he passed Madame Fabienne's parlor on his way out that it occurred to him that Madeleine *might* possibly still be his granddaughter. That thought stopped him short, but he had no time to dwell on it, for Fabienne appeared in the doorway and motioned to him.

"A message, monsieur," she said, and something in her voice touched his nape with a cold finger.

"Yes?"

"*Maître Grenouille* begs the favor of your company at midnight tomorrow. In the square before Notre Dame de Paris."

THEY DIDN'T HAVE to practice custody of the eyes in the market. In fact, Sister George—the stout nun who oversaw these expeditions, warned them in no uncertain terms to keep a sharp eye out for short weight and uncivil prices, to say nothing of pickpockets.

"Pickpockets, Sister?" Mercy had said, her blond eyebrows all but vanishing into her veil. "But we are nuns—more or less," she added hastily. "We have nothing to steal!"

Sister George's big red face got somewhat redder, but she kept her patience.

"Normally that would be true," she agreed. "But we—or I, rather—have the money with which to buy our food, and once we've bought it, you will be carrying it. A pickpocket steals to eat, *n'est-ce pas*? They don't care whether you have money or food, and most of them are so depraved that they would willingly steal from God himself, let alone a couple of chick-headed postulants."

For Joan's part, she wanted to see *everything*, pickpockets included. To her delight, the market was the one she'd passed with Michael on her first day in Paris. True, the sight of it brought back the horrors and doubts of that first day, too—but, for the moment, she pushed those aside and followed Sister George into the fascinating maelstrom of color, smells, and shouting.

Filing away a particularly entertaining expression that she planned to make Sister Philomène explain to her—Sister Philomène was a little older than Joan, but painfully shy and with such delicate skin that she blushed like an apple at the least excuse—she followed Sister George and Sister Mathilde through the fishmonger's section, where Sister George bargained shrewdly for a great quantity of sand dabs, scallops, tiny gray translucent shrimp, and an enormous sea salmon, the pale spring light shifting through its scales in colors that faded so subtly from pink to blue to silver and back that some of them had no name at all—so beautiful even in its death that it made Joan catch her breath with joy at the wonder of creation.

"Oh, *bouillabaisse* tonight!" said Mercy, under her breath. *"Délicieuse!"*

"What is *bouillabaisse*?" Joan whispered back.

"Fish stew—you'll like it, I promise!" Joan had no doubt of it; brought up in the Highlands during the poverty-stricken years following the Rising, she'd been staggered by the novelty, deliciousness, and sheer abundance of the convent's food. Even on Fridays, when the community fasted during the day, supper was simple but mouthwatering, toasted sharp cheese on nutty brown bread with sliced apples.

Luckily, the salmon was so huge that Sister George arranged for the fish seller to deliver it to the convent, along with the other briny purchases; thus they had room in their baskets for fresh vegetables and fruit and so passed from Neptune's realm to that of Demeter. Joan hoped it wasn't sacrilegious to think of Greek gods, but she couldn't forget the book of myths that Da had read to Marsali and her when they were young, with wonderful hand-colored illustrations.

After all, she told herself, you needed to know about the Greeks if you studied medicine. She had some trepidation at the thought of working in the hospital, but God called people to do things, and if it was his will, then—

The thought stopped short as she caught sight of a neat dark tricorne with a curled blue feather bobbing slowly through the tide of people. Was it—it was! Léonie, the sister of Michael Murray's dead wife. Moved by curiosity, Joan glanced at Sister George, who was engrossed in a huge display of fungus—dear God, people *ate* such things?—and slipped around a barrow billowing with green sallet herbs.

She meant to speak to Léonie, ask her to tell Michael that she needed to talk to him. Perhaps he could contrive a way to visit the convent . . . But before Joan could get close enough, Léonie looked furtively over her shoulder, as though fearing discovery, then ducked behind a curtain that hung across the back of a small caravan.

Joan had seen gypsies before, though not often. A dark-skinned man loitered nearby, talking with a group of others; their eyes passed over her habit without pausing, and she sighed with relief. Being a nun was as good as having a cloak of invisibility in most circumstances, she thought.

She looked round for her companions and saw that Sister Mathilde had been called into consultation regarding a big warty lump of something that looked like the excrement of a seriously diseased hog. Good, she could wait for a minute longer.

In fact, it took very little more than that before Léonie slipped out from behind the curtain, tucking something into the small basket on her arm. For the first time, it struck Joan as unusual that someone like Léonie should be shopping without a servant to push back crowds and carry purchases—or even be in a public market. Michael had told her about his own household during the voyage—how Madame Hortense, the cook, went to the markets at dawn to be sure of getting the freshest things. What would a lady like Léonie be buying, alone?

Joan slithered as best she could through the rows of stalls and wagons, following the bobbing blue feather. A sudden stop allowed her to come up behind Léonie, who had paused by a flower stall, fingering a bunch of white jonquils.

It occurred suddenly to Joan that she had no idea what Léonie's last name was, but she couldn't worry about politeness now.

"Ah . . . madame?" she said tentatively. "Mademoiselle, I mean?" Léonie swung round, eyes huge and face pale. Finding herself faced with a nun, she blinked, confused.

"Er . . . it's me," Joan said, diffident, resisting the impulse to pull off her veil. "Joan MacKimmie?" It felt odd to say it, as though "Joan MacKimmie" were truly someone else. It took a moment for the name to register, but then Léonie's shoulders relaxed a little.

"Oh." She put a hand to her bosom and mustered a small smile. "Michael's cousin. Of course. I didn't . . . er . . . How nice to see you!" A small frown wrinkled the skin between her brows. "Are you . . . alone?"

"No," Joan said hurriedly. "And I mustn't stop. I only saw you, and I wanted to ask—" It seemed even stupider than it had a moment ago, but no help for it. "Would you tell Monsieur Murray that I must talk to him? I know something—something important—that I have to tell him."

"Soeur Gregory?" Sister George's stentorian tones boomed through the higher-pitched racket of the market, making Joan jump. She could see the top of Sister Mathilde's head, with its great white sails, turning to and fro in vain search.

"I have to go," she said to the astonished Léonie. "Please. Please tell him!" Her heart was pounding, and not only from the sudden meeting. She'd been looking at Léonie's basket, where she caught the glint of a brown glass bottle half hidden beneath a thick bunch of what even Joan recognized as black hellebores. Lovely cup-shaped flowers of an eerie greenish-white—and deadly poison.

She dodged back across the market to arrive breathless and apologizing at Sister Mathilde's side, wondering if . . . She hadn't spent much time at all with Da's wife—but she *had* heard her talking with Da as she wrote down receipts in a book, and she'd mentioned black hellebore as something women used to make themselves miscarry. If Léonie were pregnant . . . Holy Mother of God, could she be with child by *Michael*? The thought struck her like a blow in the stomach.

No. No, she couldn't believe it. He was still in love with his wife, anyone could see that, and even if not, she'd swear he wasn't the sort to . . . But what did she ken about men, after all?

Well, she'd ask him when she saw him, she decided, her mouth clamping tight. And 'til then . . . Her hand went to the rosary at her waist and she said a quick, silent prayer for Léonie. Just in case.

As she was bargaining doggedly in her execrable French for six aubergines (wondering meanwhile what on earth they were for, medicine or food?), she became aware of someone standing at her elbow. A handsome man of middle age, taller than she was, in a well-cut dove-gray coat. He smiled at her and, touching one of the peculiar vegetables, said in slow, simple French, "You don't want the big ones. They're tough. Get small ones, like that." A long finger tapped an aubergine half the size of the ones the vegetable seller had been urging on her, and the vegetable seller burst into a tirade of abuse that made Joan step back, blinking.

Not so much because of the expressions being hurled at her—she didn't understand one word in ten—but because a voice in plain English had just said clearly, *"Tell him not to do it."*

She felt hot and cold at the same time.

"I . . . er . . . *je suis* . . . um . . . *merci beaucoup, monsieur!*" she blurted, and, turning, ran, scrambling back between piles of paper narcissus bulbs and fragrant spikes of hyacinth, her shoes skidding on the slime of trodden leaves.

"Soeur Gregory!" Sister Mathilde loomed up so suddenly in front of her that she nearly ran into the massive nun. "What are you doing? Where is Sister Miséricorde?"

"I . . . oh." Joan swallowed, gathering her wits. "She's—over there." She spoke with relief, spotting Mercy's small head in the forefront of a crowd by the meat-pie wagon. "I'll get her!" she blurted, and walked hastily off before Sister Mathilde could say more.

"Tell him not to do it." That's what the voice had said about Charles Pépin. What was going on? she thought wildly. Was M. Pépin engaged in something awful with the man in the dove-gray coat?

As though thought of the man had reminded the voice, it came again.

"Tell him not to do it," the voice repeated in her head, with what seemed like particular urgency. *"Tell him he must not!"*

"Hail Mary, full of grace, the Lord is with thee, blessed art thou among women . . ." Joan clutched at her rosary and gabbled the words, feeling the blood leave her face. There he was, the man in the dove-gray coat, looking curiously at her over a stall of Dutch tulips and sprays of yellow forsythia.

She couldn't feel the pavement under her feet but was moving toward him. *I have to,* she thought. *It doesn't matter if he thinks I'm mad. . . .*

"Don't do it," she blurted, coming face-to-face with the astonished gentleman. "You mustn't do it!"

And then she turned and ran, rosary in hand, apron and veil flapping like wings.

HE COULDN'T HELP thinking of the cathedral as an entity. An immense version of one of its own gargoyles, crouched over the city. In protection or threat?

Notre Dame de Paris rose black above him, solid, obliterating the light of the stars, the beauty of the night. Very appropriate. He'd always thought that the church blocked one's sight of God. Nonetheless, the sight of the monstrous stone creature made him shiver as he passed under its shadow, despite the warm cloak.

Perhaps it was the cathedral's stones themselves that gave him the sense of menace? He stopped, paused for a heartbeat, and then strode up to the church's wall and pressed his palm flat against the cold limestone. There was no immediate sense of anything, just the cold roughness of the rock. Impulsively, he shut his eyes and tried to feel his way into the rock. At first, nothing. But he waited, pressing with his mind, a repeated question. *Are you there?*

He would have been terrified to receive an answer but was obscurely disappointed not to. Even so, when he finally opened his eyes and took his hands away, he saw a trace of blue light, the barest trace, glowing briefly between his knuckles. That frightened him, and he hurried away, hiding his hands beneath the shelter of the cloak.

Surely not, he assured himself. He'd done that before, made the light happen when he held the jewels he used for travel and said the words over them—his own version of consecration, he supposed. He didn't know if the words were necessary, but Mélisande had used them; he was afraid not to. And yet. He had felt *something* here. The sense of something heavy, inert. Nothing resembling thought, let alone speech, thank God. By reflex, he crossed himself, then shook his head, rattled and irritated.

But something. Something immense and very old. Did God have the voice of a stone? He was further unsettled by the thought. The stones there in the chalk mine, the noise they made—was it after all God that he'd glimpsed, there in that space between?

A movement in the shadows banished all such thoughts in an instant. The frog! Rakoczy's heart clenched like a fist.

"Monsieur le Comte," said an amused, gravelly voice. "I see the years have been kind to you."

Raymond stepped into the starlight, smiling. The sight of him was disconcerting; Rakoczy had imagined this meeting for so long that the reality seemed oddly anticlimactic. Short, broad-shouldered, with long, loose hair that swept back from a massive forehead. A broad, almost lipless mouth. Raymond the frog.

"Why are you here?" Rakoczy blurted.

Maître Raymond's brows were black—surely they had been white thirty years ago? One of them lifted in puzzlement.

"I was told that you were looking for me, monsieur." He spread his hands, the gesture graceful. "I came!"

"Thank you," Rakoczy said dryly, beginning to regain some composure. "I meant—why are you in Paris?"

"Everyone has to be somewhere, don't they? They can't be in the same place." This should have sounded like badinage but didn't. It sounded serious, like a statement of scientific principle, and Rakoczy found it unsettling.

"Did you come looking for me?" he asked boldly. He moved a little, trying to get a better view of the man. He was nearly sure that the frog appeared *younger* than he had when last seen. Surely his flowing hair was darker, his step more elastic? A spurt of excitement bubbled in his chest.

"For you?" The frog seemed amused for a moment, but then the look faded. "No. I'm searching for a lost daughter."

Rakoczy was surprised and disconcerted.

"Yours?"

"More or less." Raymond seemed uninterested in explaining further. He moved a little to one side, eyes narrowing as he sought to make out Rakoczy's face in the darkness. "You can hear stones, then, can you?"

"I—what?"

Raymond nodded at the façade of the cathedral. "They do speak. They move, too, but very slowly."

An icy chill shot up Rakoczy's spine at the thought of the grinning gargoyles perched high above him and the implication that one might at any moment choose to spread its silent wings and hurtle down upon him, teeth still bared in carnivorous hilarity. Despite himself, he looked up, over his shoulder.

"Not that fast." The note of amusement was back in the frog's voice. "You would never see them. It takes them millennia to move the slightest fraction of an inch—unless of course they are propelled or melted. But you don't want to see them do that, of course. Much too dangerous."

This kind of talk struck him as frivolous, and Rakoczy was bothered by it but for some reason not irritated. Troubled, with a sense that there was something under it, something that he simultaneously wanted to know— and wanted very much to avoid knowing. The sensation was novel, and unpleasant.

He cast caution to the wind and demanded boldly, "Why did you not kill me?"

Raymond grinned at him; Rakoczy could see the flash of teeth and felt yet another shock: he was sure—almost sure—that the frog had *had* no teeth when last seen.

"If I had wanted you dead, son, you wouldn't be here talking to me," he said. "I wanted you to be out of the way, that's all; you obliged me by taking the hint."

"And just why did you want me 'out of the way'?" Had he not needed to find out, Rakcozy would have taken offense at the man's tone.

The frog lifted one shoulder.

"You were something of a threat to the lady."

Sheer astonishment brought Rakoczy to his full height.

"The lady? You mean the woman—La Dame Blanche?"

"They did call her that." The frog seemed to find the notion amusing.

It was on the tip of Rakoczy's tongue to tell Raymond that La Dame

Blanche still lived, but he hadn't lived as long as he had by blurting out everything he knew—and he didn't want Raymond thinking that he himself might be still a threat to her.

"What is the ultimate goal of an alchemist?" the frog said very seriously.

"To transform matter," Rakoczy replied automatically.

The frog's face split in a broad amphibian grin.

"Exactly!" he said. And vanished.

He *had* vanished. No puffs of smoke, no illusionist's tricks, no smell of sulfur—the frog was simply gone. The square stretched empty under the starlit sky; the only thing that moved was a cat that darted mewing out of the shadows and brushed past Rakoczy's leg.

Rakoczy was so shaken—and so excited—by the encounter that he wandered without knowing where he was going, crossed bridges without noticing, lost his way among the maze of twisting streets and allées on the Left Bank and did not reach his house till nearly dawn, footsore and exhausted but with his mind buzzing with speculation.

Younger. He was sure of it. Raymond the frog was *younger* than he had been thirty years before. So it could be done—somehow.

He was convinced now that Raymond was indeed a traveler, like him. It had to be the travel: specifically, traveling forward in time. But how? He'd tried, more than once. To go back was dangerous, and the journey depleted you physically, but it was possible. If you had the right combinations of stones, you could even arrive at a certain time—more or less. But you needed also a focus, someone or something upon which to fix the mind; without that, you might still end up at some random point. And that, he thought, was the problem in going forward: it wasn't possible to focus on something you didn't know was there.

But Master Raymond had done it.

How, then, to persuade the frog to share the secret? Raymond did not seem to be hostile to him, but neither did he seem friendly; Rakoczy would hardly have expected him to be.

A lost daughter, the frog had said. And he had poisoned Rakoczy to remove him as a threat to the Fraser woman, La Dame Blanche. And the woman had glowed with blue light—because she had touched him, when handing him the cup? He couldn't remember. But she had glowed, he was positive.

So. If he was right, then she, too, was a traveler.

"*Merveilleuse,*" he whispered. He had already been interested in the woman; now he was possessed. Not only did he want—need—to know what she knew; she was important to Raymond in some way, perhaps connected with the lost daughter—perhaps she *was* the lost daughter?

If he could but lay hands on her . . . He had made a few cautious inquiries, but no one in the Court of Miracles, or among his more respectable connections, had heard anything of Claire Fraser in the last thirty years. Her husband had been political, had died, he thought, in Scotland. But if she had gone to Scotland with him, how did Raymond come to be searching for her in Paris?

These thoughts, and many more like them, ran round in his head like a pack of fleas, raising itching welts of curiosity.

The sky had begun to lighten, though the stars still burned dimly above the rooftops. The scent of fresh woodsmoke touched him, and a whiff of yeast: the boulangeries firing their ovens for the day's bread. A distant clop of hooves, as the farmers' wagons came in from the country, full of vegetables, fresh meat, eggs, and flowers. The city was beginning to stir.

His own house, his own bed. His mind had slowed now, and the thought of sleep was overwhelming. There was a gray cat sitting on the stoop of his house, washing its paws.

"Bonjour," he said to it, and in his drowsy, exhausted state, almost expected it to answer him. It didn't, though, and when the butler opened the door it vanished, so quickly that he wondered whether it had ever really been there.

WORN OUT WITH constant walking, Michael slept like the dead these days, without dreams or motion, and woke when the sun came up. His valet, Robert, heard him stir and came in at once, one of the *femmes de chambre* on his heels with a bowl of coffee and some pastry.

He ate slowly, suffering himself to be brushed, shaved, and tenderly tidied into fresh linen. Robert kept up a soothing murmur of the sort of conversation that doesn't require response and smiled encouragingly when presenting the mirror. Rather to Michael's surprise, the image in the mirror looked quite normal. Hair neatly clubbed—he wore his own, without powder—suit modest in cut but of the highest quality. Robert hadn't asked him what he required but had dressed him for an ordinary day of business. He supposed that was all right. What, after all, did clothes matter? It wasn't as though there was a costume *de rigueur* for calling upon the sister of one's deceased wife, who had come uninvited into one's bed in the middle of the night.

He had spent the last two days trying to think of some way never to see or speak to Léonie again, but, really, there was no help for it. He'd have to see her.

But what was he to say to her, he wondered, as he made his way through the streets toward the house where Léonie lived with an aged aunt, Eugenie Galantine. He wished he could talk the situation over with Sister Joan, but that wouldn't be appropriate, even were she available.

He'd hoped that walking would give him time to come up at least with a *point d'appui,* if not an entire statement of principle, but instead he found himself obsessively counting the flagstones of the market as he crossed it, counting the bongs of the public horologe as it struck the hour of three, and—for lack of anything else—counting his own footsteps as he approached her door. *Six hundred and thirty-seven, six hundred and thirty-eight . . .*

As he turned into the street, though, he abruptly stopped counting. He stopped walking, too, for an instant—then began to run. Something was wrong at the house of Madame Galantine.

He pushed his way through the crowd of neighbors and vendors clustered near the steps and seized the butler, whom he knew, by a sleeve.

"What?" he barked. "What's happened?" The butler, a tall, cadaverous man named Hubert, was plainly agitated but settled a bit on seeing Michael.

"I don't know, sir," he said, though a sideways slide of his eyes made it clear that he did. "Mademoiselle Léonie . . . she's ill. The doctor . . ."

He could smell the blood. Not waiting for more, he pushed Hubert aside and sprinted up the stairs, calling for Madame Eugenie, Léonie's aunt.

Madame Eugenie popped out of a bedroom, her cap and wrapper neat in spite of the uproar.

"Monsieur Michel!" she said, blocking him from entering the room. "It's all right, but you must not go in."

"Yes, I must." His heart was thundering in his ears, and his hands felt cold.

"You may *not,*" she said firmly. "She's ill. It isn't proper."

"Proper? A young woman tries to make away with herself and you tell me it isn't *proper*?"

A maid appeared in the doorway, a basket piled with bloodstained linen in her arms, but the look of shock on Madame Eugenie's broad face was more striking.

"Make away with herself?" The old lady's mouth hung open for a moment, then snapped shut like a turtle's. "Why would you think such a thing?" She was regarding him with considerable suspicion. "And what are you doing here, for that matter? Who told you she was ill?"

A glimpse of a man in a dark robe, who must be the doctor, decided Michael that little was to be gained by engaging further with Madame Eugenie. He took her gently but firmly by the elbows, picked her up—she uttered a small shriek of surprise—and set her aside.

He went in and shut the bedroom door behind him.

"Who are you?" The doctor looked up, surprised. He was wiping out a freshly used bleeding-bowl, and his case lay open on the boudoir's settee.

Léonie's bedroom must lie beyond; the door was open, and Michael caught a glimpse of the foot of a bed but could not see the bed's inhabitant.

"It doesn't matter. How is she?"

The doctor eyed him narrowly, but after a moment nodded.

"She will live. As for the child . . ." He made an equivocal motion of the hand. "I've done my best. She took a great deal of the—"

"The *child*?" The floor shifted under his feet, and the dream of the night before flooded him, that queer sense of something half wrong, half familiar. It was the feeling of a small, hard swelling pressed against his bum; that's what it was. Lillie had not been far gone with child when she died, but he remembered all too well the feeling of a woman's body in early pregnancy.

"It's yours? I beg your pardon, I shouldn't ask." The doctor put away his bowl and fleam and shook out his black velvet turban.

"I want—I need to talk to her. Now."

The doctor opened his mouth in automatic protest but then glanced thoughtfully over his shoulder.

"Well . . . you must be careful not to—" But Michael was already inside the bedroom, standing by the bed.

She was pale. They had always been pale, Lillie and Léonie, with the soft glow of cream and marble. This was the paleness of a frog's belly, of a rotting fish, blanched on the shore.

Her eyes were ringed with black, sunk in her head. They rested on his face, flat, expressionless, as still as the ringless hands that lay limp on the coverlet.

"Who?" he said quietly. "Charles?"

"Yes." Her voice was as dull as her eyes, and he wondered whether the doctor had drugged her.

"Was it his idea—to try to foist the child off on me? Or yours?"

She did look away then, and her throat moved.

"His." The eyes came back to him. "I didn't want to, Michel. Not—not that I find you disgusting, not that . . ."

"Merci," he muttered, but she went on, disregarding him.

"You were Lillie's husband. I didn't envy her you," she said frankly, "but I envied what you had together. It couldn't be like that between you and me, and I didn't like betraying her. But"—her lips, already pale, compressed to invisibility—"I didn't have much choice."

He was obliged to admit that she hadn't. Charles couldn't marry her; he had a wife. Bearing an illegitimate child was not a fatal scandal in high court circles, but the Galantines were of the emerging bourgeoisie, where respectability counted for almost as much as money. Finding herself pregnant, she would have had two alternatives: find a complaisant husband quickly, or . . . He tried not to see that one of her hands rested lightly across the slight swell of her stomach.

The child . . . He wondered what he would have done had she come to him and told him the truth, asked him to marry her for the sake of the child. But she hadn't. And she wasn't asking now.

It would be best—or at least easiest—were she to lose the child. And she might yet.

"I couldn't wait, you see," she said, as though continuing a conversation. "I would have tried to find someone else, but I thought she knew. She'd tell you as soon as she could manage to see you. So I had to, you see, before you found out."

"She? Who? Tell me what?"

"The nun," Léonie said, and sighed deeply, as though losing interest. "She saw me in the market and rushed up to me. She said she had to talk to you—that she had something important to tell you. I saw her look into my basket, though, and her face . . . thought she must realize . . ."

Her eyelids were fluttering, whether from drugs or fatigue, he couldn't tell. She smiled faintly, but not at him; she seemed to be looking at something a long way off.

"So funny," she murmured. "Charles said it would solve everything— that the comte would pay him such a lot for her, it would solve everything. But how can you solve a baby?"

Michael jerked as though her words had stabbed him.

"What? Pay for whom?"

"The nun."

He grabbed her by the shoulders.

"Sister Joan? What do you mean, pay for her? What did Charles tell you?"

She made a whiny sound of protest. Michael wanted to shake her hard enough to break her neck but forced himself to withdraw his hand. She settled into the pillow like a bladder losing air, flattening under the bedclothes. Her eyes were closed, but he bent down, speaking directly into her ear.

"The comte, Léonie. What is his name? Tell me his name."

A faint frown rippled the flesh of her brow, then passed.

"St. Germain," she murmured, scarcely loud enough to be heard. "The Comte St. Germain."

HE WENT INSTANTLY to Rosenwald and, by dint of badgering and the promise of extra payment, got him to finish the engraving on the chalice at once. Michael waited impatiently while it was done and, scarcely pausing for the cup and paten to be wrapped in brown paper, flung money to the goldsmith and made for les Couvent des Anges, almost running.

With great difficulty, he restrained himself while making the presentation of the chalice, and with great humility, he inquired whether he might ask the great favor of seeing Sister Gregory, that he might convey a message to her from her family in the Highlands. Sister Eustacia looked surprised and somewhat disapproving—postulants were not normally permitted visits—but after all . . . in view of Monsieur Murray's and Monsieur Fraser's great generosity to the convent . . . perhaps just a few moments, in the visitor's parlor, and in the presence of Sister herself . . .

HE TURNED AND blinked once, his mouth opening a little. He looked shocked. Did she look so different in her robe and veil?

"It's me," Joan said, and tried to smile reassuringly. "I mean . . . still me."

His eyes fixed on her face, and he let out a deep breath and smiled, as if she'd been lost and he'd found her again.

"Aye, so it is," he said softly. "I was afraid it was Sister Gregory. I mean, the . . . er . . ." He made a sketchy, awkward gesture indicating her gray robes and white postulant's veil.

"It's only clothes," she said, and put a hand to her chest, defensive.

"Well, no," he said, looking her over carefully, "I dinna think it is, quite. It's more like a soldier's uniform, no? Ye're doing your job when ye wear it, and everybody as sees it kens what ye are and knows what ye do."

Kens what I am. I suppose I should be pleased it doesn't *show,* she thought, a little wildly.

"Well . . . aye, I suppose." She fingered the rosary at her belt. She coughed. "In a way, at least."

Ye've got to tell him. It wasn't one of the voices, just the voice of her own conscience, but that was demanding enough. She could feel her heart beating, so hard that she thought the bumping must show through the front of her habit.

He smiled encouragingly at her.

"Léonie told me ye wanted to see me."

"Michael . . . can I tell ye something?" she blurted.

He seemed surprised. "Well, of course ye can," he said. "Whyever not?"

"Whyever not," she said, half under her breath. She glanced over his shoulder, but Sister Eustacia was on the far side of the room, talking to a very young, frightened-looking French girl and her parents.

"Well, it's like this, see," she said, in a determined voice. "I hear voices."

She stole a look at him, but he didn't appear shocked. Not yet.

"In my head, I mean."

"Aye?" He sounded cautious. "Um . . . what do they say, then?"

She realized she was holding her breath, and let a little of it out.

"Ah . . . different things. But they now and then tell me something's going to happen. More often, they tell me I should say thus-and-so to someone."

"Thus-and-so," he repeated attentively, watching her face. "What . . . *sort* of thus-and-so?"

"I wasna expecting the Spanish Inquisition," she said, a little testily. "Does it matter?"

His mouth twitched.

"Well, I dinna ken, now, do I?" he pointed out. "It might give a clue as to who's talkin' to ye, might it not? Or do ye already know that?"

"No, I don't," she admitted, and felt a sudden lessening of tension. "I—I was worrit—a bit—that it might be demons. But it doesna really . . . well, they dinna tell me *wicked* sorts of things. Just . . . more like when something's going to happen to a person. And sometimes it's no a good thing—but sometimes it is. There was wee Annie MacLaren, her wi' a big belly by the third month, and by six lookin' as though she'd burst, and she was frightened she was goin' to die come her time, like her ain mother did, wi' a babe too big to be born—I mean, *really* frightened, not just like all women are. And I met her by St. Ninian's Spring one day, and one of the voices said to me, '*Tell her it will be as God wills and she will be delivered safely of a son.*' "

"And ye did tell her that?"

"Yes. I didna say how I knew, but I must have sounded like I *did* know, because her poor face got bright all of a sudden, and she grabbed on to my hands and said, 'Oh! From your lips to God's ear!' "

"And was she safely delivered of a son?"

"Aye—and a daughter, too." Joan smiled, remembering the glow on Annie's face.

Michael glanced aside at Sister Eustacia, who was bidding farewell to the new postulant's family. The girl was white-faced and tears ran down her cheeks, but she clung to Sister Eustacia's sleeve as though it were a lifeline.

"I see," he said slowly, and looked back at Joan. "Is that why—is it the voices told ye to be a nun, then?"

She blinked, surprised by his apparent acceptance of what she'd told him but more so by the question.

"Well . . . no. They never did. Ye'd think they would have, wouldn't ye?"

He smiled a little.

"Maybe so." He coughed, then looked up, a little shyly. "It's no my business, but what *did* make ye want to be a nun?"

She hesitated, but why not? She'd already told him the hardest bit.

"Because of the voices. I thought maybe—maybe I wouldna hear them in here. Or . . . if I still did, maybe somebody—a priest, maybe?—could tell me what they were and what I should do about them."

Sister Eustacia was comforting the new girl, half-sunk on one knee to bring her big, homely, sweet face close to the girl's. Michael glanced at them, then back at Joan, one eyebrow raised.

"I'm guessing ye havena told anyone yet," he said. "Did ye reckon ye'd practice on me first?"

Her own mouth twitched.

"Maybe." His eyes were dark but had a sort of warmth to them, as if they drew it from the heat of his hair. She looked down; her hands were pleating the edge of her blouse, which had come untucked. "It's no just that, though."

He made the sort of noise in his throat that meant, *"Aye, then, go on."* Why didn't French people do like that? she wondered. So much easier. But she pushed the thought aside; she'd made up her mind to tell him, and now was the time to do it.

"I told ye because—that man," she blurted. "The Comte." He squinted at her. "The Comte St. Germain?"

"Well, I dinna ken his name, now, do I?" she snapped. "But when I saw him, one of the voices pops up and says to me, *'Tell him not to do it. Tell him he must not.'*"

"It did?"

"Aye, and it was verra firm about it. I mean—they are, usually. It's no just an opinion, take it or leave it. But this one truly meant it." She spread her hands, helpless to explain the feeling of dread and urgency. She swallowed.

"And then . . . your friend. Monsieur Pépin. The first time I saw him, one o' the voices said *'Tell him not to do it.'*"

Michael's thick red eyebrows drew together.

"D'ye think it's the same thing they're not supposed to do?" He sounded startled. "Well, I don't know, now, do I?" she said, a little exasperated. "The voices didn't say. But I saw that the man on the ship was going to die, and I didna say anything, because I couldn't think what to say. And then he *did* die, and maybe he wouldn't have if I'd spoken . . . so I—well, I thought I'd best say something to *someone*."

He thought about that for a moment, then nodded uncertainly.

"Aye. All right. I'll—well, I dinna ken what to do about it, either, to be honest. But I'll talk to them both and I'll have that in my mind, so maybe I'll think of something. D'ye want me to tell them, *'Don't do it'*?"

She grimaced and looked at Sister Eustacia. There wasn't much time.

"I already told the comte. Just . . . maybe. If ye think it might help.

Now—" Her hand darted under her apron and she passed him the slip of paper, fast. "We're only allowed to write to our families twice a year," she said, lowering her voice. "But I wanted Mam to know I was all right. Could ye see she gets that, please? And . . . and maybe tell her a bit, yourself, that I'm weel and—and happy. Tell her I'm happy," she repeated, more firmly.

Sister Eustacia was now standing by the door, emanating an intent to come and tell them it was time for Michael to leave.

"I will," he said. He couldn't touch her, he knew that, so bowed instead and bowed deeply to Sister Eustacia, who came toward them, looking benevolent.

"I'll come to Mass at the chapel on Sundays, how's that?" he said rapidly. "If I've a letter from your mam, or ye have to speak to me, gie me a wee roll of the eyes or something—I'll figure something out."

TWENTY-FOUR HOURS LATER, Sister Gregory, postulant in the Convent of Angels, regarded the bum of a large cow. The cow in question was named Mirabeau and was of uncertain temper, as evidenced by the nervously lashing tail.

"She's kicked three of us this week," said Sister Anne-Joseph, eyeing the cow resentfully. "*And* spilt the milk twice. Sister Jeanne-Marie was most upset."

"Well, we canna have that, now, can we?" Joan murmured in English. "*N'inquiétez-vous pas,*" she added in French, hoping that was at least somewhat grammatical. "Let me do it."

"Better you than me," Sister Anne-Joseph said, crossing herself, and vanished before Sister Joan might think better of the offer.

A week spent working in the cowshed was intended as punishment for her flighty behavior in the marketplace, but Joan was grateful for it. There was nothing better for steadying the nerves than cows.

Granted, the convent's cows were not quite like her mother's sweet-tempered, shaggy red Hieland coos, but if you came right down to it, a cow was a cow, and even a French-speaking wee besom like the present Mirabeau was no match for Joan MacKimmie, who'd driven kine to and from the shielings for years and fed her mother's kine in the byre beside the house with sweet hay and the leavings from supper.

With that in mind, she circled Mirabeau thoughtfully, eyeing the steadily champing jaws and the long slick of blackish-green drool that hung down from slack pink lips. She nodded once, slipped out of the cowshed, and made her way down the allée behind it, picking what she could find. Mirabeau, presented with a bouquet of fresh grasses, tiny daisies, and—delicacy of all delicacies—fresh sorrel, bulged her eyes half out of her head, opened her massive jaw, and inhaled the sweet stuff. The ominous tail ceased its lashing and the massive creature stood as if turned to stone, aside from the ecstatically grinding jaws.

Joan sighed in satisfaction, sat down, and, resting her head on Mirabeau's monstrous flank, got down to business. Her mind, released, took up the next worry of the day.

Had Michael spoken to his friend Pépin? And if so, had he told him what she'd said, or just asked whether he kent the Comte St. Germain? Because if *"tell him not to do it"* referred to the same thing, then plainly the two men must be acquent with each other.

She had got thus far in her own ruminations when Mirabeau's tail began to switch again. She hurriedly stripped the last of the milk from Mirabeau's teats and snatched the bucket out of the way, standing up in a hurry. Then she saw what had disturbed the cow.

The man in the dove-gray coat was standing in the door to the shed, watching her. She hadn't noticed before, in the market, but he had a handsome dark face, though rather hard about the eyes, and with a chin that brooked no opposition. He smiled pleasantly at her, though, and bowed.

"Mademoiselle. I must ask you, please, to come with me."

MICHAEL WAS IN the warehouse, stripped to his shirtsleeves and sweating in the hot, wine-heady atmosphere, when Jared appeared, looking disturbed.

"What is it, cousin?" Michael wiped his face on a towel, leaving black streaks; the crew was clearing the racks on the southeast wall, and there were years of filth and cobwebs behind the most ancient casks.

"Ye haven't got that wee nun in your bed, have ye, Michael?" Jared lifted a beetling gray brow at him.

"Have I what?"

"I've just had a message from the Mother Superior of le Couvent des Anges, saying that one Sister Gregory appears to have been abducted from their cowshed, and wanting to know whether you might possibly have anything to do with the matter."

Michael stared at his cousin for a moment, unable to take this in.

"Abducted?" he said stupidly. "Who would be kidnapping a nun? What for?"

"Well, now, there ye have me." Jared was carrying Michael's coat over his arm and at this point handed it to him. "But maybe best ye go to the convent and find out."

"FORGIVE ME, MOTHER," Michael said carefully. Mother Hildegarde looked as though a breath would make her roll across the floor, wizened as a winter apple. "Did ye think . . . is it possible that Sister J— Sister Gregory might have . . . left of her own accord?"

The old nun gave him a look that revised his opinion of her state of health instantly.

"We did," she said dryly. "It happens. However"—she raised a sticklike finger—"one: there were signs of a considerable struggle in the cowshed. A full bucket of milk not merely spilt but apparently *thrown* at something, the manger overturned, the door left open, and two of the cows escaped into the herb garden." Another finger. "Two: had Sister Gregory experienced doubt regarding her vocation, she was quite free to leave the convent after speaking with me, and she knew that."

One more finger, and the old nun's black eyes bored into his. "And three: had she felt it necessary to leave suddenly and without informing us, where would she go? To you, Monsieur Murray. She knows no one else in Paris, does she?"

"I—well, no, not really." He was flustered, almost stammering, confusion and a burgeoning alarm for Joan making it difficult to think.

"But you have not seen her since you brought us the chalice and paten—and I thank you and your cousin with the deepest sentiments of gratitude, monsieur—which would be yesterday afternoon?"

"No." He shook his head, trying to clear it. "No, Mother."

Mother Hildegarde nodded, her lips nearly invisible, pressed together amid the lines of her face.

"Did she say anything to you on that occasion? Anything that might assist us in discovering her?"

"I—well . . ." Jesus, should he tell her what Joan had said about the voices she heard? It couldn't have anything to do with this, surely, and it wasna his secret to share. On the other hand, Joan *had* said she meant to tell Mother Hildegarde about them . . .

"You'd better tell me, my son." The reverend mother's voice was somewhere between resignation and command. "I see she told you *something*."

"Well, she did, then, Mother," he said, rubbing a hand over his face in distraction. "But I canna see how it has anything to do—she hears voices," he blurted, seeing Mother Hildegarde's eyes narrow dangerously.

The eyes went round.

"She what?"

"Voices," he said helplessly. "They come and say things to her. She thinks maybe they're angels, but she doesn't know. And she can see when folk are going to die. Sometimes," he added dubiously. "I don't know whether she can always say."

"Par le sang sacré de Jésus Christ," the old nun said, sitting up straight as an oak sapling. "Why did she not—well, never mind about that. Does anyone else know this?"

He shook his head. "She was afraid to tell anyone. That's why—well, one reason why—she came to the convent. She thought you might believe her."

"I might," Mother Hildegarde said dryly. She shook her head rapidly, making her veil flap. "*Nom de Dieu!* Why did her mother not tell me this?"

"Her mother?" Michael said stupidly.

"Yes! She brought me a letter from her mother, very kind, asking after my health and recommending Joan to me—but surely her mother would have known!"

"I don't think she—wait." He remembered Joan fishing out the carefully folded note from her pocket. "The letter she brought—it was from Claire Fraser. That's the one you mean?"

"Of course!"

He took a deep breath, a dozen disconnected pieces falling suddenly into a pattern. He cleared his throat and raised a tentative finger.

"One, Mother: Claire Fraser is the wife of Joan's stepfather. But she's not Joan's mother."

The sharp black eyes blinked once.

"And two: my cousin Jared tells me that Claire Fraser was known as a—a White Lady, when she lived in Paris many years ago."

Mother Hildegarde clicked her tongue angrily.

"She was no such thing. Stuff! But it is true that there was a common rumor to that effect," she admitted grudgingly. She drummed her fingers on the desk; they were knobbed with age but surprisingly nimble, and he remembered that Mother Hildegarde was a musician.

"Mother . . ."

"Yes?"

"I don't know if it has anything to do—do you know of a man called the Comte St. Germain?"

The old nun was already the color of parchment; at this, she went white as bone and her fingers gripped the edge of the desk.

"I do," she said. "Tell me—and quickly—what he has to do with Sister Gregory."

JOAN GAVE THE very solid door one last kick, for form's sake, then turned and collapsed with her back against it, panting. The room was huge, extending across the entire top floor of the house, though pillars and joists here and there showed where walls had been knocked down. It smelled peculiar and looked even more peculiar.

"Blessed Michael, protect me," she whispered to herself, reverting to the Gaelic in her agitation. There was a very fancy bed in one corner, piled with feather pillows and bolsters, with writhing corner posts and heavy swags and curtains of cloth embroidered in what looked like gold and silver thread. Did the comte—he'd told her his name, or at least his title, when she asked—haul young women up here for wicked ends on a regular basis? For surely he hadn't set up this establishment solely in anticipation of her arrival—the area near the bed was equipped with all kinds of solid, shiny furniture with marble tops and alarming gilt feet that looked like they'd come off some kind of beast or bird with great curving claws.

He'd told her in the most matter-of-fact way that he was a sorcerer, too, and not to touch anything. She crossed herself and averted her gaze from the table with the nastiest-looking feet; maybe he'd charmed the furniture, and it came to life and walked round after dark. The thought made her move hastily off to the farther end of the room, rosary clutched tight in one hand.

This side of the room was scarcely less alarming, but at least it didn't look as though any of the big colored glass balls and jars and tubes could move on their own. It *was* where the worst smells were coming from, though: something that smelled like burnt hair and treacle, and something else very sharp that curled the hairs in your nose, like it did when someone dug out a jakes for the saltpeter. But there *was* a window near the long table where all this sinister stuff was laid out, and she went to this at once.

The big river—the Seine, Michael had called it—was right there, and the sight of boats and people made her feel a bit steadier. She put a hand on the table to lean closer but set it on something sticky and jerked it back. She swallowed and leaned in more gingerly. The window was barred on the inside. Glancing round, she saw that all the others were, too.

What in the name of the Blessed Virgin did that man expect would try to get in? Gooseflesh raced right up the curve of her spine and spread down her arms, her imagination instantly conjuring a vision of flying demons hovering over the street in the night, beating leathery wings against the window. *Or—dear Lord in heaven!—was it to keep the furniture in?*

There was a fairly normal-looking stool; she sank down on this and, closing her eyes, prayed with great fervor. After a bit, she remembered to

breathe, and after a further bit, began to be able to think again, shuddering only occasionally.

He hadn't threatened her. Nor had he hurt her, really, just put a hand
over her mouth and his other arm round her body and pulled her along,
then boosted her into his coach with a shockingly familiar hand under her
bottom, though it hadn't been done with any sense that he was wanting
to interfere with her.

In the coach, he'd introduced himself, apologized briefly for the
inconvenience—*inconvenience? The cheek of him*—and then had grasped
both her hands in his, staring intently into her face as he clasped them
tighter and tighter. He'd raised her hands to his face, so close she'd
thought he meant to smell them or kiss them, but then had let go, his
brow deeply furrowed.

He'd ignored all her questions and her insistence upon being returned
to the convent. In fact, he almost seemed to forget she was there, leaving
her huddled in the corner of the seat while he thought intently about
something, lips pursing in and out. She'd thought of jumping out—had
almost got up her nerve to reach for the door-handle, though the coach
was rattling on at such a pace she was almost sure to be killed—but then
his eyes had fastened on her again, pinning her to the seat as though he'd
stabbed her through the chest with a knitting-needle.

"The frog," he'd said, intent. "You know the frog, don't you?"

"Any number of them," she'd said, thinking that if he was mad, she'd
best humour him. "Green ones, mostly."

His nostrils had flared in sudden anger, and she'd shrunk back into the
seat. But then he had snorted, and relapsed into a sort of brooding stare,
emerging from this only to say, "The rats didn't all die," in a sort of accusing tone, as though it were her fault.

Her mouth was so dry that she could barely speak, but had managed to
say, "Oh? Did ye try rat's-bane, then?" But she'd spoken in English, too
rattled to summon any French, and he didn't seem to take any note. And
then he had lugged her up here, told her briefly that she wouldn't be hurt,
added the bit about being a sorcerer in a very offhand sort of a way, and
locked her in!

She was terrified, and indignant, too. But now that she'd calmed down
a wee bit, she thought that she wasn't really afraid of *him,* and that seemed
odd. Surely she should be?

But she'd believed him when he said he meant her no harm. He hadn't
threatened her or tried to frighten her. But if that was true . . . what did
he want of her?

*He likely wants to know what ye meant by rushing up to him in the mar-
ket and telling him not to do it,* her common sense—lamentably absent to
this point—remarked.

"Oh," she said aloud. That made some sense. Naturally, he'd be curious about that. But if so, why hadn't he asked her, instead of dragging her off? And what had he gone off to do now?

He had something in mind, and she didn't want to think what.

She got up again and explored the room, thinking. She couldn't tell him any more than she had, though; that was the thing. Would he believe her, about the voices? Even if so, he'd try to find out more, and there wasn't any more to find out. What then?

Don't wait about to see, advised her common sense.

Having already come to this conclusion, she didn't bother replying. She'd found a heavy marble mortar and pestle; that might do. Wrapping the mortar in her apron, she went to the window that overlooked the street. She'd break the glass, then shriek 'til she got someone's attention. Even so high up, she thought, someone would hear. Pity it was a quiet street. But—

She stiffened like a bird dog. A coach was stopped outside one of the houses opposite, and Michael Murray was getting out of it! He was just putting on his hat—no mistaking that flaming red hair.

"Michael!" she shouted at the top of her lungs. But he didn't look up; the sound wouldn't pierce glass. She swung the cloth-wrapped mortar at the window, but it bounced off the bars with a ringing *clang!* She took a deep breath and a better aim; this time, she hit one of the panes and cracked it. Encouraged, she tried again, with all the strength of muscular arms and shoulders, and was rewarded with a small crash, a shower of glass, and a rush of mud-scented air from the river.

"Michael!" But he had disappeared. A servant's face showed briefly in the open door of the house opposite, then vanished as the door closed. Through a red haze of frustration, she noticed the swag of black crepe hanging from the knob. Who was dead?

CHARLES'S WIFE, EULALIE, was in the small parlor, surrounded by a huddle of women. All of them turned to see who had come, many of them lifting their handkerchiefs automatically in preparation for a fresh outbreak of tears. All of them blinked at Michael, then turned to Eulalie, as though for an explanation.

Eulalie's eyes were red but dry. She looked as though she had been dried in an oven, all the moisture and color sucked out of her, her face paper-white and drawn tight over her bones. She, too, looked at Michael, but without much interest. He thought she was too much shocked for anything to matter much. He knew how she felt.

"Monsieur Murray," she said tonelessly, as he bowed over her hand. "How kind of you to call."

"I . . . offer my condolences, madame, mine and my cousin's. I hadn't . . . heard. Of your grievous loss." He was almost stuttering, trying to grasp the reality of the situation. What the devil had happened to Charles?

Eulalie's mouth twisted.

"Grievous loss," she repeated. "Yes. Thank you." Then her dull self-absorption cracked a little and she looked at him more sharply. "You hadn't heard. You mean—you didn't know? You came to *see* Charles?"

"Er . . . yes, madame," he said awkwardly. A couple of the women gasped, but Eulalie was already on her feet.

"Well, you might as well see him, then," she said, and walked out of the room, leaving him with no choice but to follow her.

"They've cleaned him up," she remarked, opening the door to the large parlor across the hall. She might have been talking about a messy domestic incident in the kitchen.

Michael thought it must in fact have been very messy. Charles lay on the large dining table, this adorned with a cloth and wreaths of greenery and flowers. A woman clad in gray was sitting by the table, weaving more wreaths from a basket of leaves and grasses; she glanced up, her eyes going from Eulalie to Michael and back.

"Leave," said Eulalie with a flip of the hand, and the woman got up at once and went out. Michael saw that she'd been making a wreath of laurel leaves and had the sudden absurd thought that she meant to crown Charles with it, in the manner of a Greek hero.

"He cut his throat," Eulalie said. "The coward." She spoke with an eerie calmness, and Michael wondered what might happen when the shock that surrounded her began to dissipate.

He made a respectful sort of noise in his throat and, touching her arm gently, went past her to look down at his friend.

"Tell him not to do it."

The dead man didn't look peaceful. There were lines of stress in his countenance that hadn't yet smoothed out, and he appeared to be frowning. The undertaker's people had cleaned the body and dressed him in a slightly worn suit of dark blue; Michael thought that it was probably the only thing he'd owned that was in any way appropriate in which to appear dead, and suddenly missed his friend's frivolity with a surge that brought unexpected tears to his eyes.

"Tell him not to do it." He hadn't come in time. *If I'd come right away, when she told me—would it have stopped him?*

He could smell the blood, a rusty, sickly smell that seeped through the freshness of the flowers and leaves. The undertaker had tied a white neck-cloth for Charles—he'd used an old-fashioned knot, nothing that Charles himself would have worn for a moment. The black stitches showed above it, though, the wound harsh against the dead man's livid skin.

His own shock was beginning to fray, and stabs of guilt and anger poked through it like needles.

"Coward?" he said softly. He didn't mean it as a question, but it seemed more courteous to say it that way. Eulalie snorted, and, looking up, Michael met the full charge of her eyes. No, not shocked any longer.

"You'd know, wouldn't you," she said, and it wasn't at all a question, the way she said it. "You knew about your slut of a sister-in-law, didn't you? And Babette?" Her lips curled away from the name. "His *other* mistress?"

"I—no. I mean . . . Léonie told me yesterday. That was why I came to talk to Charles." Well, he would certainly have mentioned Léonie. And he wasn't going anywhere near the mention of Babette, whom he'd known about for quite some time. But, Jesus, what did the woman think he could have done about it?

"Coward," she said, looking down at Charles's body with contempt. "He made a mess of everything—*everything!*—and then couldn't deal with it, so he runs off and leaves me alone, with children, penniless!"

"Tell him not to do it."

Michael looked to see if this was an exaggeration, but it wasn't. She was burning now, but with fear as much as anger, her frozen calm quite vanished.

"The . . . house . . . ?" he began, with a rather vague wave around the expensive, stylish room. He knew it was her family house; she'd brought it to the marriage.

She snorted.

"He lost it in a card game last week," she said bitterly. "If I'm lucky, the new owner will let me bury him before we have to leave."

"Ah." The mention of card games jolted him back to an awareness of his reason for coming here. "I wonder, madame, do you know an acquaintance of Charles's—the Comte St. Germain?" It was crude, but he hadn't time to think of a graceful way to come to it.

Eugenia blinked, nonplussed.

"The comte? Why do you want to know about *him*?" Her expression sharpened into eagerness. "Do you think he owes Charles money?"

"I don't know, but I'll certainly find out for you," Michael promised her. "If you can tell me where to find Monsieur le Comte."

She didn't laugh, but her mouth quirked in what might in another mood have been humor.

"He lives across the street." She pointed toward the window. "In that big pile of—where are you going?"

But Michael was already through the door and into the hallway, boot heels clattering on the parquet in his haste.

THERE WERE FOOTSTEPS coming up the stairs; Joan started away from the window but then craned back, desperately willing the door across the street to open and let Michael out. What was he *doing* there?

That door didn't open, but a key rattled in the lock of the door to the room. In desperation, she tore the rosary from her belt and pushed it through the hole in the window, then dashed across the room and threw herself into one of the repulsive chairs.

It was the comte. He glanced round, worried for an instant, and then his face relaxed when he saw her. He came toward her, holding out his hand.

"I'm sorry to have kept you waiting, mademoiselle," he said, very courtly. "Come, please. I have something to show you."

"I don't want to see it." She stiffened a little and tucked her feet under her, to make it harder for him to pick her up. If she could just delay him until Michael came out! But he might well not see her rosary or, even if he did, know it was hers. Why should he? All nuns' rosaries looked the same!

She strained her ears, hoping to hear the sounds of departure on the other side of the street—she'd scream her lungs out. In fact . . .

The comte sighed a little but bent and took her by the elbows, lifting her straight up, her knees still absurdly bent. He was really very strong. She put her feet down, and there she was, her hand tucked into the crook of his elbow, being led across the room toward the door, docile as a cow on its way to be milked! She made her mind up in an instant, yanked free, and ran to the smashed window.

"HELP!" she bellowed through the broken pane. "Help me, help me! *Au secours,* I mean! *AU SECOU—*" The comte's hand clapped across her mouth, and he said something in French that she was sure must be bad language. He scooped her up, so fast that the wind was knocked out of her, and had her through the door before she could make another sound.

MICHAEL DIDN'T PAUSE for hat or cloak but burst into the street, so fast that his driver started out of a doze and the horses jerked and neighed in protest. He didn't pause for that, either, but shot across the cobbles and pounded on the door, a big bronze-coated affair that boomed under his fists.

It couldn't have been very long but seemed an eternity. He fumed, pounded again, and, pausing for breath, caught sight of the rosary on the pavement. He ran to catch it up, scratched his hand, and saw that it lay in a scatter of glass fragments. At once he looked up, searching, and saw the broken window just as the big door opened.

He sprang at the butler like a wildcat, seizing him by the arms.

"Where is she? Where, damn you?"

"She? But there is no 'she,' monsieur. . . . Monsieur le Comte lives quite alone. You—"

"Where is Monsieur le Comte?" Michael's sense of urgency was so great, he felt that he might strike the man. The man apparently felt he might, too, because he turned pale and, wrenching himself loose, fled into the depths of the house. With no more than an instant's hesitation, Michael pursued him.

The butler, his feet fueled by fear, flew down the hall, Michael in grim pursuit. The man burst through the door to the kitchen; Michael was dimly aware of the shocked faces of cooks and maids, and then they were out into the kitchen garden. The butler slowed for an instant going down the steps, and Michael launched himself at the man, knocking him flat.

They rolled together on the graveled path, then Michael got on top of the smaller man, seized him by the shirtfront, and, shaking him, shouted, "WHERE IS HE?"

Thoroughly undone, the butler covered his face with one arm and pointed blindly toward a gate in the wall.

Michael leapt off the supine body and ran. He could hear the rumble of coach wheels, the rattle of hooves—he flung open the gate in time to see the back of a coach rattling down the allée and a gaping servant paused in the act of sliding to the doors of a carriage house. He ran, but it was clear that he'd never catch the coach on foot.

"JOAN!" he bellowed after the vanishing equipage. "I'm coming!"

He didn't waste time in questioning the servant but ran back, pushing his way through the maids and footmen gathered round the cowering butler, and burst out of the house, startling his own coachman afresh.

"That way!" he shouted, pointing toward the distant conjunction of the street and the allée, where the comte's coach was just emerging. "Follow that coach! *Vite!*"

"*VITE!*" THE COMTE urged his coachman on, then sank back, letting fall the hatch in the roof. The light was fading; his errand had taken longer than he'd expected, and he wanted to be out of the city before night fell. The city streets were dangerous at night.

His captive was staring at him, her eyes enormous in the dim light. She'd lost her postulant's veil, and her dark hair was loose on her shoulders. She looked charming but very scared. He reached into the bag on the floor and pulled out a flask of brandy.

"Have a little of this, *chérie*." He removed the cork and handed it to her. She took it but looked uncertain what to do with it, nose wrinkling at the hot smell.

"Really," he assured her. "It will make you feel better."

"That's what they all say," she said in her slow, awkward French.

"All of whom?" he asked, startled.

"The Auld Ones. I don't know what you call them in French, exactly. The folk that live in the hills—*souterrain?*" she added doubtfully. "Underground?"

"Underground? And they give you brandy?" He smiled at her, but his heart gave a sudden thump of excitement. Perhaps she *was*. He'd doubted his instincts when his touch failed to kindle her, but clearly she was *something*.

"They give you food and drink," she said, putting the flask down between the squab and the wall. "But if you take any, you lose time."

The spurt of excitement came again, stronger.

"Lose time?" he repeated, encouraging. "How do you mean?"

She struggled to find words, smooth brow furrowed with the effort.

"They . . . you . . . one who is enchanted by them—he, it? No, he—goes into the hill, and there's music and feasting and dancing. But in the morning, when he goes . . . back, it's two hundred years later than it was when he went to feast with the . . . the Folk. Everybody he knew has turned to dust."

"How interesting!" he said. It was. He also wondered, with a fresh spasm of excitement, whether the old paintings, the ones far back in the bowels of the chalk mine, might have been made by these Folk, whoever they were.

She observed him narrowly, apparently for an indication that he was a faerie. He smiled at her, though his heart was now thumping audibly in his ears. *Two hundred years!* For that was what Mélisande—*Damn her,* he thought briefly, with a pang at the reminder of Madeleine—had told him was the usual period when one traveled through stone. It could be changed by use of gemstones or blood, she said, but that was the usual. And it had been, the first time he went back.

"Don't worry," he said to the girl, hoping to reassure her. "I only want you to look at something. Then I'll take you back to the convent—assuming that you still want to go there?" He lifted an eyebrow, half-teasing. It really wasn't his intent to frighten her, though he already had, and he feared that more fright was unavoidable. He wondered just what she might do when she realized that he was in fact planning to take her underground.

———

MICHAEL KNELT ON the seat, his head out the window of the coach, urging it on by force of will and muscle. It was nearly full dark, and the comte's coach was visible only as a distantly moving blot. They were out of the city, though; there were no other large vehicles on the road, nor likely to be—and there were very few turnings where such a large equipage might leave the main road.

The wind blew in his face, tugging strands of hair loose so they beat about his face. It blew the faint scent of decay, too—they'd pass the cemetery in a few minutes.

He wished passionately that he'd thought to bring a pistol, a smallsword—anything! But there was nothing in the coach with him, and he had nothing on his person save his clothes and what was in his pockets: this consisting, after a hasty inventory, of a handful of coins, a used handkerchief—the one Joan had given back to him, in fact, and he crumpled it tightly in one hand—a tinderbox, a mangled paper spill, a stub of sealing wax, and a small stone he'd picked up in the street, pinkish with a yellow stripe. Perhaps he could improvise a sling with the handkerchief, he thought wildly, and paste the comte in the forehead with the stone, à la David and Goliath. And then cut off the comte's head with the penknife he discovered in his breast pocket, he supposed.

Joan's rosary was also in that pocket; he took it out and wound it round his left hand, holding the beads for comfort—he was too distracted to pray, beyond the words he repeated silently over and over, hardly noticing what he said.

Let me find her in time!

———

"TELL ME," THE COMTE asked curiously, "why did you speak to me in the market that day?"

"I wish I hadn't," Joan replied briefly. She didn't trust him an inch—still less since he'd offered her the brandy. It hadn't struck her before that that he really *might* be one of the Auld Ones. They could walk about, looking just like people. Her own mother had been convinced for years—and even some of the Murrays thought so—that Da's wife, Claire, was one. She herself wasn't sure; Claire had been kind to her, but no one said the Folk *couldn't* be kind if they wanted to.

Da's wife. A sudden thought paralyzed her: the memory of her first meeting with Mother Hildegarde, when she'd given the Reverend Mother Claire's letter. She'd said, *"ma mère,"* unable to think of a word that might mean "stepmother." It hadn't seemed to matter; why should anyone care?

"Claire Fraser," she said aloud, watching the comte carefully. "Do you know her?"

His eyes widened, showing white in the gloaming. Oh, aye, he kent her, all right!

"I do," he said, leaning forward. "Your mother, is she not?"

"No!" Joan said, with great force, and repeated it in French, several times for emphasis. "No, she's not!"

But she observed, with a sinking heart, that her force had been misplaced. He didn't believe her; she could tell by the eagerness in his face. He thought she was lying to put him off.

"I told you what I did in the market because the voices told me to!" she blurted, desperate for anything that might distract him from the horrifying notion that she was one of the Folk. Though if *he* was one, her common sense pointed out, he ought to be able to recognize her. Oh, Jesus, Lamb of God—that's what he'd been trying to do, holding her hands so tight and staring into her face.

"Voices?" he said, looking rather blank. "What voices?"

"The ones in my head," she said, heaving an internal sigh of exasperation. "They tell me things now and then. About other people, I mean. You know," she went on, encouraging him, "I'm a—a"—St. Jerome on a bannock, what was the *word*?!?—"someone who sees the future," she ended weakly. "Er . . . some of it. Sometimes. Not always."

The comte was rubbing a finger over his upper lip; she didn't know if he was expressing doubt or trying not to laugh, but either way it made her angry.

"So one of them told me to tell ye that, and I did!" she said, lapsing into Scots. "I dinna ken what it is ye're no supposed to do, but I'd advise ye not to do it!"

It occurred to her belatedly that perhaps killing her was the thing he wasn't supposed to do, and she was about to put this notion to him, but by the time she had disentangled enough grammar to have a go at it, the coach was slowing, bumping from side to side as it turned off the main road. A sickly smell seeped into the air, and she sat up straight, her heart in her throat.

"Mary, Joseph, and Bride," she said, her voice no more than a squeak. "Where *are* we?"

MICHAEL LEAPT FROM the coach almost before it had stopped moving. He daren't let them get too far ahead of him; his driver had nearly missed the turning, as it was, and the comte's coach had come to a halt minutes before his own reached it.

"Talk to the other driver," he shouted at his own, half visible on the box. "Find out why the comte has come here! Find out what he's doing!"

Nothing good. He was sure of that. Though he couldn't imagine why anyone would kidnap a nun and drag her out of Paris in the dark, only to stop at the edge of a public cemetery. Unless . . . half-heard rumors of depraved men who murdered and dismembered their victims, even those who *ate* . . . His wame rose and he nearly vomited, but it wasn't possible to vomit and run at the same time, and he could see a pale splotch on the darkness that he thought—he hoped, he feared—must be Joan.

Suddenly the night burst into flower. A huge puff of green fire bloomed in the darkness, and by its eerie glow he saw her clearly, her hair flying in the wind.

He opened his mouth to shout, to call out to her, but he had no breath, and before he could recover it she vanished into the ground, the comte following her, torch in hand.

He reached the shaft moments later, and he saw below the faintest green glow, just vanishing down a tunnel. Without an instant's hesitation, he flung himself down the ladder.

"DO YOU HEAR anything?" the comte kept asking her as they stumbled along the white-walled tunnels, he grasping her so hard by the arm that he'd surely leave bruises on her skin.

"No," she gasped. "What . . . am I listening for?"

He merely shook his head in a displeased way, but more as though he was listening for something himself than because he was angry with her for not hearing it.

She had some hopes that he'd meant what he said and would take her back. He did mean to go back himself; he'd lit several torches and left them burning along their way. So he wasn't about to disappear into the hill altogether, taking her with him to the lighted ballroom where people danced all night with the Fine Folk, unaware that their own world slipped past beyond the stones of the hill.

The comte stopped abruptly, hand squeezing harder round her arm.

"Be still," he said very quietly, though she wasn't making any noise. "Listen."

She listened as hard as possible—and thought she did hear something.

What she thought she heard, though, was footsteps, far in the distance. Behind them. Her heart seized up for a moment.

"What—what do *you* hear?" she thought of asking. He glanced down at her, but not as though he really saw her.

"Them," he said. "The stones. They make a buzzing sound, most of the time. If it's close to a fire feast or a sun feast, though, they begin to sing."

"Do they?" she said faintly. He was hearing *something,* and evidently it wasn't the footsteps she'd heard. The footsteps had stopped now, as though whoever followed was waiting, maybe stealing along, one step at a time, careful to make no sound.

"Yes," he said, and his face was intent. He looked at her sharply again, and this time he saw her.

"You don't hear them," he said with certainty, and she shook her head. He pressed his lips tight together but after a moment lifted his chin, gesturing toward another tunnel, where there seemed to be something painted on the chalk.

He paused there to light another torch—this one burned a brilliant yellow and stank of sulfur—and she saw by its light the wavering shape of the Virgin and Child. Her heart lifted at the sight, for surely faeries would have no such thing in their lair.

"Come," he said, and now took her by the hand. His own was cold.

MICHAEL CAUGHT A glimpse of them as they moved into a side tunnel. The comte had lit another torch, a red one this time—how did he do that?—and it was easy to follow its glow.

How far down in the bowels of the earth were they? He had long since lost track of the turnings, though he might be able to get back by following the torches—assuming they hadn't all burned out.

He still had no plan in mind, other than to follow them until they stopped. Then he'd make himself known and . . . well, take Joan away, by whatever means proved necessary.

Swallowing hard, rosary still wrapped around his left hand and penknife in his right, he stepped into the shadows.

THE CHAMBER WAS round and quite large. Big enough that the torchlight didn't reach all the edges, but it lit the pentagram inscribed into the floor in the center.

The noise was making Rakoczy's bones ache, and as often as he had heard it, it never failed to make his heart race and his hands sweat. He let go of the nun's hand for a moment to wipe his palm on the skirts of his coat, not wanting to disgust her. She looked scared but not terrified, and if she heard it, surely she—

Her eyes had widened suddenly.

"Who's *that*?" she said.

He whirled, to see Raymond standing tranquilly in the center of the pentagram.

"Bon soir, mademoiselle," the frog said, bowing politely.

"Ah . . . *bon soir,*" the girl replied faintly.

"What the devil are you doing here?" Rakoczy interposed his body between Raymond and the nun.

"Very likely the same thing you are," the frog replied. "Might you introduce your *petite amie,* sir?"

Shock, anger, and sheer confusion robbed Rakoczy of speech for a moment. What was the infernal creature *doing* here? Wait—the girl! The lost daughter he'd mentioned: the nun was the daughter! He'd discovered her whereabouts and somehow followed them to this place. Rakoczy took hold of the girl's arm again, firmly.

"She is a Scotch," he said. "And, as you see, a nun. No concern of yours."

The frog looked amused, cool and unruffled. Rakoczy was sweating, the noise beating against his skin in waves. He could feel the little bag of stones in his pocket, a hard lump against his heart. They seemed to be warm, warmer even than his skin.

"I doubt that she is, really," said Raymond. "Why is she a concern of yours, though?"

"That's also none of your business." He was trying to think. He couldn't lay out the stones, not with the damned frog standing there. Could he just leave with the girl? But if the frog meant him harm . . . and if the girl truly wasn't . . .

Raymond ignored the incivility and bowed again to the girl.

"I am Master Raymond, my dear," he said. "And you?"

"Joan Mac—" she said. "Er . . . Sister Gregory, I mean." She tried to pull away from Rakoczy's grip. "Um. If I'm not the concern of either of you gentlemen—"

"She's my concern, gentlemen." The voice was high with nerves, but firm. Rakoczy looked round, shocked to see the young wine merchant walk into the chamber, disheveled and dirty but eyes fixed on the girl. At Rakoczy's side, the nun gasped.

"Sister." The merchant bowed. He was white-faced but not sweating. He looked as though the chill of the cavern had seeped into his bones, but he put out a hand, from which the beads of a wooden rosary swung. "You dropped your rosary."

JOAN THOUGHT SHE might faint from sheer relief. Her knees wobbled from terror and exhaustion, but she summoned enough strength to wrench free of the comte and run, stumbling, into Michael's arms. He grabbed her and hauled her away from the comte, half-dragging her.

The comte made an angry sound and took a step in Joan's direction, but Michael said, "Stop right there, ye wicked bugger!" just as the little froggy-faced man said sharply, "Stop!"

The comte swung toward first one and then the other. He looked . . . crazed. Joan swallowed and nudged Michael, urging him toward the chamber's door, only then noticing the penknife in his hand.

"What were ye going to do wi' *that*?" she whispered. "Shave him?"

"Let the air out of him," Michael muttered. He lowered his hand but didn't put the knife away and kept his eyes on the two men.

"Your daughter," the comte said hoarsely to the man who called himself Master Raymond. "You were looking for a lost daughter. I've found her for you."

Raymond's brows shot up, and he glanced at Joan.

"Mine?" he said, astonished. "She isn't one of mine. Can't you tell?"

The comte drew a breath so deep it cracked in his throat.

"Tell? But—"

The frog looked impatient.

"Can you not see auras? The electrical fluid that surrounds people," he elucidated, waving a hand around his own head.

The comte rubbed a hand hard over his face. "I can't—"

"For goodness sake, come in here!" Raymond stepped to the edge of the star, reached across, and seized the comte's hand.

RAKOCZY STIFFENED AT the touch. Blue light exploded from their linked hands, and he gasped, feeling a surge of energy such as he had never before experienced. Raymond pulled hard, and Rakoczy stepped across the line into the pentagram.

Silence. The buzzing had stopped. He nearly wept with the relief of it.

"I—you—" he stammered, looking at the linked hands.

"You didn't know?" Raymond looked surprised.

"That you were a—" He waved at the pentagram. "I thought you might be."

"Not that," Raymond said, almost gently. "That you were one of mine."

"Yours?" Rakoczy looked down again; the blue light was pulsing gently now, surrounding their fingers.

"Everyone has an aura of some kind," Raymond said. "But only my . . . people . . . have *this*."

In the blessed silence, it was possible to think again. And the first thing that came to mind was the Star Chamber, the king looking on as they had faced each other over a poisoned cup. And now he knew why the frog hadn't killed him.

HIS MIND BUBBLED with questions. La Dame Blanche, blue light, Mélisande, and Madeleine . . . Thought of Madeleine and what grew in her womb nearly stopped him, but the urge to find out, to *know* at last, was too strong.

"Can you—can we—go forward?"

Raymond hesitated a moment, then nodded.

"Yes. But it's not safe. Not safe at all."

"Will you show me?"

"I mean it." The frog's grip tightened on his. "It's not a safe thing to know, let alone to do."

Rakoczy laughed, feeling all at once exhilarated, full of joy. Why should he fear knowledge? Perhaps the passage would kill him—but he had a pocket full of gems, and, besides, what was the point of waiting to die slowly?

"Tell me!" he said, squeezing the other's hand. "For the sake of our shared blood!"

JOAN STOOD STOCK-STILL, amazed. Michael's arm was still around her, but she scarcely noticed.

"He *is*!" she whispered. "He truly is! They both are!"

"Are what?" Michael gaped at her.

"Auld Folk! Faeries!"

He looked wildly back at the scene before them. The two men stood face-to-face, hands locked together, their mouths moving in animated conversation—in total silence. It was like watching mimes but even less interesting.

"I dinna care *what* they are. Loons, criminals, demons, angels . . . Come on!" He dropped his arm and seized her hand, but she was planted solid as an oak sapling, her eyes growing wide and wider.

She gripped his hand hard enough to grind the bones and shrieked at the top of her lungs, *"Don't do it!!"*

He whirled round just in time to see them vanish.

THEY STUMBLED TOGETHER down the long, pale passages, bathed in the flickering light of dying torches, red, yellow, blue, green, a ghastly purple that made Joan's face look drowned.

"Des feux d'artifice," Michael said. His voice sounded queer, echoing in the empty tunnels. "A conjurer's trick."

"What?" Joan looked drugged, her eyes black with shock.

"The fires. The . . . colors. Have ye never heard of fireworks?"

"No."

"Oh." It seemed too much a struggle to explain, and they went on in silence, hurrying as much as they could, to reach the shaft before the light died entirely.

At the bottom, he paused to let her go first, thinking too late that he should have gone first—she'd think he meant to look up her dress. . . . He turned hastily away, face burning.

"D'ye think he was? That *they* were?" She was hanging on to the ladder, a few feet above him. Beyond her, he could see the stars, serene in a velvet sky.

"Were what?" He looked at her face, so as not to risk her modesty. She was looking better now but very serious.

"Were they Auld Folk? Faeries?"

"I suppose they must ha' been." His mind was moving very slowly; he didn't want to have to try to think. He motioned to her to climb and followed her up, his eyes tightly shut. If they were Auld Ones, then likely so was Auntie Claire. He truly didn't want to think about *that*.

He drew the fresh air gratefully into his lungs. The wind was toward the city now, coming off the fields, full of the resinous cool scent of pine trees and the breath of grass and cattle. He felt Joan breathe it in, sigh deeply, and then she turned to him, put her arms around him, and rested her forehead on his chest. He put his arms round her and they stood for some time, in peace.

Finally, she stirred and straightened up.

"Ye'd best take me back, then," she said. "The sisters will be half out o' their minds."

He was conscious of a sharp sense of disappointment but turned obediently toward the coach, standing in the distance. Then he turned back.

"Ye're sure?" he said. "Did your voices tell ye to go back?"

She made a sound that wasn't quite a rueful laugh.

"I dinna need a voice to tell me that." She brushed a hand through her hair, smoothing it off her face. "In the Highlands, if a man's widowed, he takes another wife as soon as he can get one; he's got to have someone to mend his shirt and rear his bairns. But Sister Philomène says it's different in Paris; that a man might mourn for a year."

"He might," he said, after a short silence. Would a year be enough, he wondered, to heal the great hole where Lillie had been? He knew he would never forget—never stop looking for her—but he didn't forget what Ian had told him, either.

"But after a time, ye find ye're in a different place than ye were. A different person than ye were. And then ye look about and see what's there with ye. Ye'll maybe find a use for yourself."

Joan's face was pale and serious in the moonlight, her mouth gentle.

"It's a year before a postulant makes up her mind. Whether to stay and become a novice—or . . . or leave. It takes time. To know."

"Aye," he said softly. "Aye, it does."

He turned to go, but she stopped him, a hand on his arm.

"Michael," she said. "Kiss me, aye? I think I should maybe know *that,* before I decide."

A PLAGUE OF ZOMBIES

INTRODUCTION

THE THING ABOUT LORD JOHN'S SITUATION AND career—unmarried, no fixed establishment, discreet political connections, fairly high-ranking officer—is that he can easily take part in far-flung adventures rather than being bound to a pedestrian daily life. To be honest, once I started doing "bulges" (that is, shorter pieces of fiction) involving him, I just looked at which year it was and then consulted one of my historical timeline references to see what kinds of interesting events happened in that year. That's how he happened to find himself in Quebec for the battle there.

In terms of this story, though, the impetus came from two different sources, both "trails" leading back from the main book of the series—*Voyager,* in this case. To wit: I knew that Lord John was the governor of Jamaica in 1766, when Claire met him aboard the *Porpoise;* it wasn't by any means impossible for a man with connections and no experience to be appointed to such a post—but it was more likely for a man who *had* had experience in the territory to which he was appointed. "Plague" is set in 1761, and is the story of how Lord John gained that experience. I knew also that Geillis Duncan wasn't dead and where she was. And, after all, with a story set in Jamaica, how could I possibly resist zombies?

THERE WAS A SNAKE on the drawing-room table. A small snake, but still. Lord John Grey wondered whether to say anything about it.

The governor, appearing quite oblivious of the coiled reptile's presence, picked up a cut-crystal decanter that stood not six inches from the snake. Perhaps it was a pet, or perhaps the residents of Jamaica were accustomed to keeping a tame snake in residence, to kill rats. Judging from the number of rats Grey had seen since leaving the ship, this was sensible—though this particular snake didn't appear large enough to take on even your average mouse.

The wine was decent, but served at body heat, and it seemed to pass directly through Grey's gullet and into his blood. He'd had nothing to eat since before dawn and felt the muscles of his lower back begin to tingle and relax. He put the glass down; he wanted a clear head.

"I cannot tell you, sir, how happy I am to receive you," said the governor, putting down his own glass, empty. "The position is acute."

"So you said in your letter to Lord North. The situation has not changed appreciably since then?" It had been nearly three months since that letter was written; a lot could change in three months.

He thought Governor Warren shuddered, despite the temperature in the room.

"It has become worse," the governor said, picking up the decanter. "Much worse."

Grey felt his shoulders tense, but spoke calmly.

"In what way? Have there been more—" He hesitated, searching for the right word. "More demonstrations?" It was a mild word to describe the burning of cane fields, the looting of plantations, and the wholesale liberation of slaves.

Warren gave a hollow laugh. His handsome face was beading with sweat. There was a crumpled handkerchief on the arm of his chair, and he picked it up to mop at his skin. He hadn't shaved this morning—or, quite possibly, yesterday; Grey could hear the faint rasp of his dark whiskers on the cloth.

"Yes. More destruction. They burnt a sugar press last month, though still in the remoter parts of the island. Now, though . . ." He paused, licking dry lips as he poured more wine. He made a cursory motion toward Grey's glass, but Grey shook his head.

"They've begun to move toward Kingston," Warren said. "It's deliberate; you can see it. One plantation after another, in a line coming straight down the mountain." He sighed. "I shouldn't say straight. Nothing in this bloody place is straight, starting with the landscape."

That was true enough; Grey had admired the vivid green peaks that soared up from the centre of the island, a rough backdrop for the amazingly blue lagoon and the white-sand shore.

"People are terrified," Warren went on, seeming to get a grip on himself, though his face was once again slimy with sweat, and his hand shook on the decanter. It occurred to Grey, with a slight shock, that the *governor* was terrified. "I have merchants—and their wives—in my office every day, begging, demanding protection from the blacks."

"Well, you may assure them that protection will be provided them," Grey said, sounding as reassuring as possible. He had half a battalion with him—three hundred infantry troops and a company of artillery, equipped with small cannon. Enough to defend Kingston, if necessary. But his brief from Lord North was not merely to reassure the merchants and defend the shipping of Kingston and Spanish Town—nor even to provide protection to the larger sugar plantations. He was charged with putting down the slave rebellion entirely. Rounding up the ringleaders and stopping the violence altogether.

The snake on the table moved suddenly, uncoiling itself in a languid manner. It startled Grey, who had begun to think it was a decorative sculpture. It was exquisite: only seven or eight inches long and a beautiful pale yellow marked with brown, a faint iridescence in its scales like the glow of good Rhenish wine.

"It's gone further now, though," Warren was going on. "It's not just burning and property destruction. Now it's come to murder."

That brought Grey back with a jerk.

"Who has been murdered?" he demanded.

"A planter named Abernathy. Murdered in his own house, last week. His throat cut."

"Was the house burnt?"

"No, it wasn't. The maroons ransacked it but were driven off by Abernathy's own slaves before they could set fire to the place. His wife survived by submerging herself in a spring behind the house, concealed by a patch of reeds."

"I see." He could imagine the scene all too well. "Where is the plantation?"

"About ten miles out of Kingston. Rose Hall, it's called. Why?" A bloodshot eye swivelled in Grey's direction, and he realised that the glass of wine the governor had invited him to share had not been his first of the day. Nor, likely, his fifth.

Was the man a natural sot? he wondered. Or was it only the pressure of the current situation that had caused him to take to the bottle in such a blatant manner? He surveyed the governor covertly; the man was perhaps in his late thirties and, while plainly drunk at the moment, showed none of the signs of habitual indulgence. He was well built and attractive; no bloat, no soft belly straining at his silk waistcoat, no broken veins in cheeks or nose . . .

"Have you a map of the district?" Surely it hadn't escaped Warren that if indeed the maroons were burning their way straight toward Kingston, it should be possible to predict where their next target lay and to await them with several companies of armed infantry?

Warren drained the glass and sat panting gently for a moment, eyes fixed on the tablecloth, then pulled himself together.

"Map," he repeated. "Yes, of course. Dawes—my secretary—he'll . . . he'll find you one."

Motion caught Grey's eye. Rather to his surprise, the tiny snake, after casting to and fro, tongue tasting the air, had started across the table in what appeared a purposeful, if undulant, manner, headed straight for him. By reflex, he put up a hand to catch the little thing, lest it plunge to the floor.

The governor saw it, uttered a loud shriek, and flung himself back from the table. Grey looked at him in astonishment, the tiny snake curling over his fingers.

"It's not venomous," he said, as mildly as he could. At least, he didn't *think* so. His friend Oliver Gwynne was a natural philosopher and mad for snakes; Gwynne had shown him all the prizes of his collection during the course of one hair-raising afternoon, and Grey seemed to recall Gwynne telling him that there were no venomous reptiles at all on the island of Jamaica. Besides, the nasty ones all had triangular heads, while the harmless kinds were blunt-headed, like this fellow.

Warren was indisposed to listen to a lecture on the physiognomy of snakes. Shaking with terror, he backed against the wall.

"Where?" he gasped. "Where did it come from?"

"It's been sitting on the table since I came in. I . . . um . . . thought it was . . ." Well, plainly it wasn't a pet, let alone an intended part of the table décor. He coughed and got up, meaning to put the snake outside through the French doors that led onto the terrace.

Warren mistook his intent, though, and, seeing Grey come closer, snake writhing through his fingers, he burst through the French doors, crossed the terrace in a mad leap, and pelted down the flagstoned walk, coattails flying as though the devil himself were in pursuit.

Grey was still staring after him in disbelief when a discreet cough from the inner door made him turn.

"Gideon Dawes, sir." The governor's secretary was a short, tubby man with a round pink face that probably was rather jolly by nature. At the moment, it bore a look of profound wariness. "You are Lieutenant-Colonel Grey?"

Grey thought it unlikely that there were a plethora of men wearing the uniform and insignia of a lieutenant-colonel on the premises of King's House at that very moment but nonetheless bowed, murmuring, "Your servant, Mr. Dawes. I'm afraid Mr. Warren has been taken . . . er . . ." He nodded toward the open French doors. "Perhaps someone should go after him?"

Mr. Dawes closed his eyes with a look of pain, then sighed and opened them again, shaking his head.

"He'll be all right," he said, though his tone lacked any real conviction. "I've just been discussing commissary and billeting requirements with your Major Fettes; he wishes you to know that all the arrangements are quite in hand."

"Oh. Thank you, Mr. Dawes." In spite of the unnerving nature of the governor's departure, Grey felt a sense of pleasure. He'd been a major himself for years; it was astonishing how pleasant it was to know that someone else was now burdened with the physical management of troops. All *he* had to do was give orders.

That being so, he gave one, though it was phrased as a courteous request, and Mr. Dawes promptly led him through the corridors of the rambling house to a small clerk's hole near the governor's office, where maps were made available to him.

He could see at once that Warren had been right regarding both the devious nature of the terrain and the trail of attacks. One of the maps was marked with the names of plantations, and small notes indicated where maroon raids had taken place. It was far from being a straight line, but, nonetheless, a distinct sense of direction was obvious.

The room was warm, and he could feel sweat trickling down his back.

Still, a cold finger touched the base of his neck lightly when he saw the name *Twelvetrees* on the map.

"Who owns this plantation?" he asked, keeping his voice level as he pointed at the paper.

"What?" Dawes had fallen into a sort of dreamy trance, looking out the window into the green of the jungle, but blinked and pushed his spectacles up, bending to peer at the map. "Oh, Twelvetrees. It's owned by Philip Twelvetrees—a young man; inherited the place from a cousin only recently. Killed in a duel, they say—the cousin, I mean," he amplified helpfully.

"Ah. Too bad." Grey's chest tightened unpleasantly. He could have done without *that* complication. If . . . "The cousin—was he named Edward Twelvetrees, by chance?"

Dawes looked mildly surprised.

"I do believe that was the name. I didn't know him, though; no one here did. He was an absentee owner; ran the place through an overseer."

"I see." He wanted to ask whether Philip Twelvetrees had come from London to take possession of his inheritance, but didn't. He didn't want to draw any attention by singling out the Twelvetrees family. Time enough for that.

He asked a few more questions regarding the timing of the raids, which Mr. Dawes answered promptly, but when it came to an explanation of the inciting causes of the rebellion, the secretary proved suddenly unhelpful—which Grey thought interesting.

"Really, sir, I know almost nothing of such matters," Mr. Dawes protested, when pressed on the subject. "You would be best advised to speak with Captain Cresswell. He's the superintendent in charge of the maroons."

Grey was surprised at this.

"Escaped slaves? They have a superintendent?"

"Oh. No, sir." Dawes seemed relieved to have a more straightforward question with which to deal. "The maroons are not escaped slaves. Or rather," he corrected himself, "they are *technically* escaped slaves, but it is a pointless distinction. These maroons are the descendants of slaves who escaped during the last century and took to the mountain uplands. They have settlements up there. But as there is no way of identifying any current owner . . ." And as the government lacked any means of finding them and dragging them back, the Crown had wisely settled for installing a white superintendent, as was usual for dealing with native populations. The superintendent's business was to be in contact with the maroons and deal with any matter that might arise pertaining to them.

Which raised a question, Grey thought: why had this Captain Cresswell not been brought to meet him at once? He had sent word of his arrival as soon as the ship docked at daylight, not wishing to take Derwent Warren unawares.

"Where is Captain Cresswell presently?" he asked, still polite. Mr. Dawes looked unhappy.

"I, um, am afraid I don't know, sir," he said, casting down his gaze behind his spectacles.

There was a momentary silence, in which Grey could hear the calling of some bird from the jungle nearby.

"Where is he *normally*?" Grey asked, with slightly less politesse.

Dawes blinked.

"I don't know, sir. I believe he has a house near the base of Guthrie's Defile—there is a small village there. But he would of course go up into the maroon settlements from time to time, to meet with the . . ." He waved a small, fat hand, unable to find a suitable word. "The headmen. He did buy a new hat in Spanish Town earlier this month," Dawes added, in the tones of someone offering a helpful observation.

"A *hat*?"

"Yes. Oh—but of course you would not know. It is customary among the maroons, when some agreement of importance is made, that the persons making the agreement shall exchange hats. So you see—"

"Yes, I do," Grey said, trying not to let annoyance show in his voice. "Will you be so kind, Mr. Dawes, as to send to Guthrie's Defile, then—and to any other place in which you think Captain Cresswell might be discovered? Plainly I must speak with him, and as soon as possible."

Dawes nodded vigorously, but before he could speak, the rich sound of a small gong came from somewhere in the house below. As though it had been signaled, Grey's stomach emitted a loud gurgle.

"Dinner in half an hour," Mr. Dawes said, looking happier than Grey had yet seen him. He almost scurried out the door, Grey in his wake.

"Mr. Dawes," he said, catching up at the head of the stair. "Governor Warren. Do you think—"

"Oh, he will be present at dinner," Dawes assured him. "I'm sure he is quite recovered now; these small fits of excitement never last very long."

"What causes them?" A savoury smell, rich with currants, onion, and spice, wafted up the stair, making Grey hasten his step.

"Oh . . ." Dawes, hastening along as well, glanced sideways at him. "It is nothing. Only that His Excellency has a, um, somewhat morbid fancy concerning reptiles. Did he see a snake in the drawing room or hear something concerning one?"

"He did, yes—though a remarkably small and harmless one." Vaguely, Grey wondered what had happened to the little yellow snake. He thought he must have dropped it in the excitement of the governor's abrupt exit and hoped it hadn't been injured.

Mr. Dawes looked troubled and murmured something that sounded like, "Oh, dear, oh, dear . . ." but then he merely shook his head and sighed.

GREY MADE HIS way to his room, meaning to freshen himself before dinner; the day was warm, and he smelled strongly of ship's reek—this composed in equal parts of sweat, seasickness, and sewage, well marinated in salt water—and horse, having ridden up from the harbour to Spanish Town. With any luck, his valet would have clean linen aired for him by now.

King's House, as all royal governors' residences were known, was a rambling old wreck of a mansion, perched on a high spot of ground on the edge of Spanish Town. Plans were afoot for an immense new Palladian building, to be erected in the town's centre, but it would be another year at least before construction could commence. In the meantime, efforts had been made to uphold His Majesty's dignity by means of beeswax polish, silver, and immaculate linen, but the dingy printed wallpaper peeled from the corners of the rooms, and the dark-stained wood beneath exhaled a mouldy breath that made Grey want to hold his own whenever he walked inside.

One good feature of the house, though, was that it was surrounded on all four sides by a broad terrace and was overhung by large, spreading trees that cast lacy shadows on the flagstones. A number of the rooms opened directly onto this terrace—Grey's did—and it was therefore possible to step outside and draw a clean breath, scented by the distant sea or the equally distant upland jungles. There was no sign of his valet, but there *was* a clean shirt on the bed. He shucked his coat, changed his shirt, and then threw the French doors open wide.

He stood for a moment in the centre of the room, mid-afternoon sun spilling through the open doors, and enjoyed the sense of a solid surface under his feet after seven weeks at sea and seven hours on horseback. Enjoyed even more the transitory sense of being alone. Command had its prices, and one of those was a nearly complete loss of solitude. He therefore seized it when he found it, knowing it wouldn't last for more than a few moments, but valuing it all the more for that.

Sure enough, it didn't last more than two minutes this time. He called out, "Come," at a rap on the door frame and, turning, was struck by a visceral sense of attraction such as he had not experienced in months.

The man was young, perhaps twenty, and slender in his blue and gold livery, but with a breadth of shoulder that spoke of strength and a head and neck that would have graced a Greek sculpture. Perhaps because of the heat, he wore no wig, and his tight-curled hair was clipped so close that the finest modelling of his skull was apparent.

"Your servant, sah," he said to Grey, bowing respectfully. "The governor's compliments, and dinner will be served in ten minutes. May I see you to the dining room?"

"You may," Grey said, reaching hastily for his coat. He didn't doubt that he could find the dining room unassisted, but the chance to watch this young man walk . . .

"You *may*," Tom Byrd corrected, entering with his hands full of grooming implements, "once I've put his lordship's hair to rights." He fixed Grey with a minatory eye. "You're not a-going in to dinner like that, me lord, and don't you think it. You sit down there." He pointed sternly to a stool, and Lieutenant-Colonel Grey, commander of His Majesty's forces in Jamaica, meekly obeyed the dictates of his twenty-one-year-old valet. He didn't *always* allow Tom free rein but in the current circumstance was just as pleased to have an excuse to sit still in the company of the young black servant.

Tom laid out all his implements neatly on the dressing table, from a pair of silver hairbrushes to a box of powder and a pair of curling tongs, with the care and attention of a surgeon arraying his knives and saws. Selecting a hairbrush, he leaned closer, peering at Grey's head, then gasped. "Me lord! There's a big huge spider—walking right up your temple!"

Grey smacked his temple by reflex, and the spider in question—a clearly visible brown thing nearly a half inch long—shot off into the air, striking the looking glass with an audible tap before dropping to the surface of the dressing table and racing for its life.

Tom and the black servant uttered identical cries of horror and lunged for the creature, colliding in front of the dressing table and falling over in a thrashing heap. Grey, strangling an almost irresistible urge to laugh, stepped over them and dispatched the fleeing spider neatly with the back of his other hairbrush.

He pulled Tom to his feet and dusted him off, allowing the black servant to scramble up by himself. He brushed off all apologies, as well, but asked whether the spider had been a deadly one.

"Oh, yes, sah," the servant assured him fervently. "Should one of those bite you, sah, you would suffer excruciating pain at once. The flesh around the wound would putrefy, you would commence to be fevered within an hour, and, in all likelihood, you would not live past dawn."

"Oh, I see," Grey said mildly, his flesh creeping briskly. "Well, then. Perhaps you would not mind looking about the room while Tom is at his work? In case such spiders go about in company?"

Grey sat and let Tom brush and plait his hair, watching the young man as he assiduously searched under the bed and dressing table, pulled out Grey's trunk, and pulled up the trailing curtains and shook them.

"What is your name?" he asked the young man, noting that Tom's fingers were trembling badly and hoping to distract him from thoughts of the hostile wildlife with which Jamaica undoubtedly teemed. Tom was fearless in the streets of London and perfectly willing to face down ferocious dogs or foaming horses. Spiders, though, were quite another matter.

"Rodrigo, sah," said the young man, pausing in his curtain-shaking to bow. "Your servant, sah."

He seemed quite at ease in company and conversed with them about the town, the weather—he confidently predicted rain in the evening, at about ten o'clock, leading Grey to think that he had likely been employed as a servant in good families for some time. Was the man a slave, he wondered, or a free black?

His admiration for Rodrigo was, he assured himself, the same that he might have for a marvellous piece of sculpture, an elegant painting. And one of his friends did in fact possess a collection of Greek amphorae decorated with scenes that gave him quite the same sort of feeling. He shifted slightly in his seat, crossing his legs. He would be going in to dinner soon. He resolved to think of large, hairy spiders and was making some progress with this subject when something huge and black dropped down the chimney and rushed out of the disused hearth.

All three men shouted and leapt to their feet, stamping madly. This time it was Rodrigo who felled the intruder, crushing it under one sturdy shoe.

"What the devil was that?" Grey asked, bending over to peer at the thing, which was a good three inches long, gleamingly black, and roughly ovoid, with ghastly long, twitching antennae.

"Only a cockroach, sah," Rodrigo assured him, wiping a hand across a sweating ebony brow. "They will not harm you, but they *are* most disagreeable. If they come into your bed, they feed upon your eyebrows."

Tom uttered a small, strangled cry. The cockroach, far from being destroyed, had merely been inconvenienced by Rodrigo's shoe. It now extended thorny legs, heaved itself up, and was proceeding about its business, though at a somewhat slower pace. Grey, the hairs prickling on his arms, seized the ash shovel from among the fireplace implements and, scooping up the insect on its blade, jerked open the door and flung the nasty creature as far as he could—which, given his state of mind, was some considerable distance.

Tom was pale as custard when Grey came back in, but he picked up his employer's coat with trembling hands. He dropped it, though, and with a mumbled apology bent to pick it up again, only to utter a strangled shriek, drop it once more, and run backwards, slamming so hard against the wall that Grey heard a crack of laths and plaster.

"What the devil?" He bent, reaching gingerly for the fallen coat.

"Don't touch it, me lord!" Tom cried, but Grey had seen what the trouble was: a tiny yellow snake slithered out of the crimson-velvet folds, head moving to and fro in slow curiosity.

"Well, hallo, there." He reached out a hand, and the little snake tasted his skin with a flickering tongue, then wove its way up into the palm of his hand. He stood up, cradling it carefully.

Tom and Rodrigo were standing like men turned to stone, staring at him.

"It's quite harmless," he assured them. "At least I think so. It must have fallen into my pocket earlier."

Rodrigo was regaining a bit of his nerve. He came forward and looked at the snake but declined an offer to touch it, putting both hands firmly behind his back.

"That snake likes you, sah," he said, glancing curiously from the snake to Grey's face, as though trying to distinguish a reason for such odd particularity.

"Possibly." The snake had made its way upwards and was now wrapped round two of Grey's fingers, squeezing with remarkable strength. "On the other hand, I believe he may be attempting to kill and eat me. Do you know what his natural food might be?"

Rodrigo laughed at that, displaying very beautiful white teeth, and Grey had such a vision of those teeth, those soft mulberry lips, applied to—he coughed, hard, and looked away.

"He would eat anything that did not try to eat him first, sah," Rodrigo assured him. "It was probably the sound of the cockroach that made him come out. He would hunt those."

"What a very admirable sort of snake. Could we find him something to eat, do you think? To encourage him to stay, I mean."

Tom's face suggested strongly that if the snake was staying, he was not. On the other hand . . . he glanced toward the door, whence the cockroach had made its exit, and shuddered. With great reluctance, he reached into his pocket and extracted a rather squashed bread roll containing ham and pickle.

The snake was placed on the floor with this object before it. It inspected the roll gingerly, ignored the bread and pickle, but twined itself carefully about a chunk of ham, squeezing it fiercely into limp submission. Then, opening its jaw to an amazing extent, the snake engulfed its prey, to general cheers. Even Tom clapped his hands, and, if not ecstatic at Grey's suggestion that the snake might be accommodated in the dark space beneath the bed for the sake of preserving Grey's eyebrows, he uttered no objections to this plan, either. The snake being ceremoniously installed and left to digest its meal, Grey was about to ask Rodrigo further questions regarding the natural fauna of the island but was forestalled by the faint sound of a distant gong.

"Dinner!" he exclaimed, reaching for his now snakeless coat.

"Me lord! Your hair's not even powdered!"

Grey refused to wear a wig, to Tom's ongoing dismay, but was obliged in the present instance to submit to powder. This toiletry accomplished in haste, he shrugged into his coat and fled, before Tom could suggest any further refinements to his appearance.

THE GOVERNOR APPEARED, as Mr. Dawes had predicted, calm and dignified at the dinner table. All trace of sweat, hysteria, and drunkenness had vanished, and beyond a brief word of apology for his abrupt disappearance, no reference was made to his earlier departure.

Major Fettes and Grey's adjutant, Captain Cherry, also appeared at table. A quick glance at them assured Grey that all was well with the troops. Fettes and Cherry couldn't be more diverse physically—the latter resembling a ferret and the former a block of wood—but both were extremely competent and well liked by the men.

There was little conversation to begin with; the three soldiers had been eating ship's biscuit and salt beef for weeks. They settled down to the feast before them with the single-minded attention of ants presented with a loaf of bread; the magnitude of the challenge had no effect upon their earnest willingness. As the courses gradually slowed, though, Grey began to instigate conversation—his prerogative, as senior guest and commanding officer.

"Mr. Dawes explained to me the position of superintendent," he said, keeping his attitude superficially pleasant. "How long has Captain Cresswell held this position, sir?"

"For approximately six months, Colonel," the governor replied, wiping crumbs from his lips with a linen napkin. The governor was quite composed, but Grey had Dawes in the corner of his eye and thought the secretary stiffened a little. That was interesting; he must get Dawes alone again and go into this matter of superintendents more thoroughly.

"And was there a superintendent before Captain Cresswell?"

"Yes . . . in fact, there were two of them, were there not, Mr. Dawes?"

"Yes, sir. Captain Ludgate and Captain Perriman." Dawes was assiduously not meeting Grey's eye.

"I should like very much to speak with those gentlemen," Grey said pleasantly.

Dawes jerked as though someone had run a hatpin into his buttock. The governor finished chewing a grape, swallowed, and said, "I'm so sorry, Colonel. Both Ludgate and Perriman have left their offices."

"Why?" John Fettes asked bluntly. The governor hadn't been expecting that, and blinked.

"I expect Major Fettes wishes to know whether they were replaced in their offices because of some peculation or corruption," Bob Cherry put in chummily. "And if that be the case, were they allowed to leave the island rather than face prosecution? And if so—"

"Why?" Fettes put in neatly.

Grey repressed a smile. Should peace break out on a wide scale and an army career fail them, Fettes and Cherry could easily make a living as a music-hall knockabout cross-talk act. As interrogators, they could reduce almost any suspect to incoherence, confusion, and confession in nothing flat.

Governor Warren, though, appeared to be made of tougher stuff than the usual regimental miscreant. Either that or he had nothing to hide, Grey considered, listening to him explain with tired patience that Ludgate had retired because of ill health and that Perriman had inherited money and gone back to England.

No. He watched the governor's hand twitch and hover indecisively over the fruit bowl. *He's got something to hide. And so does Dawes. Is it the same thing, though? And has it got anything to do with the present trouble?*

The governor could easily be hiding some peculation or corruption of his own—and likely was, Grey thought dispassionately, taking in the lavish display of silver on the sideboard. Such corruption was—within limits—considered more or less a perquisite of office. But if that were the case, it was not Grey's concern—unless it was in some way connected to the maroons and their rebellion.

Entertaining as it was to watch Fettes and Cherry at their work, he cut them off with a brief nod and turned the conversation firmly back to the rebellion.

"What communications have you had from the rebels, sir?" he asked the governor. "For I believe that, in these cases, rebellion arises usually from some distinct source of grievance. What is it?"

Warren looked at him, jaw agape. He closed his mouth, slowly, and hesitated for a moment before replying. Grey surmised he was considering how much Grey might discover from other avenues of inquiry.

Everything I bloody can, Grey thought, assuming an expression of neutral interest.

"Why, as to that, sir . . . the incident that began the . . . um . . . the difficulties . . . was the arrest of two young maroons, accused of stealing from a warehouse in Kingston." The two had been whipped in the town square and committed to prison, after which—

"Following a trial?" Grey interrupted.

The governor's gaze rested on him, red-rimmed but cool. "No, Colonel. They had no right to a trial."

"You had them whipped and imprisoned on the word of . . . whom? The affronted merchant?"

Warren drew himself up a little and lifted his chin. Grey saw that he had been shaved, but a patch of black whisker had been overlooked; it showed in the hollow of his cheek like a blemish, a hairy mole.

"*I* did not, no, sir," he said coldly. "The sentence was imposed by the magistrate in Kingston."

"Who is?"

Dawes had closed his eyes with a small grimace.

"Judge Samuel Peters."

Grey nodded thanks.

"Captain Cherry will visit Mr. Judge Peters tomorrow," he said pleasantly. "And the prisoners, as well. I take it they are still in custody?"

"No, they aren't," Mr. Dawes put in, suddenly emerging from his impersonation of a dormouse. "They escaped, within a week of their capture."

The governor shot a brief, irritated glance at his secretary but nodded reluctantly. With further prodding, it was admitted that the maroons had sent a protest at the treatment of the prisoners, via Captain Cresswell. The prisoners having escaped before the protest was received, though, it had not seemed necessary to do anything about it.

Grey wondered briefly whose patronage had got Warren his position but dismissed the thought in favour of further explorations. The first violence had come without warning, he was told, with the burning of cane fields on a remote plantation. Word of it had reached Spanish Town several days later, by which time another plantation had suffered similar depredation.

"Captain Cresswell rode at once to investigate the matter, of course," Warren said, lips tight.

"And?"

"He didn't return. The maroons have not demanded ransom for him, nor have they sent word that he is dead. He may be with them; he may not. We simply don't know."

Grey could not help looking at Dawes, who appeared unhappy but gave the ghost of a shrug. It wasn't his place to tell more than the governor wanted told, was it?

"Let me understand you, sir," Grey said, not bothering to hide the edge in his voice. "You have had *no* communication with the rebels since their initial protest? And you have taken no action to achieve any?"

Warren seemed to swell slightly but replied in an even tone.

"In fact, Colonel, I have. I sent for you." He smiled, very slightly, and reached for the decanter.

THE EVENING AIR hung damp and viscid, trembling with distant thunder. Unable to bear the stifling confines of his uniform any longer, Grey flung it off, not waiting for Tom's ministrations, and stood naked in the middle of the room, eyes closed, enjoying the touch of air from the terrace on his bare skin.

There was something remarkable about the air. Warm as it was, it had a silken touch that spoke of the sea and clear blue water, even indoors. He couldn't see the water from his room; even had it been visible from Spanish Town, his room faced a hillside covered with jungle. He could feel it, though, and had a sudden longing to wade out through surf and immerse himself in the clean coolness of the ocean. The sun had nearly set now, and the cries of parrots and other birds were growing intermittent.

He peered underneath the bed but didn't see the snake. Perhaps it was far back in the shadows; perhaps it had gone off in search of more ham. He straightened, stretched luxuriously, then shook himself and stood blinking, feeling stupid from too much wine and food and lack of sleep—he had slept barely three hours out of the preceding four-and-twenty, what with the arrival, disembarkation, and the journey to King's House.

His mind appeared to have taken French leave for the moment; no matter; it would be back shortly. Meanwhile, though, its abdication had left his body in charge—not at all a responsible course of action.

He felt exhausted, but restless, and scratched idly at his chest. The wounds there were solidly healed, slightly raised pink weals under his fingers, crisscrossing through the blond hair. One had passed within an inch of his left nipple; he'd been lucky not to lose it.

An immense pile of gauze cloth lay upon his bed. This must be the mosquito netting described to him by Mr. Dawes at dinner—a draped contraption meant to enclose the entire bed, thus protecting its occupant from the depredations of bloodthirsty insects.

He'd spent some time with Fettes and Cherry after dinner, laying plans for the morrow. Cherry would call upon Judge Peters and obtain details of the maroons who had been captured. Fettes would send men into Kingston in a search for the location of the retired Mr. Ludgate, erstwhile superintendent; if Ludgate could be found, Grey would like to know this gentleman's opinion of his successor. As for that successor—if Dawes did not manage to unearth Captain Cresswell by the end of tomorrow . . . Grey yawned involuntarily, then shook his head, blinking. Enough.

The troops would all be billeted by now, some granted their first liberty in months. He spared a glance at the small sheaf of maps and reports he had extracted from Mr. Dawes earlier, but those could wait till morning, and better light. He'd think more clearly after a good night's sleep.

He leaned against the frame of the open door, after a quick glance down the terrace showed him that the rooms nearby seemed unoccupied. Clouds were beginning to drift in from the sea, and he remembered what Rodrigo had said about the rain at night. He thought perhaps he could feel a slight coolness in the air, whether from rain or oncoming night, and the hair on his body prickled and rose.

From here he could see nothing but the deep green of a jungle-clad hill, glowing like a sombre emerald in the twilight. From the other side of the house, though, as he left dinner, he'd seen the sprawl of Spanish Town below, a puzzle of narrow, aromatic streets. The taverns and the brothels would be doing a remarkable business tonight, he imagined.

The thought brought with it a rare feeling of something that wasn't quite resentment. Any one of the soldiers he'd brought, from the lowliest private soldier to Fettes himself, could walk into any brothel in Spanish Town—and there were a good many, Cherry had told him—and relieve the stresses caused by a long voyage without the slightest comment or even the slightest attention. Not him.

His hand had dropped lower as he watched the light fade, idly kneading his flesh. There were accommodations for men such as himself in London, but it had been many years since he'd had recourse to such a place.

He had lost one lover to death, another to betrayal. The third . . . His lips tightened. Could you call a man who would never touch you—would recoil from the very thought of touching you—your lover? No. But at the same time, what would you call a man whose *mind* touched yours, whose prickly friendship was a gift, whose character, whose very existence, helped to define your own?

Not for the first time—and surely not for the last—he wished briefly that Jamie Fraser were dead. It was an automatic wish, though, at once dismissed from mind. The colour of the jungle had died to ash, and insects were beginning to whine past his ears.

He went in and began to worry the folds of the gauze on his bed, until Tom came in to take it away from him, hang the mosquito netting, and ready him for the night.

HE COULDN'T SLEEP. Whether it was the heavy meal, the unaccustomed place, or simply the worry of his new and so-far-unknown command, his mind refused to settle, and so did his body. He didn't waste time in useless thrashing, though; he'd brought several books. Reading a bit of *The History of Tom Jones, A Foundling* would distract his mind and let sleep steal in upon him.

The French doors were covered with sheer muslin curtains, but the moon was nearly full, and there was enough light by which to find his tinderbox, striker, and candlestick. The candle was good beeswax, and the flame rose pure and bright—and instantly attracted a small cloud of inquisitive gnats, mosquitoes, and tiny moths. He picked it up, intending to take it to bed with him, but then thought better.

Was it preferable to be gnawed by mosquitoes or to be incinerated? Grey debated the point for all of three seconds, then set the lit candlestick back on the desk. The gauze netting would go up in a flash if the candle fell over in bed.

Still, he needn't face death by bloodletting or be covered in itching bumps simply because his valet didn't like the smell of bear grease. He wouldn't get it on his clothes, in any case.

He flung off his nightshirt and knelt to rummage in his trunk, with a guilty look over his shoulder. Tom, though, was safely tucked up somewhere amid the attics or outbuildings of King's House and almost certainly sound asleep. Tom suffered badly with seasickness, and the voyage had been hard on him.

The heat of the Indies hadn't done the battered tin of bear grease any good, either; the rancid fat nearly overpowered the scent of the peppermint and other herbs mixed into it. Still, he reasoned, if it repelled him, how much more a mosquito, and he rubbed it into as much of his flesh as he could reach. Despite the stink, he found it not unpleasant. There was enough of the original smell left as to remind him of his usage of the stuff in Canada. Enough to remind him of Manoke, who had given it to him. Anointed him with it, in a cool blue evening on a deserted sandy isle in the St. Lawrence River.

Finished, he put down the tin and touched his rising prick. He didn't suppose he'd ever see Manoke again. But he did remember. Vividly.

A little later, he lay gasping on the bed under his netting, heart thumping slowly in counterpoint to the echoes of his flesh. He opened his eyes, feeling pleasantly relaxed, his head finally clear. The room was close; the servants had shut the windows, of course, to keep out the dangerous night air, and sweat misted his body. He felt too slack to get up and open the French doors onto the terrace, though; in a moment would do.

He closed his eyes again—then opened them abruptly and leapt out of bed, reaching for the dagger he'd laid on the table. The servant called

Rodrigo stood pressed against the door, the whites of his eyes showing in his black face.

"What do you want?" Grey put the dagger down but kept his hand on it, his heart still racing.

"I have a message for you, sah," the young man said. He swallowed audibly.

"Yes? Come into the light, where I can see you." Grey reached for his banyan and slid into it, still keeping an eye on the man.

Rodrigo peeled himself off the door with evident reluctance, but he'd come to say something, and say it he would. He advanced into the dim circle of candlelight, hands at his sides, nervously clutching air.

"Do you know, sah, what an Obeah man is?"

"No."

That disconcerted Rodrigo visibly. He blinked and twisted his lips, obviously at a loss as how to describe this entity. Finally, he shrugged his shoulders helplessly and gave up.

"He says to you, beware."

"Does he?" Grey said dryly. "Of anything specific?"

That seemed to help; Rodrigo nodded vigorously.

"You don't be close to the governor. Stay right away, as far as you can. He's going to—I mean . . . something bad might happen. Soon. He—" The servant broke off, apparently realising that he could be dismissed—if not worse—for talking about the governor in this loose fashion. Grey was more than curious, though, and sat down, motioning to Rodrigo to take the stool, which he did with obvious reluctance.

Whatever an Obeah man was, Grey thought, he clearly had considerable power, to force Rodrigo to do something he so plainly didn't want to do. The young man's face shone with sweat, and his hands clenched mindlessly on the fabric of his coat.

"Tell me what the Obeah man said," Grey said, leaning forward, intent. "I promise you, I will tell no one."

Rodrigo gulped but nodded. He bent his head, looking at the table as though he might find the right words written in the grain of the wood.

"Zombie," he muttered, almost inaudibly. "The zombie come for him. For the governor."

Grey had no notion what a zombie might be, but the word was spoken in such a tone as to make a chill flicker over his skin, sudden as distant lightning.

"Zombie," he said carefully. Mindful of the governor's reaction earlier, he asked, "Is a zombie perhaps a snake of some kind?"

Rodrigo gasped but then seemed to relax a little.

"No, sah," he said seriously. "Zombie are dead people." He stood up then, bowed abruptly, and left, his message delivered.

NOT SURPRISINGLY, Grey did not fall asleep immediately in the wake of this visit.

Having encountered German night-hags, Indian ghosts, and having spent a year or two in the Scottish Highlands, he had more acquaintance than most with picaresque superstition. While he wasn't inclined to give instant credence to local custom and belief, neither was he inclined to discount such belief out of hand. Belief made people do things that they otherwise wouldn't—and whether the belief had substance or not, the consequent actions certainly did.

Obeah men and zombies notwithstanding, plainly there was some threat to Governor Warren—and Grey rather thought the governor knew what it was.

How exigent was the threat, though? He pinched out the candle flame and sat in darkness for a moment, letting his eyes adjust, then rose and went soft-footed to the French doors, through which Rodrigo had vanished.

The guest bedchambers of King's House were merely a string of boxes, all facing the long terrace and each opening directly onto it through a pair of French doors. Grey paused for a moment, hand on the muslin drape; if anyone was watching his room, they would see the curtain being drawn aside.

Instead, he turned and went to the inner door of the room. This opened onto a narrow service corridor, completely dark at the moment—and completely empty, if his senses could be trusted. He closed the door quietly, glancing over his shoulder at the French doors. It was interesting, he thought, that Rodrigo had come to the front door, so to speak, when he could have approached Grey unseen.

But Rodrigo had said the Obeah man sent him. Plainly he wanted it to be seen that he had obeyed his order. Which in turn meant that someone was likely watching to see that he had.

The logical conclusion would be that the same someone—or someones—was watching to see what Grey might do next.

His body had reached its own conclusions already and was reaching for breeches and shirt before he had quite decided that if something were about to happen to Warren, it was clearly his duty to stop it, zombies or not. He stepped out of the French doors onto the terrace, moving quite openly.

There was an infantryman posted at either end of the terrace, as he'd expected; Robert Cherry was nothing if not meticulous. On the other hand, the bloody sentries had plainly not seen Rodrigo entering his room, and he wasn't at all pleased about that. Recriminations could wait, though; the nearer sentry saw *him* and challenged him with a sharp "Who goes there?"

"It's me," Grey said briefly, and, without ceremony, dispatched the sentry with orders to alert the other soldiers posted around the house, then send two men into the house, where they should wait in the hall until summoned.

Grey then went back into his room, through the inner door, and down the dark service corridor. He found a dozing black servant behind a door at the end of it, minding the fire under the row of huge coppers that supplied hot water to the household.

The man blinked and stared when shaken awake but eventually nodded in response to Grey's demand to be taken to the governor's bedchamber. He led Grey into the main part of the house and up a darkened stair lit only by the moonlight streaming through the tall casements. Everything was quiet on the upper floor save for slow, regular snoring coming from what the slave said was the governor's room.

The man was swaying with weariness; Grey dismissed him, with orders to let in and send up the soldiers who should now be at the door. The man yawned hugely, and Grey watched him stumble down the stairs into the murk of the hall below, hoping he would not fall and break his neck. The house was very quiet. He was beginning to feel somewhat foolish. And yet . . .

The house seemed to breathe around him, almost as though it were a sentient thing and aware of him. He found the fancy unsettling.

Ought he to wake Warren? he wondered. Warn him? Question him? No, he decided. There was no point in disturbing the man's rest. Questions could wait for the morning.

The sound of feet coming up the stair dispelled his sense of uneasiness, and he gave his orders quietly. The sentries were to keep guard on this door until relieved in the morning; at any sound of disturbance within, they were to enter at once. Otherwise . . .

"Stay alert. If you see or hear *anything,* I wish to know about it."

He paused, but Warren continued to snore, so he shrugged and made his way downstairs, out into the silken night, and back to his own room.

He smelled it first. For an instant he thought he had left the tin of bear-grease ointment uncovered—and then the reek of sweet decay took him by the throat, followed instantly by a pair of hands that came out of the dark and fastened on said throat.

He fought back in blind panic, striking and kicking wildly, but the grip on his windpipe didn't loosen, and bright lights began to flicker at the corners of what would have been his vision if he'd had any. With a tremendous effort of will, he made himself go limp. The sudden weight surprised his assailant and jerked Grey free of the throttling grasp as he fell. He hit the floor and rolled.

Bloody hell, where was the man? If it was a man. For even as his mind reasserted its claim to reason, his more-visceral faculties were recalling Rodrigo's parting statement: *'Zombie are dead people.'* And whatever was here in the dark with him seemed to have been dead for several days, judging from its smell.

He could hear the rustling of something moving quietly toward him. Was it breathing? He couldn't tell for the rasp of his own breath, harsh in his throat, and the blood-thick hammering of his heart in his ears.

He was lying at the foot of a wall, his legs half under the dressing table's bench. There was light in the room, now that his eyes were accustomed; the French doors were pale rectangles in the dark, and he could make out the shape of the thing that was hunting him. It was man-shaped but oddly hunched and swung its head and shoulders from side to side, almost as though it meant to smell him out. Which wouldn't take it more than two more seconds, at most.

He sat up abruptly, seized the small padded bench, and threw it as hard as he could at the thing's legs. It made a startled *oof!* noise that was undeniably human, then it staggered, waving its arms for balance. The noise reassured Grey, and he rolled up onto one knee and launched himself at the creature, bellowing incoherent abuse.

He butted it around chest height, felt it fall backwards, then lunged for the pool of shadow where he thought the table was. It was there and, feeling frantically over the surface, he found his dagger, still where he'd left it. He snatched it up and turned just in time to face the thing, which closed on him at once, reeking and making a disagreeable gobbling noise. He slashed at it and felt his knife skitter down the creature's forearm, bouncing off bone. It screamed, releasing a blast of foul breath directly into his face, then turned and rushed for the French doors, bursting through them in a shower of glass and flying muslin.

Grey charged after it, onto the terrace, shouting for the sentries. But the sentries, as he recalled belatedly, were in the main house, keeping watch over the governor, lest that worthy's rest be disturbed by . . . whatever sort of thing this was. Zombie?

Whatever it was, it was gone.

He sat down abruptly on the stones of the terrace, shaking with reaction. No one had come out in response to the noise. Surely no one could have slept through that; perhaps no one else was housed on this side of the mansion.

He felt ill and breathless and rested his head for a moment on his knees, before jerking it up to look round, lest something else be stealing up on him. But the night was still and balmy. The only noise was an agitated rustling of leaves in a nearby tree, which for a shocked second he thought might be the creature, climbing from branch to branch in search of refuge. Then he heard soft chitterings and hissing squeaks. *Bats,* said the calmly rational part of his mind—what was left of it.

He gulped and breathed, trying to get clean air into his lungs to replace the disgusting stench of the creature. He'd been a soldier most of his life; he'd seen the dead on battlefields, and smelled them, too. Had buried fallen comrades in trenches and burned the bodies of his enemies. He knew what graves and rotting flesh smelled like. And the thing that had had its hands round his throat had almost certainly come from a recent grave.

He was shivering violently, despite the warmth of the night. He rubbed a hand over his left arm, which ached from the struggle; he had been badly wounded three years before, at Crefeld, and had nearly lost the arm. It worked but was still a good deal weaker than he'd like. Glancing at it, though, he was startled. Dark smears befouled the pale sleeve of his banyan, and, turning over his right hand, he found it wet and sticky.

"Jesus," he murmured, and brought it gingerly to his nose. No mistaking *that* smell, even overlaid as it was by grave reek and the incongruous scent of night-blooming jasmine from the vines that grew in tubs by the terrace. Rain was beginning to fall, pungent and sweet—but even that could not obliterate the smell.

Blood. Fresh blood. Not his, either.

He rubbed the rest of the blood from his hand with the hem of his banyan, and the cold horror of the last few minutes faded into a glowing coal of anger, hot in the pit of his stomach.

He'd been a soldier most of his life; he'd killed. He'd seen the dead on battlefields. And one thing he knew for a fact. Dead men don't bleed.

FETTES AND CHERRY had to know, of course. So did Tom, as the wreckage of his room couldn't be explained as the result of a nightmare. The four of them gathered in Grey's room, conferring by candlelight as Tom went about tidying the damage, white to the lips.

"You've never heard of zombie—or zombies? I have no idea whether the term is plural or not." Heads were shaken all round. A large square bottle of excellent Scotch whisky had survived the rigours of the voyage in the bottom of his trunk, and he poured generous tots of this, including Tom in the distribution.

"Tom—will you ask among the servants tomorrow? Carefully, of course. Drink that; it will do you good."

"Oh, I'll be careful, me lord," Tom assured him fervently. He took an obedient gulp of the whisky before Grey could warn him. His eyes bulged and he made a noise like a bull that has sat on a bumblebee, but managed somehow to swallow the mouthful, after which he stood still, opening and closing his mouth in a stunned sort of way.

Bob Cherry's mouth twitched, but Fettes maintained his usual stolid imperturbability.

"Why the attack upon you, sir, do you suppose?"

"If the servant who warned me about the Obeah man was correct, I can only suppose that it was a consequence of my posting sentries to keep guard upon the governor. But you're right." He nodded at Fettes's implication. "That means that whoever was responsible for this"—he waved a hand to indicate the disorder of his chamber, which still smelled of its recent intruder, despite the rain-scented wind that came through the shattered doors and the burnt-honey smell of the whisky—"either was watching the house closely, or—"

"Or lives here," Fettes said, and took a meditative sip. "Dawes, perhaps?"

Grey's eyebrows rose. That small, tubby, genial man? And yet he'd known a number of small, wicked men.

"Well," he said slowly, "it was not he who attacked me; I can tell you that much. Whoever it was was taller than I am and of a very lean build—not corpulent at all."

Tom made a hesitant noise, indicating that he had had a thought, and Grey nodded at him, giving permission to speak.

"You're quite sure, me lord, as the man who went for you . . . er . . . *wasn't* dead? Because by the smell of him, he's been buried for a week, at least."

A reflexive shudder went through all of them, but Grey shook his head.

"I am positive," he said, as firmly as he could. "It was a live man—though certainly a peculiar one," he added, frowning.

"Ought we to search the house, sir?" Cherry suggested.

Grey shook his head reluctantly.

"He—or it—went away into the garden. He left discernible footmarks." He did not add that there had been sufficient time for the servants—if they were involved—to hide any traces of the creature by now. If there was involvement, he thought, the servant Rodrigo was his best avenue of inquiry—and it would not serve his purposes to alarm the house and focus attention on the young man ahead of time.

"Tom," he said, turning to his valet. "Does Rodrigo appear to be approachable?"

"Oh, yes, me lord. He was friendly to me over supper," Tom assured him, brush in hand. "D'ye want me to talk to him?"

"Yes, if you will. Beyond that . . ." He rubbed a hand over his face, feeling the sprouting beard-stubble on his jaw. "I think we will proceed with the plans for tomorrow. But, Captain Cherry, will you also find time to question Mr. Dawes? You may tell him what transpired here tonight; I should find his response to that most interesting."

"Yes, sir." Cherry finished his whisky, coughed, and sat blinking for a moment, then cleared his throat. "The, um, the governor, sir . . . ?"

"I'll speak to him myself," Grey said. "And then I propose to ride up into the hills, to pay a visit to a couple of plantations, with an eye to defensive postings. For we must be seen to be taking prompt and decisive action. If there's offensive action to be taken against the maroons, it will wait until we see what we're up against." Fettes and Cherry nodded; life-long soldiers, they had no urgent desire to rush into combat.

The meeting dismissed, Grey sat down with a fresh glass of whisky, sipping it as Tom finished his work in silence.

"You're sure as you want to sleep in this room tonight, me lord?" he said, putting the dressing-table bench neatly back in its spot. "I could find you another place, I'm sure."

Grey smiled at him with affection.

"I'm sure you could, Tom. But so could our recent friend, I expect. No, Captain Cherry will post a double guard on the terrace, as well as inside the house. It will be perfectly safe." And even if it wasn't, the thought of hiding, skulking away from whatever the thing was that had visited him . . . No. He wouldn't allow them—whoever they were—to think they had shaken his nerve.

Tom sighed and shook his head but reached into his shirt and drew out a small cross, woven of wheat stalks and somewhat battered, suspended on a bit of leather string.

"All right, me lord. But you'll wear this, at least."

"What is it?"

"A charm, me lord. Ilsa gave it to me, in Germany. She said it would protect me against evil—and so it has."

"Oh, no, Tom—surely you must keep—"

Mouth set in an expression of obstinacy that Grey knew well, Tom leaned forward and put the leather string over Grey's head. The mouth relaxed.

"There, me lord. Now *I* can sleep, at least."

GREY'S PLAN TO speak to the governor at breakfast was foiled, as that gentleman sent word that he was indisposed. Grey, Cherry, and Fettes all exchanged looks across the breakfast table, but Grey said merely,

"Fettes? *And* you, Captain Cherry, please." They nodded, a look of subdued satisfaction passing between them. He hid a smile; they loved questioning people.

The secretary, Dawes, was present at breakfast but said little, giving all his attention to the eggs and toast on his plate. Grey inspected him carefully, but he showed no sign, either of nocturnal excursions or of clandestine knowledge. Grey gave Cherry an eye. Both Fettes and Cherry brightened perceptibly.

For the moment, though, his own path lay clear. He needed to make a public appearance, as soon as possible, and to take such action as would make it apparent to the public that the situation was under control—and would make it apparent to the maroons that attention was being paid and that their destructive activities would no longer be allowed to pass unchallenged.

He summoned one of his other captains after breakfast and arranged for an escort. Twelve men should make enough of a show, he decided.

"And where will you be going, sir?" Captain Lossey asked, squinting as he made mental calculations regarding horses, pack mules, and supplies.

Grey took a deep breath and grasped the nettle.

"A plantation called Twelvetrees," he said. "Twenty miles or so into the uplands above Kingston."

PHILIP TWELVETREES was young, perhaps in his mid-twenties, and good-looking in a sturdy sort of way. He didn't stir Grey personally, but nonetheless Grey felt a tightness through his body as he shook hands with the man, studying his face carefully for any sign that Twelvetrees recognised his name or attributed any importance to his presence beyond the present political situation.

Not a flicker of unease or suspicion crossed Twelvetrees's face, and Grey relaxed a little, accepting the offer of a cooling drink. This turned out to be a mixture of fruit juices and wine, tart but refreshing.

"It's called *sangria*," Twelvetrees remarked, holding up his glass so the soft light fell glowing through it. "Blood, it means. In Spanish."

Grey did not speak much Spanish but did know that. However, blood seemed as good a *point d'appui* as any, concerning his business.

"So you think we might be next?" Twelvetrees paled noticeably beneath his tan. He hastily swallowed a gulp of sangria and straightened his shoulders, though. "No, no. I'm sure we'll be all right. Our slaves are loyal, I'd swear to that."

"How many have you? And do you trust them with arms?"

"One hundred and sixteen," Twelvetrees replied automatically. Plainly he was contemplating the expense and danger of arming some fifty men—for at least half his slaves must be women or children—and setting them essentially at liberty upon his property. Not to mention the vision of an unknown number of maroons, also armed, coming suddenly out of the night with torches. He drank a little more sangria. "Perhaps . . . what did you have in mind?" he asked abruptly, setting down his glass.

Grey had just finished laying out his suggested plans, which called for the posting of two companies of infantry at the plantation, when a flutter of muslin at the door made him lift his eyes.

"Oh, Nan!" Philip put a hand over the papers Grey had spread out on the table and shot Grey a quick warning look. "Here's Colonel Grey come to call. Colonel, my sister, Nancy."

"Miss Twelvetrees." Grey had risen at once and now took two or three steps toward her, bowing over her hand. Behind him, he heard the rustle as Twelvetrees hastily shuffled maps and diagrams together.

Nancy Twelvetrees shared her brother's genial sturdiness. Not pretty in the least, she had intelligent dark eyes—and these sharpened noticeably at her brother's introduction.

"Colonel Grey," she said, waving him gracefully back to his seat as she took her own. "Would you be connected with the Greys of Ilford, in Sussex? Or perhaps your family are from the London branch . . . ?"

"My brother has an estate in Sussex, yes," he said hastily. Forbearing to add that it was his half-brother Paul, who was not in fact a Grey, having been born of his mother's first marriage. Forbearing also to mention that his elder full brother was the Duke of Pardloe, and the man who had shot one Nathaniel Twelvetrees twenty years before. Which would logically expose the fact that Grey himself . . .

Philip Twelvetrees rather obviously did not want his sister alarmed by any mention of the present situation. Grey gave him the faintest of nods in acknowledgement, and Twelvetrees relaxed visibly, settling down to exchange polite social conversation.

"And what it is that brings you to Jamaica, Colonel Grey?" Miss Twelvetrees asked eventually. Knowing this was coming, Grey had devised an answer of careful vagueness, having to do with the Crown's concern for shipping. Halfway through this taradiddle, though, Miss Twelvetrees gave him a very direct look and demanded, "Are you here because of the governor?"

"Nan!" said her brother, shocked.

"Are you?" she repeated, ignoring her brother. Her eyes were very bright, and her cheeks flushed.

Grey smiled at her.

"What makes you think that that might be the case, may I ask, ma'am?"

"Because if you haven't come to remove Derwent Warren from his office, then *someone* should!"

"Nancy!" Philip was nearly as flushed as his sister. He leaned forward, grasping her wrist. "Nancy, please!"

She made as though to pull away, but then, seeing his pleading face, contented herself with a simple "Hmph!" and sat back in her chair, mouth set in a thin line.

Grey would dearly have liked to know what lay behind Miss Twelvetrees's animosity toward the governor, but he couldn't well inquire directly. Instead, he guided the conversation smoothly away, inquiring of Philip regarding the operations of the plantation and of Miss Twelvetrees regarding the natural history of Jamaica, for which she seemed to have some feeling, judging by the rather good watercolours of plants and animals that hung about the room, all neatly signed *N. T.*

Gradually, the sense of tension in the room relaxed, and Grey became aware that Miss Twelvetrees was focusing her attentions upon him. Not quite flirting—she was not built for flirtation—but definitely going out of her way to make him aware of her as a woman. He didn't quite know what she had in mind—he was presentable enough but didn't think she was truly attracted to him. Still, he made no move to stop her; if Philip should leave them alone together, he might be able to find out why she had said that about Governor Warren.

A quarter hour later, a mulatto man in a well-made suit put his head in at the door to the drawing room and asked if he might speak with Philip. He cast a curious eye toward Grey, but Twelvetrees made no move to introduce them, instead excusing himself and taking the visitor—who, Grey conceived, must be an overseer of some kind—to the far end of the large, airy room, where they conferred in low voices.

He at once seized the opportunity to fix his attention on Miss Nancy, in hopes of turning the conversation to his own ends.

"I collect you are acquainted with the governor, Miss Twelvetrees?" he asked, to which she gave a short laugh.

"Better than I might wish, sir."

"Really?" he said, in as inviting a tone as possible.

"Really," she said, and smiled unpleasantly. "But let us not waste time in discussing a . . . a person of such low character." The smile altered, and she leaned towards him, touching his hand, which surprised him. "Tell me, Colonel, does your wife accompany you? Or does she remain in London, from fear of fevers and slave uprisings?"

"Alas, I am unmarried, ma'am," he said, thinking that she likely knew a good deal more than her brother wished her to.

"Really," she said again, in an altogether different tone.

Her touch lingered on his hand, a fraction of a moment too long. Not long enough to be blatant, but long enough for a normal man to perceive it—and Grey's reflexes in such matters were much better developed than a normal man's, from necessity.

He barely thought consciously but smiled at her, then glanced at her brother, then back, with the tiniest of regretful shrugs. He forbore to add the lingering smile that would have said, *"Later."*

She sucked her lower lip in for a moment, then released it, wet and reddened, and gave him a look under lowered lids that said, *"Later,"* and a good deal more. He coughed, and out of the sheer need to say *something* completely free of suggestion asked abruptly, "Do you by chance know what an Obeah man is, Miss Twelvetrees?"

Her eyes sprang wide, and she lifted her hand from his arm. He managed to move out of her easy reach without actually appearing to shove his chair backwards and thought she didn't notice; she was still looking at him with great attention, but the nature of that attention had changed. The sharp vertical lines between her brows deepened into a harsh eleven.

"Where did you encounter that term, Colonel, may I ask?" Her voice was quite normal, her tone light—but she also glanced at her brother's turned back, and she spoke quietly.

"One of the governor's servants mentioned it. I see you are familiar with the term—I collect it is to do with Africans?"

"Yes." Now she was biting her upper lip, but the intent was not sexual. "The Koromantyn slaves—you know what those are?"

"No."

"Negroes from the Gold Coast," she said, and putting her hand once more on his sleeve, pulled him up and drew him a little away, toward the far end of the room. "Most planters want them, because they're big and strong and usually very well formed." Was it—no, he decided, it was *not* his imagination; the tip of her tongue had darted out and touched her lip in the fraction of an instant before she'd said "well formed." He thought Philip Twelvetrees had best find his sister a husband, and quickly.

"Do you have Koromantyn slaves here?"

"A few. The thing is, Koromantyns tend to be intractable. Very aggressive and hard to control."

"Not a desirable trait in a slave, I collect," he said, making an effort to keep any edge out of his tone.

"Well, it can be," she said, surprising him. She smiled briefly. "If your slaves are loyal—and ours are, I'd swear it—then you don't mind them being a bit bloody-minded toward . . . anyone who might want to come and cause trouble."

He was sufficiently shocked at her language that it took him a moment to absorb her meaning. The tongue tip flickered out again, and had she had dimples, she would certainly have employed them.

"I see," he said carefully. "But you were about to tell me what an Obeah man is. Some figure of authority, I take it, among the Koromantyns?"

The flirtatiousness vanished abruptly, and she frowned again.

"Yes. *Obi* is what they call their . . . religion, I suppose one must call it. Though from what little I know of it, no minister or priest would allow it that name."

Loud screams came from the garden below, and Grey glanced out, to see a flock of small, brightly coloured parrots swooping in and out of a big, lacy tree with yellowish fruit. Like clockwork, two small black children, naked as eggs, shot out of the shrubbery and aimed slingshots at the birds. Rocks spattered harmless among the branches, but the birds rose in a feathery vortex of agitation and flapped off, shrieking their complaints.

Miss Twelvetrees ignored the interruption, resuming her explanation directly the noise subsided.

"An Obeah man talks to the spirits. He, or she—there are Obeah women, too—is the person that one goes to, to . . . arrange things."

"What sorts of things?"

A faint hint of her former flirtatiousness reappeared.

"Oh . . . to make someone fall in love with you. To get with child. To get *without* child"—and here she looked to see whether she had shocked him again, but he merely nodded—"or to curse someone. To cause them ill luck or ill health. Or death."

This was promising.

"And how is this done, may I ask? Causing illness or death?"

Here, however, she shook her head.

"I don't know. It's really not safe to ask," she added, lowering her voice still further, and now her eyes were serious. "Tell me—the servant who spoke to you, what did he say?"

Aware of just how quickly gossip spreads in rural places, Grey wasn't about to reveal that threats had been made against Governor Warren. Instead, he asked, "Have you ever heard of zombies?"

She went quite white.

"No," she said abruptly.

It was a risk, but he took her hand to keep her from turning away.

"I cannot tell you why I need to know," he said, very low-voiced, "but please believe me, Miss Twelvetrees—Nancy." Callously, he pressed her hand. "It's extremely important. Any help that you can give me would be . . . well, I should appreciate it extremely."

Her hand was warm; the fingers moved a little in his, and not in an effort to pull away. Her colour was coming back.

"I truly don't know much," she said, equally low-voiced. "Only that zombies are dead people who have been raised by magic to do the bidding of the person who made them."

"The person who made them—this would be an Obeah man?"

"Oh! No," she said, surprised. "The Koromantyns don't make zombies. In fact, they think it quite an unclean practice."

"I'm entirely of one mind with them," he assured her. "Who *does* make zombies?"

"Nancy!" Philip had concluded his conversation with the overseer and was coming toward them, a hospitable smile on his broad, perspiring face. "I say, can we not have something to eat? I'm sure the colonel must be famished, and I'm most extraordinarily clemmed myself."

"Yes, of course," Miss Twelvetrees said, with a quick warning glance at Grey. "I'll tell Cook." Grey tightened his grip momentarily on her fingers, and she smiled at him.

"As I was saying, Colonel, you must call on Mrs. Abernathy at Rose Hall. She would be the person best equipped to inform you."

"Inform you?" Twelvetrees, curse him, chose this moment to become inquisitive. "About what?"

"Customs and beliefs among the Ashanti, my dear," his sister said blandly. "Colonel Grey has a particular interest in such things."

Twelvetrees snorted briefly.

"Ashanti, my left foot! Ibo, Fulani, Koromantyn—baptise 'em all proper Christians and let's hear no more about what heathen beliefs they may have brought with 'em. From the little *I* know, you don't want to hear about that sort of thing, Colonel. Though if you *do*, of course," he added hastily, recalling that it was not his place to tell the lieutenant-colonel who would be protecting Twelvetrees's life and property his business, "then my sister's quite right—Mrs. Abernathy would be best placed to advise you. Almost all her slaves are Ashanti. She . . . er . . . she's said to . . . um . . . take an interest."

To Grey's own interest, Twelvetrees's face went a deep red, and he hastily changed the subject, asking Grey fussy questions about the exact disposition of his troops. Grey evaded direct answers, beyond assuring Twelvetrees that two companies of infantry would be dispatched to his plantation as soon as word could be sent to Spanish Town.

He wished to leave at once, for various reasons, but was obliged to remain for tea, an uncomfortable meal of heavy, stodgy food, eaten under the heated gaze of Miss Twelvetrees. For the most part, he thought he had handled her with tact and delicacy, but toward the end of the meal she began to give him little pursed-mouth jabs. Nothing one could—or should—overtly notice, but he saw Philip blink at her once or twice in frowning bewilderment.

"Of course, I could not pose as an authority regarding any aspect of life on Jamaica," she said, fixing Grey with an unreadable look. "We have lived here barely six months."

"Indeed," he said politely, a wodge of undigested Savoy cake settling heavily in his stomach. "You seem very much at home—and a very lovely home it is, Miss Twelvetrees. I perceive your most harmonious touch throughout."

This belated attempt at flattery was met with the scorn it deserved; the eleven was back, hardening her brow.

"My brother inherited the plantation from his cousin, Edward Twelvetrees. Edward lived in London himself." She levelled a look like the barrel of a musket at him. "Did you know him, Colonel?"

And just what would the bloody woman do if he told her the truth? he wondered. Clearly, she thought she knew something, but . . . No, he thought, watching her closely. She couldn't know the truth but had heard some rumour. So this poking at him was an attempt—and a clumsy one—to get him to say more.

"I know several Twelvetrees casually," he said very amiably. "But if I met your cousin, I do not think I had the pleasure of speaking with him at any great length." *You bloody murderer!* and *Fucking sodomite!* not really constituting conversation, if you asked Grey.

Miss Twelvetrees blinked at him, surprised, and he realised what he should have seen much earlier. She was drunk. He had found the sangria light, refreshing—but had drunk only one glass himself. He had not noticed her refill her own, and yet the pitcher stood nearly empty.

"My dear," said Philip, very kindly. "It is warm, is it not? You look a trifle pale and indisposed." In fact, she was flushed, her hair beginning to come down behind her rather large ears—but she did indeed look indisposed. Philip rang the bell, rising to his feet, and nodded to the black maid who came in.

"I am not indisposed," Nancy Twelvetrees said, with some dignity. "I'm—I simply—that is—" But the black maid, evidently used to this office, was already hauling Miss Twelvetrees toward the door, though with sufficient skill as to make it look as though she merely assisted her mistress.

Grey rose, perforce, and took Miss Nancy's hand, bowing over it.

"Your servant, Miss Twelvetrees," he said. "I hope—"

"We know," she said, staring at him from large, suddenly tear-filled eyes. "Do you hear me? *We know.*" Then she was gone, the sound of her unsteady steps a ragged drumbeat on the parquet floor.

There was a brief, awkward silence between the two men. Grey cleared his throat just as Philip Twelvetrees coughed.

"Didn't really like cousin Edward," he said.

"Oh," said Grey.

They walked together to the yard, where Grey's horse browsed under a tree, its sides streaked with parrot droppings.

"Don't mind Nancy, will you?" Twelvetrees said quietly, not looking at him. "She had . . . a disappointment, in London. I thought she might get over it more easily here, but—well, I made a mistake, and it's not easy to unmake." He sighed, and Grey had a strong urge to pat him sympathetically on the back.

In lieu of that, he made an indeterminate noise in his throat, nodded, and mounted.

"The troops will be here the day after tomorrow, sir," he said. "You have my word upon it."

GREY HAD INTENDED to return to Spanish Town, but instead paused on the road, pulled out the chart Dawes had given him, and calculated the distance to Rose Hall. It would mean camping on the mountain overnight, but they were prepared for that—and beyond the desirability of hearing firsthand the details of a maroon attack, he was now more than curious to speak with Mrs. Abernathy regarding zombies.

He called his aide, wrote out instructions for the dispatch of troops to Twelvetrees, then sent two men back to Spanish Town with the message and two more on ahead to discover a good campsite. They reached this as the sun was beginning to sink, glowing like a flaming pearl in a soft pink sky.

"What is that?" he asked, glancing up abruptly from the cup of gunpowder tea Corporal Sansom had handed him. Sansom looked startled, too, and stared up the slope where the sound had come from.

"Don't know, sir," he said. "It sounds like a horn of some kind."

It did. Not a trumpet or anything of a standard military nature. Definitely a sound of human origin, though. The men stood quiet, waiting. A moment or two, and the sound came again.

"That's a different one," Sansom said, sounding alarmed. "It came from over there"—pointing up the slope—"didn't it?"

"Yes, it did," Grey said absently. "Hush!"

The first horn sounded again, a plaintive bleat almost lost in the noises of the birds settling for the night, and then fell silent.

Grey's skin tingled, his senses alert. They were not alone in the jungle. Someone—some*ones*—were out there in the oncoming night, signalling to each other. Quietly, he gave orders for the building of a hasty fortification, and the camp fell at once into the work of organising defence. The men with him were mostly veterans and, while wary, not at all panicked. Within a very short time, a redoubt of stone and brush had been thrown up, sentries were posted in pairs around camp, and every man's weapon was loaded and primed, ready for an attack.

Nothing came, though, and while the men lay on their arms all night, there was no further sign of human presence. Such presence was there, though; Grey could feel it. Them. Watching.

He ate his supper and sat with his back against an outcrop of rock, dagger in his belt and loaded musket to hand. Waiting.

But nothing happened, and the sun rose. They broke camp in an orderly fashion, and if horns sounded in the jungle, the sound was lost in the shriek and chatter of the birds.

HE HAD NEVER been in the presence of anyone who repelled him so acutely. He wondered why that was; there was nothing overtly ill-favoured or ugly about her. If anything, she was a handsome Scotchwoman of middle age, fair-haired and buxom. And yet the widow Abernathy chilled him, despite the warmth of the air on the terrace where she had chosen to receive him at Rose Hall.

She was not dressed in mourning, he saw, nor did she make any obvious acknowledgement of the recent death of her husband. She wore white muslin, embroidered in blue about the hems and cuffs.

"I understand that I must congratulate you upon your survival, madam," he said, taking the seat she gestured him to. It was a somewhat callous thing to say, but she looked hard as nails; he didn't think it would upset her, and he was right.

"Thank you," she said, leaning back in her own wicker chair and looking him frankly up and down in a way that he found unsettling. "It was bloody cold in that spring, I'll tell ye that for nothing. Like to died myself, frozen right through."

He inclined his head courteously.

"I trust you suffered no lingering ill effects from the experience? Beyond, of course, the lamentable death of your husband," he hurried to add.

She laughed coarsely.

"Glad to get shot o' the wicked sod."

At a loss how to reply to this, Grey coughed and changed the subject.

"I am told, madam, that you have an interest in some of the rituals practised by slaves."

Her somewhat bleared green glance sharpened at that.

"Who told you that?"

"Miss Nancy Twelvetrees." There was no reason to keep the identity of his informant secret, after all.

"Oh, wee Nancy, was it?" She seemed amused by that, and shot him a sideways look. "I expect she liked *you*, no?"

He couldn't see what Miss Twelvetrees's opinion of him might have to do with the matter, and politely said so.

Mrs. Abernathy merely smirked, waving a hand. "Aye, well. What is it ye want to know, then?"

"I want to know how zombies are made."

Shock wiped the smirk off her face, and she blinked at him stupidly for a moment before picking up her glass and draining it.

"Zombies," she said, and looked at him with a certain wary interest. "Why?"

He told her. From careless amusement, her attitude changed, interest piqued. She made him repeat the story of his encounter with the thing in his room, asking pointed questions regarding its smell particularly.

"Decayed flesh," she said. "Ye'd ken what that smells like, would ye?"

It must have been her accent that brought back the battlefield at Culloden and the stench of burning corpses. He shuddered, unable to stop himself.

"Yes," he said abruptly. "Why?"

She pursed her lips in thought.

"There are different ways to go about it, aye? One way is to give the *afile* powder to the person, wait until they drop, and then bury them atop a recent corpse. Ye just spread the earth lightly over them," she explained, catching his look. "And make sure to put leaves and sticks over the face afore sprinkling the earth, so as the person can still breathe. When the poison dissipates enough for them to move again and sense things, they see they're buried, they smell the reek, and so they ken they must be dead." She spoke matter-of-factly, as though she had been telling him her private recipe for apple pandowdy or treacle cake. Weirdly enough, that steadied him, and he was able to speak calmly past his revulsion.

"Poison. That would be the *afile* powder? What sort of poison is it, do you know?"

Seeing the spark in her eye, he thanked the impulse that had led him to add "do you know?" to that question—for if not for pride, he thought, she might not have told him. As it was, she shrugged and answered off-hand.

"Oh . . . herbs. Ground bones—bits o' other things. But the main thing, the one thing ye *must* have, is the liver of a *fugu* fish."

He shook his head, not recognising the name. "Describe it, if you please." She did; from her description, he thought it must be one of the odd puffer fish that blew themselves up like bladders if disturbed. He made a silent resolve never to eat one. In the course of the conversation, though, something was becoming apparent to him.

"But what you are telling me—your pardon, madam—is that in fact a zombie is *not* a dead person at all? That they are merely drugged?"

Her lips curved; they were still plump and red, he saw, younger than her face would suggest. "What good would a dead person be to anyone?"

"But plainly the widespread belief is that zombies *are* dead."

"Aye, of course. The zombies think they're dead, and so does everyone else. It's not true, but it's effective. Scares folk rigid. As for 'merely drugged,' though . . ." She shook her head. "They don't come back from it, ye ken. The poison damages their brains and their nervous systems. They can follow simple instructions, but they've no real capacity for thought anymore—and they mostly move stiff and slow."

"Do they?" he murmured. The creature—well, the man, he was now sure of that—who had attacked him had not been stiff and slow, by any means. Ergo . . .

"I'm told, madam, that most of your slaves are Ashanti. Would any of them know more about this process?"

"No," she said abruptly, sitting up a little. "I learnt what I ken from a *houngan*—that would be a sort of . . . practitioner, I suppose ye'd say. He wasna one of my slaves, though."

"A practitioner of *what*, exactly?"

Her tongue passed slowly over the tips of her sharp teeth, yellowed but still sound.

"Of magic," she said, and laughed softly, as though to herself. "Aye, magic. African magic. Slave magic."

"You believe in magic?" He asked it as much from curiosity as anything else.

"Don't you?" Her brows rose, but he shook his head.

"I do not. And from what you have just told me yourself, the process of creating—if that's the word—a zombie is *not* in fact magic but merely the administration of poison over a period of time, added to the power of suggestion." Another thought struck him. "Can a person recover from such poisoning? You say it does not kill them."

She shook her head.

"The poison doesn't, no. But they always die. They starve, for one thing. They lose all notion of will and canna do anything save what the *houngan* tells them to do. Gradually they waste away to nothing, and—" Her fingers snapped silently.

"Even were they to survive," she went on practically, "the people would kill them. Once a person's been made a zombie, there's nay way back."

Throughout the conversation, Grey had become aware that Mrs. Abernathy spoke from what seemed a much closer acquaintance with the notion than one might acquire from an idle interest in natural philosophy. He wanted to get away from her but obliged himself to sit still and ask one more question.

"Do you know of any particular significance attributed to snakes, madam? In African magic, I mean."

She blinked, somewhat taken aback by that.

"Snakes," she repeated slowly. "Aye. Well . . . snakes ha' wisdom, they say. And some o' the *loas* are snakes."

"*Loas?*"

She rubbed absently at her forehead, and he saw, with a small prickle of revulsion, the faint stippling of a rash. He'd seen that before: the sign of advanced syphilitic infection.

"I suppose ye'd call them spirits," she said, and eyed him appraisingly. "D'ye see snakes in your dreams, Colonel?"

"Do I—no. I don't." He didn't, but the suggestion was unspeakably disturbing. She smiled.

"A *loa* rides a person, aye? Speaks through them. And I see a great huge snake lyin' on your shoulders, Colonel." She heaved herself abruptly to her feet.

"I'd be careful what ye eat, Colonel Grey."

THEY RETURNED TO Spanish Town two days later. The ride back gave Grey time for thought, from which he drew certain conclusions. Among these conclusions was the conviction that maroons had not, in fact, attacked Rose Hall. He had spoken to Mrs. Abernathy's overseer, who seemed reluctant and shifty, very vague on the details of the presumed attack. And later . . .

After his conversations with the overseer and several slaves, he had gone back to the house to take formal leave of Mrs. Abernathy. No one had answered his knock, and he had walked round the house in search of a servant. What he had found instead was a path leading downward from the house, with a glimpse of water at the bottom.

Out of curiosity, he had followed this path and found the infamous spring in which Mrs. Abernathy had presumably sought refuge from the murdering intruders. Mrs. Abernathy was in the spring, naked, swimming with slow composure from one side to the other, white-streaked fair hair streaming out behind her.

The water was crystalline; he could see the fleshy pumping of her buttocks, moving like a bellows that propelled her movements—and glimpsed the purplish hollow of her sex, exposed by the flexion. There were no banks of concealing reeds or other vegetation; no one could have failed to see the woman if she'd been in the spring—and, plainly, the temperature of the water was no dissuasion to her.

So she'd lied about the maroons. He had a cold certainty that Mrs. Abernathy had murdered her husband, or arranged it—but there was little he was equipped to do with that conclusion. Arrest her? There were no witnesses—or none who could legally testify against her, even if they wanted to. And he rather thought that none of her slaves would want to; those he had spoken with had displayed extreme reticence with regard to their mistress. Whether that was the result of loyalty or fear, the effect would be the same.

What the conclusion *did* mean to him was that the maroons were in fact likely not guilty of murder, and that was important. So far, all reports of mischief involved only property damage—and that, only to fields and equipment. No houses had been burned, and while several plantation owners had claimed that their slaves had been taken, there was no proof of this; the slaves in question might simply have taken advantage of the chaos of an attack to run.

This spoke to him of a certain amount of care on the part of whoever led the maroons. Who did? he wondered. What sort of man? The impression he was gaining was not that of a rebellion—there had been no declaration, and he would have expected that—but of the boiling over of a long-simmering frustration. He *had* to speak with Captain Cresswell. And he hoped that bloody secretary had managed to find the superintendent by the time he reached King's House.

IN THE EVENT, he reached King's House long after dark and was informed by the governor's butler—appearing like a black ghost in his nightshirt—that the household were asleep.

"All right," he said wearily. "Call my valet, if you will. And tell the governor's servant in the morning that I will require to speak to His Excellency after breakfast, no matter what his state of health may be."

Tom was sufficiently pleased to see Grey in one piece as to make no protest at being awakened and had him washed, nightshirted, and tucked up beneath his mosquito netting before the church bells of Spanish Town tolled midnight. The doors of his room had been repaired, but Grey made Tom leave the window open and fell asleep with a silken wind caressing his cheeks and no thought of what the morning might bring.

He was roused from an unusually vivid erotic dream by an agitated banging. He pulled his head out from under the pillow, the feel of rasping red hairs still rough on his lips, and shook his head violently, trying to re-orient himself in space and time. Bang, bang, bang, bang, *bang!* Bloody hell . . . ? Oh. Door.

"What? Come in, for God's sake! What the devil—oh. Wait a moment, then." He struggled out of the tangle of bedclothes and discarded nightshirt—good Christ, had he really been doing what he'd been dreaming about doing?—and flung his banyan over his rapidly detumescing flesh.

"What?" he demanded, finally getting the door open. To his surprise, Tom stood there, saucer-eyed and trembling, next to Major Fettes.

"Are you all right, me lord?" Tom burst out, cutting off Major Fettes's first words.

"Do I appear to be spurting blood or missing any necessary append-ages?" Grey demanded, rather irritably. "What's happened, Fettes?"

Now that he'd got his eyes properly open, he saw that Fettes looked almost as disturbed as Tom. The major—veteran of a dozen major cam-paigns, decorated for valour, and known for his coolness—swallowed vis-ibly and braced his shoulders.

"It's the governor, sir. I think you'd best come and see."

"WHERE ARE THE MEN who were assigned to guard him?" Grey asked calmly, stepping out of the governor's bedroom and closing the door gently behind him. The doorknob slid out of his fingers, slick under his hand. He knew the slickness was his own sweat, and not blood, but his stomach gave a lurch and he rubbed his fingers convulsively against the leg of his breeches.

"They're gone, sir." Fettes had got his voice, if not quite his face, back under control. "I've sent men to search the grounds."

"Good. Would you please call the servants together? I'll need to ques-tion them."

Fettes took a deep breath.

"They're gone, too."

"What? All of them?"

"Yes, sir."

He took a deep breath himself—and let it out again, fast. Even outside the room, the stench was gagging. He could feel the smell, thick on his skin, and rubbed his fingers on his breeches once again, hard. He swal-lowed and, holding his breath, jerked his head to Fettes—and to Cherry, who had joined them, shaking his head mutely in answer to Grey's raised brow. No sign of the vanished sentries, then. God damn it; a search would have to be made for their bodies. The thought made him cold, despite the growing warmth of the morning.

He went down the stairs, his officers only too glad to follow. By the time he reached the foot, he had decided where to begin, at least. He stopped and turned to Fettes and Cherry.

"Right. The island is under military law as of this moment. Notify the officers, but tell them there is to be no public announcement yet. And *don't* tell them why." Given the flight of the servants, it was more than likely that news of the governor's death would reach the inhabitants of Spanish Town within hours—if it hadn't already. But if there was the slightest chance that the populace might remain in ignorance of the fact that Governor Warren had been killed and partially devoured in his own residence, while under the guard of His Majesty's army, Grey was taking it.

"What about the secretary?" he asked abruptly, suddenly remembering. "Dawes. Is he gone, too? Or dead?"

Fettes and Cherry exchanged a guilty look.

"Don't know, sir," Cherry said gruffly. "I'll go and look."

"Do that, if you please."

He nodded in return to their salutes and went outside, shuddering in relief at the touch of the sun on his face, the warmth of it through the thin linen of his shirt. He walked slowly around the terrace toward his room, where Tom had doubtless already managed to assemble and clean his uniform.

Now what? Dawes, if the man was still alive—and he hoped to God he was . . . A surge of saliva choked him, and he spat several times on the terrace, unable to swallow for the memory of that throat-clenching smell.

"Tom," he said urgently, coming into the room. "Did you have an opportunity to speak to the other servants? To Rodrigo?"

"Yes, me lord." Tom waved him onto the stool and knelt to put his stockings on. "They all knew about zombies—said they were dead people, just like Rodrigo said. A *houngan*—that's a . . . well, I don't quite know, but folk are right scared of 'em. Anyway, one of those who takes against somebody—or what's paid to do so, I reckon—will take the somebody and kill them, then raise 'em up again to be his servant, and that's a zombie. They were all dead scared of the notion, me lord," he said earnestly, looking up.

"I don't blame them in the slightest. Did any of them know about my visitor?"

Tom shook his head.

"They said not, but I think they did, me lord. They weren't a-going to say. I got Rodrigo off by himself and he admitted he knew about it, but he said he didn't think it was a zombie what came after you, because I told him how you fought it and what a mess it made of your room." He narrowed his eyes at the dressing table, with its cracked mirror.

"Really? What did he think it was?"

"He wouldn't quite say, but I pestered him a bit, and he finally let on as it might have been a *houngan,* just pretending to be a zombie."

Grey digested that possibility for a moment. Had the creature who attacked him meant to kill him? If so, why? But if not, the attack might only have been meant to pave the way for what had now happened, by making it seem that there were zombies lurking about King's House in some profusion. That made a certain amount of sense, save for the fact . . .

"But I'm told that zombies are slow and stiff in their movements. Could one of them have done what . . . was done to the governor?" He swallowed.

"I dunno, me lord. Never met one." Tom grinned briefly at him, rising from fastening his knee buckles. It was a nervous grin, but Grey smiled back, heartened by it.

"I suppose I will have to go and look at the body again," he said, rising. "Will you come with me, Tom?" His valet was very observant, especially in matters pertaining to the body, and had been of help to him before in interpreting postmortem phenomena.

Tom paled noticeably but gulped and nodded and, squaring his shoulders, followed Lord John out onto the terrace.

On their way to the governor's room, they met Major Fettes, gloomily eating a slice of pineapple scavenged from the kitchen.

"Come with me, Major," Grey ordered. "You can tell me what discoveries you and Cherry have made in my absence."

"I can tell you one such, sir," Fettes said, putting down the pineapple and wiping his hands on his waistcoat. "Judge Peters has gone to Eleuthera."

"What the devil for?" That was a nuisance; he'd been hoping to discover more about the original incident that had incited the rebellion, and as he was obviously not going to learn anything from Warren . . . He waved a hand at Fettes; it hardly mattered why Peters had gone.

"Right. Well, then—" Breathing through his mouth as much as possible, Grey pushed open the door. Tom, behind him, made an involuntary sound but then stepped carefully up and squatted beside the body.

Grey squatted beside him. He could hear thickened breathing behind him.

"Major," he said, without turning round. "If Captain Cherry has found Mr. Dawes, would you be so kind as to fetch him in here?"

THEY WERE HARD at it when Dawes came in, accompanied by both Fettes and Cherry, and Grey ignored all of them.

"The bite marks *are* human?" he asked, carefully turning one of Warren's lower legs toward the light from the window. Tom nodded, wiping the back of his hand across his mouth.

"Sure of it, me lord. I been bitten by dogs—nothing like this. Besides—" He inserted his forearm into his mouth and bit down fiercely, then displayed the results to Grey. "See, me lord? The teeth go in a circle, like."

"No doubt of it." Grey straightened and turned to Dawes, who was sagging at the knees to such an extent that Captain Cherry was obliged to hold him up. "Do sit down, please, Mr. Dawes, and give me your opinion of matters here."

Dawes's round face was blotched, his lips pale. He shook his head and tried to back away but was prevented by Cherry's grip on his arm.

"I know nothing, sir," he gasped. "Nothing at all. Please, may I go? I, I . . . really, sir, I grow faint!"

"That's all right," Grey said pleasantly. "You can lie down on the bed if you can't stand up."

Dawes glanced at the bed, went white, and sat down heavily on the floor. Saw what was on the floor beside him and scrambled hurriedly to his feet, where he stood swaying and gulping.

Grey nodded at a stool, and Cherry propelled the little secretary, not ungently, onto it.

"What's he told you, Fettes?" Grey asked, turning back toward the bed. "Tom, we're going to wrap Mr. Warren up in the counterpane, then lay him on the floor and roll him up in the carpet. To prevent leakage."

"Right, me lord." Tom and Captain Cherry set gingerly about this process, while Grey walked over and stood looking down at Dawes.

"Pled ignorance, for the most part," Fettes said, joining Grey and giving Dawes a speculative look. "He did tell us that Derwent Warren had seduced a woman called Nancy Twelvetrees, in London. Threw her over, though, and married the heiress to the Atherton fortune."

"Who had better sense than to accompany her husband to the West Indies, I take it? Yes. Did he know that Miss Twelvetrees and her brother had inherited a plantation on Jamaica and were proposing to emigrate here?"

"No, sir." Dawes's voice was little more than a croak. He cleared his throat and spoke more firmly. "He was entirely surprised to meet the Twelvetrees at his first assembly."

"I daresay. Was the surprise mutual?"

"It was. Miss Twelvetrees went white, then red, then removed her shoe and set about the governor with the heel of it."

"I wish I'd seen that," Grey said, with real regret. "Right. Well, as you can see, the governor is no longer in need of your discretion. I, on the other hand, am in need of your loquacity. You can start by telling me why he was afraid of snakes."

"Oh." Dawes gnawed his lower lip. "I cannot be sure, you understand—"

"Speak up, you lump," growled Fettes, leaning menacingly over Dawes, who recoiled.

"I—I—" he stammered. "Truly, I don't know the details. But it—it had to do with a young woman. A young black woman. He—the governor, that is—women were something of a weakness for him . . ."

"And?" Grey prodded.

The young woman, it appeared, was a slave in the household. And not disposed to accept the governor's attentions. The governor was not accustomed to take "no" for an answer—and didn't. The young woman had vanished the next day, run away, and had not been recaptured as yet. But the day after, a black man in a turban and loincloth had come to King's House and had requested audience.

"He wasn't admitted, of course. But he wouldn't go away, either." Dawes shrugged. "Just squatted at the foot of the front steps and waited."

When Warren had at length emerged, the man had risen, stepped forward, and in formal tones informed the governor that he was herewith cursed.

"Cursed?" said Grey, interested. "How?"

"Well, now, there my knowledge reaches its limits, sir," Dawes replied. He had recovered some of his self-confidence by now and straightened up a little. "For, having pronounced the fact, he then proceeded to speak in an unfamiliar tongue—I think some of it may have been Spanish, though it wasn't all like that. I must suppose that he was, er, administering the curse, so to speak?"

"I'm sure I don't know." By now Tom and Captain Cherry had completed their disagreeable task, and the governor reposed in an innocuous cocoon of carpeting. "I'm sorry, gentlemen, but there are no servants to assist us. We're going to take him down to the garden shed. Come, Mr. Dawes; you can be assistant pallbearer. And tell us on the way where the snakes come into it."

Panting and groaning, with the occasional near slip, they manhandled the unwieldy bundle down the stairs. Mr. Dawes, making ineffectual grabs at the carpeting, was prodded by Captain Cherry into further discourse.

"Well, I *thought* that I caught the word 'snake' in the man's tirade," he said. "And then . . . the snakes began to come."

Small snakes, large snakes. A snake was found in the governor's bath. Another appeared under the dining table, to the horror of a merchant's lady who was dining with the governor and who had hysterics all over the dining room before fainting heavily across the table. Mr. Dawes appeared to find something amusing in this, and Grey, perspiring heavily, gave him a glare that returned him more soberly to his account.

"Every day, it seemed, and in different places. We had the house searched, repeatedly. But no one could—or would, perhaps—detect the source of the reptiles. And while no one was bitten, still the nervous strain of not knowing whether you would turn back your coverlet to discover something writhing amongst your bedding . . ."

"Quite. Ugh!" They paused and set down their burden. Grey wiped his forehead on his sleeve. "And how did you make the connection, Mr. Dawes, between this plague of snakes and Mr. Warren's mistreatment of the slave girl?"

Dawes looked surprised and pushed his spectacles back up his sweating nose.

"Oh, did I not say? The man—I was told later that he was an Obeah man, whatever that may be—spoke her name, in the midst of his denunciation. Azeel, it was."

"I see. All right, ready? One, two, three—up!"

Dawes had given up any pretence of helping but scampered down the garden path ahead of them to open the shed door. He had quite lost any lingering reticence and seemed anxious to provide any information he could.

"He did not tell me directly, but I believe he had begun to dream of snakes and of the girl."

"How do—you know?" Grey grunted. "That's my foot, Major!"

"I heard him . . . er . . . speaking to himself. He had begun to drink rather heavily, you see. Quite understandable under the circumstances, don't you think?"

Grey wished he could drink heavily but had no breath left with which to say so.

There was a sudden cry of startlement from Tom, who had gone in to clear space in the shed, and all three officers dropped the carpet with a thump, reaching for nonexistent weapons.

"Me lord, me lord! Look who I found, a-hiding in the shed!" Tom was leaping up the path toward Grey, face abeam with happiness, the youth Rodrigo coming warily behind him. Grey's heart leapt at the sight, and he felt a most unaccustomed smile touch his face.

"Your servant, sah." Rodrigo, very timid, made a deep bow.

"I'm very pleased to see you, Rodrigo. Tell me—did you see anything of what passed here last night?"

The young man shuddered and turned his face away.

"No, sah," he said, so low-voiced Grey could barely hear him. "It was zombies. They . . . eat people. I heard them, but I know better than to look. I ran down into the garden and hid myself."

"You heard them?" Grey said sharply. "What did you hear, exactly?"

Rodrigo swallowed, and if it had been possible for a green tinge to show on skin such as his, he would undoubtedly have turned the shade of a sea turtle.

"Feet, sah," he said. "Bare feet. But they don't walk, *step-step,* like a person. They only shuffle, *sh-sh, sh-sh.*" He made small pushing motions with his hands in illustration, and Grey felt a slight lifting of the hairs on the back of his neck.

"Could you tell how many . . . men . . . there were?"

Rodrigo shook his head. "More than two, from the sound."

Tom pushed a little forward, round face intent. "Was there anybody else with 'em, d'you think? Somebody with a regular step, I mean?"

Rodrigo looked startled and then horrified.

"You mean a *houngan*? I don't know." He shrugged. "Maybe. I didn't hear shoes. But . . ."

"Oh. Because—" Tom stopped abruptly, glanced at Grey, and coughed. "Oh."

Despite more questions, this was all that Rodrigo could contribute, and so the carpet was picked up again—this time, with the servant helping—and bestowed in its temporary resting place. Fettes and Cherry chipped away a bit more at Dawes, but the secretary was unable to offer any further information regarding the governor's activities, let alone speculate as to what malign force had brought about his demise.

"Have you heard of zombies before, Mr. Dawes?" Grey inquired, mopping his face with the remains of his handkerchief.

"Er . . . yes," the secretary replied cautiously. "But surely you don't believe what the servant . . . Oh, surely not!" He cast an appalled glance at the shed.

"Are zombies in fact reputed to devour human flesh?"

Dawes resumed his sickly pallor.

"Well, yes. But . . . oh, dear!"

"Sums it up nicely," muttered Cherry, under his breath. "I take it you don't mean to make a public announcement of the governor's demise, then, sir?"

"You are correct, Captain. I don't want public panic over a plague of zombies at large in Spanish Town, whether that is actually the case or not. Mr. Dawes, I believe we need trouble you no more for the moment; you are excused." He watched the secretary stumble off, before beckoning his officers closer. Tom moved a little away, discreet as always, and took Rodrigo with him.

"Have you discovered anything else that might have bearing on the present circumstance?"

They glanced at each other, and Fettes, wheezing gently, nodded to Cherry. Cherry strongly resembled that eponymous fruit, but, being younger and more slender than Fettes, had more breath than his superior.

"Yes, sir. I went looking for Ludgate, the old superintendent. Didn't find him—he's buggered off to Canada, they said—but I got a right earful concerning the present superintendent."

Grey groped for a moment for the name.

"Cresswell?"

"That's him."

"Peculation or corruption" appeared to sum up the subject of Captain Cresswell's tenure as superintendent very well, according to Cherry's informants in Spanish Town and Kingston. Amongst other abuses, he had arranged trade between the maroons on the uplands and the merchants below, in the form of bird skins, snakeskins, and other exotica, timber from the upland forests, and so on—but had, by report, accepted payment on behalf of the maroons but failed to deliver it.

"Had he any part in the arrest of the two young maroons accused of theft?"

Cherry's teeth flashed in a grin.

"Odd you should ask, sir. Yes, they said—well, some of them did—that the two young men had come down to complain about Cresswell's behaviour, but the governor wouldn't see them. They were heard to declare they would take back their goods by force—so when a substantial chunk of the contents of one warehouse went missing, it was assumed that was what they'd done. They—the maroons—insisted they hadn't touched the stuff, but Cresswell seized the opportunity and had them arrested for theft."

Grey closed his eyes, enjoying the momentary coolness of a breeze from the sea.

"The governor wouldn't see the young men, you said. Is there any suggestion of an improper connection between the governor and Captain Cresswell?"

"Oh, yes," said Fettes, rolling his eyes. "No proof yet—but we haven't been looking long, either."

"I see. And we still do not know the whereabouts of Captain Cresswell?"

Cherry and Fettes shook their heads in unison.

"The general conclusion is that Accompong scragged him," Cherry said.

"Who?"

"Oh. Sorry, sir," Cherry apologised. "That's the name of the maroon's headman, so they say. *Captain* Accompong, he calls himself, if you please." Cherry's lips twisted a little.

Grey sighed. "All right. No reports of any further depredations by the maroons, by whatever name?"

"Not unless you count murdering the governor," said Fettes.

"Actually," Grey said slowly, "I don't think that the maroons are responsible for this particular death." He was somewhat surprised to hear himself say so, in truth—and yet he found that he *did* think it.

Fettes blinked, this being as close to an expression of astonishment as he ever got, and Cherry looked openly sceptical. Grey did not choose to go into the matter of Mrs. Abernathy nor yet to explain his conclusions about the maroons' disinclination for violence. Strange, he thought. He had heard Captain Accompong's name only moments before, but with that name his thoughts began to coalesce around a shadowy figure. Suddenly there was a mind out there, someone with whom he might engage.

In battle, the personality and temperament of the commanding officer was nearly as important as the number of troops he commanded. So. He needed to know more about Captain Accompong, but that could wait for the moment.

He nodded to Tom, who approached respectfully, Rodrigo behind him.

"Tell them what you discovered, Tom."

Tom cleared his throat and folded his hands at his waist.

"Well, we . . . er . . . disrobed the governor"—Fettes flinched, and Tom cleared his throat again before going on—"and had a close look. And the long and the short of it, sir, and sir," he added, with a nod to Cherry, "is that Governor Warren was stabbed in the back."

Both officers looked blank.

"But . . . the place is covered with blood and filth and nastiness," Cherry protested. "It smells like that place where they put the bloaters they drag out of the Thames!"

"Footprints," Fettes said, giving Tom a faintly accusing look. "There were footprints. Big, bloody, *bare* footprints."

"I do not deny that something objectionable was present in that room," Grey said dryly. "But whoever—or whatever—gnawed the governor probably did not kill him. He was almost certainly dead when the . . . er . . . subsequent damage occurred."

Rodrigo's eyes were huge. Fettes was heard to observe under his breath that he would be damned, but both Fettes and Cherry were good men and did not argue with Grey's conclusions, any more than they had taken issue with his order to hide Warren's body: they could plainly perceive the desirability of suppressing rumour of a plague of zombies.

"The point, gentlemen, is that after several months of incident, there has been nothing for the last month. Perhaps Mr. Warren's death is meant to be incitement, but if it was not the work of the maroons, then the question is . . . what are the maroons waiting for?"

Tom lifted his head, eyes wide.

"Why, me lord, I'd say—they're waiting for *you*. What else?"

WHAT ELSE, INDEED. Why had he not seen that at once? Of course Tom was right. The maroons' protest had gone unanswered, their complaint unremedied. So they had set out to attract attention in the most noticeable—if not the best—way open to them. Time had passed, nothing was done in response, and then they had heard that soldiers were coming. Lieutenant-Colonel Grey had now appeared. Naturally they were waiting to see what he would do.

What had he done so far? Sent troops to guard the plantations that were the most likely targets of a fresh attack. That was not likely to encourage the maroons to abandon their present plan of action, though it might cause them to direct their efforts elsewhere.

He walked to and fro in the wilderness of the King's House garden, thinking, but there were few alternatives.

He summoned Fettes and informed him that he, Fettes, was, until further notice, acting governor of the island of Jamaica.

Fettes looked more like a block of wood than usual.

"Yes, sir," he said. "If I might ask, sir . . . where are you going?"

"I'm going to talk to Captain Accompong."

"ALONE, SIR?" Fettes was appalled. "Surely you cannot mean to go up there *alone*!"

"I won't be," Grey assured him. "I'm taking my valet and the servant boy. I'll need someone who can translate for me, if necessary."

Seeing the mulish cast settling upon Fettes's brow, he sighed.

"To go there in force, Major, is to invite battle, and that is not what I want."

"No, sir," Fettes said dubiously, "but surely a proper escort . . . !"

"No, Major." Grey was courteous but firm. "I wish to make it clear that

I am coming to *speak* with Captain Accompong, and nothing more. I go alone."

"Yes, sir." Fettes was beginning to look like a block of wood that someone had set about with a hammer and chisel.

"As you wish, sir."

Grey nodded and turned to go into the house, but then paused and turned back.

"Oh, there is one thing that you might do for me, Major."

Fettes brightened slightly.

"Yes, sir?"

"Find me a particularly excellent hat, would you? With gold lace, if possible."

THEY RODE FOR nearly two days before they heard the first of the horns. A high, melancholy sound in the twilight, it seemed far away, and only a sort of metallic note made Grey sure that it was not in fact the cry of some large exotic bird.

"Maroons," Rodrigo said under his breath, and crouched a little, as though trying to avoid notice, even in the saddle. "That's how they talk to one another. Every group has a horn; they all sound different."

Another long, mournful falling note. Was it the same horn? Grey wondered. Or a second, answering the first?

"Talk to one another, you say. Can you tell what they're saying?"

Rodrigo had straightened up a bit in his saddle, putting a hand automatically behind him to steady the leather box that held the most ostentatious hat available in Spanish Town.

"Yes, sah. They're telling one another we're here."

Tom muttered something under his own breath, which sounded like, "Could have told you that meself for free," but declined to repeat or expand upon his sentiment when invited to do so.

They camped for the night under the shelter of a tree, so tired that they merely sat in silence as they ate, watching the nightly rainstorm come in over the sea, then crawled into the canvas tent Grey had brought. The young men fell asleep instantly to the pattering of rain above them.

Grey lay awake for a little, fighting tiredness, his mind reaching upwards. He had worn uniform, though not full dress, so that his identity would be apparent. And his gambit so far had been accepted; they had not been challenged, let alone attacked. Apparently Captain Accompong would receive him.

Then what? He wasn't sure. He did hope that he might recover his men—the two sentries who had disappeared on the night of Governor

Warren's murder. Their bodies had not been discovered, nor had any of their uniform or equipment turned up—and Captain Cherry had had the whole of Spanish Town *and* Kingston turned over in the search. If they had been taken alive, though, that reinforced his impression of Accompong—and gave him some hope that this rebellion might be resolved in some manner not involving a prolonged military campaign fought through jungles and rocks and ending in chains and executions. But if . . . Sleep overcame him, and he lapsed into incongruous dreams of bright birds, whose feathers brushed his cheeks as they flew silently past.

Grey woke in the morning to the feel of sun on his face. He blinked for a moment, confused, and then sat up. He was alone. Truly alone.

He scrambled to his feet, heart thumping, reaching for his dagger. It was there in his belt, but that was the only thing still where it should be. His horse—all the horses—were gone. So was his tent. So was the pack mule and its panniers. And so were Tom and Rodrigo.

He saw this at once—the blankets in which they'd lain the night before were still there, tumbled into the bushes—but he called for them anyway, again and again, until his throat was raw with shouting.

From somewhere high above him, he heard one of the horns, a long-drawn-out hoot that sounded mocking to his ears.

He understood the present message instantly. *You took two of ours; we have taken two of yours.*

"And you don't think I'll come and get them?" he shouted upwards into the dizzying sea of swaying green. "Tell Captain Accompong I'm coming! I'll have my young men back, and back *safe*—or I'll have his head!"

Blood rose in his face, and he thought he might burst but had better sense than to punch something, which was his very strong urge. He was alone; he couldn't afford to damage himself. He had to arrive among the maroons with everything that still remained to him, if he meant to rescue Tom and resolve the rebellion—and he did mean to rescue Tom, no matter what. It didn't matter that this might be a trap; he was going.

He calmed himself with an effort of will, stamping round in a circle in his stockinged feet until he had worked off most of his anger. That's when he saw them, sitting neatly side by side under a thorny bush.

They'd left him his boots. They did expect him to come.

HE WALKED FOR three days. He didn't bother trying to follow a trail; he wasn't a particularly skilled tracker, and finding any trace among the rocks and dense growth was a vain hope in any case. He simply climbed and listened for the horns.

The maroons hadn't left him any supplies, but that didn't matter. There were numerous small streams and pools, and while he was hungry, he didn't starve. Here and there he found trees of the sort he had seen at Twelvetrees, festooned with small yellowish fruits. If the parrots ate them, he reasoned, the fruits must be at least minimally comestible. They were mouth-puckeringly sour, but they didn't poison him.

The horns had increased in frequency since dawn. There were now three or four of them, signaling back and forth. Clearly, he was getting close. To what, he didn't know, but close.

He paused, looking up. The ground had begun to level out here; there were open spots in the jungle, and in one of these small clearings he saw what were plainly crops: mounds of curling vines that might be yams, beanpoles, the big yellow flowers of squash or gourds. At the far edge of the field, a tiny curl of smoke rose against the green. Close.

He took off the crude hat he had woven from palm leaves against the strong sun and wiped his face on the tail of his shirt. That was as much preparation as it was possible to make. The gaudy gold-laced hat he'd brought was presumably still in its box—wherever that was. He put his palm-leaf hat back on and limped toward the curl of smoke.

As he walked, he became aware of people fading slowly into view. Dark-skinned people, dressed in ragged clothing, coming out of the jungle to watch him with big, curious eyes. He'd found the maroons.

A SMALL GROUP of men took him further upwards. It was just before sunset, and the sunlight slanted gold and lavender through the trees when they led him into a large clearing, where there was a compound consisting of a number of huts. One of the men accompanying Grey shouted, and from the largest hut emerged a man who announced himself with no particular ceremony as Captain Accompong.

Captain Accompong was a surprise. He was very short, very fat, and hunchbacked, his body so distorted that he did not so much walk as proceed by a sort of sideways lurching. He was attired in the remnants of a splendid coat, now buttonless and with its gold lace half missing, the cuffs filthy with wear.

He peered from under the drooping brim of a ragged felt hat, eyes bright in its shadow. His face was round and much creased, lacking a good many teeth—but giving the impression of great shrewdness and perhaps good humor. Grey hoped so.

"Who are you?" Accompong asked, peering up at Grey like a toad under a rock.

Everyone in the clearing very plainly knew his identity; they shifted

from foot to foot and nudged one another, grinning. He paid no attention
to them, though, and bowed very correctly to Accompong.

"I am the man responsible for the two young men who were taken on
the mountain. I have come to get them back—along with my soldiers."

A certain amount of scornful hooting ensued, and Accompong let it go
on for a few moments before lifting his hand. He sat down, carefully, sighing as he settled.

"You say so? Why you think I have anything to do with these young
men?"

"I do not say that you do. But I know a great leader when I see one—
and I know that you can help me to find my young men. If you will."

"Phu!" Accompong's face creased into a gap-toothed smile. "You think
you flatter me and I help?"

Grey could feel some of the smaller children stealing up behind him; he
heard muffled giggles but didn't turn round.

"I ask for your help. But I do not offer you only my good opinion in
return."

A small hand reached under his coat and rudely tweaked his buttock.
There was an explosion of laughter and mad scampering behind him. He
didn't move.

Accompong chewed slowly at something in the back of his capacious
mouth, one eye narrowed.

"Yes? What do you offer, then? Gold?" One corner of his thick lips
turned up.

"Do you have any need of gold?" Grey asked. The children were whispering and giggling again behind him, but he also heard shushing noises
from some of the women—they were getting interested. Maybe.

Accompong thought for a moment, then shook his head.

"No. What else you offer?"

"What do you want?" Grey parried.

"Captain Cresswell's head!" said a woman's voice, very clearly. There
was a shuffle and smack, a man's voice rebuking in Spanish, a heated
crackle of women's voices in return. Accompong let it go on for a minute
or two, then raised one hand. Silence fell abruptly.

It lengthened. Grey could feel the pulse beating in his temples, slow
and labouring. Ought he to speak? He came as a suppliant already; to
speak now would be to lose face, as the Chinese put it. He waited.

"The governor is dead?" Accompong asked at last.

"Yes. How do you know of it?"

"You mean did I kill him?" The bulbous yellowed eyes creased.

"No," Grey said patiently. "I mean do you know how he died?"

"The zombies kill him." The answer came readily—and seriously. There
was no hint of humor in those eyes now.

"Do you know who made the zombies?"

A most extraordinary shudder ran through Accompong, from his ragged hat to the horny soles of his bare feet.

"You do know," Grey said softly, raising a hand to prevent the automatic denial. "But it wasn't you, was it? Tell me."

The captain shifted uneasily from one buttock to the other but didn't reply. His eyes darted toward one of the huts, and after a moment he raised his voice, calling something in the maroons' patois, wherein Grey thought he caught the word "Azeel." He was puzzled momentarily, finding the word familiar but not knowing why. Then the young woman emerged from the hut, ducking under the low doorway, and he remembered.

Azeel. The young slave woman whom the governor had taken and misused, whose flight from King's House had presaged the plague of serpents.

Seeing her as she came forward, he couldn't help but see what had inspired the governor's lust, though it was not a beauty that spoke to him. She was small but not inconsequential. Perfectly proportioned, she stood like a queen, and her eyes burned as she turned her face to Grey. There was anger in her face—but also something like a terrible despair.

"Captain Accompong says that I will tell you what I know—what happened."

Grey bowed to her.

"I should be most grateful to hear it, madam."

She looked hard at him, obviously suspecting mockery, but he'd meant it, and she saw that. She gave a brief, nearly imperceptible nod.

"Well, then. You know that beast"—she spat neatly on the ground—"forced me? And I left his house?"

"Yes. Whereupon you sought out an Obeah man, who invoked a curse of snakes upon Governor Warren, am I correct?"

She glared at him and gave a short nod. "The snake is wisdom, and that man had none. None!"

"I think you're quite right about that. But the zombies?"

There was a general intake of breath among the crowd. Fear, distaste—and something else. The girl's lips pressed together, and tears glimmered in her large dark eyes.

"Rodrigo," she said, and choked on the name. "He—and I—" Her jaw clamped hard; she couldn't speak without weeping and would not weep in front of him. He cast down his gaze to the ground, to give her what privacy he could. He could hear her breathing through her nose, a soft, snuffling noise. Finally, she heaved a deep breath.

"He was not satisfied. He went to a *houngan*. The Obeah man warned him, but—" Her entire face contorted with the effort to hold in her feelings. "The *houngan*. He had zombies. Rodrigo paid him to kill the beast."

Grey felt as though he had been punched in the chest. Rodrigo. Rodrigo, hiding in the garden shed at the sound of shuffling bare feet in the night—or Rodrigo, warning his fellow servants to leave, then unbolting the doors, following a silent horde of ruined men in clotted rags up the stairs . . . or running up before them, in apparent alarm, summoning the sentries, drawing them outside, where they could be taken.

"And where is Rodrigo now?" Grey asked sharply. There was a deep silence in the clearing. None of the people even glanced at one another; every eye was fixed on the ground. He took a step toward Accompong. "Captain?"

Accompong stirred. He raised his misshapen face to Grey and a hand toward one of the huts.

"We do not like zombies, Colonel," he said. "They are unclean. And to kill a man using them . . . this is a great wrong. You understand this?"

"I do, yes."

"This man, Rodrigo . . ." Accompong hesitated, searching out words. "He is not one of us. He comes from Hispaniola. They . . . do such things there."

"Such things as make zombies? But presumably it happens here, as well." Grey spoke automatically; his mind was working furiously in light of these revelations. The thing that had attacked him in his room—it would be no great trick for a man to smear himself with grave dirt and wear rotted clothing . . .

"Not among us," Accompong said very firmly. "Before I say more, my colonel—do you believe what you have heard so far? Do you believe that we—that *I*—had nothing to do with the death of your governor?"

Grey considered that one for a moment. There was no evidence, only the story of the slave girl. Still . . . he did have evidence. The evidence of his own observations and conclusions regarding the nature of the man who sat before him.

"Yes," he said abruptly. "So?"

"Will your king believe it?"

Well, not as baldly stated, no, Grey thought. The matter would need a little tactful handling . . .

Accompong snorted faintly, seeing the thoughts cross Grey's face.

"This man, Rodrigo. He has done us great harm by taking his private revenge in a way that . . . that . . ." Accompong groped for the word.

"That incriminates you," Grey finished for him. "Yes, I see that. What have you done with him?"

"I cannot give this man to you," Accompong said at last. His thick lips pressed together briefly, but he met Grey's eye. "He is dead."

The shock hit Grey like a musket ball, a thump that knocked him off-balance and the sickening knowledge of irrevocable damage done.

"How?" he said, short and sharp. "What happened to him?"

The clearing was still silent. Accompong stared at the ground in front of him. After a long moment, a sigh, a whisper, drifted from the crowd.

"Zombie."

"Where?" he barked. "Where is he? Bring him to me. Now!"

The crowd shrank away from the hut, and a sort of moan ran through them. Women snatched up their children, pushed back so hastily that they stepped on the feet of their companions. The door opened.

"Anda!" said a voice from inside. *Walk,* it meant, in Spanish. Grey's numbed mind had barely registered this when the darkness inside the hut changed and a form appeared at the door.

It was Rodrigo. But then again—it wasn't. The glowing skin had gone pale and muddy, almost waxen. The firm, soft mouth hung loose, and the eyes—oh, God, the eyes! They were sunken, glassy, and showed no comprehension, no movement, not the least sense of awareness. They were a dead man's eyes. And yet . . . he walked.

This was the worst of all. Gone was every trace of Rodrigo's springy grace, his elegance. This creature moved stiffly, shambling, feet dragging, almost lurching from foot to foot. Its clothing hung upon its bones like a scarecrow's rags, smeared with clay and stained with dreadful liquids. The odour of putrefaction reached Grey's nostrils, and he gagged.

"Alto," said the voice softly, and Rodrigo stopped abruptly, arms hanging like a marionette's. Grey looked up then at the hut. A tall, dark man stood in the doorway, burning eyes fixed on Grey.

The sun was all but down; the clearing lay in deep shadow, and Grey felt a convulsive shiver go through him. He lifted his chin and, ignoring the horrid thing standing stiff before him, addressed the tall man.

"Who are you, sir?"

"Call me Ishmael," said the man, in an odd, lilting accent. He stepped out of the hut, and Grey was conscious of a general shrinking, everyone pulling away from the man, as though he suffered from some deadly contagion. Grey wanted to step back, too, but didn't.

"You did . . . this?" Grey asked, flicking a hand at the remnant of Rodrigo.

"I was paid to do it, yes." Ishmael's eyes flicked toward Accompong, then back to Grey.

"And Governor Warren—you were paid to kill him, as well, were you? By this man?" A brief nod at Rodrigo; he could not bear to look directly at him.

"The zombies think they're dead, and so does everyone else."

A frown drew Ishmael's brows together, and with the change of expression, Grey noticed that the man's faced was scarred, with apparent deliberation, long channels cut in cheeks and forehead. He shook his head.

"No. This"—he nodded at Rodrigo—"paid me to bring my zombies. He says to me that he wishes to terrify a man. And zombies will do that," he added, with a wolfish smile. "But when I brought them into the room and the *buckra* turned to flee, this one"—the flick of a hand toward Rodrigo—"sprang upon him and stabbed him. The man fell dead, and Rodrigo then *ordered* me"—his tone of voice made it clear what he thought of anyone ordering him to do anything—"to make my zombies feed upon him. And I did," he ended abruptly.

Grey swung round to Captain Accompong, who had sat silently through this testimony.

"And then you paid this . . . this—"

"Houngan," Ishmael put in helpfully.

"—to do *that*?!" He pointed at Rodrigo, and his voice shook with outraged horror.

"Justice," said Accompong, with simple dignity. "Don't you think so?"

Grey found himself temporarily bereft of speech. While he groped for something possible to say, the headman turned to a lieutenant and said, "Bring the other one."

"The *other*—" Grey began, but before he could speak further, there was another stir among the crowd, and from one of the huts a maroon emerged, leading another man by a rope around his neck. The man was wild-eyed and filthy, his hands bound behind him, but his clothes had originally been very fine. Grey shook his head, trying to dispel the remnants of horror that clung to his mind.

"Captain Cresswell, I presume?" he said.

"Save me!" the man panted, and collapsed on his knees at Grey's feet. "I beg you, sir—whoever you are—save me!"

Grey rubbed a hand wearily over his face and looked down at the erstwhile superintendent, then at Accompong.

"Does he need saving?" he asked. "I don't want to—I know what he's done—but it *is* my duty."

Accompong pursed his lips, thinking.

"You know what he is, you say. If I give him to you, what would you do with him?"

At least there was an answer to that one.

"Charge him with his crimes and send him to England for trial. If he is convicted, he would be imprisoned—or possibly hanged. What would happen to him here?" he asked curiously.

Accompong turned his head, looking thoughtfully at the *houngan,* who grinned unpleasantly.

"No!" gasped Cresswell. "No, please! Don't let him take me! I can't—I can't—oh, GOD!" He glanced, appalled, at the stiff figure of Rodrigo, then fell face-first onto the ground at Grey's feet, weeping convulsively.

Numbed with shock, Grey thought for an instant that it *would* probably resolve the rebellion . . . but no. Cresswell couldn't countenance the possibility of being handed over to Ishmael, and neither could Grey.

"Right," said Grey, and swallowed before turning to Accompong. "He *is* an Englishman, and, as I said, it's my duty to see that he's subject to English laws. I must therefore ask that you give him into my custody and take my word that I will see he receives justice. Our sort of justice," he added, giving the evil look back to the *houngan*.

"And if I don't?" Accompong asked, blinking genially at him.

"Well, I suppose I'll have to fight you for him," Grey said. "But I'm bloody tired and I really don't want to." Accompong laughed at this, and Grey followed swiftly up with "I will, of course, appoint a new superintendent—and, given the importance of the office, I will bring the new superintendent here so that you may meet him and approve of him."

"If I don't approve?"

"There are a bloody lot of Englishmen on Jamaica," Grey said, impatient. "You're bound to like *one* of them."

Accompong laughed out loud, his little round belly jiggling under his coat.

"I like you, Colonel," he said. "You want to be superintendent?"

Grey suppressed the natural answer to this and instead said, "Alas, I have a duty to the army which prevents my accepting the offer, amazingly generous though it is." He coughed. "You have my word that I will find you a suitable candidate, though."

The tall lieutenant who stood behind Captain Accompong lifted his voice and said something sceptical in a patois that Grey didn't understand—but from the man's attitude, his glance at Cresswell, and the murmur of agreement that greeted his remark, Grey had no trouble in deducing what had been said.

What is the word of an Englishman worth?

Grey gave Cresswell, grovelling and snivelling at his feet, a look of profound disfavour. It would serve the man right if—then he caught the faint reek of corruption wafting from Rodrigo's still form, and shuddered. No, nobody deserved *that*.

Putting aside the question of Cresswell's fate for the moment, Grey turned to the question that had been in the forefront of his mind since he'd come in sight of that first curl of smoke.

"My men," he said. "I want to see my men. Bring them out to me, please. At once." He didn't raise his voice, but he knew how to make a command sound like one.

Accompong tilted his head a little to one side, as though considering, but then waved a hand casually. There was a stirring in the crowd, an expectation. A turning of heads, then bodies, and Grey looked toward the rocks where their focus lay. An explosion of shouts, catcalls, and laughter, and the two soldiers and Tom Byrd came out of the defile. They were roped together by the necks, their ankles hobbled and hands tied in front of them, and they shuffled awkwardly, bumping into one another, turning their heads to and fro like chickens, in a vain effort to avoid the spitting and the small clods of earth thrown at them.

Grey's outrage at this treatment was overwhelmed by his relief at seeing Tom and his young soldiers, all plainly scared but uninjured. He stepped forward at once so they could see him, and his heart was wrung by the pathetic relief that lighted their faces.

"Now, then," he said, smiling. "You didn't think I would leave you, surely?"

"*I* didn't, me lord," Tom said stoutly, already yanking at the rope about his neck. "I told 'em you'd be right along, the minute you got your boots on!" He glared at the little boys, naked but for shirts, who were dancing round him and the soldiers, shouting, *"Buckra! Buckra!"* and making not-quite-pretend jabs at the men's genitals with sticks. "Can you make 'em leave off that filthy row, me lord? They been at it ever since we got here."

Grey looked at Accompong and politely raised his brows. The headman barked a few words of something not quite Spanish, and the boys reluctantly fell back, though they continued to make faces and rude arm-pumping gestures.

Captain Accompong put out a hand to his lieutenant, who hauled the fat little headman to his feet. He dusted fastidiously at the skirts of his coat, then walked slowly around the small group of prisoners, stopping at Cresswell. He contemplated the man, who had now curled himself into a ball, then looked up at Grey.

"Do you know what a *loa* is, my colonel?" he asked quietly.

"I do, yes," Grey replied warily. "Why?"

"There is a spring, quite close. It comes from deep in the earth, where the *loas* live, and sometimes they will come forth and speak. If you will have back your men—I ask you to go there and speak with whatever *loa* may find you. Thus we will have truth, and I can decide."

Grey stood for a moment, looking back and forth from the fat old man to Cresswell, whose back heaved with silent sobs, to the young girl Azeel, who had turned her head to hide the hot tears coursing down her cheeks. He didn't look at Tom. There didn't seem much choice.

"All right," he said, turning back to Accompong. "Let me go now, then."

Accompong shook his head.

"In the morning," he said. "You do not want to go there at night."

"Yes, I do," Grey said. "Now."

"QUITE CLOSE" was a relative term, apparently. Grey thought it must be near midnight by the time they arrived at the spring—Grey, the *houngan* Ishmael, and four maroons bearing torches and armed with the long cane knives called machetes.

Accompong hadn't told him it was a *hot* spring. There was a rocky overhang and what looked like a cavern beneath it, from which steam drifted out like dragon's breath. His attendants—or guards, as one chose to look at it—halted as one, a safe distance away. He glanced at them for instruction, but they were silent.

He'd been wondering what the *houngan*'s role in this peculiar undertaking was. The man was carrying a battered canteen; now he uncorked this and handed it to Grey. It smelled hot, though the tin of the heavy canteen was cool in his hands. Raw rum, he thought, from the sweetly searing smell of it—and doubtless a few other things.

"*. . . Herbs. Ground bones—bits o' other things. But the main thing, the one thing ye must have, is the liver of a fugu fish . . . They don't come back from it, ye ken. The poison damages their brains . . .*"

"Now we drink," Ishmael said. "And we enter the cave."

"Both of us?"

"Yes. I will summon the *loa*. I am a priest of Damballa." The man spoke seriously, with none of the hostility or smirking he had displayed earlier. Grey noticed, though, that their escort kept a safe distance from the *houngan*, and a wary eye upon him.

"I see," said Grey, though he didn't. "This . . . Damballa. He, or she—"

"Damballa is the great serpent," Ishmael said, and smiled, teeth flashing briefly in the torchlight. "I am told that snakes speak to you." He nodded at the canteen. "Drink."

Repressing the urge to say, "You first," Grey raised the canteen to his lips and drank slowly. It was *very* raw rum, with a strange taste, sweetly acrid, rather like the taste of fruit ripened to the edge of rot. He tried to keep any thought of Mrs. Abernathy's casual description of *afile* powder out of mind—she hadn't, after all, mentioned how the stuff might taste. And surely Ishmael wouldn't simply poison him . . . ? He hoped not.

He sipped the liquid until a slight shift of the *houngan*'s posture told him it was enough, then he handed the canteen to Ishmael, who drank from it without hesitation. Grey supposed he should find this comforting, but his head was beginning to swim in an unpleasant manner, his heartbeat throbbing audibly in his ears, and something odd was happening to his vision: it went intermittently dark, then returned with a brief flash of light, and when he looked at one of the torches, it had a halo of coloured rings around it.

He barely heard the *clunk* of the canteen, dropped on the ground, and watched, blinking, as the *houngan*'s white-clad back wavered before him. A dark blur of face as Ishmael turned to him.

"Come." The man disappeared into the veil of water.

"Right," he muttered. "Well, then . . ." He removed his boots, unbuckled the knee bands of his breeches, and peeled off his stockings. Then Grey shucked his coat and stepped cautiously into the steaming water.

It was hot enough to make him gasp, but within a few moments he had got used to the temperature and made his way across a shallow, steaming pool toward the mouth of the cavern, shifting gravel hard under his bare feet. He heard whispering from his guards, but no one offered any alternative suggestions.

Water poured from the overhang but not in the manner of a true waterfall—slender streams, like jagged teeth. The guards had pegged the torches into the ground at the edge of the spring; the flames danced like rainbows in the drizzle of the falling water as he passed beneath the overhang.

The hot, wet air pressed his lungs and made it hard to breathe. After a short while he couldn't feel any difference between his skin and the moist air through which he walked; it was as though he had melted into the darkness of the cavern.

And it *was* dark. Completely. A faint glow came from behind him, but he could see nothing at all before him and was obliged to feel his way, one hand on the rough rock wall. The sound of falling water grew fainter, replaced by the heavy thump of his own heartbeat, struggling against the pressure on his chest. Once he stopped and pressed his fingers against his eyelids, taking comfort in the coloured patterns that appeared there; he wasn't blind, then. When he opened his eyes again, though, the darkness was still complete.

He thought the walls were narrowing—he could touch them on both sides by stretching out his arms—and had a nightmare moment when he seemed to *feel* them drawing in upon him. He forced himself to breathe, a deep, explosive gasp, and forced the illusion back.

"Stop there." The voice was a whisper. He stopped.

There was silence for what felt like a long time.

"Come forward," said the whisper, sounding suddenly quite near him. "There is dry land, just before you."

He shuffled forward, felt the floor of the cave rise beneath him, and stepped out carefully onto bare rock. Walked slowly forward until again the voice bade him stop.

Silence. He thought he could make out breathing but wasn't sure; the sound of the water was still faintly audible in the distance. *All right,* he thought. *Come along, then.*

It hadn't been precisely an invitation, but what came into his mind was Mrs. Abernathy's intent green eyes, staring at him as she said, *"I see a great, huge snake lyin' on your shoulders, Colonel."*

With a convulsive shudder, he realised that he felt a weight on his shoulders. Not a dead weight but something live. It moved, just barely.

"Jesus," he whispered, and thought he heard the ghost of a laugh from somewhere in the cave. He stiffened and fought back against the mental image, for surely this was nothing more than imagination, fuelled by rum. Sure enough, the illusion of green eyes vanished—but the weight rested on him still, though he couldn't tell whether it lay upon his shoulders or his mind.

"So," said the low voice, sounding surprised. "The *loa* has come already. The snakes *do* like you, *buckra*."

"And if they do?" he asked. He spoke in a normal tone of voice; his words echoed from the walls around him.

The voice chuckled briefly, and he felt rather than heard movement nearby, the rustle of limbs and a soft thump as something struck the floor near his right foot. His head felt immense, throbbing with rum, and waves of heat pulsed through him, though the depths of the cave were cool.

"See if this snake likes you, *buckra*," the voice invited. "Pick it up."

He couldn't see a thing but slowly moved his foot, feeling his way over the silty floor. His toes touched something and he stopped. Whatever he had touched moved abruptly, recoiling from him. Then he felt the tiny flicker of a snake's tongue on his toe, tasting him.

Oddly, the sensation steadied him. Surely this wasn't his friend, the tiny yellow constrictor—but it was a serpent much like that one in general size, so far as he could tell. Nothing to fear from that.

"Pick it up," the voice invited again. "The krait will tell us if you speak the truth."

"Will he, indeed?" Grey said dryly. "How?"

The voice laughed, and he thought he heard two or three more chuckling behind it—but perhaps it was only echoes.

"If you die . . . you lied."

Grey gave a small, contemptuous snort. There were no venomous snakes on Jamaica. He cupped his hand and bent at the knee, but hesitated. He had an instinctive aversion to being bitten by a snake, venomous or not. And how did he know how the man—or men—sitting in the shadows would take it if the thing *did* bite him?

"I trust this snake," said the voice softly. "Krait comes with me from Africa. Long time now."

Grey's knees straightened abruptly. Africa! Now he placed the name, and cold sweat broke out on his face. *Krait.* A fucking *African* krait. Gwynne had had one. Small, no bigger than the circumference of a man's little finger. *"Bloody deadly,"* Gwynne had crooned, stroking the thing's back with the tip of a goose quill—an attention to which the snake, a slender, nondescript brown thing, had seemed oblivious.

This one was squirming languorously over the top of Grey's foot; he had to restrain a strong urge to kick it away and stamp on it. What the devil was it about him that attracted *snakes,* of all ungodly things? He supposed it could be worse; it might be cockroaches. Instantly he felt a hideous crawling sensation upon his forearms and rubbed them hard reflexively, seeing—yes, he bloody *saw* them, here in the dark—thorny jointed legs and wriggling, inquisitive antennae brushing his skin.

He might have cried out. Someone laughed.

If he thought at all, he wouldn't be able to do it. He stooped and snatched the thing and, rising, hurled it into the darkness. There was a yelp and a scrabbling, then a brief, shocked scream.

He stood panting and trembling from reaction, checking and rechecking his hand—but felt no pain, could find no puncture wounds. The scream had been succeeded by a low stream of unintelligible curses, punctuated by the deep gasps of a man in terror. The voice of the *houngan*—if that's who it was—came urgently, followed by another voice, doubtful, fearful. Behind him, before him? He had no sense of direction anymore.

Something brushed past him, the heaviness of a body, and he fell against the wall of the cave, scraping his arm. He welcomed the pain; it was something to cling to, something real.

More urgency in the depths of the cave, sudden silence. And then a swishing *thunk!* as something struck hard into flesh, and the sheared-copper smell of fresh blood came strong over the scent of hot rock and rushing water. No further sound.

He was sitting on the muddy floor of the cave; he could feel the cool dirt under him. He pressed his hands flat against it, getting his bearings. After a moment, he heaved himself to his feet and stood, swaying and dizzy.

"I don't lie," he said, into the dark. "And I *will* have my men."

Dripping with sweat and water, he turned back, toward the rainbows.

THE SUN HAD barely risen when he came back into the mountain compound. The smoke of cooking fires hung among the huts, and the smell of food made his stomach clench painfully, but all that could wait. He strode as well as he might—his feet were so badly blistered that he hadn't been able to get his boots back on and had walked back barefoot, over rocks and thorns—to the largest hut, where Captain Accompong sat placidly waiting for him.

Tom and the soldiers were there, too, no longer roped together but still bound, kneeling by the fire. And Cresswell, a little way apart, appearing wretched but at least upright.

Accompong looked at one of his lieutenants, who stepped forward with a big cane knife and cut the prisoners' bonds with a series of casual but fortunately accurate swipes.

"Your men, my colonel," he said magnanimously, flipping one fat hand in their direction. "I give them back to you."

"I am deeply obliged to you, sir." Grey bowed. "There is one missing, though. Where is Rodrigo?"

There was a sudden silence. Even the shouting children hushed instantly, melting back behind their mothers. Grey could hear the trickling of water down the distant rock face and the pulse beating in his ears.

"The zombie?" Accompong said at last. He spoke mildly, but Grey sensed some unease in his voice. "He is not yours."

"Yes," Grey said firmly. "He is. He came to the mountain under my protection—and he will leave the same way. It is my duty."

The squatty headman's expression was hard to interpret. None of the crowd moved or murmured, though Grey caught glimpses from the corner of his eyes of the faint turning of heads, as folk asked silent questions of one another.

"It is my duty," Grey repeated. "I cannot go without him." He carefully omitted any suggestion that it might not be his choice whether to go or not. Still, why would Accompong return the white men to him if he planned to kill or imprison Grey?

The headman pursed fleshy lips, then turned his head and said something questioning. Movement in the hut where Ishmael had emerged the night before. There was a considerable pause, but, once more, the *houngan* came out.

His face was pale, and one of his feet was wrapped in a bloodstained wad of fabric, bound tightly. Amputation, Grey thought with interest, recalling the metallic *thunk* that had seemed to echo through his own flesh in the cave. It was the only sure way to keep a snake's venom from spreading through the body.

"Ah," said Grey, voice light. "So the krait liked me better, did he?"

He thought Accompong laughed under his breath, but he didn't really pay attention. The *houngan*'s eyes flashed hate at him, and Grey regretted his wit, fearing that it might cost Rodrigo more than had already been taken from him.

Despite his shock and horror, though, he clung to what Mrs. Abernathy had told him. The young man was *not* truly dead. He swallowed. Could Rodrigo perhaps be restored? The Scotchwoman had said not—but perhaps she was wrong. Clearly Rodrigo had not been a zombie for more than a few days. And she did say that the drug dissipated over time. Perhaps . . .

Accompong spoke sharply, and the *houngan* lowered his head.

"Anda," he said sullenly. There was stumbling movement in the hut, and he stepped aside, half-pushing Rodrigo out into the light, where he came to a stop, staring vacantly at the ground, mouth open.

"You want this?" Accompong waved a hand at Rodrigo. "What for? He's no good to you surely? Unless you want to take him to bed—he won't say no to you!"

Everyone thought that very funny; the clearing rocked with laughter. Grey waited it out. From the corner of his eye, he saw the girl Azeel watching him with something like a fearful hope in her eyes.

"He is under my protection," he repeated. "Yes, I want him."

Accompong nodded and took a deep breath, sniffing appreciatively at the mingled scents of cassava porridge, fried plantain, and frying pig meat.

"Sit down, Colonel," he said, "and eat with me."

Grey sank slowly down beside him, weariness throbbing through his legs. Looking around, he saw Cresswell dragged roughly off but left sitting on the ground against a hut, unmolested. Tom and the two soldiers, looking dazed, were being fed at one of the cook fires. Then he saw Rodrigo, still standing like a scarecrow, and struggled to his feet.

He took the young man's tattered sleeve and said, "Come with me." Rather to his surprise, Rodrigo did, turning like an automaton. He led the young man through the staring crowd to the girl Azeel, and said, "Stop." He lifted Rodrigo's hand and offered it to the girl, who, after a moment's hesitation, took firmly hold of it.

"Look after him, please," Grey said to her. Only as he turned away did it register upon him that the arm he had held was wrapped with a bandage. Ah. Dead men don't bleed.

Returning to Accompong's fire, he found a wooden platter of steaming food awaiting him. He sank down gratefully upon the ground again and closed his eyes—then opened them, startled, as he felt something descend upon his head and found himself peering out from under the drooping felt brim of the headman's ragged hat.

"Oh," he said. "Thank you." He hesitated, looking round, either for the leather hatbox or for his ragged palm-frond hat, but didn't see either one.

"Never mind," said Accompong, and, leaning forward, slid his hands carefully over Grey's shoulders, palms up, as though lifting something heavy. "I will take your snake, instead. You have carried him long enough, I think."

AUTHOR'S NOTES

MY SOURCE FOR THE THEORETICAL BASIS OF MAK-
ing zombies was *The Serpent and the Rainbow: A Harvard Scientist's Astonishing Journey into the Secret Societies of Haitian Voodoo,
Zombis, and Magic,* by Wade Davis, which I'd read many years ago.
Information on the maroons of Jamaica, the temperament, beliefs,
and behaviour of Africans from different regions, and on historical
slave rebellions came chiefly from *Black Rebellion: Five Slave Revolts,*
by Thomas Wentworth Higginson. This manuscript (originally a series of articles published in *Atlantic Monthly, Harper's* magazine,
and *Century*) also supplied a number of valuable details regarding
terrain and personalities.

Captain Accompong was a real maroon leader—I took his physical description from this source—and the custom of trading hats
upon conclusion of a bargain also came from *Black Rebellion.* General background, atmosphere, and the importance of snakes came
from Zora Neale Hurston's *Tell My Horse* and a number of less important books dealing with voodoo. (By the way, I now have most of
my reference collection—some 2,500 books—listed on LibraryThing
and cross-indexed by topic, in case you're interested in pursuing anything like, say, Scotland, magic, or the American Revolution.)

A LEAF ON THE WIND
OF ALL HALLOWS

INTRODUCTION

ONE OF THE INTERESTING THINGS YOU CAN DO with a "bulge" (i.e., one of the novellas or short stories in the Outlander universe) is to follow mysteries, hints, and loose ends from the main books of the series. One such trail follows the story of Roger MacKenzie's parents.

In *Outlander,* we learn that Roger was orphaned during World War II, and then adopted by his great-uncle, the Reverend Reginald Wakefield, who tells his friends, Claire and Frank Randall, that Roger's mother was killed in the Blitz, and that his father was a Spitfire pilot "shot down over the Channel."

In *Drums of Autumn,* Roger tells his wife, Brianna, the moving story of his mother's death in the collapse of a Tube station during the bombing of London.

But in *An Echo in the Bone,* there is a poignant conversation in the moonlight between Claire and Roger, during which we encounter *this* little zinger:

Her hands wrapped his, small and hard and smelling of medicine.

"I don't know what happened to your father," she said. "But it wasn't what they told you [. . .]

"Of course things happen," she said, as though able to read his thoughts. "Accounts get garbled, too, over time and distance. Whoever told your mother might have been mistaken; she might have said something that the reverend misconstrued. All those things are possible. But during the War, I had letters from Frank—he wrote as often as he could, up until they recruited him into MI6. After that, I often wouldn't hear anything for months. But just before that, he wrote to me, and mentioned—just as casual chat, you know—that he'd run into something strange in the reports he was handling. A Spitfire had gone down, crashed—not shot down; they thought it must have been an engine failure—in Northumbria, and while it hadn't burned, for a wonder, there was no sign of the pilot. None. And he did mention the

name of the pilot, because he thought Jeremiah rather an appropriately doomed sort of name."

"Jerry," Roger said, his lips feeling numb. "My mother always called him Jerry."

"Yes," she said softly. "And there are circles of standing stones scattered all over Northumbria."

So what *really* happened to Jerry MacKenzie and his wife, Marjorie (known to her husband as Dolly)? Read on.

IT WAS TWO WEEKS yet to Hallowe'en, but the gremlins were already at work.

Jerry MacKenzie turned *Dolly II* onto the runway full throttle, shoulder hunched, blood thumping, already halfway up Green leader's arse—pulled back on the stick and got a choking shudder instead of the giddy lift of takeoff. Alarmed, he eased back, but before he could try again, there was a bang that made him jerk by reflex, smacking his head against the Perspex. It hadn't been a bullet, though; the off tyre had blown, and a sickening tilt looped them off the runway, bumping and jolting into the grass.

There was a strong smell of petrol, and Jerry popped the Spitfire's hood and hopped out in panic, envisioning imminent incineration, just as the last plane of Green flight roared past him and took wing, its engine fading to a buzz within seconds.

A mechanic was pelting down from the hangar to see what the trouble was, but Jerry'd already opened Dolly's belly and the trouble was plain: the fuel line was punctured. Well, thank Christ he hadn't got into the air with it, that was one thing, but he grabbed the line to see how bad the puncture was, and it came apart in his hands and soaked his sleeve nearly to the shoulder with high-test petrol. Good job the mechanic hadn't come loping up with a lit cigarette in his mouth.

He rolled out from under the plane, sneezing, and Gregory the mechanic stepped over him.

"Not flying her today, mate," Greg said, squatting down to look up into the engine, and shaking his head at what he saw.

"Aye, tell me something I don't know." He held his soaked sleeve gingerly away from his body. "How long to fix her?"

Greg shrugged, eyes squinted against the cold wind as he surveyed Dolly's guts.

"Half an hour for the tyre. You'll maybe have her back up tomorrow, if the fuel line's the only engine trouble. Anything else we should be looking at?"

"Aye, the left wing-gun trigger sticks sometimes. Gie' us a bit o' grease, maybe?"

"I'll see what the canteen's got in the way of leftover dripping. You best hit the showers, Mac. You're turning blue."

He was shivering, right enough, the rapidly evaporating petrol wicking his body heat away like candlesmoke. Still, he lingered for a moment, watching as the mechanic poked and prodded, whistling through his teeth.

"Go on, then," Greg said in feigned exasperation, backing out of the engine and seeing Jerry still there. "I'll take good care of her."

"Aye, I know. I just—aye, thanks." Adrenaline from the aborted flight was still surging through him, thwarted reflexes making him twitch. He walked away, suppressing the urge to look back over his shoulder at his wounded plane.

JERRY CAME OUT of the pilots' WC half an hour later, eyes stinging with soap and petrol, backbone knotted. Half his mind was on Dolly, the other half with his mates. Blue and Green were up this morning, Red and Yellow resting. Green flight would be out over Flamborough Head by now, hunting.

He swallowed, still restless, dry-mouthed by proxy, and went to fetch a cup of tea from the canteen. That was a mistake; he heard the gremlins laughing as soon as he walked in and saw Sailor Malan.

Malan was Group Captain and a decent bloke overall. South African, a great tactician—and the most ferocious, most persistent air fighter Jerry'd seen yet. Rat terriers weren't in it. Which was why he felt a beetle skitter briefly down his spine when Malan's deep-set eyes fixed on him.

"Lieutenant!" Malan rose from his seat, smiling. "The very man I had in mind!"

The Devil he had, Jerry thought, arranging his face into a look of respectful expectancy. Malan couldn't have heard about Dolly's spot of bother yet, and without that, Jerry would have scrambled with A squadron on their way to hunt 109s over Flamborough Head. Malan hadn't been looking for Jerry; he just thought he'd do, for whatever job was up. And the fact that the Group Captain had called him by his rank, rather than his name, meant it probably wasn't a job anyone would volunteer for.

He didn't have time to worry about what that might be, though; Malan was introducing the other man, a tallish chap in army uniform with dark hair and a pleasant, if sharp, look about him. Eyes like a good sheepdog's, he thought, nodding in reply to Captain Randall's greeting. Kindly, maybe, but he won't miss much.

"Randall's come over from Ops at Ealing," Sailor was saying over his shoulder. He hadn't waited for them to exchange polite chat, but was already leading them out across the tarmac, heading for the Flight Command offices. Jerry grimaced and followed, casting a longing glance downfield at Dolly, who was being towed ignominiously into the hangar. The rag doll painted on her nose was blurred, the black curls partially dissolved by weather and spilled petrol. Well, he'd touch it up later, when he'd heard the details of whatever horrible job the stranger had brought.

His gaze rested resentfully on Randall's neck, and the man turned suddenly, glancing back over his shoulder as though he'd felt the stress of Jerry's regard. Jerry felt a qualm in the pit of his stomach, as half-recognised observations—the lack of insignia on the uniform, that air of confidence peculiar to men who kept secrets—gelled with the look in the stranger's eye.

Ops at Ealing, my Aunt Fanny, he thought. He wasn't even surprised, as Sailor waved Randall through the door, to hear the Group Captain lean close and murmur in his ear, "Careful—he's a funny bugger."

Jerry nodded, stomach tightening. Malan didn't mean Captain Randall was either humorous or a Freemason. "Funny bugger" in this context meant only one thing. MI6.

CAPTAIN RANDALL *WAS* from the secret arm of British Intelligence. He made no bones about it, once Malan had deposited them in a vacant office and left them to it.

"We're wanting a pilot—a good pilot," he added with a faint smile, "to fly solo reconnaissance. A new project. Very special."

"Solo? Where?" Jerry asked warily. Spitfires normally flew in four-plane flights, or in larger configurations, all the way up to an entire squadron, sixteen planes. In formation, they could cover one another to some extent against the heavier Heinkels and Messerschmitts. But they seldom flew alone by choice.

"I'll tell you that a bit later. First—are you fit, do you think?"

Jerry reared back a bit at that, stung. What did this bloody boffin think he— Then he caught a glance at his reflection in the windowpane. Eyes red as a mad boar's, his wet hair sticking up in spikes, a fresh red bruise spreading on his forehead, and his blouson stuck to him in damp patches where he hadn't bothered to dry off before dressing.

"Extremely fit," he snapped. "Sir."

Randall lifted a hand half an inch, dismissing the need for *sir*s.

"I meant your knee," he said mildly.

"Oh," Jerry said, disconcerted. "That. Aye, it's fine."

He'd taken two bullets through his right knee a year before, when he'd dived after a 109 and neglected to see another one that popped out of nowhere behind him and peppered his arse.

On fire, but terrified of bailing out into a sky filled with smoke, bullets, and random explosions, he'd ridden his burning plane down, both of them screaming as they fell out of the sky, *Dolly I*'s metal skin so hot it had seared his left forearm through his jacket, his right foot squelching in the blood that filled his boot as he stamped the pedal. Made it, though, and had been on the sick-and-hurt list for two months. He still limped very noticeably, but he didn't regret his smashed patella; he'd had his second month's sick leave at home—and wee Roger had come along nine months later.

He smiled broadly at the thought of his lad, and Randall smiled back in involuntary response.

"Good," he said. "You're all right to fly a long mission, then?"

Jerry shrugged. "How long can it be in a Spitfire? Unless you've thought up a way to refuel in the air." He'd meant that as a joke, and was further disconcerted to see Randall's lips purse a little, as though thinking whether to tell him they *had*.

"It is a Spitfire ye mean me to fly?" he asked, suddenly uncertain. Christ, what if it was one of the experimental birds they heard about now and again? His skin prickled with a combination of fear and excitement. But Randall nodded.

"Oh, yes, certainly. Nothing else is maneuverable enough, and there may be a good bit of ducking and dodging. What we've done is to take a Spitfire II, remove one pair of wing guns, and refit it with a pair of cameras."

"One pair?"

Again, that slight pursing of lips before Randall replied.

"You might need the second pair of guns."

"Oh. Aye. Well, then . . ."

The immediate notion, as Randall explained it, was for Jerry to go to Northumberland, where he'd spend two weeks being trained in the use of the wing cameras, taking pictures of selected bits of landscape at different altitudes. And where he'd work with a support team who were meant to be trained in keeping the cameras functioning in bad weather. They'd teach him how to get the film out without ruining it, just in case he had to. After which . . .

"I can't tell you yet exactly where you'll be going," Randall said. His manner through the conversation had been intent, but friendly, joking now and then. Now all trace of joviality had vanished; he was dead serious. "Eastern Europe is all I can say just now."

Jerry felt his inside hollow out a little and took a deep breath to fill the empty space. He could say no. But he'd signed up to be an RAF flier, and that's what he was.

"Aye, right. Will I—maybe see my wife once, before I go, then?"

Randall's face softened a little at that, and Jerry saw the Captain's thumb touch his own gold wedding ring in reflex.

"I think that can be arranged."

MARJORIE MACKENZIE—Dolly, to her husband—opened the blackout curtains. No more than an inch . . . well, two inches. It wouldn't matter; the inside of the little flat was dark as the inside of a coal scuttle. London outside was equally dark; she knew the curtains were open only because she felt the cold glass of the window through the narrow crack. She leaned close, breathing on the glass, and felt the moisture of her breath condense, cool near her face. Couldn't see the mist, but felt the squeak of her fingertip on the glass as she quickly drew a small heart there, the letter *J* inside.

It faded at once, of course, but that didn't matter; the charm would be there when the light came in, invisible but there, standing between her husband and the sky.

When the light came, it would fall just so, across his pillow. She'd see his sleeping face in the light: the jackstraw hair, the fading bruise on his temple, the deep-set eyes, closed in innocence. He looked so young, asleep. Almost as young as he really was. Only twenty-two; too young to have such lines in his face. She touched the corner of her mouth but couldn't feel the crease the mirror showed her—her mouth was swollen, tender, and the ball of her thumb ran across her lower lip, lightly, to and fro.

What else, what else? What more could she do for him? He'd left her with something of himself. Perhaps there would be another baby—something he gave her, but something she gave him, as well. Another baby. Another child to raise alone?

"Even so," she whispered, her mouth tightening, face raw from hours of stubbled kissing; neither of them had been able to wait for him to shave. "Even so."

At least he'd got to see Roger. Hold his little boy—and have said little boy sick up milk all down the back of his shirt. Jerry'd yelped in surprise, but hadn't let her take Roger back; he'd held his son and petted him until the wee mannie fell asleep, only then laying him down in his basket and stripping off the stained shirt before coming to her.

It was cold in the room, and she hugged herself. She was wearing nothing but Jerry's string vest—he thought she looked erotic in it, "lewd," he said, approving, his Highland accent making the word sound really dirty—and the thought made her smile. The thin cotton clung to her breasts, true enough, and her nipples poked out something scandalous, if only from the chill.

She wanted to go crawl in next to him, longing for his warmth, longing to keep touching him for as long as they had. He'd need to go at eight, to catch the train back; it would barely be light then. Some puritanical impulse of denial kept her hovering there, though, cold and wakeful in the dark. She felt as though if she denied herself, her desire, offered that denial as sacrifice, it would strengthen the magic, help to keep him safe and bring him back. God knew what a minister would say to that bit of superstition, and her tingling mouth twisted in self-mockery. And doubt.

Still, she sat in the dark, waiting for the cold blue light of the dawn that would take him.

Baby Roger put an end to her dithering, though; babies did. He rustled in his basket, making the little waking-up grunts that presaged an outraged roar at the discovery of a wet nappy and an empty stomach, and she hurried across the tiny room to his basket, breasts swinging heavy, already letting down her milk. She wanted to keep him from waking Jerry, but stubbed her toe on the spindly chair, and sent it over with a bang.

There was an explosion of bedclothes as Jerry sprang up with a loud "FUCK!" that drowned her own muffled "Damn!" and Roger topped them both with a shriek like an air-raid siren. Like clockwork, old Mrs. Munns in the next flat thumped indignantly on the thin wall.

Jerry's naked shape crossed the room in a bound. He pounded furiously on the partition with his fist, making the wallboard quiver and boom like a drum. He paused, fist still raised, waiting. Roger had stopped screeching, impressed by the racket.

Dead silence from the other side of the wall, and Marjorie pressed her mouth against Roger's round little head to muffle her giggling. He smelled of baby scent and fresh pee, and she cuddled him like a large hot-water bottle, his immediate warmth and need making her notions of watching over her men in the lonely cold seem silly.

Jerry gave a satisfied grunt and came across to her.

"Ha," he said, and kissed her.

"What d'ye think you are?" she whispered, leaning into him. "A gorilla?"

"Yeah," he whispered back, taking her hand and pressing it against him. "Want to see my banana?"

"Dzień dobry."

JERRY HALTED IN the act of lowering himself into a chair, and stared at a smiling Frank Randall.

"Oh, aye," he said. "Like that, is it? *Niech sie pan odpierdoli.*" It meant, "Fuck off, sir," in formal Polish, and Randall, taken by surprise, broke out laughing.

"Like that," he agreed. He had a wodge of papers with him, official forms, all sorts, the bumf, as the pilots called it—Jerry recognised the one you signed that named who your pension went to, and the one about what to do with your body if there was one and anyone had time to bother. He'd done all that when he signed up, but they made you do it again, if you went on special service. He ignored the forms, though, eyes fixed instead on the maps Randall had brought.

"And here's me thinkin' you and Malan picked me for my bonny face," he drawled, exaggerating his accent. He sat and leaned back, affecting casualness. "It is Poland, then?" So it hadn't been coincidence, after all—or only the coincidence of Dolly's mishap sending him into the building early. In a way, that was comforting; it wasn't the bloody Hand of Fate tapping him on the shoulder by puncturing the fuel line. The Hand of Fate had been in it a good bit earlier, putting him in Green flight with Andrej Kolodziewicz.

Andrej was a real guid yin, a good friend. He'd copped it a month before, spiralling up away from a Messerschmitt. Maybe he'd been blinded by the sun, maybe just looking over the wrong shoulder. Left wing shot to hell, and he'd spiralled right back down and into the ground. Jerry hadn't seen the crash, but he'd heard about it. And got drunk on vodka with Andrej's brother after.

"Poland," Randall agreed. "Malan says you can carry on a conversation in Polish. That true?"

"I can order a drink, start a fight, or ask directions. Any of that of use?"

"The last one might be," Randall said, very dry. "But we'll hope it doesn't come to that."

The MI6 agent had pushed aside the forms and unrolled the maps. Despite himself, Jerry leaned forward, drawn as by a magnet. They were official maps, but with markings made by hand—circles, X's.

"It's like this," Randall said, flattening the maps with both hands. "The Nazis have had labour camps in Poland for the last two years, but it's not common knowledge among the public, either home or abroad. It would be very helpful to the war effort if it *were* common knowledge. Not just the camps' existence, but the kind of thing that goes on there." A shadow crossed the dark, lean face—anger, Jerry thought, intrigued. Apparently, Mr. MI6 knew what kind of thing went on there, and he wondered how.

"If we want it widely known and widely talked about—and we do—

we need documentary evidence," Randall said matter-of-factly. "Photographs."

There'd be four of them, he said, four Spitfire pilots. A flight—but they wouldn't fly together. Each one of them would have a specific target, geographically separate, but all to be hit on the same day.

"The camps are guarded, but not with anti-aircraft ordnance. There are towers, though; machine-guns." And Jerry didn't need telling that a machine-gun was just as effective in someone's hands as it was from an enemy plane. To take the sort of pictures Randall wanted would mean coming in low—low enough to risk being shot from the towers. His only advantage would be the benefit of surprise; the guards might spot him, but they wouldn't be expecting him to come diving out of the sky for a low pass just above the camp.

"Don't try for more than one pass, unless the cameras malfunction. Better to have fewer pictures than none at all."

"Yes, sir." He'd reverted to "sir," as Group Captain Malan was present at the meeting, silent but listening intently. Got to keep up appearances.

"Here's the list of the targets you'll practise on in Northumberland. Get as close as you think reasonable, without risking—" Randall's face did change at that, breaking into a wry smile. "Get as close as you can manage with a chance of coming back, all right? The cameras may be worth even more than you are."

That got a faint chuckle from Malan. Pilots—especially trained pilots—were valuable. The RAF had plenty of planes now, but nowhere near enough pilots to fly them.

He'd be taught to use the wing cameras and to unload the film safely. If he was shot down but was still alive and the plane didn't burn, he was to get the film out and try to get it back over the border.

"Hence the Polish." Randall ran a hand through his hair, and gave Jerry a crooked smile. "If you have to walk out, you may need to ask directions." They had two Polish-speaking pilots, he said—one Pole and a Hungarian who'd volunteered, and an Englishman with a few words of the language, like Jerry.

"And it is a volunteer mission, let me reiterate."

"Aye, I know," Jerry said irritably. "Said I'd go, didn't I? Sir."

"You did." Randall looked at him for a moment, dark eyes unreadable, then lowered his gaze to the maps again. "Thanks," he said softly.

THE CANOPY SNICKED shut over his head. It was a dank, damp Northumberland day, and his breath condensed on the inside of the Perspex hood within seconds. He leaned forward to wipe it away, emitting a sharp yelp as several strands of his hair were ripped out. He'd forgotten to duck. Again. He shoved the canopy release with a muttered oath and the light brown strands that had caught in the seam where the Perspex closed flew away, caught up by the wind. He closed the canopy again, crouching, and waiting for the signal for takeoff.

The signalman wig-wagged him, and he turned up the throttle, feeling the plane begin to move.

He touched his pocket automatically, whispering, "Love you, Dolly," under his breath. Everyone had his little rituals, those last few moments before takeoff. For Jerry MacKenzie, it was his wife's face and his lucky stone that usually settled the worms in his belly. She'd found it in a rocky hill on the Isle of Lewis, where they'd spent their brief honeymoon—a rough sapphire, she said, very rare.

"Like you," he'd said, and kissed her.

No need for worms just the now, but it wasn't a ritual if you only did it sometimes, was it? And even if it wasn't going to be combat today, he'd need to be paying attention.

He went up in slow circles, getting the feel of the new plane, sniffing to get her scent. He wished they'd let him fly *Dolly II,* her seat stained with his sweat, the familiar dent in the console where he'd slammed his fist in exultation at a kill—but they'd already modified this one with the wing cameras and the latest thing in night sights. It didn't do to get attached to the planes, anyway; they were almost as fragile as the men flying them, though the parts could be reused.

No matter; he'd sneaked out to the hangar the evening before and done a quick rag doll on the nose to make it his. He'd know *Dolly III* well enough by the time they went into Poland.

He dived, pulled up sharp, and did Dutch rolls for a bit, wig-wagging through the cloud layer, then complete rolls and Immelmanns, all the while reciting Malan's Rules to focus his mind and keep from getting airsick.

The Rules were posted in every RAF barracks now: the Ten Commandments, the fliers called them—and not as a joke.

TEN OF MY RULES FOR AIR FIGHTING, the poster said in bold black type. Jerry knew them by heart.

"Wait until you see the whites of his eyes," he chanted under his breath. "Fire short bursts of one to two seconds only when your sights are definitely 'ON.' " He glanced at his sights, suffering a moment's disorientation. The camera wizard had relocated them. Shite.

"Whilst shooting, think of nothing else, brace the whole of your body: have both hands on the stick: concentrate on your ring sight." Well, away to fuck, then. The buttons that operated the camera weren't on

the stick; they were on a box connected to a wire that ran out the window; the box itself was strapped to his knee. He'd be bloody looking out the window anyway, not using sights—unless things went wrong and he had to use the guns. In which case . . .

"Always keep a sharp lookout. 'Keep your finger out.'" Aye, right, *that one was still good.*

"Height gives you the initiative." Not in this case. *He'd be flying low, under the radar, and not be looking for a fight. Always the chance one might find him, though. If any German craft found him flying solo in Poland, his best chance was likely to head straight for the sun and fall in. That thought made him smile.*

"Always turn and face the attack." He snorted and flexed his bad knee, which ached with the cold. *Aye, if you saw it coming in time.*

"Make your decisions promptly. It is better to act quickly even though your tactics are not the best." He'd learnt that one fast. His body often was moving before his brain had even notified his consciousness that he'd seen something. *Nothing to see just now, nor did he expect to, but he kept looking by reflex.*

"Never fly straight and level for more than thirty seconds in the combat area." Definitely out. *Straight and level was just what he was going to have to do. And slowly.*

"When diving to attack, always leave a proportion of your formation above to act as a top guard." Irrelevant; *he wouldn't have a formation—and that was a thought that gave him the cold grue. He'd be completely alone, no help coming if he got into bother.*

"INITIATIVE, AGGRESSION, AIR DISCIPLINE, and TEAM WORK are words that MEAN something in Air Fighting." Yeah, they *did. What meant something in reconnaissance? Stealth, Speed, and Bloody Good Luck, more like. He took a deep breath, and dived, shouting the last of the Ten Commandments so it echoed in his Perspex shell.*

"Go in quickly—Punch hard—GET OUT!"

Rubbernecking, they called it, but Jerry usually ended a day's flying feeling as though he'd been cast in concrete from the shoulder blades up. He bent his head forward now, ferociously massaging the base of his skull to ease the growing ache. He'd been practising since dawn, and it was nearly teatime. *Ball bearings, set, for the use of pilots, one,* he thought. Ought to add that to the standard equipment list. He shook his head like a wet dog, hunched his shoulders, groaning, then resumed the sector-by-sector scan of the sky around him that every pilot did religiously, three hundred and sixty degrees, every moment in the air. All the live ones, anyway.

Dolly'd given him a white silk scarf as a parting present. He didn't know how she'd managed the money for it and she wouldn't let him ask, just settled it round his neck inside his flight jacket. Somebody'd told her the Spitfire pilots all wore them, to save the constant collar chafing, and she meant him to have one. It felt nice, he'd admit that. Made him think of her touch when she'd put it on him. He pushed the thought hastily aside; the last thing he could afford to do was start thinking about his wife, if he ever hoped to get back to her. And he did mean to get back to her.

Where was that bugger? Had he given up?

No, he'd not; a dark spot popped out from behind a bank of cloud just over his left shoulder and dived for his tail. Jerry turned, a hard, high spiral, up and into the same clouds, the other after him like stink on shite. They played at dodgem for a few moments, in and out of the drifting clouds—he had the advantage in altitude, could play the coming-out-of-the-sun trick, if there was any sun, but it was autumn in Northumberland and there hadn't been any sun in days . . .

Gone. He heard the buzzing of the other plane, faintly, for a moment—or thought he had. Hard to tell above the dull roar of his own engine. Gone, though; he wasn't where Jerry'd expected him to be.

"Oh, like that, is it?" He kept on looking, ten degrees of sky every second; it was the only way to be sure you didn't miss any— A glimpse of something dark, and his heart jerked along with his hand. Up and away. It was gone then, the black speck, but he went on climbing, slowly now, looking. Wouldn't do to get too low, and he wanted to keep the altitude . . .

The cloud was thin here, drifting waves of mist, but getting thicker. He saw a solid-looking bank of cloud moving slowly in from the west, but still a good distance away. It was cold, too; his face was chilled. He might be picking up ice if he went too hi— There.

The other plane, closer and higher than he'd expected. The other pilot spotted him at the same moment and came roaring down on him, too close to avoid. He didn't try.

"Aye, wait for it, ye wee bugger," he murmured, hand tight on the stick. One second, two, almost on him—and he buried the stick in his balls, jerked it hard left, turned neatly over, and went off in a long, looping series of barrel rolls that put him right away out of range.

His radio crackled and he heard Paul Rakoczy chortling through his hairy nose.

"*Kurwa twoja mac!* Where you learn that, you Scotch fucker?"

"At my mammy's tit, *dupek*," he replied, grinning. "Buy me a drink, and I'll teach it to ye."

A burst of static obscured the end of an obscene Polish remark, and Rakoczy flew off with a wig-wag of farewell. Ah, well. Enough skylarking, then; back to the fucking cameras.

Jerry rolled his head, worked his shoulders and stretched as well as could be managed in the confines of a II's cockpit—it had minor improvements over the Spitfire I, but roominess wasn't one of them—had a glance at the wings for ice—no, that was all right—and turned farther inland.

It was too soon to worry over it, but his right hand found the trigger that operated the cameras. His fingers twiddled anxiously over the buttons, checking, rechecking. He was getting used to them, but they didn't work like the gun triggers; he didn't have them wired in to his reflexes yet. Didn't like the feeling, either. Tiny things, like typewriter keys, not the snug feel of the gun triggers.

He'd had the left-handed ones only since yesterday; before that, he'd been flying a plane with the buttons on the right. Much discussion with Flight and the MI6 button-boffin, whether it was better to stay with the right, as he'd had practice already, or change for the sake of his cack-handedness. When they'd finally got round to asking him which he wanted, it had been too late in the day to fix it straight off. So he'd been given a couple of hours' extra flying time today, to mess about with the new fix-up.

Right, there it was. The bumpy grey line that cut through the yellowing fields of Northumberland like a perforation, same as you might tear the countryside along it, separating north from south as neat as tearing a piece of paper. Bet the emperor Hadrian wished it was that easy, he thought, grinning, as he swooped down along the line of the ancient wall.

The cameras made a loud *clunk-clunk* noise when they fired. *Clunk-clunk, clunk-clunk!* Okay, sashay out, bank over, come down . . . *clunk-clunk, clunk-clunk* . . . He didn't like the noise, not the same satisfaction as the vicious short *Brrpt!* of his wing guns. Made him feel wrong, like something gone with the engine . . . Aye, there it was coming up, his goal for the moment.

Mile-castle 37.

A stone rectangle, attached to Hadrian's Wall like a snail on a leaf. The old Roman legions had made these small, neat forts to house the garrisons that guarded the wall. Nothing left now but the outline of the foundation, but it made a good target.

He circled once, calculating, then dived and roared over it at an altitude of maybe fifty feet, cameras clunking like an army of stampeding robots. Pulled up sharp and hared off, circling high and fast, pulling out to run for the imagined border, circling up again . . . and all the time his heart thumped and the sweat ran down his sides, imagining what it would be like when the real day came.

Mid-afternoon, it would be, like this. The winter light just going, but still enough to see clearly. He'd circle, find an angle that would let him cross the whole camp and please God, one that would let him come out of the sun. And then he'd go in.

One pass, Randall had said. Don't risk more than one, unless the cameras malfunction.

The bloody things did malfunction, roughly every third pass. The buttons were slippery under his fingers. Sometimes they worked on the next try; sometimes they didn't.

If they didn't work on the first pass over the camp, or didn't work often enough, he'd have to try again.

"*Niech to szlag,*" he muttered, *Fuck the Devil,* and pressed the buttons again, one-two, one-two. "Gentle but firm, like you'd do it to a lady's privates," the boffin had told him, illustrating a brisk twiddle. He'd never thought of doing that . . . Would Dolly like it? he wondered. And where exactly did you do it? Aye, well, women did come with a button, maybe that was it—but then, two fingers? . . . *Clunk-clunk. Clunk-clunk. Crunch.*

He reverted to English profanity, and smashed both buttons with his fist. One camera answered with a startled *clunk!* but the other was silent.

He poked the button again and again, to no effect. "Bloody fucking arse-buggering . . ." He thought vaguely that he'd have to stop swearing once this was over and he was home again—bad example for the lad.

"FUCK!" he bellowed, and ripping the strap free of his leg, he picked up the box and hammered it on the edge of the seat, then slammed it back onto his thigh—visibly dented, he saw with grim satisfaction—and pressed the balky button.

Clunk, the camera answered meekly.

"Aye, well, then, just you remember that!" he said, and, puffing in righteous indignation, gave the buttons a good jabbing.

He'd not been paying attention during this small temper-tantrum, but had been circling upward—standard default for a Spitfire flier. He started back down for a fresh pass at the mile-castle, but within a minute or two, began to hear a knocking sound from the engine.

"No!" he said, and gave it more throttle. The knocking got louder; he could feel it vibrating through the fuselage. Then there was a loud *clang!* from the engine compartment right by his knee, and with horror he saw tiny droplets of oil spatter on the Perspex in front of his face. The engine stopped.

"Bloody, bloody . . ." He was too busy to find another word. His lovely agile fighter had suddenly become a very clumsy glider. He was going down and the only question was whether he'd find a relatively flat spot to crash in.

His hand groped automatically for the landing gear but then drew back—no time, belly landing, where was the bottom? Jesus, he'd been distracted, hadn't seen that solid bank of cloud move in; it must have come faster than he . . . Thoughts flitted through his mind, too fast for words. He glanced at the altimeter, but what it told him was of limited use, because he didn't know what the ground under him was like: crags, flat meadow, water? He hoped and prayed for a road, a grassy flat spot, anything short of—God, he was at five hundred feet and still in cloud!

"Christ!"

The ground appeared in a sudden burst of yellow and brown. He jerked the nose up, saw the rocks of a crag dead ahead, swerved, stalled, nose-dived, pulled back, pulled back, not enough, *Oh, God—*

HIS FIRST CONSCIOUS thought was that he should have radioed base when the engine went.

"Stupid fucker," he mumbled. "Make your decisions promptly. It is better to act quickly even though your tactics are not the best. Clot-heid."

He seemed to be lying on his side. That didn't seem right. He felt cautiously with one hand—grass and mud. What, had he been thrown clear of the plane?

He had. His head hurt badly, his knee much worse. He had to sit down on the matted wet grass for a bit, unable to think through the waves of pain that squeezed his head with each heartbeat.

It was nearly dark, and rising mist surrounded him. He breathed deep, sniffing the dank, cold air. It smelt of rot and old mangelwurzels—but what it didn't smell of was petrol and burning fuselage.

Right. Maybe she hadn't caught fire when she crashed, then. If not, and if her radio was still working . . .

He staggered to his feet, nearly losing his balance from a sudden attack of vertigo, and turned in a slow circle, peering into the mist. There was nothing *but* mist to his left and behind him, but to his right, he made out two or three large, bulky shapes, standing upright.

Making his way slowly across the lumpy ground, he found that they were stones. Remnants of one of those prehistoric sites that littered the ground in northern Britain. Only three of the big stones were still standing, but he could see a few more, fallen or pushed over, lying like bodies in the darkening fog. He paused to vomit, holding on to one of the stones. Christ, his head was like to split! And he had a terrible buzzing in his ears . . . He pawed vaguely at his ear, thinking somehow he'd left his headset on, but felt nothing but a cold, wet ear.

He closed his eyes again, breathing hard, and leaned against the stone for support. The static in his ears was getting worse, accompanied by a sort of whine. Had he burst an eardrum? He forced himself to open his eyes, and was rewarded with the sight of a large, dark irregular shape, well beyond the remains of the stone circle. Dolly!

The plane was barely visible, fading into the swirling dark, but that's what it had to be. Mostly intact, it looked like, though very much nose-down with her tail in the air—she must have ploughed into the earth. He staggered on the rock-strewn ground, feeling the vertigo set in again, with a vengeance. He waved his arms, trying to keep his balance, but his head spun, and Christ, the bloody *noise* in his head . . . He couldn't think, oh, Jesus, he felt as if his bones were dissolv—

IT WAS FULL DARK when he came to himself, but the clouds had broken and a three-quarter moon shone in the deep black of a country sky. He moved, and groaned. Every bone in his body hurt—but none was broken. That was something, he told himself. His clothes were sodden with damp, he was starving, and his knee was so stiff he couldn't straighten his right leg all the way, but that was all right; he thought he could make shift to hobble as far as a road.

Oh, wait. Radio. Yes, he'd forgotten. If Dolly's radio were intact, he could . . .

He stared blankly at the open ground before him. He'd have sworn it was—but he must have got turned round in the dark and fog—no.

He turned quite round, three times, before he stopped, afraid of becoming dizzy again. The plane was gone.

It *was* gone. He was sure it had lain about fifty feet beyond that one stone, the tallest one; he'd taken note of it as a marker, to keep his bearings. He walked out to the spot where he was sure Dolly had come down, walked slowly round the stones in a wide circle, glancing to one side and then the other in growing confusion.

Not only was the plane gone, it didn't seem ever to have been there. There was no trace, no furrow in the thick meadow grass, let alone the kind of gouge in the earth that such a crash would have made. Had he been imagining its presence? Wishful thinking?

He shook his head to clear it—but in fact, it *was* clear. The buzzing and whining in his ears had stopped, and while he still had bruises and a mild headache, he was feeling much better. He walked slowly back around the stones, still looking, a growing sense of deep cold curling through his wame. It wasn't fucking there.

HE WOKE IN the morning without the slightest notion where he was. He was curled up on grass; that much came dimly to him—he could smell it. Grass that cattle had been grazing, because there was a large cow pat just by him, and fresh enough to smell that, too. He stretched out a leg, cautious. Then an arm. Rolled onto his back, and felt a hair better for having something solid under him, though the sky overhead was a dizzy void.

It was a soft, pale blue void, too. Not a trace of cloud.

How long . . . ? A jolt of alarm brought him up onto his knees, but a bright yellow stab of pain behind his eyes sat him down again, moaning and cursing breathlessly.

Once more. He waited 'til his breath was coming steady, then risked cracking one eye open.

Well, it was certainly still Northumbria, the northern part, where England's billowing fields crash onto the inhospitable rocks of Scotland. He recognised the rolling hills, covered with sere grass and punctuated by towering rocks that shot straight up into sudden toothy crags. He swallowed, and rubbed both hands hard over his head and face, assuring himself he was still real. He didn't feel real. Even after he'd taken a careful count of fingers, toes, and private bits—counting the last twice, just in case—he still felt that something important had been misplaced, torn off somehow, and left behind.

His ears still rang, rather like they did after an especially active trip. Why, though? What had he heard?

He found that he could move a little more easily now, and managed to look all round the sky, sector by sector. Nothing up there. No memory of anything up there. And yet the inside of his head buzzed and jangled, and the flesh on his body rippled with agitation. He chafed his arms, hard, to make it go.

Horripilation. That's the proper word for gooseflesh; Dolly'd told him that. She kept a little notebook and wrote down words she came across in her reading; she was a great one for the reading. She'd already got wee Roger sitting in her lap to be read to after tea, round-eyed as Bonzo at the coloured pictures in his rag book.

The thought of his family got him up onto his feet, swaying, but all right now, better, yes, definitely better, though he still felt as though his skin didn't quite fit. The plane, where was that?

He looked round him. No plane was visible. Anywhere. Then it came back to him, with a lurch of the stomach. Real, it was real. He'd been sure in the night that he was dreaming or hallucinating, had lain down to recover himself, and must have fallen asleep. But he was awake now, no mistake; there was a bug of some kind down his back, and he slapped viciously to try to squash it.

His heart was pounding unpleasantly and his palms were sweating. He wiped them on his trousers and scanned the landscape. It wasn't flat, but neither did it offer much concealment. No trees, no bosky dells. There was a small lake off in the distance—he caught the shine of water—but if he'd ditched in water, surely to God he'd be wet?

Maybe he'd been unconscious long enough to dry out, he thought. Maybe he'd imagined that he'd seen the plane near the stones. Surely he couldn't have walked this far from the lake and forgotten it? He'd started walking toward the lake, out of sheer inability to think of anything more useful to do. Clearly time had passed; the sky had cleared like magic. Well, they'd have little trouble finding him, at least; they knew he was near the wall. A truck should be along soon; he couldn't be more than two hours from the airfield.

"And a good thing, too," he muttered. He'd picked an especially god-forsaken spot to crash—there wasn't a farmhouse or a paddock anywhere in sight, not so much as a sniff of chimney smoke.

His head was becoming clearer now. He'd circle the lake—just in case— then head for the road. Might meet the support crew coming in.

"And tell them I've lost the bloody plane?" he asked himself aloud. "Aye, right. Come on, ye wee idjit, think! Now, where did ye see it last?"

HE WALKED FOR a long time. Slowly, because of the knee, but that began to feel easier after a while. His mind was not feeling easier. There was something wrong with the countryside. Granted, Northumbria was a ragged sort of place, but not *this* ragged. He'd found a road—but it wasn't the B road he'd seen from the air. It was a dirt track, pocked with stones and showing signs of being much travelled by hooved animals with a heavily fibrous diet.

Wished he hadn't thought of diet. His wame was flapping against his backbone. Thinking about breakfast was better than thinking about other things, though, and for a time, he amused himself by envisioning the powdered eggs and soggy toast he'd have got in the mess, then going on to the lavish breakfasts of his youth in the Highlands: huge bowls of steaming parritch, slices of black pudding fried in lard, bannocks with marmalade, gallons of hot, strong tea . . .

An hour later, he found Hadrian's Wall. Hard to miss, even grown over with grass and all-sorts like it was. It marched stolidly along, just like the Roman legions who'd built it, stubbornly workmanlike, a grey seam stitching its way up hill and down dale, dividing the peaceful fields to the south from those marauding buggers up north. He grinned at the thought and sat down on the wall—it was less than a yard high, just here—to massage his knee.

He hadn't found the plane, or anything else, and was beginning to doubt his own sense of reality. He'd seen a fox, any number of rabbits, and a pheasant that'd nearly given him heart failure by bursting out from right under his feet. No people at all, though, and that was giving him a queer feeling in his water.

Aye, there was a war on, right enough, and many of the menfolk were gone, but the farmhouses hadn't been sacrificed to the war effort, had they? The women were running the farms, feeding the nation, all that—he'd heard the PM on the radio praising them for it only last week. So where the bloody hell was everybody?

The sun was getting low in the sky when at last he saw a house. It was flush against the wall, and struck him as somehow familiar, though he knew he'd never seen it before. Stone-built and squat, but quite large, with a ratty-looking thatch. There was smoke coming from the chimney, though, and he limped toward it as fast as he could go.

There was a person outside—a woman in a ratty long dress and an apron, feeding chickens. He shouted, and she looked up, her mouth falling open at the sight of him.

"Hey," he said, breathless from hurry. "I've had a crash. I need help. Are ye on the phone, maybe?"

She didn't answer. She dropped the basket of chicken feed and ran right away, round the corner of the house. He sighed in exasperation. Well, maybe she'd gone to fetch her husband. He didn't see any sign of a vehicle, not so much as a tractor, but maybe the man was—

The man was tall, stringy, bearded, and snaggletoothed. He was also dressed in a dirty shirt and baggy short pants that showed his hairy legs and bare feet—and accompanied by two other men in similar comic attire. Jerry instantly interpreted the looks on their faces, and didn't stay to laugh.

"Hey, nay problem, mate," he said, backing up, hands out. "I'm off, right?"

They kept coming, slowly, spreading out to surround him. He hadn't liked the looks of them to start with, and was liking them less by the second. Hungry, they looked, with a speculative glitter in their eyes.

One of them said something to him, a question of some kind, but the Northumbrian accent was too thick for him to catch more than a word. "Who" was the word, and he hastily pulled his dog tags from the neck of his blouson, waving the red and green disks at them. One of the men smiled, but not in a nice way.

"Look," he said, still backing up. "I didna mean to—"

The man in the lead reached out a horny hand and took hold of Jerry's forearm. He jerked back, but the man, instead of letting go, punched him in the belly.

He could feel his mouth opening and shutting like a fish's, but no air came in. He flailed wildly, but they all were on him then. They were calling out to each other, and he didn't understand a word, but the intent was plain as the nose he managed to butt with his head.

It was the only blow he landed. Within two minutes, he'd been efficiently beaten into pudding, had his pockets rifled, been stripped of his jacket and dog tags, been frog-marched down the road and heaved bodily down a steep, rocky slope.

He rolled, bouncing from one outcrop to the next, until he managed to fling out an arm and grab on to a scrubby thornbush. He came to a scraping halt and lay with his face in a clump of heather, panting and thinking incongruously of taking Dolly to the pictures, just before he'd joined up. They'd seen *The Wizard of Oz,* and he was beginning to feel creepily like the lass in that film—maybe it was the resemblance of the Northumbrians to scarecrows and lions.

"At least the fucking lion spoke English," he muttered, sitting up. "Jesus, now what?"

It occurred to him that it might be a good time to stop cursing and start praying.

London, two years later

SHE'D BEEN HOME from her work no more than five minutes. Just time to meet Roger's mad charge across the floor, shrieking "MUMMY!," she pretending to be staggered by his impact—not so much a pretence; he was getting big. Just time to call out to her own mum, hear the muffled reply from the kitchen, sniff hopefully for the comforting smell of tea, and catch a tantalising whiff of tinned sardines that made her mouth water—a rare treat.

Just time to sit down for what seemed the first time in days, and take off her high-heeled shoes, relief washing over her feet like seawater when the tide comes in. She noticed with dismay the hole in the heel of her stocking, though. Her last pair, too. She was just undoing her garter, thinking that she'd have to start using leg-tan like Maisie, drawing a careful seam up the back of each leg with an eyebrow pencil, when there came a knock at the door.

"Mrs. MacKenzie?" The man who stood at the door of her mother's flat was tall, a dark silhouette in the dimness of the hall, but she knew at once he was a soldier.

"Yes?" She couldn't help the leap of her heart, the clench of her stomach. She tried frantically to damp it down, deny it, the hope that had sprung up like a struck match. A mistake. There'd been a mistake. He hadn't been killed, he'd been lost somehow, maybe captured, and now they'd found hi— Then she saw the small box in the soldier's hand and her legs gave way under her.

Her vision sparkled at the edges, and the stranger's face swam above her, blurred with concern. She could hear, though—hear her mum rush through from the kitchen, slippers slapping in her haste, voice raised in agitation. Heard the man's name, Captain Randall, Frank Randall. Hear Roger's small, husky voice warm in her ear, saying "Mummy? Mummy?" in confusion.

Then she was on the swaybacked davenport, holding a cup of hot water that smelt of tea—they could change the tea leaves only once a week, and this was Friday, she thought irrelevantly. He should have come on Sunday, her mum was saying, they could have given him a decent cuppa. But perhaps he didn't work on Sundays?

Her mum had put Captain Randall in the best chair, near the electric fire, and had switched on two bars as a sign of hospitality. Her mother was chatting with the Captain, holding Roger in her lap. Her son was more interested in the little box sitting on the tiny piecrust table; he kept reaching for it, but his grandmother wouldn't let him have it. Marjorie recognised the intent look on his face. He wouldn't throw a fit—he hardly ever did—but he wouldn't give up, either.

He didn't look a lot like his father, save when he wanted something badly. She pulled herself up a bit, shaking her head to clear the dizziness, and Roger looked up at her, distracted by her movement. For an instant, she saw Jerry look out of his eyes, and the world swam afresh. She closed her own, though, and gulped her tea, scalding as it was.

Mum and Captain Randall had been talking politely, giving her time to recover herself. Did he have children of his own? Mum asked.

"No," he said, with what might have been a wistful look at wee Roger. "Not yet. I haven't seen my wife in two years."

"Better late than never," said a sharp voice, and she was surprised to discover that it was hers. She put down the cup, pulled up the loose stocking that had puddled round her ankle, and fixed Captain Randall with a look. "What have you brought me?" she said, trying for a tone of calm dignity. Didn't work; she sounded brittle as broken glass, even to her own ears.

Captain Randall eyed her cautiously, but took up the little box and held it out to her.

"It's Lieutenant MacKenzie's," he said. "An MID oakleaf cluster. Awarded posthumously for—"

With an effort, she pushed herself away, back into the cushions, shaking her head.

"I don't want it."

"Really, Marjorie!" Her mother was shocked.

"And I don't like that word. Pos—posth—don't say it."

She couldn't overcome the notion that Jerry was somehow inside the box—a notion that seemed dreadful at one moment, comforting the next. Captain Randall set it down, very slowly, as though it might blow up.

"I won't say it," he said gently. "May I say, though . . . I knew him. Your husband. Very briefly, but I did know him. I came myself, because I wanted to say to you how very brave he was."

"Brave." The word was like a pebble in her mouth. She wished she could spit it at him.

"Of course he was," her mother said firmly. "Hear that, Roger? Your dad was a good man, and he was a brave one. You won't forget that."

Roger was paying no attention, struggling to get down. His gran set him reluctantly on the floor and he lurched over to Captain Randall, taking a firm grip on the Captain's freshly creased trousers with both hands—hands greasy, she saw, with sardine oil and toast crumbs. The Captain's lips twitched, but he didn't try to detach Roger, just patted his head.

"Who's a good boy, then?" he asked.

"Fith," Roger said firmly. "Fith!"

Marjorie felt an incongruous impulse to laugh at the Captain's puzzled expression, though it didn't touch the stone in her heart.

"It's his new word," she said. " 'Fish.' He can't say 'sardine.' "

"Thar . . . DEEM!" Roger said, glaring at her. "Fitttthhhhh!"

The Captain laughed out loud, and pulling out a handkerchief, carefully wiped the spittle off Roger's face, casually going on to wipe the grubby little paws as well.

"Of course it's a fish," he assured Roger. "You're a clever lad. And a big help to your mummy, I'm sure. Here, I've brought you something for your tea." He groped in the pocket of his coat and pulled out a small pot of jam. Strawberry jam. Marjorie's salivary glands contracted painfully. With the sugar rationing, she hadn't tasted jam in . . .

"He's a great help," her mother put in stoutly, determined to keep the conversation on a proper plane despite her daughter's peculiar behaviour. She avoided Marjorie's eyes. "A lovely boy. His name's Roger."

"Yes, I know." He glanced at Marjorie, who'd made a brief movement. "Your husband told me. He was—"

"Brave. You told me." Suddenly something snapped. It was her half-hooked garter, but the pop of it made her sit up straight, fists clenched in the thin fabric of her skirt. "Brave," she repeated. "They're all brave, aren't they? Every single one. Even you—or are you?"

She heard her mother's gasp, but went on anyway, reckless.

"You all have to be brave and noble and—and—perfect, don't you? Because if you were weak, if there were any cracks, if anyone looked like being not quite the thing, you know—well, it might all fall apart, mightn't it? So none of you will, will you? Or if somebody did, the rest of you would cover it up. You won't ever not do something, no matter what it is, because you can't not do it; all the other chaps would think the worse of you, wouldn't they, and we can't have that, oh, no, we can't have that!"

Captain Randall was looking at her intently, his eyes dark with concern. Probably thought she was a nutter—probably she was, but what did it matter?

"Marjie, Marjie, love," her mother was murmuring, horribly embarrassed. "You oughtn't to say such things to—"

"You made him do it, didn't you?" She was on her feet now, looming over the Captain, making him look up at her. "He told me. He told me about you. You came and asked him to do—whatever it was that got him killed. Oh, don't trouble yourself, he didn't tell me your bloody precious secrets—not him, he wouldn't do that. He was a flier." She was panting with rage and had to stop to draw breath. Roger, she saw dimly, had shrunk into himself and was clinging to the Captain's leg; Randall put an arm about the boy automatically, as though to shelter him from his mother's wrath. With an effort she made herself stop shouting, and, to her horror, felt tears begin to course down her face.

"And now you come and bring me—and bring me . . ."

"Marjie." Her mother came up close beside her, her body warm and soft and comforting in her worn old pinny. She thrust a tea towel into Marjorie's hands, then moved between her daughter and the enemy, solid as a battleship.

"It's kind of you to've brought us this, Captain," Marjorie heard her saying, and felt her move away, bending to pick up the little box. Marjorie sat down blindly, pressing the tea towel to her face, hiding.

"Here, Roger, look. See how it opens? See how pretty? It's called— what did you say it was again, Captain? Oh, oakleaf cluster. Yes, that's right. Can you say 'medal,' Roger? *Meh-dul.* This is your dad's medal."

Roger didn't say anything. Probably scared stiff, poor little chap. She had to pull herself together. But she'd gone too far. She couldn't stop.

"He cried when he left me." She muttered the secret into the folds of the tea towel. "He didn't want to go." Her shoulders heaved with a convulsive, unexpected sob, and she pressed the towel hard against her eyes, whispering to herself, "You said you'd come back, Jerry, you said you'd come *back*."

She stayed hidden behind her flour-sacking fortress, while renewed offers of tea were made and, to her vague surprise, accepted. She'd thought Captain Randall would seize the chance of her retreat to make his own. But he stayed, chatting calmly with her mother, talking slowly to Roger while her mother fetched the tea, ignoring her embarrassing performance entirely, keeping up a quiet, companionable presence in the shabby room.

The rattle and bustle of the tea tray's arrival gave her the opportunity to drop her cloth façade, and she meekly accepted a slice of toast spread with a thin scrape of margarine and a delectable spoonful of the strawberry jam.

"There, now," her mother said, looking on with approval. "You'll not have eaten anything since breakfast, I daresay. Enough to give anyone the wambles."

Marjorie shot her mother a look, but in fact it was true; she hadn't had any luncheon because Maisie was off with "female trouble"—a condition that afflicted her roughly every other week—and she'd had to mind the shop all day.

Conversation flowed comfortably around her, a soothing stream past an immoveable rock. Even Roger relaxed with the introduction of jam. He'd never tasted any before, and sniffed it curiously, took a cautious lick—and then took an enormous bite that left a red smear on his nose, his moss-green eyes round with wonder and delight. The little box, now open, sat on the piecrust table, but no one spoke of it or looked in that direction.

After a decent interval, Captain Randall got up to go, giving Roger a shiny sixpence in parting. Feeling it the least she could do, Marjorie got up to see him out. Her stockings spiralled down her legs, and she kicked them off with contempt, walking bare-legged to the door. She heard her mother sigh behind her.

"Thank you," she said, opening the door for him. "I . . . appreciate—"
To her surprise, he stopped her, putting a hand on her arm.

"I've no particular right to say this to you—but I will," he said, low-voiced. "You're right; they're not all brave. Most of them—of us—we're just . . . there, and we do our best. Most of the time," he added, and the corner of his mouth lifted slightly, though she couldn't tell whether it was in humor or bitterness.

"But your husband—" He closed his eyes for a moment and said, "The bravest are surely those who have the clearest vision of what is before them, glory and danger alike, and yet notwithstanding, go out to meet it. He did that, every day, for a long time."

"You sent him, though," she said, her voice as low as his. "You did."
His smile was bleak.

"I've done such things every day . . . for a long time."

The door closed quietly behind him, and she stood there swaying, eyes closed, feeling the draft come under it, chilling her bare feet. It was well into the autumn now, and the dark was smudging the windows, though it was just past teatime.

I've done what I do every day for a long time, too, she thought. *But they don't call it brave when you don't have a choice.*

Her mother was moving through the flat, muttering to herself as she closed the curtains. Or not so much to herself.

"He liked her. Anyone could see that. So kind, coming himself to bring the medal and all. And how does she act? Like a cat that's had its tail stepped on, all claws and caterwauling, that's how. How does she ever expect a man to—"

"I don't want a man," Marjorie said loudly. Her mother turned round, squat, solid, implacable.

"You need a man, Marjorie. And little Rog needs a father."

"He has a father," she said through her teeth. "Captain Randall has a wife. And I don't need anyone."

Anyone but Jerry.

Northumbria

HE LICKED HIS lips at the smell. Hot pastry, steaming, juicy meat. There was a row of fat little pasties ranged along the sill, covered with a clean cloth in case of birds, but showing plump and rounded through it, the odd spot of gravy soaking through the napkin.

His mouth watered so fiercely that his salivary glands ached and he had to massage the underside of his jaw to ease the pain.

It was the first house he'd seen in two days. Once he'd got out of the ravine, he'd circled well away from the mile-castle and eventually struck a small cluster of cottages, where the people were no more understandable, but did give him some food. That had lasted him a little while; beyond that, he'd been surviving on what he could glean from hedges and the odd vegetable patch. He'd found another hamlet, but the folk there had driven him away.

Once he'd got enough of a grip on himself to think clearly, it became obvious that he needed to go back to the standing stones. Whatever had happened to him had happened there, and if he really *was* somewhere in the past—and hard as he'd tried to find some alternative explanation, none was forthcoming—then his only chance of getting back where he belonged seemed to lie there, too.

He'd come well away from the drover's track, though, seeking food, and as the few people he met didn't understand him any more than he understood them, he'd had some difficulty in finding his way back to the wall. He thought he was quite close, now, though—the ragged country was beginning to seem familiar, though perhaps that was only delusion.

Everything else had faded into unimportance, though, when he smelt food.

He circled the house at a cautious distance, checking for dogs. No dog.

Aye, fine, then. He chose an approach from the side, out of view of any of the few windows. Darted swiftly from bush to ploughshare to midden to house, and plastered himself against the grey stone wall, breathing hard—and breathing in that delicious, savoury aroma. Shite, he was drooling. He wiped his sleeve hastily across his mouth, slithered round the corner, and reached out a hand.

As it happened, the farmstead did boast a dog, which had been attending its absent master in the barn. Both these worthies returning unexpectedly at this point, the dog at once spotted what it assumed to be jiggery-pokery taking place, and gave tongue in an altogether proper manner. Alerted in turn to felonious activity on his premises, the householder instantly joined the affray, armed with a wooden spade, with which he batted Jerry over the head.

As he staggered back against the wall of the house, he had just wit enough left to notice that the farmwife—now sticking out of her window and shrieking like the Glasgow Express—had knocked one of the pasties to the ground, where it was being devoured by the dog, who wore an expression of piety and rewarded virtue that Jerry found really offensive.

Then the farmer hit him again, and he stopped being offended.

IT WAS A well-built byre, the stones fitted carefully and mortared. He wore himself out with shouting and kicking at the door until his gammy leg gave way and he collapsed onto the earthen floor.

"Now bloody what?" he muttered. He was damp with sweat from his effort, but it was cold in the byre, with that penetrating damp cold peculiar to the British Isles, that seeps into your bones and makes the joints ache. His knee would give him fits in the morning. The air was saturated with the scent of manure and chilled urine. "Why would the bloody Jerries want the damn place?" he said, and, sitting up, huddled into his shirt. It was going to be a frigging long night.

He got up onto his hands and knees and felt carefully round inside the byre, but there was nothing even faintly edible—only a scurf of mouldy hay. Not even the rats would have that; the inside of the place was empty as a drum and silent as a church.

What had happened to the cows? he wondered. Dead of a plague, eaten, sold? Or maybe just not yet back from the summer pastures—though it was late in the year for that, surely.

He sat down again, back against the door, as the wood was marginally less cold than the stone walls. He'd thought about being captured in battle, made prisoner by the Germans—they all had, now and then, though chaps mostly didn't talk about it. He thought about POW camps, and those camps in Poland, the ones he'd been meant to photograph. Were they as bleak as this? Stupid thing to think of, really.

But he'd got to pass the time 'til morning one way or another, and there were lots of things he'd rather not think about just now. Like what would happen once morning came. He didn't think breakfast in bed was going to be part of it.

The wind was rising. Whining past the corners of the cow byre with a keening noise that set his teeth on edge. He still had his silk scarf; it had slipped down inside his shirt when the bandits in the mile-castle had attacked him. He fished it out now and wrapped it round his neck, for comfort, if not warmth.

He'd brought Dolly breakfast in bed now and then. She woke up slow and sleepy, and he loved the way she scooped her tangled curly black hair off her face, peering out slit-eyed, like a small, sweet mole blinking in the light. He'd sit her up and put the tray on the table beside her, and then he'd shuck his own clothes and crawl in bed, too, cuddling close to her soft, warm skin. Sometimes sliding down in the bed, and her pretending not to notice, sipping tea or putting marmite on her toast while he burrowed under the covers and found his way up through the cottony layers of sheets and nightie. He loved the smell of her, always, but especially when he'd made love to her the night before, and she bore the strong, musky scent of him between her legs.

He shifted a little, roused by the memory, but the subsequent thought—that he might never see her again—quelled him at once.

Still thinking of Dolly, though, he put his hand automatically to his pocket, and was alarmed to find no lump there. He slapped at his thigh, but failed to find the small, hard bulge of the sapphire. Could he have put it in the other pocket by mistake? He delved urgently, shoving both hands deep into his pockets. No stone—but there was something in his right-hand pocket. Something powdery, almost greasy . . . what the devil?

He brought his fingers out, peering as closely at them as he could, but it was too dark to see more than a vague outline of his hand, let alone anything on it. He rubbed his fingers gingerly together; it felt something like the thick soot that builds up inside a chimney.

"Jesus," he whispered, and put his fingers to his nose. There was a distinct smell of combustion. Not petrolish at all, but a scent of burning so intense he could taste it on the back of his tongue. Like something out of a volcano. What in the name of God Almighty could burn a rock and leave the man who carried it alive?

The sort of thing he'd met among the standing stones, that was what.

He'd been doing all right with the not feeling too afraid until now, but . . . he swallowed hard, and sat down again, quietly.

"Now I lay me down to sleep," he whispered to the knees of his trousers. "I pray the Lord my soul to keep . . ."

He did in fact sleep eventually, in spite of the cold, from simple exhaustion. He was dreaming about wee Roger, who for some reason was a grown man now, but still holding his tiny blue bear, minuscule in a broad-palmed grasp. His son was speaking to him in Gaelic, saying something urgent that he couldn't understand, and he was growing frustrated, telling Roger over and over for Christ's sake to speak English, couldn't he?

Then he heard another voice through the fog of sleep and realised that someone was in fact talking somewhere close by.

He jerked awake, struggling to grasp what was being said and failing utterly. It took him several seconds to realise that whoever was speaking—there seemed to be two voices, hissing and muttering in argument—really was speaking in Gaelic.

He had only a smattering of it himself; his mother had had it, but—he was moving before he could complete the thought, panicked at the notion that potential assistance might get away.

"Hoy!" he bellowed, scrambling—or trying to scramble—to his feet. His much-abused knee wasn't having any, though, and gave way the instant he put weight on it, catapulting him face-first toward the door.

He twisted as he fell and hit it with his shoulder. The booming thud put paid to the argument; the voices fell silent at once.

"Help! Help me!" he shouted, pounding on the door. "Help!"

"Will ye for God's sake hush your noise?" said a low, annoyed voice on the other side of the door. "Ye want to have them all down on us? Here, then, bring the light closer."

This last seemed to be addressed to the voice's companion, for a faint glow shone through the gap at the bottom of the door. There was a scraping noise as the bolt was drawn, and a faint grunt of effort, then a *thunk!* as the bolt was set down against the wall. The door swung open, and Jerry blinked in a sudden shaft of light as the slide of a lantern grated open.

He turned his head aside and closed his eyes for an instant, deliberate, as he would if flying at night and momentarily blinded by a flare or by the glow of his own exhaust. When he opened them again, the two men were in the cow byre with him, looking him over with open curiosity.

Biggish buggers, both of them, taller and broader than he was. One fair, one black-haired as Lucifer. They didn't look much alike, and yet he had the feeling that they might be related—some fleeting glimpse of bone, a similarity of expression, maybe.

"What's your name, mate?" said the dark chap, softly. Jerry felt the nip of wariness at his nape, even as he felt a thrill in the pit of his stomach. It was regular speech, perfectly understandable. A Scots accent, but—

"MacKenzie, J. W.," he said, straightening up to attention. "Lieutenant, Royal Air Force. Service number—"

An indescribable expression flitted across the dark bloke's face. An urge to laugh, of all bloody things, and a flare of excitement in his eyes—really striking eyes, a vivid green that flashed suddenly in the light. None of that mattered to Jerry; what was important was that the man plainly knew. He *knew*.

"Who are you?" he asked, urgent. "Where d'ye come from?"

The two exchanged an unfathomable glance, and the other answered. "Inverness."

"Ye know what I mean!" He took a deep breath. *"When?"*

The two strangers were much of an age, but the fair one had plainly had a harder life; his face was deeply weathered and lined.

"A lang way from you," he said quietly, and, despite his own agitation, Jerry heard the note of desolation in his voice. "From now. Lost."

Lost. Oh, God. But still—

"Jesus. And where are we now? Wh-when?"

"Northumbria," the dark man answered briefly, "and I don't bloody know for sure. Look, there's no time. If anyone hears us—"

"Aye, right. Let's go, then."

The air outside was wonderful after the smells of the cow byre, cold and full of dying heather and turned earth. He thought he could even smell the moon, a faint green sickle above the horizon; he tasted cheese at the thought, and his mouth watered. He wiped a trickle of saliva away and hurried after his rescuers, hobbling as fast as he could.

The farmhouse was black, a squatty black blot on the landscape. The dark bloke grabbed him by the arm as he was about to go past it, quickly licked a finger, and held it up to test the wind.

"The dogs," he explained in a whisper. "This way."

They circled the farmhouse at a cautious distance, and found themselves stumbling through a ploughed field. Clods burst under Jerry's boots as he hurried to keep up, lurching on his bad knee with every step.

"Where we going?" he panted, when he thought it safe to speak.

"We're taking ye back to the stones near the lake," the dark man said tersely. "That has to be where ye came through." The fair one just snorted, as though this wasn't his notion—but he didn't argue.

Hope flared up in Jerry like a bonfire. They knew what the stones were, how it worked. They'd show him how to get back!

"How—how did ye find me?" He could hardly breathe, such a pace they kept up, but he had to know. The lantern was shut and he couldn't see their faces, but the dark man made a muffled sound that might have been a laugh.

"I met an auld wifie wearing your dog tags. Very proud of them, she was."

"Ye've got them?" Jerry gasped.

"Nay, she wouldna give them up." It was the fair man, sounding definitely amused. "Told us where she'd got them, though, and we followed your trail backward. Hey!" He caught Jerry's elbow, just as his foot twisted out from under him. The sound of a barking dog broke the night—some way away, but distinct. The fair man's hand clenched tight on his arm. "Come on, then—hurry!"

Jerry had a bad stitch in his side, and his knee was all but useless by the time the little group of stones came in sight, a pale huddle in the light of the waning moon. Still, he was surprised at how near the stones were to the farmhouse; he must have circled round more than he thought in his wanderings.

"Right," said the dark man, coming to an abrupt halt. "This is where we leave you."

"Ye do?" Jerry panted. "But—but you—"

"When ye came . . . through. Did ye have anything on you? A gemstone, any jewellery?"

"Aye," Jerry said, bewildered. "I had a raw sapphire in my pocket. But it's gone. It's like it—"

"Like it burnt up," the blond man finished for him, grim-voiced. "Aye. Well, so?" This last was clearly addressed to the dark man, who hesitated. Jerry couldn't see his face, but his whole body spoke of indecision. He wasn't one to dither, though—he stuck a hand into the leather pouch at his waist, pulled something out, and pressed it into Jerry's hand. It was faintly warm from the man's body, and hard in his palm. A small stone of some kind. Faceted, like the stone in a ring.

"Take this; it's a good one. When ye go through," the dark man was speaking urgently to him, "think about your wife, about Marjorie. Think hard; see her in your mind's eye, and walk straight through. Whatever the hell ye do, though, don't think about your son. Just your wife."

"What?" Jerry was gob-smacked. "How the bloody hell do you know my wife's name? And where've ye heard about my son?"

"It doesn't matter," the man said, and Jerry saw the motion as he turned his head to look back over his shoulder.

"Damn," said the fair one, softly. "They're coming. There's a light."

There was: a single light, bobbing evenly over the ground, as it would if someone carried it. But look as he might, Jerry could see no one behind it, and a violent shiver ran over him.

"Tannasg," said the other man under his breath. Jerry knew that word well enough—spirit, it meant. And usually an ill-disposed one. A haunt.

"Aye, maybe." The dark man's voice was calm. "And maybe not. It's near Samhain, after all. Either way, ye need to go, man, and now. Remember, think of your wife."

Jerry swallowed, his hand closing tight around the stone.

"Aye. Aye . . . right. Thanks, then," he added awkwardly, and heard the breath of a rueful laugh from the dark man.

"Nay bother, mate," he said. And with that, they were both off, making their way across the stubbled meadow, two lumbering shapes in the moonlight.

Heart thumping in his ears, Jerry turned toward the stones. They looked just like they'd looked before. Just stones. But the echo of what he'd heard in there . . . He swallowed. It wasn't like there was much choice.

"Dolly," he whispered, trying to summon up a vision of his wife. "Dolly. Dolly, help me!"

He took a hesitant step toward the stones. Another. One more. Then nearly bit his tongue off as a hand clamped down on his shoulder. He whirled, fist up, but the dark man's other hand seized his wrist.

"I love you," the dark man said, his voice fierce. Then he was gone again, with the *shoof-shoof* sounds of boots in dry grass, leaving Jerry with his mouth agape.

He caught the other man's voice from the darkness, irritated, half-amused. He spoke differently from the dark man, a much thicker accent, but Jerry understood him without difficulty.

"Why did ye tell him a daft thing like that?"

And the dark one's reply, soft-spoken, in a tone that terrified him more than anything had so far.

"Because he isn't going to make it back. It's the only chance I'll ever have. Come on."

THE DAY WAS DAWNING when he came to himself again, and the world was quiet. No birds sang, and the air was cold with the chill of November and winter coming on. When he could stand up, he went to look, shaky as a newborn lamb.

The plane wasn't there, but there was still a deep gouge in the earth where it had been. Not raw earth, though; furred over with grass and meadow plants—not just furred, he saw, limping over to have a closer look. Matted. Dead stalks from earlier years' growth.

If he'd been where he thought he'd been, if he'd truly gone . . . back . . . then he'd come forward again, but not to the same place he'd left. How long? A year, two? He sat down on the grass, too drained to stand up any longer. He felt as though he'd walked every second of the time between then and now.

He'd done what the green-eyed stranger had said. Concentrated fiercely on Dolly. But he hadn't been able to keep from thinking of wee Roger, not altogether. How could he? The picture he had most vividly of Dolly was her holding the lad, close against her breast; that's what he'd seen. And yet he'd made it. He thought he'd made it. Maybe.

What might have happened? he wondered. There hadn't been time to ask. There'd been no time to hesitate, either; more lights had come bobbing across the dark, with uncouth Northumbrian shouts behind them, hunting him, and he'd hurled himself into the midst of the standing stones and things went pear-shaped again, even worse. He hoped the strangers who'd rescued him had got away.

Lost, the fair man had said, and even now, the word went through him like a bit of jagged metal. He swallowed.

He thought he wasn't where he had been, but was he still lost, himself? Where was he now? Or rather, when?

He stayed for a bit, gathering his strength. In a few minutes, though, he heard a familiar sound—the low growl of engines, and the swish of tyres on asphalt. He swallowed hard, and, standing up, turned away from the stones, toward the road.

HE WAS LUCKY—for once, he thought wryly. There was a line of troop transports passing, and he swung aboard one without difficulty. The soldiers looked startled at his appearance—he was rumpled and stained, bruised and torn about and with a two-week beard—but they instantly assumed he'd been off on a tear and was now trying to sneak back to his base without being detected. They laughed and nudged him knowingly, but were sympathetic, and when he confessed he was skint, they had a quick whip-round for enough cash to buy a train ticket from Salisbury, where the transport was headed.

He did his best to smile and go along with the ragging, but soon enough they tired of him and turned to their own conversations, and he was allowed to sit, swaying on the bench, feeling the thrum of the engine through his legs, surrounded by the comfortable presence of comrades.

"Hey, mate," he said casually to the young soldier beside him. "What year is it?"

The boy—he couldn't be more than seventeen, and Jerry felt the weight of the five years between them as though they were fifty—looked at him wide-eyed, then whooped with laughter.

"What've you been having to drink, Dad? Bring any away with you?"

That led to more ragging, and he didn't try asking again.

Did it matter?

HE REMEMBERED almost nothing of the journey from Salisbury to London. People looked at him oddly, but no one tried to stop him. It didn't matter; nothing mattered but getting to Dolly. Everything else could wait.

London was a shock. There was bomb damage everywhere. Streets were scattered with shattered glass from shop windows, glinting in the pale sun, other streets blocked off by barriers. Here and there a stark black notice: Do Not Enter—UNEXPLODED BOMB.

He made his way from Saint Pancras on foot, needing to see, his heart rising into his throat fit to choke him as he did see what had been done. After a while, he stopped seeing the details, perceiving bomb craters and debris only as blocks to his progress, things stopping him from reaching home.

And then he did reach home.

The rubble had been pushed off the street into a heap, but not taken away. Great blackened lumps of shattered stone and concrete lay like a cairn where Montrose Terrace had once stood.

All the blood in his heart stopped dead, congealed by the sight. He groped, pawing mindlessly for the wrought-iron railing to keep himself from falling, but it wasn't there.

Of course not, his mind said, quite calmly. It's gone for the war, hasn't it? Melted down, made into planes. Bombs.

His knee gave way without warning, and he fell, landing hard on both knees, not feeling the impact, the crunch of pain from his badly mended kneecap quite drowned out by the blunt, small voice inside his head.

Too late. Ye went too far.

"Mr. MacKenzie, Mr. MacKenzie!" He blinked at the blurred thing above him, not understanding what it was. Something tugged at him, though, and he breathed, the rush of air in his chest ragged and strange.

"Sit up, Mr. MacKenzie, do." The anxious voice was still there, and hands—yes, it was hands—tugging at his arm. He shook his head, screwed his eyes shut hard, then opened them again, and the round thing became the houndlike face of old Mr. Wardlaw, who kept the corner shop.

"Ah, there you are." The old man's voice was relieved, and the wrinkles in his baggy old face relaxed their anxious lines. "Had a bad turn, did you?"

"I—" Speech was beyond him, but he flapped his hand at the wreckage.

He didn't think he was crying, but his face was wet. The wrinkles in Wardlaw's face creased deeper in concern, then the old grocer realised what he meant, and his face lit up.

"Oh, dear!" he said. "Oh, no! No, no, no—they're all right, sir, your family's all right! Did you hear me?" he asked anxiously. "Can you breathe? Had I best fetch you some salts, do you think?"

It took Jerry several tries to make it to his feet, hampered both by his knee and by Mr. Wardlaw's fumbling attempts to help him, but by the time he'd got all the way up, he'd regained the power of speech.

"Where?" he gasped. "Where are they?"

"Why—your missus took the little boy and went to stay with her mother, sometime after you left. I don't recall quite where she said . . ." Mr. Wardlaw turned, gesturing vaguely in the direction of the river. "Camberwell, was it?"

"Bethnal Green." Jerry's mind had come back, though it felt still as though it was a pebble rolling round the rim of some bottomless abyss, its balance uncertain. He tried to dust himself off, but his hands were shaking. "She lives in Bethnal Green. You're sure—you're sure, man?"

"Yes, yes." The grocer was altogether relieved, smiling and nodding so hard that his jowls trembled. "She left—must be more than a year ago, soon after she—soon after she . . ." The old man's smile faded abruptly and his mouth slowly opened, a flabby dark hole of horror.

"But you're dead, Mr. MacKenzie," he whispered, backing away, hands held up before him. "Oh, God. You're dead."

"THE FUCK I AM, the fuck I am, the *fuck* I am!" He caught sight of a woman's startled face and stopped abruptly, gulping air like a landed fish. He'd been weaving down the shattered street, fists pumping, limping and staggering, muttering his private motto under his breath like the Hail Marys of a rosary. Maybe not as far under his breath as he'd thought.

He stopped, leaning against the marble front of the Bank of England, panting. He was streaming with sweat and the right leg of his trousers was heavily streaked with dried blood from the fall. His knee was throbbing in time with his heart, his face, his hands, his thoughts. *They're alive. So am I.*

The woman he'd startled was down the street, talking to a policeman; she turned, pointing at him. He straightened up at once, squaring his shoulders. Braced his knee and gritted his teeth, forcing it to bear his weight as he strode down the street, officerlike. The very last thing he wanted just now was to be taken up as drunk.

He marched past the policeman, nodding politely, touching his forehead in lieu of cap. The policeman looked taken aback, made to speak but couldn't quite decide what to say, and a moment later, Jerry was round the corner and away.

It was getting dark. There weren't many cabs in this area at the best of times—none at all, now, and he hadn't any money, anyway. The Tube. If the lines were open, it was the fastest way to Bethnal Green. And surely he could cadge the fare from someone. Somehow. He went back to limping, grimly determined. He had to reach Bethnal Green by dark.

IT WAS SO much changed. Like the rest of London. Houses damaged, halfway repaired, abandoned, others no more than a blackened depression or a heap of rubble. The air was thick with cold dust, stone dust, and the smells of paraffin and cooking grease, the brutal, acrid smell of cordite.

Half the streets had no signs, and he wasn't so familiar with Bethnal Green to begin with. He'd visited Dolly's mother just twice, once when they went to tell her they'd run off and got married—she hadn't been best pleased, Mrs. Wakefield, but she'd put a good face on it, even if the face had a lemon-sucking look to it.

The second time had been when he signed up with the RAF; he'd gone alone to tell her, to ask her to look after Dolly while he was gone. Dolly's mother had gone white. She knew as well as he did what the life expectancy was for fliers. But she'd told him she was proud of him, and held his hand tight for a long moment before she let him leave, saying only, "Come back, Jeremiah. She needs you."

He soldiered on, skirting craters in the street, asking his way. It was nearly full dark, now; he couldn't be on the streets much longer. His anxiety began to ease a little as he started to see things he knew, though. Close, he was getting close.

And then the sirens began, and people began to pour out of the houses.

He was being buffeted by the crowd, borne down the street as much by their barely controlled panic as by their physical impact. There was shouting, people calling for separated family members, wardens bellowing directions, waving their torches, their flat, white helmets pale as mushrooms in the gloom. Above it, through it, the air-raid siren pierced him like a sharpened wire, thrust him down the street on its spike, ramming him into others likewise skewered by fright.

The tide of it swept round the next corner, and he saw the red circle with its blue line over the entrance to the Tube station, lit up by a warden's flashlight. He was sucked in, propelled through sudden bright lights, hurtling down the stair, the next, onto a platform, deep into the earth, into safety. And all the time the whoop and moan of the sirens still filling the air, barely muffled by the dirt above.

There were wardens moving among the crowd, pushing people back against the walls, into the tunnels, away from the edge of the track. He brushed up against a woman with two toddlers, picked one—a little girl with round eyes and a blue teddy bear—out of her arms and turned his shoulder into the crowd, making a way for them. He found a small space in a tunnel-mouth, pushed the woman into it, and gave her back the little girl. Her mouth moved in thanks, but he couldn't hear her above the noise of the crowd, the sirens, the creaking, the—

A sudden monstrous thud from above shook the station, and the whole crowd was struck silent, every eye on the high arched ceiling above them.

The tiles were white, and as they looked, a dark crack appeared suddenly between two rows of them. A gasp rose from the crowd, louder than the sirens. The crack seemed to stop, to hesitate—and then it zigzagged suddenly, parting the tiles, in different directions.

He looked down from the growing crack, to see who was below it—the people still on the stair. The crowd at the bottom was too thick to move, everyone stopped still by horror. And then he saw her, partway up the stair.

Dolly. *She's cut her hair,* he thought. It was short and curly, black as soot—black as the hair of the little boy she held in her arms, close against her, sheltering him. Her face was set, jaw clenched. And then she turned a bit, and saw him.

Her face went blank for an instant and then flared like a lit match, with a radiant joy that struck him in the heart and flamed through his being.

There was a much louder *thud!* from above, and a scream of terror rose from the crowd, louder, much louder than the sirens. Despite the shrieking, he could hear the fine rattle, like rain, as dirt began to pour from the crack above. He shoved with all his might, but couldn't get past, couldn't reach them. Dolly looked up, and he saw her jaw set hard again, her eyes ablaze with determination. She shoved the man in front of her, who stumbled and fell down a step, squashing into the people in front of him. She swung Roger down into the little space she'd made, and with a twist of her shoulders and the heave of her whole body, hurled the little boy up, over the rail—toward Jerry.

He saw what she was doing and was already leaning, pushing forward, straining to reach . . . The boy struck him high in the chest like a lump of concrete, little head smashing painfully into Jerry's face, knocking his head back. He had one arm round the child, falling back on the people behind him, struggling to find his footing, get a firmer hold—and then something gave way in the crowd around him, he staggered into an open space, and then his knee gave way and he plunged over the lip of the track.

He didn't hear the crack of his head against the rail or the screams of the people above; it was all lost in a roar like the end of the world as the roof over the stair fell in.

—————

THE LITTLE BOY was still as death, but he wasn't dead; Jerry could feel his heartbeat, thumping fast against his own chest. It was all he could feel. Poor little bugger must have had his wind knocked out.

People had stopped screaming, but there was still shouting, calling out. There was a strange silence underneath all the racket. His blood had stopped pounding through his head, his own heart no longer hammering. Perhaps that was it.

The silence underneath felt alive, somehow. Peaceful, but like sunlight on water, moving, glittering. He could still hear the noises above the silence, feet running, anxious voices, bangs and creakings—but he was sinking gently into the silence; the noises grew distant, though he could still hear voices.

"Is that one—?"

"Nay, he's gone—look at his head, poor chap, caved in something horrid. The boy's well enough, I think, just bumps and scratches. Here, lad, come up . . . no, no, let go, now. It's all right, just let go. Let me pick you up, yes, that's good, it's all right now, hush, hush, there's a good boy . . ."

"What a look on that bloke's face. I never saw anything like—"

"Here, take the little chap. I'll see if the bloke's got any identification."

"Come on, big man, yeah, that's it, that's it, come with me. Hush, now, it's all right, it's all right . . . is that your daddy, then?"

"No tags, no service book. Funny, that. He's RAF, though, isn't he? AWOL, d'ye think?"

He could hear Dolly laughing at that, felt her hand stroke his hair. He smiled and turned his head to see her smiling back, the radiant joy spreading round her like rings in shining water . . .

"Rafe! The rest of it's going! Run! *Run!*"

AUTHOR'S NOTES

BEFORE Y'ALL GET TANGLED UP IN YOUR UNDER-wear about it being All Hallows' Eve when Jeremiah leaves, and "nearly Samhain" (aka All Hallows' Eve) when he returns—bear in mind that Great Britain changed from the Julian to the Gregorian calendar in 1752, this resulting in a "loss" of twelve days. And for those of you who'd like to know more about the two men who rescue him, more of their story can be found in *An Echo in the Bone*.

"Never have so many owed so much to so few." This was Winston Churchill's acknowledgement to the RAF pilots who protected Britain during World War II—and he was about right.

Adolph Gysbert Malan—known as Sailor (probably because Adolph was not a popular name at the time)—was a South African flying ace who became the leader of the famous No. 74 Squadron RAF. He was known for sending German bomber pilots home with dead crews, to demoralize the Luftwaffe, and I would have mentioned this gruesomely fascinating detail in the story, had there been any good way of getting it in, but there wasn't. His Ten Commandments for Air Fighting are as given in the text.

While the mission that Captain Frank Randall recruits Jerry MacKenzie for is fictional, the situation wasn't. The Nazis did have labor camps in Poland long before anyone in the rest of Europe became aware of them, and the eventual revelation did much to rally anti-Nazi feeling.

I'd like particularly to acknowledge the assistance of Maria Szybek in the delicate matter of Polish vulgarities (any errors in grammar, spelling, or accent marks are entirely mine), and of Douglas Watkins in the technical descriptions of small-plane maneuvers (also the valuable suggestion of the malfunction that brought Jerry's Spitfire down).

VIRGINS

INTRODUCTION

WHILE MANY OF THE STORIES IN THIS BOOK SHOW you an alternate view of events seen in the main novels or explore the stories of heretofore minor characters, "Virgins" is a straightforward prequel. Set about three years prior to the events recounted in *Outlander*, this story explains what happened to Jamie Fraser after his escape from Fort William. He's suddenly an outlaw, wounded and with a price on his head, his family and home left in shambles, and his only choice is to seek refuge outside of Scotland with his best friend and blood brother, Ian Murray.

As young mercenaries in France, neither Ian nor Jamie has yet killed a man or bedded a lass—but they're trying.

IAN MURRAY KNEW FROM the moment he saw his best friend's face that something terrible had happened. The fact that he was seeing Jamie Fraser's face at all was evidence enough of that, never mind the look of the man.

Jamie was standing by the armorer's wagon, his arms full of the bits and pieces Armand had just given him, white as milk and swaying back and forth like a reed on Loch Awe. Ian reached him in three paces and took him by the arm before he could fall over.

"Ian." Jamie looked so relieved at seeing him that Ian thought he might break into tears. "God, Ian."

Ian seized Jamie in an embrace and felt him stiffen and draw in his breath at the same instant that Ian felt the bandages beneath Jamie's shirt.

"Jesus!" he began, startled, but then coughed and said, "Jesus, man, it's good to see ye." He patted Jamie's back gently and let go. "Ye'll need a bit to eat, aye? Come on, then."

Plainly they couldn't talk now, but he gave Jamie a quick private nod, took half the equipment from him, and then led him to the fire, to be introduced to the others.

Jamie'd picked a good time of day to turn up, Ian thought. Everyone was tired but happy to sit down, looking forward to their supper and the daily ration of whatever was going in the way of drink. Ready for the possibilities a new fish offered for entertainment, but without the energy to include the more physical sorts of entertainment.

"That's Big Georges over there," Ian said, dropping Jamie's gear and gesturing toward the far side of the fire. "Next to him, the wee fellow wi' the warts is Juanito; doesna speak much French and nay English at all."

"Do any of them speak English?" Jamie likewise dropped his gear and sat heavily on his bedroll, tucking his kilt absently down between his knees. His eyes flicked round the circle, and he nodded, half-smiling in a shy sort of way.

"I do." The captain leaned past the man next to him, extending a hand to Jamie. "I'm *le capitaine*—Richard D'Eglise. You'll call me Captain. You look big enough to be useful—your friend says your name is Fraser?"

"Jamie Fraser, aye."

Ian was pleased to see that Jamie knew to meet the captain's eye square and had summoned the strength to return the handshake with due force.

"Know what to do with a sword?"

"I do. And a bow, forbye." Jamie glanced at the unstrung bow by his feet and the short-handled ax beside it. "Havena had much to do wi' an ax before, save chopping wood."

"That's good," one of the other men put in, in French. "That's what you'll use it for." Several of the others laughed, indicating that they at least understood English, whether they chose to speak it or not.

"Did I join a troop of soldiers, then, or charcoal-burners?" Jamie asked, raising one brow. He said that in French—very good French, with a faint Parisian accent—and a number of eyes widened. Ian bent his head to hide a smile, in spite of his anxiety. The wean might be about to fall face-first into the fire, but nobody—save maybe Ian—was going to know it, if it killed him.

Ian *did* know it, though, and kept a covert eye on Jamie, pushing bread into his hand so the others wouldn't see it shake, sitting close enough to catch him if he should in fact pass out. The light was fading into gray now, and the clouds hung low and soft, pink-bellied. Going to rain, likely, by the morning. He saw Jamie close his eyes, just for an instant, saw his throat move as he swallowed, and felt the trembling of Jamie's thigh, near his own.

What the devil's happened? he thought in anguish. *Why are ye here?*

IT WASN'T UNTIL everyone had settled for the night that Ian got an answer.

"I'll lay out your gear," he whispered to Jamie, rising. "You stay by the fire that wee bit longer—rest a bit, aye?" The firelight cast a ruddy glow on Jamie's face, but Ian thought his friend was likely still white as a sheet; he hadn't eaten much.

Coming back, he saw the dark spots on the back of Jamie's shirt, blotches where fresh blood had seeped through the bandages. The sight filled him with fury, as well as fear. He'd seen such things; the wean had been flogged. Badly, and recently. *Who? How?*

"Come on, then," he said roughly, and, bending, slipped an arm under Jamie's and got him to his feet and away from the fire and the other men. He was alarmed to feel the clamminess of Jamie's hand and hear his shallow breath.

"What?" he demanded, the moment they were out of earshot. "What happened?"

Jamie sat down abruptly.

"I thought one joined a band of mercenaries because they didna ask ye questions."

Ian gave him the snort this statement deserved and was relieved to hear a breath of laughter in return.

"Eejit," he said. "D'ye need a dram? I've got a bottle in my sack."

"Wouldna come amiss," Jamie murmured. They were camped at the edge of a wee village, and D'Eglise had arranged for the use of a byre or two, but it wasn't cold out, and most of the men had chosen to sleep by the fire or in the field. Ian had put their gear down a little distance away and, with the possibility of rain in mind, under the shelter of a plane tree that stood at the side of a field.

Ian uncorked the bottle of whisky—it wasn't good, but it *was* whisky— and held it under his friend's nose. When Jamie reached for it, though, Ian pulled it away.

"Not a sip do ye get until ye tell me," he said. "And ye tell me *now, a charaid.*"

Jamie sat hunched, a pale blur on the ground, silent. When the words came at last, they were spoken so softly that Ian thought for an instant he hadn't really heard them.

"My father's dead."

He tried to believe he *hadn't* heard, but his heart had; it froze in his chest.

"Oh, Jesus," he whispered. "Oh, God, Jamie." He was on his knees then, holding Jamie's head fierce against his shoulder, trying not to touch his hurt back. His thoughts were in confusion, but one thing was clear to him—Brian Fraser's death hadn't been a natural one. If it had, Jamie would be at Lallybroch. Not here, and not in this state.

"Who?" he said hoarsely, relaxing his grip a little. "Who killed him?"

More silence, then Jamie gulped air with a sound like fabric being ripped.

"I did," he said, and began to cry, shaking with silent, tearing sobs.

IT TOOK SOME TIME to winkle the details out of Jamie—and no wonder, Ian thought. He wouldn't want to talk about such things, either, or to remember them. The English dragoons who'd come to Lallybroch to loot and plunder, who'd taken Jamie away with them when he'd fought them. And what they'd done to him then, at Fort William.

"A hundred lashes?" he said in disbelief and horror. "For protecting your *home*?"

"Only sixty the first time." Jamie wiped his nose on his sleeve. "For escaping."

"The *first* ti— Jesus, God, man! What . . . how . . ."

"Would ye let go my arm, Ian? I've got enough bruises; I dinna need any more." Jamie gave a small, shaky laugh, and Ian hastily let go but wasn't about to let himself be distracted.

"Why?" he said, low and angry. Jamie wiped his nose again, sniffing, but his voice was steadier.

"It was my fault," he said. "It—what I said before. About my . . ." He had to stop and swallow, but went on, hurrying to get the words out before they could bite him in a tender place. "I spoke chough to the commander. At the garrison, ken. He—well, it's nay matter. It was what I said to him made him flog me again, and Da—he—he'd come. To Fort William, to try to get me released, but he couldn't, and he—he was there, when they . . . did it."

Ian could tell from the thicker sound of his voice that Jamie was weeping again but trying not to, and he put a hand on the wean's knee and gripped it, not too hard, just so as Jamie would ken he was there, listening.

Jamie took a deep, deep breath and got the rest out.

"It was . . . hard. I didna call out, or let them see I was scairt, but I couldna keep my feet. Halfway through it, I fell into the post, just—just hangin' from the ropes, ken, wi' the blood . . . runnin' down my legs. They thought for a bit that I'd died—and Da must ha' thought so, too. They told me he put his hand to his head just then and made a wee noise, and then . . . he fell down. An apoplexy, they said."

"Mary, Mother o' God, have mercy on us," Ian said. "He—died right there?"

"I dinna ken was he dead when they picked him up or if he lived a bit after that." Jamie's voice was desolate. "I didna ken a thing about it; no one told me until days later, when Uncle Dougal got me away." He coughed and wiped the sleeve across his face again. "Ian . . . would ye let go my knee?"

"No," Ian said softly, though he did indeed take his hand away. Only so he could gather Jamie gently into his arms, though. "No. I willna let go, Jamie. Bide. Just . . . bide."

JAMIE WOKE DRY-MOUTHED, thickheaded, and with his eyes half swollen shut by midgie bites. It was also raining, a fine, wet mist coming down through the leaves above him. For all that, he felt better than he had in the last two weeks, though he didn't at once recall why that was—or where he was.

"Here." A piece of half-charred bread rubbed with garlic was shoved under his nose. He sat up and grabbed it.

Ian. The sight of his friend gave him an anchor, and the food in his belly another. He chewed slower now, looking about. Men were rising, stumbling off for a piss, making low rumbling noises, rubbing their heads and yawning.

"Where are we?" he asked. Ian gave him a look.

"How the devil did ye find us if ye dinna ken where ye are?"

"Murtagh brought me," he muttered. The bread turned to glue in his mouth as memory came back; he couldn't swallow and spat out the half-chewed bit. Now he remembered it all, and wished he didn't. "He found the band but then left; said it would look better if I came in on my own."

His godfather had said, in fact, *"The Murray lad will take care of ye now. Stay wi' him, mind—dinna come back to Scotland. Dinna come back, d'ye hear me?"* He'd heard. Didn't mean he meant to listen.

"Oh, aye. I wondered how ye'd managed to walk this far." Ian cast a worried look at the far side of the camp, where a pair of sturdy horses was being brought to the traces of a canvas-covered wagon. "*Can* ye walk, d'ye think?"

"Of course. I'm fine." Jamie spoke crossly, and Ian gave him the look again, even more slit-eyed than the last.

"Aye, right," he said, in tones of rank disbelief. "Well. We're near Bèguey, maybe twenty miles from Bordeaux; that's where we're going. We're takin' the wagon yon to a Jewish moneylender there."

"Is it full of money, then?" Jamie glanced at the heavy wagon, interested.

"No," Ian said. "There's a wee chest, verra heavy, so it's maybe gold, and there are a few bags that clink and might be silver, but most of its rugs."

"Rugs?" He looked at Ian in amazement. "What sort of rugs?"

Ian shrugged. "Couldna say. Juanito says they're Turkey rugs and verra valuable, but I dinna ken that he knows. He's Jewish, too," Ian added, as an afterthought. "Jews are—" He made an equivocal gesture, palm flattened. "But they dinna really hunt them in France, or exile them anymore, and the captain says they dinna even arrest them, so long as they keep quiet."

"And go on lending money to men in the government," Jamie said cynically. Ian looked at him, surprised, and Jamie gave him the *I went to the Université in Paris and ken more than you do* smart-arse look, fairly sure that Ian wouldn't thump him, seeing he was hurt.

Ian looked tempted but had learned enough merely to give Jamie back the *I'm older than you and ye ken well ye havena sense enough to come in out of the rain, so dinna be trying it on* look instead. Jamie laughed, feeling better.

"Aye, right," he said, bending forward. "Is my shirt verra bloody?"

Ian nodded, buckling his sword belt. Jamie sighed and picked up the leather jerkin the armorer had given him. It would rub, but he wasn't wanting to attract attention.

HE MANAGED. The troop kept up a decent pace, but it wasn't anything to trouble a Highlander accustomed to hill-walking and running down the odd deer. True, he grew a bit light-headed now and then, and sometimes his heart raced and waves of heat ran over him—but he didn't stagger any more than a few of the men who'd drunk too much for breakfast.

He barely noticed the countryside but was conscious of Ian striding along beside him, and Jamie took pains now and then to glance at his friend and nod, in order to relieve Ian's worried expression. The two of them were close to the wagon, mostly because he didn't want to draw attention by lagging at the back of the troop but also because he and Ian were taller than the rest by a head or more, with a stride that eclipsed the others, and he felt a small bit of pride in that. It didn't occur to him that possibly the others didn't *want* to be near the wagon.

The first inkling of trouble was a shout from the driver. Jamie had been trudging along, eyes half closed, concentrating on putting one foot ahead of the other, but a bellow of alarm and a sudden loud *bang!* jerked him to attention. A horseman charged out of the trees near the road, slewed to a halt, and fired his second pistol at the driver.

"What—" Jamie reached for the sword at his belt, half fuddled but starting forward; the horses were neighing and flinging themselves against the traces, the driver cursing and on his feet, hauling on the reins. Several of the mercenaries ran toward the horseman, who drew his own sword and rode through them, slashing recklessly from side to side. Ian seized Jamie's arm, though, and jerked him round. "Not there! The back!"

He followed Ian at the run, and, sure enough, there was the captain on his horse at the back of the troop, in the middle of a mêlée, a dozen strangers laying about with clubs and blades, all shouting.

"Caisteal DHOON!" Ian bellowed, and swung his sword over his head

and flat down on the head of an attacker. It hit the man a glancing blow, but he staggered and fell to his knees, where Big Georges seized him by the hair and kneed him viciously in the face.

"Caisteal DHOON!" Jamie shouted as loud as he could, and Ian turned his head for an instant, a big grin flashing.

It was a bit like a cattle raid but lasting longer. Not a matter of hit hard and get away; he'd never been a defender before and found it heavy going. Still, the attackers were outnumbered and began to give way, some glancing over their shoulders, plainly thinking of running back into the wood.

They began to do just that, and Jamie stood panting, dripping sweat, his sword a hundredweight in his hand. He straightened, though, and caught the flash of movement from the corner of his eye.

"Dhoon!" he shouted, and broke into a lumbering, gasping run. Another group of men had appeared near the wagon and were pulling the driver's body quietly down from his seat, while one of their number grabbed at the lunging horses' bridles, pulling their heads down. Two more had got the canvas loose and were dragging out a long rolled cylinder—one of the rugs, he supposed.

He reached them in time to grab another man trying to mount the wagon, yanking him clumsily back onto the road. The man twisted, falling, and came to his feet like a cat, knife in hand. The blade flashed, bounced off the leather of Jamie's jerkin, and cut upward, an inch from his face. Jamie squirmed back, off-balance, narrowly keeping his feet, and two more of the bastards charged him.

"On your right, man!" Ian's voice came suddenly at his shoulder, and without a moment's hesitation Jamie turned to take care of the man to his left, hearing Ian's grunt of effort as he laid about with a broadsword.

Then something changed; he couldn't tell what, but the fight was over. The attackers melted away, leaving one or two of their number lying in the road.

The driver wasn't dead; Jamie saw him roll half over, an arm across his face. Then he himself was sitting in the dust, black spots dancing before his eyes. Ian bent over him, panting, hands braced on his knees. Sweat dripped from his chin, making dark spots in the dust that mingled with the buzzing spots that darkened Jamie's vision.

"All . . . right?" Ian asked.

He opened his mouth to say yes, but the roaring in his ears drowned it out, and the spots merged suddenly into a solid sheet of black.

HE WOKE TO find a priest kneeling over him, intoning the Lord's Prayer in Latin. Not stopping, the priest took up a little bottle and poured oil into the palm of one hand, then dipped his thumb into the puddle and made a swift sign of the cross on Jamie's forehead.

"I'm no dead, aye?" Jamie said, then repeated this information in French. The priest leaned closer, squinting nearsightedly.

"Dying?" he asked.

"Not that, either."

The priest made a small, disgusted sound but went ahead and made crosses on the palms of Jamie's hands, his eyelids, and his lips. *"Ego te absolvo,"* he said, making a final quick sign of the cross over Jamie's supine form. "Just in case you've killed anyone." Then he rose swiftly to his feet and disappeared behind the wagon in a flurry of dark robes.

"All right, are ye?" Ian reached down a hand and hauled him into a sitting position.

"Aye, more or less. Who was that?" He nodded in the direction of the recent priest.

"Père Renault. This is a verra well-equipped outfit," Ian said, boosting him to his feet. "We've got our own priest, to shrive us before battle and give us Extreme Unction after."

"I noticed. A bit over-eager, is he no?"

"He's blind as a bat," Ian said, glancing over his shoulder to be sure the priest wasn't close enough to hear. "Likely thinks better safe than sorry, aye?"

"D'ye have a surgeon, too?" Jamie asked, glancing at the two attackers who had fallen. The bodies had been pulled to the side of the road; one was clearly dead, but the other was beginning to stir and moan.

"Ah," Ian said thoughtfully. "That would be the priest, as well."

"So if I'm wounded in battle, I'd best try to die of it, is that what ye're sayin'?"

"I am. Come on, let's find some water."

~~~

THEY FOUND A rock-lined irrigation ditch running between two fields, a little way off the road. Ian pulled Jamie into the shade of a tree and, rummaging in his rucksack, produced a spare shirt, which he shoved into his friend's hands.

"Put it on," he said, low-voiced. "Ye can wash yours out; they'll think the blood on it's from the fightin'." Jamie looked surprised, but grateful, and with a nod skimmed out of the leather jerkin and peeled the sweaty, stained shirt gingerly off his back. Ian grimaced; the bandages were filthy and coming loose, save where they stuck to Jamie's skin, crusted black with old blood and dried pus.

"Shall I pull them off?" he muttered in Jamie's ear. "I'll do it fast."

Jamie arched his back in refusal, shaking his head.

"Nay, it'll bleed more if ye do." There wasn't time to argue; several more of the men were coming. Jamie ducked hurriedly into the clean shirt and knelt to splash water on his face.

"Hey, Scotsman!" Alexandre called to Jamie. "What's that you two were shouting at each other?" He put his hands to his mouth and hooted, "GOOOOOON!" in a deep, echoing voice that made the others laugh.

"Have ye never heard a war cry before?" Jamie asked, shaking his head at such ignorance. "Ye shout it in battle, to call your kin and your clan to your side."

"Does it mean anything?" Petit Philippe asked, interested.

"Aye, more or less," Ian said. "Castle Dhuni's the dwelling place of the chieftain of the Frasers of Lovat. *Caisteal Dhuin* is what ye call it in the *Gàidhlig*—that's our own tongue."

"And that's our clan," Jamie clarified. "Clan Fraser, but there's more than one branch, and each one will have its own war cry and its own motto." He pulled his shirt out of the cold water and wrung it out; the bloodstains were still visible but faint brown marks now, Ian saw with approval. Then he saw Jamie's mouth opening to say more.

Don't say it! he thought, but, as usual, Jamie wasn't reading his mind, and Ian closed his eyes in resignation, knowing what was coming.

"Our clan motto's in French, though," Jamie said, with a small air of pride. *"Je suis prêt."*

It meant "I am ready" and was, as Ian had foreseen, greeted with gales of laughter and a number of crude speculations as to just what the young Scots might be ready for. The men were in good humor from the fight, and it went on for a bit. Ian shrugged and smiled, but he could see Jamie's ears turning red.

"Where's the rest of your queue, Georges?" Petit Philippe demanded, seeing Big Georges shaking off after a piss. "Someone trim it for you?"

"Your wife bit it off," Georges replied, in a tranquil tone indicating that this was common badinage. "Mouth like a sucking pig, that one. And a *cramouille* like a—"

This resulted in a further scatter of abuse, but it was clear from the sidelong glances that it was mostly performance for the benefit of the two Scots. Ian ignored it. Jamie had gone squiggle-eyed; Ian wasn't sure his friend had ever heard the word *"cramouille"* before, but he likely figured what it meant.

Before Jamie could get them in more trouble, though, the conversation by the stream was stopped dead by a strangled scream beyond the scrim of trees that hid them from the roadside.

"The prisoner," Alexandre murmured after a moment.

Ian knelt by Jamie, water dripping from his cupped hands. He knew what was happening; it curdled his wame. He let the water fall and wiped his hands on his thighs.

"The captain," he said softly to Jamie. "He'll . . . need to know who they were. Where they came from."

"Aye." Jamie's lips pressed tight at the sound of muted voices, the sudden meaty smack of flesh and a loud grunt. "I know." He splashed water fiercely onto his face.

The jokes had stopped. There was little conversation now, though Alexandre and Josef-from-Alsace began a random argument, speaking loudly, trying to drown out the noises from the road. Most of the men finished their washing and drinking in silence and sat hunched in the shade, shoulders pulled in.

"Père Renault!" The captain's voice rose, calling for the priest. Père Renault had been performing his own ablutions a discreet distance from the men but stood at this summons, wiping his face on the hem of his robe. He crossed himself and headed for the road, but on the way he paused by Ian and motioned toward his drinking cup.

"May I borrow this from you, my son? Only for a moment."

"Aye, of course, Father," Ian said, baffled. The priest nodded, bent to scoop up a cup of water, and went on his way. Jamie looked after him, then at Ian, brows raised.

"They say he's a Jew," Juanito said nearby, very quietly. "They want to baptize him first." He knelt by the water, fists curled tight against his thighs.

Hot as the air was, Ian felt a spear of ice run right through his chest. He stood up fast and made as though to follow the priest, but Big Georges snaked out a hand and caught him by the shoulder.

"Leave it," he said. He spoke quietly, too, but his fingers dug hard into Ian's flesh.

He didn't pull away but stayed standing, holding Georges's eyes. He felt Jamie make a brief, convulsive movement, but said, "No!" under his breath, and Jamie stopped.

They could hear French cursing from the road, mingled with Père Renault's voice. *"In nomine Patris, et Filii . . ."* Then struggling, spluttering, and shouting, the prisoner, the captain, and Mathieu, and even the priest, all using such language as made Jamie blink. Ian might have laughed if not for the sense of dread that froze every man by the water.

"No!" shouted the prisoner, his voice rising above the others, anger lost in terror. "No, please! I told you all I—" There was a small sound, a hollow noise like a melon being kicked in, and the voice stopped.

"Thrifty, our captain," Big Georges said, under his breath. "Why waste a bullet?" He took his hand off Ian's shoulder, shook his head, and knelt down to wash his hands.

THERE WAS A ghastly silence under the trees. From the road, they could hear low voices—the captain and Mathieu speaking to each other, and over that, Père Renault repeating, *"In nomine Patris, et Filii . . ."* but in a very different tone. Ian saw the hairs on Jamie's arms rise, and Jamie rubbed the palms of his hands against his kilt, maybe feeling a slick from the chrism oil still there.

Jamie plainly couldn't stand to listen and turned to Big Georges at random.

"Queue?" he said with a raised brow. "That what ye call it in these parts, is it?"

Big Georges managed a crooked smile.

"And what do you call it? In your tongue?"

"Bot," Ian said, shrugging. There were other words, but he wasn't about to try one like *clipeachd* on them.

"Mostly just cock," Jamie said, shrugging, too.

"Or penis, if ye want to be all English about it," Ian chimed in.

Several of the men were listening now, willing to join in any sort of conversation to get away from the echo of the last scream, still hanging in the air like fog.

"Ha," Jamie said. "Penis isna even an English word, ye wee ignoramus. It's Latin. And even in Latin, it doesna mean a man's closest companion—it means 'tail.'"

Ian gave him a long, slow look.

"Tail, is it? So ye canna even tell the difference between your cock and your arse, and ye're preachin' to me about *Latin*?"

The men roared. Jamie's face flamed up instantly, and Ian laughed and gave him a good nudge with his shoulder. Jamie snorted but elbowed Ian back and laughed, too, reluctantly.

"Aye, all right, then." He looked abashed; he didn't usually throw his education in Ian's face. Ian didn't hold it against him; he'd floundered for a bit, too, his first days with the company, and that was the sort of thing you did, trying to get your feet under you by making a point of what you were good at. But if Jamie tried rubbing Mathieu's or Big Georges's face in his Latin and Greek, he'd be proving himself with his fists, and fast, too. Right this minute, he didn't look as though he could fight a rabbit and win.

The renewed murmur of conversation, subdued as it was, dried up at once with the appearance of Mathieu through the trees. Mathieu was a big man, though broad rather than tall, with a face like a mad boar and a character to match. Nobody called him "Pig-face" *to* his face.

"You, cheese rind—go bury that turd," he said to Jamie, adding with a narrowing of red-rimmed eyes, "far back in the wood. And go before I put a boot in your arse. Move!"

Jamie got up—slowly—eyes fixed on Mathieu with a look Ian didn't care for. He came up quick beside Jamie and gripped him by the arm.

"I'll help," he said. "Come on."

"WHY DO THEY want this one buried?" Jamie muttered to Ian. "Giving him a *Christian* burial?" He drove one of the trenching spades Armand had lent them into the soft leaf mold, with a violence that would have told Ian just how churned up his friend was if he hadn't known already.

"Ye kent it's no a verra civilized life, *a charaid*," Ian said. He didn't feel any better about it himself, after all, and spoke sharp. "Not like the *Université*."

The blood flamed up Jamie's neck like tinder taking fire, and Ian held out a palm, in hopes of quelling him. He didn't want a fight, and Jamie couldn't stand one.

"We're burying him because D'Eglise thinks his friends might come back to look for him, and it's better they don't see what was done to him, aye? Ye can see by looking that the other fellow was just killed fightin'. Business is one thing; revenge is another."

Jamie's jaw worked for a bit, but gradually the hot flush faded and his clench on the shovel loosened.

"Aye," he muttered, and resumed digging. The sweat was running down his neck in minutes, and he was breathing hard. Ian nudged him out of the way with an elbow and finished the digging. Silent, they took the dead man by the oxters and ankles and dragged him into the shallow pit.

"D'ye think D'Eglise found out anything?" Jamie asked, as they scattered matted chunks of old leaves over the raw earth.

"I hope so," Ian replied, eyes on his work. "I wouldna like to think they did that for nothing."

He straightened up and they stood awkwardly for a moment, not quite looking at each other. It seemed wrong to leave a grave, even that of a stranger and a Jew, without a word of prayer. But it seemed worse to say a Christian prayer over the man—more insult than blessing, in the circumstances.

At last Jamie grimaced and, bending, dug about under the leaves, coming out with two small stones. He gave one to Ian, and one after the other, they squatted and placed the stones together atop the grave. It wasn't much of a cairn, but it was something.

IT WASN'T THE captain's way to make explanations or to give more than brief, explicit orders to his men. He had come back into camp at evening, his face dark and his lips pressed tight. But three other men had heard the interrogation of the Jewish stranger, and by the usual metaphysical processes that happen around campfires, everyone in the troop knew by the next morning what he had said.

"Ephraim bar-Sefer," Ian said to Jamie, who had come back late to the fire, after going off quietly to wash his shirt out again. "That was his name." Ian was a bit worrit about the wean. His wounds weren't healing as they should, and the way he'd passed out . . . He'd a fever now; Ian could feel the heat coming off his skin, but he shivered now and then, though the night wasn't bitter.

"Is it better to know that?" Jamie asked bleakly.

"We can pray for him by name," Ian pointed out. "That's better, is it not?"

Jamie wrinkled up his brow, but after a moment he nodded.

"Aye, it is. What else did he say, then?"

Ian rolled his eyes. Ephraim bar-Sefer had confessed that the band of attackers were professional thieves, mostly Jews, who—

"Jews?" Jamie interrupted. "Jewish *bandits*?" For some reason, the thought struck Jamie as funny, but Ian didn't laugh.

"Why not?" he asked briefly, and went on without waiting for an answer. The men gained advance knowledge of valuable shipments and made a practice of lying in wait, to ambush and rob. "It's mostly other Jews they rob, so there's nay much danger of being pursued by the French army or a local judge."

"Oh. And the advance knowledge—that's easier come by, too, I suppose, if the folk they rob are Jews. Jews live close by one another in groups," Jamie explained, seeing the look of surprise on Ian's face. "They all read and write, though, and they write letters all the time; there's a good bit of information passed to and fro between the groups. Wouldna be that hard to learn who the moneylenders and merchants are and intercept their correspondence, would it?"

"Maybe not," Ian said, giving Jamie a look of respect. "Bar-Sefer said they got notice from someone—he didna ken who it was himself—who kent a great deal about valuables comin' and goin'. The person who knew wasna one of their group, though; it was someone outside, who got a percentage o' the proceeds."

That, however, was the total of the information bar-Sefer had divulged. He wouldn't give up the names of any of his associates—D'Eglise didn't care so much about that—and had died stubbornly insisting that he knew nothing of future robberies planned.

"D'ye think it might ha' been one of ours?" Jamie asked, low-voiced.

"One of—oh, our Jews, ye mean?" Ian frowned at the thought. There were three Spanish Jews in D'Eglise's band—Juanito, Big Georges, and Raoul—but all three were good men and fairly popular with their fellows. "I doubt it. All three o' them fought like fiends. When I noticed," he added fairly.

"What I want to know is how the thieves got away wi' that rug," Jamie said reflectively. "Must have weighed what, ten stone?"

"At least that," Ian assured him, flexing his shoulders at the memory. "I helped load the wretched things. I suppose they must have had a wagon somewhere nearby, for their booty. Why?"

"Well, but . . . *rugs?* Who steals rugs? Even valuable ones. And if they kent ahead of time that we were comin', presumably they kent what we carried."

"Ye're forgettin' the gold and silver," Ian reminded him. "It was in the front of the wagon, under the rugs. They had to pull the rugs out to get at it."

"Mmphm." Jamie looked vaguely dissatisfied—and it was true that the bandits had gone to the trouble to carry the rug away with them. But there was nothing to be gained by more discussion, and when Ian said he was for bed, Jamie came along without argument.

They settled down in a nest of long yellow grass, wrapped in their plaids, but Ian didn't sleep at once. He was bruised and tired, but the excitements of the day were still with him, and he lay looking up at the stars for some time, remembering some things and trying hard to forget others—like the look of Ephraim bar-Sefer's head. Maybe Jamie was right and it was better not to have kent his right name.

He forced his mind into other paths, succeeding to the extent that he was surprised when Jamie shifted, cursing under his breath as the movement hurt him.

"Have ye ever done it?" Ian asked suddenly.

There was a small rustle as Jamie hitched himself into a more comfortable position.

"Have I ever done what?" he asked. His voice sounded that wee bit hoarse but none so bad. "Killed anyone? No."

"Nay, lain wi' a lass."

"Oh, that."

"Aye, *that*. Gowk." Ian rolled toward Jamie and aimed a feint toward his middle.

Despite the darkness, Jamie caught his wrist before the blow landed. "Have you?"

"Oh, ye haven't, then." Ian detached the grip without difficulty. "I thought ye'd be up to your ears in whores and poetesses in Paris."

"Poetesses?" Jamie was beginning to sound amused. "What makes ye think women write poetry? Or that a woman who writes poetry would be wanton?"

"Well, o' course they are. Everybody kens that. The words get into their heads and drive them mad, and they go looking for the first man who—"

"Ye've bedded a poetess?" Jamie's fist struck him lightly in the middle of the chest. "Does your mam ken that?"

"Dinna be telling my mam anything about poetesses," Ian said firmly. "No, but Big Georges did, and he told everyone about her. A woman he met in Marseilles. He has a book of her poetry and read some out."

"Any good?"

"How would I ken? There was a good bit o' swooning and swellin' and bursting goin' on, but it seemed to do wi' flowers, mostly. There was a good wee bit about a bumblebee, though, doin' the business wi' a sunflower. Pokin' it, I mean. With its snout."

There was a momentary silence as Jamie absorbed the mental picture.

"Maybe it sounds better in French," he said.

"I'LL HELP YE," Ian said suddenly, in a tone that was serious to the bone.

"Help me . . . ?"

"Help ye kill this Captain Randall."

Jamie lay silent for a moment, feeling his chest go tight.

"Jesus, Ian," he said, very softly. He lay for several minutes, eyes fixed on the shadowy tree roots near his face.

"No," he said at last. "Ye can't. I need ye to do something else for me, Ian. I need ye to go home."

"Home? What—"

"I need ye to go home and take care of Lallybroch—and my sister. I—I canna go. Not yet." He bit his lower lip hard.

"Ye've got tenants and friends enough there," Ian protested. "Ye need me here, man. I'm no leavin' ye alone, aye? When ye go back, we'll go together." And he turned over in his plaid with an air of finality.

Jamie lay with his eyes tight closed, ignoring the singing and conversation near the fire, the beauty of the night sky over him, and the nagging pain in his back. He should perhaps be praying for the soul of the dead Jew, but he had no time for that just now. He was trying to find his father.

Brian Fraser's soul must still exist, and he was positive that his father was in heaven. But surely there must be some way to reach him, to sense him. When first Jamie had left home, to foster with Dougal at Beannachd, he'd been lonely and homesick, but Da had told him he would be and not to trouble overmuch about it.

"Ye think of me, Jamie, and Jenny and Lallybroch. Ye'll not see us, but we'll be here nonetheless and thinking of you. Look up at night, and see the stars, and ken we see them, too."

He opened his eyes a slit, but the stars swam, their brightness blurred. He squeezed his eyes shut again and felt the warm glide of a single tear down his temple. He couldn't think about Jenny. Or Lallybroch. The homesickness at Dougal's had stopped. The strangeness when he went to Paris had eased. This wouldn't stop, but he'd have to go on living anyway.

Where are ye, Da? he thought in anguish. *Da, I'm sorry!*

HE PRAYED AS he walked next day, making his way doggedly from one Hail Mary to the next, using his fingers to count the rosary. For a time, it kept him from thinking and gave him a little peace. But eventually the slippery thoughts came stealing back, memories in small flashes, quick as sun on water. Some he fought off—Captain Randall's voice, playful as he took the cat in hand—the fearful prickle of the hairs on his body in the cold wind when he took his shirt off—the surgeon's *"I see he's made a mess of you, boy. . . ."*

But some memories he seized, no matter how painful they were. The feel of his da's hands, hard on his arms, holding him steady. The guards had been taking him somewhere—he didn't recall and it didn't matter— when suddenly his da was there before him, in the yard of the prison, and he'd stepped forward fast when he saw Jamie, a look of joy and eagerness on his face, this blasted into shock the next moment, when he saw what they'd done to him.

"Are ye bad hurt, Jamie?"

"No, Da, I'll be all right."

For a minute, he had been. So heartened by seeing his father, sure it would all come right—and then he'd remembered Jenny, taking yon *cro-chaire* into the house, sacrificing herself for—

He cut that one off short, too, saying "Hail Mary, full of grace, the Lord is with thee!" savagely out loud, to the startlement of Petit Philippe, who was scuttling along beside him on his short bandy legs.

"Blessed art thou amongst women . . ." Philippe chimed in obligingly. "Pray for us sinners, now and at the hour of our death, amen!"

"Hail Mary," said Père Renault's deep voice behind him, taking it up, and within seconds seven or eight of them were saying it, marching solemnly to the rhythm, and then a few more . . . Jamie himself fell silent, unnoticed. But he found the wall of prayer a barricade between himself and the wicked sly thoughts and, closing his eyes briefly, felt his father walk beside him and Brian Fraser's last kiss soft as the wind on his cheek.

THEY REACHED BORDEAUX just before sunset, and D'Eglise took the wagon off with a small guard, leaving the other men free to explore the delights of the city—though such exploration was somewhat constrained by the fact that they hadn't yet been paid. They'd get their money after the goods were delivered next day.

Ian, who'd been in Bordeaux before, led the way to a large, noisy tavern with drinkable wine and large portions.

"The barmaids are pretty, too," he observed, as he stood watching one of these creatures wend her way deftly through a crowd of groping hands.

"Is it a brothel upstairs?" Jamie asked, out of curiosity, having heard a few stories.

"I dinna ken," Ian said, with what sounded like regret, though Jamie was almost sure he'd never been to a brothel, out of a mixture of penury and fear of catching the pox. "D'ye want to go and find out later?"

Jamie hesitated.

"I—well. No, I dinna think so." He turned his face toward Ian and spoke very quietly. "I promised Da I wouldna go wi' whores, when I went to Paris. And now . . . I couldna do it without . . . thinkin' of him, ken?"

Ian nodded, his face showing as much relief as disappointment.

"Time enough another day," he said philosophically, and signaled for another jug. The barmaid didn't see him, though, and Jamie snaked out a long arm and tugged at her apron. She whirled, scowling, but seeing Jamie's face, wearing its best blue-eyed smile, chose to smile back and take the order.

Several other men from D'Eglise's band were in the tavern, and this byplay didn't pass unnoticed.

Juanito, at a nearby table, glanced at Jamie, raised a derisive eyebrow, then said something to Raoul in the Jewish sort of Spanish they called Ladino; both men laughed.

"You know what causes warts, friend?" Jamie said pleasantly—in biblical Hebrew. "Demons inside a man, trying to emerge through the skin." He spoke slowly enough that Ian could follow this, and Ian in turn broke out laughing—as much at the looks on the two Jews' faces as at Jamie's remark.

Juanito's lumpy face darkened, but Raoul looked sharply at Ian, first at his face, then, deliberately, at his crotch. Ian shook his head, still grinning, and Raoul shrugged but returned the smile, then took Juanito by the arm, tugging him off in the direction of the back room, where dicing was to be found.

"What did you say to him?" the barmaid asked, glancing after the departing pair, then looking back wide-eyed at Jamie. "And what tongue did you say it in?"

Jamie was glad to have the wide brown eyes to gaze into; it was causing his neck considerable strain to keep his head from tilting farther down in order to gaze into her décolletage. The charming hollow between her breasts drew the eye . . .

"Oh, nothing but a little *bonhomie,*" he said, grinning down at her. "I said it in Hebrew." He wanted to impress her, and he did, but not the way he'd meant to. Her half smile vanished, and she edged back a little.

"Oh," she said. "Your pardon, sir, I'm needed . . ." and with a vaguely apologetic flip of the hand, she vanished into the throng of customers, pitcher in hand.

"Eejit," Ian said. "What did ye tell her that for? Now she thinks ye're a Jew."

Jamie's mouth fell open in shock. "What, me? How, then?" he demanded, looking down at himself. He'd meant his Highland dress, but Ian looked critically at him and shook his head.

"Ye've got the lang neb and the red hair," he pointed out. "Half the Spanish Jews I've seen look like that, and some of them are a good size, too. For all yon lass kens, ye stole the plaid off somebody ye killed."

Jamie felt more nonplussed than affronted. Rather hurt, too.

"Well, what if I was a Jew?" he demanded. "Why should it matter? I wasna askin' for her hand in marriage, was I? I was only talkin' to her, for God's sake!"

Ian gave him that annoyingly tolerant look. He shouldn't mind, he knew; he'd lorded it over Ian often enough about things he kent and Ian didn't. He did mind, though; the borrowed shirt was too small and chafed him under the arms, and his wrists stuck out, bony and raw-looking. He didn't look like a Jew, but he looked like a gowk and he knew it. It made him cross-grained.

"Most o' the Frenchwomen—the Christian ones, I mean—dinna like to go wi' Jews. Not because they're Christ-killers, but because of their . . . um . . ." He glanced down, with a discreet gesture at Jamie's crotch. "They think it looks funny."

"It doesna look *that* different."

"It does."

"Well, aye, when it's . . . but when it's—I mean, if it's in a state that a lassie would be lookin' at it, it isna . . ." He saw Ian opening his mouth to ask just how he happened to know what an erect circumcised cock looked like. "Forget it," he said brusquely, and pushed past his friend. "Let's be goin' down the street."

AT DAWN, the band gathered at the inn where D'Eglise and the wagon waited, ready to escort it through the streets to its destination—a warehouse on the banks of the Garonne. Jamie saw that the captain had changed into his finest clothes, plumed hat and all, and so had the four men—among the biggest in the band—who had guarded the wagon during the night. They were all armed to the teeth, and Jamie wondered whether this was only to make a good show or whether D'Eglise intended to have them stand behind him while he explained why the shipment was one rug short, to discourage complaint from the merchant receiving the shipment.

Jamie was enjoying the walk through the city, though keeping a sharp eye out, as he'd been instructed, against the possibility of ambush from alleys or thieves dropping from a roof or balcony onto the wagon. He thought the latter possibility remote but dutifully looked up now and then. Upon lowering his eyes from one of these inspections, he found that the captain had dropped back and was now pacing beside him on his big gray gelding.

"Juanito says you speak Hebrew," D'Eglise said, looking down at him as though he'd suddenly sprouted horns. "Is this true?"

"Aye," he said cautiously. "Though it's more I can read the Bible in Hebrew—a bit—there not bein' so many Jews in the Highlands to converse with." There had been a few in Paris, but he knew better than to talk about the *Université* and the study of philosophers like Maimonides. They'd scrag him before supper.

The captain grunted but didn't look displeased. He rode for a time in silence but kept his horse to a walk, pacing at Jamie's side. This made Jamie nervous, and after a few moments, impulse made him jerk his head to the rear and say, "Ian can, too. Read Hebrew, I mean."

D'Eglise looked down at him, startled, and glanced back. Ian was clearly visible, as he stood a head taller than the three men with whom he was conversing as he walked.

"Will wonders never cease?" the captain said, as though to himself. But he nudged his horse into a trot and left Jamie in the dust.

IT WASN'T UNTIL the next afternoon that this conversation returned to bite Jamie in the arse. They'd delivered the rugs and the gold

and silver to the warehouse on the river, D'Eglise had received his payment, and consequently the men were scattered down the length of an
allée that boasted cheap eating and drinking establishments, many of these
with a room above or behind where a man could spend his money in other
ways.

Neither Jamie nor Ian said anything further regarding the subject of
brothels, but Jamie found his mind returning to the pretty barmaid. He
had his own shirt on now and had half a mind to find his way back and tell
her he wasn't a Jew.

He had no idea what she might do with that information, though, and
the tavern was clear on the other side of the city.

"Think we'll have another job soon?" he asked idly, as much to break
Ian's silence as to escape from his own thoughts. There had been talk
around the fire about the prospects; evidently there were no good wars at
the moment, though it was rumored that the King of Prussia was beginning to gather men in Silesia.

"I hope so," Ian muttered. "Canna bear hangin' about." He drummed
long fingers on the tabletop. "I need to be movin'."

"That why ye left Scotland, is it?" He was only making conversation
and was surprised to see Ian dart him a wary glance.

"Didna want to farm, wasna much else to do. I make good money here.
And I mostly send it home."

"Still, I dinna imagine your da was pleased." Ian was the only son; Auld
John was probably still livid, though he hadn't said much in Jamie's hearing during the brief time he'd been home, before the redcoats—

"My sister's marrit. Her husband can manage, if . . ." Ian lapsed into a
moody silence.

Before Jamie could decide whether to prod Ian or not, the captain appeared beside their table, surprising them both.

D'Eglise stood for a moment, considering them. Finally he sighed and
said, "All right. The two of you, come with me."

Ian shoved the rest of his bread and cheese into his mouth and rose,
chewing. Jamie was about to do likewise when the captain frowned at him.

"Is your shirt clean?"

He felt the blood rise in his cheeks. It was the closest anyone had come
to mentioning his back, and it was too close. Most of the wounds had
crusted over long since, but the worst ones were still infected; they broke
open with the chafing of the bandages or if he bent too suddenly. He'd
had to rinse his shirt almost every night—it was constantly damp, and that
didn't help—and he knew fine that the whole band knew but nobody'd
spoken of it.

"It is," he replied shortly, and drew himself up to his full height, staring
down at D'Eglise, who merely said, "Good, then. Come on."

THE NEW POTENTIAL client was a physician named Dr. Hasdi, reputed to be a person of great influence among the Jews of Bordeaux. The last client had made the introduction, so apparently D'Eglise had managed to smooth over the matter of the missing rug.

Dr. Hasdi's house was discreetly tucked away in a decent but modest side street, behind a stuccoed wall and locked gates. Ian rang the bell, and a man dressed like a gardener promptly appeared to let them in, gesturing them up the walk to the front door. Evidently, they were expected.

"They don't flaunt their wealth, the Jews," D'Eglise murmured out of the side of his mouth to Jamie. "But they have it."

Well, these did, Jamie thought. A manservant greeted them in a plain tiled foyer but then opened the door into a room that made the senses swim. It was lined with books in dark-wood cases, carpeted thickly under- foot, and what little of the walls was not covered with books was adorned with small tapestries and framed tiles that he thought might be Moorish. But above all, the scent! He breathed it in to the bottom of his lungs, feel- ing slightly intoxicated, and, looking for the source of it, finally spotted the owner of this earthly paradise sitting behind a desk and staring—at him. Or maybe him and Ian both; the man's eyes flicked back and forth between them, round as sucked toffees.

He straightened up instinctively and bowed. "We greet thee, lord," Jamie said, in carefully rehearsed Hebrew. "Peace be on your house."

The man's mouth fell open. Noticeably so; he had a large, bushy dark beard, going white near the mouth. An indefinable expression—surely it wasn't amusement?—ran over what could be seen of his face.

A small sound that certainly *was* amusement drew Jamie's attention to one side. A small brass bowl sat on a round, tile-topped table, with smoke wandering lazily up from it through a bar of late-afternoon sun. Between the sun and the smoke, he could just make out the form of a woman standing in the shadows. She stepped forward, materializing out of the gloom, and his heart jumped.

She inclined her head gravely to the soldiers, addressing them impar- tially.

"I am Rebekah bat-Leah Hauberger. My grandfather bids me make you welcome to our home, gentlemen," she said, in perfect French, though the old gentleman hadn't spoken. Jamie drew in a great breath of relief; he wouldn't have to try to explain their business in Hebrew, after all. The breath was so deep, though, that it made him cough, the perfumed smoke tickling his chest.

As he tried to strangle the cough, he could feel his face going red and Ian glancing sidelong at him. The girl—yes, she was young, maybe his own age—swiftly took up a cover and clapped it on the bowl, then rang a bell and told the servant something in what sounded like Spanish. *Ladino?* he thought.

"Do please sit, sirs," she said, waving gracefully toward a chair in front of the desk, then turning to fetch another standing by the wall.

"Allow me, mademoiselle!" Ian leapt forward to assist her. Jamie, still choking as quietly as possible, followed suit.

She had dark hair, very wavy, bound back from her brow with a rose-colored ribbon but falling loose down her back, nearly to her waist. He had actually raised a hand to stroke it before catching hold of himself. Then she turned around. Pale skin, big dark eyes, and an oddly knowing look in those eyes when she met his own—which she did, very directly, when he set the third chair down before her.

Annalise. He swallowed, hard, and cleared his throat. A wave of dizzy heat washed over him, and he wished suddenly that they'd open a window.

D'Eglise, too, was visibly relieved at having a more reliable interpreter than Jamie and launched into a gallant speech of introduction, much decorated with French flowers, bowing repeatedly to the girl and her grandfather in turn.

Jamie wasn't paying attention to the talk; he was still watching Rebekah. It was her passing resemblance to Annalise de Marillac, the girl he'd loved in Paris, that had drawn his attention—but now he came to look, she was quite different.

Quite different. Annalise had been tiny and fluffy as a kitten. This girl was small—he'd seen that she came no higher than his elbow; her soft hair had brushed his wrist when she sat down—but there was nothing either fluffy or helpless about her. She'd noticed him watching her and was now watching *him*, with a faint curve to her red mouth that made the blood rise in his cheeks. He coughed and looked down.

"What's amiss?" Ian muttered out of the side of his mouth. "Ye look like ye've got a cocklebur stuck betwixt your hurdies."

Jamie gave an irritable twitch, then stiffened as he felt one of the rawer wounds on his back break open. He could feel the fast-cooling spot, the slow seep of pus or blood, and sat very straight, trying not to breathe deep, in hopes that the bandages would absorb the liquid before it got onto his shirt.

This niggling concern had at least distracted his mind from Rebekah bat-Leah Hauberger, and to distract himself from the aggravation of his back, he returned to the three-way conversation between D'Eglise and the Jews.

The captain was sweating freely, whether from the hot tea or the strain of persuasion, but he talked easily, gesturing now and then toward his matched pair of tall, Hebrew-speaking Scots, now and then toward the window and the outer world, where vast legions of similar warriors awaited, ready and eager to do Dr. Hasdi's bidding.

The doctor watched D'Eglise intently, occasionally addressing a soft rumble of incomprehensible words to his granddaughter. It did sound like the Ladino that Juanito spoke, more than anything else; certainly it sounded nothing like the Hebrew that Jamie had been taught in Paris.

Finally the old Jew glanced among the three mercenaries, pursed his lips thoughtfully, and nodded. He rose and went to a large blanket chest that stood under the window, where he knelt and carefully gathered up a long, heavy cylinder wrapped in oiled cloth. Jamie could see that it was remarkably heavy for its size, from the slow way the old man rose with it, and his first thought was that it must be a gold statue of some sort. His second thought was that Rebekah smelled like rose petals and vanilla pods. He breathed in, very gently, feeling the shirt stick to his back.

The thing, whatever it was, jingled and chimed softly as it moved. Some sort of Jewish clock? Dr. Hasdi carried the cylinder to the desk and set it down, then curled a finger to invite the soldiers to step near.

Unwrapped with a slow and solemn sense of ceremony, the object emerged from its layers of linen, canvas, and oiled cloth. It *was* gold, in part, and not unlike statuary but made of wood and shaped like a prism, with a sort of crown at one end. While Jamie was still wondering what the devil it might be, the doctor's arthritic fingers touched a small clasp and the box opened, revealing yet more layers of cloth, from which yet another delicate, spicy scent emerged. All three soldiers breathed deep, in unison, and Rebekah made that small sound of amusement again.

"The case is cedar wood," she said. "From Lebanon."

"Oh," D'Eglise said respectfully. "Of course!"

The bundle inside was dressed—there was no other word for it; it was wearing a sort of caped mantle and a belt, with a miniature buckle—in velvet and embroidered silk. From one end, two massive golden finials protruded like twin heads. They were pierced work and looked like towers, adorned in the windows and along their lower edges with a number of tiny bells.

"This is a *very* old Torah scroll," Rebekah said, keeping a respectful distance. "From Spain."

"A priceless object, to be sure," D'Eglise said, bending to peer closer.

Dr. Hasdi grunted and said something to Rebekah, who translated:

"Only to those whose Book it is. To anyone else, it has a very obvious and attractive price. If this were not so, I would not stand in need of your services." The doctor looked pointedly at Jamie and Ian. "A respectable man—a Jew—will carry the Torah. It may not be touched. But you will safeguard it—and my granddaughter."

"Quite so, your honor." D'Eglise flushed slightly but was too pleased to look abashed. "I am deeply honored by your trust, sir, and I assure you . . ." But Rebekah had rung her bell again, and the manservant came in with wine.

The job offered was simple; Rebekah was to be married to the son of the chief rabbi of the Paris synagogue. The ancient Torah was part of her dowry, as was a sum of money that made D'Eglise's eyes glisten. The doctor wished to engage D'Eglise to deliver all three items—the girl, the scroll, and the money—safely to Paris; the doctor himself would travel there for the wedding but later in the month, as his business in Bordeaux detained him. The only things to be decided were the price for D'Eglise's services, the time in which they were to be accomplished, and the guarantees D'Eglise was prepared to offer.

The doctor's lips pursed over this last; his friend Ackerman, who had referred D'Eglise to him, had not been entirely pleased at having one of his valuable rugs stolen en route, and the doctor wished to be assured that none of *his* valuable property—Jamie saw Rebekah's soft mouth twitch as she translated this—would go missing between Bordeaux and Paris. The captain gave Ian and Jamie a stern look, then altered this to earnest sincerity as he assured the doctor that there would be no difficulty; his best men would take on the job, and he would offer whatever assurances the doctor required. Small drops of sweat stood out on his upper lip.

Between the warmth of the fire and the hot tea, Jamie was sweating, too, and could have used a glass of wine. But the old gentleman stood up abruptly and, with a courteous bow to D'Eglise, came out from behind his desk and took Jamie by the arm, pulling him up and tugging him gently toward a doorway.

He ducked, just in time to avoid braining himself on a low archway, and found himself in a small, plain room, with bunches of drying herbs hung from its beams. What—

But before he could formulate any sort of question, the old man had got hold of his shirt and was pulling it free of his plaid. He tried to step back, but there was no room, and willy-nilly, he found himself set down on a stool, the old man's horny fingers pulling loose the bandages. The doctor made a deep sound of disapproval, then shouted something in which the words *"agua caliente"* were clearly discernible, back through the archway.

He daren't stand up and flee—and risk D'Eglise's new arrangement. And so he sat, burning with embarrassment, while the physician probed, prodded, and—a bowl of hot water having appeared—scrubbed at his back with something painfully rough. None of this bothered Jamie nearly as much as the appearance of Rebekah in the doorway, her dark eyebrows raised.

"My grandfather says your back is a mess," she told him, translating a remark from the old man.

"Thank ye. I didna ken that," he muttered in English, but then repeated the remark more politely in French. His cheeks burned with mortification, but a small, cold echo sounded in his heart. *"I see he's made a mess of you, boy."*

The surgeon at Fort William had said it when the soldiers dragged Jamie to him after the flogging, legs too wobbly to stand by himself. The surgeon had been right, and so was Dr. Hasdi, but it didn't mean Jamie wanted to hear it again.

Rebekah, evidently interested to see what her grandfather meant, came round behind Jamie. He stiffened, and the doctor poked him sharply in the back of the neck, making him bend forward again. The two Jews were discussing the spectacle in tones of detachment; he felt the girl's small, soft fingers trace a line between his ribs and nearly shot off the stool, his skin erupting in goose flesh.

"Jamie?" Ian's voice came from the hallway, sounding worried. "Are ye all right?"

"Aye!" he managed, half strangled. "Don't—ye needn't come in."

"Your name is Jamie?" Rebekah was now in front of him, leaning down to look into his face. Her own was alive with interest and concern. "James?"

"Aye. James." He clenched his teeth as the doctor dug a little harder, clicking his tongue.

"Diego," she said, smiling at him. "That's what it would be in Spanish—or Ladino. And your friend?"

"He's called Ian. That's"—he groped for a moment and found the English equivalent—"John. That would be . . ."

"Juan. Diego and Juan." She touched him gently on the bare shoulder. "You're friends? Brothers? I can see you come from the same place—where is that?"

"Friends. From . . . Scotland. The—the—Highlands. A place called Lallybroch." He'd spoken unwarily, and a pang shot through him at the name, sharper than whatever the doctor was scraping his back with. He looked away; the girl's face was too close—he didn't want her to see.

She didn't move away. Instead, she crouched gracefully beside him and took his hand. Hers was very warm, and the hairs on his wrist rose in response, in spite of what the doctor was doing to his back.

"It will be done soon," she promised. "He's cleaning the infected parts; he says they will scab over cleanly now and stop draining." A gruff question from the doctor. "He asks, do you have fever at night? Bad dreams?"

Startled, he looked back at her, but her face showed only compassion. Her hand tightened on his in reassurance.

"I . . . yes. Sometimes."

A grunt from the doctor, more words, and Rebekah let go his hand with a little pat and went out, skirts a-rustle. He closed his eyes and tried to keep the scent of her in his mind—he couldn't keep it in his nose, as the doctor was now anointing him with something vile-smelling. He could smell himself, too, and his jaw prickled with embarrassment; he reeked of stale sweat, campfire smoke, and fresh blood.

He could hear D'Eglise and Ian talking in the parlor, low-voiced, discussing whether to come and rescue him. He would have called out to them, save that he couldn't bear the captain to see . . . He pressed his lips together tight. Aye, well, it was nearly done; he could tell from the doctor's slower movements, almost gentle now.

"Rebekah!" the doctor called, impatient, and the girl appeared an instant later, a small cloth bundle in one hand. The doctor let off a short burst of words, then pressed a thin cloth of some sort over Jamie's back; it stuck to the nasty ointment.

"Grandfather says the cloth will protect your shirt until the ointment is absorbed," she told him. "By the time it falls off—don't peel it off, let it come off by itself—the wounds will be scabbed, but the scabs should be soft and not crack."

The doctor took his hand off Jamie's shoulder, and Jamie shot to his feet, looking round for his shirt. Rebekah handed it to him. Her eyes were fastened on his naked chest, and he was—for the first time in his life—embarrassed by the fact that he possessed nipples. An extraordinary but not unpleasant tingle made the curly hairs on his body stand up.

"Thank you—ah, I mean . . . *gracias, señor.*" His face was flaming, but he bowed to the doctor with as much grace as he could muster. "*Muchas gracias.*"

"*De nada,*" the old man said gruffly, with a dismissive wave of one hand. He pointed at the small bundle in his granddaughter's hand. "Drink. No fever. No dream." And then, surprisingly, he smiled.

"*Shalom,*" he said, and made a shooing gesture.

D'EGLISE, LOOKING PLEASED with the new job, left Ian and Jamie at a large tavern called *Le Poulet Gai,* where some of the other mercenaries were enjoying themselves—in various ways. The Cheerful Chicken most assuredly did boast a brothel on the upper floor, and slatternly women in various degrees of undress wandered freely through the lower rooms, picking up new customers with whom they vanished upstairs.

The two tall young Scots provoked a certain amount of interest from the women, but when Ian solemnly turned his empty purse inside out in front of them—he having put his money inside his shirt for safety—they left the lads alone.

"Couldna look at one of those," Ian said, turning his back on the whores and devoting himself to his ale. "Not after seein' the wee Jewess up close. Did ye ever seen anything like?"

Jamie shook his head, deep in his own drink. It was sour and fresh and went down a treat, parched as he was from the ordeal in Dr. Hasdi's surgery. He could still smell the ghost of Rebekah's scent, vanilla and roses, a fugitive fragrance among the reeks of the tavern. He fumbled in his sporran, bringing out the little cloth bundle Rebekah had given him.

"She said—well, the doctor said—I was to drink this. How, d'ye think?" The bundle held a mixture of broken leaves, small sticks, and a coarse powder, and smelled strongly of something he'd never smelled before. Not bad; just odd.

Ian frowned at it. "Well . . . ye'd brew a tea of it, I suppose," he said. "How else?"

"I havena got anything to brew it in," Jamie said. "I was thinkin' . . . maybe put it in the ale?"

"Why not?"

IAN WASN'T PAYING much attention; he was watching Mathieu Pig-face, who was standing against a wall, summoning whores as they passed by, looking them up and down, and occasionally fingering the merchandise before sending each one on with a smack on the rear.

He wasn't really tempted—the women scairt him, to be honest—but he was curious. If he ever *should* . . . how did ye start? Just grab, like Mathieu was doing, or did ye need to ask about the price first, to be sure you could afford it? And was it proper to bargain, like ye did for a loaf of bread or a flitch of bacon, or would the woman kick ye in the privates and find someone less mean?

He shot a glance at Jamie, who, after a bit of choking, had got his herbed ale down all right and was looking a little glazed. He didn't think Jamie knew, either, but he didn't want to ask, just in case he did.

"I'm goin' to the privy," Jamie said abruptly, and stood up. He looked pale.

"Have ye got the shits?"

"Not yet." With this ominous remark, he was off, bumping into tables in his haste, and Ian followed, pausing long enough to thriftily drain the last of Jamie's ale as well as his own.

Mathieu had found one he liked; he leered at Ian and said something obnoxious as he ushered his choice toward the stairs. Ian smiled cordially and said something much worse in *Gàidhlig*.

By the time Ian got to the yard at the back of the tavern, Jamie had disappeared. Figuring Jamie would be back as soon as he rid himself of his trouble, Ian leaned tranquilly against the back wall of the building, enjoying the cool night air and watching the folk in the yard.

There were a couple of torches burning, stuck in the ground, and it looked a bit like a painting he'd seen of the Last Judgment, with angels on the one side blowing trumpets, and sinners on the other going down to hell in a tangle of naked limbs and bad behavior. It was mostly sinners out here, though now and then he thought he saw an angel floating past the corner of his eye. He licked his lips thoughtfully, wondering what was in the stuff Dr. Hasdi had given Jamie.

Jamie himself emerged from the privy at the far side of the yard, looking a little more settled in himself. Spotting Ian, he made his way through the small knots of drinkers sitting on the ground singing and the others wandering to and fro, smiling vaguely as they looked for something, not knowing what they were looking for.

Ian was seized by a sudden sense of revulsion, almost terror: a fear that he would never see Scotland again, would die here, among strangers.

"We should go home," he said abruptly, as soon as Jamie was in earshot. "As soon as we've finished this job."

"Home?" Jamie looked strangely at Ian, as though he were speaking some incomprehensible language.

"Ye've business there, and so have I. We—"

A skelloch and the thud and clatter of a falling table with its burden of dishes interrupted them. The back door of the tavern burst open and a woman ran out, yelling in a sort of French that Ian didn't understand but knew fine was bad words from the tone of it. Similar words in a loud male voice, and Mathieu charged out after her.

He caught her by the shoulder, spun her round, and cracked her across the face with the back of one meaty hand. Ian flinched at the sound, and Jamie's hand tightened on his wrist.

"What—" Jamie began, but then stopped dead.

"Putain de . . . merde . . . tu fais . . . chien," Mathieu panted, slapping her with each word. She shrieked some more, trying to get away, but he had her by the arm and now jerked her round and pushed her hard in the back, knocking her to her knees.

Jamie's hand loosened, and Ian grabbed his arm, tight.

"Don't," he said tersely, and yanked Jamie back into the shadow.

"I wasn't," Jamie said, but under his breath and not noticing much what he was saying, because his eyes were fixed on what was happening, as much as Ian's were.

The light from the door spilled over the woman, glowing off her hanging breasts, bared in the ripped neck of her shift. Glowing off her wide round buttocks, too; Mathieu had shoved her skirts up to her waist and was behind her, jerking at his flies one-handed, the other hand twisted in her hair so her head pulled back, throat straining and her face white-eyed as a panicked horse.

"Pute!" he said, and gave her arse a loud smack, open-handed. "Nobody says no to me!" He'd got his cock out now, in his hand, and shoved it into the woman with a violence that made her hurdies wobble and knotted Ian from knees to neck.

"Merde," Jamie said, still under his breath. Other men and a couple of women had come out into the yard and were gathered round with the others, enjoying the spectacle as Mathieu set to work in a businesslike manner. He let go of the woman's hair in order to grasp her by the hips, and her head hung down, hair hiding her face. She grunted with each thrust, panting bad words that made the onlookers laugh.

Ian was shocked—and shocked as much at his own arousal as at what Mathieu was doing. He'd not seen open coupling before, only the heaving and giggling of things happening under a blanket, now and then a wee flash of pale flesh. This . . . He ought to look away, he knew that fine. But he didn't.

Jamie took in a breath, but no telling whether he meant to say something. Mathieu threw back his big head and howled like a wolf, and the watchers all cheered. Then his face convulsed, gapped teeth showing in a grin like a skull's, and he made a noise like a pig gives out when you knock it clean on the head and collapsed on top of the whore.

The whore squirmed out from under his bulk, abusing him roundly. Ian understood what she was saying now and would have been shocked anew if he'd had any capacity for being shocked left. She hopped up, evidently not hurt, and kicked Mathieu in the ribs once, then twice, but having no shoes on, she didn't hurt him. She reached for the purse still tied at his waist, stuck her hand in, and grabbed a handful of coins, then kicked him once more for luck and stomped off into the house, holding up the neck of her shift. Mathieu lay sprawled on the ground, his breeks around his thighs, laughing and wheezing.

Ian heard Jamie swallow and realized he was still gripping Jamie's arm. Jamie didn't seem to have noticed. Ian let go. His face was burning all the way down to the middle of his chest, and he didn't think it was just torchlight on Jamie's face, either.

"Let's . . . go someplace else," he said.

"I WISH WE'D . . . done something," Jamie blurted. They hadn't spoken at all after leaving *Le Poulet Gai*. They'd walked clear to the other end of the street and down a side alley, eventually coming to rest in a small tavern, fairly quiet. Juanito and Raoul were there, dicing with some locals, but gave Ian and Jamie no more than a glance.

"I dinna see what we *could* have done," Ian said reasonably. "I mean, we could maybe have taken on Mathieu together and got off with only bein' maimed. But ye ken it would ha' started a kebbie-lebbie, wi' all the others there." He hesitated and gave Jamie a quick glance before returning his gaze to his cup. "And . . . she *was* a whore. I mean, she wasna a—"

"I ken what ye mean." Jamie cut him off. "Aye, ye're right. And she did go with the man, to start. God knows what he did to make her take against him, but there's likely plenty to choose from. I wish—ah, feck it. D'ye want something to eat?"

Ian shook his head. The barmaid brought them a jug of wine, glanced at them, and dismissed them as negligible. It was rough wine that took the skin off the insides of your mouth, but it had a decent taste to it, under the resin fumes, and wasn't too much watered. Jamie drank deep and faster than he generally did; he was uneasy in his skin, prickling and irritable, and wanted the feeling to go away.

There were a few women in the place, not many. Jamie had to think that whoring maybe wasn't a profitable business, wretched as most of the poor creatures looked, raddled and half toothless. Maybe it wore them down, having to . . . He turned away from the thought and, finding the jug empty, waved to the barmaid for another.

Juanito gave a joyful whoop and said something in Ladino. Looking in that direction, Jamie saw one of the whores who'd been lurking in the shadows come gliding purposefully in, bending down to give Juanito a congratulatory kiss as he scooped in his winnings. Jamie snorted a little, trying to blow the smell of her out of his neb—she'd passed by close enough that he'd got a good whiff of her, a stink of rancid sweat and dead fish. Alexandre had told him that was from unclean privates, and he believed it.

He went back to the wine. Ian was matching him, cup for cup, and likely for the same reason. His friend wasn't usually irritable or crankit, but if he was well put out, he'd often stay that way until the next dawn—a good sleep erased his bad temper, but 'til then you didn't want to rile him.

He shot a sidelong glance at Ian. He couldn't tell Ian about Jenny. He just . . . couldn't. But neither could he think about her, left alone at Lallybroch . . . maybe with ch—

"Oh, God," he said, under his breath. "No. Please. No."

"Dinna come back," Murtagh had said, and plainly meant it. Well, he *would* go back—but not yet a while. It wouldn't help his sister, him going back just now and bringing Randall and the redcoats straight to her like flies to a fresh-killed deer . . . He shoved that analogy hastily out of sight, horrified. The truth was, it made him sick with shame to think about Jenny, and he tried not to—and was the more ashamed because he mostly succeeded.

Ian's gaze was fixed on another of the harlots. She was old, in her thirties at least, but had most of her teeth and was cleaner than most. She was flirting with Juanito and Raoul, too, and Jamie wondered whether she'd mind if she found out they were Jews. Maybe a whore couldn't afford to be choosy.

His treacherous mind at once presented him with a picture of his sister, obliged to follow that walk of life to feed herself, made to take any man who . . . Blessed Mother, what would the folk, the tenants, the servants, do to her if they found out what had happened? The talk . . . He shut his eyes tight, hoping to block the vision.

"That one's none sae bad," Ian said meditatively, and Jamie opened his eyes. The better-looking whore had bent over Juanito, deliberately rubbing her breast against his warty ear. "If she doesna mislike a Jew, maybe she'd . . ."

The blood flamed up in Jamie's face.

"If ye've got any thought to my sister, ye're no going to—to—pollute yourself wi' a French whore!"

Ian's face went blank but then flooded with color in turn.

"Oh, aye? And if I said your sister wasna worth it?"

Jamie's fist caught him in the eye and he flew backward, overturning the bench and crashing into the next table. Jamie scarcely noticed, the agony in his hand shooting fire and brimstone from his crushed knuckles up his forearm. He rocked to and fro, injured hand clutched between his thighs, cursing freely in three languages.

Ian sat on the floor, bent over, holding his eye and breathing through his mouth in short gasps. After a minute, he straightened up. His eye was puffing already, leaking tears down his lean cheek. He got up, shaking his head slowly, and put the bench back in place. Then he sat down, picked up his cup and took a deep gulp, put it down and blew out his breath. He took the snot-rag Jamie was holding out to him and dabbed at his eye.

"Sorry," Jamie managed. The agony in his hand was beginning to subside, but the anguish in his heart wasn't.

"Aye," Ian said quietly, not meeting his eye. "I wish we'd done something, too. Ye want to share a bowl o' stew?"

TWO DAYS LATER, they set off for Paris. After some thought, D'Eglise had decided that Rebekah and her maid, Marie, would travel by coach, escorted by Jamie and Ian. D'Eglise and the rest of the troop would take the money, with some men sent ahead in small groups to wait, both to check the road and so that they could ride in shifts, not stopping anywhere along the way. The women obviously would have to stop, but if they had nothing valuable with them, they'd be in no danger.

It was only when they went to collect the women at Dr. Hasdi's residence that they learned the Torah scroll and its custodian, a sober-looking man of middle age introduced to them as Monsieur Peretz, would be traveling with Rebekah. "I trust my greatest treasures to you, gentlemen," the doctor told them, through his granddaughter, and gave them a formal little bow.

"May you find us worthy of trust, lord," Jamie managed in halting Hebrew, and Ian bowed with great solemnity, hand on his heart. Dr. Hasdi looked from one to the other, gave a small nod, and then stepped forward to kiss Rebekah on the forehead.

"Go with God, child," he whispered, in something close enough to Spanish that Jamie understood it.

ALL WENT WELL for the first day and the first night. The autumn weather held fine, with no more than a pleasant tang of chill in the air, and the horses were sound. Dr. Hasdi had provided Jamie with a purse to cover the expenses of the journey, and they all ate decently and slept at a very respectable inn—Ian being sent in first to inspect the premises and insure against any nasty surprises.

The next day dawned cloudy, but the wind came up and blew the clouds away before noon, leaving the sky clean and brilliant as a sapphire overhead. Jamie was riding in the van, Ian post, and the coach was making good time, in spite of a rutted, winding road.

As they reached the top of a small rise, though, Jamie brought his horse to a sudden stop, raising a hand to halt the coach, and Ian reined up alongside him. A small stream had run through the roadbed in the dip below, making a bog some ten feet across.

"What—" Jamie began, but was interrupted. The driver had pulled his team up for an instant, but at a peremptory shout from inside the coach, now snapped the reins over the horses' backs and the coach lunged forward, narrowly missing Jamie's horse, which shied violently, flinging its rider off into the bushes.

"Jamie! Are ye all right?" Torn between concern for his friend and for his duty, Ian held his horse, glancing to and fro.

"Stop them! Get them! *Ifrinn!*" Jamie scuttled crabwise out of the weeds, face scratched and bright red with fury. Ian didn't wait but kicked his horse and lit out in pursuit of the heavy coach, this now lurching from side to side as it ran down into the boggy bottom. Shrill feminine cries of protest from inside were drowned by the driver's exclamation of *"Ladrones!"*

That was one word he kent in Spanish—"thieves." One of the *ladrones* was already skittering up the side of the coach like an eight-legged cob, and the driver promptly dived off the box, hit the ground, and ran for it.

"Coward!" Ian bellowed, and gave out with a Hieland screech that set the coach horses dancing, flinging their heads to and fro, and giving the would-be kidnapper fits with the reins. He forced his own horse—which hadn't liked the screeching any better than the coach horses did—through the narrow gap between the brush and the coach and, as he came even with the driver, had his pistol out. He drew down on the fellow—a young chap with long yellow hair—and shouted at him to pull up.

The man glanced at him, crouched low, and slapped the reins on the horses' backs, shouting at them in a voice like iron. Ian fired and missed—but the delay had let Jamie catch them up; he saw Jamie's red head poke up as he climbed the back of the coach, and there were more screams from inside as Jamie pounded across the roof and launched himself at the yellow-haired driver.

Leaving that bit of trouble to Jamie to deal with, Ian kicked his horse forward, meaning to get ahead and seize the reins, but another of the thieves had beat him to it and was hauling down on one horse's head. Aye, well, it worked once. Ian inflated his lungs as far as they'd go and let rip.

The coach horses bolted in a spray of mud. Jamie and the yellow-haired driver fell off the box, and the whoreson in the road disappeared, possibly trampled into the mire. Ian hoped so. Blood in his eye, he reined up his own agitated mount, drew his broadsword, and charged across the road, shrieking like a *ban-sidhe* and slashing wildly. Two thieves stared up at him openmouthed, then broke and ran for it.

He chased them a wee bit into the brush, but the going was too thick for his horse, and he turned back to find Jamie rolling about in the road, earnestly hammering the yellow-haired laddie. Ian hesitated—help him, or see to the coach? A loud crash and horrible screams decided him at once, and he charged down the road.

The coach, driver-less, had run off the road, hit the bog, and fallen sideways into a ditch. From the clishmaclaver coming from inside, he thought the women were likely all right and, swinging off his horse, wrapped the reins hastily round a tree and went to take care of the coach horses before they killed themselves.

It took no little while to disentangle the mess single-handed—luckily the horses had not managed to damage themselves significantly—and his efforts were not aided by the emergence from the coach of two agitated and very disheveled women carrying on in an incomprehensible mix of French and Ladino.

Just as well, he thought, giving them a vague wave of a hand he could ill spare at the moment. *It wouldna help to hear what they're saying.* Then he picked up the word "dead" and changed his mind. Monsieur Peretz was normally so silent that Ian had in fact forgotten his presence, in the confusion of the moment. He was even more silent now, Ian learned, having broken his neck when the coach overturned.

"Oh, Jesus," he said, running to look. But the man was undeniably dead, and the horses were still creating a ruckus, slipping and stamping in the mud of the ditch. He was too busy for a bit to worry about how Jamie was faring, but as he got the second horse detached from the coach and safely tethered to a tree, he did begin to wonder where the wean was.

He didn't think it safe to leave the women; the banditti might come back, and a right numpty he'd look if they did. There was no sign of their driver, who had evidently abandoned them out of fright. He told the ladies to sit down under a sycamore tree and gave them his canteen to drink from, and, after a bit, they stopped talking quite so fast.

"Where is Diego?" Rebekah said, quite intelligibly.

"Och, he'll be along presently," Ian said, hoping it was true. He was beginning to be worrit himself.

"Perhaps he's been killed, too," said the maidservant, who shot an ill-tempered glare at her mistress. "How would you feel then?"

"I'm sure he wouldn't—I mean, he's not. I'm sure," Rebekah repeated, not sounding all that sure.

She was right, though; no sooner had Ian decided to march the women back along the road to have a keek when Jamie came shambling around the bend and sank down in the dry grass, closing his eyes.

"Are you all right?" Rebekah asked, bending down anxiously to look at him from under the brim of her straw traveling hat. He didn't look very peart, Ian thought.

"Aye, fine." He touched the back of his head, wincing slightly. "Just a wee dunt on the heid. The fellow who fell down in the road," he explained to Ian, closing his eyes again. "He got up again and hit me from behind. Didna knock me clean out, but it distracted me for a wee bit, and when I got my wits back, they'd both gone—the fellow that hit me, and the one I was hittin'."

"Mmphm," said Ian, and, squatting in front of his friend, thumbed up one of Jamie's eyelids and peered intently into the bloodshot blue eye behind it. He had no idea what to look for, but he'd seen Père Renault do that, after which he usually applied leeches somewhere. As it was, both that eye and the other one looked fine to him; just as well, as he hadn't any leeches. He handed Jamie the canteen and went to look the horses over.

"Two of them are sound enough," he reported, coming back. "The light bay's lame. Did the bandits take your horse? And what about the driver?"

Jamie looked surprised.

"I forgot I had a horse," he confessed. "I dinna ken about the driver—didna see him lyin' in the road, at least." He glanced vaguely round. "Where's Monsieur Pickle?"

"Dead. Stay there, aye?"

Ian sighed, got up, and loped back down the road, where there was no sign of the driver, though he walked to and fro calling for a while. Fortunately, he did come across Jamie's horse peaceably cropping grass by the verge. He rode it back and found the women on their feet, discussing something in low voices, now and then looking down the road or standing on their toes in a vain attempt to see through the trees.

Jamie was still sitting on the ground, eyes closed—but at least upright.

"Can ye ride, man?" Ian asked softly, squatting down by his friend. To his relief, Jamie opened his eyes at once.

"Oh, aye. Ye're thinkin' we should ride into Saint-Aulaye and send someone back to do something about the coach and Peretz?"

"What else is there to do?"

"Nothing I can think of. I dinna suppose we can take him with us." Jamie got to his feet, swaying a little but without needing to hold on to the tree. "Can the women ride, d'ye think?"

Marie could, it turned out—at least a little. Rebekah had never been on a horse. After more discussion than Ian would have believed possible on the subject, he got the late M. Peretz decently laid out on the coach's seat with a handkerchief over his face against flies, and the rest of them finally mounted: Jamie on his horse with the Torah scroll in its canvas wrappings bound behind his saddle—between the profanation of its being touched by a Gentile and the prospect of its being left in the coach for anyone happening by to find, the women had reluctantly allowed the former—the maid on one of the coach horses, with a pair of saddlebags fashioned from the covers of the coach's seats, these filled with as much of the women's luggage as they could cram in, and Ian with Rebekah on the saddle before him.

Rebekah looked like a wee dolly, but she was surprisingly solid, as he found when she put her foot in his hands and he tossed her up into the saddle. She didn't manage to swing her leg over and instead lay across the saddle like a dead deer, waving her arms and legs in agitation. Wrestling her into an upright position and getting himself set behind her left him red-faced and sweating, far more than dealing with the horses had.

Jamie gave him a raised eyebrow, as much jealousy as amusement in it, and he gave Jamie a squinted eye in return and put his arm round Rebekah's waist to settle her against him, hoping that he didn't stink too badly.

IT WAS DARK by the time they made it into Saint-Aulaye and found an inn that could provide them with two rooms. Ian talked to the landlord and arranged that someone should go in the morning to retrieve M. Peretz's body and bury it; the women weren't happy about the lack of proper preparation of the body, but as they insisted he must be buried before the next sundown, there wasn't much else to be done. Then he inspected the women's room, looked under the beds, rattled the shutters in a confident manner, and bade them good night. They looked that wee bit frazzled.

Going back to the other room, he heard a sweet chiming sound and found Jamie on his knees, pushing the bundle that contained the Torah scroll under the single bed.

"That'll do," he said, sitting back on his heels with a sigh. He looked nearly as done up as the women, Ian thought, but didn't say so.

"I'll go and have some supper sent up," he said. "I smelled a joint roasting. Some of that, and maybe—"

"Whatever they've got," Jamie said fervently. "Bring it all."

THEY ATE HEARTILY, and separately, in their rooms. Jamie was beginning to feel that the second helping of *tarte tatin* with clotted cream had been a mistake, when Rebekah came into the men's room, followed by her maid carrying a small tray with a jug on it, wisping aromatic steam. Jamie sat up straight, restraining a small cry as pain flashed through his head. Rebekah frowned at him, gull-winged brows lowering in concern.

"Your head hurts very much, Diego?"

"No, it's fine. No but a wee bang on the heid." He was sweating and his wame was wobbly, but he pressed his hands flat on the table and was sure he looked steady. She appeared not to agree and came close, bending down to gaze searchingly into his eyes.

"I don't think so," she said. "You look . . . clammy."

"Oh. Aye?" he said, rather feebly.

"If she means ye resemble a fresh-shucked clam, then, aye, ye do," Ian informed him. "Shocked, ken? All pale and wet and—"

"I ken what clammy means, aye?" He glowered at Ian, who gave him half a grin—damn, he must look awful; Ian was actually worried. He swallowed, groping for something witty to say in reassurance, but his gorge rose suddenly and he was obliged to shut both mouth and eyes tightly, concentrating fiercely to make it go back down.

"Tea," Rebekah was saying firmly. She took the jug from her maid and poured a cup, then folded Jamie's hands about it and, holding his hands with her own, guided the cup to his mouth. "Drink. It will help."

He drank, and it did. At least he felt less queasy at once. He recognized the taste of the tea, though he thought this cup had a few other things in it, too.

"Again." Another cup was presented; he managed to drink this one alone, and by the time it was down, he felt a good bit better. His head still throbbed with his heartbeat, but the pain seemed to be standing a little apart from him, somehow.

"You shouldn't be left alone for a while," Rebekah informed him, and sat down, sweeping her skirts elegantly around her ankles. He opened his mouth to say that he wasn't alone, Ian was there—but caught Ian's eye in time and stopped.

"The bandits," she was saying to Ian, her pretty brow creased, "who do you think that they were?"

"Ah . . . well, depends. If they kent who ye were and wanted to abduct ye, that's one thing. But could be they were no but random thieves and saw the coach and thought they'd chance it for what they might get. Ye didna recognize any of them, did ye?"

Her eyes sprang wide. They weren't quite the color of Annalise's, Jamie thought hazily. A softer brown . . . like the breast feathers on a grouse.

"Know who I was?" she whispered. "Wanted to abduct me?" She swallowed. "You . . . think that's possible?" She gave a little shudder.

"Well, I dinna ken, of course. Here, *a nighean,* ye ought to have a wee nip of that tea, I'm thinkin'." Ian stretched out a long arm for the jug, but she moved it back, shaking her head.

"No, it's medicine—and Diego needs it. Don't you?" she said, leaning forward to peer earnestly into Jamie's eyes. She'd taken off the hat but had her hair tucked up—mostly—in a lacy white cap with pink ribbon. He nodded obediently.

"Marie—bring some brandy, please. The shock . . ." She swallowed again and wrapped her arms briefly around herself. Jamie noticed the way it pushed her breasts up, so they swelled just a little above her stays. There was a bit of tea left in his cup; he drank it automatically.

Marie came with the brandy and poured a glass for Rebekah—then one for Ian, at Rebekah's gesture, and when Jamie made a small polite noise in his throat, half-filled his cup, pouring in more tea on top of it. The taste was peculiar, but he didn't really mind. The pain had gone off to the far side of the room; he could see it sitting over there, a wee glowering sort of purple thing with a bad-tempered expression on its face. He laughed at it, and Ian frowned at him.

"What are ye giggling at?"

Jamie couldn't think how to describe the pain beastie, so he just shook his head, which proved a mistake—the pain looked suddenly gleeful and shot back into his head with a noise like tearing cloth. The room spun and he clutched the table with both hands.

"Diego!" Chairs scraped and there was a good bit of clishmaclaver that he paid no attention to. Next thing he knew, he was lying on the bed, staring at the ceiling beams. One of them seemed to be twining slowly, like a vine growing.

". . . and he told the captain that there was someone among the Jews who kent about . . ." Ian's voice was soothing, earnest and slow so Rebekah would understand him—though Jamie thought she maybe understood more than she said. The twining beam was slowly sprouting small green leaves, and he had the faint thought that this was unusual, but a great sense of tranquillity had come over him and he didn't mind it a bit.

Rebekah was saying something now, her voice soft and worried, and with some effort he turned his head to look. She was leaning over the table toward Ian, and he had both big hands wrapped round hers, reassuring her that he and Jamie would let no harm come to her.

A different face came suddenly into his view: the maid, Marie, frowning down at him. She rudely pulled back his eyelid and peered into his eye, so close he could smell the garlic on her breath. He blinked hard, and she let go with a small "hmph!" then turned to say something to Rebekah, who replied in quick Ladino. The maid shook her head dubiously but left the room.

Her face didn't leave with her, though. He could still see it, frowning down at him from above. It had become attached to the leafy beam, and he now realized that there was a snake up there, a serpent with a woman's head, and an apple in its mouth—that couldn't be right, surely it should be a pig?—and it came slithering down the wall and right over his chest, pressing the apple close to his face. It smelled wonderful, and he wanted to bite it, but before he could, he felt the weight of the snake change, going soft and heavy, and he arched his back a little, feeling the distinct imprint of big round breasts squashing against him. The snake's tail—she was mostly a woman now, but her back end seemed still to be snake-ish—was delicately stroking the inside of his thigh.

He made a very high-pitched noise, and Ian came hurriedly to the bed.

"Are ye all right, man?"

"I—oh. Oh! Oh, Jesus, do that again."

"Do *what*—" Ian was beginning, when Rebekah appeared, putting a hand on Ian's arm.

"Don't worry," she said, looking intently at Jamie. "He's all right. The medicine—it gives men strange dreams."

"He doesna look like he's asleep," Ian said dubiously.

In fact, Jamie was squirming—or thought he was squirming—on the bed, trying to persuade the lower half of the snake woman to change, too. He *was* panting; he could hear himself.

"It's a waking dream," Rebekah said reassuringly. "Come, leave him. He'll fall quite asleep in a bit, you'll see."

Jamie didn't think he'd fallen asleep, but it was evidently some time later that he emerged from a remarkable tryst with the snake demon—he didn't know how he knew she was a demon, but clearly she was—who had not changed her lower half but had a very womanly mouth about her. The tryst also included a number of her friends, these being small female demons who licked his ears—and other things—with great enthusiasm.

He turned his head on the pillow to allow one of these better access and saw, with no sense of surprise, Ian kissing Rebekah. The brandy bottle had fallen over, empty, and Jamie seemed to see the wraith of its perfume rise swirling through the air like smoke, wrapping the two of them in a mist shot with rainbows.

He closed his eyes again, the better to attend to the snake lady, who now had a number of new and interesting acquaintances. When he opened his eyes some time later, Ian and Rebekah were gone.

At one point he heard Ian give a sort of strangled cry and wondered dimly what had happened, but it didn't seem important, and the thought drifted away. He slept.

HE WOKE FEELING limp as a frostbitten cabbage leaf, but the pain in his head was gone. He just lay there for a bit, enjoying the feeling. It was dark in the room, and it was some time before he realized from the smell of brandy that Ian was lying beside him.

Memory came back to him. It took a little while to disentangle the real memories from the memory of dreams, but he was quite sure he'd seen Ian embracing Rebekah—and her, him. What the devil had happened *then*?

Ian wasn't asleep; he could tell. His friend lay rigid as one of the tomb figures in the crypt at Saint Denis, and his breathing was rapid and shaky, as though he'd just run a mile uphill. Jamie cleared his throat, and Ian jerked as though stabbed with a brooch pin.

"Aye, so?" he whispered, and Ian's breathing stopped abruptly. He swallowed audibly.

"If ye breathe a word of this to your sister," he said in an impassioned whisper, "I'll stab ye in your sleep, cut off your heid, and kick it to Arles and back."

Jamie didn't want to think about his sister, and he did want to hear about Rebekah, so he merely repeated, "Aye. So?"

Ian made a small grunting noise, indicative of thinking how best to begin, and turned over in his plaid, facing Jamie.

"Aye, well. Ye raved a bit about the naked she-devils ye were havin' it away with, and I didna think the lass should have to be hearing that manner o' thing, so I said we should go into the other room, and—"

"Was this before or after ye started kissing her?" Jamie asked.

Ian inhaled strongly through his nose. "After," he said tersely. "And she was kissin' me back, aye?"

"Aye, I noticed that. So then . . . ?" He could feel Ian squirming slowly, like a worm on a hook, but Jamie waited. It often took Ian a moment to find words, but it was usually worth waiting for. Certainly in this instance.

He was a little shocked—and frankly envious—and he did wonder what might happen when the lass's affianced discovered she wasn't a virgin, but he supposed the man might not find out; she seemed a clever lass. It might be wise to leave D'Eglise's troop, though, and head south, just in case . . .

"D'ye think it hurts a lot to be circumcised?" Ian asked suddenly.

"I do. How could it not?" His hand sought out his own member, protectively rubbing a thumb over the bit in question. True, it wasn't a very big bit, but . . .

"Well, they do it to wee bairns," Ian pointed out. "Canna be that bad, can it?"

"Mmphm," Jamie said, unconvinced, though fairness made him add, "Aye, well, and they did it to Christ, too."

"Aye?" Ian sounded startled. "Aye, I suppose so—I hadna thought o' that."

"Well, ye dinna think of Him bein' a Jew, do ye? But He was, to start."

There was a momentary, meditative silence before Ian spoke again.

"D'ye think Jesus ever did it? Wi' a lass, I mean, before he went to preachin'?"

"I think Père Renault's goin' to have ye for blasphemy, next thing."

Ian twitched, as though worried that the priest might be lurking in the shadows.

"Père Renault's nowhere near here, thank God."

"Aye, but ye'll need to confess yourself to him, won't ye?"

Ian shot upright, clutching his plaid around him.

"What?"

"Ye'll go to hell, else, if ye get killed," Jamie pointed out, feeling rather smug. There was moonlight through the window and he could see Ian's face drawn in anxious thought, his deep-set eyes darting right and left from Scylla to Charybdis. Suddenly Ian turned his head toward Jamie, having spotted the possibility of an open channel between the threats of hell and Père Renault.

"I'd only go to hell if it was a mortal sin," he said. "If it's no but venial, I'd only have to spend a thousand years or so in purgatory. That wouldna be so bad."

"Of course it's a mortal sin," Jamie said, cross. "Anybody kens fornication's a mortal sin, ye numpty."

"Aye, but . . ." Ian made a "wait a bit" gesture with one hand, deep in thought. "To be a *mortal* sin, though, ye've got the three things. Requirements, like." He put up an index finger. "It's got to be seriously wrong." Middle finger. "Ye've got to *know* it's seriously wrong." Ring finger. "And ye've got to give full consent to it. That's the way of it, aye?" He put his hand down and looked at Jamie, brows raised.

"Aye, and which part of that did ye not do? The full consent? Did she rape ye?" He was chaffing, but Ian turned his face away in a manner that gave him a sudden doubt. "Ian?"

"Noo . . ." his friend said, but it sounded doubtful, too. "It wasna like that—exactly. I meant more the seriously wrong part. I dinna think it was . . ." His voice trailed off.

Jamie flung himself over, raised on one elbow.

"Ian," he said, steel in his voice. "What did ye *do* to the lass? If ye took her maidenheid, it's seriously wrong. Especially with her betrothed. Oh—" A thought occurred to him, and he leaned a little closer, lowering his voice. "Was she no a virgin? Maybe that's different." If the lass was an out-and-out wanton, perhaps . . . she probably *did* write poetry, come to think . . .

Ian had now folded his arms on his knees and was resting his forehead on them, his voice muffled in the folds of his plaid. ". . . dinna ken . . ." emerged in a strangled croak.

Jamie reached out and dug his fingers hard into Ian's calf. His friend unfolded with a startled cry that made someone in a distant chamber shift and grunt in their sleep.

"What d'ye mean ye dinna ken? How could ye not notice?" he gibed.

"Ah . . . well . . . she . . . erm . . . she did me wi' her hand," Ian blurted. "Before I could . . . well."

"Oh." Jamie rolled onto his back, somewhat deflated in spirit, if not in flesh. His cock seemed still to want to hear the details.

"Is that seriously wrong?" Ian asked, turning his face toward Jamie again. "Or—well, I canna say I really gave full *consent* to it, because that wasna what I had in mind doing at all, but . . ."

"I think ye're headed for the Bad Place," Jamie assured him. "Ye meant to do it, whether ye managed or not. And how did it happen, come to that? Did she just . . . take hold?"

Ian let out a long, long sigh and sank his head in his hands. He looked as though it hurt.

"Well, we kissed for a bit, and there was more brandy—lots more. She . . . er . . . she'd take a mouthful and kiss me and, er . . . put it into my mouth, and—"

"*Ifrinn!*"

"Will ye not say, 'Hell!' like that, please? I dinna want to think about it."

"Sorry. Go on. Did she let ye feel her breasts?"

"Just a bit. She wouldna take her stays off, but I could feel her nipples through her shift—did ye say something?"

"No," Jamie said with an effort. "What then?"

"Well, she put her hand under my kilt and then pulled it out again like she'd touched a snake."

"And had she?"

"She had, aye. She was shocked. Will ye no snort like that?" he said, annoyed. "Ye'll wake the whole house. It was because it wasna circumcised."

"Oh. Is that why she wouldna . . . er . . . the regular way?"

"She didna say so, but maybe. After a bit, though, she wanted to look at it, and that's when . . . well."

"Mmphm." Naked demons versus the chance of damnation or not, Jamie thought Ian had had well the best of it this evening. A thought occurred to him. "Why did ye ask if being circumcised hurts? Ye werena thinking of doing it, were ye? For her, I mean?"

"I wouldna say the thought hadna occurred to me," Ian admitted. "I mean . . . I thought I should maybe marry her, under the circumstances. But I suppose I couldna become a Jew, even if I got up the nerve to be circumcised—my mam would tear my heid off if I did."

"No, ye're right," Jamie agreed. "She would. *And* ye'd go to hell." The thought of the rare and delicate Rebekah churning butter in the yard of a Highland croft or waulking urine-soaked wool with her bare feet was slightly more ludicrous than the vision of Ian in a skullcap and whiskers— but not by much. "Besides, ye havena got any money, have ye?"

"A bit," Ian said thoughtfully. "Not enough to go and live in Timbuktu, though, and I'd have to go at least that far."

Jamie sighed and stretched, easing himself. A meditative silence fell— Ian no doubt contemplating perdition, Jamie reliving the better bits of his opium dreams but with Rebekah's face on the snake lady. Finally he broke the silence, turning to his friend.

"So . . . was it worth the chance of goin' to hell?"

Ian sighed long and deep once more, but it was the sigh of a man at peace with himself.

"Oh, aye."

JAMIE WOKE AT DAWN, feeling altogether well and in a much better frame of mind. Some kindly soul had brought a jug of sour ale and some bread and cheese. He refreshed himself with these as he dressed, pondering the day's work.

He'd have to collect a few men to go back and deal with the coach.

He thought the coach wasn't badly damaged; they might get it back up on the road again by noon. . . . How far might it be to Bonnes? That was the next town with an inn. If it was too far, or the coach too badly hurt, or he couldn't find a Jew to dispose decently of M. Peretz, they'd need to stay the night here again. He fingered his purse but thought he had enough for another night and the hire of men; the doctor had been generous.

He was beginning to wonder what was keeping Ian and the women. Though he kent women took more time to do anything than a man would, let alone getting dressed—well, they had stays and the like to fret with, after all . . . He sipped ale, contemplating a vision of Rebekah's stays and the very vivid images his mind had been conjuring ever since Ian's description of his encounter with the lass. He could all but see her nipples through the thin fabric of her shift, smooth and round as pebbles . . .

Ian burst through the door, wild-eyed, his hair standing on end.

"They're gone!"

Jamie choked on his ale.

"What? How?"

Ian understood what he meant and was already heading for the bed.

"No one took them. There's nay sign of a struggle, and their things are gone. The window's open, and the shutters aren't broken."

Jamie was on his knees alongside Ian, thrusting first his hands and then his head and shoulders under the bed. There was a canvas-wrapped bundle there, and he was flooded with a momentary relief—which disappeared the instant Ian dragged it into the light. It made a noise, but not the gentle chime of golden bells. It rattled, and when Jamie seized the corner of the canvas and unrolled it, the contents were shown to be naught but sticks and stones, these hastily wrapped in a woman's petticoat to give the bundle the appropriate bulk.

"Cramouille!" he said, this being the worst word he could think of on

short notice. And very appropriate, too, if what he thought had happened really had. He turned on Ian.

"She drugged me and seduced you, and her bloody maid stole in here and took the thing whilst ye had your fat heid buried in her . . . er . . ."

"Charms," Ian said succinctly, and flashed him a brief, evil grin. "Ye're only jealous. Where d'ye think they've gone?"

It was the truth, and Jamie abandoned any further recriminations, rising and strapping on his belt, hastily arranging dirk, sword, and ax in the process.

"Not to Paris, would be my guess. Come on, we'll ask the ostler."

The ostler confessed himself at a loss; he'd been the worse for drink in the hay shed, he said, and if someone had taken two horses from the shelter, he hadn't waked to see it.

"Aye, right," said Jamie, impatient, and, grabbing the man's shirtfront, lifted him off his feet and slammed him into the inn's stone wall. The man's head bounced once off the stones and he sagged in Jamie's grip, still conscious but dazed. Jamie drew his dirk left-handed and pressed the edge of it against the man's weathered throat.

"Try again," he suggested pleasantly. "I dinna care about the money they gave you—keep it. I want to know which way they went and when they left."

The man tried to swallow but abandoned the attempt when his Adam's apple hit the edge of the dirk.

"About three hours past moonrise," he croaked. "They went toward Bonnes. There's a crossroads no more than three miles from here," he added, now trying urgently to be helpful.

Jamie dropped him with a grunt. "Aye, fine," he said in disgust. "Ian—oh, ye've got them." For Ian had gone straight for their own horses while Jamie dealt with the ostler and was already leading one out, bridled, the saddle over his arm. "I'll settle the bill, then."

The women hadn't made off with his purse; that was something. Either Rebekah bat-Leah Hauberger had some vestige of conscience—which he doubted very much—or she just hadn't thought of it.

IT WAS STILL EARLY; the women had perhaps six hours' lead.

"Do we believe the ostler?" Ian asked, settling himself in the saddle.

Jamie dug in his purse, pulled out a copper penny, and flipped it, catching it on the back of his hand.

"Tails we do, heads we don't?" He took his hand away and peered at the coin. "Heads."

"Aye, but the road back is straight all the way through Yvrac," Ian pointed out. "And it's nay more than three miles to the crossroads, he said. Whatever ye want to say about the lass, she's no a fool."

Jamie considered that one for a moment, then nodded. Rebekah couldn't have been sure how much lead she'd have—and unless she'd been lying about her ability to ride (which he wouldn't put past her, but such things weren't easy to fake and she was gey clumsy in the saddle), she'd want to reach a place where the trail could be lost before her pursuers could catch up with her. Besides, the ground was still damp with dew; there might be a chance . . .

"Aye, come on, then."

LUCK WAS WITH THEM. No one had passed the inn during the late-night watches, and while the roadbed was trampled with hoof marks, the recent prints of the women's horses showed clear, edges still crumbling in the damp earth. Once sure they'd got upon the track, the men galloped for the crossroads, hoping to reach it before other travelers obscured the marks.

No such luck. Farm wagons were already on the move, loaded with produce headed for Parcoul or La Roche-Chalais, and the crossroads was a maze of ruts and hoofprints. But Jamie had the bright thought of sending Ian down the road that lay toward Parcoul, while he took the one toward La Roche-Chalais, catching up the incoming wagons and questioning the drivers. Within an hour, Ian came pelting back with the news that the women had been seen, riding slowly and cursing volubly at each other, toward Parcoul.

"And *that*," he said, panting for breath, "is not all."

"Aye? Well, tell me while we ride."

Ian did. He'd been hurrying back to find Jamie when he'd met Josef-from-Alsace, just short of the crossroads, come in search of them.

"D'Eglise was held up near La Teste-de-Buch," Ian reported in a shout. "The same band of men that attacked us at Bèguey—Alexandre and Raoul both recognized some of them. Jewish bandits."

Jamie was shocked and slowed for a moment to let Ian catch him up. "Did they get the dowry money?"

"No, but they had a hard fight. Three men wounded badly enough to need a surgeon, and Paul Martan lost two fingers of his left hand. D'Eglise pulled them into La Teste-de-Buch and sent Josef to see if all was well wi' us."

Jamie's heart bounced into his throat. "Jesus. Did ye tell him what happened?"

"I did not," Ian said tersely. "I told him we'd had an accident wi' the

coach, and ye'd gone ahead with the women; I was comin' back to fetch
something left behind."

"Aye, good." Jamie's heart dropped back into his chest. The last thing
he wanted was to have to tell the captain that they'd lost the girl and the
Torah scroll. And he'd be damned if he would.

THEY TRAVELED FAST, stopping only to ask questions now and
then, and by the time they pounded into the village of Aubeterre-sur-
Dronne, they were sure that their quarry lay no more than an hour ahead
of them—if the women had passed on through the village.

"Oh, those two?" said a woman, pausing in the act of scrubbing her
steps. She stood up slowly, stretching her back. "I saw them, yes. They
rode right by me and went down the lane there." She pointed.

"I thank you, madame," Jamie said, in his best Parisian French. "What
lies down that lane, please?"

She looked surprised that they didn't know and frowned a little at such
ignorance.

"Why, the chateau of the Vicomte Beaumont, to be sure!"

"To be sure," Jamie repeated, smiling at her, and Ian saw a dimple appear in her cheek in reply. *"Merci beaucoup, madame!"*

"WHAT THE DEVIL . . . ?" Ian murmured. Jamie reined up beside
him, pausing to look at the place. It was a small manor house, somewhat
run down but pretty in its bones. And the last place anyone would think
to look for a runaway Jewess, he'd say that for it.

"What shall we do now, d'ye think?" he asked, and Jamie shrugged and
kicked his horse.

"Go knock on the door and ask, I suppose."

Ian followed his friend up to the door, feeling intensely conscious of his
grubby clothes, sprouting beard, and general state of uncouthness. Such
concerns vanished, though, when Jamie's forceful knock was answered.

"Good day, gentlemen!" said the yellow-haired bugger Ian had last
seen locked in combat in the roadbed with Jamie the day before. The man
smiled broadly at them, cheerful despite an obvious black eye and a freshly
split lip. He was dressed in the height of fashion, in a plum velvet suit; his
hair was curled and powdered, and his yellow beard was neatly trimmed.
"I hoped we would see you again. Welcome to my home!" he said, stepping back and raising his hand in a gesture of invitation.

"I thank you, monsieur . . . ?" Jamie said slowly, giving Ian a sidelong glance. Ian lifted one shoulder in the ghost of a shrug. Did they have a choice?

The yellow-haired bugger bowed. "Pierre Robert Heriveaux d'Anton, Vicomte Beaumont, by the grace of the Almighty, for one more day. And you, gentlemen?"

"James Alexander Malcolm MacKenzie Fraser," Jamie said, with a good attempt at matching the other's grand manner. Only Ian would have noticed the faint hesitation or the slight tremor in his voice when he added, "Laird of Broch Tuarach."

"Ian Alastair Robert MacLeod Murray," Ian said, with a curt nod, and straightened his shoulders. "His . . . er . . . the laird's . . . tacksman."

"Come in, please, gentlemen." The yellow-haired bugger's eyes shifted just a little, and Ian heard the crunch of gravel behind them, an instant before he felt the prick of a dagger in the small of his back. No, they didn't have a choice.

Inside, they were relieved of their weapons, then escorted down a wide hallway and into a commodious parlor. The wallpaper was faded, and the furniture was good but shabby. By contrast, the big Turkey carpet on the floor glowed like it was woven from jewels. A big roundish thing in the middle was green and gold and red, and concentric circles with wiggly edges surrounded it in waves of blue and red and cream, bordered in a soft, deep red, and the whole of it so ornamented with unusual shapes it would take you a day to look at them all. He'd been so taken with it the first time he saw it, he'd spent a quarter of an hour looking at them, before Big Georges caught him at it and shouted at him to roll the thing up, they hadn't all day.

"Where did ye get this?" Ian asked abruptly, interrupting something the vicomte was saying to the two rough-clad men who'd taken their weapons.

"What? Oh, the carpet! Yes, isn't it wonderful?" The vicomte beamed at him, quite unself-conscious, and gestured the two roughs away toward the wall. "It's part of my wife's dowry."

"Your wife," Jamie repeated carefully. He darted a sideways glance at Ian, who took the cue.

"That would be Mademoiselle Hauberger, would it?" he asked. The vicomte blushed—actually blushed—and Ian realized that the man was no older than he and Jamie were.

"Well. It—we—we have been betrothed for some time, and in Jewish custom, that is almost like being married."

"Betrothed," Jamie echoed again. "Since . . . when, exactly?"

The vicomte sucked in his lower lip, contemplating them. But whatever caution he might have had was overwhelmed in what were plainly vei , high spirits.

"Four years," he said. And, unable to contain himself, he beckoned them to a table near the window and proudly showed them a fancy document covered with colored scrolly sorts of things and written in some very odd language that was all slashes and tilted lines.

"This is our *ketubah*," he said, pronouncing the word very carefully. "Our marriage contract."

Jamie bent over to peer closely at it. "Aye, verra nice," he said politely. "I see it's no been signed yet. The marriage hasna taken place, then?"

Ian saw Jamie's eyes flick over the desk and could sense him passing the possibilities through his mind: grab the letter opener off the desk and take the vicomte hostage? Then find the sly wee bitch, roll her up in one of the smaller rugs, and carry her to Paris? That would doubtless be his own job, Ian thought.

A slight movement as one of the roughs shifted his weight, catching Ian's eye, and he thought, *Don't do it, eejit!* at Jamie, as hard as he could. For once, the message seemed to get through; Jamie's shoulders relaxed a little and he straightened up.

"Ye do ken the lass is meant to be marrying someone else?" he asked baldly. "I wouldna put it past her not to tell ye."

The vicomte's color became higher. "Certainly I know!" he snapped. "She was promised to me first, by her father!"

"How long have ye been a Jew?" Jamie asked carefully, edging round the table. "I dinna think ye were born to it. I mean—ye *are* a Jew now, aye? For I kent one or two, in Paris, and it's my understanding that they dinna marry people who aren't Jewish." His eyes flicked round the solid, handsome room. "It's my understanding that they mostly aren't aristocrats, either."

The vicomte was quite red in the face by now. With a sharp word, he sent the roughs out—though they were disposed to argue. While the brief discussion was going on, Ian edged closer to Jamie and whispered rapidly to him about the rug in *Gàidhlig*.

"Holy God," Jamie muttered in the same language. "I didna see him or either of those two at Bèguey, did you?"

Ian had no time to reply and merely shook his head, as the roughs reluctantly acquiesced to Vicomte Beaumont's imperious orders and shuffled out with narrowed eyes aimed at Ian and Jamie. One of them had Jamie's dirk in his hand and drew this slowly across his neck in a meaningful gesture as he left.

Aye, they might manage in a fight, Ian thought, returning the slit-eyed glare, *but not that wee velvet gomerel.* Captain D'Eglise wouldn't have taken on the vicomte, and neither would a band of professional highwaymen, Jewish or not.

"All right," the vicomte said abruptly, leaning his fists on the desk. "I'll tell you."

And he did. Rebekah's mother, the daughter of Dr. Hasdi, had fallen in love with a Christian man and run away with him. The doctor had declared his daughter dead, as was the usual way in such a situation, and done formal mourning for her. But she was his only child, and he had not been able to forget her. He had arranged to have information brought to him and knew about Rebekah's birth.

"Then her mother died. That's when I met her—about that time, I mean. Her father was a judge, and my father knew him. She was fourteen and I sixteen; I fell in love with her. And she with me," he added, giving the Scots a hard eye, as though daring them to disbelieve it. "We were betrothed, with her father's blessing. But then her father caught a flux and died in two days. And—"

"And her grandfather took her back," Jamie finished. "And she became a Jew?"

"By Jewish belief, she was born Jewish; it descends through the mother's line. And . . . her mother had told her, privately, about her lost heritage. She embraced it, once she went to live with her grandfather."

Ian stirred and cocked a cynical eyebrow. "Aye? Why did ye not convert then, if ye're willing to do it now?"

"I said I would!" The vicomte had one fist curled round his letter opener as though he would strangle it. "The miserable old wretch said he did not believe me. He thought I would not give up my—my—this life." He waved a hand dismissively around the room, encompassing, presumably, his title and property, both of which would be confiscated by the government the moment his conversion became known.

"He said it would be a sham conversion and that the moment I had her I would become a Christian again and force Rebekah to be Christian, too. Like her father," he added darkly.

Despite the situation, Ian was beginning to have some sympathy for the wee popinjay. It was a very romantic tale, and he was partial to those. Jamie, however, was still reserving judgment. He gestured at the rug beneath their feet.

"Her dowry, ye said?"

"Yes," said the vicomte, but sounded much less certain. "She says it belonged to her mother. She had some men bring it here last week, along with a chest and a few other things. Anyway," he said, resuming his self-confidence and glowering at them, "when the old beast arranged her marriage to that fellow in Paris, I made up my mind to—to—"

"To abduct her. By arrangement, aye? Mmphm," Jamie said, his noise indicating his opinion of the vicomte's skills as a highwayman. He raised one red brow at Pierre's black eye but forbore to make any more remarks, thank God. It hadn't escaped Ian that they were prisoners, though it maybe had Jamie.

"May we speak with Mademoiselle Hauberger?" Ian asked politely. "Just to be sure she's come of her own free will, aye?"

"Rather plainly she did, since you followed her here." The vicomte hadn't liked Jamie's noise. "No, you may not. She's busy." He raised his hands and clapped them sharply, and the rough fellows came back in, along with a half dozen or so male servants as reinforcement, led by a tall, severe-looking butler armed with a stout walking-stick.

"Go with Ecrivisse, gentlemen. He'll see to your comfort."

"COMFORT" PROVED TO be the chateau's wine cellar, which was fragrant but cold. Also dark. The vicomte's hospitality did not extend so far as a candle.

"If he meant to kill us, he'd have done it already," Ian reasoned.

"Mmphm." Jamie sat on the stairs, the fold of his plaid pulled up around his shoulders against the chill. There was music coming from somewhere outside: the faint sound of a fiddle and the tap of a little hand drum. It started, then stopped, then started again.

Ian wandered restlessly to and fro; it wasn't a very large cellar. If he didn't mean to kill them, what did the vicomte intend to do with them?

"He's waiting for something to happen," Jamie said suddenly, answering the thought. "Something to do wi' the lass, I expect."

"Aye, reckon." Ian sat down on the stairs, nudging Jamie over. "*A Dhia*, that's cold!"

"Mm," said Jamie absently. "Maybe they mean to run. If so, I hope he leaves someone behind to let us out and doesna leave us here to starve."

"We wouldna starve," Ian pointed out logically. "We could live on wine for a good long time. Someone would come before it ran out." He paused a moment, trying to imagine what it would be like to stay drunk for several weeks.

"That's a thought." Jamie got up, a little stiff from the cold, and went off to rummage the racks. There was no light to speak of, save what seeped through the crack at the bottom of the door to the cellar, but Ian could hear Jamie pulling out bottles and sniffing the corks.

He came back in a bit with a bottle and, sitting down again, drew the cork with his teeth and spat it to one side. He took a sip, then another, and tilted back the bottle for a generous swig, then handed it to Ian.

"No bad," he said.

It wasn't, and there wasn't much conversation for the next little while. Eventually, though, Jamie set the empty bottle down, belched gently, and said, "It's her."

"What's her? Rebekah, ye mean. I daresay." Then after a moment, "What's her?"

"It's her," Jamie repeated. "Ken what the Jew said—Ephraim bar-Sefer? About how his gang knew where to strike, because they got information from some outside source? It's her. She told them."

Jamie spoke with such certainty that Ian was staggered for a moment, but then he marshaled his wits.

"That wee lass? Granted, she put one over on us—and I suppose she at least kent about Pierre's abduction, but . . ."

Jamie snorted. "Aye, Pierre. Does the mannie strike ye either as a criminal or a great schemer?"

"No, but—"

"Does she?"

"Well . . ."

"Exactly."

Jamie got up and wandered off into the racks again, this time returning with what smelled to Ian like one of the very good local red wines. It was like drinking his mam's strawberry preserves on toast with a cup of strong tea, he thought approvingly.

"Besides," Jamie went on, as though there'd been no interruption in his train of thought, "mind what ye told me the maid said, when I got my heid half-stove in? *'Perhaps he's been killed, too. How would you feel then?'* Nay, she'd planned the whole thing—to have Pierre and his lads stop the coach and make away with the women and the scroll and doubtless Monsieur Pickle, too. *But,*" he added, sticking up a finger in front of Ian's face to stop him interrupting, "then Josef-from-Alsace tells ye that thieves— and the *same* thieves as before, or some of them—attacked the band wi' the dowry money. Ye ken well that canna have been Pierre. It had to be her who told them."

Ian was forced to admit the logic of this. Pierre had enthusiasm but couldn't possibly be considered a professional highwayman.

"But a lass . . ." he said helplessly. "How could she—"

Jamie grunted. "D'Eglise said Dr. Hasdi's a man much respected among the Jews of Bordeaux. And plainly he's kent as far as Paris, or how else did he make the match for his granddaughter? But he doesna speak French. Want to bet me that she didna manage his correspondence?"

"No," Ian said, and took another swallow. "Mmphm."

Some minutes later he said, "That rug. And the other things Monsieur le Vicomte mentioned—her *dowry*."

Jamie made an approving noise. "Aye. Her percentage of the take, more like. Ye can see our lad Pierre hasna got much money, and he'd lose all his property when he converted. She was feathering their nest, like— makin' sure they'd have enough to live on. Enough to live *well* on."

"Well, then," Ian said, after a moment's silence. "There ye are."

THE AFTERNOON dragged on. After the second bottle, they agreed to drink no more for the time being, in case a clear head should be neces- sary if or when the door at last opened, and aside from going off now and then to have a pee behind the farthest wine racks, they stayed huddled on the stairs.

Jamie was singing softly along to the fiddle's distant tune when the door finally *did* open. He stopped abruptly and lunged awkwardly to his feet, nearly falling, his knees stiff with cold.

"Monsieurs?" said the butler, peering down at them. "If you will be so kind as to follow me, please?"

To their surprise, the butler led them straight out of the house and down a small path, in the direction of the distant music. The air outside was fresh and wonderful after the must of the cellar, and Jamie filled his lungs with it, wondering what the devil . . . ?

Then they rounded a bend in the path and saw a garden court before them, lit by torches driven into the ground. Somewhat overgrown, but with a fountain tinkling away in the center—and just by the fountain a sort of canopy, its cloth glimmering pale in the dusk. There was a little knot of people standing near it, talking, and as the butler paused, holding them back with one hand, Vicomte Beaumont broke away from the group and came toward them, smiling.

"My apologies for the inconvenience, gentlemen," he said, a huge smile splitting his face. He looked drunk, but Jamie thought he wasn't—no smell of spirits. "Rebekah had to prepare herself. And we wanted to wait for nightfall."

"To do what?" Ian asked suspiciously, and the vicomte giggled. Jamie didn't mean to wrong the man, but it was a giggle. He gave Ian an eye and Ian gave it back. Aye, it was a giggle.

"To be married," Pierre said, and while his voice was still full of *joie de vivre,* he said the words with a sense of deep reverence that struck Jamie somewhere in the chest. Pierre turned and waved a hand toward the dark- ening sky, where the stars were beginning to prick and sparkle. "For luck, you know—that our descendants may be as numerous as the stars."

"Mmphm," Jamie said politely.

"But come with me, if you will." Pierre was already striding back to the knot of . . . well, Jamie supposed they must be wedding guests. The vicomte beckoned to the Scots to follow.

Marie the maid was there, along with a few other women; she gave Jamie and Ian a wary look. But it was the men with whom the vicomte was concerned. He spoke a few words to his guests, and three men with enormous beards came back with him, all dressed formally, if somewhat oddly, with little velvet skullcaps decorated with beads.

"May I present Monsieur Gershom Sanders and Monsieur Levi Champfleur. Our witnesses. And Reb Cohen, who will officiate."

The men shook hands, murmuring politeness. Jamie and Ian exchanged looks. Why were *they* here?

The vicomte caught the look and interpreted it correctly.

"I wish you to return to Dr. Hasdi," he said, the effervescence in his voice momentarily supplanted by a note of steel, "and tell him that everything—everything!—was done in accordance with proper custom and according to the Law. This marriage will not be undone. By anyone."

"Mmphm," said Ian, less politely.

And so it was that a few minutes later they found themselves standing among the male wedding guests—the women stood on the other side of the canopy—watching as Rebekah came down the path, jingling faintly. She wore a dress of deep red silk; Jamie could see the torchlight shift and shimmer through its folds as she moved. There were gold bracelets on both wrists, and she had a veil over her head and face, with a little headdress sort of thing made of gold chains that dipped across her forehead, strung with small medallions and bells—it was this that made the jingling sound. It reminded him of the Torah scroll, and he stiffened a bit at the thought.

Pierre stood with the rabbi under the canopy; as Rebekah approached, he stepped apart, and she came to him. She didn't touch him, though, but proceeded to walk round him. And round him, and round him. Seven times she circled him, and the hairs rose a little on the back of Jamie's neck; it had the faint sense of magic about it—or witchcraft. Something she did to bind the man.

She came face-to-face with Jamie as she made each turn and plainly could see him in the light of the torches, but her eyes were fixed straight ahead; she made no acknowledgment of anyone—not even Pierre.

But then the circling was done and she came to stand by the vicomte's side. The rabbi said a few words of welcome to the guests and then, turning to the bride and groom, poured out a cup of wine, and said what appeared to be a Hebrew blessing over it. Jamie made out the beginning— *"Blessed are you, Adonai our God"*—but then lost the thread.

Pierre reached into his pocket when Reb Cohen stopped speaking, removed a small object—clearly a ring—and, taking Rebekah's hand in his, put it on the forefinger of her right hand, smiling down into her face with a tenderness that, despite everything, rather caught at Jamie's heart. Then Pierre lifted her veil, and Jamie caught a glimpse of the answering tenderness on Rebekah's face in the instant before her husband kissed her.

The congregation sighed as one.

The rabbi picked up a sheet of parchment from a little table nearby. The thing he'd called a *ketubah,* Jamie saw—the wedding contract.

The rabbi read the thing out, first in a language Jamie didn't recognize, and then again in French. It wasn't so different from the few marriage contracts he'd seen, laying out the disposition of property and what was due to the bride and all—though he noted with disapproval that it provided for the possibility of divorce. His attention wandered a bit then; Rebekah's face glowed in the torchlight like pearl and ivory, and the roundness of her bosom showed clearly as she breathed. In spite of everything he thought he now knew about her, he experienced a brief wave of envy toward Pierre.

The contract read and carefully laid aside, the rabbi recited a string of blessings; Jamie kent it was blessings because he caught the words "Blessed are you, Adonai . . ." over and over, though the subject of the blessings seemed to be everything from the congregation to Jerusalem, so far as he could tell. The bride and groom had another sip of wine.

A pause then, and Jamie expected some official word from the rabbi, uniting husband and wife, but it didn't come. Instead, one of the witnesses took the wineglass, wrapped it in a linen napkin, and placed it on the ground in front of Pierre. To the Scots' astonishment, he promptly stamped on the thing—and the crowd burst into applause.

For a few moments, everything seemed quite like a country wedding, with everyone crowding round, wanting to congratulate the happy couple. But within moments, the happy couple was moving off toward the house, while the guests all streamed toward tables that had been set up at the far side of the garden, laden with food and drink.

"Come on," Jamie muttered, and caught Ian by the arm. They hastened after the newly wedded pair, Ian demanding to know what the devil Jamie thought he was doing. "I want to talk to her—alone. You stop him, keep him talking for as long as ye can."

"I—how?"

"How would I know? Ye'll think of something."

They had reached the house, and ducking in close upon Pierre's heels, Jamie saw that by good luck the man had stopped to say something to a servant. Rebekah was just vanishing down a long hallway; he saw her put her hand to a door.

"The best of luck to ye, man!" Jamie said, clapping Pierre so heartily on the shoulder that the groom staggered.

Before Pierre could recover, Ian, very obviously commending his soul to God, stepped up and seized him by the hand, which he wrung vigorously, meanwhile giving Jamie a private *"Hurry the bloody hell up!"* sort of look.

Grinning, Jamie ran down the short hallway to the door where he'd seen Rebekah disappear. The grin faded as his hand touched the doorknob, though, and the face he presented to her as he entered was as grim as he could make it.

Her eyes widened in shock and indignation at sight of him.

"What are you doing here? No one is supposed to come in here but my husband and me!"

"He's on his way," Jamie assured her. "The question is—will he get here?"

Her little fist curled up in a way that would have been comical if he didn't know as much about her as he did.

"Is that a threat?" she said, in a tone as incredulous as it was menacing. "Here? You dare threaten me *here*?"

"Aye, I do. I want that scroll."

"Well, you're not getting it," she snapped. He saw her glance flicker over the table, probably in search of either a bell to summon help or something to bash him on the head with, but the table held nothing but a platter of stuffed rolls and exotic sweeties. There *was* a bottle of wine, and he saw her eye light on that with calculation, but he stretched out a long arm and got hold of it before she could.

"I dinna want it for myself," he said. "I mean to take it back to your grandfather."

"Him?" Her face hardened. "No. It's worth more to him than *I* am," she added bitterly, "but at least that means I can use it for protection. As long as I have it, he won't try to hurt Pierre or drag me back, for fear I might damage it. I'm keeping it."

"I think he'd be a great deal better off without ye, and doubtless he kens that fine," Jamie informed her, and had to harden himself against the sudden look of hurt in her eyes. He supposed even spiders might have feelings, but that was neither here nor there.

"Where's Pierre?" she demanded. "If you've harmed a hair on his head, I'll—"

"I wouldna touch the poor gomerel, and neither would Ian—Juan, I mean. When I said the question was whether he got to ye or not, I meant whether he thinks better of his bargain."

"What?" He thought she paled a little, but it was hard to tell.

"You give me the scroll to take back to your grandfather—a wee letter of apology to go with it wouldna come amiss, but I willna insist on that—or Ian and I take Pierre out back and have a frank word regarding his new wife."

"Tell him what you like!" she snapped. "He wouldn't believe any of your made-up tales!"

"Oh, aye? And if I tell him exactly what happened to Ephraim bar-Sefer? And why?"

"Who?" she said, but now she really had gone pale to the lips and put out a hand to the table to steady herself.

"Do ye ken yourself what happened to him? No? Well, I'll tell ye, lass." And he did so, with a terse brutality that made her sit down suddenly, tiny pearls of sweat appearing round the gold medallions that hung across her forehead.

"Pierre already kens at least a bit about your wee gang, I think—but maybe not what a ruthless, grasping wee besom ye really are."

"It wasn't me! I didn't kill Ephraim!"

"If not for you, he'd no be dead, and I reckon Pierre would see that. I can tell him where the body is," he added, more delicately. "I buried the man myself."

Her lips were pressed so hard together that nothing showed but a straight white line.

"Ye havena got long," he said, quietly now, but keeping his eyes on hers. "Ian canna hold him off much longer, and if he comes in—then I tell him everything, in front of you, and ye do what ye can then to persuade him I'm a liar."

She stood up abruptly, her chains and bracelets all a-jangle, and stamped to the door of the inner room. She flung it open, and Marie jerked back, shocked.

Rebekah said something to her in Ladino, sharp, and with a small gasp the maid scurried off.

"All *right*," Rebekah said through gritted teeth, turning back to him. "Take it and be damned, you *dog*."

"Indeed I will, ye bloody wee bitch," he replied with great politeness.

Her hand closed round a stuffed roll, but instead of throwing it at him, she merely squeezed it into paste and crumbs, slapping the remains back on the tray with a small exclamation of fury.

The sweet chiming of the Torah scroll presaged Marie's hasty arrival, the precious thing clasped in her arms. She glanced at her mistress and, at Rebekah's curt nod, delivered it with great reluctance into the arms of the Christian dog.

Jamie bowed, first to maid and then mistress, and backed toward the door.

"Shalom," he said, and closed the door an instant before the silver platter hit it with a ringing thud.

———

"DID IT HURT a lot?" Ian was asking Pierre with interest, when Jamie came up to them.

"My God, you have no idea," Pierre replied fervently. "But it was worth it." He divided a beaming smile between Ian and Jamie and bowed to them, not even noticing the canvas-wrapped bundle in Jamie's arms. "You must excuse me, gentlemen; my bride awaits me!"

"Did what hurt a lot?" Jamie inquired, leading the way hastily out through a side door. No point in attracting attention, after all.

"Ye ken he was born a Christian but converted in order to marry the wee besom," Ian said. "So he had to be circumcised." He crossed himself at the thought, and Jamie laughed.

"What is it they call the stick-insect things where the female one bites off the head of the male one after he's got the business started?" Jamie asked, nudging the door open with his bum.

Ian's brow creased for an instant. "Praying mantis, I think. Why?"

"I think our wee friend Pierre may have a more interesting wedding night than he expects. Come on."

Bordeaux

IT WASN'T THE worst thing he'd ever had to do, but he wasn't looking forward to it. Jamie paused outside the gate of Dr. Hasdi's house, the Torah scroll in its wrappings in his arms. Ian was looking a bit worm-eaten, and Jamie reckoned he kent why. Having to tell the doctor what had happened to his granddaughter was one thing; telling him to his face with the knowledge of what said granddaughter's nipples felt like fresh in the mind . . . or the hand . . .

"Ye dinna have to come in, man," he said to Ian. "I can do it alone."

Ian's mouth twitched, but he shook his head and stepped up next to Jamie.

"On your right, man," he said simply.

Jamie smiled. When he was five years old, Ian's da, Auld John, had persuaded his own da to let Jamie handle a sword cack-handed, as he was wont to do. "And you, lad," he'd said to Ian, very serious, "it's your duty to stand on your laird's right hand and guard his weak side."

"Aye," Jamie said. "Right, then." And rang the bell.

AFTERWARD, THEY WANDERED slowly through the streets of Bordeaux, making their way toward nothing in particular, not speaking much.

Dr. Hasdi had received them courteously, though with a look of mingled horror and apprehension on his face when he saw the scroll. This look had faded to one of relief at hearing—the manservant had had enough French to interpret for them—that his granddaughter was safe, then to shock, and finally to a set expression that Jamie couldn't read. Was it anger, sadness, resignation?

When Jamie had finished the story, they sat uneasily, not sure what to do next. Dr. Hasdi sat at his desk, head bowed, his hands resting gently on the scroll. Finally, he raised his head and nodded to them both, one and then the other. His face was calm now, giving nothing away.

"Thank you," he said in heavily accented French. *"Shalom."*

"ARE YE HUNGRY?" Ian motioned toward a small *boulangerie*, whose trays bore filled rolls and big, fragrant round loaves. He was starving himself, though half an hour ago, his wame had been in knots.

"Aye, maybe." Jamie kept walking, though, and Ian shrugged and followed.

"What d'ye think the captain will do when we tell him?" Ian wasn't all that bothered. There was always work for a good-sized man who kent what to do with a sword. And he owned his own weapons. They'd have to buy Jamie a sword, though. Everything he was wearing, from pistols to ax, belonged to D'Eglise.

He was busy enough calculating the cost of a decent sword against what remained of their pay that he didn't notice Jamie not answering him. He did notice that his friend was walking faster, though, and, hurrying to catch up, he saw what they were heading for. The tavern where the pretty brown-haired barmaid had taken Jamie for a Jew.

Oh, like that, is it? he thought, and hid a grin. Aye, well, there was one sure way the lad could prove to the lass that he wasn't a Jew.

The place was moiling when they walked in, and not in a good way; Ian sensed it instantly. There were soldiers there, army soldiers, and other fighting men, mercenaries like themselves, and no love wasted between them. You could cut the air with a knife, and judging from a splotch of half-dried blood on the floor, somebody had already tried.

There were women but fewer than before, and the barmaids kept their eyes on their trays, not flirting tonight.

Jamie wasn't taking heed of the atmosphere; Ian could see him looking round for her, but the brown-haired lass wasn't on the floor. They might have asked after her—if they'd known her name.

"Upstairs, maybe?" Ian said, leaning in to half-shout into Jamie's ear over the noise. Jamie nodded and began forging through the crowd, Ian bobbing in his wake, hoping they found the lass quickly so he could eat while Jamie got on with it.

THE STAIRS WERE crowded—with men coming down. Something was amiss up there, and Jamie shoved someone into the wall with a thump, pushing past. Some nameless anxiety shot jolts down his spine, and he was half prepared before he pushed through a little knot of onlookers at the head of the stairs and saw them.

Mathieu and the brown-haired girl. There was a big open room here, with a hallway lined with tiny cubicles leading back from it; Mathieu had the girl by the arm and was boosting her toward the hallway with a hand on her bum, despite her protests.

"Let go of her!" Jamie said, not shouting but raising his voice well enough to be heard easily. Mathieu paid not the least attention, though everyone else, startled, turned to look at Jamie.

He heard Ian mutter, "Joseph, Mary, and Bride preserve us," behind him, but he paid no heed. He covered the distance to Mathieu in three strides and kicked him in the arse.

He ducked, by reflex, but Mathieu merely turned and gave him a hot eye, ignoring the whoops and guffaws from the spectators.

"Later, little boy," he said. "I'm busy now."

He scooped the young woman into one big arm and kissed her sloppily, rubbing his stubbled face hard over hers so she squealed and pushed at him to get away.

Jamie drew the pistol from his belt.

"I said, let her go." The noise dropped suddenly, but he barely noticed for the roaring of blood in his ears.

Mathieu turned his head, incredulous. Then he snorted with contempt, grinned unpleasantly, and shoved the girl into the wall so her head struck with a thump, pinning her there with his bulk.

The pistol was primed.

"Salop!" Jamie roared. *"*Don't touch her! Let her go!" He clenched his teeth and aimed with both hands, rage and fright making his hands tremble.

Mathieu didn't even look at him. The big man half-turned away, a casual hand on the girl's breast. She squealed as he twisted it, and Jamie fired. Mathieu whirled, the pistol he'd had concealed in his own belt now in hand, and the air shattered in an explosion of sound and white smoke.

There were shouts of alarm, excitement—and another pistol went off, somewhere behind Jamie. *Ian?* he thought dimly, but, no, Ian was running toward Mathieu, leaping for the massive arm rising, the second pistol's barrel making circles as Mathieu struggled to fix it on Jamie. It discharged, and the ball hit one of the lanterns that stood on the tables, which exploded with a *whuff* and a bloom of flame.

Jamie had reversed his pistol and was hammering at Mathieu's head with the butt before he was conscious of having crossed the room. Mathieu's mad-boar eyes were almost invisible, slitted with the glee of fighting, and the sudden curtain of blood that fell over his face did nothing but enhance his grin, blood running down between his teeth. He shook Ian off with a shove that sent him crashing into the wall, then wrapped one big arm almost casually around Jamie's body and, with a snap of his head, butted him in the face.

Jamie had turned his head reflexively and thus avoided a broken nose, but the impact crushed the flesh of his jaw into his teeth, and his mouth filled with blood. His head was spinning with the force of the blow, but he got a hand under Mathieu's jaw and shoved upward with all his strength, trying to break the man's neck. His hand slipped off the sweat-greased flesh, though, and Mathieu let go his grip in order to try to knee Jamie in the stones. A knee like a cannonball struck Jamie a numbing blow in the thigh as he squirmed free, and he staggered, grabbing Mathieu's arm just as Ian came dodging in from the side, seizing the other. Without a moment's hesitation, Mathieu's huge forearms twisted; he seized the Scots by the scruffs of their necks and cracked their heads together.

Jamie couldn't see and could barely move but kept moving anyway, groping blindly. He was on the floor, could feel boards, wetness . . . His pawing hand struck flesh, and he lunged forward and bit Mathieu as hard as he could in the calf of the leg. Fresh blood filled his mouth, hotter than his own, and he gagged but kept his teeth locked in the hairy flesh, clinging stubbornly as the leg kicked in frenzy. His ears were ringing, he was vaguely aware of screaming and shouting, but it didn't matter.

Something had come upon him, and nothing mattered. Some small remnant of his consciousness registered surprise, and then that was gone, too. No pain, no thought. He was a red thing, and while he saw other things—faces, blood, bits of room—they didn't matter. Blood took him, and when some sense of himself came back, he was kneeling astride the man, hands locked around the big man's neck, fingers throbbing with a pounding pulse—his or his victim's, he couldn't tell.

Him. Him. He'd lost the man's name. His eyes were bulging, the ragged mouth slobbered and gaped, and there was a small, sweet *crack* as something broke under Jamie's thumbs. He squeezed with all he had, squeezed and squeezed and felt the huge body beneath him go strangely limp.

He went on squeezing, couldn't stop, until a hand seized him by the arm and shook him, hard.

"Stop," a voice croaked, hot in his ear. "Jamie. Stop."

He blinked up at the white bony face, unable to put a name to it. Then drew breath—the first he could remember drawing for some time—and with it came a thick stink, blood and shit and reeking sweat, and he became suddenly aware of the horrible spongy feeling of the body he was sitting on. He scrambled awkwardly off, sprawling on the floor as his muscles spasmed and trembled.

Then he saw her.

She was lying crumpled against the wall, curled into herself, her brown hair spilling across the boards. He got to his knees, crawling to her.

He was making a small whimpering noise, trying to talk, having no words. Got to the wall and gathered her into his arms, limp, her head lolling, striking his shoulder, her hair soft against his face, smelling of smoke and her own sweet musk.

"*A nighean,*" he managed. "Christ, *a nighean.* Are ye . . ."

"Jesus," said a voice by his side, and he felt the vibration as Ian—thank God, the name had come back, of course it was Ian—collapsed next to him. His friend had a bloodstained dirk still clutched in his hand. "Oh, Jesus, Jamie."

He looked up, puzzled, desperate, and then looked down as the girl's body slipped from his grasp and fell back across his knees with impossible boneless grace, the small dark hole in her white breast stained with only a little blood. Not much at all.

HE'D MADE JAMIE come with him to the cathedral of Saint André and insisted he go to Confession. Jamie had balked—no great surprise.

"No. I can't."

"We'll go together." Ian had taken him firmly by the arm and very literally dragged him over the threshold. He was counting on the atmosphere of the place to keep Jamie there, once inside.

His friend stopped dead, the whites of his eyes showing as he glanced warily around.

The stone vault of the ceiling soared into shadow overhead, but pools of colored light from the stained-glass windows lay soft on the worn slates of the aisle.

"I shouldna be here," Jamie muttered under his breath.

"Where better, eejit? Come on," Ian muttered back, and pulled Jamie down the side aisle to the chapel of Saint Estèphe. Most of the side chapels were lavishly furnished, monuments to the importance of wealthy families. This one was a tiny, undecorated stone alcove, containing little more than an altar, a faded tapestry of a faceless saint, and a small stand where candles could be placed.

"Stay here." Ian planted Jamie dead in front of the altar and ducked out, going to buy a candle from the old woman who sold them near the main door. He'd changed his mind about trying to make Jamie go to Confession; he knew fine when ye could get a Fraser to do something and when ye couldn't.

He worried a bit that Jamie would leave and hurried back to the chapel, but Jamie was still there, standing in the middle of the tiny space, head down, staring at the floor.

"Here, then," Ian said, pulling him toward the altar. He plunked the candle—an expensive one, beeswax and large—on the stand and pulled the paper spill the old lady had given him out of his sleeve, offering it to Jamie. "Light it. We'll say a prayer for your da. And . . . and for her."

He could see tears trembling on Jamie's lashes, glittering in the red glow of the sanctuary lamp that hung above the altar, but Jamie blinked them back and firmed his jaw.

"All right," he said, low-voiced, but he hesitated.

Ian sighed, took the spill out of his hand, and, standing on tiptoe, lit it from the sanctuary lamp. "Do it," he whispered, handing the spill to Jamie, "or I'll gie ye a good one in the kidney, right here."

Jamie made a sound that might have been the breath of a laugh and lowered the lit spill to the candle's wick. The fire rose up, a pure high flame with blue at its heart, then settled as Jamie pulled the spill away and shook it out in a plume of smoke.

They stood for some time, hands clasped loosely in front of them, watching the candle burn. Ian prayed for his mam and da, his sister and her bairns . . . with some hesitation (was it proper to pray for a Jew?) for Rebekah bat-Leah, and, with a sidelong glance at Jamie to be sure he wasn't looking, for Jenny Fraser. Then for the soul of Brian Fraser . . . and finally, eyes tight shut, for the friend beside him.

The sounds of the church faded, the whispering stones and echoes of wood, the shuffle of feet and the rolling gabble of the pigeons on the roof. Ian stopped saying words but was still praying. And then that stopped, too, and there was only peace and the soft beating of his heart.

He heard Jamie sigh, from somewhere deep inside, and opened his eyes. Without speaking, they went out, leaving the candle to keep watch.

"Did ye not mean to go to Confession yourself?" Jamie asked, stopping near the church's main door. There was a priest in the confessional; two or three people stood a discreet distance away from the carved wooden stall, out of earshot, waiting.

"It'll bide," Ian said, with a shrug. "If ye're goin' to hell, I might as well go, too. God knows, ye'll never manage alone."

Jamie smiled—a wee bit of a smile, but still—and pushed the door open into sunlight.

They strolled aimlessly for a bit, not talking, and found themselves eventually on the river's edge, watching the Garonne's dark waters flow past, carrying debris from a recent storm.

"It means 'peace,' " Jamie said at last. "What he said to me. The doctor. *'Shalom.'* "

Ian kent that fine. "Aye," he said. "But peace is no our business now, is it? We're soldiers." He jerked his chin toward the nearby pier, where a packet boat rode at anchor. "I hear the King of Prussia needs a few good men."

"So he does," said Jamie, and squared his shoulders. "Come on, then."

A FUGITIVE GREEN

1

SURVIVAL

Paris, April 1744

MINNIE RENNIE HAD SECRETS. Some were for sale and some were strictly her own. She touched the bosom of her dress and glanced toward the latticework door at the rear of the shop. Still closed, the blue curtains behind it drawn firmly shut.

Her father had secrets, too; Andrew Rennie (as he called himself in Paris) was outwardly a dealer in rare books but more privately a collector of letters whose writers had never meant them to be read by any but the addressee. He also kept a stock of more fluid information, this soaked out of his visitors with a combination of tea, wine, small amounts of money, and his own considerable charm.

Minnie had a good head for wine, needed no money, and was impervious to her father's magnetism. She did, however, have a decently filial respect for his powers of observation.

The murmur of voices from the back room didn't have the rhythm of leave-taking, no scraping of chairs . . . She nipped across the book-crammed shop to the shelves of tracts and sermons.

Taking down a red-calf volume with marbled endpapers, titled *Collected Sermons of the Reverend George V. Sykes,* she snatched the letter from the bosom of her dress, tucked it between the pages, and slid the book back into place. Just in time: there was movement in the back room, the putting down of cups, the slight raising of voices.

Heart thumping, she took one more glance at the Reverend Sykes and saw to her horror that she'd disturbed the dust on the shelf—there was a clear track pointing to the oxblood-leather spine. She darted back to the main counter, seized the feather duster kept under it, and had the entire section flicked over in a matter of moments.

She took several deep breaths; she mustn't look flushed or flustered. Her father was an observant man—a trait that had (he often said, when instructing her in the art) kept him alive on more than one occasion.

But it was all right; the voices had changed again—some new point had come up.

She strolled composedly along the shelves and paused to look through the stacks of unsorted volumes that sat on a large table against the west wall. A strong scent of tobacco rose from the books, along with the usual smell of leather, buckram, glue, paper, and ink. This batch had plainly belonged to a man who liked a pipe when he read. She was paying little attention to the new stock, though; her mind was still on the letter.

The carter who had delivered this latest assemblage of books—the library of a deceased professor of history from Exeter—had given her a nod and a wink, and she'd slipped out with a market basket, meeting him round the corner by a fruiterer's shop. A *livre tournois* to the carter, and five *sous* for a wooden basket of strawberries, and she'd been free to read the letter in the shelter of the alley before sauntering back to the shop, fruit in hand to explain her absence.

No salutation, no signature, as she'd requested—only the information: *Have found her,* it read simply. *Mrs. Simpson, Chapel House, Parson's Green, Peterborough Road, London.*

Mrs. Simpson. A name, at last. A name and a place, mysterious though both were.

Mrs. Simpson.

It had taken months, months of careful planning, choosing the men among the couriers her father used who might be amenable to making a bit extra on the side and a bit more for keeping her inquiries quiet.

She didn't know what her father might do should he find out that she'd been looking for her mother. But he'd refused for the last seventeen years to say a word about the woman; it was reasonable to assume he wouldn't be pleased.

Mrs. Simpson. She said it silently, feeling the syllables in her mouth. Mrs. Simpson . . . Was her mother married again, then? Did she have other children?

Minnie swallowed. The thought that she might have half brothers or sisters was at once horrifying, intriguing . . . and startlingly painful. That someone else might have had her mother—hers!—for all those years . . .

"This will *not* do," she said aloud, though under her breath. She had no idea of *Mrs. Simpson*'s personal circumstances, and it was pointless to waste emotion on something that might not exist. She blinked hard to refocus her mind and suddenly saw it.

The thing sitting atop a pigskin-bound edition of Volume III of *History of the Papacy* (Antwerp) was as long as her thumb and, for a cockroach, remarkably immobile. Minnie had been staring at it unwittingly for nearly a minute, and it hadn't so much as twitched an antenna. Perhaps it was dead? She picked a ratty quill out of the collection in the Chinese jar and gingerly poked the thing with the quill's pointy end.

The thing hissed like a teakettle and she let out a small yelp, dropping the quill and leaping backward. The roach, disturbed, turned round in a slow, huffy circle, then settled back on the gilt-embossed capital "P" and tucked its thorny legs back under itself, obviously preparing to resume its nap.

"Oh, I don't *think* so," she said to it, and turned to the shelves in search of something heavy enough to smash it but with a cover that wouldn't show the stain. She'd set her hand on a Vulgate Bible with a dark-brown pebble-grain cover when the secret door beside the shelves opened, revealing her father.

"Oh, you've met Frederick?" he said, stepping forward and taking the Bible out of her hand. "You needn't worry, my dear; he's quite tame."

"Tame? Who would trouble to domesticate a cockroach?"

"The inhabitants of Madagascar, or so I'm told. Though the trait is heritable; Frederick here is the descendant of a long and noble line of hissing cockroaches but has never set foot on the soil of his native land. He was born—or hatched, I suppose—in Bristol."

Frederick had suspended his nap long enough to nuzzle inquiringly at her father's thumb, extended as one might hold out one's knuckles to a strange dog. Evidently finding the scent acceptable, the roach strolled up the thumb and onto the back of her father's hand. Minnie twitched, unable to keep the gooseflesh from rippling up her arms.

Mr. Rennie edged carefully toward the big shelves on the east wall, hand cradled next to his chest. These shelves contained the salable but less-valuable books: a jumble of everything from *Culpeper's Herbal* to tattered copies of Shakespeare's plays and—by far the most popular—a large collection of the more lurid gallows confessions of an assortment of highwaymen, murderers, forgers, and husband-slayers. Amid the volumes and pamphlets was scattered a miscellany of small curiosities, ranging from a toy bronze cannon and a handful of sharp-edged stones said to be used at the dawn of time for scraping hides to a Chinese fan that showed erotic scenes when spread. Her father picked a wicker cricket cage from the detritus and decanted Frederick neatly into it.

"Not before time, either, old cock," he said to the roach, now standing on its hind legs and peering out through the wickerwork. "Here's your new master, just coming."

Minerva peered round her father and her heart jumped a little; she recognized that tall, broad-shouldered silhouette automatically ducking beneath the lintel in order to avoid being brained.

"Lord Broch Tuarach!" Her father stepped forward, beaming, and inclined his head to the customer.

"Mr. Fraser will do," he said, as always, extending a hand. "Your servant, sir."

He'd brought a scent of the streets inside with him: the sticky sap of the plane trees, dust, manure and offal, and Paris's pervasive smell of piss, lightly perfumed by the orange-sellers outside the theater down the street. He carried his own deep tang of sweat, wine, and oak casks, as well; he often came from his warehouse. She inhaled appreciatively, then let her breath out as he turned, smiling, from her father toward her.

"Mademoiselle Rennie," he said, in a deep Scotch accent that rolled the "R" delightfully. He seemed a bit surprised when she held out her hand, but he obligingly bent over it, breathing courteously on her knuckles. *If I were married, he'd kiss it,* she thought, her grip tightening unconsciously on his. He blinked, feeling it, but straightened up and bowed to her, as elegantly as any courtier.

Her father made a slight sound in his throat and tried to catch her eye, but she ignored him, picking up the feather duster and heading industriously for the shelves behind the counter—the ones containing a select assortment of erotica from a dozen different countries. She knew perfectly well what his glance would have said.

"Frederick?" she heard Mr. Fraser say, in a bemused tone of voice. "Does he answer to his name?"

"I—er—I must admit that I've never called him to heel," her father replied, a little startled. "But he's very tame; will come to your hand." Evidently her father had unlatched the cricket cage in order to demonstrate Frederick's talents, for she heard a slight shuffle of feet.

"Nay, dinna bother," Mr. Fraser—his Christian name was James; she'd seen it on a bill of sale for a calf-bound octavo of *Persian Letters* with gilt impressions—said, laughing. "The beastie's not my pet. A gentleman of my acquaintance wants something exotic to present to his mistress—she's a taste for animals, he says."

Her sensitive ear easily picked up the delicate hesitation before "gentleman of my acquaintance." So had her father, for he invited James Fraser to take coffee with him, and in the next instant the two of them had vanished behind the latticework door that concealed her father's private lair and she was blinking at Frederick's stubby antennae, waving inquisitively from the cricket cage her father had dropped onto the shelf in front of her.

"Put up a bit of food for Mr. Fraser to take along," her father called back to her from behind the screen. "For Frederick, I mean."

"What does he eat?" she called.

"Fruit!" came a faint reply, and then a door closed behind the screen.

She caught one more glimpse of Mr. Fraser when he left half an hour later, giving her a smile as he took the parcel containing Frederick and the insect's breakfast of strawberries. Then he ducked once more beneath the lintel, the afternoon sun glinting off his bright hair, and was gone. She stood staring at the empty door.

Her father had emerged from the back room, as well, and was regarding her, not without sympathy.

"Mr. Fraser? He'll never marry you, my dear—he has a wife, and quite a striking woman she is, too. Besides, while he's the best of the Jacobite agents, he doesn't have the scope you'd want. He's only concerned with the Stuarts, and the Scottish Jacobites will never amount to anything. Come, I've something to discuss with you." Without waiting, he turned and headed for the Chinese screen.

A wife. Striking, eh? While the word "wife" was undeniably a blow to the liver, Minnie's next thought was that she didn't necessarily need to *marry* Jamie Fraser. And if it came to striking, she could deal a man a good, sharp buffet in the cods herself. She twirled a lock of ripe-wheat hair around one finger and tucked it behind her ear.

She followed her father, finding him at the little satinwood table. The coffee cups had been pushed aside, and he was pouring wine; he handed her a glass and nodded for her to sit.

"Don't you think of it, my girl." Her father was watching her over his own glass, not unkindly. "After you're married, you do what you like. But you need to keep your virginity until we've got you settled. The English are notorious bores about virginity, and I have my heart set on an Englishman for you."

She made a dismissive noise with her lips and took a delicate sip of the wine.

"What makes you think I haven't already . . . ?"

He lifted one eyebrow and tapped the side of his nose.

"*Ma chère,* I could smell a man on you a mile away. And even when I'm not here . . . I'm here." He lifted the other eyebrow and stared at her. She sniffed, drained her glass, and poured another.

Was he? She sat back and examined him, her own face carefully bland. True, he had informants everywhere; after listening to him do business all day behind the latticework, she dreamed of spiders all night, busy in their webs. Spinning, climbing, hunting along the sleek silk paths that ran hidden through the sticky stuff. And sometimes just hanging there, round as marbles in the air, motionless. Watching with their thousands of eyes.

But the spiders had their own concerns, and for the most part she wasn't one of them. She smiled suddenly at her father, dimpling, and was pleased to see a flicker of unease in his eyes. She lowered her lashes and buried the smile in her wine.

He coughed.

"So," he said, sitting up straight. "How would you like to visit London, my darling?"

London . . .

She tilted her head from side to side, considering.

"The food's terrible, but the beer's not bad. Still, it rains all the time."

"You could have a new dress."

That was interesting—not purely a book-buying excursion, then—but she feigned indifference.

"Only one?"

"That depends somewhat on your success. You might need . . . something special."

That made something twitch behind her ears.

"Why do you bother with this nonsense?" she demanded, putting her glass down with a thump. "You know you can't cozen me into things anymore. Just tell me what you have in mind, and we'll discuss it. Like rational beings."

That made him laugh but not unkindly.

"You do know that women aren't rational, don't you?"

"I do. Neither are men."

"Well, you have a point," he admitted, patting a dribble of wine off his chin with a napkin. "But they do have patterns. And women's patterns are . . ." He paused, squinting over the gold rims of his spectacles, in search of the word.

"More complex?" she suggested, but he shook his head.

"No, no—superficially they seem chaotic, but in fact women's patterns are brutally simple."

"If you mean the influence of the moon, I might point out that every lunatic I've met has been a man."

His eyebrows rose. They were beginning to thicken and gray, to grow unruly; she saw of a sudden that he was becoming elderly, and her heart gave a small lurch at the thought.

He didn't ask how many lunatics she'd met—in the book business, such people were a weekly occurrence—but shook his head.

"No, no, such things are mere physical calendar-keeping. I mean the patterns that cause women to do what they do. And those all come down to survival."

"The day I marry a man merely to survive . . ." She didn't bother finishing the sentence but flicked her fingers scornfully and rose to take the steaming kettle off its spirit lamp and refresh the teapot. Two glasses of wine were her strict limit—particularly when dealing with her father—and today of all days she wanted her wits about her.

"Well, you do have rather higher standards than most women." Her father took the cup of tea she brought him, smiling at her over it. "And—I flatter myself—more resources with which to support them. But the fact remains that you are a woman. Which means that you can conceive. And that, my dear, is where a woman's pattern becomes brutal indeed."

"Really," she said, but not in a tone to invite him to expand upon his point. It was London she wanted to hear about. She'd need to be careful, though.

"What are we looking for, then?" she asked, pouring tea into her own cup so she could keep her eyes fixed on the amber stream. "In London, I mean."

"Not we," her father corrected. "Not this time. I have a bit of business to do in Sweden—speaking of Jacobites. You—"

"There are Swedish Jacobites?"

Her father sighed and rubbed his temples with the forefingers of each hand.

"My dear, you have no idea. They spring up like weeds—and like the grass of the field, in the evening they are cut down and wither. Just when you think they're finally dead, though, something happens, and suddenly— but that's of no matter to you. You're to deliver a package to a particular gentleman and to receive information from a list of contacts that I'll give you. You needn't question them, just take whatever they hand over. And naturally—"

"Tell them nothing," she finished. She dropped a sugar lump into her own tea. "Of course not, Father; what sort of nincompoop do you think I am?"

That made him laugh, deep lines of amusement creasing his eyes almost shut.

"Where did you get that word?"

"Everyone says nincompoop," she informed him. "You hear it in the street in London a dozen times a day."

"Oh, I doubt it," he said. "Know where it comes from, do you?"

"Samuel Johnson told me it was from *non compos mentis*."

"Oh, that's where you got it." He'd stopped laughing but still looked amused. "Well, Mr. Johnson would know. You're still corresponding with him? He's an Englishman, I grant you, but not at all what I have in mind for you, my girl. Bats in the belfry and not a penny to his name. Married, too," he added as an afterthought. "Lives on his wife's money."

That surprised her, and not in a pleasant way. But he was entirely straightforward; his tone was the same as he used when instructing her closely in some important aspect of the work. They didn't fence or mess each other about when it came to the work, and she sat back a little, indi- cating by the inclination of her head that she was ready to listen.

"Mind you," her father said, raising one ink-stained finger, "many folk would tell you that women have nothing on their minds but clothes, or parties, or what Lady Whatnot said about Sir Fart-Catcher at yesterday's salon. And that's a reasonable observation, but it's only an observation. When you see something like that, you ask what's behind it. Or, perhaps, under it," he admitted judiciously. "Push the wine over, sweetheart. I'm done with business for the day."

"I daresay you are," she said tartly, and plunked the decanter of Madeira in front of him. He'd been out all morning, nominally visiting booksellers and collectors of rarities but in reality talking—talking and listening. And he never drank alcohol when working.

He refilled his glass and made to top hers up, as well, but she shook her head and reached for the teapot. She'd been right about needing her wits.

"Chalk up another woman's pattern there," she said, sardonic. "They can't hold drink in the quantities that men do—but they're much less likely to become drunk."

"Clearly you've never been down Gropecunt Lane in London after dark, my dear," her father said imperturbably. "Not that I recommend it, mind. Women drink for the same reasons men do: in order to ignore circumstance or to obliterate themselves. Given the right circumstance, either sex will drown itself. Women care much more about staying alive than men do, though. But enough talk—cut me a fresh pen, my dear, and let me tell you who you'll see in London."

He reached into one of the pigeonholes along the wall and came out with a shabby notebook.

"Ever heard of the Duke of Pardloe?"

Précis: Harold Grey, Duke of Pardloe

Family background: Gerard Grey, Earl of Melton, was given the Title Duke of Pardloe (with considerable Estates) in Reward for his raising of a Regiment (46th Foot, which served with distinction during the Jacobite Rebellions of 1715 and 1719, seeing Combat at Preston and Sheriffmuir). However, the Duke's Allegiance to the Crown appeared to waver during the Reign of George II, and Gerard Grey was implicated in the Cornbury Plot. While he escaped Arrest at that time, a later Plot caused a Warrant for his Arrest on a Charge of Treason to be issued. Hearing of this, Pardloe shot himself in the Conservatory of his Country Estate before the Arrest could be made.

Pardloe's eldest son, Harold Grey, succeeded to the Title at the Age of twenty-one, upon his Father's Death. While the Title was not formally attainted, the younger Grey considered the Title stained with Treason and refused to adopt it, preferring to be known by the older Family Title, Earl of Melton. Married to Esmé Dufresne (a younger Daughter of the Marquis de Robillard) shortly before his Father's Suicide.

The present Duke has publicly and violently rejected all Jacobite Associations (from necessity), but this does not mean such Associations have rejected him, nor that such Rejection reflects his true Inclination. There is considerable Interest in some Quarters as to the Duke's political Leanings and Affiliations, and any Letters, known Meetings with Persons of interest (List attached), or Private Conversations that might give Indications of Jacobite Leanings would be valuable.

Précis: Sir Robert Abdy, Baronet

Succeeded to the Title at the Age of Three, and while living a personally (and regrettably) virtuous Life, became heavily involved in Jacobite Politics and, Last Year, was so injudicious as to sign his Name to a Petition sent to Louis of France, urging French Invasion of Britain in support of a Stuart Restoration. Needless to say, this is not generally known in Britain, and it would not be a good Idea to mention it directly to Sir Robert. Neither should you approach him, though he is active in Society and you may encounter him. If so, we are particularly interested in his present Associations—names only, for the Present. Don't get too close.

Précis: Henry Scudamore, Duke of Beaufort

The fourth-richest Man in England, and likewise a Signatory to the French Petition. Very much seen in Society and makes little Secret of his political Inclinations.

His private Life is much less virtuous than Sir Robert's, I'm afraid. Having adopted his Wife's Surname by Act of Parliament, he sued last Year to divorce her on Grounds of Adultery (true: she was having an adulterous Relationship with William Talbot, Heir to Earl Talbot, and she wasn't discreet about it). The Lady—her Name is Frances—

promptly countersued on Grounds that the Duke was impotent. The Duke, who is no shrinking Violet, demonstrated before several Court-appointed Examiners that he was capable of having an Erection, won his Divorce, and is now presumably enjoying his Freedom.

Don't get too close. Associates, Names only for the Present.

Précis: Mr. Robert Willimot

Lord Mayor of London until 1741. Presently associated with . . .

2

COLD HONEY AND SARDINES

London, May 1744
Argus House, Residence of the Duke of Pardloe

THE ROOM SMELLED OF dead flowers. It was raining heavily, but Hal seized the window sash and shoved, regardless. The action *was* regardless; the wood had swelled with the damp and the window remained shut. He tried twice more, then stood breathing heavily.

The chiming of the little carriage clock on the mantelpiece brought him to an awareness that he'd been standing in front of the closed window with his mouth half open, watching rain run down the glass, for a quarter of an hour, unable to make up his mind whether to call a footman to open the damn thing or just put his fist through it.

He turned away and, chilled, made his way by instinct toward the fire. He'd felt as though he were moving through cold honey ever since he'd forced himself out of bed, and now he collapsed joint by joint into his father's chair.

His father's chair. Blast. He closed his eyes, trying to summon the will to stand up and move. The leather was cold and stiff under his fingers, under his legs, hard against his back. He could feel the fire, a few feet away in its hearth, but the heat didn't reach him.

"I've brought your coffee, my lord." Nasonby's voice cut through the cold honey, as did the smell of the coffee. Hal opened his eyes. The footman had already put the tray down on the little marquetry table and was setting out the spoons, unlidding the sugar bowl, placing the tongs just so, tenderly removing the napkin folded about the jug of warm milk—the cream was in its twin jug at the other side, keeping cold. He found the symmetry and Nasonby's quiet, deft movements soothing.

"Thank you," he managed to say, and made a small gesture indicating that Nasonby should see to the details. This Nasonby did, and the cup was placed in his limp, waiting hands. He took a mouthful—it was perfect, very hot but not so much as to burn his mouth, sweet and milky—and nodded. Nasonby vanished.

For a little while, he could just drink coffee. He didn't have to think. Halfway through the cup, he briefly considered getting up and sitting in another chair, but by then the leather had warmed and molded to his body. He could almost imagine his father's touch on his shoulder, the brief squeeze the duke had always used to express affection for his sons. *Damn you.* His throat closed suddenly, and he set the cup down.

How was John managing? he wondered. He'd be safe enough in Aberdeen, surely. Still, he ought to write to his brother. Cousin Kenneth and Cousin Eloise were incredible bores, so rigidly Presbyterian that they didn't even countenance card-playing and disapproved of any activity on the Sabbath other than reading the Bible.

On the one occasion he and Esmé had stayed with them, Eloise had politely asked Esmé to read to them after the stodgy Sunday dinner of roast mutton and bashed neeps. Ignoring the text for the day, bookmarked with a handmade lace strip, Em had blithely thumbed through the book and settled on the story of Jephthah, who had sworn that if the Lord would grant him victory in battle against the sons of Ammon, then Jephthah would sacrifice to the Lord the first thing to greet him when he returned home.

"Really," said Esmé, swallowing the "R" in a particularly fetching French way. She looked up, frowning. "What if it should have been his dog? What do you say, Mercy," she said, addressing Hal's twelve-year-old cousin, Mercy. "If your papa should come home one day and announce that he was going to kill Jasper there"—the spaniel looked up from his rug, hearing his name—"just because he'd told God he would, what would you do?"

Mercy's eyes went round with horror and her lip quivered as she looked at the dog.

"But—but—he wouldn't," she said. But then she glanced at her father, doubt in her eyes. "You *wouldn't*, would you, Papa?"

"But if you had promised God?" Esmé put in helpfully, looking up at

Kenneth with her large blue eyes. Hal was enjoying the look on Kenneth's face, but Eloise was going a bit red round the jowls, so he coughed—and with a distinct, exhilarating sense that he was driving a carriage over a cliff said, "But Jephthah didn't meet his dog, did he? What *did* happen? Do remind me—been some time since I've read the Old Testament." In fact, he'd never read it, but Esmé loved to read it and tell him the stories—with her own inimitable commentary.

Esmé had carefully not looked at him but turned the page with delicate fingers and cleared her throat.

"And Jephthah came to Mizpeh unto his house, and, behold, his daughter came out to meet him with timbrels and with dances: and she was his only child; beside her he had neither son nor daughter.

"And it came to pass, when he saw her, that he rent his clothes, and said, Alas, my daughter! thou hast brought me very low, and thou art one of them that trouble me: for I have opened my mouth unto the Lord, and I cannot go back.

"And she said unto him, My father, if thou hast opened thy mouth unto the Lord, do to me according to that which hath proceeded out of thy mouth; forasmuch as the Lord hath taken vengeance for thee of thine enemies, even of the children of Ammon.

"And she said unto her father, Let this thing be done for me: let me alone two months, that I may go up and down upon the mountains, and bewail my virginity, I and my fellows.

"And he said, Go. And he sent her away for two months: and she went with her companions, and bewailed her virginity upon the mountains.

"And it came to pass at the end of two months, that she returned unto her father, who did with her according to his vow which he had vowed: and she knew no man. And it was a custom in Israel that the daughters of Israel went yearly to lament the daughter of Jephthah the Gileadite four days in a year."

Then she'd laughed, closing the book.

"I don't think I would have bewailed my virginity for long, me. I would have come home without it"—*then* she'd met his eyes, with a spark that had ignited his vitals—"and see whether my dear papa still considered me a suitable sacrifice."

His eyes were closed; he was breathing hard and dimly aware that tears were leaking out between his lids.

"You bitch," he whispered. "Em, you *bitch*!"

He breathed until the memory passed and the echo of her voice faded from his ear. When he opened his eyes, he found that his chin was resting in his hands, elbows on his knees, and that he was staring at the hearth rug. An expensive bit of carpet for such a use. Soft white wool, tufted, with the Grey family coat of arms in the center and an extravagantly worked "H" and "E" in black silk on either side. She'd had it made for him—a wedding present.

He'd given her a diamond pendant. And buried it with her and her child, a month ago.

He closed his eyes again. And breathed.

AFTER A TIME, he got up and wandered down the hall to the nook he'd taken over as his study. It was cramped as an eggshell, but he didn't need much space—and the close confines seemed to help him think better, shutting out some of the outside world.

He plucked a quill from the jar and bit it absently, tasting the bitter tang of dried ink. He should cut a new one but couldn't summon up the energy to find his penknife, and after all, what did it matter? John wouldn't mind a few blots.

Paper . . . There was a half quire of the parchment sheets he'd used to reply to the expressions of sympathy about Esmé. They'd come in by the bushelful—unlike the spatter of embarrassed notes that had followed his father's suicide three years before. He'd written the replies himself, in spite of his mother's offer to help. He'd been filled with something like the electric fluid natural philosophers talked about, something that numbed him to any natural need like food or sleep, that filled his brain and body with a manic need to move, to do something—though God knew there was nothing more he could have done after killing Nathaniel Twelvetrees. Not that he hadn't tried . . .

The paper felt gritty with dust; he didn't let anyone touch his desk. He held up a sheet and blew at it, shook it a bit, and set it down, then dipped his quill.

J— he wrote, and stopped dead. What was there to say? *I hope to God you're not dead? Have you seen anyone strange asking questions? How are you finding Aberdeen? Other than cold, wet, dreary, and gray . . .*

After twiddling the quill for a while, he gave up, wrote, *Luck. –H,* sanded the sheet, folded it, and, taking up the candle, dribbled smoke-stained wax onto the paper and stamped it firmly with his signet. A swan, flying, neck outstretched, across a full moon.

He was still sitting at his desk an hour later. There was progress: John's letter sat there, squared to the corner of the desk, sealed and with the

Armstrongs' direction in Aberdeen neatly written—with a freshly cut pen. The quire of parchment had been shaken free of dust, tapped into alignment, and put away in a drawer. And he'd found the source of the dead-flower smell: a bunch of rotting carnations left in a pottery mug on the windowsill. He'd managed to open *that* window and throw them out and then had summoned a footman to take the mug away to be washed. He was exhausted.

He became aware of noises in the distance: the sound of the front door opening, voices. That was all right; Sylvester would take care of whoever it was.

To his surprise, the butler seemed to have been overcome by the intruder; there were raised voices and a determined step coming rapidly toward his sanctum.

"What the devil are you doing, Melton?" The door was flung open and Harry Quarry's broad face glowered in at him.

"Writing letters," Hal said, with what dignity he could summon. "What does it look like?"

Harry strode into the room, lit a taper from the fire, and touched it to the candlestick on the desk. Hal hadn't noticed it growing dark, but it must be teatime, at least. His friend lifted the candlestick and examined him critically by its light.

"You don't want to know what you look like," said Harry, shaking his head. He put down the candle. "You didn't recall that you were meant to be meeting with Washburn this afternoon, I take it."

"Wash—oh, Jesus." He'd risen halfway out of his chair at the name and now sank back, feeling hollow at mention of his solicitor.

"I've spent the last hour with him, after meeting with Anstruther and Josper—you remember, the adjutant from the Fourteenth?" He spoke with a strong note of sarcasm.

"I do," Hal said shortly, and rubbed a hand hard over his face, trying to rouse his wits.

"I'm sorry, Harry," he said, and shook his head. He rose, pulling his banyan round him. "Call Nasonby, will you? Have him bring us tea in the library. I have to change and wash."

Washed, dressed, brushed, and feeling some semblance of ability, he came into the library a quarter hour later to find the tea trolley already in place; a wisp of aromatic steam rose from the teapot's spout to mingle with the spicy scents of ham and sardines and the unctuous sweetness of a currant sponge, oozing cream and butter.

"When's the last time you ate anything?" Harry demanded, watching Hal consume sardines on toast with the single-mindedness of a starving cat.

"Yesterday. Maybe. I forget." He reached for his cup and washed the sardines down far enough to make cake feasible as the next step. "Tell me what Washburn said."

Harry disposed of his own cake, swallowed, and replied.

"Well, you can't actually be tried in open court. Whatever you think about your damned title—no, don't tell me, I've heard it." He held out the palm of his hand in prevention, picking up a gherkin with the other.

"Whether you choose to call yourself the Duke of Pardloe, the Earl of Melton, or plain Harold Grey, you're still a peer. You can't be tried by anything save a jury *of* your peers—to wit, the House of Lords. And I didn't really require Washburn to tell me that the odds of a hundred no-blemen agreeing that you should be either imprisoned or hanged for chal-lenging the man who seduced your wife to a duel, and killing him as a result, is roughly a thousand to one—but he did tell me so."

"Oh." Hal hadn't given the matter a moment's thought but if he had would likely have reached a similar conclusion. Still, he felt some relief at hearing that the Honorable Lawrence Washburn, KC, shared it.

"Mind you—are you going to eat that last slice of ham?"

"Yes." Hal took it and reached for the mustard pot. Harry took an egg sandwich instead.

"Mind you," he repeated, mouth half full of deviled egg and thin white bread, "that doesn't mean you aren't in trouble."

"You mean with Reginald Twelvetrees, I suppose." Hal kept his eyes on his plate, carefully cutting the ham into pieces. "That isn't news to me, Harry."

"I shouldn't have thought so, no," Harry agreed. "I meant with the king."

Hal set down his fork and stared at Harry.

"The king?"

"Or, to be more exact, the army." Harry delicately plucked an almond biscuit from the wreckage of the tea trolley. "Reginald Twelvetrees has sent a petition to the secretary at war, asking that you be brought to a court-martial for the unlawful killing of his brother and, further, that you be removed as colonel of the Forty-sixth and the regiment refused perma-nent re-commission, on grounds that your behavior is so deranged as to constitute a danger to the readiness and ability of said regiment. That being where His Majesty comes in."

"Balderdash," Hal said shortly. But his hand trembled slightly as he lifted the teapot, and the lid rattled. He saw Harry notice, and he set it down carefully.

What the king giveth, the king also taketh away. It had taken months of painstaking work to have his father's regiment provisionally re-commissioned and more—much more—to find decent officers willing to join it.

"The scribblers—" Harry began, but Hal made a quick, violent gesture, cutting him off.

"I know."

"No, you don't—"

"I do! Don't bloody talk about it."

Harry made a soft growling noise but subsided. He picked up the pot and filled both cups, pushing Hal's toward him.

"Sugar?"

"Please."

The regiment—in its resurrected form—had not yet seen service anywhere; it had barely half its complement of men, and most of those didn't know one end of a musket from the other. He had only a skeleton staff, and while most of his officers were good, solid men, only a handful, like Harry Quarry, had any personal allegiance to him. Any pressure, any hint of scandal—well, any *more* scandal—and the whole structure could collapse. The remnants to be greedily scooped up or trampled on by Reginald Twelvetrees, Hal's father's blackened memory left forever dishonored as a traitor, and his own name dragged further through the mud—painted by the scribblers of the press not only as a cuckold but a murderer and lunatic.

The handle of his porcelain teacup broke off suddenly and shot across the table, striking the pot with a *tink!* The cup itself had cracked right through, and tea ran down his arm, soaking his cuff.

He carefully put down the two pieces of the cup and shook tea off his hand. Harry said nothing but raised one bushy black brow at him.

Hal closed his eyes and breathed through his nose for several moments.

"All right," he said, and opened his eyes. "One—Twelvetrees's petition. It hasn't been granted yet?"

"It has not." Harry was beginning to relax a little, which gave Hal a bit more confidence in his own assumption of composure.

"Well, then. That's the first thing—stop that petition. Do you know the secretary personally?"

Harry shook his head. "You?"

"I've met him once, at Ascot. Friendly wager. I won, though."

"Ah. Too bad." Harry drummed his fingers on the cloth for a moment, then darted a glance at Hal. "Ask your mother?"

"Absolutely not. She's in France, anyway, and she's not coming back."

Harry knew *why* the Dowager Countess of Melton was in France—and why John was in Aberdeen—and nodded reluctantly. Benedicta Grey knew a great many people, but the suicide of her husband on the eve of his being arrested as a Jacobite traitor had barred her from the sort of circles where Hal might otherwise have found influence.

There was a long silence, unbroken by Nasonby's appearance with a new teacup. He filled this, took up the shattered bits of the old one, and vanished as he'd come, soft-footed as a cat.

"What does this petition say, exactly?" Hal asked finally.

Harry grimaced but settled himself to answer.

"That you killed Nathaniel Twelvetrees because you had conceived the unfounded notion that he had been, er . . . dallying with your wife. In the grip of this delusion, you then assassinated him. And thus you are plainly mentally unfit to hold command over—"

"Unfounded?" Hal said blankly. *"Assassinated?"*

Harry reached out quickly and took the cup from his hand.

"You know as well as I do, Melton—it's not what's true; it's what you can make people believe." He set the full cup gingerly on its saucer. "The hound was damned discreet about it, and apparently so was Esmé. There wasn't a breath of gossip until the news that you'd shot him on his own croquet lawn."

"*He* chose the ground! *And* the weapons!"

"I know that," Harry said patiently. "I was there, remember?"

"What do you think I am?" Hal snapped. "An idiot?"

Harry ignored that.

"I'll say what I know, of course—that it was a legitimate challenge and that Nathaniel Twelvetrees accepted it. But his second—that chap Buxton—was killed last month in a carriage accident near Smithfield. And no one else was on that croquet lawn. That's doubtless what gave Reginald the notion of trying to nobble you this way—no independent witnesses."

"Oh . . . *hell*." The sardines were stirring in his guts.

Harry took a breath that strained the seams of his uniform and looked down at the table.

"I—forgive me. But . . . is there any proof?"

Hal managed a laugh, dry as sawdust.

"Of the affair? Do you think I'd have killed him if I hadn't been sure?"

"No, of course not. I only mean—well . . . bloody hell . . . did she just . . . *tell* you? Or perhaps you . . . er . . . saw . . ."

"No." Hal was feeling dizzy. He shook his head, closed his eyes, and tried a deep breath of his own. "No, I never caught them together. And she didn't—didn't *quite* tell me. There were—there were letters."

She'd left them where she knew he'd find them. But why? That was one of the things that killed him, over and over again. She'd never told him why. Was it simple guilt? Had she grown tired of the affair but lacked the courage to end it herself? Worse—had she *wanted* him to kill Nathaniel?

No. Her face when he'd come back that day, when he told her what he'd done . . .

His face was resting on the white cloth and there were black and white spots swarming before his eyes. He could smell starch and spilled tea, sardines with their tang of the sea. Of Esmé's birth waters. And her blood. *Oh, God, don't let me vomit. . . .*

3

IRISH ROVERS

London, May 1744

MINNIE LAY IN BED, the remains of breakfast on a tray beside her, and contemplated the shape of her first day in London. She'd arrived late the night before and had barely taken notice of the rooms her father had engaged for her—she had a suite in a townhouse on Great Ryder Street, "convenient to everything," as he'd assured her, complete with a housemaid and meals provided from the kitchen in the basement.

She had been filled with an intoxicating sense of freedom from the moment she'd taken an affectionate leave of her father on the dock at Calais. She could still feel the pleasure of it, bubbling in the slow, pleasant fashion of a crock of fermenting cabbage under her stays, but her innate caution kept a lid on it.

She'd done small jobs on her own before, sometimes outside of Paris, but those had been simple things like calling on the relatives of a dead bibliophile and sympathetically relieving them of their burdensome inheritance—she'd noticed that almost no one felt that a library was much of a legacy—and even then she'd had an escort, usually a stout, middle-aged, long-married man still capable of hoisting boxes and deflecting nuisances but unlikely to make improper advances to a young woman of seventeen.

Monsieur Perpignan would not, of course, be a suitable escort for London. Aside from a tendency to seasickness, a fondness for his wife, and a disgust for British cooking, he didn't speak English and had no sense of direction. She'd been a bit surprised that her father would let her stay in London entirely on her own—but of course he hadn't. He had Made Arrangements: his specialty.

"I've arranged a chaperone for you," her father had said, handing over a neat docket of notes, addresses, maps, and English money. "A Lady Buford, a widow of slender means but good connections. She'll arrange a social life for you, introduce you to the right sorts of people, take you to plays and salons, that sort of thing."

"What fun," she'd said politely, and he laughed.

"Oh, I expect you'll find some, my dear," he said. "That's why I've also arranged two . . . shall we call them bodyguards?"

"So much more tactful than minders, or wardens. Two?"

"Yes, indeed. They'll run errands for you, as well as accompany you when you visit clients." He reached into one of the pigeonholes of his desk and drew out a folded sheet of paper, which he handed her. "This is a précis of what I told you about the Duke of Pardloe—and a few others. I didn't mention him to Lady Buford, and you should be somewhat discreet about your interest in him. There's a great deal of scandal attached to that family, and you—"

"Don't touch pitch until you're ready to set light to it," she finished, with no more than a slight roll of the eyes.

"Travel safe, my dear." He'd kissed her forehead and embraced her briefly. "I'll miss you."

"I'll miss you, too, Papa," she murmured now, climbing out of bed. "But not *that* much."

She glanced at the secretaire, where she'd put all the lists and documents. Time enough for the chaste Duke of Pardloe and the randy Duke of Beaufort when she came within sight of them. Lady Buford had left a card, saying that she would meet Minnie at Rumm's Tea-Room in Piccadilly at four o'clock for tea. *Wear something pretty, modest, and not over-elaborate,* Lady Buford had added, with welcome practicality. The pink muslin, then, with the little jacket.

There were three appointments already scheduled for the early afternoon—routine book business—and the two bodyguards were meant to come and introduce themselves at eleven. She glanced at her little traveling clock, which showed half-eight. A quick wash, a simple dress, stout boots for walking, and London was hers—alone!—for two hours.

THEY'D LIVED IN London for a time, when she was much younger. And she'd come with her father twice for brief visits, when she was four-teen and fifteen. She had a general idea of the city's shape but had never needed to find her own way.

She was accustomed to exploring a new place, though, and within the first hour had discovered a decent-looking ordinary for quick meals out-

side her rooms, a baker's shop for cakes, and the nearest church. Her father had nothing to do with religion, and so far as she knew, she'd never
even been christened—but it was as well to look the part you played, and
pious, modest young women went to church on Sunday. Besides, she liked
the music.

The day was bright, the air tangy with spring sap, and the streets were
full of an exuberant bustle, quite different from Paris or Prague. There was
really no place like London. Particularly as no other city contained her
mother. But that small matter would need to wait for a bit; much as she
longed to rush off to Parson's Green at once and see this Mrs. Simpson, it
was too important. She needed to reconnoiter, to calculate her approach.
To be hasty or importunate might ruin everything.

She headed toward Piccadilly, which housed a good many booksellers.
On the way, though, were Regent and then Oxford Streets, charmingly
studded with expensive shops. She must ask Lady Buford about dress-
makers.

She had a little French watch pinned to her fichu—it didn't do to be
late for appointments—and when it told her in a tiny silver voice that it
was now half-ten, she sighed and turned back toward Great Ryder Street.
As she crossed the corner of Upper St. James's Park, though, she began to
have an odd feeling at the back of her neck.

She reached the corner, made as though to step into the street, then
suddenly darted sideways, across a lane, and into the park itself. She
whipped behind a large tree and stood in the shadow, frozen, watching.
Sure enough, a young man came hurtling into the lane, looking sharp
from side to side. He was roughly dressed, brown hair tied back with
string—perhaps an apprentice or a laborer.

He halted for an instant, then walked fast down the lane, out of sight.
She was just about to slide out of her shelter and run for the street when
she heard him whistle loudly. An answering whistle came *from* the street,
and she pressed herself against the tree, heart hammering.

Bloody, bloody hell, she thought. *If I'm raped and murdered, I'll never
hear the end of it!*

She swallowed and made up her mind. It would be somewhat harder
for anyone to abduct her off a busy street than to winkle her out of her
precarious hiding spot. A couple of gentlemen were coming along the
path toward her, deep in conversation. As they passed, she stepped out on
the path directly behind them, keeping so close that she was obliged to
hear a very scabrous story concerning one man's father-in-law and what
had happened when he chose to celebrate his birthday in a bawdy house.
Before the end was reached, though, the street was reached, and she
stepped away, walking fast down Ryder Street, with a sense of relief.

She was perspiring, in spite of the cool morning, and the pin thrust through her straw hat had loosened. She paused, took off the hat, and was dabbing her face with a handkerchief when a male voice spoke in her ear.

"So here ye are!" it said triumphantly. "Jaysus God!" This last was the result of her having whipped the eight-inch hatpin from its moorings and aimed it at his breast.

"Who the blood helly are you, and what do you mean by following me?" Minnie demanded, glaring at him. Then she saw his eyes lift, noticing something over her shoulder, and the words "two bodyguards" dropped into her mind like pebbles dropped in water. *Merde!*

"Two," she said flatly, and lowered the hatpin. "Mister O'Higgins, I presume? And . . . Mr. O'Higgins, as well?" she added, turning toward the other young man, who had come up behind her. He grinned at her and bowed extravagantly, sweeping off his cap.

"Raphael Thomas O'Higgins, me lady," he said. "Blood helly? Would that be a French expression, at all?"

"If you like," she said, still annoyed. "And you?" She swung back to face the first pursuer, who was also grinning from ear to ear.

"Michael Seamas O'Higgins, miss," he said, with a bob of the head. "Mick, to me friends, and me brother there is Rafe. Ye were expecting us, I see?"

"Hmph. How long have you been following me?"

"Since ye left the house, sure," Rafe said easily. "What was it spooked ye, would ye tell me? I thought we'd kept well back."

"To be honest, I don't know," she said. The rush of fright and flight was fading from her blood, and her annoyance with it. "I just suddenly had a . . . feeling. Just something at the back of my neck. But I didn't *know* someone was following me until I ran into the park and you"—nodding at Mick—"ran in after me."

The brothers O'Higgins exchanged a glance with lifted brows but seemed to take this at face value.

"Aye, then," Rafe said. "Well, we were to introjuice ourselves to ye at eleven o' the clock, and I hear the bells sayin' that's just what it is now . . . so, miss, is there anything we can be doin' for you today? Any errands to be run, parcels picked up, perhaps the little small quiet murder on the side . . . ?"

"How much is my father paying you?" she asked, beginning to be amused. "I doubt it extends to procuring murder."

"Oh, we come cheap," Mick assured her, straight-faced. "Though if it was to be anything of a fancy nature—beheading, say, or hiding multiple bodies—well, I won't say but what that might not run into money."

"That's all right," she assured him. "Should it come to that, I have a bit of my own. And speaking of that"—the idea came to her as she re-pinned her hat—"I have several letters of credit, drawn on the Bankers on the Strand—you know the place? That's what you can do today: come with me to the bank and back again. I'll need cash in hand for one or two of my afternoon appointments."

4

REGIMENTAL BUSINESS

W INSTEAD TERRACE WAS A small row of discreetly fine townhouses that faced a similar terrace on the other side of a private park, its privacy protected by a tall fence of black iron and a locked gate.

Hal reached through the iron bars of the fence and carefully broke a twig from one of the small trees that pressed against it.

"What are you doing?" Harry demanded, stopping in mid-stride. "Picking a posy for your buttonhole? I don't think Grierson's much of a dandy."

"Nor am I," said Hal equably. "I wanted to see if this is what I thought it was, but it is."

"And what's that, pray?" Harry came back a step to look at the twig in Hal's hand. The foliage was cool on his fingers; it had rained a bit earlier and the leaves and flowers were still wet, water droplets sliding down his wrist, disappearing into the cloth of his frilled cuff.

He transferred the twig to his other hand and shook the water off, absently wiping his hand on his coat. He liked good linen and a well-fitting suit, but in fact he wasn't a dandy. It *was* necessary to impress Donald Grierson favorably, though, and to that end, he and Harry were both wearing semi-dress uniform, with a discreet but visible amount of gold lace.

"Cockspur," he said, showing Harry the two-inch thorns protruding from the twig. "It's a hawthorn of sorts."

"I thought hawthorns were hedges." Harry jerked his head toward the terrace, and Hal nodded, coming along.

"They can be. Or shrubs or trees. Interesting plant—the leaves are said to taste like bread and cheese, though I haven't tried."

Harry looked amused.

"I'll remember that, next time I'm in the country and not a pub in sight. Ready, are you?"

Hal might have felt annoyed at Harry's solicitousness, but his friend was—all too clearly—honestly worried for him. He drew breath and straightened his shoulders, admitting to himself that, *in* all honesty, he couldn't dismiss that worry as unfounded. He was getting better, though. He had to—there was the devil of a lot of work to be done if he had any hope of getting the regiment on its feet and ready to fight. And Major Grierson was going to help him do it.

"There's something else about hawthorn," he said, as they reached Grierson's door.

"What's that?" Harry was wearing his bird-dog look, alert and intent on the prey to be flushed, and Hal smiled privately to see it.

"Well, the green of the leaves symbolizes constancy, of course, but the flowers are said to—and I quote—'have the scent of a woman sexually aroused.'"

Harry's intent look switched instantly to the flowering twig in Hal's hand. Hal laughed, brushed the flowers under his own nose, then handed them to Harry, turning to lift the brass boar's-head knocker.

Good lord, it's true. The whiff of insinuating musk so distracted him that he scarcely noticed when the door opened. How the devil could something smell . . . slippery? He closed his fist involuntarily, with the very disconcerting feeling that he had touched his wife.

"My lord?" The servant who had opened the door was looking at him with a slightly puzzled frown.

"Oh," Hal said, snapping back to himself. "Yes. I am. I mean—"

"Major Grierson is expecting his lordship, I think?" Harry inserted himself between Hal and the inquiring face, which nodded obligingly and withdrew into the house, gesturing them to follow.

There were voices coming from the morning room to which they were escorted: a woman, and at least two men. Perhaps Grierson was married and his wife was accepting callers . . . ?

"Lord Melton!" Grierson himself—a big, bluff-looking, sandy-haired chap—rose from a settee and came to meet him, smiling. Hal's heart rose; he'd not met Grierson before, but his reputation was stellar. He'd served with a famous regiment of foot for years, fought at Dettingen, and was known as much for his organizational abilities as his courage. And organization was what the fledgling 46th needed, above all.

"So pleased to meet you," Grierson was saying. "Everyone's buzzing about this new regiment, and I want to hear all about it. Pansy, my dear, may I present his lordship, the Earl of Melton?" He half-turned, extending a hand to a small, darkly pretty woman of about his own age—which Hal estimated as thirty-five. "Lord Melton, my wife, Mrs. Grierson."

"Charmed, Mrs. Grierson."

Hal made a leg to Mrs. Grierson, who smiled at the attention—but his own attention was slightly distracted by Harry, behind him. Instead of advancing to be introduced and pay his own compliments, Harry had uttered a sort of throaty noise that might have been a growl in less-civil company.

Hal glanced in Harry's direction, saw what Harry was seeing, and felt as though he'd been punched in the stomach.

"We've met," said Reginald Twelvetrees, as Grierson turned to introduce him. Twelvetrees rose to his feet, cold-eyed.

"Indeed?" said Grierson, still smiling but now glancing warily between Hal and Twelvetrees. "I'd no idea. I trust you have no objection to Colonel Twelvetrees meeting with us, Lord Melton? And I trust that you, sir"—with a deferential nod to Twelvetrees—"have no objection to my inviting Colonel Lord Melton to join us?"

"Not in the slightest," said Twelvetrees, with a twitch in one cheek that was by no means a token smile. Still, he sounded as though he meant that "not in the slightest," and Hal began to feel a certain tightness in his chest.

"By all means," he said coolly, meeting Twelvetrees's stony gaze with one of his own. Reginald's eyes were the same color that Nathaniel's had been, a brown so dark as to seem black in some lights. Nathaniel's had been black as pitch, facing him in the dawn.

Mrs. Grierson excused herself and went out, saying that she would have refreshments brought, and the men settled, in the uneasy fashion of seabirds jealous of their rocky perches.

"Quite to my surprise, gentlemen, I find myself in the enviable position of being a valuable commodity," Grierson said, leaning affably forward. "As you may know, I fell ill in Prussia, was shipped home to recover, and fortunately did so. But it was a long convalescence, and by the time I was fit, my regiment had . . . well . . . I'm sure you know the general situation; I won't go into the particulars just now."

All three of his guests made small grunts of assent, with a few murmurs of decent sympathy. What had happened was that Grierson had been bloody lucky in falling ill when he did. There had been a truly scandalous mutiny a month after his removal to England, and when the mess had been cleaned up, half the surviving officers had been court-martialed, fifteen mutineers had been hanged, and the remnants dispersed to four other regiments. The original regiment had formally ceased to exist, and Grierson's commission with it.

The normal thing for a man in his position to do would be to buy a commission in another regiment. But Grierson was, as he bluntly put it, a valuable commodity. Not only was he a very capable administrator and a good commander—he was popular, with other officers, with the War Office, and with the press.

Hal needed Grierson's expertise; he needed even more Grierson's connections. With Grierson on his staff, he could attract officers of a much higher caliber than he could do with money alone.

As to what Twelvetrees, colonel of a long established and very solid artillery regiment, might want with him, that was fairly obvious, too: he wanted Hal not to have Grierson.

"So, Lord Melton, tell me how things stand with you," Grierson said, once they'd got stuck into the wine and biscuits that Mrs. Grierson had sent in. "Who are your staff officers, to begin with?"

Hal set down his glass carefully and told him, in a calm voice, exactly who they were. Competent men, so far as he knew—but almost all of them quite young, with no experience of foreign campaigns.

"Of course," Harry put in helpfully, "that means that you would be quite senior in the regiment: have your pick of companies, postings, aides . . ."

"Just how many troops have you on your muster roll, Colonel?" Reginald didn't bother trying to sound neutral, and Grierson glanced at him. Not with disapproval, Hal saw, and his heart sped up a little.

"I cannot tell you exactly, sir," he said, with exquisite politeness. Sweat had begun to dampen his collar, though the room was cool. "We are conducting a major campaign of recruitment at the moment, and our numbers rise—substantially—each day." On a good day, they might get three new men—one of whom would not abscond with the bounty for signing— and from the smirk on Twelvetrees's face, Hal knew he was aware of this.

"Indeed," said Twelvetrees. "Untrained recruits. The Royal Artillery is at full strength presently. My company commanders have been with me for at least a decade."

Hal kept his temper, though he was beginning to feel slightly breathless from suppressed rage.

"In that case, Major Grierson may have less space in which to distinguish himself," he riposted smartly. "Whereas with us, sir . . ." He bowed to Grierson and felt momentarily giddy when he raised his head. "With us," he repeated more strongly, "you would have the satisfaction of helping to shape a fine regiment in . . . your own likeness, so to speak."

Harry chuckled in support, and Grierson smiled but politely. He'd also have the not-inconsiderable risk of failure and knew it.

Hal felt Harry stir uncomfortably next to him and took a deep breath, preparing to say something forceful about . . . about . . . The word had gone. Simply gone. He'd breathed in, and a trace of scent from the cockspur in Harry's buttonhole had touched his brain. He closed his eyes abruptly.

Major Grierson had luckily asked a question; Hal could hear Twelve-trees replying in a gruff, matter-of-fact way. Grierson said something else and Twelvetrees's voice relaxed a little, and quite suddenly it was Nathaniel's voice, and he opened his eyes and saw nothing of the cozy morning room, of the men there with him. He was cold, shaking with cold . . .

And his fingers were squeezing the cold pistol in his hand so hard the metal would leave marks on his palm. He'd fucked Esmé before he left to kill her lover. Waked her in the dark and taken her, and she'd wanted him—ferociously—or perhaps she had pretended it was Nathaniel in the dark. He knew it was the last time . . .

"Colonel?" A voice, a dim voice. "Lord Melton!"

"Hal?" Harry's voice, full of alarm. Harry, with him on the lawn, rain running down his face in a sunless dawn. He swallowed, tried to swallow, tried to breathe, but there was no air.

His eyes were open, but he couldn't see anything. The cold was spreading down the sides of his jaws, and he realized suddenly that . . .

He looked straight into Nathaniel's eyes and felt the bang and then it was . . .

HARRY HAD INSISTED on calling a carriage to take them home. Hal refused brusquely and strode—knees shaking, but he could walk, he *would* walk, dammit—away from Winstead Terrace.

He made it to the far side of the private garden—well away from the cockspur tree—where he stopped and gripped the cold black iron of the fence and carefully lowered himself to the pavement. His mouth tasted of brandy; Grierson had forced it down him, when he could breathe again.

"I've never bloody fainted in my *life*," he said. He was sitting, back against the fence, forehead on his knees. "Not even when they told me about Father."

"I know." Harry had sat down beside him. Hal thought briefly what flats they must look, two young soldiers got up in scarlet and gold lace, sitting on the pavement like a pair of beggars. He really didn't care.

"Actually," Hal said after a minute, "that's not true, is it? I passed out in the ham at tea last week, didn't I?"

"You just felt a bit queasy," Harry said stoutly. "Not eating for days, then two dozen sardines—enough to fell anyone."

"Two dozen?" Hal asked, and laughed despite everything. Not much of a laugh, but he turned his head and looked at Harry. Harry's face was creased with anxiety but relaxed a little when he saw Hal looking at him.

"At least that many. With mustard, too."

They sat a few moments, feeling easier. Neither of them wanted to say anything about what had just happened, and they didn't, but each could tell the other was thinking of it—how could they not?

"If it falls apart . . ." Harry began at last, then bent and looked at him searchingly. "You going to faint again?"

"No." Hal swallowed twice, then took a shallow breath—the only kind he could manage—and pushed himself to his feet, holding on to the iron fence. He had to let Harry know he could go, that he didn't have to try to carry on with this doomed enterprise, this fool's game. Though the thought of it made his throat close. He cleared it, hard, and repeated Harry's words: "If it does fall apart—"

Harry's hand on his arm stopped him. Harry's face was six inches from his own, the brown eyes clear and steady.

"Then we'll start again, old man," he said. "That's all. Come on; I need a drink, and so do you."

5

STRATEGY AND TACTICS

I T TOOK LESS THAN five minutes over the cake plate at Rumm's for Minnie to realize the depths of her father's treachery.

"Your style is very good, my dear," said Lady Buford. The chaperone was a thin, gray-haired lady with an aristocratically long nose and sharp gray eyes under heavy lids that had probably been languorously appealing in her youth. She gave a small, approving nod at the delicate white daisies embroidered on Minnie's pink linen jacket. "I had thought, with your portion, that we might set our sights on a London merchant, but with your personal attractions, it *might* be possible to aim a little higher."

"My . . . portion?"

"Yes, five thousand pounds is quite attractive—we'll have a good selection, I assure you. You could have your pick of army officers"—she made an elegantly dismissive gesture, then wrapped long, bony fingers around the handle of her teacup—"and there are a few that are *quite* appealing, I admit. But there's the perpetual absences to be considered . . . and postings in insalubrious spots, should your husband wish you to accompany him. Now, if he's killed, there's a reasonable pension, but it's nothing to what a sound merchant might leave—and if he should be wounded to such an extent as to exclude him from service . . ." She took a long, considering sip, then shook her head.

"No. We can certainly do better than the army. Or the navy, God help us. Sailors tend to be somewhat . . . un. *Couth*," she said, leaning toward Minnie and pursing her wrinkled lips in a whisper.

"God help us," Minnie repeated in a pious tone, though her fist was knotted in the folds of the tablecloth. *You utter weasel!* she thought toward her absent father. *Establish a social life for me, eh?*

Despite her astonished annoyance, though, she had to admit to being somewhat impressed. Five thousand pounds?

If he actually meant it . . . the cynical part of her mind put in. But he likely did. It would be *just* like him. He'd see it as killing two birds with one stone: getting her access to likely sources of salable information and simultaneously marrying her off to one of them, with Lady Buford as his unwitting accomplice.

And he had, to be fair, told her that he wanted an Englishman for her. She just hadn't thought he'd meant *now*. Really, she had to admire her father's twisted genius; who but a marriage procuress would know more— and have less hesitation in revealing what she knew—about the intimate familial and financial details of wealthy men?

Taking a deep breath, she let go of the fistful of tablecloth and did her best to look interested, in a demure sort of way.

"We'll avoid the navy, then," she said. "Do you think . . . I hope I am not immodest in suggesting it, but after all, five thousand pounds . . . What about minor—very minor," she added hastily, "members of the peerage?"

Lady Buford blinked but not as though taken aback; merely reordering her mental index, Minnie thought.

"Well, there are impoverished knights and baronets by the score," she said. "And if you are set on a title . . . But really, my dear, I wouldn't recommend that avenue unless you will have independent means of your own. Your portion would be instantly swallowed in sustaining some crumbling manor and you yourself would molder inside it, never getting to London or having a new dress from one year's end to the next."

"To be sure. I, um, *do* possess a, er . . . small competence, shall we say?"

"Indeed." Lady Buford's wispy brows rose in interest. "How small?"

"A thousand a year," Minnie said, wildly exaggerating the income from her small private ventures, which totaled less than a tenth of that sum. Still, it hardly mattered, as she wasn't actually marrying any of these theoretical impoverished baronets; she only needed to enter the social circles they—they and their more interesting brethren—inhabited.

"Hmm." Lady Buford assumed an inward look and drank tea. After a few moments' contemplation, she set down the cup with decision.

"You speak good French, your father says?"

"Mais oui."

Lady Buford looked at her sharply, but Minnie kept a straight face.

"Well, then. We'll begin with Lady Jonas's Thursday *salon*. It's literary and intellectual, but she usually has a good mix of available gentlemen, including European—though your father *did* specify an Englishman. . . . Well, we'll see. Then perhaps a play on Saturday evening. . . . We'll have a box; it's important that you be seen—have you something appropriate to wear?"

"I don't know," Minnie said honestly. "I've never been to a play; what *is* appropriate?"

Half an hour, two pots of China tea, and a dozen tea cakes (with cream) later, she made her way out into the street, a scribbled list of engagements in her hand and her head spinning with tippets, panniers, mantuas, swags, fans—she had a nice fan, luckily—and other items necessary to the pursuit and bagging of a wealthy and influential husband.

"A gun would be simpler," she muttered, thrusting the list into her pocket. "And certainly less expensive."

"What kind of gun?" said Mick O'Higgins with interest, appearing out of a nearby doorway.

"Never mind," she said. "We're going to a milliner's."

"Oh, a milliner's, is it?" He bowed and offered her his arm. "Nay bother, then. Sure, the bird'll be dead before they put it on your hat."

A week later . . .

HER APPOINTMENT BOOK was a pleasure to look at, a glory to hold. Made in Florence, the leather cover was the color of rich chocolate, with a pressed gilt design of looping vines and a glorious, explosive-looking flower in the center. Her father had informed her that the Chinese called it *"Chu"* and that it was a symbol of happiness. He'd given her the book for her seventeenth birthday.

He'd given her another one, too, before she left Paris: a rough-cut notebook such as an artist might use for sketching notes—and sketches were just what decorated its pages, made by her own hand. And coded into the sketches were the appointments made for those clients whose names were never spoken aloud.

The first few pages were decoys; the first *aide-memoire* was on the fifth page (the appointment being for the fifth of the month): a sketch of trees overhanging a path, with the legend *Vauxhall Gardens* underneath. There were footprints on the path, leading the way into the shadows—three of them clearly marked, and half of another. Half-three in Vauxhall Gardens, on the third of June. On the facing page, a sketch of a wrapped parcel, like a birthday present. To be received . . .

That was for tomorrow. She set the sketchbook aside and picked up the chuppointment book, where the less-private clients were listed—those merely wanting to buy or sell books. Eight ticked off since her arrival in London; she'd been very efficient.

She rubbed a thumb gently over the exuberant bloom on the cover. She'd never seen a real *chu* flower. Perhaps she might come across a botanist in London who would have such a plant; she'd love to know what they smelled like.

At the back of the appointment book, between the creamy blank pages and the soft leather cover, was the letter. She had written and rewritten it several times. Wanting to be sure, but knowing there could be no surety in this.

In the morning, she'd give it to one of the O'Higginses. She'd known them long enough now to be sure they'd carry out her errands without question—well, without a *lot* of questions. She sent a good many notes and letters in the course of business; there was no reason why this one should seem at all odd.

Mrs. Simpson, Parson's Green, Peterborough Road

Her fingers were damp; she put the letter back before the ink of the direction should smear and closed the book upon it.

From the Chu Diary

Monday, June 1

11:00—Mr. H. R. Wallace, to view *Philologus Hebraeus* (Johannes Leusden). Offer also *Histoire de la Guerre des Juifs Contre les Romains* (Joseph Flavius) and *De Sacrificiis Libri Duo Quorum Altero Explicantur Omnia Judæorum, Nonnulla Gentium Profanarum Sacrificia* (William Owtram)

1:00—Misses Emma and Pauline Jones, to discuss catalog of late father's library. In Swansea(!) How blood helly will I get those shipped?

2:00—fitting at Myers, peach silk suit

4:00—Lady Buford, tea here, then Mrs. Montague's salon
8:00—Drury Lane Theatre, *Mahomet the Imposter*

Tuesday, June 2

9:00—bath
10:00—hairdresser
1:00—Lady Buford, for Viscountess Baldo's luncheon
5:00—the Hon. Horace Walpole, to view Italian titles
        (arrange tea)

Wednesday, June 3

10:00—boating on Thames with Sir George Vance, Kt.,
        luncheon
3:30—Deer Park
7:00—Mrs. Annabelle Wrigley's rout

Note: Sir George young but boring; told L. Buford to cross
him off. Met a promising gentleman named Hanksleigh at
rout, knowledgeable about finance; seeing him for tea next
week.

Note: Vauxhall Gardens charming (visit again next week)

Thursday, June 4

9:00—bath
10:00—body groomer (ouch)
11:00—hairdresser
1:00—measurements, Madame Alexander's, eau-de-nil ball
        gown
3:00—promenade in Hyde Park with Sir Robert Abdy, Bt.
8:00—supper party, Lady Wilford

Note: Lady Wilford's party well supplied. Two engagements
for next week, and a promising conversation with the Mar-
quess of Tewksbury about hocus-pocus in House of Lords.

Note: Also met Duke of Beaufort at supper, chatted briefly
over asparagus mayonnaise. Asked me to ride with him in

Rotten Row next Tuesday. Declined on grounds that I have no horse, only to have him offer me one. Accepted. How hard can it be?

Friday, June 5

11:00—Baron Edgerly, to view French titles, elephant folio atlas
1:30—Visit Mr. Smethurst, bookseller in Piccadilly, worm list
    of clients out of him if poss.
4:30—Lady Buford, tea with Mrs. Randolph and her
    two daughters

Note: supper alone, thank God. Don't want to hear one more word spoken. Randolph girls complete *emmerdeuses*.

Note: reply from Mrs. Simpson. Monday, two o'clock.

Saturday, June 6

Beginning to attract clients desiring information rather than books. Father's work. Two this week. Said no to one, yes to Sir Roger Barrymore (request re character of man seeking to wed his daughter; met said man last week and could have told Sir Roger he's a wrong 'un on the spot, but will give him news next week to justify bill).

Sunday, June 7

Morning service, St. George's, Hanover Square, with Mr. Jaken (Exchange)—fond of organ music

4:00—tea, Lady Buford, review of progress
7:00—Evensong, St. Clement's, Mr. Hopworth, banker

6

UNEXPECTED INTRODUCTIONS

Monday, June 8

MINERVA RUBBED HER HANDS nervously on her petticoat to dry them, then poked for the dozenth time at her hair, though knowing it to be pinned up as securely as hair *could* be pinned; the skin of her face felt stretched, her eyebrows ludicrously arched. She glanced into the glass quickly—for the dozenth time—to assure herself that this was in fact not the case.

Would Mrs. Simpson come? She'd dithered about her mother all the way to London and for the two weeks since her arrival—and she hated dithering above all things. Make up one's mind and be done with it!

So she had, but for once, decision had not removed doubt. Maybe she should have gone to her mother's residence, appeared on the doorstep without warning. That had been her first impulse, and it was still strong. She'd finally decided instead to send a note—phrased with the utmost simplicity and the barest of facts—requesting the pleasure of Mrs. Simpson's company in her rooms in Great Ryder Street at two o'clock on Monday, the eighth of June.

She'd thought of sending a note asking permission to call upon Mrs. Simpson; that might have seemed more polite. But she feared the receipt of a rejection—or, still worse, silence—and so had issued an invitation instead. If her mother didn't come this afternoon, the doorstep option was still open. And by God, she would do it . . .

The note crackled in her pocket, and she pulled it out—again—unfolding it to read the message, written in a firm round hand—presumably Mrs. Simpson's—without salutation or signature, promise or rebuke.

Do you think this is wise? it said.

"Well, obviously not," she said aloud, cross, and shoved it back into her pocket. "What does that matter?"

The knock on the door nearly stopped her heart. She was here! She was early—it lacked a quarter hour of two o'clock—but perhaps Mrs. Simpson had been as eager as herself for the meeting, despite the cool reserve of the note.

The maid—Eliza, a solid middle-aged woman in a high state of starch, who had been engaged with the rooms—glanced at her and, at her nod, went down the hall to answer the door. Minnie glanced in the looking glass again (*God, I look quite wild*), smoothed her embroidered overskirt, and assumed an aloof-but-cordial expression.

"Colonel Quarry, ma'am," said the maid, coming in and stepping aside to admit the visitor.

"Who?" said Minnie blankly. The tall gentleman who had appeared in the doorway had paused to look her over with interest; she lifted her chin and returned his regard.

He was wearing his scarlet uniform—infantry—and was quite handsome in a blunt sort of way. Dark and dashing—and well aware of it, she thought, concealing an inward smile. She knew how to handle this sort and allowed the smile to blossom.

"Your servant, ma'am," he said, with an answering flash of good teeth. He made her a very graceful leg, straightened, and said, "How old are you?"

"Nineteen," she said, adding two years without hesitation. "And you, sir?"

He blinked. "Twenty-one. Why?"

"I have an interest in numerology," she said, straight-faced. "Are you acquainted with the science?"

"Er . . . no." He was still eyeing her with interest, but the interest was of a different type now.

"What is your date of birth, sir?" she asked, sidling behind the small gilt desk and taking up a quill. "If you please?" she added politely.

"The twenty-third of April," he said, lips twitching slightly.

"So," she said, scratching briskly, "that is two plus three, which is five, plus four—April being the fourth month, of course," she informed him kindly. "Which makes nine, and then we add the digits of your year of birth, which makes . . . one plus seven plus two plus three? Yes, just so . . . totaling twenty-two. We then add both twos together and end with four."

"Apparently so," he agreed, coming round the desk to look over her shoulder at the paper, where she had written a large four, circling it. He emitted a noticeable amount of heat, standing so close. "What does this signify?"

She relaxed slightly against the tightness of her stays. Now she had him. Once they got curious, you could get them to tell you anything.

"Oh, the four is the most masculine of numbers," she assured him— quite truthfully. "It designates an individual of marked strength and stability. Dependable, and exceedingly trustworthy."

He'd put his shoulders back half an inch.

"You're very punctual," she said, giving him a sidelong look from beneath her lashes. "Healthy . . . strong . . . you notice details and are very good in controlling complex affairs. And you're loyal—very loyal to those you care for." She gave him a small but admiring smile to go with this.

Fours were capable and persistent but not swift thinkers, and, once again, she was surprised at just how often the numbers turned out to be right.

"Indeed," he said, and cleared his throat, looking mildly embarrassed but undeniably pleased.

At this point, she heard the subdued ticking of the longcase clock behind her and a bolt of apprehension shot through her. She needed to get rid of him, and promptly.

"But I doubt that a desire to learn the science of numerology accounts for the pleasure of your visit, sir."

"Well." He looked her up and down in an effort at assessment, but she could have told him it was far too late for that. "Well . . . to be blunt, madam, I wish to employ you. In a matter of . . . some discretion."

That gave her another small jolt. So he knew who—or rather what—she was. Still, that wasn't really unusual. It was, after all, a business in which all connections were by word of mouth. And she was certainly known by now to at least three gentlemen in London who might move in the circles to which Colonel Quarry had access.

No point in beating round the bush or being coy; she was interested in him but more interested in his leaving. She gave him a small bow and looked inquiring. He nodded back and took a deep breath. *Some discretion, indeed . . .*

"The situation is this, madam: I have a good friend whose wife recently died in childbed."

"I'm sorry to hear it," Minnie said quite honestly. "How very tragic."

"Yes, it was." Quarry's face showed what he was thinking, and the trouble was clear in his eyes. "The more so, perhaps, in that my friend's wife had been . . . well . . . having an affair with a friend of his for some months prior."

"Oh, dear," Minnie murmured. "And—forgive me—was the child . . . ?"

"My friend doesn't know." Quarry grimaced but relaxed a little, indicating that the most difficult part of his business had been communicated. "Bad enough, you might say . . ."

"Oh, I would."

"But the further difficulty—well, without going into the reasons why, we . . . I . . . would like to engage you to find proof of that affair."

That confused her.

"Your friend—he isn't sure that she *was* having an affair?"

"No, he's positive," Quarry assured her. "There were letters. But—

well, I can't really explain why this is necessary, but he requires proof of the affair for a . . . a . . . legal reason, and he will not countenance the idea of letting anyone read his wife's letters, no matter that she is beyond the reach of public censure nor that the consequences to himself if the affair is *not* proved may be disastrous."

"I see." She eyed him with interest. Was there really a friend, or was this perhaps his own situation, thinly disguised? She thought not; he was clearly grieved and troubled but not flushed—not ashamed or angry in the least. And he hadn't the look of a married man. At all.

As though her invisible thought had struck him on the cheek like a flying moth, he looked sharply at her, meeting her eyes directly. No, not a married man. And not so grieved or troubled that a spark didn't show clearly in those deep-brown eyes. She looked modestly down for a moment, then up, resuming her businesslike manner.

"Well, then. Have you specific suggestions as to how the inquiry might proceed?"

He shrugged, a little embarrassed.

"Well . . . I thought . . . perhaps you could make the acquaintance of some of Esmé's—that was her name, Esmé Grey, Countess Melton—some of her friends. And . . . er . . . perhaps some of . . . *his* . . . particular friends. The, um, man who . . ."

"And the man's name?" Picking up the quill, she wrote *Countess Melton,* then looked up expectantly.

"Nathaniel Twelvetrees."

"Ah. Is he a soldier, too?"

"No," and here Quarry *did* blush, surprisingly. "A poet."

"I see," Minnie murmured, writing it down. "All right." She put down the quill and came out from behind the desk, passing him closely so that he was obliged to turn toward her—and toward the door. He smelled of bay rum and vetiver, though he didn't wear a wig or powder in his hair.

"I'm willing to undertake your inquiry, sir—though, of course, I can't guarantee results."

"No, no. Of course."

"Now, I have a prior engagement at two o'clock"—he glanced at the clock, as did she: four minutes to the hour—"but if you would perhaps make a list of the friends you think might be helpful and send it round? Once I've assessed the possibilities, I can inform you of my terms." She hesitated. "May I approach Mr. Twelvetrees? Very discreetly, of course," she assured him.

He made a grimace, half shock and half amusement.

"Afraid not, Miss Rennie. My friend shot him. I'll send the list," he promised, and, with a deep bow, left her.

The door had barely closed behind him before there was another knock. The maid popped out of the boudoir, where she had been discreetly lurking, and glided silently over the thick red Turkey carpet.

Minnie felt her stomach lurch and her throat tighten, as though she'd been dropped out of a high window and caught by the neck at the last moment.

Voices. Men's voices. Disconcerted, she hurried into the hall, to find the maid stolidly confronting a pair of what were not quite gentlemen.

"Madam is—" the maid was saying firmly, but one of the men spotted Minnie and brushed past the maid.

"Miss Rennie?" he inquired politely, and at her jerky nod bowed with surprising style for one dressed so plainly.

"We have come to escort you to Mrs. Simpson," he said. And, turning to the maid, "Be so kind as to fetch the lady's things, if you please."

The maid turned, wide-eyed, and Minnie nodded to her. Her arms prickled with gooseflesh and her face felt numb.

"Yes," she said. "If you please." And her fingers closed on the paper in her pocket, damp with handling.

Do you think this is wise?

THERE WAS A coach outside, waiting. Neither of the men spoke, but one opened the door for her; the other took her by the elbow and helped her politely up into the conveyance. Her heart was pounding and her head full of her father's warnings about dealing with unvouched-for strangers— these warnings accompanied by a number of vividly detailed accounts of things that had happened to incautious persons of his own acquaintance as a result of unwariness.

What if these men had nothing to do with her mother but knew who her father was? There *were* people who—

With phrases like *"And they only found her* head . . ." echoing in her mind, it was several moments before she could take notice of the two gentlemen, both of whom had entered the coach behind her and were now sitting on the squabs opposite, watching her like a pair of owls. Hungry owls.

She took a deep breath and pressed a hand to her middle, as though to ease her stays. Yes, the small dagger was still reassuringly tucked inside her placket; the way she was sweating, it would be quite rusted by the time she had to use it. *If,* she corrected herself. *If* she had to use it . . .

"Are you all right, madam?" one of the men asked, leaning forward. His voice cracked sharply on "madam," and she actually looked at him properly for the first time. Sure enough, he was a beardless boy. Taller than his companion, and pretty well grown, but a lad nonetheless—and his guileless face showed nothing but concern.

"Yes," she said, and, swallowing, pulled a small fan from her sleeve and snapped it open. "Just . . . a little warm."

The older man—in his forties, slender and dark, with a cocked hat balanced on his knee—at once reached into his pocket and produced a flask: a lovely object made in chased silver, adorned with a sizable chrysoberyl, she saw with surprise.

"Try this," he said in a pleasant voice. "It is orange-flower water, with sugar, herbs, the juice of blood oranges, and just a touch of gin, for refreshment."

"Thank you." She repressed the *"drugged and raped"* murmuring in her brain and accepted the flask. She passed it unobtrusively under her nose, but there was no telltale scent of laudanum. In fact, it smelled divine and tasted even better.

Both of the men saw the expression on her face and smiled. Not with the smile of satisfied entrapment, but with genuine pleasure that she enjoyed their offering. She took a deep breath, another sip, and began to relax. She smiled back at them. On the other hand . . . her mother's address lay in Parson's Green, and she had just noticed that they were heading steadily in the opposite direction. Or at least she thought so . . .

"Where are we going?" she asked politely. They looked surprised, looked at each other, eyebrows raised, then back at her.

"Why . . . to see Mrs. Simpson," the older gentleman said. The boy nodded and bowed awkwardly to her.

"Mrs. Simpson," he murmured, blushing.

And that was all anyone said for the remainder of the journey. She occupied herself with sipping the refreshing orange drink and with surreptitious observation of her . . . not captors, presumably. Escorts?

The gentleman who had given her the flask spoke excellent English, but with a touch of foreign sibilance: Italian, perhaps, or Spanish?

The younger man—he didn't really seem a boy, in spite of smooth cheeks and cracking voice—had a strong face and, regardless of his blushing, an air of confidence about him. He was fair and yellow-eyed, yet that brief glimpse when the two had looked at her in question had shown her a faint, vanishing resemblance between the two of them. Father and son? Perhaps so.

She flipped quickly through the ledger she carried in her head, in search of any such pair among her father's clients—or enemies—but found no one who met the description of her escorts. She took a deep breath, another sip, and resolved to think of nothing until they arrived at their destination.

Half an hour later, the flask was nearly empty and the coach lurched to a stop in what she thought was possibly Southwark.

Their destination was a small inn standing in a street of shops dominated by Kettrick's Eel-Pye House, this being evidently a successful eating place, judging by the crowds of people and the strong scent of jellied eels. Her belly rumbled as she got down from the carriage, but the sound was lost in the noises of the street. The boy bowed and offered her his arm; she took it, and putting on her most blandly pleasant face, she went with him inside.

IT WAS SHADOWY inside, light coming through two narrow, curtained windows. She noticed the smell of the place—hyacinths, how odd—but nothing more. Everything was a blur; all she felt was the beating of her heart and the solidness of the boy's arm.

Then a hallway, then a door, and then . . .

A woman. Blue dress. Soft-brown hair looped up behind her ears. Eyes. Pale-green eyes. Not blue like her own.

Minnie stopped dead, not breathing. For the moment, she felt an odd disappointment; the woman looked nothing like the picture she had carried with her all her life. This one was tall and thin, almost lean, and while her face was arresting, it wasn't the face Minnie saw in her mirror.

"Minerva?" the woman said, in a voice little more than a whisper. She coughed, cleared her throat explosively, and, coming toward Minnie, said much louder, "Minerva? Is it truly you?"

"Well, yes," said Minnie, not sure quite what to do. *She must be; she knows my real name.* "That's my name. And you are . . . Mrs. . . . Simpson?" Her own voice broke quite absurdly, the final syllable uttered like the squeak of a bat.

"Yes." The woman turned her head and gave the two who had brought her a brief nod. The boy vanished at once, but the older man touched the woman's shoulder gently and gave Minnie a smile before following suit, leaving Minnie and Mrs. Simpson frankly staring at each other.

Mrs. Simpson was dressed well but quietly. She pursed her lips, looked sidelong at Minnie, as though estimating the possibility that she might be armed, then sighed, her square shoulders slumping.

"I'm not your mother, child," she said quietly.

Quiet as they were, the words struck Minnie like fists, four solid blows in the pit of her stomach.

"Well, who the bloody hell *are* you?" she demanded, taking a step backward. Every cautionary word she'd ignored came flooding back in her father's voice.

"*. . . kidnapped . . . sold to a brothel . . . shipped off to the colonies . . . murdered for sixpence . . .*"

"I'm your aunt, my dear," Mrs. Simpson said. The nettle grasped, she had regained some of her starch. "Miriam Simpson. Your mother is my sister, Hélène."

"Hélène," Minnie repeated. The name struck a spark in her soul. She had that much, at least. *Hélène.* A Frenchwoman? She swallowed.

"Is she dead?" she asked, as steadily as she could. Mrs. Simpson pursed her lips again, unhappy, but shook her head.

"No," she said, with obvious reluctance. "She lives. But . . ."

Minnie wished she'd brought a pocket pistol instead of a knife. If she had, she'd fire a shot into the ceiling right this minute. Instead, she took a step forward, so that her eyes were no more than inches from the green ones that didn't look like hers.

"Take me to her. Right now," she said. "You can tell me the story on the way."

7

ANNUNCIATION

THE COACH CROSSED OVER the cobbles of a bridge with a great clattering of hooves and wheels. The racket was as nothing to the noise inside Minnie's head.

"A nun," Minnie said, as they passed onto a dirt road and the noise decreased. She sounded as blank as she felt. "My mother . . . was a *nun*?"

Mrs. Simpson—her aunt, Aunt Simpson, Aunt Miriam . . . she must get used to thinking of her that way—took a deep breath and nodded. With that bit of news out of the way, she had regained some of her composure.

"Yes. A sister of the Order of Divine Mercy, in Paris. You know of them?"

Minnie shook her head. She had thought she was prepared to hear anything, but she hadn't been, by a long chalk.

"What—what do they look like?" It was the first thing to come into her head. "Black, gray, white . . . ?"

Mrs. Simpson relaxed a little, bracing her back against the blue cushions to counter the jolting of the coach.

"Their habit is white, with a gray veil. They are a contemplative order but not cloistered."

"What does that mean, contemplative?" Minnie burst out. "What are they *contemplating*? Not their vows of chastity, apparently."

Her aunt looked startled, but her mouth twitched a little.

"Apparently not," she said. "Their chief occupation is prayer. Contemplation of God's mercy and His divine nature."

The day was cool enough, but Minnie felt hot blood rise from her chest to her ears.

"I see. So she—my mother—had an encounter with the Holy Spirit during a particularly intense prayer, did she?" She'd meant it sarcastically, but perhaps . . . "Wait a moment. My father *is* my father, isn't he?"

Her aunt overlooked the gibe.

"You are the daughter of Raphael Wattiswade, I assure you," she said dryly, with a glance at Minnie's face.

One of the small knots of doubt in Minnie's chest loosened. The possibility of this all being a hoax—if nothing more sinister—receded. Very few people knew her father's real name. If this woman did, then perhaps . . .

She sat back, crossed her arms, and fixed Mrs. Simpson with a hard look.

"So. What happened? And where are we going?" she added belatedly.

"To your mother," her aunt said tersely. "As to what happened . . . it was a book."

"Of course it was." Minnie's confidence in the woman's story moved up another small notch. "What book?"

"A Book of Hours." Mrs. Simpson waved away an inquisitive wasp that had flown in through the window. "I said that the order's chief occupation is prayer. They have others. Some of the nuns are scribes; some are artists. Soeur Emmanuelle—that's the name Hélène took when she entered the convent—was both," she explained, seeing Minnie's momentary confusion. "The order produces very beautiful books—things of a religious nature, of course, Bibles, devotionals—and sells them in order to support the community."

"And my father learned about this?"

Her aunt shrugged. "It's no secret. The order's books are well known, as are their skills. I imagine Raphael had dealt with the convent before. He—"

"He's never dealt with them, so far as I know, or I would have heard of them."

"Do you think he would risk your finding out?" her aunt said bluntly. "Whatever his defects of character, I will say the man knows how to keep a secret. He severed all connection with the order, after . . ." Her mouth pressed tight and she made a flicking gesture with one hand that had nothing to do with the wasp.

Minnie's teeth were clenched, but she managed to get a few words out.

"Bloody tell me what happened!"

Her aunt looked at her searchingly, the frills on her cap trembling with the vibration of the coach, then shrugged.

"*Bon,*" she said.

What had happened ("in brief," said Mrs. Simpson) was that Raphael Wattiswade had acquired a very rare Book of Hours, made more than a century before. It was beautiful but in poor condition. The cover could be repaired, its missing jewels replaced—but some of the illustrations had suffered badly from the effects of time and use.

"And so Raphael came to the abbess of the order—a woman he knew well, in the course of business—and asked whether one of their more talented scribes might be able to restore the illustrations. For a price, of course."

Normally the book would simply be taken away to the scriptorium for examination and work, but in this case, some pages had been completely obliterated. Raphael, however, had discovered several letters from the original owner, rhapsodizing to a friend about his new acquisition and giving detailed descriptions of the more important illustrations.

"And he couldn't just give the letters to the abbess?" Minnie asked skeptically. Not that she could think why her father would purposely set out to seduce a nun he'd never heard of or set eyes on . . .

Mrs. Simpson shook her head.

"I said the book was from a previous age? The letters were written in German, and a very archaic form of that barbarous language. No one in the order was able to translate it."

Given that and the fragile state of the book, Soeur Emmanuelle was allowed to travel to Raphael's workshop—"With a proper *chaperon,* to be sure," Mrs. Simpson added, with a fresh pressing of the lips.

"To be sure."

Her aunt gave a very Gallic shrug. "But things happen, don't they?"

"Evidently they *do.*" She eyed Mrs. Simpson, who, she thought, seemed tolerably free with her father's Christian name.

"*C'est vrai.* And what happened, of course, was you."

There was no good response to that, and Minnie didn't try to find one.

"She was only nineteen," her aunt finally said, looking down at her clasped hands, and speaking in a voice so soft that Minnie hardly heard it over the rumble of the coach. And how old had her father been? she wondered. He was forty-five now . . . twenty-eight. Maybe twenty-seven, allowing for the length of a pregnancy.

"Bloody old enough to know better," Minnie muttered, but under her breath. "I suppose she—my mother"—she forced herself to say the words, which now felt shocking in her mouth— "was obliged to leave the order? I mean, you can't be pregnant in a convent, surely."

"You might be surprised," her aunt observed cynically. "But in this case, you're right. They sent her away, to a sort of asylum in Rouen—a terrible place." A flush had begun to burn on Mrs. Simpson's high cheekbones. "I heard nothing of it until Raphael appeared at my door one night, very distraught, to tell me she was gone."

"What did you do?"

"We went and got her," her aunt said simply. "What else?"

"You said 'we.' Do you mean you and . . . my father?"

Her aunt blinked, shocked.

"No, of course not. My husband and myself." She breathed deep, clearly trying to calm herself. "It—she—it was most distressing."

Soeur Emmanuelle, torn from the community that had been her home since she entered the convent as a twelve-year-old novice, treated as an object of shame, having no knowledge or experience of pregnancy, without friend or family, and locked up in an establishment that sounded very like a prison, had been first hysterical, then had gradually withdrawn into a state of despair and finally of stone-like silence, sitting and staring all day at the blank wall, taking no notice even of food.

"She was skin and bones when I found her," Mrs. Simpson said, her voice shaking with remembered fury. "She didn't even know me!"

Soeur Emmanuelle had very gradually been brought back to a cognizance of the world—but not the world she had left.

"I don't know whether it was leaving her order—they were her family!—or the shock of being with child, but . . ." She shook her head, desolation draining the color from her face. "She lost her reason entirely. Took no notice of her state and believed herself to be back in the convent, going about her usual work."

They had humored her, given her a habit, provided her with paint and brushes, vellum and parchment, and she had shown some signs of being aware of her surroundings—would talk sometimes and knew her sister. But then the birth had come, inexorable.

"She had refused to think about it," Mrs. Simpson said, with a sigh. "But there you were . . . pink and slimy and loud." Soeur Emmanuelle, unable to cope with the situation, lost her tentative grip on sanity and reverted to her earlier state of blank detachment.

So I drove my own mother to insanity and destroyed her life. Her heart had risen into her throat, a hard, pulsing lump that hurt with each beat. Still, she had to speak.

"The shock, you said." She licked dry lips. "Was it just . . . me? I mean, was it rape, do you think?"

To Minnie's infinite relief, Mrs. Simpson looked aghast at the word.

"*Nom de Dieu!* No. No, certainly not." Her mouth twisted a little as she recovered from the brief shock. "Say what you will about Raphael, I'm sure he's never taken a woman who wasn't willing. Mind, he can make them willing in very short order."

Minnie didn't want to hear one word about willing women and her father.

"Where, exactly, are we going?" she asked in a firm voice. "Where *is* my mother?"

"In her own world, *ma chère.*"

IT WAS A modest farm cottage, standing by itself at the edge of a broad, sunny field, though the house itself was sheltered by well-grown oaks and beeches. Perhaps a quarter mile farther on was a small village that boasted a surprisingly large stone church, with a tall spire.

"I wanted her to be close enough to hear the bells," Mrs. Simpson explained, nodding toward the distant church as their coach came to a halt outside the cottage. "They don't keep the hours of praise as a Catholic abbey would, of course, but she doesn't usually realize that, and the sound gives her comfort."

She looked at Minnie for a long moment, biting her lip, doubt plain in her eyes. Minnie touched her aunt's hand, as gently as she could, though the pulse beating in her ears nearly deafened her.

"I won't hurt her," she whispered in French. "I promise you."

The look of doubt didn't leave her aunt's eyes, but her face relaxed a little and she nodded to the groom outside, who opened the door and offered his arm to help her down.

An anchorite, her aunt had said; Sister Emmanuelle believed herself to be an anchorite. A hermitess, fixed in place, her only duty that of prayer. "She feels . . . secure, I think," Mrs. Simpson had said, though the creases in her brow showed the shadow of long worry. "Safe, you know?"

"Safe from the world?" Minnie had asked. Her aunt had given her a very direct look, and the creases in her brow grew deeper.

"Safe from everything," she had said. "And everyone."

And so Minerva now followed her aunt to the door, filled with a mixture of anxiety, astonishment, sorrow, and—unavoidably—hope.

She'd *heard* of anchorites, of course; they were mentioned frequently in religious histories—of saints, monasteries, persecutions, reformations—but at the moment the word conjured up only a ridiculous vision of St. Simeon Stylites, who had lived on top of a pillar for thirty years—and, when his niece was orphaned, generously set *her* up with her very own pillar, next to his. After a few years of this life, the niece had reportedly climbed down and decamped with a man, much to the disapproval of the history's author.

The door of the cottage opened, revealing a large, cheerful-looking woman who greeted Miriam Simpson warmly and looked with pleasant inquiry at Minnie.

"This is Miss Rennie," Mrs. Simpson said, gesturing toward Minnie. "I've brought her to see my sister, Mrs. Budger."

Mrs. Budger's sparse gray brows rose toward her cap, but she made a brief bob in Minnie's direction.

"Your servant, mum," she said, and flapped her apron at a large calico cat. "Shoo, cat. The lady's none o' your business. He knows it's nearly time for Sister's tea," she explained. "Come in, ladies, the kettle's a-boiling already."

Minnie was in a fever of impatience, this interrupted by stabs of icy terror.

"Soeur Emmanuelle, she still calls herself," Mrs. Simpson had explained on the way. "She spends her days—and often her nights"—her wide brow had creased at the words—"in prayer, but she does have visitors. People who've heard of her, who come to ask her prayers for one thing or another.

"At first, I was afraid," she'd said, and turned to look out the coach window at a passing farm wagon, "that they'd upset her, telling her their troubles. But she seems . . . better when she's listened to someone."

"Does she . . . talk to them?" Minnie had asked. Her aunt had glanced at her, then paused for a few seconds too long before saying, "Sometimes," and turning toward the window again.

It doesn't matter, she told herself, clenching her fists in the folds of her skirt to avoid strangling Mrs. Budger, who was slowly, slowly puttering around the hearth, assembling a few slices of buttered bread, a wedge of cheese, and a mug on a tray, at the same time fetching down a chipped teapot and three more stone mugs, a dented tin tea caddy, and a small, sticky blue pot of honey. *It doesn't matter if she won't speak to me. It doesn't even matter if she can't hear me. I just want to see her!*

8

THE BOOK OF HOURS

IT WAS A TINY stone building with a thatch; Minnie thought it must once have been a lambing shed or something of the kind. The thought made her inhale, nostrils flaring—and she blinked in surprise. There was certainly a smell, but it wasn't the warm agricultural fug of animals; it was the faint tang of incense.

Mrs. Simpson glanced up at the sun, halfway down the sky.

"You won't have long," she said, grunting a little as she lifted the heavy bar from the door. "It's almost time for None—what she thinks is None. When she hears the bells, she won't do anything until the prayer is done, and often she's silent afterward."

"None?"

"The hours," Mrs. Simpson said, pushing the door open. "Hurry, if you want her to speak with you."

Minnie was bewildered, but she did certainly want her mother to speak with her. She nodded briefly and ducked under the lintel into a sort of glowing gloom.

The glow came from a single large candle set in a tall iron stand and from a brazier on the floor next to it. Fragrant smoke rose from both, drifting near the sooty beams of the low ceiling. A dim light suffused the room, seeming to gather around the figure of a woman dressed in white robes, kneeling at a crude prie-dieu.

The woman turned, startled at the sound of Minnie's entry, and froze at sight of her.

Minnie felt much the same but forced herself to walk forward, slowly. Instinctively, she held out a hand, like one does to a strange dog, presenting her knuckles to be sniffed.

The woman rose with a slow rustling of coarse cloth. She wasn't veiled, which surprised Minnie—her hair had been roughly cropped but had grown out somewhat; it curved just under her ears, cupping the angles of her jaw. Thick, smooth, the color of wheat in a summer field.

Mine, Minnie thought, with a thump of the heart, and stared into the woman's eyes. Mrs. Simpson had been right. *Mine, too . . .*

"Sister?" she said tentatively, in French. "Soeur Emmanuelle?"

The woman said nothing, but her eyes had gone quite round. They traveled down Minnie's body and returned to her face, intent. She turned her head and addressed a crucifix that hung on the plastered wall behind her.

"*Est-ce une vision, Seigneur?*" she said, in the rusty voice of one who seldom speaks aloud. "Is this a vision, Lord?" She sounded uncertain, perhaps frightened. Minnie didn't hear a reply from Christ on the cross, but Sister Emmanuelle apparently did. She turned back to face Minnie, drawing herself upright, and crossed herself.

"Erm . . . *Comment ca va?*" Minnie asked, for lack of anything better. Sister Emmanuelle blinked but didn't reply. Perhaps that wasn't the right sort of thing for a vision to say.

"I hope I see you well," Minnie added politely.

Mother, she thought suddenly, with a pang as she saw the grubby hem of the rough habit, the streaks of food on breast and skirt. *Oh, Mother . . .*

There was a book on the prie-dieu. Swallowing the lump in her throat, she walked past her mother to look at it but glanced up and saw the crucifix—it was a rich one, she saw, polished ebony with mother-of-pearl edging. The corpus had been made by another, truer hand, though—the body of Christ glowed in the candlelight, contorted in the grip of a knotted chunk of some dark wood, rubbed smooth. His face was turned away, invisible, but the thorns were carved sharp and vivid, sharp enough to prick your finger if you touched them. The outflung arms were only half freed from the wood, but the sense of entrapment, of unendurable agony, struck Minnie like a blow to the chest.

"*Mon Dieu,*" she said aloud. She said it in shock, rather than by way of prayer, but vaguely heard the woman behind her let go a held breath. She heard the rustle of cloth and straw—she hadn't noticed when she came in, but the floor was covered in clean straw—and forced herself to stand quite still, heart beating in her ears, though she longed to turn and embrace Sister Emmanuelle, seize and carry her, drag her, bring her out into the world. After a long moment during which she could hear the woman's breathing, she felt a touch on her shoulder. She turned round slowly.

Her mother was close now, close enough that Minnie could smell her. Surprisingly, she smelled sweet—a tang of sweat, the smell of clothes worn too long without washing, but incense perfumed her hair, the cloth of her robe, and the hand that touched Minnie's cheek. Her flesh smelled warm and . . . pure.

"Are you an angel?" Emmanuelle asked suddenly. Doubt and fear had come into her face again, and she edged back a step. "Or a demon?"

So close, Minnie could see the lines in her face—crow's-feet, the gentle crease from nose to mouth—but the face itself was a blurred mirror of the one she saw in her looking glass. She took a breath and stepped closer.

"I'm an angel," she said firmly. She'd spoken in English, without think-ing, and Emmanuelle's eyes flew wide in shock. She took an awkward step backward and sank to her knees.

"Oh, no! Don't do that!" Minnie cried, distressed. "I didn't mean it—I mean, *Je ne veux pas . . .* " She stooped to raise her mother to her feet, but Emmanuelle had clapped her hands to her eyes and wouldn't be moved, only swaying to and fro, making small whimpering noises.

Then Minnie realized that they weren't just noises. Her mother was whispering, "RaphaelRaphaelRaphael," over and over. Panicked, she seized her mother's wrists and pulled her hands away from her face.

"Stop! *Arrêtez!* Please stop!"

Her mother stopped, gasping for breath, looking up at her. *"Est-ce qu'il vous a envoyé? Raphael L'Archange? Êtes-vous l'un des siens?"* "Did he send you? Raphael the archangel? Are you his?" Her voice quivered, but she had calmed a little; she wasn't struggling, and Minnie cautiously let go.

"No, no one sent me," she said, as soothingly as possible. "I came on my own, to visit you." Groping for something else to say, she blurted, *"Je m'appelle Minerve."*

Emmanuelle's face went quite blank.

What is it? Does she know that name? Mrs. Simpson hadn't said whether her mother might know her name.

And then she realized that the bells of the distant church were ringing. Perhaps her mother hadn't even heard her speak.

Helpless, she watched as Emmanuelle got laboriously to her feet, step-ping on the hem of her robe and staggering. Minnie made to take the woman's arm, but Emmanuelle regained her balance and went to the prie-dieu, quickly but with no sense of panic. Her face was composed, all her attention focused on the book lying on the prie-dieu.

Seeing it now, Minnie realized at last what her aunt had meant by "None" and "hours." The book was a small, elegant volume with an aged green cover, set with tiny rounded cabochon jewels. And as Emmanuelle opened it, Minnie saw inside the glow of beautiful paintings, pictures of angels speaking to the Virgin, to a man with a crown, to a crowd of peo-ple, to Christ on the cross . . .

It was a Book of Hours, a devotional volume meant for rich lay people, made during the last age, with the psalms and prayers intended to be said during the monastic hours of worship: Matins, Lauds, Prime, Terce, Sext, None, Vespers, and Compline. None was the ninth hour—the prayer said at three o'clock in the afternoon.

Emmanuelle's head was bent over the open book, and she was praying aloud, her voice soft but audible. Minnie hesitated, not sure whether she should leave . . . but no. She wasn't ready to say goodbye to her mother—

the more so as the woman probably wouldn't notice her trying to take her leave. Instead, she came quietly to the prie-dieu and knelt down beside Emmanuelle, in the straw.

She knelt close enough that the pink linen of her gown nearly brushed the white habit. It wasn't cold in the shed, not with the brazier going, but nonetheless she could feel her mother's warmth and, for just a moment, surrendered to the vain hope she had brought here—of being seen, accepted, wrapped in her mother's love.

She closed her eyes against the starting tears and listened to Emmanuelle's voice, soft and husky but sure. Minnie swallowed and opened her eyes, making an effort to follow the Latin.

"Deus, in adjutorium meum intende; Domine, ad adjuvandum me festina . . ." "O God, come to my assistance; O Lord, make haste to help me . . ."

As the recitation of the Office of None went on, Minnie joined timidly in the prayers she could read adequately. Her mother took no notice, but Emmanuelle's voice got stronger, her back straighter, as though she felt the support of her imagined community around her.

Minnie could see that the book was very old—at least a hundred years, maybe more—and then realized with a small shock that she had seen it before. Her father had sold it—or one very like it—to Mother Hildegarde, the abbess of le Couvent des Anges, a hospital order of nuns. Minnie had delivered it to the good mother herself a year or so before. How had it come here?

In spite of the rawness of her own emotions, she found a small sense of peace in the words, even when she didn't understand them all. Emmanuelle seemed to grow both quieter and stronger as she spoke, and when she had finished, she stayed motionless, gazing up at the crucifix, an expression of the greatest tenderness on her face.

Minnie was afraid to rise, not wanting to disturb the sense of peace in the room, but her knees couldn't stand much more kneeling on the stones of the floor, straw covering or no. She took a deep breath and eased herself up. The nun seemed not to have noticed, still deep in communion with Jesus.

Minnie tiptoed toward the door, which, she saw, was now open a crack. She could see a movement of something blue through the gap—undoubtedly Mrs. Simpson, come to remove her. She turned suddenly, on impulse, and went back quickly to the prie-dieu.

"Soeur Emmanuelle?" she said very softly, and gently, slowly, laid her hands on her mother's shoulders, fragile under the white cloth. She swallowed hard, so her voice wouldn't shake. "You are forgiven."

Then she lifted her hands and went quickly away, the glow of the straw a blur of light around her.

9

WELL PAST MIDNIGHT

I T WAS TIME.
Argus House had fourteen bedrooms, not counting the servants' quarters. So far, Hal had not been able to bring himself to sleep in any of them. Not his own. He hadn't lain there since the dawn when he'd risen from Esmé's warm body and gone out in the rain to face Nathaniel.

"On your bloody croquet lawn!" he said aloud, but under his breath. It was after midnight, and he didn't want to wake any inquisitive servant. "You pretentious nit!"

Not Esmé's chaste blue and white boudoir next door, either. He couldn't bring himself even to open the door, not sure whether her ghost might still linger in the scented air or whether the room would be a cold and empty shell. Afraid to find out, either way.

He was standing now at the head of the stairs, the long corridor of bedrooms lit at this late hour by only three of the dozen sconces, the colors of a half dozen Turkey rugs melting into shadow. He shook his head and, turning, went downstairs.

He generally didn't sleep at night, anyway. Went out occasionally and roamed the dark paths of Hyde Park, sometimes stopping briefly to share a fire with some of the vagrants who camped there. More often sat up reading in the library 'til the wax from melting candles pattered onto tables and floors and Nasonby or Wetters came silently in with scrapers and new candles, even though he'd ordered the footmen to go to bed.

Then he'd read stubbornly on by the new light—Tacitus, Marcus Aurelius, Cicero, Pliny, Julius Caesar—losing himself in distant battles and the thoughts of long-dead men. Their fellowship comforted him, and he'd fall asleep with the dawn, curled up on the blue settee or sprawled on the cool marble floor, his head cushioned on the white hearth rug.

Someone would come silently and cover him. He'd usually wake to find someone standing over him with a luncheon tray and would rise with aching limbs and a foggy mind that took 'til teatime to clear again.

"This will *not* do," he said aloud, pausing at the door to the library. Not tonight.

He didn't go into the library, though it was brightly lit in expectation of his presence. Instead, he reached into the bosom of his shirt and pulled out the note. He'd been carrying it ever since it had arrived at teatime, reading it again and again—and now opened it to read again, as though the words might have altered or disappeared.

His Royal Highness the Prince of Wales is pleased to invite you to visit him to discuss your proposals regarding the re-commissioning of the 46th Regiment of Foot, a project which is of the deepest interest to him. It would perhaps be most convenient for you to attend the princess's garden fête at the White House on Sunday, 21 June. A formal invitation will be sent you this week; should the arrangement be agreeable to you, please reply in the usual fashion.

"Agreeable," he said aloud, and felt an unaccustomed tingle of excitement, as he had every time he'd read the note. "Agreeable, he says!"

Agreeable, indeed—if dangerous. The prince had a good deal of power, a good deal of influence in military circles, including with the secretary at war. But he wasn't the king. And king and prince most assuredly did *not* agree. The king and his heir had been estranged—if not actually at loggerheads—for several years, and to court the favor of the one was to invite coldness from the other.

Still . . . it might be possible to tread the narrow line between the two and emerge with the support of both. . . .

But he knew he was in no sort of shape to undertake that kind of finesse, exhausted as he was in mind and body.

Besides. It was time. He knew it. He cast a brief, regretful look into the library, then reached out and gently closed the door on his book-lined refuge.

The house was quiet, and his footsteps made no sound on the thick rugs as he came back—at last—to Esmé's room. He opened the door without hesitation and went in.

There was no light and he left the door open behind him, crossing the room to draw back the drapes from the big double window. A pale wash of moonlight fell over him and he went back and closed the door, silently. Then slid the bolt.

The room was cold, and clean. A faint smell of beeswax polish and fresh linen lingered. No trace of her perfume.

He made his way half blind to the dressing table in her closet and felt about in the darkness until he found the chunky crystal bottle. He felt the smooth ground-glass stopper grate softly as he took it out and dabbed a drop of her scent inside his wrist—just as he'd seen her do it, a hundred times and more.

It was a scent made just for her, and for the instant she lived again within it: complex and heady, spicy and bitter—cinnamon and myrrh, green oranges and oil of carnations. Leaving the bottle open, he walked back into the bedroom and came slowly to the curtained white bed. Put back the drapes and sat down.

Everything in her chamber was white or blue; the room was filled with shadow. Even the Bible on her nightstand was covered in white leather. Only the glints of gold or silver in jewel box and candlestick caught the light of the moon.

Without the hiss and crackle of a fire or the melting of candles, the air lay quiet. He could hear his own heart, beating slow and heavy. There was only him. And her.

"Em," he said softly, eyes closed. "I'm sorry." And whispered, so low he barely heard the words, "I miss you. God, I miss you."

Finally, finally, he let grief take him and wept for her then, for a long time.

"Forgive me," he said.

And at last lay down upon her white bed and let sleep take him, too, to whatever dreams it would.

10

DOWN TO BUSINESS

O VER THE NEXT TWO weeks, Minnie threw herself determinedly into the pursuit of business. She tried not to think of Soeur Emmanuelle, but thought of her mother hovered near her, like an angel on her shoulder, and after a bit she accepted this. There was, after all, nothing she could do about it, and at least now she knew her mother was alive. Perhaps even content.

Between increasing business—of both kinds—and Lady Buford's determined social agenda, Minnie scarcely had a minute to herself. When she wasn't going to view a collection of moldy hymnals in a garret down by the Thames or accepting sealed documents from her father's mysterious client in the Vauxhall Gardens, she was dressing for a card party in Fulham. The O'Higginses, faithful Irish wolfhounds, either accompanied or trailed her to every destination, their visibility depending on her errand.

She was pleased, therefore, to be able to combine Colonel Quarry's commission with Lady Buford's husband-hunting. Rather to Minnie's surprise, the latter involved a great deal of socializing with females.

"To be desirable, it is necessary to be talked about, my dear," Lady Buford told her over a glass of iced negus at Largier's tea shop (Madame Largier was French and thought tea itself a distinctly second-class beverage). "But you must be talked about *in the right way.* You must not suggest any hint of scandal, and—just as important—you must not cause jealousy. Be sweet and unassuming, always admire your companions' frocks and dismiss your own, and do not bat your eyes at their sons or brothers, should such be present."

"I've never batted my eyes at anyone in my life!" Minnie said indignantly.

"It isn't a difficult technique to master," Lady Buford said dryly. "But I trust you take my point."

Minnie did, and as she had no intention whatever of attracting a potential husband, she was extremely popular with the young women of society. Which turned out to be an unexpectedly good thing, because most young women had no discretion whatever, very little judgment, and would tell you the most unspeakable things without batting a single one of their own eyes.

They hadn't the least hesitation in telling her all about Esmé Grey; the late Countess Melton was a prime subject of gossip. But it wasn't the sort of gossip Minnie had expected to hear.

After a week's gentle prodding, Minnie had formed the distinct impression that women in general had not really liked Esmé—most of them had been afraid of her or envious of her—but that most men very definitely *had* liked her; hence, the envy. That being so, the lack of any hint of scandal was surprising.

There was quite a bit of public sympathy for Esmé; she *was* dead, and the poor little baby, too. . . . It was a tragic story, and people did love tragedy, as long as it wasn't theirs.

And certainly there was a good deal of talk (in lowered tones) about Lord Melton having shot poor Mr. Twelvetrees, which threw the countess into such a state of shock that she had gone into labor too early and died—but, surprisingly, there was no indication that Esmé's affair with Nathaniel had been noticed.

There was a great deal of speculation as to Lord Melton's motive for assassinating Mr. Twelvetrees—but apparently Esmé had been more than discreet, and there was no talk at all about Mr. Twelvetrees having paid her attention or even having been seen alone with her on any occasion.

There *was* a whisper of gossip to the effect that Lord Melton had killed Nathaniel because of an intrigue over an Italian singer, but the general opinion was that it had been over a matter of business; Nathaniel had been a failed curate who then became a stockbroker ("though he wrote the most *divine* poetry, my dear!"), and there had been a rumor of considerable losses incurred by the Grey family, attributed to Nathaniel's incompetence.

But as she continued to poke and prod, Minnie discovered an increasing sentiment along the lines that Colonel Quarry had mentioned: people were beginning to whisper that Lord Melton had killed Nathaniel in a fit of madness. After all, the duke ("though I'm told we mustn't call him by his title; he won't have it—and if *that's* not proof of madness . . .") had appeared nowhere in public since the death of his wife.

Given that the countess's death had occurred only two months earlier, Minnie thought this reticence perhaps reasonable, even admirable.

But as Lady Buford had been present during one of these exchanges, Minnie took the opportunity in the carriage going home to ask her chaperone's opinion of the Duke—or not—of Pardloe's marriage.

Lady Buford pursed her lips and tapped her closed fan against them in a considering manner.

"Well, there was a great deal of scandal over the first duke's death—had you heard about that?"

Minnie shook her head, in hopes of hearing more than her father's précis had provided, but Lady Buford was one who could tell the difference between facts and gossip, and her account of the first duke's supposed Jacobite associations was even briefer than Minnie's father's had been.

"It was quixotic at best—do you know that word, my dear?"

"I do, yes. You're speaking of—the second duke, would he be—Harold? He repudiated his title, is that what you mean?"

Lady Buford gave a small sniff and put away her fan in her capacious sleeve.

"It's actually not possible to repudiate a title, unless the king should give one leave to do so. But he did decline to use it, which amused some people, disgusted others who thought it affectation, and quite shocked society in general. Still . . . he'd been married a year before the first duke died, so Esmé had wed him with the expectation that he'd eventually succeed to the title. She hadn't given any indication that she regretted his decision—or even that she'd noticed it. That girl knew the meaning of 'aloof,'" Lady Buford added with approval.

"Were they in love, do you think?" Minnie asked, with genuine interest.

"Yes, I do," Lady Buford said, without hesitation. "She was French, of course, and quite striking—exotic, you might say. And Harold Grey is certainly an odd—well, I shouldn't say that, perhaps I merely mean unusual—young man. Their peculiarities seemed to complement each other. And neither one of them gave a single thought to what anyone else said or thought about *them*."

Lady Buford's sharp eyes had softened slightly, looking into memory, and she shook her head, making the ring-necked dove on her hat bob precariously.

"It really was a tragedy," she said, with evident regret.

And that, despite further discreet inquiry, was apparently that.

SHE MET COLONEL Quarry, by arrangement, at a concert of sacred music in St. Martin-in-the-Fields. There were enough people there that it was possible to sit inconspicuously in one of the galleries; she could see the back of Quarry's head at the far end of the gallery, bent in apparent rapt attention to the music being performed below.

She normally enjoyed music of any kind, but as the vibration of the organ's pipes ceased rumbling through the boards underfoot and a single high, pure voice rose from the silence in a *Magnificat,* she felt a sudden sense of acute sorrow, seeing in memory a room of shadows and candle-light, the dirty hem of a white habit, a bent head and a slender neck be-neath a bell of hair as golden as clean straw.

Her throat was tight and she bent her own head, shielding her face from view with a spread fan; it was a warm day, and whenever the music paused, the air in the gallery whispered with the movement of fans. No one noticed.

At last it was over, and she stood with the others, lingering by the rail-ing as people filed out in a buzz of conversation that rose above the last strains of the recessional.

Quarry came strolling toward her—exaggeratedly casual, but, after all, he likely wasn't used to intrigue, and if someone *did* notice, "intrigue" (in the vulgar meaning of the term) was exactly what they'd think it was.

"Miss Rennie!" he said, as though surprised by her presence, and swept her a bow. "Your most obedient servant, ma'am!"

"Why, Colonel Quarry!" she said, fluttering her fan coquettishly. "*What* a surprise! I'd no notion that you enjoyed sacred music."

"Can't stand it," he said amiably. "I'd have gone mad in another min-ute if they hadn't stopped that caterwauling. What the devil have you found out?"

She told him without preamble what her researches had discovered—or, rather, had *not* discovered.

"Damn," he said, then hunched his shoulders as two women going past gave him a shocked look.

"I mean," he said, lowering his voice, "my friend is quite certain that it actually happened. The, um . . ."

"Affair. Yes, you said he had letters proving it but that he wouldn't let anyone read them. Reasonably enough." She wasn't sure why she was interested in this business, but there was something oddly fascinating about it. She ought just to give him a bill for her time and leave it at that, but . . .

"Do you know where he keeps these letters?" she asked.

"Why . . . I suppose they're in his father's library desk. He usually keeps correspondence there. Wh—" He stopped abruptly, looking hard at her. She shrugged a little.

"I told you what the talk is, about your friend's state of mind. And if the letters are the only proof that he had a reason—and an honorable one—for what he did . . ." She paused delicately. Quarry's face darkened, and she felt the shift in his body as his hands curled.

"Are you suggesting that—that I take the—I could never do such a thing! It's dishonorable, impossible! He's my friend, dammit!" He looked aside, swallowing, and unclenched his fists.

"For God's sake, if he found that I'd done such a thing, I . . . I think he'd—" He stopped, all too clearly envisioning the possible results of such a discovery. The blood was draining from his cheeks, and a wash of pale-blue light from a stained-glass window made him look suddenly corpse-like.

"I wasn't suggesting that, sir," Minnie said, as meekly as possible. "Not at all! Naturally a gentleman such as yourself, and a devoted friend, couldn't—wouldn't—*ever* do such a thing." *And if you did,* she thought, watching his face, *he'd know it the second he looked at you. You couldn't lie your way out of a children's tea party, poor sod.*

"But," she said, and glanced deliberately around, so that he could see they were now alone in the gallery, save for a group of women at the far side, leaning over the rail and waving to acquaintances in the nave below. *"But,"* she repeated in a low voice, "if the letters were simply to . . . be delivered anonymously to . . . ?" She paused and cocked a brow.

He swallowed again, audibly, and looked at her for a long moment.

"The secretary at war," he blurted, as though trying to get the words out before he thought better.

"I see," she said, relaxing inwardly. "Well. That does seem very . . . drastic. Perhaps I can think of some other avenue of inquiry. There must be some intimate friend of the late countess that I haven't yet discovered." She put a hand very lightly on his arm.

"Leave the matter with me for another few days, Colonel. I'm sure something useful will occur to one of us."

11

GARDEN PARTY

> *1 June, AD 1744*
> *Paris*

My Dearest,

*Having heard nothing to the contrary, I assume that all is well
with you. I've received a special Request, through a Friend;
an English Collector by the Name of Mr. Bloomer wishes to discuss
a special Commission. His Letter, with Details of his Requirements,
a List of Resources with which to meet those Requirements, and a
Note of acceptable Payment, will follow under separate Covers.*

> *Your most affectionate Father,*
> *R. Rennie*

"MR. BLOOMER" HAD SPECIFIED His Royal Highness
the Prince of Wales's residence at Kew for their meeting, on the
twenty-first of June—Midsummer's Day. Minnie's diary carried a sketch
of various flowers and fruits to mark the occasion; the White House (as it
was casually known) had notable gardens, and a private tea (*Admission by
Invitation Only*) was being held in said gardens by Princess Augusta, in
support of one of that lady's favorite charities.

It was a little *outré* for an unmarried young woman to go alone to such
an event, Minnie reflected, dressing for the occasion, but Mr. Bloomer
had specified that the agent do just that, sending a single ticket of invitation with his letter. Of course, he probably hadn't realized that the agent
would *be* a young woman.

It was a fine day out, and Minnie stepped down from the hansom at the
end of the long avenue that led along the riverbank and up to the—quite
large, if not quite palatial—house.

"I'll walk from here," she said to Rafe O'Higgins, who had accompanied her. "You can watch 'til I get in to the house, if you think you really
must." A number of colored parasols, broad-brimmed hats, and belled silk
skirts were swaying slowly along the walks that edged a huge reflecting
pool in the distance, like a parade of animated flowers—*very appropriate
to a garden party,* she thought, amused.

"I'll be picking ye up just here, then," Rafe said, ignoring her gibe. He pointed to a carved-stone horse tank that stood in a small lay-by. "Just here," he repeated, and looked at the sun. "It's just gone two—will ye be done with your business by four, d'ye think?"

"I've no idea," she said, standing on tiptoe to look as far as she could over the sea of green surrounding the house. Ornamental domes and shiny bits that might be glass or metal were visible through the trees, and she heard faint strains of music in the distance. She meant to explore the delights of Their Highnesses' royal residence and its gardens to the full, once she'd dealt with Mr. Bloomer.

Rafe rolled his eyes but good-naturedly.

"Aye, then. If ye're not here at four, I'll come back on the hour 'til I find you." He leaned down to address her nose to nose, hazel eyes boring into hers. "And if ye're not here by seven, I'm comin' in after you. Got that, have ye, Lady Bedelia?"

"Oh, piffle," she said, but in a genial manner. She'd bought a modest parasol of ruffled green silk and now unfurled it with a flourish, turning her back on him. "I'll see you anon."

"And's when anon, then?" he shouted behind her.

"Whenever I'm bloody ready!" she called back over her shoulder and strolled on, gently twirling.

The crowd was funneling in to a large central hall, where Princess Augusta—or so Minnie assumed the pretty, bejeweled woman with the big blue eyes and the incipient double chin to be—was greeting her guests, supported by several other gorgeously dressed ladies. Minnie casually faded into the crowd and bypassed the receiving line; no need to call attention to herself.

There were enormous refreshment tables at the back of the house, and she graciously accepted a glass of sherbet and an iced cake offered her by a servant; she nibbled as she wandered out into the gardens, with an eye to its design and the locations of various landmarks. She was to meet Mr. Bloomer at three o'clock, in the "first of the glasshouses." Wearing green.

Green she was, from head to toe: a pale-green muslin gown, with a jacket and overskirt in a printed French calico. And, of course, the parasol, which she erected again once outside the house.

It was clever of Mr. Bloomer to choose green, she thought; she was very visible among the much more common pinks and blues and whites the other women wore, though not so uncommon as to cause staring. Green didn't suit many complexions, but beyond that, green fabric tended to fade badly: Monsieur Vernet—an artist friend of her father's, quite obsessed with whales—had told her once that green was a fugitive color, a notion that delighted her.

Perhaps that was why trees changed the color of their leaves in autumn? The green slipped away somehow, leaving them to fade into a brownish death. But why, then, did they have that momentary blaze of red and yellow?

Such concerns were far from the plants surrounding her; it was mid-summer, and everything was so verdant that, far from being conspicuous, had she stopped moving in the midst of all this burgeoning flora, she would have been almost invisible.

She found the glasshouses without difficulty. There were five of them, all in a row, glittering like diamonds in the afternoon sun, each one linked to its fellow by a short covered passageway. She was a bit early, but that shouldn't matter. She furled the parasol and joined the people passing in.

Inside, the air was heavy and damp, luscious with the smell of ripening fruit and heady blossom. She'd seen the king's Orangerie at Versailles once; this was much less impressive but much more appealing. Oranges and lemons and limes, plums, peaches and apricots, pears . . . and the in-toxicating scent of citrus blossom floating over everything.

She sighed happily and drifted down the graveled pathways that led among the rows, murmuring apology or acknowledgment as she brushed someone in passing, never meeting anyone's eyes, and, finding herself mo-mentarily alone beneath a canopy of quince trees, stopped to breathe the perfume of the solid yellow fruits overhead, the size of cricket balls.

A flash of red caught her own eye through the trees, and for an instant she thought it was an exotic bird, lured by the astonishing abundance of peculiar fruits. Then she heard male voices above the well-bred hum of the largely female guests, and a moment later her red bird stepped out into the wide graveled patch where the pathways intersected. A soldier, in full-dress uniform—a blaze of scarlet and gold, with shining black boots to the knee and a sword at his belt.

He wasn't tall; in fact, he was rather slight, with a fine-boned face seen in profile as he turned to say something to his companion. He stood very straight, though, shoulders square and head up, and there was something about him that reminded her of a bantam cock—something deeply fierce, innately proud, and completely unaware of its relative size. Ready to take on all comers, spurs first.

The thought entertained her so much that it was a moment before she noticed his interlocutor. The companion wasn't dressed as a soldier but was certainly very fine, too, in ocher velvet with a blue satin sash and some large medallion pinned to his chest—the Order of Something-or-Other, she supposed. He did, however, strongly resemble a frog, wide-lipped and pale, with rather big, staring eyes.

The sight of the two of them, rooster and frog, engaged in convivial conversation, made her smile behind her fan, and she didn't notice the gentleman who had come up behind her until he spoke.

"Are you fond of opuntioid cacti . . . madam?"

"I might be, if I knew what they were," she replied, swinging round to see a youngish gentleman in a plum-colored suit gazing at her intently. He cleared his throat and cocked an eyebrow.

"Um . . . actually, I prefer succulents," she said, giving the agreed-upon countersign. She cleared her throat, as well, hoping she remembered the word. "Particularly the, um, euphorbias."

The question in his eyes vanished, replaced by amusement. He looked her up and down in a manner that might in other circumstances have been insulting. She flushed but held his gaze and raised her brows.

"Mr. Bloomer, I presume?"

"If you like," he said, smiling, and offered her his arm. "Do let me show you the euphorbias, Miss . . . ?"

A moment of panic: who should she be, or admit to being?

"Houghton," she said, seizing Rafe's mocking nickname. "Lady Bedelia Houghton."

"Of course you are," he said, straight-faced. "Charmed to make your acquaintance, Lady Bedelia."

He bowed slightly, she took his arm, and together they walked slowly into the wilderness.

They passed through minor jungles of philodendrons—but philodendrons that had never graced anything so plebeian as a parlor, with ragged leaves each half as large as Minnie herself, and a thing with great veined leaves the color of green ink and the look of watered silk.

"They're rather poisonous, philodendrons," Mr. Bloomer said, with a casual nod. "All of them. Did you know?"

"I shall make a note of it."

And then trees—ficus, Mr. Bloomer informed her (perhaps he hadn't chosen his *nom de guerre* at random, after all), with twisted stems and thick leaves and a sweet, musty smell, some of them with vines climbing their trunks with convulsive force, sturdy root-like hairs clinging to the thin bark.

And then, sure enough: the bloody euphorbias, in person.

She hadn't known things like that existed. Many of them didn't even look like proper plants, and some that did were strange perversions of the plant kingdom, with thick bare stems studded with cruel thorns, things that resembled lettuce—but a ruffled white lettuce with dark-red edgings that made it look as though someone had used it to mop up blood—

"They're rather poisonous, too, the euphorbias, but it's more the sap. Won't kill you, but you don't want to get it in your eyes."

"I'm sure I don't." Minnie took a better grip on her parasol, ready to unfurl it in case any of the plants should take it into mind to spit at her; several of them looked as though they'd like nothing better.

"They call that one 'crown of thorns,'" Mr. Bloomer said, nodding at one particularly horrid thing with long black spikes sticking out in all directions. "Apt." He noticed her expression at this point and smiled, tilting his head toward the next house. "Come along; you'll like the next collection better."

"Oh," she said, in a small voice. Then, *"Oh!"* much louder. The new glasshouse was much bigger than the others, with a high, vaulted roof that filled the air with sun and lit the thousand—at least!—orchids that sprang from tables and spilled from trees in cascades of white and gold and purple and red and . . .

"Oh, my." She sighed in bliss, and Mr. Bloomer laughed.

They weren't alone in their appreciation. All of the glasshouses were popular—there had been a fair number of people exclaiming at the spiny, the grotesque, and the poisonous—but the orchid house was packed with guests, and the air was filled with a hum of amazement and delight.

Minnie inhaled as much as she could, sniffing. The air was scented with a variety of fragrances, enough to make her head swim.

"You don't want to smell that one." Mr. Bloomer, guiding her from one delight to the next, put out a shielding hand toward a large pot of rather dull green orchids with thick petals. "Rotting meat."

She took a cautious sniff and recoiled.

"And why on earth would an orchid want to smell like rotting meat?" she demanded.

He gave her a slightly queer look but smiled.

"Flowers put on the color and scent they require to attract the insects that pollinate them. Our friend the *Satyrium* there"—he nodded at the green things—"depends upon the services of carrion flies. Come, this one smells of coconut—have you ever smelt a coconut?"

They took their time in the orchid house—they could hardly do otherwise, given the slow-moving crowd—and despite Minnie's regret at leaving the exotic loveliness, she was relieved to pass into the last glasshouse in the row and find it nearly deserted. It was also cool, by contrast with the tropical heat created by so many bodies, and she breathed deep. The scents in here were subtle and modest by contrast, the plants small and ordinary-seeming, and quite suddenly she realized Mr. Bloomer's strategy.

The orchid house served as a sieve or barrier. Here they were quite alone, though standing in the open, where they could easily see anyone coming in time to alter their conversation to innocuous chat.

"To business, then?" she said, and Mr. Bloomer smiled again.

"Just so. You first or me?"

"You." It would be an exchange rather than a sale, but her half of the bargain was concrete, and his was not. "Tell it to me," she said, focusing her concentration on his face—rather narrow but not displeasing; she could see humor in the creases near his mouth.

"You're quite sure you can remember?" he said dubiously.

"Certainly."

He drew breath, gave a short nod of his own, and began to talk.

Once more she took his arm, and they paced the aisles of the glass-house, walking through patches of sun and shadow, while he told her various bits of information. She memorized these, repeating them back to him, now and again asking for clarification or repetition.

Most of the information had to do with financial matters, banking and the Exchange, the movement of money—between persons and between countries. A few tidbits of political gossip, but not many.

That surprised her; the information he was dealing *for* was all political in nature, and quite specific. Mr. Bloomer was hunting Jacobites. Particularly in England and Paris.

I can't think why, her father had remarked in the margin of his list. *It's true, Charles Stuart has come to Paris, but that's common Knowledge, and besides, everyone knows he'll never get anywhere; the Man's an Idiot. Still, you don't make Money by refusing to sell People what they want. . . .*

She was relieved when Mr. Bloomer finished. It hadn't been a long nor yet a complicated account, and she was sure that she had all the names and the necessary numbers securely fixed in mind.

"All right," she said, and took her own list—sealed—from the secret pocket sewn inside her jacket. She handed it over, making sure to meet his eyes as she did so. Her heart was beating fast and her palm was slightly moist, but he didn't appear suspicious.

Not that there was really anything wrong with what she'd done—she wasn't cheating Mr. Bloomer. Not exactly. Everything on her list was just as her father had specified . . . save that when she'd written it out fair, she'd left out James Fraser's name and the bits of information regarding his movements and interactions with Charles Stuart and his followers. She felt rather possessive, not to say protective, of Mr. Fraser.

Mr. Bloomer wasn't a fool; he opened the document and read it through, at least twice. Then he folded it up and smiled at her.

"Thank you, my dear. A pleasure to—"

He stopped suddenly and drew back a little. She turned to see what had struck him and saw the soldier, the bantam cock, coming in from the passage that led from the orchid house. He was alone, but his scarlet and gold made him glow like a tropical parrot as he stepped through a patch of sun.

"Someone you know?" she asked, low-voiced. *And someone you don't want to meet, I daresay.*

"Yes," Mr. Bloomer replied, and retired into the shadows of a tree fern.

"Will you do me a service, my dear? Go engage His Grace there in conversation for a few moments, while I take my leave."

He nodded encouragingly toward the advancing soldier, and as she took a hesitant step in that direction, he blew her a kiss and stepped round behind the tree fern.

There wasn't time to think what to say.

"Good afternoon," she said, smiling and bowing to the officer. "Isn't it pleasant in here, after all that crush?"

"Crush?" he said, looking faintly puzzled, and then his eyes cleared, focusing on her for the first time, and she realized that he hadn't actually seen her until she spoke to him.

"In the orchid house," she said, nodding toward the doorway he'd just come through. "I thought perhaps you'd come in here as I did, for refuge from the Turkish bath."

He was in fact sweating visibly in his heavy uniform, a bead of perspiration rolling down his temple. He wore his own hair—dark, she saw, in spite of the remnants of rice powder clinging to it. He seemed to realize that he'd been socially remiss, for he made her a deep bow, hand to his heart.

"Your servant, ma'am. I beg your pardon; I was . . ." Straightening, he trailed off with a vague gesture at the plants around them. "It is cooler here, is it not?"

Mr. Bloomer was still visible, near the door leading to the orchid house. He'd stopped, to her surprise, and she was somewhat displeased to realize that he was listening to her conversation—insipid as it was. She narrowed her eyes at him; he saw, and one corner of his long mouth turned up.

She moved closer to the soldier and touched his arm. He stiffened slightly, but there was no sign of repulsion on his face—quite the opposite, which was reassuring—and she said chattily, "Do you know what any of these plants are? Beyond orchids and roses, I'm afraid I'm a complete ignoramus."

"I know . . . some of them," he said. He hesitated for a moment, then said, "I actually came in here to see a particular flower that His Highness recommended to me just now."

"Oh, indeed?" she said, impressed. Her recollections of the frog in the ocher coat were undergoing a rapid readjustment, and she felt slightly faint at the thought that she'd been that close to the Prince of Wales. "Er . . . which flower was that, do you mind telling me?"

"Not at all. Pray let me show it to you. If I can find it." He smiled quite unexpectedly, bowed again, and gave her his arm, which she took with a small thrill, turning her back on the distant Mr. Bloomer.

"Go engage His Grace . . ." That's what he'd said: "His Grace." It had been a long time since she'd lived in London, and she'd rarely had occa-

sion to use English titles, but she was almost sure that you said "Your Grace" only to a duke.

She stole a quick sideways look at him; he wasn't tall but had a good six inches on her. Young, though . . . She'd always thought of dukes (when she thought of them at all) as gouty old men with paunches and dewlaps. This one couldn't be more than five-and-twenty. He was slender, though he still radiated that rooster-like fierceness, and he had a very striking face, but there were deep shadows under his eyes, and his cheeks had lines and hollows that made him seem older than she thought he probably was.

She felt suddenly sorry for him, and her hand squeezed his arm, quite without her meaning to do it.

He glanced down at her, surprised, and she snatched her hand back, diving into her pocket for a handkerchief that she pressed to her lips, feigning a coughing fit.

"Are you all right, madam?" he asked, concerned. "Shall I fetch you—" He turned to look toward the door that led back through the line of glass-houses, then turned back, courteously straight-faced. "I fear that were I to go and fetch you an ice, you'd be dead long before I returned. Shall I thump you on the back instead?"

"You shall not," she managed to say, and giving one or two small, lady-like hacks, dabbed her lips with the handkerchief and tucked it away. "Thank you, anyway."

"Not at all." He bowed but didn't offer her his arm again, instead nodding her to precede him toward a low table filled with an assortment of beautiful chinoiserie. *One more amazement,* she thought, seeing the array of delicate blue and white and gilded porcelain. Any one of these delicately painted bowls would cost a fortune, and here they were, filled with *dirt,* and used to display quite unremarkable flowers.

"These?" she said, turning to look at His Grace—ought she to ask his name? Offer hers?

"Yes," he said, though his voice now seemed hesitant, and she saw him very briefly clench his fists before advancing to the edge of the table. "They were brought from China—very . . . very rare."

She glanced at him, surprised at the catch in his voice.

"What are they, do you know?"

"They have a Chinese name . . . I don't recall it. I know a botanist, a Swedish fellow . . . he calls them chrysanthemum. *Chrystos*—gold, that is—and *anth, anthemon.* Means . . . flower."

She saw his throat bob above the edge of his leather stock as he swallowed and noticed with alarm that he was very pale.

"Sir?" she said, reaching tentatively for his arm. "Are you quite—are you well?"

"Yes, of course," he said, but his breath was coming fast, and the sweat was trickling down his neck. "I'm . . . I'll be . . . quite all ri—" He stopped suddenly, gasping, and leaned heavily on the table. The pots shifted a little and two of them chimed together, a high-pitched ringing that set her teeth on edge and made her skin jump.

"Perhaps you'd best sit down," she said, seizing him by the elbow and trying to lead him back a step, lest he fall face-first into hundreds of pounds of priceless porcelain and rare flowers. He stumbled back and sank to his knees in the gravel, clutching her arms, a heavy weight. She looked wildly about for help, but there was no one in the glasshouse. Mr. Bloomer had disappeared.

"I—" He choked, coughed, coughed harder, gulped air. His lips were slightly blue, which scared her. His eyes were open, but she thought he couldn't see; he let go of her and fumbled blindly at the skirts of his coat. "Need—"

"What is it? Is it in your pocket?" She stooped, pushed his hand away, groped through the folds of fabric, and felt something hard. There was a small pocket in the tail of his coat, and she thought for an instant that she hadn't expected it to be quite this way the first time she touched a man's buttocks, but she found her way into the pocket and extracted a blue enameled snuffbox.

"Is this what you want?" she asked dubiously, holding it out. Snuff seemed the very last thing likely to be helpful to a man in his state, surely. . . .

He took it from her, hands shaking, and tried to open the box. She took it back and opened it for him, only to find a tiny corked vial inside. With no idea what to do—she glanced wildly toward the entrance again, but no help appeared—she took the vial in hand, pulled the cork, and gasped, recoiling as the stinging fumes of ammonia rushed out.

She held the vial to his nose, and he gasped in turn, sneezed—all over her hand—then grabbed her hand and held the vial closer, taking one heroic breath before he dropped it.

He sat down heavily in the gravel, hunched over, and wheezed and snorted and gulped, as she surreptitiously wiped her hand on her petticoat.

"Sir . . . I'm going to go and find someone to help," she said, and made to do so, but his hand had shot out and grasped the fabric of her skirt. He shook his head, speechless, but after a moment got enough breath to say, "No. Be . . . all . . . right now."

She doubted that very much. Still, being conspicuous was the last thing she wanted, and he did seem, if not exactly *better,* at least less in danger of dying on the spot.

She nodded uncertainly, though she didn't think he saw her, and after looking about helplessly for a moment sat down gingerly on the rim of a raised bed full of what looked like pincushions, varying from things that would have fit in the palm of her hand (had they not been equipped with quite so many thorns) to ones much larger than her head. Her stays felt tight, and she tried to slow her breathing.

As her alarm subsided, she became aware of the distant chatter in the orchid house, which had just become noticeably louder and higher-pitched.

"Fred . . . rick," said the hunched form at her feet.

"What?" She bent over to look at him. He was still a bad color and breathing noisily, but he *was* breathing.

"Prince . . ." He flipped a hand toward the distant noise.

"Oh." She thought he meant that the Prince of Wales had come in to view the orchids, this causing the rising tide of excitement next door. In that case, she thought, they were probably safe from interruption for the present—no one would abandon His Royal Highness in order to look at pincushions and Chinese . . . whatever-they-weres.

His Grace had closed his eyes and appeared to be concentrating on breathing, which she thought a good thing. Moved by the desire to do something other than stare at the poor man, she rose and went over to the Chinese bowls.

All her attention had been for the porcelain, to start with, but now she examined the bowls' contents. Chrysanthemum, that's what he'd said. Most of the flowers were smallish, little tufty ball-like blossoms in cream or gold, with long stems and dark-green leaves. One was a pretty rusty color, though, and another bowl held a profusion of small purple blossoms. Then she saw a larger version, snowy white, and realized what she was looking at.

"Oh!" she said, quite loud. She glanced guiltily over her shoulder, then put out a hand and touched the flower very gently. There it was: the curved, symmetrical petals, tightly layered but airy, as though the flower floated above its leaves. It—they—had a noticeable fragrance, so close to. Nothing like the voluptuous, fleshy scents of the orchids; this was a delicate, bitter perfume—but perfume, nonetheless.

"Oh," she said again, more quietly, and breathed it in. It was clean and fresh and made her think of cold wind and pure skies and high mountains.

"Chu," said the man sitting in the gravel behind her.

"Bless you," she said absently. "Are you feeling better?"

"The flowers. They're called *chu*. In Chinese. I apologize."

That made her turn round. He'd made it up onto one knee but was swaying a bit, plainly gathering his strength to try to rise. She reached down and gripped his hand as solidly as she could. His fingers were cold, but his grip was firm. He looked surprised but nodded and, with a wheezing gasp, staggered to his feet, releasing her hand as he did so.

"I apologize," he said again, and inclined his head an inch. More than that and he might have fallen again, she thought, bracing herself uneasily to catch him if he did. "For discommoding you, madam."

"Not at all," she said politely. His eyes were rather unfocused, and she could hear his breath creaking in his chest. "Er . . . what the devil just happened to you? If you don't mind my asking."

He shook his head, then stopped abruptly, eyes closed.

"I—nothing. I shouldn't have come in here. Knew better."

"You're going to fall down again, I think," she said, and took him by the hand once more, guiding him to the raised bed, where she made him sit and sat beside him.

"You *should* have stayed at home," she said reprovingly, "if you knew you were ill."

"I'm not ill." He ran a trembling hand over the sweat on his face, which he then wiped carelessly on the skirts of his coat. "I—I just . . ."

She sighed and glanced at the doorway, then behind her. No other way out, and the chatter in the orchid house was still going strong.

"You just *what*?" she said. "I'm not dragging it out of you one word at a time. Tell me what's the matter with you, or I'm going in there and fetching His Highness out to look after you."

He gave her an astonished look, then started to laugh. And to wheeze. He stopped, fist to his mouth, and panted a bit, catching more breath.

"If you must know . . ." he said, and gulped air, "my father shot himself in the conservatory at our house. Three years ago . . . today. I . . . saw him. His body. Among the glass, all the plants, the—the light—" He looked up at the panes overhead, blinding with sun, then down at the gravel, patterned with the same light, and closed his eyes briefly. "It . . . disturbed me. I wouldn't have come—" He paused to cough. "Pardon me. I wouldn't have come here today, save that His Highness invited me, and I needed very much to meet him." His eyes, bloodshot and watering, met hers directly. They were blue, pale blue.

"In the unlikely event that you haven't heard the story: my father was accused of treason; he shot himself the night before they planned to arrest him."

"That's *very* terrible," Minnie said, appalled. Terrible in a number of ways—not least in the realization that this must be the Duke of Pardloe, the one her father had in mind as a potential . . . source. She avoided even thinking the word "victim."

"It was. He was *not* a traitor, as it happens, but there you are. The family was disgraced, naturally. His regiment—the one he had raised, had built himself—was disbanded. I mean to raise it again." He spoke with a simple matter-of-factness and paused to mop his face with his hand again.

"Haven't you got a handkerchief? Here, have mine." She squirmed on the rough stones, digging for her pocket.

"Thank you." He wiped his face more thoroughly, coughed once, and shook his head. "I need support—patronage from high quarters—in that endeavor, and a friend managed an introduction to His Highness, who was kind enough to listen to me. I think he'll help," he added, in a meditative sort of way. Then he glanced at her and smiled ruefully. "Wouldn't help my cause to be found writhing on the ground like a worm directly after speaking to him, though, would it?"

"No, I can see that." She considered for a moment, then ventured a cautious question. "The *sal volatile*—" She gestured at the vial, fallen to the ground a few feet away. "Do you often feel faint? Or did you just . . . think you might need it today?"

His lips pressed tight at that, but he answered.

"Not often." He pushed himself to his feet. "I'm quite all right now. I'm sorry to have interrupted your day. Would you . . ." He hesitated, looking toward the orchid house. "Would you like me to present you to His Highness? Or to Princess Augusta, if you like; I know her."

"Oh. No, no, that's quite all right," Minnie said hastily, getting up, too. Regardless of her own desires, which didn't involve coming to the notice of royalty, she could see that the very last thing *he* wanted to do was to go anywhere near people, disheveled, shaken, and wheezing as he was. Still, he was pulling himself together before her eyes, firmness straightening his body. He coughed once more and shook his head doggedly, trying to rid himself of it.

"Your friend," he said, with the decisive air of one changing the subject, "do you know him well?"

"My fr—oh, the, um, gentleman I was talking to earlier?" Apparently Mr. Bloomer hadn't been quite fast enough in his disappearing act. "He isn't a friend. I met him by the euphorbias"—she gestured airily, as though she and the euphorbias were quite good chums—"and he began telling me about the plants, so we walked on together. I don't even know his name."

That made him look sharply at her, but it was, after all, the truth, and her look of innocence was apparently convincing.

"I see," he said, and it was obvious that he saw a good deal more than Minnie did. He thought for a moment, then made up his mind.

"I do know him," he said carefully, and wiped a hand under his nose. "And while I would not presume to tell you how to choose your friends, I don't think he's a good man with whom to associate. Should you meet him again, I mean." He stopped, considering, but that was all he had to say on the subject of Mr. Bloomer. Minnie would have liked to know Bloomer's real name but didn't feel she could ask.

There was a short, awkward silence, in which they stared at each other, half-smiling and trying to think what to say next.

"I—" Minnie began.

"You—" he began.

The smiles became genuine.

"What?" she asked.

"I was going to say that I think the prince has likely left the orchids to their own devices by now. You ought to go along, before anyone comes in. You don't want to be seen alone in my company," he added, rather stiffly.

"I don't?"

"No, you don't," he said, his voice softer, regretful but still firm. "Not if you have any desire to be accepted in society. I meant what I said about my father and the family. I mean to change that, but for now . . ." Reaching out, he took her hands and drew her toward him, turning so they faced the entrance to the orchids. He was right; the conversation there had subsided to the mildly threatening hum of bumblebees.

"Thank you," he said, still more softly. "You're very kind."

There was a smudge of rice powder on his cheek; she stood a-tiptoe and wiped it off, showing him the white on her thumb.

He smiled, took her hand again, and, to her surprise, kissed the tip of her thumb.

"Go," he said, his voice very low, and let go her hand. She drew a deep breath and curtsied.

"I—all right. I'm . . . very happy to have made your acquaintance, Your Grace."

His face changed like lightning, startling her terribly. Just as fast, he got it—whatever "it" was—under control and was once more the civil king's officer. For that split second, though, he'd been pure rooster, an enraged cock ready to throw himself at an enemy.

"Don't call me that. Please," he added, and bowed formally. "I have not taken my father's title."

"I—yes, I see," she said, still shaken.

"I doubt it," he said quietly. "Goodbye."

He turned his back on her, took a few steps toward the Chinese bowls and their mysterious flowers, and stood still, gazing down at them.

Minnie seized her fallen fan and parasol, and fled.

12

WERY WENGEFUL

Dear Miss Rennie,

May I beg the Honour of an Appointment with you at your earliest convenience? I wish to propose a Commission that I think very well suited to your considerable Talents.

Your Most Humble Servant,
Edward Twelvetrees

MINNIE FROWNED AT THE note. It was commendably brief but odd. This Twelvetrees spoke of her "talents" in a most familiar sort of way; clearly he knew what those talents were—and yet he gave no introduction, supplied no reference from one of her existing clients or connections. It made her uneasy.

Still, there was no sense of threat in the note, and she *was* in business. No harm in seeing him, she supposed. She'd be under no obligation to accept his commission if it, or he, seemed fishy.

She hesitated over whether to allow him to come to her rooms—but, after all, he had sent the note here; plainly he knew where she lived. She wrote back, offering to see him next day at three o'clock but making a mental note to tell one of the O'Higginses to come a bit early and hide in the boudoir, just in case.

"OH," SHE SAID, opening the door. "So that's it. I thought there was something a trifle odd about your note."

"If you feel yourself offended, Miss Rennie, I willingly apologize." Mr. Bloomer—alias Edward Twelvetrees, evidently—stepped in, not waiting for invitation, and obliging her to take a step back. "But I imagine a woman of your undoubted sense and experience might be willing to overlook a bit of professional subterfuge?"

He smiled at her, and, despite herself, she smiled back.

"I might," she said. "A professional, are you?"

"It takes one to know one," he said, with a small bow. "Shall we sit down?"

She shrugged slightly and gave Eliza a nod, indicating that she might bring in a tray of refreshments.

Mr. Twelvetrees accepted a cup of tea and an almond biscuit but left the latter lying on his saucer and the former steaming away unstirred.

"I shan't waste your time, Miss Rennie," he said. "When I left you in the princess's glasshouse, I abandoned you—rather cavalierly, I'm afraid—to the company of His Grace, the Duke of Pardloe. Given the scandal attached to his family, I assumed at the time that you knew who he was, but from your manner when I observed you speaking with him, I revised this opinion. Was I right in thinking that you did *not* know him?"

"I didn't," Minnie said, keeping her composure. "But it was quite all right. We exchanged a few pleasantries, and I left." *Just how long were you watching us?* she wondered.

"Ah." He'd been watching her face intently but at this broke off his inspection long enough to add cream and sugar to his tea and stir it. "Well, then. The commission for which I wish to engage your services has to do with this gentleman."

"Indeed," she said politely, and picked up her own cup.

"I wish you to abstract certain letters from the duke's possession and deliver them to me."

She nearly dropped the cup but tightened her hold just in time.

"What letters?" she asked sharply. Now she knew what it was about his note that had struck her oddly. *Twelvetrees.* That was the name of the Countess of Melton's lover: Nathaniel Twelvetrees. All too plainly, this Edward was some relation.

And she heard in memory Colonel Quarry's words when she'd asked if she might speak with Nathaniel: *"Afraid not, Miss Rennie. My friend shot him."*

"Correspondence between the late Countess Melton and my brother Nathaniel Twelvetrees."

She sipped her tea, feeling Edward's gaze as hot on her skin as the breath from her cup. She set the cup down carefully and looked up. His face had an expression she'd seen on the faces of hawks fixing on their prey. But it wasn't she who was the prey here.

"That might be possible," she said coolly, though her heart had sped up noticeably. "Forgive me, though—are you sure such correspondence exists?"

He uttered a short laugh, quite without humor.

"It *did* exist, I'm sure of that."

"I'm sure you are," she said politely. "But if the correspondence is of the nature I surmise you mean—I *have* heard certain speculations—would the duke not have burned any such letters, following the death of his wife?"

Mr. Twelvetrees lifted one shoulder and let it fall, his eyes still fixed on hers.

"He might have done," he said. "And your immediate task would of course be to discover whether that is the case. But I have reason to believe that the correspondence still exists—and if it does, I want it, Miss Rennie. And I'll pay for it. Handsomely."

WHEN THE DOOR closed behind Edward Twelvetrees, she stood frozen for a moment, until she heard the door of her boudoir open, across the hall.

"Well, that's a rum cove," Rafe O'Higgins observed, with a nod toward the closed front door. Eliza, who had come in to take away the tray, inclined her head in sober agreement.

"Wengeful," she said. "Wery wengeful, 'e is. But oo'd blame him?"

Oo, indeed? Minnie thought, and suppressed the urge to laugh. Not from humor so much as from nerves.

"Aye, mibbe," Rafe said. He went to the window and, lifting the edge of the blue velvet curtain, looked carefully down into the street, where Edward Twelvetrees was presumably vanishing into the distance. "I'd say your man's inclined toward vengeance, sure. But what d'ye think he'd be after doing with these letters, if there are any?"

There was a brief silence, as all three of them contemplated the possibilities.

"Put 'em on broadsheets and sell 'em at a ha'penny a go?" Eliza suggested. "Could make a bit o' money out o' that, I s'pose."

"Make a lot more out of the duke," Rafe said, shaking his head. "Blackmail, aye? If the letters are juicy enough, I daresay His Grace would pay through the nose to keep just that from happening."

"I imagine so," Minnie said absently, though the echoes of her conversation with Colonel Quarry drowned out further suggestions.

"*. . . he requires proof of the affair for a . . . a . . . legal reason, and he will not countenance the idea of letting anyone read his wife's letters, no matter that she is beyond the reach of public censure nor that the consequences to himself if the affair is* not *proved may be disastrous.*"

What if numerology was less penetrating an art than usual and Harry Quarry wasn't a bluff, transparent four, after all? What if his care for Lord Melton was a charade? Twelvetrees had just openly engaged her to be his cat's-paw; what if Quarry had the same end in mind but was playing a double game?

If so . . . were the two men playing the *same* game? And if so, were they in it together or working in opposition, whether known to each other or not?

She brought Quarry to mind, reliving their conversations and analyzing them, word for word, watching the emotions play out in memory across his broad, crudely handsome face.

No. One of the chief tenets of her family credo was "Trust no one," but one did have to make judgments. And she was as sure as it was possible to be that Harry Quarry's motive was what he had said: to protect his friend. And after all . . . Harry Quarry not only was convinced of the letters' existence but had a good notion of their location. True, he hadn't asked her to steal the letters, not explicitly, but had certainly done everything but.

She had promised Edward Twelvetrees nothing beyond an attempt to find out whether the letters *did* exist; if so, she'd said, then they could discuss further terms.

Well, then. The next step, at least, was clear.

"Rafe," she said, interrupting an argument between Rafe and Eliza as to whether Mr. Twelvetrees more resembled a ferret or an obelisk (she assumed they meant "basilisk" but didn't stop to find out), "I have a job for you and Mick."

13

THE LETTERS

MR. VAUXHALL GARDENS (alias Mr. Hosmer Thornapple, a wealthy broker on the Exchange, as Minnie had discovered by the simple expedient of having Mick O'Higgins follow him home) had proved to be not only an excellent client, with an insatiable appetite for Lithuanian illuminated manuscripts and Japanese erotica, but also a most valuable connection. Through him, she had acquired (besides a thin sheaf of sealed documents intended for her father's eyes) two fifteenth-century incunabula—one in excellent condition, the other needing some repair— and a tattered but originally beautiful small book by María Anna Águeda de San Ignacio, an abbess from New Spain, with handwritten annotations said to be in the hand of the nun herself.

Minnie hadn't enough Spanish to make out much of the content, but it was the sort of small book that gave one pleasure simply to hold, and she had paused in her labors to do just that.

The sturdy sideboard in her parlor was stacked on one side with books and on the other with more books, these wrapped in soft cloth, then a layer of felt, one of lambswool, and then an outer skin of oiled silk, tied with tarred twine. Piles of packing materials were arrayed on the dining table, and several large wooden crates were wedged under it.

She trusted no one else to handle or pack the books for shipment back to Paris and was in consequence dust-stained and sweaty, in spite of the breeze from the open window. Just past Midsummer's Day, the weather had kept fine for a whole week, much to the astonishment of every Londoner she'd spoken to.

La Vida de la Alma. Close enough to the Latin to translate as "The Life of the Soul." It was soft-bound in a thin oxblood leather, worn by years—a lifetime?—of reading, with a stamped pattern of tiny pecten shells, each one edged with gilt. She touched one gently, feeling a great sense of peace. Books always had something to say, beyond the words inside, but it was rare to find one with so strong a character.

She opened it carefully; the paper inside was thin, and the ink had begun to fade with age but not to blur. The book had few illustrations, and those few, simple: a cross, the Lamb of God, the pecten shell, drawn larger—she'd seen that once or twice before, in Spanish manuscripts, but didn't know the significance. She must remember to ask her father. . . .

"Ah," she said, compressing her lips. "Father." She'd been trying not to think of him, not until she'd had time to sort out her emotions and consider what on earth she might say to him about her mother.

She'd thought of the woman called Sister Emmanuelle many times since leaving her in her hay-filled womb of light. The shock had faded, but the images of that meeting were printed on her mind as indelibly as the black ink inside this book. She still felt the sting of loss and the ache of sorrow—but the sense of peace from the book seemed somehow to shelter her, like a covering wing.

"Are you an angel?"

She sighed and set the book gently into its nest of cloth and felt. She'd have to talk to her father, yes. But what on earth would she say?

"Raphael . . ."

"If *you* have any answers," she said to the book and its author, "please pray for me. For us."

She wasn't crying, but her eyes were damp, and she wiped her face with the hem of her dusty apron. Before she could settle to work again, though, there came a knock at the door.

Eliza had gone out to do the shopping, so Minnie opened the door just as she was. Mick and Rafe O'Higgins stood shoulder to shoulder in the hall, both of them smudged with soot and excited as terriers smelling a rat.

"We've got the letters, Bedelia!" Rafe said.

"*All* the letters!" Mick added, proudly holding up a leather bag.

"WE WAITED FOR the butler's day out," Mick explained, laying his booty out ceremoniously before her. "It's the butler what arranges for the sweeps to come in when needed, aye? So when we come to the door with our brooms and cloths—not to worry, we borrowed 'em, ye'll not have to pay—and said Mr. Sylvester had sent for us to attend to the library chimney . . ."

"Well, the housekeeper looked a bit squint-eyed," Rafe chimed in, "but she showed us along, and when we began to bang about and shout up the chimney and kick up soot, she left us quite to ourselves. And so . . ."

He swept a hand out over the table. All the letters, indeed. The bag had disgorged a small, flat wooden case, a leather folder, and a thin stack of letters, soberly bound with black grosgrain ribbon.

"Well done!" Minnie told them sincerely. She felt a flutter of excitement at sight of the letters, though a cautious excitement. The O'Higginses had, of course, brought away every letter they could find. They must have more than the countess's letters here, and she wondered for a brief moment whether some of the extras might be valuable . . . but dismissed the thought for now. As long as they'd found Esmé's . . .

"Did you get paid for sweeping the chimney?" she asked, out of curiosity.

"Sure and ye wound us, Lady Bedelia," Rafe said, clasping a battered hat over his heart and trying to look wounded. There was smut on his nose.

"O' course we did," Mick said, grinning. "T'wouldn't have been convincing, otherwise, would it?"

They were cock-a-hoop over their success, and it took nearly half a bottle of Madeira to celebrate said success enough for them to leave, but at last she closed the door upon them, rubbed at a smudge on the white doorjamb with her thumb, and walked slowly back to the table to see what she had.

She took the letters from their various wrappings and set them out in three neat piles. The letters from Esmé, Lady Melton, to her lover, Nathaniel Twelvetrees: those were the ones in the wooden box. The letters in the beribboned bundle were from said Nathaniel Twelvetrees to Esmé. And the leather folder held quite unexpected letters—from Harold, Lord Melton, to his wife.

Minnie had never felt the slightest reservation in reading someone else's letters. It was simply part of the work, and if she occasionally met someone in those pages whose voice struck her mind or heart, someone real—that was a bonus, something to treasure privately, with a sweet regret that she would never know the writer face-to-face.

Well, she'd certainly never know Esmé or Nathaniel face-to-face, she thought. As for Harold, Lord Melton—just looking at the untidy pile of crumpled, smoothed-out, ink-blotted sheets made the hairs prickle at the back of her neck.

Esmé first, she decided. Esmé was the center of it all. And it was Esmé's letters she'd been commissioned—more or less—to steal. A faint hint of perfume rose from the wooden box, something slightly bitter, fresh, and mysterious. Myrrh? Nutmeg? Dried lemon? Not sweet at all, she thought—nor, likely, was Esmé Grey.

Not all of the letters had dates, but she sorted them as best she could. All on the same stationery, an expensive linen rag paper, thick to the touch and pure white. The sentiments inscribed upon them were not pure at all.

Mon cher . . . Dois-je vous dire ce que je voudrais que vous me fassiez? "Shall I tell you what I want you to do to me?"

Minnie had read her way with interest through her father's entire stock of erotica when she was fourteen, accidentally discovering in the process that one didn't necessarily need a partner in order to experience the sensations so euphorically described therein. Esmé hadn't much literary style, but her imagination—surely some of it must *be* imagination?—was remarkable and expressed with a blunt freedom that made Minnie want to squirm, ever so slightly, in her seat.

Not that they were all like that. One was a simple two-line note making an assignation, another was a more thoughtful—and, surprisingly, a more intimate—letter describing Esmé's visit to—*oh, God,* Minnie thought, and wiped her hand on her skirt, as she'd begun to perspire—Princess Augusta and her fabulous garden.

Esmé had noted carelessly that she had no liking for the princess, whom she thought heavy in both body and mind, but that Melton had asked her to accept the invitation to tea in order to—and here Minnie translated Esmé's idiomatic French expression—"drench in melted butter" the vulgar woman and pave the way for Melton to discuss his military designs with the prince.

She then mentioned walking through the glass conservatories with the princess, paused to make comical, if offhandedly complimentary, comparisons between her lover's physical parts and various exotic plants—she mentioned the euphorbias, Minnie noted—and ended with a brief remark about the Chinese flowers called *chu*. She was attracted—Minnie snorted, reading this—by the "purity and stillness" of the blooms.

"*À les regarder, mon âme s'est apaisée,*" she had written. "It soothed my soul to look at them."

Minnie set the letter down, as gently as if it might break, and closed her eyes.

"You poor man," she whispered.

———

THERE WAS A DECANTER of wine on the sideboard. She poured a small glass, very carefully, and stood sipping it, looking at the desk and its burden of letters.

Someone real. She had to admit that Esmé Grey was definitely real. The impact of her personality was as palpable as though she'd reached out of the paper and stroked her correspondent's face. Teasing, erotic . . .

"Cruel," Minnie said aloud, though softly. To write to your lover and mention your husband?

"Hmph," she said.

And Esmé's partner in this criminal conversation? She glanced at the bundle of Nathaniel Twelvetrees's letters to his mistress. What bizarre quirk of mind had made Melton keep them? Was it guilt, a sort of hair shirt of the spirit?

And if so . . . guilt for killing Nathaniel Twelvetrees? Or guilt over Esmé's death? She wondered how quickly the one event had followed the other—had the shock of hearing of her lover's death brought on a miscarriage, or a fatally early labor, as gossip said?

Likely she'd never learn the answers to those questions, but while Melton had killed Nathaniel, he'd left the poet his voice; Nathaniel Twelvetrees could speak for himself.

She poured another glass of the wine—a heavy, aromatic Bordeaux; she felt she needed ballast—and unfolded the first of Nathaniel's letters.

For a poet, Nathaniel was a surprisingly pedestrian writer. His sentiments were expressed in sufficiently passionate language but a very common prose, and while he made a distinct effort to meet Esmé on her own ground, he was clearly not her match, in either imagination or expression.

Still, he was a poet, not a novelist; perhaps it wasn't fair to judge him by his prose style alone. In two of his letters, he mentioned an enclosure, a poem written in honor of his beloved. She checked the box: no poems. Maybe Melton had burned those—or Esmé had. Nathaniel's tone in presenting these literary gifts reminded Minnie very much of a naturalist's description she had read—of a type of male spider who brought his chosen mate an elaborately silk-wrapped parcel containing an insect and then leapt upon her whilst she was absorbed in unwrapping her snack, hastily achieving his purpose before she could finish eating and have him for dessert.

"She scared him," Minnie murmured to herself, with a sense of sympathy but one tempered with a mild contempt. "Poor worm." She was somewhat shocked to realize that contempt—and the more so to realize that Esmé had very likely felt the same.

Hence her invoking Melton's name in the letters to Twelvetrees? An attempt to sting him into greater ardor? She'd done it more than once; in fact—Minnie turned again to Esmé's letters—yes, she'd mentioned her husband, by name or reference, in every letter, even the two-line assignation: *My husband will be gone on his regimental business—come to me tomorrow in the oratory at four o'clock.*

"Huh," Minnie said, and sat back, eyeing the letters as she sipped her wine. They lay in stacks and single sheets and fans before her, with the as-yet-unread folder that held Melton's letters in the center. It looked not unlike a layout of the tarot—she'd had her own cards read several times in Paris, by an acquaintance of her father's named Jacques, who was practicing the art.

"Sometimes it's quite subtle," Jacques had said, shuffling the gaudy cards. "Especially the minor arcana. But then—sometimes it's obvious at first glance." This said, smiling, as he laid Death in front of her.

She had no opinion regarding the truth laid out in tarot cards, considering that to be no more than the reflection of the client's mind at the time of the reading. But she had definite opinions regarding letters, and she touched the two-line assignation thoughtfully.

Where had Esmé's letters come from? Would the Twelvetrees family have sent them to Lord Melton following Nathaniel's death? They might, she thought. What could be more painful to him? Though that argued both a subtlety of mind and a sense of refined cruelty that she saw no trace of in Nathaniel's letters and that she hadn't noticed in most English people.

Besides . . . what had made Melton challenge Twelvetrees in the first place? Surely Esmé hadn't confessed the affair to him. No . . . Colonel Quarry had said, or at least intimated, that Melton had found incriminating letters *written by his wife,* and that that was what . . .

She picked up the countess's pile again, frowning at the letters. Looking carefully, she could see that each one had a blot of ink or the occasional smear—one appeared to have had water spilled over the bottom edge. So . . . these were drafts of letters, later copied fair to be sent to Nathaniel? If so, though, why not throw the drafts into the fire? Why keep them and risk discovery?

"Or invite it," she said aloud, surprising herself. She sat up straight and read the letters through again, then set them down.

My husband will be gone . . . Every one. Every one of them noted Melton's absence—and his preoccupation with his nascent regiment.

Jacques was right; sometimes it was obvious.

Minnie shook her head, the wine fumes mingling with the dead countess's bitter perfume.

"Pauvre chienne," she said softly. "Poor bitch."

14

NOTORIOUS BORES

IT WASN'T NECESSARY TO read Lord Melton's letters, but she couldn't possibly have stopped herself from doing so, and she picked one up as though it were a lit grenade that might go off in her hand.

It did. She read the five letters through without stopping. None were dated, and there was no way of telling the order in which they had been written; time had plainly been of no consequence to the writer—and yet it had meant everything. This was the voice of a man pushed off a cliff into the abyss of eternity and documenting his fall.

I will love you forever, I cannot do otherwise, but by God, Esmé, I will hate you forever, with all the power of my soul, and had I you before me and your long white neck in my hands I would strangle you like a fucking swan and fuck you as you died, you . . .

He might as well have picked up the inkwell and flung it at the page. The words were scrawled and blotted, big and black, and there were ragged holes torn through the paper where here and there he had stabbed the page with his quill.

She took a deep, gasping breath when she came to the end, feeling as though she hadn't breathed once in the reading. She didn't weep, but her hands were shaking, and the last letter slipped from her fingers and floated to the floor. Weighted with loss and a grief that didn't cut but clawed and, merciless, tore its prey to bloody ribbons.

SHE DIDN'T READ the letters again. It would have felt like a desecration. As it was, there was no need to read them over; she thought she would never forget a word of any of them.

She had to leave her rooms and walk for some time to regain any sense of composure. Now and then she felt tears run down her cheeks and hastily blotted them before any passerby should notice and ask her trouble. She felt as though she'd wept for days or as though someone had beaten her. And yet it was nothing to do with her.

She felt one of the O'Higgins brothers following somewhere behind her, but he tactfully hung back. She walked from one end to the other of St. James's Park, and all the way around the lake, but finally sat down on a bench near a flotilla of swans, exhausted in mind and body both. Someone sat down on the other end of the bench—Mick, she saw, from the corner of her eye.

It was teatime; the bustle of the streets was dying down as people hurried home or dropped into a tavern or an ordinary to refresh themselves after a long day's labor. Mick coughed in a meaning manner.

"I'm not hungry," she said. "You go on, if you like."

"Now, Bedelia. Ye know fine I'm not goin' anywhere you don't go." He'd scooted along the bench and sat at her elbow, slouched and companionable. "Shall I be fetchin' ye a pie, now? Whatever's the trouble, it'll seem better on a full belly."

She wasn't hungry, but she *was* empty and, after a moment's indecision, gave in and let him buy her a meat pie from a pie man. The smell of it was so strong and good that she felt somewhat restored just from holding it. She nibbled the crust, felt the rich flood of juice and flavor in her mouth, and, closing her eyes, gave herself over to the pie.

"There, now." Mick, having long since finished his own pie, sat gazing benevolently at her. "Better, is it not?"

"Yes," she admitted. At least she could now think about the matter, rather than drowning in it. And while she hadn't been conscious of actually *thinking* at any time since leaving her rooms, evidently some back chamber of her mind had been turning things over.

Esmé and Nathaniel were dead. Harold, theoretical Duke of Pardloe, wasn't. That's what it came down to. She could do something about him. And she found that she was determined to do it.

"What, though?" she asked, having explained the matter to Mick in general terms. "I can't send those letters to the secretary at war—there's no way His Grace wouldn't find out, and I think it would kill him to know anyone had read them, let alone people who . . . who had any power over him, you know."

Mick pulled a face but allowed that this might be so.

"So what is it ye want to happen, Lady Bedelia?" he asked. "There's maybe another way of it?"

She drew a breath that went down to her shoes and let it out slowly.

"I suppose I want what Captain Quarry wants: to scotch the notion that His Grace is insane and to get his regiment re-commissioned. I think I have to do both those things. But how?"

"And ye can't—or ye won't—do it with the letters. . . ." He eyed her sideways, to see if she might be convinced otherwise, but she shook her head at him.

"Get a false witness?" he suggested. "Bribe someone to say there was an affair betwixt the countess and the poet?"

Minnie shook her head dubiously.

"I'm not saying I couldn't find someone who would take a bribe," she said. "But not one who'd be believed. Most young women aren't good liars at all."

"No," he agreed. "You're one of a kind, so ye are." It was said with admiration, and she nodded briefly at the compliment but went on with her train of thought.

"The other thing is that it's easy enough to start a rumor, but once it's started, it's quite likely to take on a life of its own. You can't control it, I mean. If I got someone—man or woman—to say he or she knew about the affair, it wouldn't stop there. And because it wouldn't be the truth to start with, there's no telling where it might go. You don't set light to a fuse without knowing where it's laid," she added, raising a brow at him. "My father always told me that."

"A wise man, your father." Mick touched the brim of his hat in respect. "If it's not to be bribery and false witness, then . . . what might his honor, your da, recommend?"

"Well . . . forgery, most likely," she said with a shrug. "But I don't think writing a false version of those letters would be a great deal better than showing the originals, in terms of effect." She rubbed her thumb across her fingers, feeling the faint slick of lard from the piecrust. "Get me another pie, will you, Mick? Thinking is hungry work."

She finished the second pie and, thus fortified, reluctantly began to mentally revisit Esmé's letters. It was, after all, Countess Melton who was the *fons et origo* of all this misery.

Would you think it was worth it, I wonder? she thought toward the absent Esmé. Likely the woman had only wanted to make her husband jealous; she probably hadn't had the slightest intent of causing her husband to shoot one of his friends; most certainly she hadn't had any intent of dying, along with her child. That circumstance struck Minnie with a particular poignancy and, for some odd reason, made her think of her mother.

I don't suppose you intended anything that happened, either, she thought with compassion. *You certainly didn't intend me.* Still, she thought her mother's situation, while very regrettable, wasn't the theatrical tragedy that Esmé's had been. *I mean, we both survived.*

And speaking only for myself, she added, *I'm quite glad to be here. I'm reasonably sure that Father's pleased about that, too.*

A slight sound pulled her from her thoughts, and she perceived that Mick had adjusted his position, indicating silently that he thought it was getting late and best they begin walking back to Great Ryder Street.

He was right; the shadows of the huge trees had begun to edge across the path like a seeping stain of spilled tea. And the sounds had changed, too: the cawing laughter of the society women with their parasols had mostly vanished, replaced by the male voices of soldiers and businessmen and clerks, all heading for their tea with the single-mindedness of donkeys headed for their mangers.

She stood up and shook her skirts back into place, retrieved her hat and pinned it firmly to her hair. She nodded to Mick and indicated with a small movement of the hand that he should walk with her, rather than follow. She was wearing a decent but very demure blue gingham with a plain straw hat; she might easily pass for an upper housemaid walking out with an admirer, as long as they didn't meet anyone she knew—and that wasn't likely at this hour.

"This chap what his lordship shot," Mick said, after half a block. "They say he was a poet, was he?"

"So I'm told."

"Have ye maybe read any of his poems, like?"

She glanced at him, surprised.

"No. Why?"

"Well, it was just ye mentioned your da thinkin' highly o' forgery in some situations. I was wonderin' what ye might forge that would help, and it struck me—what if your man Twelvetrees had written a poem of an incriminatin' nature about the countess? Or, rather," he added, in case she was missing his point, which she wasn't, "what if ye were to write one for him?"

"It's a thought," she said slowly. "Perhaps quite a good thought, too— but let's turn it over for a bit, shall we?"

"Aye," said Mick, beginning to grow enthused. "Well, first off, o' course: what class of a forger might ye be, at all?"

"Not inspired," she admitted. "I mean, no hope of me doing a proper banknote. And I've really not done much in the way of true forgery, either—copying the writing of a real person, I mean. It's mostly writing a false letter but one that's meant for a person who doesn't know the sender. And only now and then, not often."

Mick emitted a low humming noise.

"Still, ye have got some of the man's letters to work from," he pointed out. "Could ye maybe trace a few words here and there and add in, between-like?"

"Maybe," she said dubiously. "But there's more to a good forgery than only the handwriting, you know. If it's going to a person who knows the sender, then the style needs to be a decent facsimile—has to resemble the real person's, I mean," she added quickly, seeing his lips start to shape "facsimile."

"And his style writing a poem could be different to what he'd do writing a letter?" Mick turned that over for a moment, considering.

"Yes. What if he was only known to write sonnets, I mean, and I wrote a sestina? Someone might smell a rat."

"I'll take yer word for it. Though I shouldn't think your man was in the habit of writin' love poems to the secretary at war, eh?"

"No," she said, a little tersely. "But if I wrote something shocking enough to justify his lordship shooting the man who wrote it, what are the chances that the secretary would show it to somebody else? Who might tell somebody else, and . . . and so on." She flipped a hand. "If it got to someone who could tell that Nathaniel Twelvetrees didn't write it, then what?"

Mick nodded soberly. "Then they'd maybe think your lordship did it himself, ye mean?"

"That's one possibility." On the other hand, the *other* possibility was undeniably fascinating.

They had reached Great Ryder Street and the scrubbed white steps that led up to her door. The scent of brewing tea floated up from the servants' areaway beside the steps, and her stomach curled in a pleasantly anticipatory fashion.

"It's a good idea, Mick," she said, and touched his hand lightly. "Thank you. I'll ask Lady Buford whether Nathaniel published any of his poetry. If I could read a bit of it, just to see . . ."

"Me money's on you, Lady Bedelia," Mick said, and, smiling at her, raised her hand and kissed it.

"NATHANIEL TWELVETREES?" Lady Buford was surprised and peered closely at Minnie through her quizzing glass. "I don't believe so. He was much given to declaiming his poetry at salons and I believe went so far as to give a theatrical reading at one point, but from what little I heard of his poetry—well, what little I hear of what people *said* of his poetry—I doubt that most printers would have considered it a promising financial venture."

She resumed watching the stage, this presently featuring a mediocre performance of "Charming Country Songs, by a Duette of Two Ladies," but tapped her closed fan now and then against her closed lips, an indication of continued thought.

"I believe," she said at once, when the next pause in the entertainment came, "that Nathaniel *did* have some of his poems privately printed. For the edification of his friends," she added, with a delicate lift of one strong gray brow. "Why do you ask?"

Fortunately the pause had given Minnie time enough to foresee that one, and she answered readily enough.

"Sir Robert Abdy was speaking of Mr. Twelvetrees at Lady Scroggs's rout the other night—rather scornfully," she added, with her own delicacy. "But as Sir Robert has his own pretensions in that line . . ."

Lady Buford laughed, a deep, engaging laugh that made people in the box next them turn round to look, and proceeded to say a few scornful— and deeply amusing—things of her own about Sir Robert.

But Minnie continued to think, through the appearances of a pair of Italian fire-eaters, a dancing pig (which disgraced itself onstage, to the delight of the audience), two purportedly Chinese gentlemen who sang a purportedly comic song, and several more acts of a similar ilk.

Privately printed. For the edification of his friends. There were at least two poems, written expressly for the edification of Esmé, Countess Melton. Where were they?

"I wonder," she said quite casually, as they began to make their way out through the throngs of theatergoers, "if Countess Melton was fond of poetry?"

Lady Buford was only half attending, being occupied in trying to catch the eye of an acquaintance on the far side of the theater, and replied absently, "Oh, I don't think so. Woman never read a book in her life, save the Bible."

"The Bible?" Minnie asked, incredulous. "I wouldn't have thought her a . . . a religious person." Lady Buford had succeeded in attracting the friend, who was wading forcefully toward them through the crowd, and spared a cynic smile for Minnie.

"She wasn't. But she did like to read the Bible and make fun of it to shock people. Only too easy to do, I'm afraid."

⟶

"SHE WOULDN'T HAVE thrown the poems away," Minnie argued to Rafe, who was disposed to be dubious. "They were *to* her, *about* her. No woman would throw away a poem that a man she cared for wrote about her—and most especially not a woman like Esmé."

"Has any man ever written you a love poem, Lady Bedelia?" he asked, teasing.

"No," she said primly, but felt herself blushing. A few men had done just that—and she'd kept the poems, even though she didn't care all that much for the men who'd written them. Still . . .

"Mmm," Rafe conceded, with a waggle of his head. "But maybe your man Melton burnt them. *I* would, if some smellsmock had been sending my wife that class of thing."

"If he didn't burn the letters," Minnie said, "he wouldn't have burnt the poems, either. The poems couldn't possibly have contained anything worse."

Why didn't *he burn the letters?* she wondered, for at least the hundredth time. And to have kept *all* the letters—Esmé's, Nathaniel's . . . and his own.

Perhaps it was guilt, the need to suffer for what he'd done, obsessively reading them over. Perhaps it was confusion—some need or hope of making sense of what had happened, what they'd *all* done, in making this tragedy. He was the only one left to do it, after all.

Or . . . perhaps it was only that he still loved his wife and his friend, mourned them both, and couldn't bear to part with these last personal relics. His own letters were certainly filled with a heartbreaking grief, easily visible amongst the blots of rage.

"I think that she deliberately left the letters where her husband would find them," Minnie said slowly, watching a line of half-grown cygnets sailing after their mother. "But the poems . . . maybe those didn't have any pointed references to Lord Melton in them. If they were only about *her*, she might have kept them private, put them away somewhere safe, I mean."

"So?" Rafe was beginning to look wary. "We'll not get back in Argus House, ye know. Every servant in the place saw us last time."

"Ye-es." She stretched out a leg, considering her new calf-leather court shoes. "But I was wondering . . . might you have a . . . a sister, say, or perhaps a cousin, who wouldn't mind earning . . . say . . . five pounds?" Five pounds was half a year's pay for a house servant.

Rafe stopped dead and stared at her.

"Are ye wanting us to burgle the house or burn it down, for all love?"

"Nothing at all dangerous," she assured him, and batted her eyes, just once. "I just want you—or, rather, your female accomplice—to steal the countess's Bible."

IN THE END, stealing the book hadn't been necessary. Cousin Aoife, in her guise as a newly hired chambermaid, had simply gone through the Bible, this still resting chastely on the night table beside the countess's bereft bed, removed from it a handful of folded papers, pocketed these, walked down the stairs and out to the privy behind the house, from whence she had modestly disappeared through a hole in the hedge, never to return.

"Anything ye can use, Lady Bedelia?" Mick and Rafe had both come up to her rooms the day after they'd delivered their prize and collected Aoife's wages.

"Yes." She hadn't slept at all the night before, and everything around her had a slightly dream-like quality, including the two Irishmen. She yawned, spreading her fan just in time, and blinked at them, then reached into her pocket and drew out a parchment cover, sealed with black wax and addressed to *Sir William Yonge, Secretary at War.*

"Can you ensure—and I do mean make *sure*—that Sir William will get this? I know," she said dryly, seeing Rafe make doe's eyes at her, "I wound you. Do it, though."

They laughed and went, leaving her to the silence of her room and the company of paper. Small barricades of books protected the table on which she'd made her magic, summoning the shade of her father with half a glass of Madeira, crossing herself and asking the blessing of her mother's prayers before picking up her quill.

Nathaniel Twelvetrees, bless his erotically inclined heart, had waxed lascivious in describing his mistress's charms. He had also, in one of the poems, mentioned various aspects of the place in which the lovers had disported themselves. He hadn't signed that one—but he had written *Yours forever, darling—Nathaniel* at the bottom of the other.

After some dithering, she had at last decided to take the risk in order to put the matter beyond doubt and, after filling two foolscap pages with practice attempts, had cut a fresh quill and written—in what she *thought* was a decent version of Nathaniel's hand and style—a title for his untitled poem: *Love's Constant Flowering: in Celebration of the Seventh of April.* And at the bottom—after a lot more practice: *Yours, in the flesh and in the spirit, darling Esmé—Nathaniel.*

If she was lucky, no one would ever think to investigate where Esmé, Countess Melton, had been on the seventh of April, but one of said countess's letters had made an assignation for that date, and the details of the place given in Nathaniel's poem matched what Minnie knew of the spot chosen for said assignation.

The poem made it clear, at least, that the Duke of Pardloe would have had more than adequate grounds for challenging Nathaniel Twelvetrees to a duel. And it certainly suggested that the countess had encouraged Twelvetrees's attentions, if not more—but it didn't disclose the true heart of the matter, let alone reveal Esmé's character or the painful intimacies of her husband.

So. Now it was done.

The letters—all of them—were still arrayed on the table in their tarot spread before her, silent witnesses.

"And what am I to do with *you*?" she said to them. She filled up her glass of wine and drank it slowly, contemplating.

The simplest thing—and by far the safest—was to burn them. Two considerations stopped her, though.

One. If the poem didn't work, the letters were the only evidence of the affair. In the last resort, she could give them to Harry Quarry and let him make what use he could—or would—of them.

Two. That final thought lingered in her mind, nibbled at her heart. *Why did he keep them?* Whether for guilt, grief, repentance, solace, or reminder—His Grace had kept them. They had value to him.

It was just past Midsummer's Day; the sun still hung in the sky, though it was past eight o'clock. She heard the bells of St. James's strike the hour and, draining her glass, made up her mind.

She'd have to put them back.

WHETHER IT WAS the influence of her mother's prayers or a benign intercession by Mother María Anna Águeda de San Ignacio, it was only three days following this rash decision that the opportunity to carry it out was put into Minnie's hands.

"Such news, my dear!" Lady Buford was quite flushed, from either heat or excitement, and fanned herself rapidly. "Earl Melton is holding a ball, in honor of his mother's birthday."

"What? I didn't know he had a mother. Er . . . I mean—"

Lady Buford laughed, growing noticeably pinker.

"Even that villain Diderot has a mother, my dear. But it's true that the dowager Countess of Melton is not strongly in evidence. She wisely decamped to France following her husband's suicide and has been living very quietly there ever since."

"But . . . she's coming back?"

"Oh, I doubt it extremely," Lady Buford said, and took out a rather worn lace handkerchief, with which she dabbed her forehead. "Is there tea, my dear? I find myself in dire need of a cup; summer air is so drying."

Eliza hadn't waited for a summons. Knowing Lady Buford's attitude toward tea, she had begun brewing a pot the moment Lady B's knock was heard at the door and now came trundling down the hall with a rattling tray.

Minnie waited with what patience she could summon for the necessary ceremony of pouring: the administration of three sugar lumps—Lady Buford had very few teeth left, and no wonder—a large dollop of cream, and the acquisition of exactly two ginger biscuits. Finally restored, Lady Buford patted her lips, stifled a soft belch, and sat up straight, ready for business.

"There's tremendous talk about it, of course," she said. "It's not even four months since the countess's death. And while I'm sure his mother is not planning to appear at this affair, choosing to celebrate her birthday is . . . audacious, but audacious without committing open scandal."

"I should think the . . . er . . . his lordship has had quite enough of that," Minnie murmured. "Um . . . what do you mean by 'audacious,' though?"

Lady Buford looked pleased; she enjoyed displaying her skills.

"Well. When someone—especially a man—does something unusual, you must always ask what it was they intended by the action. Whether or not that effect is achieved, the intent usually explains much.

"And in this instance," she said, plucking another biscuit delicately from the plate and dunking it into her tea to soften, "I think that his lordship means to put himself on display, in order to prove to society at large that he is not insane—whatever else he might be," she added thoughtfully.

Minnie wasn't so sure about Lord Melton's mental state but nodded obligingly.

"You see . . ." Lady Buford paused to nibble the edge of her softened biscuit, made an approving face, and swallowed. "You see, were he simply to host a rout or ball of the normal sort, he would seem light-minded and frivolous at best, cold and unfeeling at worst. He would also expose himself to considerable risk that no one would accept an invitation."

"But as it is?" Minnie prompted.

"Well, there's the factor of curiosity, which can never be overlooked." Lady Buford's rather pointed tongue darted out to capture a stray crumb, which was whisked out of sight. "But by making the occasion in honor of his mother, he more or less commands the loyalty of her friends—who are many—and also those who were friends of his late father but who couldn't openly support him. *And,*" she added, leaning forward portentously, "there are the Armstrongs."

"Who?" Minnie asked blankly. By this time she had quite an extensive social index of London but recognized no prominent person therein named Armstrong.

"The duke's mother is an Armstrong by birth," Lady Buford explained, "though her mother was English. But the Armstrongs are a very powerful Scottish family, from the Borders. And the rumor is that Lord Fairbairn—that's the duke's maternal grandfather, only a baron but very rich—is in London and will attend the . . . er . . . function."

Minnie was beginning to think tea inadequate to the occasion and rose to fetch the decanter of Madeira from the sideboard. Lady Buford made no demur.

"Of course you must go," Lady Buford said, having downed half a glassful at one gulp.

"Really?" Minnie was experiencing that sudden visceral emptiness that attends excitement, anticipation, and panic.

"Yes," Lady Buford said, with determination, and downed the rest, setting her glass down with a thump. "Almost all of your choicest prospects will be there, and there is nothing like competition to make a gentleman declare himself."

Now the sensation was one of unalloyed panic. What with one thing and another, Minnie had quite forgotten that she was meant to be husband-hunting. Just last week, she'd had two proposals, though luckily from fairly undistinguished suitors, and Lady Buford hadn't objected to her refusing them.

She finished her own Madeira and poured another for them both.

"All right," she said, feeling a slight spinning sensation. "What do you think I should wear?"

"Your very best, my dear." Lady Buford raised her refilled glass in a sort of toast. "Lord Fairbairn is a widower."

15

BURGLARY AND OTHER DIVERSIONS

T HE *CARTE D'INVITATION* ARRIVED by messenger two days later, addressed to her simply as *Mademoiselle Wilhelmina Rennie*. Seeing her name—even a mistaken version of her assumed name—in black and white gave her a slight rippling sensation down the back. If she should be caught . . .

"Think about it, girl," said her father's logical voice, affectionate and slightly impatient. *"What if you* are *caught? Don't be afraid of unimagined possibilities; imagine the possibilities and then imagine what you'll do about them."*

Her father was, as usual, right. She wrote down every possibility she could think of, from being refused admittance to Argus House, to being recognized at the ball by one of the clients she'd met this week, to being detected by a servant while returning the letters. And then she summoned the O'Higginses and told them what she wanted.

SHE'D COME LATE, smoothly inserting herself into a group of several giggly young women and their chaperones, avoiding the notice paid to guests who arrived singly and were announced to the crowd. The dancing had started; it was simple to find a place among the wallflowers, where she could watch without being seen.

She'd learned from Lady Buford the art of drawing men's eyes. She'd already known the art of avoiding them. Despite having worn her best— the soft river-green eau-de-nil gown—so long as she kept her head modestly lowered, hung about on the edge of a group, and didn't speak, she was unlikely to get a second glance.

Her eyes, though, knew just where to look. There were a number of soldiers in lavish uniform, but she saw Lord Melton instantly, as though there was no other man in the room. He stood by the enormous hearth, absorbed in conversation with a few other men; with no sense of surprise, she recognized Prince Frederick, bulging and amiable in puce satin, and Harry Quarry, fine in his own uniform. A small, fierce-looking man with an iron-gray wig and the features of a shrike stood at Melton's elbow— that must be Lord Fairbairn, she thought.

She sensed someone behind her and turned to see the Duke of Beaufort beaming down at her. He swept her a deep bow.

"Miss Rennie! Your most humble servant, I do assure you!"

"Charmed, as always, Your Grace." She batted her eyes at him over her fan. She'd known she was likely to meet people she knew—and she'd decided what to do about it. To wit, nothing special. She knew how to flirt and disengage, moving skillfully from one partner to another without causing offense. So she gave Sir Robert her hand, joined him for two dances, sent him for an ice, and disappeared to the ladies' retiring room for a quarter of an hour—long enough for him to have given up and sought another partner.

When she came back, moving cautiously, her eyes went at once to the hearth and discovered that Lord Melton and his companions had vanished. A group of bankers and stockbrokers, many of whom she knew, had replaced them by the fire, deep in financial conversation by the look of them.

She drifted inconspicuously around the room, watching, but Hal— *Lord Melton,* she corrected herself firmly—was nowhere to be found. Nor was the prince, Harry Quarry, or the ferocious Scottish grandfather. Clearly the conversation had reached a stage where privacy was required.

Well enough. But she couldn't get on with her own job until the bloody man came back into sight. If he was having private discussions, chances were good that he was doing it in the library; she daren't risk walking in on him.

"Miss Rennie! What a vision you are! Come and dance with me, I insist!"

She smiled and raised her fan.

"Of course, Sir Robert. Charmed!"

It was more than half an hour before the men came back. The prince reappeared first, strolling to one of the refreshment tables with a look of pleased accomplishment on his face. Then Lord Fairbairn, who popped out of a door on the far side of the ballroom and stood against the wall, looking on with as amiable an expression as his forbidding features could manage.

And then Lord Melton and Harry emerged from the door that opened into the main hallway, chatting to each other with a casualness that failed entirely to cover their excitement. So, whatever Hal's business was with the prince, it had come to a successful conclusion.

Good. He'd stay here, then, celebrating.

She put down the half-finished glass of champagne and faded discreetly away in the direction of the retiring room.

She'd noted what she could—the locations of doors, mostly, and the quickest path should she need to get out fast. The library was down a side corridor, second door on the right.

The door stood open; the room warm and inviting, a good fire lit in the hearth and candles blazing, softly upholstered furniture in blue and pink against a wallpaper of wine-striped damask. She breathed deep, burped slightly, and felt the bubbles of champagne rise up the back of her nose, and, with a quick look up and down the hallway, stepped into the library and quietly closed the door behind her.

The desk was on the left side of the hearth, just as Mick had told her.

THE METAL WAS warm from being carried in her bosom, and her hands were trembling. She'd dropped the picks twice already.

"It's dead easy," Rafe had told her, handing over the two little brass instruments. "Just don't let yourself be hurried. Locks don't care for haste, and they'll defy and obstruct ye if ye try to rush them."

"Like women," Mick put in, grinning at her.

Under the O'Higginses' patient tutelage, she'd succeeded in unlocking the drawer of her own desk with the picks, several times. She'd felt confident then, but it was a lot less easy to feel confident when you were committing burglary—well, reverse burglary, but that was even worse—in a duke's private library, with said duke and two hundred carousing witnesses no more than a stone's throw away.

Theoretically, this desk had the same type of lock. It was bigger, though, a solid brass plate with a beveled edge surrounding a keyhole that looked to her as big as a gun barrel at the moment. She took a deep breath, pushed the tension pick into the hole, and, as instructed, turned it to the left.

Then insert the feeler and pull it out gently, listening to the lock. The roar of the ballroom was muffled by the intervening walls, but music thrummed in her head, making it hard to hear. She sank to her knees, pressing her ear almost to the brass of the lock as she pulled out the pick. Nothing.

She'd been holding her breath and the blood was pounding in her ears, making it even harder to hear. She sat back on her heels, making herself breathe. Had she got it wrong?

Again. She put in the tension pick and turned it to the right. As slowly as she could, she slid the feeler in. She thought she felt something, but . . . She licked her lips and pulled the feeler gently out. Yes! A tiny ripple of sound as the pins dropped.

"Don't . . . bloody . . . rush," she whispered, and, wiping her hand on her skirt, took up the feeler again.

On the third try, she'd nearly got it—she could feel that there were five pins, and she had three, each making its soft little click—and then the doorknob turned behind her, with a much louder *click!*

She sprang to her feet with a stifled shriek, startling the footman who'd come in nearly as badly as he'd startled her. He said, "Oh!" and dropped the tray he was carrying, which struck the marble floor with a loud clang and spun like a top, clattering finally to a stop.

Minnie and the footman stared at each other, equally aghast.

"I—I beg your pardon, madam," he said, and squatted, fumbling with the tray. "I didn't know anyone was in here."

"That's . . . quite all right," she said, and paused to swallow. "I—I— felt a bit faint. Thought I'd just . . . sit . . . down for a moment. Out of— of the—the crowd."

Both picks were sticking out of the lock. She took a step backward and put one hand on the desk, to support herself. It wasn't pretense; her knees had gone to water, and cold sweat was chilling the back of her neck. But the footman couldn't see the lock, screened as it was by her eau-de-nil skirts.

"Oh. Of course, madam." With his tray now held to his chest like a shield, the footman was regaining his composure. "May I bring you an ice? A glass of water?"

Jesus Lord, no!

But then she saw the small table at the far side of the hearth, flanked by two armchairs and holding a plate of savories, several glasses, and three or four decanters—one of these plainly filled with water.

"Oh," she said faintly, and gestured toward the table. "Perhaps . . . a little water?"

The instant he turned his back, she reached behind her and jerked the picks out of the lock. With trembling knees, she crossed the hearth and sank into one of the chairs, pushing the picks down beside the cushion, under cover of her skirts.

"Would you like me to fetch someone for you, ma'am?" The footman, having solicitously poured her water, was swiftly tidying away the decanters of spirit and what she now saw were used glasses onto his tray. Of course—this was where the duke had been having his meeting.

"No, no. Thank you. I'll be quite all right."

The footman glanced at her, then at the plate of savories, and, with a tiny shrug, left it on the table, bowed, and went out, pulling the door gently to behind him.

She sat quite still, forcing herself to breathe evenly. It was all right. Everything would be all right. She could smell the little savories—things wrapped in bacon, bits of anchovy and cheese. Her stomach rumbled; ought she to eat something, to steady her nerves, her hands?

No. She was still safe, but there was no time to waste. She wiped her hands on the arms of the chair, stood up, and marched back to the desk.

Tension pick. Right turn. Feeler to be sure of the pins. Probe. Raise the pins one by one, listening for each tiny metal *tink!* A pull. No. No, dammit! Try again.

Twice she had to get up, go drink water, and walk clockwise round the room—another of the O'Higginses' bits of advice—to calm herself before trying again.

But then . . . a sudden decisive metal *choonk* and it was done. Her hands were shaking so badly that she could barely get the three parcels out of her pockets, but get them she did. She yanked out the drawer and flung them in, then slammed the drawer with an exclamation of triumph.

"What the devil are you doing?" said a curious voice behind her. She shrieked and whirled round to find the Duke of Pardloe standing in the doorway and, behind him, Harry Quarry and another soldier.

"I say—" Harry began, plainly aghast.

"What's all this, then?" said the other man, peering curiously past Harry's shoulder.

"Don't trouble yourselves," the duke said, not looking back at them.

His eyes were fixed on hers, intent. "I'll take care of it." Without turning round, he grasped the edge of the door and pushed it shut in their staring faces.

For the first time, she heard the ticking of the little enamel clock on the mantelpiece and the hiss of the fire. She couldn't move.

He walked across the room to her, eyes still fixed on hers. The sweat on her body had chilled to snow and she shivered once, convulsively.

He took her carefully by the elbow and moved her to one side, then stood staring at the closed drawer and the picklocks sticking out of it, brassily accusing.

"What the *devil* have you been doing?" he said, and turned his head sharply to look at her. She barely heard him for the pounding of the blood in her ears.

"I—I—robbing you, Your Grace," she blurted. Finding that she could speak after all was a relief, and she gulped air. "So much must be obvious, surely?"

"Obvious," he repeated, with a faint tone of incredulity. "What on earth is there to steal in a library?"

This from a man whose shelves included at least half a dozen books worth a thousand pounds each; she could see them from here. Still, he had a point.

"The drawer was locked," she said. "Why would it be locked if there wasn't something valuable in it?"

He glanced instantly at the drawer and his face changed like lightning. *Oh, bloody* hell! she thought. *He'd forgotten the letters were there.* Or maybe not . . .

He turned on her then, and the air of slightly puzzled inquiry had vanished. He didn't seem to move but was suddenly much closer to her; she could smell the starch in his uniform and the faint odor of his sweat.

"Tell me who you are, 'Lady Bedelia,' " he said, "and exactly why you're here."

"I'm just a thief, Your Grace. I'm sorry." No chance of making it to the door, let alone out of the house.

"I don't believe that for an instant." He saw her glance and grasped her arm. "And you're not going anywhere until you tell me what you're here for."

She was light-headed with fear, but the faint implication that she *might* go somewhere seemed to offer at least the possibility that he wouldn't immediately summon a constable and have her arrested. On the other hand . . .

He wasn't waiting for her to make up her mind or a story. He tightened his grasp on her arm.

"Edward Twelvetrees," he said, and his voice was nearly a whisper, his face deadly white. "Did he send you?"

"No!" she said, but her heart nearly leapt out of her bodice at the name. He stared hard at her, then his eyes dropped, running the length of her shimmering green skirts.

"If I were to search you, madam—what would I find, I wonder?"

"An unclean handkerchief and a little bottle of scent," she said truthfully. Then added boldly, "If you want to search me, go ahead."

His nostrils flared a bit, and he pulled her aside.

"Stand there," he said shortly, then let go of her and yanked the picklocks from the drawer. He dipped a finger into the small pocket on his waistcoat and came out with a key, with which he unlocked the drawer and pulled it out.

Minnie's heart had changed its rhythm when he suggested searching her—no slower, but different—but now sped up to such a rate that she saw white spots at the corners of her eyes.

She hadn't put the letters back in their correct places; she couldn't—Mick hadn't taken notice. He'd know. She closed her eyes.

He said something under his breath, in . . . Latin?

She had to breathe and did so, with a gasp.

The hand was back, now gripping her shoulder.

"Open your eyes," he said, in a low, menacing voice, "and bloody look at me."

Her eyes popped open and met his, a winter blue, like ice. He was so angry that she could feel it vibrating through him like a struck tuning fork.

"What were you doing with my letters?"

"I—" Invention completely failed her, and she spoke the truth, hopelessly. "Putting them back."

He blinked. Looked at the open drawer, with the key still in the lock.

"You . . . er . . . you saw me," she said, and found enough saliva to swallow. "Saw me close the drawer, I mean. Er . . . didn't you?"

"I—" A small line had formed between his dark brows, deep as a paper cut. "I did." He let go of her shoulder and stood there, looking at her.

"How," he said carefully, "did you come to be in possession of my letters, may I ask?"

Her heart was still thundering in her ears, but some blood was coming back into her head. She swallowed again. Only the one possibility, wasn't there?

"Mr. Twelvetreees," she said. "He—he did ask me to steal the letters. I . . . wouldn't do it for him."

"You wouldn't," he repeated. One brow had risen slowly, and he was looking at her as though she were some exotic insect he'd found crawling over his chrysanthemums. He cocked his head at the drawer in question. "Why not?"

"I liked you," she blurted. "When we . . . met at the princess's garden party."

"Indeed." A faint flush rose in his cheeks and the stiffness returned to his person.

"Yes." She met his eyes straight on. "I could tell that Mr. Twelvetrees *didn't* like you."

"That's putting it mildly," he said. "So you say he asked you to steal my letters—why did he think you would be the person to employ for such a venture? Do you steal things professionally?"

"Well, not often," she said, striving for composure. "It's more that we—I—discover information that may be of value. Just . . . inquiries here and there, you know. Gossip at parties, that sort of thing."

"We?" he repeated, both brows rising now. "Who are your confederates, may I ask?"

"Just my father and me," she said hastily, lest he recall the chimney sweeps. "It's . . . the family business, you might say."

"The family business," he repeated, with a faintly incredulous air. "Well . . . putting that aside, if you refused Edward Twelvetrees's commission, how did you come to be in possession of my letters, anyway?"

She commended her soul to a God she didn't quite believe in and threw her fate to the wind.

"Someone else must have stolen them for him," she said, with as much sincerity as possible. "But I had occasion to . . . be in his house, and I found them. I . . . recognized your name. I didn't read them," she added hastily. "Not once I saw that they were personal."

He'd gone white again. No doubt envisioning Edward Twelvetrees poring greedily over his most intimate wounds.

"But I—I knew what they must be, because of what Mr. Twelvetrees had told me. So I . . . took them back."

She was breathing a little more easily now. It was much easier to lie than to tell him the truth.

"You took them back," he said, and blinked, then looked hard at her. "And then you thought you'd come put them back in my house? Why?"

"I thought you . . . might want them," she said in a small voice, and felt her own cheeks flush. *Oh, God, he'll know I read them!*

"How very kind of you," he said dryly. "Why didn't you just send them to me anonymously, if your only intent was to return them?"

She took a small, unhappy breath and told him the truth, though she knew he wouldn't believe it.

"I didn't want you to be hurt. And you would be if you thought someone had read them."

"You what?" he said, incredulous.

"Shall I prove it?" she whispered, and her hand floated up without her actually willing it, to touch his face. "Your Grace?"

"What?" he said blankly. "Prove it?"

She couldn't think of anything at all to say so merely rose on her toes, hands on his shoulders, and kissed him. Softly. But she didn't stop, and her body moved toward his—and his toward hers—with the slow certainty of plants turning toward sun.

Moments later, she was kneeling on the hearth rug, fumbling madly under folds of eau-de-nil for the tapes of her petticoats, and Hal's—she was frightened and exhilarated to realize that she was thinking of him as Hal—uniform coat had struck the floor with a muffled crash of buttons, epaulets, and gold lace, and he was ripping at his waistcoat buttons, muttering to himself in Latin.

"What?" she said, catching the word "insane." "Who's insane?"

"Plainly you are," he said, stopping for a moment to stare at her. "Do you want to change your mind? Because you have roughly ten seconds to do so."

"It will take longer than that to get at my blasted bum roll!"

Muttering *"Irrumabo"* under his breath, he dropped to his knees, rummaged her petticoats, and seized the tie of her bum roll. Rather than untie it, he jerked it, broke the tie, slid the bum roll out of her clothes like a huge sausage, and flung it onto one of the wing chairs. Then he threw off his waistcoat and pushed her onto her back.

"What does *irrumabo* mean?" she said to the hanging crystals of the chandelier overhead.

"Me, too," he said, breathless. His hands were under her skirt, very cold on her bottom.

"You, too, *what?*" The middle part of him was between her thighs, very warm, even through the moleskin breeches.

"*I'm* insane," he said, as though this should be evident—and maybe it was, she thought.

"Oh," he added, looking up from the flies of his breeches, "*irrumabo* means 'fuck.'"

Three seconds later he was alarmingly hot and terrifyingly immediate and—

"Jesus Christ!" he said, and froze, looking down at her, his eyes huge with shock.

It hurt shockingly and she froze as well, taking shallow breaths. She felt his weight shift, knew he was about to leave her, and gripped his bottom to stop him. It was tight and solid and warm, an anchor against pain and terror.

"I said I'd prove it," she whispered, and pulled him in with all her strength, arching her back. She let out a stifled shriek as he came the rest of the way, and he grabbed her and held her, keeping her from moving.

They lay face-to-face, staring at each other and gulping air like a pair of stranded fish. His heart was hammering so hard that she could feel it under the hand she had on his back.

He swallowed.

"You've proved it," he said at last. "Whatever it . . . What was it you wanted to prove again?"

Between the tightness of her stays and his weight, she hadn't enough breath to laugh, but she managed a small smile.

"That I didn't want to hurt you."

"Oh." His breathing was growing slower, deeper. *He isn't wheezing,* she thought.

"I didn't want—I didn't mean—to hurt you, either," he said softly. For an instant she saw him hesitate: should he pull away? But then decision settled on his features once more and he bent his head and kissed her. Slowly.

"It doesn't hurt that much," she assured him when he stopped.

"*Mendatrix.* That means 'liar.' Shall I—"

"No, you shan't," she said firmly. Over the first shock, her brain was now working again. "This is never going to happen again, so I mean to enjoy it—if such a thing is possible," she added, a little dubiously.

He didn't laugh, either, and his smile was only a trace—but it reached his eyes. The fire was hot on her skin.

"Yes, it is," he said. "Let me prove it."

Some little time later . . .

HE PUT OUT a hand to her and, dazed, she took it. His cold fingers closed tight on hers, and hers on his.

He took her to the back stairs, where he let go her hand—the stairs were too narrow to go side by side—and went down before her, glancing back now and then to be sure she hadn't disappeared or fallen. He looked as dazed as she felt.

Noise echoed up the wooden stairwell from the kitchens below—pots clanging, voices calling to and fro, the clash of crockery, a crash and subsequent cursing. The scent of roasting meat struck her in a gust of warm air, and she was suddenly ravenous.

He took her hand again and drew her away from the smell of food, through a plain, dim, unvarnished corridor into a larger one, with a canvas floor cloth that muffled their footsteps, into a broad corridor with a Turkey carpet in blue and gold and candles flickering in the bronze plates of reflectors that shed a bright, soft light over everything. Servants flitted past them like ghosts, carrying trays, jugs, garments, bottles, eyes averted.

It was like walking through a soundless dream: something between curiosity and nightmare, where you had no notion where you were going or what lay before you but were obliged to keep on walking.

He stopped abruptly and looked at her as though he'd found her walking through *his* dream—and perhaps it was, she thought, perhaps it was. He put a hand very lightly on her breast for an instant, fixing her in place, then vanished round a corner.

With him gone, her stunned senses began to awaken. She could hear music and voices, laughter. A strong smell of hot punch and wine; she'd drunk nothing save that first glass of champagne but now felt very drunk indeed. She opened and closed her fingers slowly, still feeling the grasp of his hand, hard and chilled.

Suddenly he was there again, and she felt his presence like a blow to her chest. He had her cape in his hand and swung it open, round her, enveloping her. As though it was part of the same movement, he took her in his arms and kissed her fiercely. Let go, panting, then did it again.

"You—" she said, but then stopped, having no idea what to say.

"I know," he said, as though he did, and with a hand under her elbow led her somewhere—she wasn't noticing anything anymore—and then there was a whoosh of cold, rainy night air and he was helping her up the step of a hansom cab.

"Where do you live?" he said, in an almost normal voice.

"Southwark," she said, sheer instinct preventing her from giving him her real address. "Bertram Street, Number Twenty-two," she added, inventing wildly.

He nodded. His face was white, his eyes dark in the night. The place between her legs burned and felt slippery. He swallowed and she saw his throat move, slick with rain and gleaming in the light from the lantern; he hadn't put on his neckcloth or his waistcoat, and his shirt was open under his scarlet coat.

He took her hand.

"I will call upon you tomorrow," he said. "To inquire after your welfare."

She didn't answer. He turned her hand over and kissed her palm. Then the door was shut and she was rattling alone over wet cobbles, her hand closed tight on the warmth of his breath.

She couldn't think. She felt wetness seep into her petticoats, with the slightly sticky feel of blood. The only thing floating through her mind was a remark of her father's. *"The English are notorious bores about virginity."*

16

SIC TRANSIT

I T WASN'T THAT HARD to disappear. The O'Higgins brothers were masters of the art, as they assured her.

"Leave it to us, sweetheart," Rafe said, taking the purse she handed him. "To a Londoner, the world beyond the end of his street is as furrin as the pope. All ye need do is keep away from the places folk are used to seein' ye."

She hadn't had much choice. She wasn't going anywhere near the Duke of Pardloe or his friend Quarry or the Twelvetrees brothers. But there was still business to be done before she could go back to Paris—books to be both sold and bought, shipments made and received—and a few bits of more-private business, as well.

So Minnie had written a note paying off Lady Buford and announcing her return to France and then stayed in Parson's Green with Aunt Simpson and her family for a month. She allowed the O'Higginses to do the more straightforward things and—with some reluctance—entrusted the more delicate acquisitions to Mr. Simpson and her cousin Joshua. There'd been two or three clients who had declined to meet with anyone save her, and though the temptation was considerable, the risk was too great, and she had simply not replied to those.

She had gone once with Aunt Simpson to the farm, to take leave of her mother. She hadn't been able to bring herself to go into Soeur Emmanuelle's chamber, though, and had only laid her head and hands against the cool wood of the door and wept silently.

But now it was all done. And she stood alone in the rain on the deck of the *Thunderbolt*, bobbing like a cork over the waves of the channel toward France. And her father.

THE LAST THING she would ever do, she vowed to herself, was to tell her father who it had been.

He knew who Pardloe was, what his family background had been, just how fragile his family's present grip on respectability. And thus Pardloe's vulnerability to blackmail.

Perhaps not outright blackmail . . . at least, she didn't want to believe her father engaged in that. He'd always told her to avoid it. Not on moral grounds—he had principles, her father, but not morals—but on the purely pragmatic grounds that it was dangerous.

"Most blackmailers are amateurs," he'd told her, handing her a small stack of letters to read—an educational exchange between a blackmailer and his victim, written in the late fifteenth century. "They don't know what it's decent to ask for, and they don't know how to quit, even if they wanted to. It doesn't take a victim long to realize that, and then . . . it's often death. For one or the other.

"In this instance"—he'd nodded at the crumbling brown-stained papers in her hand—"it was both of them. The woman being blackmailed invited the blackmailer to her home for dinner and poisoned him. But she used the wrong drug; it didn't kill him outright, but it worked fast enough for him to realize what she'd done, and he strangled her over the dessert."

No, he *probably* hadn't had any intent of blackmailing Pardloe himself.

At the same time, she was certainly intelligent enough to realize that the letters and documents her father dealt in were very often commissioned by or sold to persons who intended to *use* them for blackmail. She thought of Edward Twelvetrees and his brother and felt colder than the icy blast of the wind off the English Channel.

Were her father to realize that it was Pardloe who had debauched his daughter . . . *What on earth* would *he do?* she wondered.

He wouldn't scruple to kill Pardloe, if he could do it undetected, she was pretty sure of that. Though he *was* very pragmatic: he might just demand satisfaction of a financial nature as compensation for the loss of his daughter's virginity. That was a salable commodity, after all.

Or—the worst possibility of all—he might try to force the Duke of Pardloe to marry her.

That's what he'd wanted: to find her a rich English husband, preferably one well-placed in society.

"Over my dead body!" she said out loud, causing a passing deckhand to look at her strangely.

SHE'D REHEARSED IT on the journey back. How she'd tell her father—what she *wouldn't* tell him—what he might say, think, do . . . She had a speech composed—firm, calm, definite. She was prepared for him to shout, to rebuke, disown her, show her the door. She wasn't at all prepared for him to look at her standing in the doorway of the shop, gulp air, and burst into tears.

Flabbergasted, she said nothing and an instant later was being crushed in his arms.

"Are you all right?" He held her away from him, so he could look into her face, and swiped a sleeve across his own wet, anxious, gray-stubbled face. "Did the swine hurt you?"

She couldn't decide whether to say "What swine?" or "What are you talking about?" and instead settled on a dubious-sounding "No . . ."

He let go then and stepped back, reaching into his pocket for a handkerchief, which he handed her. She realized belatedly that she was sniffling and her own eyes were welling.

"I'm sorry," she said, all her speeches forgotten. "I didn't mean to. . . . to . . ." *But you did,* her heart reminded her. *You did mean it.* She swallowed that down with her tears and said instead, "I didn't mean to hurt you, Papa."

She hadn't called him that in years, and he made a sound as though someone had punched him in the belly.

"It's me that's sorry, girl," he said, his voice unsteady. "I let you go by yourself. I should never . . . I knew . . . Christ, I'll kill him!" Blood flooded his pale cheeks, and he slammed a fist on the counter.

"No, don't," she said, alarmed. "It was my fault. I—" *I what?*

He grabbed her by the shoulders and shook her, though not hard.

"Don't ever say that. It—whatever—however it happened, it wasn't your fault." His hands dropped away from her shoulders and he drew breath, panting as though he'd been running. "I—I—" He stopped and ran a trembling hand down his face, closing his eyes.

He took two more deep breaths, opened his eyes, and said, with some semblance of his normal calm, "Come and sit down, *ma chère.* I'll make us some tea."

She nodded and followed him, leaving her bag where it had fallen. The back room seemed at once completely familiar and quite strange, as though she had left it years ago rather than months. It smelled wrong, and she felt uneasy.

She sat down, though, and put her hands on the worn wooden tabletop. There was a spinning sensation in her head, and when she took a deep breath to try to stop it, the sense of seasickness came back, the smell of dust and ancient silk, stewed tea and the nervous sweat of many visitors curling into a greasy ball in her stomach.

"How . . . how did you find out?" she asked her father, in an effort to distract herself from the sense of clammy apprehension.

His back was to her, as he chiseled a chunk from the battered brick of tea and dropped it into the chipped Chinese pot with its blue peonies. He didn't turn around.

"How do you think?" he said evenly, and she thought suddenly of the spiders, the thousands of eyes, hanging motionless, watching . . .

"*Pardonnez-moi,*" she said, breathless, and, stumbling to her feet, blundered out into the corridor and to the alley door, where she threw up over the cobblestones outside.

She stayed outside for perhaps a quarter of an hour, letting the cold air in the shadows cool her face, letting the sounds of the city come back to her, the noise of the street a faint echo of normality. Then the bell of Sainte-Chapelle struck the hour, and all the others followed, the distant *bong* of Notre Dame de Paris telling Paris in a deep bronze voice that the hour was three o'clock.

"*It's almost time for None,*" her aunt had said. "*When she hears the bells, she won't do anything until the prayer is done, and often she's silent afterward.*"

"None?"

"*The hours,*" Mrs. Simpson had said, pushing the door open. "*Hurry, if you want her to speak with you.*"

She wiped her mouth on the hem of her skirt and went inside. Her father had finished making the tea; a fresh-poured cup sat by her place. She picked it up, took a mouthful of the steaming brew, swished it round her mouth, and spat it into the aspidistra.

"I saw my mother," she blurted.

He stared at her, so shocked that he didn't seem to breathe. After a long moment, he carefully unclenched his fists and laid his hands on the table, one atop the other.

"Where?" he said very quietly. His gaze was still fixed, intent on her face.

"In London," she said. "Did you know where she was—is?"

He'd started to think; she saw the thoughts flying behind his eyes. What did she know? Could he get away with lying? Then he blinked, took a breath, and let it out through his nose in a sigh of . . . decision, she thought.

"Yes," he said. "I . . . keep in touch with her sister. If you've met Emmanuelle, I imagine you've met Miriam, as well?" One of his unruly eyebrows went up, and she nodded.

"She said—said that you paid for her care. Have you seen her, though? Seen where they keep her, seen how she . . . is?" Emotion was rumbling through her like an approaching thunderstorm, and she had trouble keeping her voice steady.

"No," he said, and she saw he'd gone white to the lips, whether with anger or some other emotion, she couldn't tell. "I never saw her again, after she told me that she was with child." He swallowed, and his eyes went to his folded hands.

"I tried," he said, looking up as though she'd challenged him, even though she'd said nothing. "I went to the convent, spoke with the mother superior. She had me arrested." He laughed, shortly but not with humor. "Did you know that debauching a nun is a crime punishable by exposure in the pillory?"

"I imagine you bought your way out of it," she said, as nastily as she could.

"So would anyone capable of doing so, *ma chère*," he said, keeping his temper. "But I had to leave Paris. I hadn't met Miriam then, but I knew about her. I sent her word, and money, imploring her to find what they had done with Emmanuelle—to save her."

"She did."

"I know." He'd got hold of himself now and gave her a sharp look. "And if you've seen Emmanuelle, you know what her state is. She went mad when the child—"

"When *I* was born!" She slapped a hand on the table, and the cups chimed in their saucers. "Yes, I know. Do you bloody blame me for her—for what happened to her?"

"No," he said, with an obvious effort. "I don't."

"Good." She took a breath and blurted, "I'm pregnant."

He went dead white and she thought he might faint. She thought she might faint, too.

"No," he whispered. His eyes dropped to her middle, and a deep qualm there made her feel she might be sick again.

"No. I won't . . . I won't let such a thing happen to you!"

"You—" She wanted to strike him, might have done so had he not been on the other side of the table.

"Don't you dare tell me how I can get rid of it!" She swept the cup and saucer off the table, smashing them against the wall in a spray of Bohea. "I'd never do that—never, never, *never*!"

Her father took a deep breath and very consciously relaxed his posture. He was still white, and his eyes creased with emotion, but he had himself under control.

"That," he said softly, "is the last thing I would ever do. *Ma chère. Ma fille.*"

She saw that his eyes were full of tears and felt the blow in her heart. He'd come for her when she was born. Come for his child, cherished and kept her.

He saw her fists unclench and he took a step toward her, tentative, as though walking on ice. But she didn't recoil and didn't shout, and one more step and they were in each other's arms, both weeping. She'd so missed the smell of him, tobacco and black tea, ink and sweet wine.

"Papa . . ." she said, and then cried harder, because she'd never been able to say "Mama" and never would, and this tiny, helpless thing she carried would never know a father. She'd never felt so sad—but at the same time comforted.

He'd cared. He'd come for her after she was born. He'd loved her. He always would—that was what he was saying now, murmuring into her hair, sniffing back the tears. He'd never let her be persecuted and abused as her mother was, never let harm come to her or to her child.

"I know," she said. Worn out, she rested her head on his chest, holding him as he held her. "I know."

17

RED WAX AND EVERYTHING

HAL STRODE OUT OF Sir William Yonge's office, boot heels brisk on the marble tiles and head held high. He nodded cordially to the soldier outside the door and made it down the stairs, along the hall, and out into the street, dignity intact. Harry was waiting across the street, anxious.

He saw Harry's face break into an enormous grin at sight of him, and then Harry threw back his head and howled like a wolf, to the startlement of Lord Pitt and two companions, who were coming along the pavement at the moment. Hal just managed to bow to them and then was across the street, hammering Harry's back and shoulders in joy. One-handed, because the other hand was clutching the precious certificate of commission to his bosom.

"God! We did it!"

"*You* did it!"

"No," Hal insisted, and shoved Harry in exhilaration. "Us. We did it. Look!" He waved the document, covered and sealed with red wax, under Harry's nose. "King's signature and everything! Shall I read it to you?"

"Yes, every word—but not out here." Harry gripped his elbow and hailed a passing cab. "Come on—we'll go to the Beefsteak; we can get a drink there."

Mr. Bodley, the club's steward, viewed them benignly as they tumbled into the club, calling for champagne and steak and more champagne, and within moments they were installed in the deserted dining room—it being eleven o'clock in the morning—with a cold bottle to hand and steak ordered to follow.

"*. . . commissioned this day by His Royal Majesty, by the grace of God, George the second* . . . oh, my God, I can't breathe . . . such a-a-*thing* . . ."

Hal laughed at that. His own chest had felt as though it were in a vise all the time he'd been in Sir William's office—but the vise had burst when he'd seen the certificate, with its unmistakable royal seal at the bottom, and now he breathed as freely as a newborn babe.

"Isn't it, though?" He could barely stand to have the certificate out of his hand and now reached out to trace the king's signature with a possessive forefinger. "I was sure when I went in there that it was all up, that Sir William would give me some cock-and-bull story for refusal, all the time eyeing me in that way people do when they think you're off your head and might just pick up an ax and brain them unexpectedly. Not that I haven't often felt that way," he added judiciously, and drained his glass. "Drink up, Harry!"

Harry did, coughed, and poured more.

"So what *did* happen? Was Yonge friendly, matter-of-fact . . . what did he *say?*"

Hal frowned, absently enjoying the fresh burst of dry bubbles on his tongue.

"Friendly enough . . . though I don't think I could tell quite *what* his manner was. Not nervous at all. And not that wary way politicals often are with me when they're thinking of Father."

Harry made a low noise in this throat, indicating complete understanding and sympathy—he'd been by Hal's side through his father's suicide and all the bloody mess that came afterward. Hal smiled at his friend and half-lifted his glass in silent acknowledgment.

"As to what he said, he greeted me very affably, asked me to sit, and offered me a currant biscuit."

Harry whistled.

"My God, you *are* honored. I hear he only gives biscuits to the king and the first minister. Though I imagine he'd give one to the queen, too, should she choose to visit his lair."

"I think the contingency is remote." Hal emptied the bottle and turned to call for another, but Mr. Bodley's tray was already at his elbow. "Oh, thank you, Mr. Bodley." He stifled a belch and realized that his head, while not swimming, was showing a slight disposition to float. "Do you think the steak will be long in coming?"

Mr. Bodley tilted his head from side to side in equivocation.

"A little time, my lord. But the cook has some wonderful small eel pies, just out of the oven—perhaps I could tempt you with a pair while you're waiting?"

Harry sniffed the fragrant air drifting in from the kitchen and closed his eyes in anticipatory bliss. The Beefsteak made their eel pies with the usual onion, butter, and parsley but also with nutmeg and dry sherry.

"Oh, God, yes."

Hal's mouth watered a bit at the thought—but the thought also brought a tightening of his body. Harry opened his eyes and looked surprised.

"What's the matter, old man?"

"Matter? Nothing." Mr. Bodley had freed the cork from its lead seal and now loosed it deftly with a soft burp and a hiss of rising bubbles. "Thank you, Mr. Bodley. Yes, eel pies by all means!

"Eel pies," he repeated, as Mr. Bodley faded discreetly toward the kitchen. "The mention just reminded me of Kettrick's . . . and that young woman."

The thought of her—God damn it, why had he not even thought to make her tell him her real name? Lady Bedelia Houghton, for God's sake—caused its usual *frisson* of mixed emotions. Lust, curiosity, annoyance . . . longing? He didn't know if he'd put it that strongly, but he did have an intense desire to see her again, if only to find out what the devil she'd actually been doing. A desire now greatly intensified by his meeting with the secretary.

"Kettrick's?" Harry said, looking blank. "Kettrick's Eel-Pye House, you mean? And what young woman?"

Hal caught something in Harry's voice and gave his friend a sharp look.

"The girl I caught magicking the drawer of my desk, the night of the ball."

"Oh, that girl," Harry murmured, and buried his nose in his glass.

Hal looked harder at Harry. He hadn't told Harry everything—not by a long chalk, by God—but he *had* told him that he was satisfied with what she'd told him (actually, a long way from satisfied, but . . .) and that he'd sent her home in a coach and requested her address, which she'd given.

Only to discover that said address didn't exist, and when he'd tracked down the coach driver, an Irish rapscallion, the man had told him that the girl had professed to be starving—she was; he'd heard her stomach growling when he . . . oh, Jesus—and had asked him to put her down for a moment at Kettrick's. He had, and the girl had promptly walked through the house, out the back, and legged it down an alley, never to be seen again.

Which, Hal thought, was a sufficiently interesting story as to have stuck in Harry's mind. To say nothing of the fact that he'd several times mentioned the girl, as well as his efforts to find her, to Harry.

"Hmph," he said, drank more, and shook his head to clear it. "Well, regardless . . . there was a bit of cordial conversation, quite cordial, though all through it there was something . . . odd . . . in Sir William's manner.

Rather grave—that's why I thought he was working up to a refusal—but then . . . sympathetic."

"Really?" Harry's thick brows shot up. "Why, do you suppose?"

Hal shook his head again, baffled.

"I don't know. Only . . . at the end, when he'd given me the certificate and congratulated me, he shook my hand and held on to it for a moment, and . . . he gave me a brief word of condolence on my . . . my loss." He'd thought he had his emotions well in check, but the pang was sharp as ever and he was obliged to clear his throat.

"Only being decent, surely," Harry said gruffly. Hal saw, to his fascination, that the blood was rising up Harry's neck and into his cheeks.

"Yes," he said, and leaned back, casual, glass in hand, but an eye on Harry. "At the time, I was so elated that I wouldn't have cared if he'd told me that a crocodile had hold of my foot, but with more-sober thought . . ."

Harry hooted slightly at that but then settled into his glass, eyes on the tablecloth. The flush had spread to his nose, now faintly glowing.

"I wondered—actually, just now—whether perhaps it was some sort of oblique reference to that bloody petition. You know, the one Reginald Twelvetrees brought, claiming that I'd assassinated his brother while off my head."

"He—didn't actually mention the petition?"

Hal shook his head. "No."

The eel pies arrived at this moment, smoking and savory, and no more was said for a bit.

Hal wiped the last bit of juice out of the dish with a sop of bread, chewed blissfully, swallowed, then opened his eyes and gave Harry a straight look.

"What the devil do you know about that petition, Harry?"

He'd known Harry Quarry since Harry was two and himself five. Harry *could* lie, if given warning and enough time to prepare, but he couldn't lie to Hal and knew it.

Harry sighed, closed his eyes, and thought for a bit, then opened one eye cautiously. Hal raised both brows and laid his hands flat on the table, in demonstration of the fact that he wasn't about to either hit Harry or strangle him. Harry looked down and bit his lip.

"Harry," Hal said softly. "Whatever you did, I forgive you. Just bloody tell me, all right?"

Harry looked up, nodded, drew a deep breath, and did.

"Irrumabo," Hal said, more in astonishment than anger. "But you told her not to take the letters, you say. . . ."

"Yes. I swear I did, Hal." The flush had diffused and was beginning to fade. "I mean—I knew what you felt—about—"

"I believe you." Hal was feeling a bit flushed himself and looked away.

Mr. Bodley was approaching with fresh plates and silver, followed by one of the club's waiters, ceremoniously carrying a sizzling platter.

They sat quietly while the steak—accompanied by a heap of wild mushrooms, garnished with tiny boiled onions and glistening with butter—was served. Hal watched, smelled, made the appropriate noises of appreciation to Mr. Bodley, and asked for a bottle of good Bordeaux. All this was purely automatic, though; his mind was in the library, on the night of the ball.

"I didn't want you to be hurt." He could still see the look on her face when she'd said it, and he believed her now just as much as he had then, the firelight glowing in her eyes, on her skin, in the folds of her green dress. *"Shall I prove it?"*

And she had, after all, proved it. A violent shiver ran through him at the memory.

"Are you all right, old man?" Harry was looking at him anxiously, a forkful of steak halfway to his mouth.

"I—yes," he said abruptly. "But she wasn't stealing Esmé's—I mean—the letters from my desk; she was putting them *back*. I know she was; I saw her close the drawer before she saw me. So she didn't send them to Sir William, I'm sure of that."

Harry nodded slowly. "I . . . don't like to suggest such a thing," he said, looking unhappy. "I mean—I trusted her, foolish as that likely was. But could she . . . copies, perhaps? Because the way you describe Yonge's manner . . ."

Hal shook his head.

"I'd swear not. The way she . . . No. I'm sure not. If nothing else . . ." He hesitated, but it was, after all, Harry. He swallowed and went on, eyes fixed on his plate but his voice steady. "If Sir William had seen those letters, he couldn't have looked me in the face, let alone have behaved as he did. No. Something convinced him that I had cause to challenge Twelve-trees, I'm sure of that—but God alone knows what it was. Perhaps the—the girl—did find someone who . . . knew about the affair . . ." Blood burned in his cheeks, and the pattern on the fork was digging into his palm where he clutched it. "If someone of good character swore to it . . ."

Harry let out a breath, nodding.

"You're right. And—that *was* what I'd asked her to do. Er . . . ask about discreetly, I mean. Um . . . sorry."

Hal nodded but couldn't speak. He did forgive Harry, but the thought that someone—someone unknown to him—had known . . . He had a brief, vivid urge to seize a candle from the sconce and set his head on fire in order to obliterate the thought, but instead he closed his eyes and breathed deeply for a few moments. The tightness in his chest began to loosen.

Well. Nothing to be done about it now. And the regiment *was* all right. He felt a bit of his earlier euphoria return and opened his eyes. Yes, by God, it was. There was the certificate, red wax seal and all, right there on the linen cloth.

He unclenched the fork, made himself pick up the knife, and cut into his steak. Hot red juice ran out, and he saw in memory the small blood-stain on the white hearthrug. Heat washed over him as though he *had* set his hair on fire.

"One thing you could do, Harry—if you're of a mind . . ."

"Anything you like, old man."

"Help me find her."

Harry stopped, fork halfway to his half-opened mouth.

"Of course," he said slowly, and lowered the fork. "But—" But, his face said, they'd both been looking for the past three weeks. Miss Rennie had vanished as surely as though she'd gone up in smoke.

Hal suddenly laughed. Mr. Bodley had materialized with the Bordeaux, and a brimming glass sat by his elbow.

"Confusion to all Twelvetrees!" Harry said, hoisting his own glass. Hal returned the salute and drank deep. It was a gorgeous wine, deep, strong, and smelling of cherries and buttered toast. Another bottle of this—well, maybe two—and he might just feel able to deal with things.

"One thing my father always said to me, Harry: 'They can't beat you if you don't give up.' And"—he lifted the glass to his friend—"I don't."

Harry's face cleared and he gave Hal a lopsided smile, returning the toast. "No," he said. "God help us all, you don't."

18

TAKING FLIGHT

Amsterdam, Kalverstraat 18
January 3, 1745

MINNIE CAREFULLY BRUSHED powdered sugar off the ledger. The early queasiness of pregnancy had mostly passed, re-placed by the appetite of a ravening owl, according to her father.

"An *owl*?" she'd said, and he nodded, smiling. His shock had passed along with her queasiness, and his face took on a rapt look sometimes when she caught him watching her.

"You look at food, *ma chère,* and turn your head to and then fro, as though you expect it to bolt, and then you swoop on it and—*gulp!*—it's gone."

"Bah," she said now, and looked to see if there were more *oliebollen* in the pottery jar, but, no, she'd finished them. Mortimer's antics had abated and he'd fallen into a stupor, as he usually did when she ate, but she was still hungry.

"Is dinner nearly ready?" she called downstairs to her father. In the usual Amsterdam style, the house was long and narrow, the shop on the ground floor, living quarters above, and the kitchen in the basement. A savory smell of roasting chicken had been creeping up the steps for the last hour, and she was famished, in spite of the *oliebollen.*

Instead of an answer, she heard the sound of her father's feet coming up the stairs, accompanied by a rattle of stoneware and pewter.

"It's not even noon," he said mildly, setting down a tray on the counter. "Dinner won't be ready for another hour at least. But I've brought you some coffee and rolls with honey."

"Honey?" She sniffed pleasurably. Even though the queasiness had mostly gone, the acute sensitivity to smells remained, and the strong aroma of coffee with fresh buttered rolls ravished her.

"That child is nearly as big as you are now," her father observed, with an eye to her protuberant belly. "*When* did you say it will be born?"

"In about three months," she said, reaching for a roll and ignoring the implication. "And the midwife says it will be just about double in size by then." She glanced down at Mortimer's bulge. "I don't actually think such a thing is possible, but that's what she says."

Her father laughed and, leaning across the counter, rested a hand lightly on the curve of his grandchild.

"*Comment ça va, mon petit?*" he said.

"What makes you think it's a boy?" she asked, though she didn't move away. It touched her when he spoke to the baby; he always did so with the greatest tenderness.

"Well, you call him—it—Mortimer," he pointed out, and with a gentle pat withdrew his hand. "I suppose that means *you* think he's a male."

"I was just taken by the advertisement on a bottle of English patent medicine: *Mortimer's Dissolving, Resolving, and Absolving Tonic—removes stains of any kind: physical, emotional, or moral.*"

That took him aback; he wasn't sure whether she was joking. She saved him by laughing herself and waved him away to the kitchen. She loved Sundays, when Hulda, the maid of all work, stayed at home with her family, leaving the two Snyders—Willem Snyder being her father's *nom de guerre* in the Low Countries—to fend for themselves. Her father was a much better cook, and it was peaceful without Hulda's solicitous questions and repeated suggestions of "nice gentlemen" among the shop's clientele who might be willing to take on a young widow with a child, if Mr. Snyder was able to offer a sufficiently generous inducement. . . .

Frankly, she thought her father wouldn't be above it. But he wouldn't push her into anything, either. She thought he was actually loath to part with her—and Mortimer, no doubt.

She closed her eyes, savoring the contrast of bitter coffee followed by a bite of buttered roll dripping with honey. As though stimulated by the coffee, Mortimer suddenly stretched himself as far as possible, making her clutch her belly and gasp.

"You little bastard," she said to him, and paused to swallow the last of the honeyed bite. "Sorry. You're *not* a bastard." At least he wouldn't be, as far as he or the rest of the world knew. He'd be the posthumous child of . . . Well, she hadn't quite decided. For the moment he was the child of a Spanish captain of rifles named Mondragon, dead of fever in some conveniently obscure campaign, but she'd think of something better by the time Mortimer was old enough to ask questions.

Perhaps a German; there were enough small duchies and principalities among which to hide an irregular birth—though the Germans *were* annoyingly methodical about registering people. Italy—now, there was an unmethodical country for you, and it was warm. . . .

He wouldn't be an Englishman, though. She sighed and put a hand over the little foot poking inquisitively under her liver. Mortimer *could* be a girl, she supposed, but Minnie couldn't think of him as anything other than male. Because she couldn't think of him without thinking of his father.

Maybe she *would* marry. Eventually.

Time enough for such considerations. For the moment, there was an inconsistency in the accounts between September and October, and she took a fresh sheet of foolscap and picked up her quill, on the trail of an errant three guilders.

Half an hour later, the stray guilders finally captured and pinned firmly to their proper column, she stretched, groaned, and hoisted herself to her feet. Her belly, much given to odd noises of late, was gurgling in ominous fashion. If dinner wasn't ready yet, she was going to—

The bell over the door tinged briskly, and she looked up, surprised. The virtuous Protestants of Amsterdam would never think of going anywhere on Sunday but to church. The man standing in the doorway, though, was neither Dutch nor virtuous. He *was* wearing a British uniform.

"Your . . . Grace?" she said stupidly.

"Hal," he said. "My name's Hal." Then he caught full sight of her and turned as white as the spilled sugar on the counter. "Jesus Christ."

"It's not . . ." she began, sliding out from behind the counter, "what you think . . ." she ended faintly.

It didn't matter. He took an enormous breath and strode toward her. She dimly heard her father coming up the stairs but saw nothing but that bone-white face, caught between shock and determination.

He reached her, bent his knees, and picked her up.

"Jesus Christ!" he said again, this time in response to her weight, which was considerable. Clenching his teeth, he clutched her tightly and wove his way across the shop, staggering only slightly. He smelled wonderfully of bay leaves and leather.

The door stood open, with Harry Quarry holding it and a blast of cold winter air coming in. His solid, square face broke into an enormous grin as he met her eyes.

"Pleased to see you again, Miss Rennie. Hurry up, old man, somebody's coming."

"Minnie! Stop! You—" Her father's shout was cut off by the slam of the shop door, and a moment later she was dumped unceremoniously into a coach that stood waiting. Hal shot in after her, and Harry hung precariously off the coach's step, shouting at the driver, before swinging inside himself and slamming the door.

"Minnie!" Her father's shout reached her, faint but audible.

She tried to turn, to look out of the rear window, but couldn't manage it without actually standing up and rotating her entire body. Before she could even contemplate doing that, though, Hal had wriggled free of his blue military cloak and was tucking it round her. The warmth of his body surrounded her, and his face was no more than a few inches from hers, still white, the warmth of his breath on her cheek white, too, misting in the frigid air of the coach.

His hands were on her shoulders, steadying her against the jolting, and she thought he might kiss her, but a sudden lurch as the coach swung round a corner sent him staggering. He fell backward into the seat opposite, beside Harry Quarry, who was still grinning from ear to ear.

She took a deep breath and readjusted her skirts over her bulge.

"Where do you think you're taking me?"

He'd been staring at her intensely but evidently without actually seeing her, for her words made him jerk.

"What?"

"*Where* are you taking me?" she repeated, louder.

"I don't know," he said, and looked at Harry, beside him. "Where are we going?"

"Place on the Keizersgracht," Harry said with a shrug. "Called *De Gevulde Gans.*"

"The Stuffed Goose? You're taking me to a *pub?*" Her voice rose involuntarily.

"I'm taking you to be married," Hal said, frowning at her.

He was very pale, and a muscle near his mouth twitched—the only thing he couldn't control, she thought. Well, that, and her.

"I married a lady and she became a whore. I cannot complain if it should be the other way about this time."

"You think I'm a whore, do you?" She wasn't sure whether to be amused or insulted. Perhaps both.

"Do you normally sleep with your victims, madam?"

She gave him a long, level stare and folded her arms atop the rounded curve of her belly.

"I wasn't asleep, Your Grace, and if you had been, I think I would have noticed."

THE STUFFED GOOSE was a rather down-at-heel establishment, with a drunkard bundled in rags picturesquely huddled against the steps.

"Why did you pick *this* place?" she asked Harry, picking up her skirts to avoid a small heap of vomit on the stones and glancing at the grimy doorknob.

"The landlady's husband is a minister," he said reasonably, leaning to open the door for her. "And reputed not to be too fussed about things."

Things like a wedding license, she supposed. Though perhaps you didn't need one when getting married in a different country?

"Go in," said Hal impatiently, behind her. "It stinks out here."

"And you think it will be better inside?" she asked, pinching her nose in preparation. He was right, though: the breeze had shifted, and she caught the full impact of the drunkard's scent.

"Oh, God," she said, turned neatly on her heel, and threw up on the opposite side of the step.

"Oh, God," said Hal. "Never mind, I'll get you some gin. Now go inside, for God's sake." He pulled a large white handkerchief out of his sleeve, wiped her mouth briskly with it, and hustled her through the door.

Harry had already gone in and opened negotiations, in bad but serviceable Dutch, this augmented by a substantial purse, which he plonked on the bar with a loud clinking noise.

Hal, who apparently had no Dutch, interrupted Harry's conversation with the landlady behind the bar by removing a golden guinea from his pocket and tossing it onto the bar.

"Gin," he said.

Minnie had subsided onto a stool as soon as she entered and was curled over, eyes shut and Hal's handkerchief clutched in one hand, trying not to breathe. A moment later, though, the sharp, clean scent of juniper cut through the miasma of the pub and the hint of dead rat. She swallowed, made herself sit up, and took the cup of gin Hal handed her.

To her considerable surprise, it worked. The nausea subsided with the first sip, the desire to lie down on the floor faded, and within a few moments she felt relatively normal—or as normal as one might feel if six months' pregnant and on the verge of marrying Hal, she thought.

The minister, apparently rousted from bed and evidently suffering from an extreme form of *la grippe,* turned bleary eyes from Hal to Minnie, then back.

"You want to marry her?" The tone of incredulity seeped through the nasal congestion, slow and glutinous.

"Yes," said Hal. "Now, if you please."

The minister closed one eye and looked at him, then turned his head slowly to his wife, who tutted impatiently and said something rapid in Dutch, accompanied by a peremptory gesture. He hunched his shoulders against the tirade in a way indicating that such assaults were common. When she stopped speaking, he nodded in a resigned fashion, drew a sodden handkerchief from the pocket of his sagging breeches, and blew his nose.

Hal's hand tightened on Minnie's; he hadn't let go since they'd entered the pub, and she twitched, not quite pulling away. He looked down at her.

"Sorry," he said, and loosened—but didn't release—his grip.

"She's wis child," said the minister, in a reproachful tone.

"I know that," Hal said, tightening his hold once more. "Get on with it, please. At once."

"Why?" said Minnie, mildly provoked. "Do you have somewhere special you have to be?"

"No," he said, narrowing his eyes at her. "But I want the child to be legitimate, and I think you may give birth to it at any moment."

"I will *not*," she said, offended. "You *know* I'm no more than six months gone!"

"You look like a—" Catching a glimpse of her eyes at this point, he shut his mouth abruptly, coughed, and turned his attention once more to the minister. "Do please continue, sir."

The man nodded, blew his nose again, and motioned to his wife, who bent to rummage beneath the bar, eventually emerging with a battered prayer book, its cover spotted with kronk rings.

Possessed of this talisman, the minister seemed to take heart and straightened up a little.

"You heb witnesses?" he asked Hal.

"Yes," said Hal, impatient. "He's—Harry? Dammit, he went out to pay the carriage. Stay here!" he commanded Minnie, and, dropping her hand, strode out.

The minister looked dubiously after him, then at Minnie. The end of his nose was moist and scarlet, and tiny veins empurpled his cheeks.

"You are willing to marry dis man?" he asked. "I see he is rich, but maybe better to take a poor man who will treat you well."

"Ze is zes maanden zwanger, idioot," said the minister's wife. "She's six months gone with child." *"Is dit die schurk die je zwanger heeft gemaakt?"* She removed the pipe from the corner of her mouth and gestured from the door to Minnie's belly: *"He's the no-good who got you pregnant?"* A hefty kick from the occupant made Minnie grunt and double over.

"Ja, is die schurk," she assured the woman, glancing over her shoulder to the door, where Hal's shadow in the window was visible, a larger shadow that must be Harry behind him.

The men entered with a blast of winter air and the woman exchanged a look with her husband. Both shrugged, and the minister opened the book and began thumbing through it in a helpless sort of way.

Harry smiled reassuringly at Minnie and patted her hand before lining up solidly beside Hal. Oddly enough, she did feel reassured. If a man like Harry was Hal's good friend, then perhaps—just perhaps—she wasn't wrong about him.

Not that it would make any difference at this point, she thought, feeling a strangely pleasant shiver run up her back. It felt as though she were about to jump off a cliff but feeling a great pair of wings unfurling at her back, even as she looked out into the wind.

"Mag ik uw volledige naam alstublieft?" "What are your names, please?" The landlady had pulled out a ratty register book—it might be the accounts for the pub, Minnie thought, looking at the stained pages. But the woman turned to a clean, blank page at the back of the book and dipped her quill, expectant.

Hal looked blank for a moment, then said firmly, "Harold Grey."

"Only two names?" Minnie said, surprised. "No titles?"

"No," he said. "It's not the Duke of Pardloe or even the Earl of Melton you're marrying. Just me. Sorry to disappoint you, if that's what you thought," he added, in a tone that actually sounded apologetic.

"Not at all," she said politely.

"My middle name's Patricius," he blurted. "Harold Patricius Gerard Bleeker Grey."

"Really?"

"Ik na gat niet allemaal opschrijven," the woman objected. "I'm not going to write all that."

"Bleeker—*dat is Nederlands*," the minister said, in surprised approval. "Your family is Dutch?"

"My father's mother's mother," Hal said, equally surprised.

The woman shrugged and wrote down the words, repeating, "Harold . . . Bleeker . . . Grey," to herself. *"En u?"* she asked, looking up at Minnie.

Minnie would have thought her heart couldn't go any faster, but she was wrong. Loose as her stays were, she felt light-headed, and before she could gather enough breath to speak, Hal stepped in.

"She's called Wilhelmina Rennie," he told the woman.

"Actually, it's Minerva Wattiswade," she said, getting a solid breath. Hal looked down at her, frowning.

"Wattiswade? What's Wattiswade?"

"Not what," she said, with exaggerated patience. "Who. Me, in fact."

This appeared to be too much for Hal, who looked to Harry for help.

"She means her name isn't Rennie, old man. It's Wattiswade."

"Nobody's named Wattiswade," Hal objected, transferring the frown back to Minnie. "I'm not marrying you under an assumed name."

"I'm not bloody marrying *you* under an assumed name!" she said. "Gah!"

"What—"

"Your bloody baby kicked me in the liver!"

"Oh." Hal looked somewhat abashed. "You mean your name really *is* Wattiswade, then."

"Yes, I do."

He took a deep breath.

"All right. Wattiswade. Why—never mind. You'll tell me later why you've been calling yourself Rennie."

"No, I won't."

He glanced at her, brows raised high, and she could see him—for once—debating whether to say something. But then his eyes lost the look of a man talking to himself and focused on hers.

"All right," he said softly, and held out his hand to her, palm upward.

She took another breath, looked out into the void, and jumped.

"Cunnegunda," she said, and put her hand in his. "Minerva Cunnegunda Wattiswade."

He said nothing, but she could feel him vibrating slightly. She carefully didn't look at him. Harry seemed to be arguing about something with the woman—something to do with the need for a second witness, she thought, but she couldn't concentrate enough to make out the words. The smell of tobacco smoke and stale sweat was making her gorge rise again, and she swallowed hard, several times.

All right. They'd decided that Mrs. Ten Boom could be the second witness. Good. Mortimer turned a somersault, landing heavily. Perspiration had broken out on Minnie's temples, and her ears felt hot.

Suddenly she was possessed by the fear that her father would burst through the door at any moment. She wasn't afraid of his stopping this impromptu ceremony; she was quite sure Hal wouldn't let him—and that certainty steadied her. Still . . . she didn't want him here. This was hers alone.

"Hurry," she said to Hal, in a low voice. "Please, hurry."

"Get on with it," he said to the minister, in a voice that wasn't particularly loud but plainly expected to be obeyed. The Reverend Ten Boom blinked, coughed, and opened his book.

It was all in Dutch; she could have followed the words but didn't—what echoed in her ears were the never-spoken phrases from the letters.

Not Esmé's—his. Letters written to a dead wife, in passionate grief, in fury, in despair. He might as well have punctured his own wrist with the sharpened quill and written those words in blood. She looked up at him now, white as the winter sky, as though all the blood had run out of his body, leaving him drained.

But his eyes were a pale and piercing blue when he turned his dark-browed face toward her, and the fire in him was not quenched, by any means.

You didn't deserve him, she thought toward the absent Esmé and rested her free hand on her gently heaving stomach. *But you loved him. Don't fret; I'll take care of them both.*

AUTHOR'S NOTE

IF YOU NEVER READ MADELEINE L'ENGLE'S MARVELous *A Wrinkle in Time* in your younger years, it's not too late. It's a wonderful story and I highly recommend it. If you *did* read it, though, you'll certainly remember this iconic line: *There is such a thing as a tesseract.*

In fact, there is such a thing as a tesseract, both as a geometrical and a scientific concept: Putting it crudely, it's a four-dimensional construct, in which the fourth dimension is time. And it's used as a fictional device to bring two separate space/time lines together, obviating the linear time between them. Much more convenient than a clunky old time machine.

Now, it's also a well-known fact that I stink at ages. I have only the vaguest general notion as to how old anyone in these stories is at any given point, I usually don't know when their birthdays are, and I don't really care. This drives both my copy editor and the more OCD-prone of my readers to distraction, and they Aren't Going to Be Happy about this, but really, there's no choice.

When I wrote *The Scottish Prisoner*, I randomly assigned ages to Hal's and Minnie's young sons, never thinking we'd see them again until they were adults (we have in fact seen all of them at one time or another as adults in *An Echo in the Bone* and in *Written in My Own Heart's Blood*).

Now . . . I *also* noted in *The Scottish Prisoner* that Jamie Fraser had met Minnie prior to her marriage, in Paris, and that they had known each other in the context of the Jacobite plots of that time. That's something of a plot point, has to do with both their characters and their subsequent actions, and so is important.

And I allowed Minnie to tell Lord John the circumstances of her marriage to his brother Hal. That's also important, as indicating something of the relationships between Minnie and Hal and just why he calls on her for help in intelligence matters at various points in later stories.

So—those two facts are important. How old the kids are *isn't* important.

But going back to tell more of Minnie and Hal's backstory, naturally I wanted to include Minnie's acquaintance with Jamie Fraser. Okay, that *had* to take place sometime in 1744, when the Frasers were in Paris, plotting away.

Minnie's pregnancy and the impending birth of her first son, Benjamin, had much to do with the marriage between Minnie and Hal and with her feelings about it. Ergo, Benjamin has to have been conceived sometime in 1744.

As the more nitpicking sort of reader will have instantly realized, if Benjamin *was* conceived in 1744 and born in 1745—as he has to have been—then he can't have been eight years old in 1760, when *The Scottish Prisoner* takes place. Only he was.

Obviously, the only way to reconcile Benjamin's age—as well as those of his brothers, Henry and Adam—is to draw the logical conclusion that a tesseract occurred somewhere between the writing of *The Scottish Prisoner* and "A Fugitive Green," and the boys will all be full-grown men next time we see them and it won't matter. Luckily, I have full confidence in the mental ability of my Very Intelligent Readers to grasp this concept and enjoy the story without further pointless fretting.

Whale Painters

At one point, while contemplating the subtle color of her eau-de-nil dress, Minnie refers mentally to her acquaintance with a Mr. Vernet, who is a whale painter.

Whale painting was actually a thing in the eighteenth century: There was great demand for the production of romantically watery, adventurous paintings, and thus there were specialists in that production. Claude Joseph Vernet was a real historical artist whose profession consisted mostly of painting seascapes, many including whales. As such, he would also be a great expert in the delineation of water and its many colors and thus in a position to tell Minnie about the concept of "a fugitive green"—i.e., green paint at that time was made with a pigment given to fading out eventually, unlike the more robust and permanent blues and grays.

And of course you all understand the metaphorical allusion of the title. (I actually included M. Vernet in order to make it clear to readers who don't speak French and don't necessarily stop to Google unknown terms while reading that eau-de-nil is, in fact, a shade of green.)

BESIEGED

LORD JOHN GREY DIPPED a finger gingerly into the little stone pot, withdrew it, glistening, and sniffed cautiously.

"Jesus!"

"Yes, me lord. That's what I said." His valet, Tom Byrd, face carefully averted, put the lid back on the pot. "Was you to rub yourself with *that* stuff, you'd be drawing flies in their hundreds, same as if you were summat that was dead. *Long* dead," he added, and muffled the pot in a napkin for additional protection.

"Well, in justice," Grey said dubiously, "I suppose the whale *is* long dead." He looked at the far wall of his office. There were a number of flies resting along the wainscoting, as usual, fat and black as currants against the white plaster. Sure enough, a couple of them had already risen into the air, circling lazily toward the pot of whale oil. "Where did you get that stuff?"

"The owner of the Moor's Head keeps a keg of it; he burns it in his lamps—cheaper nor even tallow candles, he says, let alone proper wax ones."

"Ah. I daresay." Given the usual smell of the Moor's Head on a busy night, nobody would notice the stink of whale oil above the symphony of other reeks.

"Easier to come by on Jamaica than bear grease, I reckon," Tom remarked, picking up the pot. "D'you want me to try it with the mint, me lord? It *might* help," he added, with a dubious wrinkle of the nose.

Tom had automatically picked up the oily rag that lived on the corner of Grey's desk and, with a dexterous flick, snapped a fat fly out of the air and into oblivion.

"Dead whale garnished with mint? That should cause my blood to be especially attractive to the more discriminating biting insects in Charles

Town—to say nothing of Canada." Jamaican flies were a nuisance but seldom carnivorous, and the sea breeze and muslin window screening kept most mosquitoes at bay. The swamps of coastal America, though . . . and the deep Canadian woods, his ultimate destination . . .

"No," Grey said reluctantly, scratching his neck at the mere thought of Canadian deer flies. "I can't attend Mr. Mullryne's celebration of his new plantation house basted in whale oil. Perhaps we can get bear grease in South Carolina. Meanwhile . . . sweet oil, perhaps?"

Tom shook his head decidedly.

"No, me lord. Azeel says sweet oil draws spiders. They come and lick it off your skin whilst you're asleep."

Lord John and his valet shuddered simultaneously, recollecting last week's experience with a banana spider—a creature with a leg span the size of a child's hand—that had burst unexpectedly out of a ripe banana, followed by what appeared at the time to be several hundred small offspring, at a garden party given by Grey to mark his departure from the island and to welcome the Honorable Mr. Houghton Braythwaite, his successor as governor.

"I thought he'd have an apoplexy on the spot," Grey said, lips twitching.

"Likely wishes he had."

Grey looked at Tom, Tom at Grey, and they burst into suffocated snorts of laughter at the memory of the Honorable Mr. Braythwaite's face on this occasion.

"Come, come," Lord John said, getting himself under control. "This will never do. Have you—"

The rumble of a carriage coming up the gravel drive of King's House interrupted him.

"Oh, God, is that him now?" Grey glanced guiltily round at the disarray of his office: A gaping half-packed portmanteau lolled in the corner, and the desk was strewn with scattered documents and the remnants of lunch, in no condition to be viewed by the man who would inherit it tomorrow. "Run out and distract him, will you, Tom? Take him to the receiving room and pour rum into him. I'll come and fetch him as soon as I've done . . . something . . . about this." He waved a hand at the debris, and Tom obligingly vanished.

Grey picked up the oiled rag and disposed of an unwary fly, then seized a plate scattered with bread crusts, blobs of custard, and fruit peelings and decanted this out of the window into the garden beneath. Thrusting the empty plate out of sight under the desk, he began hurriedly to gather papers into piles but was interrupted almost at once by the reappearance of Tom, looking excited.

"Me lord! It's General Stanley!"

"Who?" Grey said blankly. His mind, occupied with the details of imminent escape, refused to deal with anything that might interfere with said escape, but "Stanley" did ring a distant, small bell.

"Might be as he's your mother's husband, me lord?" Tom said, with a becoming diffidence.

"Oh . . . *that* General Stanley. Why didn't you say so?" John hastily grabbed his coat from its hook and shrugged into it, brushing crumbs off his waistcoat as he did so. "Show him in, by all means!"

John in fact liked his mother's third husband—she having been twice widowed when she acquired the general four years before—though any military intrusion at this point was something to be regarded warily.

Wariness was, as usual, justified. The General Stanley who eventually appeared was not the bluff, jaunty, self-confident man last seen in his mother's company. This General Stanley was hobbling with a stick, his right foot bound up in an immense bandage, and his face gray with pain, effort . . . and profound anxiety.

"General!" John seized him by the arm before he could fall over and guided him to the nearest chair, hastily removing a pile of maps from it. "Do sit down, please—Tom, would you . . . ?"

"Just here, me lord." Tom had dug Grey's flask out of the open traveling bag with commendable promptitude and now thrust it into General Stanley's hand.

The general accepted this without question and drank deeply.

"Dear Lord," he said, setting the flask on his knee and breathing heavily. "I thought I shouldn't make it from the landing." He took another drink, somewhat more slowly, eyes closed.

"More brandy, Tom, if you please?" Grey said, watching this. Tom gave the general an assessing look, not sure whether he might die before more brandy could be fetched, but decided to bet on the general's survival and disappeared in search of sustenance.

"God." The general looked a good deal short of human but distinctly better than he had. He nodded thanks to John and handed back the empty flask with a trembling hand. "The doctor says I mustn't drink wine—apparently it's bad for the gout—but I don't recall his mentioning brandy."

"Good," John said, glancing at the bandaged foot. "Did he say anything about rum?"

"Not a word."

"Excellent. I'm down to my last bottle of French brandy, but we've got quite a lot of rum."

"Bring the cask." The general was beginning to show a tinge of color and, at this point, began to be cognizant of his surroundings. "You were packing to leave?"

"I *am* packing to leave, yes," John said, the feeling of wariness developing small, prickling feet inside his stomach. "I'm meant to sail tonight, for Charles Town."

"Thank God. I was afraid I shouldn't make it in time." The general breathed audibly for a moment, then gathered himself. "It's your mother."

"*What's* my mother?" The wariness turned instantly to a flare of alarm. "What's happened to her?"

"Nothing, yet. Or at least I sincerely hope not." The general patted the air in a vague gesture of reassurance that failed singularly to reassure.

"Where the devil is she? And what in God's name is she up to now?" Grey spoke with more heat than filial respect, but panic made him edgy.

"She's in Havana," General Stanley said. "Minding your cousin Olivia."

This seemed like a moderately respectable thing for an elderly lady to be doing, and Grey relaxed slightly. But only slightly.

"Is she ill?" he asked.

"I hope not. She said in her last letter that there was an outbreak of some sort of ague in the city, but she herself was in good health."

"Fine." Tom had come back with the brandy bottle, and John poured himself a small glass. "I trust she's enjoying the weather." He raised an eyebrow at his stepfather, who sighed deeply and put his hands on his knees.

"I'm sure she is. The problem, my boy, is that the British Navy is on its way to lay siege to the city of Havana, and I really think it would be a good idea if your mother wasn't *in* the city when they get there."

FOR A MOMENT, John stood frozen, glass in hand, mouth open, and his brain so congested with questions that he was unable to articulate any of them. At last, he gulped the remains of his drink, coughed, and said mildly, "Oh, I see. How does my mother come to be in Havana to start with?"

The general leaned back and let out a long breath.

"It's all the fault of that Stubbs fellow."

"Stubbs . . . ?" It sounded vaguely familiar, but stunned as he was, Grey couldn't think why.

"You know, chap who married your cousin Olivia. Looks like a builder's brick. What's his Christian name . . . Matthew? No, Malcolm, that's it. Malcolm Stubbs."

Grey reached for the brandy bottle, but Tom was already pouring a fresh glass, which he thrust into his employer's hand. He carefully avoided meeting Grey's eye.

"Malcolm Stubbs." Grey sipped brandy, to give himself time to think. "Yes, of course. I . . . take it that he's quite recovered, then?" On one level, this was good news; Malcolm Stubbs had lost a foot and part of the adjoining leg to a cannonball at the Battle of Quebec, more than two years before. By good luck, Grey had fallen over him on the field and had the presence of mind to use his belt as a tourniquet, thus preventing Stubbs from bleeding to death. He vividly recalled the splintered bone protruding from the remnants of Malcolm's shin, and the hot, wet smell of blood and shit, steaming in the cold air. He took a deeper swallow of brandy.

"Yes, quite. Got an artificial foot, gets around quite well—even rides."

"Good for him," Grey said, rather shortly. There were a few other things he recalled about Malcolm Stubbs. "Is *he* in Havana?"

The general looked surprised.

"Yes, didn't I say? He's a diplomat of some kind now—sent to Havana last September."

"A diplomat," Grey repeated. "Well, well." Stubbs probably did diplomacy well—given his demonstrated skills at lying, deceit, and dishonor. . . .

"He wanted his wife and children to join him in Havana, once he had a suitable establishment, so—"

"Children? He had only the one son when I last saw him." *Only the one* legitimate *son,* he added silently.

"Two, now—Olivia gave birth to a daughter two years ago; lovely child called Charlotte."

"How nice." His memory of the birth of Olivia's first child, Cromwell, was nearly as horrifyingly vivid as his memories of the Battle of Quebec, if for somewhat different reasons. Both had involved blood and shit, though. "But Mother—"

"Your mother offered to accompany Olivia, to help with the children. Olivia's expecting again, and a long sea voyage . . ."

"*Again?*" Well, it wasn't as though Grey didn't *know* what Stubbs's attitude toward sex was . . . and at least the man was doing it with his wife. John kept his temper with some difficulty, but the general didn't notice, continuing with his explanations.

"You see, I was meant to be sailing to Savannah in the spring—now, I mean—to advise a Colonel Folliott, who's raising a local militia to assist the governor, and your mother was going to come with me. So it seemed reasonable that she go ahead with Olivia and help her to get settled, and I would arrange for her to join me when I came."

"Very sensible," John said. "That's Mother, then. And where does the British Navy come into it?"

"Admiral Holmes, me lord," Tom said, with a faint air of reproach. "He told you last week, when you had him to dinner. He said the Duke of Albemarle was a-coming to take Martinique away from the frogs and then see to Cuba."

"Oh. Ah."

Grey recalled the dinner, which had featured a remarkable dish that he had realized—too late—was the innards of pickled sea urchins, mixed with bits of raw fish and sea lettuce that had been cured with orange juice. In his desire to keep his guests—all recently arrived from London, and all lamenting the dearth of roast beef and potatoes in the Indies—from sharing his realization, he had called for lavish and repeated applications of a native palm liquor. This had been very effective; by the second glass, they wouldn't have known they were eating whale turds, should his adventurous cook have taken it into his head to serve that as a second course. Consequently, though, his own memories of the occasion were somewhat dim.

"He didn't say Albemarle was proposing to lay siege to the place, did he?"

"No, me lord, but that must've been his meaning, don't you think?"

"God knows," said John, who knew nothing about Cuba, Havana, or the Duke of Albemarle. "Or possibly you do, sir?" He turned politely to General Stanley, who was beginning to look better, under the influence of relief and brandy. The general nodded.

"I wouldn't," he admitted frankly, "save that I shared Albemarle's table aboard his flagship for six weeks. What I don't presently know about the harbor at Havana probably isn't worth knowing, but I take no credit for the acquisition of that knowledge."

The general had learned of Albemarle's expedition only the night before the fleet sailed, when a message from the War Office had reached him, ordering him aboard.

"At that point, of course, the ship would reach Cuba long before any message I could send to your mother, so I went aboard at once—*this*"—he glowered at his bandaged foot—"notwithstanding."

"Quite." John raised a hand in brief interruption and turned to his valet. "Tom,—run—and I do mean *run*—to Admiral Holmes's residence and ask him to call upon me as soon as is convenient. And by *convenient,* I mean—"

"Right now. Yes, me lord."

"Thank you, Tom."

Despite the brandy, Grey's brain had finally grasped the situation and was busy calculating what to do about it.

If the British Navy showed up in Havana Harbor and started shelling the place, it wasn't merely physical danger threatening the Stubbs family and Lady Stanley, also known as the Dowager Duchess of Pardloe. All of them would likely become immediate hostages of Spain.

"The moment we got within sight of Martinique and joined Monckton's forces there, I . . . er . . . requisitioned a small cutter to bring me here, as quickly as possible."

"Requisitioned, sir?" John said, smiling at the general's tone.

"Well, I stole it, to be perfectly frank," the general admitted. "I don't imagine they'd bring me to a court-martial, at my age . . . and I bloody don't care if they do." He sat upright, gray-stubbled chin outthrust and a glint in his eye. "All I care about is Benedicta."

WHAT THE GENERAL knew about the harbor at Havana was, generally speaking, that it was one of the finest deepwater harbors in the world, capable of accommodating a hundred ships of the line, and that it was guarded on either side by a large fortress: Morro Castle to the east, and La Punta on the west.

"La Punta's a working fortress, purely defensive; it overlooks the city, though of course one side faces the harbor. El Morro—that's what the Spaniards call it—is a bigger place and is the administrative headquarters of Don Juan de Prado, governor of the city. It's also where the main batteries controlling the harbor are located."

"With luck, I won't need to know that," John said, pouring rum into a glass of orange juice, "but I'll make a note of it, just in case."

Tom returned toward the end of the general's remarks, to report that Admiral Holmes was aware of the planned invasion but had no details concerning it, beyond the fact that Sir James Douglas, who was due to take command of the Jamaica squadron, had sent word that he wished to rendezvous with the squadron off Haiti, at the admiral's earliest convenience.

Through all of this discussion, Lord John had been making mental notes of anything that might conceivably be useful to him—and a parallel list of things here in Jamaica that might come in handy for an impromptu expedition to an island where he didn't speak the language. When he got up to pour more orange juice for the general, he asked Tom, in an undertone, to fetch Azeel from the kitchen.

"What did you mean, you stole the cutter?" John asked curiously, topping up the orange juice with rum.

"Well, that might be a slightly dramatic way to have put it," the general admitted. "The cutter normally attends the *Warburton,* and I do believe Captain Grace, who commands her, was intending to send Lieutenant Rimes off on an errand of his own. I nipped across to Albemarle's ship, though, and . . . er . . . preempted him."

"I see. Why—oh." He caught sight of Azeel, who had arrived but was waiting respectfully in the doorway to be summoned. "Do come in, my dear; I want you to meet someone."

Azeel entered but stopped short at sight of General Stanley, the look of happy anticipation on her face turning at once to one of caution. She dropped a low curtsy to the general, modestly lowering her white-capped head.

"General, may I present Mrs. Sanchez, my housekeeper? Mrs. Sanchez, this is General Stanley, my stepfather."

"Oh!" she exclaimed in surprise, and then blushed—a lovely sight, as the color in her dark cheeks made her look like a black rose. "Your servant, sir!"

"Your most humble, madam." The general bowed as gallantly as possible while remaining seated. "You must forgive my not standing . . ." He gestured ruefully toward his bandaged foot.

She made a graceful gesture of dismissal and turned toward John.

"This is—your . . ." She groped for the word. "He is the next governor?"

"No, he's not my replacement," John said. "That's Mr. Braythwaite; you saw him at the garden party. No, the general has come to give me some disturbing news, I'm afraid. Do you think you could fetch your husband, Mrs. Sanchez? I wish to discuss the situation with you both."

She looked both astonished and concerned at this and studied him carefully to see if he meant it. He nodded, and she at once curtsied again and vanished, her sandal heels tapping on the tiles in agitation.

"Her husband?" General Stanley said, in some surprise.

"Yes. Rodrigo is . . . er . . . a sort of factotum."

"I see," said the general, who plainly didn't. "But if this Braythwaite is already on board, so to speak, won't he want to make his own domestic arrangements?"

"I imagine so. I, um, had had it in mind to take Azeel and Rodrigo with me to South Carolina. But they may be helpful to the present venture, if . . . er . . . if Rodrigo is sufficiently recovered."

"Has he been ill?" Worry creased the general's already-furrowed brow. "I hear the yellow jack comes to the West Indies at this season, but I hadn't thought Jamaica was badly affected."

"No, not ill, exactly. He had the misfortune to run afoul of a *houngan*— a sort of, um, African wizard, I believe—and was turned into a zombie."

"A what?" The look of worry was superseded by one of astonishment.

Grey drew a deep breath and took a long swallow of his drink, the sound of Rodrigo's own description echoing in his ears.

"Zombie are dead people, sah."

GENERAL STANLEY WAS still blinking in astonishment at Grey's brief description of the events that had culminated in his own appointment as military governor—Grey judiciously suppressing the facts that Azeel had commissioned an Obeah man to drive the previous governor mad and that Rodrigo had gone one step further and arranged to have the late Governor Warren killed and partially devoured—when the sound of footsteps echoed once again in the corridor. Two people this time: the clack of Azeel's sandals but now walking slowly, to accommodate the slightly limping gait of the booted person accompanying her.

Grey stood up as they came in, Azeel hovering protectively behind Rodrigo.

The young man stopped, taking a deep breath before bowing deeply to the gentlemen.

"Your . . . servant. Sah," he said to Grey, and then straightened, turned upon his axis, and repeated this process to the general, who watched him with a mixture of fascination and wariness.

Every time he saw Rodrigo, Grey's heart was torn between regret for what the young man had once been—and a cautious joy in the fact that some of that splendid young man seemed still to be present, intact, and might yet come back further.

He was still beautiful, in a way that made Grey's body tighten every time he saw that dark, finely carved head and the tall straight lines of his body. The lovely cat-like grace of him was gone, but he could walk again, almost normally, though one foot dragged a little.

It had taken weeks of careful nursing by Azeel—she was the only member of Grey's household who was not terrorized by Rodrigo's mere proximity—with help from Tom, who was afraid, too, but thought it wasn't becoming for an Englishman to admit it.

Rodrigo had been nothing more than a shell of himself when Grey had rescued him and Tom from the maroons who had kidnapped them, and no one had expected that he would survive. Zombies didn't. Drugged with zombie poison—Grey had little notion what was in the stuff, beyond the liver of some remarkably poisonous fish—and buried in a shallow grave, the person attacked by a *houngan* woke after some time to find himself apparently dead and buried.

Rising in a state of mental and physical disorientation, they numbly followed the orders of the *houngan,* until they died of starvation and the aftereffects of the drugs—or were killed. Zombies were (justifiably, Grey thought) viewed with horror by everyone, even by the people who had once loved them. Left without food, shelter, or kindness, they didn't last long.

But Grey had refused to abandon Rodrigo, and so had Azeel. She had brought him slowly, slowly back to humanity—and then had married him, to the extreme horror of everyone in King's Town.

"He's got back most of his speech," Grey explained to the general.

"But only Spanish, that being his first language. He only remembers a few scattered words of English. We"—he smiled at Azeel, who ducked her head shyly—"hope that will improve, too, given time. But for now . . . he tells his wife things in Spanish, and she translates them for me."

He explained the situation briefly to Azeel and Rodrigo—the young man could understand some English, if spoken slowly, but his wife filled in the missing bits for him.

"I would like you to go with me to Cuba," Grey said, looking from one to the other. "Rodrigo could go where I could not go, and hear and see things I couldn't. But . . . there might be some small danger, and if you choose not to go, I will give you enough money for passage to the colonies. If you do choose to come with me, I will take you from Cuba to America, and you will either remain in my employment or, if you prefer, I will find you a place there."

Man and wife exchanged a long look, and at last Rodrigo nodded.

"We . . . go," he said.

GREY HAD NEVER seen a black person turn white before. Azeel had gone the color of grimy old bones and was clutching Rodrigo's hand as though one or both of them were about to be dragged off by slavers.

"Are you given to seasickness, Mrs. Sanchez?" he asked, making his way to them through the confusion of the docks. She swallowed heavily but shook her head, unable to take her eyes off the *Otter*. Rodrigo was unable to take his eyes off her and was anxiously patting her hand. He turned to Grey, fumbling for English words.

"She . . . scare . . ." He looked helplessly back and forth between his wife and his employer. Then he nodded a bit, making up his mind, then looked at Grey while pointing to Azeel. He lowered his hand, indicating something—someone?—short. Then turned to the sea and flung his arm wide, gesturing to the horizon.

"Africa," he said, turning back to Grey and putting his arm around his wife's shoulders. His face was solemn.

"Oh, Jesus," Grey said to Azeel. "You were brought from Africa as a child? Is that what he means?"

"Yes," she said, and swallowed again. "I was . . . very . . . small."

"Your parents? Were they . . ." His voice died in his throat. He'd seen a slave ship only once, and that at a distance. He would remember the smell for as long as he lived. And the body that had bobbed up suddenly beside his own ship, thrown overboard by the slaver. It might have been dead kelp or a blood-bleached scrap from a whaling ship, bobbing in the waves, emaciated, sexless, scarcely human. The color of old bones.

Azeel shook her head. Not in negation but in a vain refusal to think of dreadful things.

"Africa," she said softly. "They are dead. In Africa."

Africa. The sound of the word prickled over Grey's skin like a centipede, and he shook himself suddenly.

"It's all right," he said to her firmly. "You are free now." At least he hoped so.

He had managed her manumission a few months before, in recognition of her services during the slave rebellion during which the late Governor Warren had been killed by zombies. Or, rather, by men under the delusion that they were zombies. Grey doubted that this distinction had been appreciated by the governor.

Grey didn't know whether the girl had been Warren's personal property, and he didn't ask her. He'd taken advantage of his own doubt to tell Mr. Dawes, the governor's erstwhile secretary, that as there was no record of her provenance, they should assume that she was technically the property of His Majesty and should thus be omitted from the list of Governor Warren's belongings.

Mr. Dawes, an excellent secretary, had made a noise like a mildly consumptive sheep and lowered his eyes in acquiescence.

Grey had then dictated a brief letter of manumission, signed this as acting military governor of Jamaica (and thus His Majesty's agent), and had Mr. Dawes affix the most imposing seal in his collection—Grey thought it was the seal of the department of weights and measures, but it was done in red wax and looked very impressive.

"You have your paper with you?" he asked. Azeel nodded, obedient. But her eyes, large and black, lingered fearfully on the ship.

The master of the cutter, having been apprised of their presence, now popped up on deck and came down the gangplank to meet them.

"Lord John?" he asked respectfully, bowing. "Lieutenant Geoffrey Rimes, commander. Your servant, sir!"

Lieutenant Rimes looked about seventeen, very blond and small for his age. He was, however, wearing proper uniform and looked both cheerful and capable.

"Thank you, Lieutenant." Grey bowed. "I understand that you . . . er . . . obliged General Stanley by bringing him here. And that you are now willing to convey me and my party to Havana?"

Lieutenant Rimes pursed his lips in thought.

"Well, I suppose I can do that, my lord. I'm to rendezvous with the fleet here in Jamaica, but as they won't likely arrive for another two weeks, I think I can deliver you safe to Havana, then skip back here to make my meeting."

A small knot formed in Grey's stomach.

"You . . . mean to leave us in Havana?"

"Well, yes, my lord," he said cheerfully. "Unless you can manage your business within two days, I'll have to. Orders, you know." He pulled a commiserating face.

"I'm not really *meant* to be going to Havana, you know," the lieutenant said, leaning forward in a confidential manner and lowering his voice. "But I hadn't any orders to stay in Jamaica, either, if you know what I mean. As written, my orders just say I'm to rendezvous here with the fleet, after delivering the message to Admiral Holmes. As I've already done that . . . well, the navy's always willing to oblige the army—when it suits," he added honestly. "And I'm thinking it wouldn't do me any harm to have a look at Havana Harbor and be able to tell Admiral Pocock about it when he gets here. The Duke of Albemarle's in command of the expedition," he added, seeing Grey look blank. "But Admiral Pocock's in charge of the ships."

"To be sure."

Grey was thinking that Lieutenant Rimes was equally likely to rise to great heights in his service or to be court-martialed and hanged at Execution Dock, but he kept these thoughts to himself.

"Wait a moment," he said, calling the lieutenant's attention— momentarily distracted by the sight of Azeel Sanchez, brilliant as a macaw in a yellow skirt and sapphire-blue bodice—to himself.

"Do you mean that you intend actually to sail *into* Havana Harbor?"

"Oh, yes, my lord."

Grey cast a glance at the *Otter*'s unmistakable British colors, lifting gently in the tropical breeze.

"You will pardon my ignorance, I hope, Lieutenant Rimes—but are we not at war with Spain just now?"

"Certainly, my lord. That's where you come in."

"That's where *I* come in?" Grey felt a sort of cold, inexorable horror rising from the base of his spine. "In what capacity, may I ask?"

"Well, my lord, the thing is, I have to bring you into Havana Harbor; it's the only real anchorage on that coast. I mean, there are fishing villages and the like, but was I to land you in one of those places, you'd have to make your way overland to Havana, and it might take longer than you've got."

"I see . . ." said John, in a tone indicating quite the opposite. Mr. Rimes noticed this and smiled reassuringly.

"So, I'll bring you in under colors—they won't shell a cutter, I don't think, not until they see what's what—and deliver you as an official visitor of some sort. The general thought perhaps you might be bringing some message to the English consul there, but of course you'll know best about that."

"Oh, indeed." *It couldn't be patricide, could it?* he thought. Strangling a stepfather, particularly under the circumstances . . .

"It's all right, me lord," Tom put in helpfully. "I've brought your full-dress uniform. Just in case you might need it."

IN THE EVENT, the officer of the battery guarding the boom chain declined to allow Mr. Rimes to pass, but neither did he offer to sink him. There were a good many curious looks directed at the cutter, but Grey's party was allowed to come ashore. The officer's English was on a par with Grey's Spanish, but after a long conversation filled with vehement gesticulations, Rodrigo convinced him to provide transport into the city.

"What did you tell him?" Grey asked curiously, when at last they were allowed to pass through the battery guarding the west side of the harbor. An imposing fortress with a tall watchtower stood on a promontory in the distance, and he wondered whether this was Morro Castle or the other one.

Rodrigo shrugged and said something to Azeel, who answered.

"He didn't understand the word 'consul'—we don't, either," she added apologetically. "So Rodrigo said you have come to visit your mother, who is sick."

Rodrigo had been following her words with great concentration and here added something else, which she translated in turn.

"He says everybody has a mother, sir."

The address General Stanley had given was the Casa Hechevarria, in Calle Yoenis. When Grey and his fellow travelers were eventually delivered to the *casa* by a wagon driver whose normal cargo appeared to be un-tanned hides, the place proved to be a large, pleasant, yellow-plastered house with a walled garden and a beehive-like air of peaceful busyness about it. Grey could hear the murmur of voices and occasional laughter within, but none of the bees seemed inclined to answer the door.

After a wait of some five minutes had failed to produce anyone—let alone his mother or something comestible—Grey left his small, queasy party on the portico and ventured round the house. Splashing noises, sharp cries, and the reek of lye soap seemed to indicate that laundry was being done at no great distance. This impression was confirmed as he came round the corner of the house into a rear courtyard and was struck in the face by a thick cloud of hot, wet air, scented with dirty linen, woodsmoke, and fried plantains.

A number of women and children were working in the vicinity of a huge cauldron, this mounted on a sort of brick hearth with a fire beneath—this in turn being fed by two or three small, mostly naked children who were poking sticks into it. Two women were stirring the mess in the cauldron with huge wooden forks, one of them bawling at the children in Spanish with what he assumed were dire warnings against being underfoot, not getting splashed with boiling water, and keeping well clear of the soap bucket.

The courtyard itself looked like Dante's Fifth Circle of Hell, with sullen gurglings from the cauldron and drifting wisps of steam and smoke giving the scene a sinister Stygian cast. More women were pinning up wet clothes on lines strung round the pillars supporting a sort of loggia, and still others were tending braziers and griddles in a corner, from which drifted the fragrant smells of food. Everyone was talking, all at once, in a Spanish punctuated by parrot-like shrieks of laughter. Knowing that his mother was much less likely to be interested in laundry than in food, he edged round the courtyard—totally ignored by everyone—toward the cooks.

He saw her at once; her back was turned to him, hair hanging casually down her back in a long, thick plait, and she was talking, waving her hands, to a coal-black woman who was squatting, barefooted, on the tiles of the courtyard, patting out some sort of dough onto a hot greased stone.

"That smells good," he said, walking up beside her. "What is it?"

"Cassava bread," she said, turning to him and raising an eyebrow. "And *platanos* and *ropa vieja*. That means 'old clothes,' and while the name is quite descriptive, it's actually very good. Are you hungry? Why do I bother asking?" she added before he could answer. "Naturally you are."

"Naturally," he said, and was, the last vestiges of seasickness vanishing in the scents of garlic and spice. "I didn't know you could speak Spanish, Mother."

"Well, I don't know about speaking, so much," she said, thumbing a straggle of graying blond hair out of her left eye, "but I gesture fluently. What are you doing here, John?"

He glanced round the courtyard; everyone was still at their work, but every eye was fixed on him, interested.

"Do any of your . . . um . . . associates here speak English? In a non-gestural sort of way?"

"A few of them speak a little, yes, and Jacinto, the butler, is pretty fluent. They won't understand you if you talk fast, though."

"I can do that," he said, lowering his voice a little. "In short, your husband sent me, and . . . but before I acquaint you with the situation,—I brought several people with me, servants, and—"

"Oh, did you bring Tom Byrd?" Her face blossomed into what could only be called a grin.

"Certainly. He, along with two . . . er . . . Well, I left them on the portico; I couldn't make anyone hear me at the door."

His mother said something in Spanish that he thought must be an indelicate expletive, as it made the black woman blink and then grin herself.

"We *have* a porter, but he's rather given to drink," his mother said apologetically, and beckoned to one of the older girls hanging laundry. "Juanita! *Aquí,* if you please."

Juanita instantly abandoned her wet laundry and hastened over, dropping a perfunctory curtsy and staring at Grey in fascination.

"*Señora.*"

"*Es mi hijo,*" his mother said, pointing at him. "*Amigos de el . . .*" She twirled a forefinger, indicating circumnavigation, and pointed toward the front of the house, then jerked a thumb at a brazier over which an earthenware pot was bubbling. "*Agua. Comida. Por favor?*"

"I'm deeply impressed," John said, as Juanita nodded, said something fast and indecipherable, and vanished, presumably to rescue Tom and the Sanchezes. "Is *comida* food, by any chance?"

"Very perceptive of you, my dear." His mother gestured to the black lady, pointed in turn to John and herself, stabbed a finger at various pots and skewers, then nodded at a door on the far side of the courtyard and took John by the arm. "*Gracias, Maricela.*"

She led him into a small, rather dark salon that smelled of citronella, candle wax, and the distinctively sewer-like aroma of small children.

"I don't suppose this is a diplomatic ambassage, is it?" she said, crossing the room to throw open a window. "I would have heard about that."

"I am for the moment incognito," he assured her. "And with any luck, we'll be out of here before anyone recognizes me. How fast can you organize Olivia and the children for travel?"

She halted abruptly, hand on the windowsill, and stared at him.

"Oh," she said. Her expression had gone in an instant from surprise to calculation. "So it's come to that already, has it? Where's George?"

⤙⟶

"WHAT DO YOU mean, has it come to that already?" Grey said, startled. He stared hard at his mother. "Do you *know* about the"—he glanced round and lowered his voice, though no one was in sight and the laughter and chittering from the patio continued unabated—"the invasion?"

Her eyes flew open wide.

"The *what?*" she said loudly, then glanced hastily over her shoulder toward the open door. "When?" she said, turning back and lowering her own voice.

"Well, now, more or less," Grey said. He got up and quietly closed the door. The racket from the patio diminished appreciably.

"General Stanley turned up on my doorstep in Jamaica a week ago, with the news that the British Navy was on its way to take Martinique and then—if all goes as planned—Cuba. He rather thought it would be a good idea for you and Olivia to leave before they get here."

"I quite agree with him." His mother closed her eyes and rubbed her hands hard over her face, then shook her head violently, as though dislodging bats, and opened her eyes again. "Where is he?" she asked, with some semblance of calm.

"Jamaica. He'd, um, managed to borrow a naval cutter while the navy was preparing to take Martinique and came ahead as fast as he could, in hopes of warning you in time."

"Yes, yes," she said impatiently, "very good of him. But why is he in Jamaica and not here?"

"Gout." And quite possibly a few other infirmities, but no point in worrying her. She looked sharply at him but didn't ask further.

"Poor George," she said, and bit her lip. "Well, then. Olivia and the children are in the country, staying with a Señora Valdez."

"How far in the country?" Grey was making hasty calculations. Three women, two children, three men . . . four, with Malcolm. Ah, Malcolm . . . "Is Malcolm with them?"

"Oh, no. I'm not sure where he *is*," she added dubiously. "He travels a good deal, and with Olivia gone, he often stays in Havana;—he has an office in La Punta—that's the fortress on the west side of the harbor. But he does sleep here now and then."

"Oh, does he?" Grey tried to keep the edge out of his voice, but his mother glanced at him sharply. He looked away. If she didn't know about Malcolm's proclivities, he wasn't going to tell her.

"I need to talk to him as quickly as possible," he said. "Meanwhile, we must fetch Olivia and the children back here, but without giving the impression that there's any sort of emergency. If you'll write a note that will accomplish that, I'll have Rodrigo and Azeel carry it—they can help Olivia to pack up and help mind the children on the way."

"Yes, of course."

There was a small secretaire, rustic in design, crouched in the shadows. He hadn't noticed it until his mother opened it and swiftly produced paper, quill, and inkwell. She uncorked the latter, found it dry, said something under her breath in Greek that sounded like a curse but probably wasn't, and, crossing the room quickly, removed a bunch of yellow flowers from a pottery vase and poured some of the water from it into the empty well.

She shook ink powder into the well and was stirring the mixture briskly with a bedraggled quill when something occurred belatedly to Grey.

"What did you mean, Mother, when you said, 'It's come to that already'? Because you didn't know about the invasion, did you?"

She glanced up at him sharply, ceasing to stir. Then she took a deep breath, like one marshaling her mental forces, visibly made a decision, and put down the quill and ink.

"No," she said, turning to him. "George had told me such a thing was being quietly discussed—but I left England with Olivia in September. War with Spain hadn't yet been declared, though anyone could have seen that it was coming. No," she repeated, and looked at him intently. "I meant the slave revolt."

John stared at his mother for the space of thirty seconds or so, then slowly sank onto a wooden pew that ran along the side of the room. He closed his eyes briefly, shook his head, and opened them.

"Is there anything to drink in this establishment, Mother?"

FED, WASHED, AND fortified with Spanish brandy, Grey left Tom to see to the unpacking and made his way on foot back through the city to the harbor, where the fortress of La Punta—smaller than El Morro (what was a *morro*? he wondered), but still impressive—guarded the western shore.

A few people glanced at him but with no more interest than he might attract in London, and upon reaching La Punta, he was surprised at the ease with which he was not only admitted but escorted promptly to the *oficina del Señor Stubbs*. Granted, the Spaniards had their own notions of military readiness, but this seemed quite lax for an island at war.

The soldier accompanying him rapped on a door, said something in Spanish, and, with a brief nod, left him.

Footsteps, and the door opened.

Malcolm Stubbs looked twenty years older than he had last time Grey had seen him. He was still broad-shouldered and thick-bodied, but he seemed to have softened and fallen in on himself, like a slightly decayed melon.

"Grey!" he said, his tired face brightening. "Wherever did you spring from?"

"Zeus's forehead, no doubt," Grey said. "Where have you come from, for that matter?" The skirts of Stubbs's coat were thick with red dust, and he smelled strongly of horse.

"Oh . . . here and there." Malcolm beat the dust perfunctorily from his coat and subsided into his chair with a groan. "Oh, God. Stick your head out and call for a servant, will you? I need a drink and some food before I perish."

Well, he did know the Spanish word for "beer" . . . Sticking his head out into the corridor as advised, he spotted two servant girls loitering by the window at the far end, evidently talking to someone in the courtyard below, their conversation accompanied by a good deal of giggling.

Interrupting this colloquy with a brief "Hoy!" he said, *"Cerveza?"* in a tone of polite inquiry, following this with scooping motions toward his mouth.

"Sí, señor!" one of the girls said, with a hasty bob, adding something else in a questioning voice.

"Certainly," he said cordially. "Er . . . I mean, *sí!* Um . . . *gracias,*" he added, wondering what he had just agreed to. Both girls curtsied and vanished in a swirl of skirts, though, presumably to fetch something edible.

"What is *pulpo*?" he asked, returning to the office and sitting down opposite Malcolm.

"Octopus," Malcolm replied, emerging from the folds of a linen towel with which he'd been wiping dirt from his face. "Why?"

"Just wondered. Putting aside the usual inquiries about your health— are you all right, by the way?" he interrupted himself, looking down at what used to be Malcolm's right foot. The boot encircled a sort of cup or stirrup, made of stiff leather with wooden reinforcements on the sides. Both wood and leather were deeply stained from long use, but there was fresh bright blood on the stocking above.

"Oh, that." Malcolm glanced down indifferently. "It's all right. My horse broke down a few miles from the city, and I had to walk some way before I got another." Bending down with a grunt, he unbuckled the appurtenance and took it off—an action that Grey found oddly more disconcerting than sight of the stump itself.

The flesh was deeply ridged from the boot, and when Malcolm peeled the ragged stocking off, Grey saw that a wide ring of skin about the calf had been flayed raw. Malcolm hissed a little and closed his eyes, gently rubbing the end of the stump, the flesh there showing the pale blue of fresh bruising.

"Did I ever thank you, by the way?" Malcolm asked, opening his eyes.

"For what?" Grey said blankly.

"Not letting me bleed to death on that field in Quebec," Malcolm said dryly. "That slipped your mind, did it?"

Actually, it had. There had been a great many things happening on and off that field in Quebec, and the frantic moments of grappling to get his belt loose and jerked tight round Malcolm's spurting leg were just fragments—though vivid ones—of a fractured space where neither time nor thought existed; he'd been actually conscious that day of nothing beyond a sense of constant thunder—of the guns, of his heart, of the hooves of the Indians' horses, all one and pounding through his blood.

"You're welcome," he said politely. "As I say—putting the social courtesies to one side for the moment, I came to inform you that a rather large

British fleet is on its way to invade and capture the island. Am I correct, by the way, in my assumption that the local commander does not yet realize that war has been declared?"

Malcolm blinked. He stopped massaging his leg, straightened up, and said, "Yes. When?" His face had changed in an instant, from exhaustion and pain to alertness.

"I think you may have as long as two weeks, but it might be less." He gave Malcolm what details he had, as concisely as he could. Malcolm nodded, a line of concentration deepening between his brows.

"So I've come to remove you and your family," Grey finished. "And my mother, of course."

Malcolm glanced at him, one eyebrow raised.

"Me? You'll take Olivia and the children, of course—I'm very much obliged to you *and* General Stanley. But I'm staying."

"What? What the devil for?" John was conscious of a sudden surge of temper. "Besides a pending invasion, my mother tells me there's a bloody slave revolt in progress!"

"Well, yes," Malcolm said calmly. "That's mine."

Before Grey could sort out a coherent response to this statement, the door opened suddenly and a sweet-faced black girl with a yellow scarf round her head and an enormous battered tin tray in her hands sidled through it.

"Señores," she said, curtsying despite the tray, and deposited it on the desk. *"Cerveza, vino rústico, y un poco comida: moros y cristianos"*—she unlidded one of the dishes, loosing a savory steam— *"maduros"*—that was fried plantains; Grey was familiar with those— *"y pulpo con tomates, aceitunas, y vinagre!"*

"Muchas gracias, Inocencia," Malcolm said, in what sounded like a surprisingly good accent. *"Es suficiente."* He waved a hand in dismissal, but instead of leaving, she came round the desk and knelt down, frowning at his mangled leg.

"Está bien," Malcolm said. *"No te preocupes."* He tried to turn away, but she put a hand on his knee, her face turned up to his, and said something rapid in Spanish, in a tone of scolding concern that made Grey raise his brows. It reminded him of the way Tom Byrd spoke to *him* when he was sick or injured—as though it were all his own fault, and he therefore ought to submit meekly to whatever frightful dose or treatment was being proposed—but there was a distinct note in the girl's voice that Tom Byrd's lacked entirely.

Malcolm shook his head and replied, his own manner dismissive but kindly, and laid his hand on the girl's yellow head for a moment. It *might* have been merely a friendly gesture, but it wasn't, and Grey stiffened.

The girl rose, shook her head reprovingly at Malcolm, and went out, with a hint of flirtation in the sway of her skirts. Grey watched the door close behind her, then turned back to Malcolm, who had plucked an olive out of one dish and was sucking it.

"Inocencia, my arse," Grey said bluntly.

Malcolm's normal complexion being brick red, he didn't flush, but neither did he meet Grey's eye.

"Quite the usual sort of names they give girls, the Spanish," he said, discarding the olive pit and picking up a serving spoon. "You find young women called all kinds of things: Assumpción, Immaculata, Concepción . . ."

"Conception, indeed." This was said in a tone cold enough to make Malcolm's wide shoulders hunch a little, though he still wouldn't look at Grey.

"They call this *moros y cristianos*—that means 'moors and Christians'—the rice being Christians and the black beans Moors, d'you see?"

"Speaking of conception—and Quebec," Grey said, ignoring the food—though it smelled remarkably good, "your son by the Indian woman . . ."

Malcolm did glance at him then. He looked back at his plate, finished chewing, swallowed, and nodded, not looking at Grey.

"Yes. I did make inquiries—once I was mended. They told me the child had died."

That struck Grey in the pit of the stomach. He swallowed, tasting bile, and plucked a bit of something out of the dish of *pulpo* at random.

"I see. How . . . regrettable."

Malcolm nodded, wordless, and helped himself liberally to the octopus.

"Was it quite recent, this news?" The shock had gone through him like an ocean breaker. He remembered vividly the day when he had taken the infant—the child's mother having died of smallpox, he had bought the boy from his grandmother for a blanket, a pound of sugar, two golden guineas, and a small cask of rum—and carried him to the little French mission in Gareon. The boy had been warm and solid in his arms, looking up at him from round, unblinking dark eyes, as though trusting him.

"Oh. No. No, it was at least two years ago."

"Ah." Grey put the piece of whatever-it-was into his mouth and chewed slowly, the sense of shock fading into an immense relief—and then a growing anger.

Not a trusting man himself, he had given the priest money for the child's needs and told him this payment would continue—but only so long as the priest sent Grey a lock of the child's hair once a year, to prove his continued existence and presumed good health.

Malcolm Stubbs's natural hair was sandy and tightly curled as sheep's wool; when left to its own devices, it exploded from its owner's head like a ruptured mattress. Consequently, Malcolm usually kept his head polled and wore a wig. He'd evidently been wearing one earlier but had taken it off and set it aside, and the inch of mad growth thus displayed strongly resembled the texture of the two small curls of dark cinnamon-colored hair that Grey had so far received from Canada, each one bound carefully with black thread and accompanied by a brief note of thanks and blessing from Father LeCarré—the latest, just before his departure for Jamaica.

The urge to bounce Malcolm's head off the desk and shove him face-down into the *pulpo* was strong, but Grey mastered it, chewing the bite of octopus—very flavorful, but in texture reminiscent of an artist's rubber—thoroughly before saying anything. He swallowed.

"Tell me about this slave revolt of yours, then."

MALCOLM DID LOOK at him now, considering. He nodded and reached, grunting, for the limp, bloodstained stocking hanging out of his artificial foot.

"We'll go up to the battlements," he said. "Not many of the servants speak any English—but that doesn't mean none of them understand it. And they do listen at doors."

Grey blinked as they emerged from the gloom of a stone stairwell into a pure and brilliant day, a blinding sky spinning with seagulls overhead. A stiff wind was coming off the water, and Grey removed his hat, tucking it under his arm lest it be carried away.

"I come up here several times a day," Malcolm said, raising his voice above the wind and the shrieks of the gulls. He had wisely left his own hat and wig below in his office. "To watch the ships." He nodded toward the expanse of the huge harbor, where several very large ships were anchored, these surrounded by coveys of smaller vessels, going to and from the shore.

"They're beautiful," Grey said, and they were. "But they're not doing anything, are they?" All sails were furled, all port lids closed. The ships lay at anchor, rocking slowly in the wind, masts and spars swaying stark and black against the blue of sea and sky.

"Yes," Malcolm said dryly. "Particularly beautiful when they're not doing anything. That's how I know the declaration of war hasn't yet been received; if it had, the decks would be black with men, and the sails would be reefed, not furled. And that's why I come up here morning, noon, and night," he added.

"Yes," Grey said slowly, "but . . . if in fact de Prado—that's the commander of the forces here?—if he *doesn't* know that war is declared,—why are these ships here already? I mean, plainly they're men of war, not merchantmen. Even I know that much."

Malcolm laughed, though without much humor.

"Yes, the cannons rather give it away, don't they? The Spanish have been expecting war to be declared for the last six months. General Hevia brought these ships in last November, and they've been lying in wait here ever since."

"Ah."

Malcolm gave him a raised brow.

"Ah, indeed. De Prado's expecting a declaration any day. That's why I sent Olivia and the children to the country. De Prado's staff all treat me with exquisite courtesy"—his mouth twitched a little—"but I can see them measuring me for leg-irons and a cell."

"Surely not, Malcolm," Grey said mildly. "You're a diplomat, not an enemy combatant. Presumably they'd either deport or detain you, but I can't see it coming to chains."

"Yes," Malcolm agreed, eyes fixed again on the ships, as though he feared they might have begun to move in the last few moments. "But if they find out about the revolt—and I really don't see how that can be avoided—I rather think that might alter their views on my claim to diplomatic immunity."

This was said with a sort of calm detachment that impressed Grey—reluctantly, but still. He glanced round to be sure they were not overheard.

There were a lot of soldiers up here but none close to them; the gray stone of the rooftop stretched away for a hundred yards in all directions. Grey could hear, faintly, shouts between an officer at the far end of the battlement and someone in the watchtower above. There was a small group of regulars—most of them black, Grey saw—stripped to the waist and sweating despite the wind, repairing a gap in the battlement with baskets of stones—and there were guards. Four guards at each corner of the battlements, stiffly upright, muskets shouldered. The fortress of La Punta was prepared.

A detachment of twelve men marched past, two by two, under the command of a young corporal shouting the Spanish equivalent of "Hup!" as they wheeled past the stubby watchtower. The corporal saluted smartly; Malcolm bowed and turned again to the vast expanse of the harbor. It was a clear day; John could just make out the great boom chain at the harbor mouth, a thin darkness in the water, like a snake.

"It was Inocencia who told me," Malcolm said abruptly, as the soldiers disappeared down a stairway at the far side of the rooftop. He cut his eyes at Grey, who said nothing. Malcolm turned his face back to the harbor and began to talk.

The revolt was planned among slaves from two of the large sugar plantations near Havana. The original plan, according to Inocencia—whose cousin was a servant at Hacienda Mendez but was having an affair with one of the house slaves, whose brother was one of the ringleaders of the plot—had been to band together and kill the owners of the haciendas, loot the houses, which were very rich, and then escape through the countryside to the Golfo de Xaguas, on the other side of the island.

"Thinking that the soldiers wouldn't pursue them, being distracted by the imminent arrival of the English on this side, you see." Malcolm appeared quite unmoved by the putative murder of the plantation owners. "It wasn't a bad plan, if they chose their moment and waited 'til the English *did* arrive. There are dozens of small islands in the *golfo;* they might have hidden there indefinitely."

"But you discovered this plan, and rather than mentioning it to the *comandante* . . ."

Malcolm shrugged.

"Well, we are at war with the Spanish, are we not? Or if we weren't, it was obvious that we would be at any moment. I met with the two leaders of the revolt and, er, convinced them that there was a better way to achieve their ends."

"Alone? I mean—you went to meet these men by yourself?"

"Of course," Malcolm said simply. "I wouldn't have got near them had I come mob-handed. Didn't have a mob to hand, anyway," he added, turning to Grey with a self-conscious grin that suddenly took years off his careworn face.

"I met Inocencia's cousin at the edge of the Saavedra plantation, and she took me to a big tobacco shed," he went on, the grin fading. "It was almost nightfall, so darkish inside. Lots of shadows, and I couldn't tell how many men were there; it felt as though the whole place was moving and whispering, but likely that was just the drying leaves—they're quite big, did you know? A plant is almost the size of a man. They hang them up, up in the rafters, and they brush against each other with this dry sort of rustle, almost like they're tittering to themselves . . . put the wind up me, a bit."

Grey tried to imagine that meeting and, surprisingly, could envision it: Malcolm, artificial foot and all, limping alone into a dark shed to convince dangerous men to forgo their own murderous plans in favor of his. In Spanish.

"You aren't dead, so they listened to you," Grey said slowly. "What did you offer them?"

"Freedom," Malcolm said simply. "I mean,—the army goes about freeing slaves who enlist—why oughtn't the navy to be similarly enlightened?"

"I'm not so sure that a sailor's life is noticeably better than that of a slave," Grey said dubiously. "In terms of food, they may be better off as they are."

"I don't mean they're to enlist, booby," Malcolm said. "But I'm sure I can persuade either Albemarle or Admiral Pocock that they should be freed in token of regard for their service. If they survive," he added thoughtfully.

Grey was beginning to think that Malcolm might actually be a decent diplomat. Still . . .

"Since you mention service—what, exactly, are you proposing that these men do?"

"Well, my first notion was that they might creep along the shoreline after dark and detach and sink the boom chain across the harbor mouth."

"A good notion," Grey said, still dubious, "but—"

"The batteries. Yes, exactly. I couldn't very well go down and ask to inspect the batteries, but . . ." He reached into his coat and withdrew a small brass telescope.

"Have a look," he said, passing this to Grey. "Wave it around a bit, so it doesn't look as though you're spying out the batteries particularly."

Grey took the telescope. His hands were chilled and the brass, warm from Malcolm's body, gave him an odd *frisson*.

He'd seen one of the batteries close to, on the way in; the one on the opposite side of the harbor was similarly equipped: six four-pounders and two mortars.

"It's not only that, of course," Grey said, handing back the telescope. "It's the—"

"Timing," Malcolm finished. "Yes. Even if the men could swim from down shore rather than come through the battery, it would have to be done with the British fleet actually in view, or the Spaniards would have time to raise the chain again." He shook his head regretfully. "No. What I'm thinking, though—and do say, if you have a better idea—is that we might be able to take El Morro."

"What?" Grey glanced across the channel at the towering hulk of Morro Castle. Set on a rocky promontory, it rose considerably higher than La Punta and commanded the entire channel, most of the harbor, and a good bit of the city, as well. "How, exactly?"

Malcolm bit his lip, not in concern but concentration. He nodded at the castle.

"I've been inside, several times. And I can make an occasion to go again. You'll go with me—it's a blessing that you should have come, John," he added, turning his head to Grey. "It makes things much easier."

"Does it, indeed?" Grey murmured. A faint uneasiness began to stir at the base of his spine. A seagull landed on the parapet near his elbow and gave him a beady yellow look, which didn't help.

"The governor's down with fever, at the moment, but he might be better tomorrow. I'll request a meeting to introduce you. While you're engaged with de Prado—or his lieutenant, if de Prado's still indisposed—I'll make an excuse, slip off, and manage to take note of the floor plan, entrances and exits, all that—" He broke off suddenly. "You did say two weeks?"

"About that. But there's no telling, is there? What if Martinique didn't surrender easily, or there was a typhoon as they left the island? It *could* be a month or more." Another thought struck him. "And then there are the volunteers from the American colonies. Lieutenant Rimes says a number of transports are meant to rendezvous with the fleet here."

Malcolm scratched his head. The clipped bronze curls rippled in the wind like shorn autumn grass.

What? John thought, quite shocked at the poetic image his errant brain had presented him with. He didn't even *like* Malcolm, let alone . . .

"I don't suppose the transports would come near the harbor until they'd joined the fleet," Malcolm pointed out. "But two weeks seems decent odds—and that's long enough to get Olivia and your mother safely off the island."

"Oh. Yes," John said, relieved at this apparent return to sanity. "I had Mother send a note to bring them back to—oh, damn. You did say you'd sent them away on purpose."

The seagull made a disapproving noise, defecated on the parapet, and launched itself into the air.

"I did, yes. I tried to persuade your mother to go with Olivia, but she insisted on staying. Said she's writing something and wanted to be left in peace for a few days." Malcolm turned his back on the harbor and stared contemplatively at the stones under his feet.

"Adelante!" A shout came from behind Grey; he turned at the sound of marching feet and clanking weaponry. Another detachment drilling. They clumped past, eyes fixed forward, but their corporal saluted Malcolm politely, including Grey with a brief nod and a sidelong glance.

Was it his imagination, or had the man's eyes lingered on his face?

"The thing is . . ." Malcolm said, waiting 'til the soldiers had receded into the distance. "I mean . . ." He coughed and fell silent.

Grey waited.

"I know you don't like me, John," Malcolm said abruptly. "Or respect me. I don't like myself all that much," he added, looking away. "But—will you help me?"

"I don't see that I have a choice," Grey said, leaving the question of liking alone. "But for what it's worth," he added formally, "I do respect you."

Malcolm's broad face lighted at this, but before he could say anything in reply, Grey became suddenly aware of a change around them. The men repairing the wall had leapt to their feet, gesturing and pointing, shouting excitedly.

Everyone was shouting, rushing toward the battlements overlooking the harbor. Caught in the crush, the two Englishmen pushed their way forward, far enough to see the ship. A small boat, a fast Spanish cutter, coming like the wind itself, its sails white as gull's wings, hurtling across the blue water toward them.

"Oh, Jesus," Grey said. "It's—is it?"

"Yes, it is. It must be." Malcolm grabbed him by the elbow and pulled him out of the crowd of excited Spaniards. "Come. Now!"

THE STAIRWELL WAS blind dark after the dazzle above, and Grey had to drag a hand along the rough stone wall to avoid falling. He *did* fall, slipping on one of the age-hollowed steps near the bottom, but was luckily saved by clutching Malcolm's sleeve.

"This way." There was more light below, bright flashes from the narrow windows at the ends of long corridors, dim flickering of lanterns on the walls, a strong smell of whale oil. Malcolm led the way down to his office, where he said something in rapid Spanish to the secretary, who rose, looking surprised, and went out. Malcolm closed the door and locked it.

"Now what?" Grey asked. His heart was beating fast, and he felt a sense of confusion: an alertness like that of impending battle, an absurd urge to flee, the urgent need to do *something* . . . but what? The first knuckle on his right hand was bleeding; he'd scraped it when he slipped on the stairs. He put it to his mouth in reflex, tasting silver blood and stone dust.

Malcolm was breathing harder than the brisk walk merited. He braced himself with both hands on the desk, looking down at the dark wood. Finally he nodded, shook himself like a dog, and straightened up.

"It's not as though I haven't been thinking about it," he said. "But I hadn't expected you to be here."

"Don't let me interfere with your plans," Grey said politely. Malcolm looked at him, startled, then laughed and seemed to settle into himself.

"Right," he said. "Well, there's the two things, aren't there? The slaves, and Olivia—and your mother, of course," he added hastily.

Grey thought he might himself have reversed those two items in order of importance, but, then, he didn't know just how dangerous the slaves might be. He nodded.

"Do you really think they'll arrest you?"

Malcolm lifted one heavy shoulder and let it fall.

"Yes, I do—but I don't know how long it might take them to get round to it. After all, I'm no particular threat, so far as they know." He went to the small window and peered out. Grey could hear shouting in the courtyard below, someone trying to create order in the midst of a rising gabble of Spanish voices.

"The thing is," Malcolm said, turning back from the window with a frown of concentration upon his face, "they'll know officially that war has been declared, as soon as the captain of that ship presents his letters to the governor. But do you think they know anything about the fleet?" He saw Grey's raised eyebrow and added hastily, "I mean,—the ship bringing the declaration—if that's truly what it is—they might have spotted the fleet or . . . —or heard word of it. In which case . . ."

Grey shook his head.

"It's a big ocean, Malcolm," he said. "And is there anything you'd do differently if the Spanish *did* know about the fleet?"

He was rather impatient with Malcolm's orderly exegesis. His own blood was up, and he needed to be moving.

"Actually, yes. Number one being, run—both of us. If they think the British are about to be on their doorstep, the second thing the Spanish will do—after putting both forts on full alert—is round up every British citizen in Havana, very likely starting with me. If they *don't* know that, we might still have a bit of time in hand."

Grey saw that Malcolm was needing to move, too; he'd begun to walk to and fro behind his desk, glancing out of the window each time he passed it. He was limping heavily; walking clearly hurt him, but he seemed oblivious to the pain.

"The Mendez slaves will be nervous—well, they are already—but they'll be bloody well stirred up by this news. I've got to go and talk to them, as quickly as possible. Reassure them, you know? If I don't, they may very well take the declaration of war as a signal to fall upon their owners and slaughter them on the spot—which, aside from being generally deplorable in terms of humanity, would be a complete waste of their value to us."

"Deplorable, yes." Grey felt a qualm at the thought of the inhabitants of Haciendas Mendez and Saavedra, sitting down peaceably to their suppers tonight, with no notion that they might be murdered at any moment by the servants bringing their food. It occurred to him—as perhaps it had to Malcolm—that the slaves of those two plantations were quite possibly not the only ones on the island of Cuba who might be inclined to take advantage of a British invasion to settle scores. But there wasn't much either Malcolm or he could do about that.

"You'd best go, then, at once. I'll see to the women and children."

Malcolm was rubbing a hand fiercely over his face, as though this might assist thought.

"Yes. You'll have to get them off the island before the fleet arrives. Here, take this." He pulled out a drawer and withdrew a small, fat leather pouch. "Spanish money—you'll attract less attention. Cojimar—I think that's your best bet."

"What and where is Cojimar?" Drums. There were drums now, beating a tattoo in the courtyard, and the clatter of boots and voices as men spilled out of the recesses of the fortress. How big was the force manning El Morro?

He didn't realize he'd spoken that last question aloud until Malcolm answered it, distracted.

"About seven hundred soldiers, maybe another three hundred support-ives—oh, and the African laborers; perhaps another three hundred of them—they don't live in the fort, though." He met Grey's eyes and nod-ded, divining his next thought. "I don't know. They might join our men, they might not. If I had time . . ." He grimaced. "But I don't. Cojimar is—oh, wait." Turning, he seized the wig he'd taken off earlier from his desk and thrust it into Grey's hands.

"Disguise," he said, and smiled briefly. "You rather take the eye, John. Best if people don't notice you on the street." He snatched up the hat and crammed it on his own bare head, then unlocked the door and pulled it open, impatiently gesturing Grey ahead of him.

John went, asking over his shoulder, "Cojimar?"

"Fishing village." Malcolm was looking up and down the corridor. "It's east of Havana, maybe ten miles. If the fleet can't get into the harbor, it's the best anchorage for them. Small bay—oh, and a small fort, too. *El Cas-tillo de Cojimar.* You'll want to keep clear of that."

"Yes, I'll do that," John said dryly. "I'll—" He'd been going to say that he'd send Tom Byrd with any news, but the words died in his throat. Mal-colm would presumably be somewhere in the countryside, tending his slaves, by the time there was any news. That, or in captivity. Or—very possibly—dead.

"Malcolm," he said.

Malcolm turned his head sharply and saw John's face. He stopped dead for a moment, then nodded.

"Olivia," he said quietly. "Will you tell her—" He broke off and looked away.

"You know I will."

He put out a hand, and Malcolm grasped it, hard enough that the bones shifted. When they let go, his skinned knuckle burned, and he saw that there was blood from it on Malcolm's palm.

They spoke no more but went out into the corridor, walking fast.

THE WIG WOULD have been much too large, given Malcolm's round-headed resemblance to an oversize muskmelon, but Grey's own hair—yellow and noticeable, as Malcolm had so tactfully noted—was thick, and with it stuffed up inside the wig, the horsehair contrivance sat securely, if uncomfortably. He hoped that Malcolm didn't suffer from lice but forgot such minor concerns as he made his way through the throngs of people in the street outside La Punta.

There was an air of curiosity in the street; people glanced at the fortress as they passed, clearly sensing some disturbance from its daily routine. But the news had not yet spread; for that matter, Grey wondered whether the news had officially reached the office of the governor—or his sickbed, as the case might be. Neither he nor Malcolm had had any doubt; only the most urgent news would have got the cutter past the boom chain with such dispatch.

The guard at the fortress's street gate had given him no more than a casual glance before waving him through; as was the case in peacetime, there were nearly as many civilians as soldiers inside the fort, and there were plenty of fair-skinned, blue-eyed Spaniards. The cut of his suit was not in the Spanish style, but it was discreet and sober in color.

He was going to need a horse—that was the first thing. He could walk ten miles, but doing so in his court shoes would be both slow and painful—and making the round-trip of twenty miles on foot . . . He glanced up at the sky; it was well past noon. Granted, in this latitude, the sun wouldn't set before eight or nine o'clock, but . . .

"Why the devil didn't I ask Stubbs what the word for 'horse' is?" he muttered under his breath, threading his way through a district of fragrant market stalls filled with fruit—he recognized plantains, of course, and papayas, mangoes, coconuts, and pineapples, but there were odd dark-green things that he'd not seen before, with pebbly skins, and lighter-green objects that he thought *might* be custard apples—whatever they were, they smelled delicious. His stomach growled—despite the octopus, he was starving—but then his head snapped round as he smelled something of a distinctly different nature. Fresh manure.

IT WAS VERY LATE by the time he finally returned to Casa Heche-varria that night. A full moon sailed high overhead, and the air was thick with smoke and orange blossom and the smell of slowly roasting meat. He'd eaten in Cojimar easily enough, merely pointing at things in the tiny market square and offering what appeared to be the smaller coins in his pouch, but Cojimar was no more than a sunstruck distant memory, and he was starving again.

He slid off the rented mule, wrapped the creature's reins over the railing in front of the house, and went to hammer on the door. His arrival had been noticed, though, and soft lantern light flooded out upon him as he came up the shallow wooden steps.

"Is that you, me lord?" Tom Byrd, bless him, stood framed in the open doorway, lantern in hand and round face creased with worry.

"What's left of me," Grey said. He cleared his throat, clogged with dust, spat into the flowering bush by the portico, and limped into the house. "Get someone to see to the mule, will you, Tom?"

"Right away, me lord. What's amiss with your foot, though?" Tom fixed an accusing gaze on Grey's right foot.

"Nothing." Grey made his way into the *sala,* dimly lit by a small candle before a holy picture of some sort—there were things with wings in it, which must be angels—and sat down with a sigh of relief. "The heel of my shoe came off whilst I was helping the mule out of a rocky ditch."

"He fell into a ditch with you, me lord?" Tom was deftly lighting more candles with a spill and now lifted this in order to examine Grey more closely. "I thought mules was meant to be sure-footed."

"There's nothing wrong with his feet, either," Grey assured him, leaning back and closing his eyes for a moment. The candlelight made red patterns on the insides of his eyelids. "I'd stopped for a piss, and he took the opportunity of my inattention to walk down into said ditch, which he did without the slightest difficulty, by the way. There were some of these things growing on the bushes there that he wanted to eat." Fumbling in his pocket, Grey produced three or four small, smooth green fruits.

"I tried to lure him out with a handful, but he was happy as he was, and eventually I was obliged to resort to force." Said force being applied by two young black women passing by, who had laughed at Grey's predicament but then resolved it, one of the women tugging at the reins and addressing the mule in what sounded like deeply pejorative terms while her friend prodded it sternly in the backside with a stick. Grey yawned hugely. At least he'd learned the word for mule—*mula,* which seemed very reasonable—along with a few other things that might come in handy.

"Is there any food, Tom?"

"Those are guavas, me lord," Tom said, nodding at the little fruits, which Grey placed on a side table. "You make jelly from 'em, but they maybe won't poison you if you eat 'em raw." He'd knelt and got Grey's shoes off in a matter of seconds, then stood and deftly plucked the battered wig off Grey's head, viewing it with an expression of deep disapproval. "I mean, if you can't wait while I go rouse the cook."

"Don't do that. It must be past midnight." Grey dubiously prodded one of the guavas, which seemed unripe—it was hard as a golf ball.

"Never mind, me lord, there'll be cold stuff in the larder," Tom assured him. "Oh—" he added, stopping at the door, wig dangling from one hand, "I forgot to say as Her Grace is gone."

"Her Gr—what? Where the devil has she gone?" Grey sat up straight, all thoughts of food, bed, and sore feet vanishing.

"A note came from a Señora Valdez late this morning, me lord, saying as how Mrs. Stubbs and her little girl was both ill with fever and asking would Her Grace please come. So she went," he added unnecessarily, and vanished, too. *"Chingado huevón!"* Grey said, standing up.

"What did you say, me lord?" Tom's voice came from somewhere down the hall.

"I don't know. Never mind. Get the food, please, Tom. And beer, if there is any."

A faint laugh, cut off by the muffled thump of a swinging door. He looked round the room, wanting to do something violent, but an ancient cat curled up on the back of a stuffed chair opened its great green eyes and glared at him out of the twilight, disconcerting him.

"Bloody hell," he muttered, and turned away. So, not only were Olivia and family *not* headed back to Havana, his mother had decamped—how long ago had she left? She couldn't have made it to the Valdez plantation before dark; she must be somewhere on the road—and as for Rodrigo and Azeel, God knew where *they* were. Had they even reached Olivia's rural hideaway yet?

He strode restlessly to and fro, the stone-tiled floor cool through his stockings. He had no idea in which direction the Valdez plantation lay; how far might it be from Cojimar?

Not that it mattered, if Olivia and her daughter were too ill to travel. A moment ago, his mind had been as exhausted as his body, empty of thought. Now he felt as though his head were filled with ants, all rushing in different directions, each with tremendous determination.

He could find a wagon. But how sick were they? He couldn't load desperately ill people into a wagon, drive them ten, twenty, thirty miles over rocky trails, and then decant them into a boat, which might take *how* long to reach a safe haven. . . . —What about food and water? The *peón*—that's what someone had called him, he had no idea what it meant—with whom he'd arranged to rent a small boat had promised water;—he could buy food, but—Jesus, how many people could he get aboard? Could he leave Rodrigo and Azeel, to be rescued later? No, he'd need them to talk with the boatman, and to help, if half his passengers were prostrate and heaving, needing to be tended. What if more of the party fell ill on the way?

What if the boatman succumbed to fever? What if his mother caught the fever and died at sea?

He could all too easily envision himself making landfall on some god-forsaken shore of the southern colonies with a boatload of his dead or dying family and servants . . .

"No!" he said aloud, clenching his fists. "No, that's bloody not going to happen."

"What's not going to happen?" Tom inquired, backing into the room with a small wheeled table, festooned with edibles. "There's a *lot* of beer, me lord. You could bathe in it, should the fancy take you."

"Don't tempt me." He closed his eyes briefly and took several deep breaths. "Thank you, Tom."

Plainly, he couldn't do anything tonight, and no matter what he did in the morning, he'd do it better if he had food and rest.

Hungry as he'd been half an hour before, his appetite seemed now to have deserted him. He sat down, though, and forced himself to eat. There were small patties of some kind of blood sausage, made with onions and rice, a hard cheese, the light, thin-crusted Cuban bread—he thought he'd heard someone call it a *flauta,* could that be right? Pickled vegetables of some kind. Beer. More beer.

Tom was hovering nearby, quiet but watchful.

"Go to bed, Tom. I'll be fine."

"That's good, me lord." Tom didn't bother trying to look as though he believed Grey; there was a deep crease between his valet's brows. "Is Captain Stubbs all right, me lord?"

Grey took a deep breath and another mouthful of beer.

"He was quite well when we parted this afternoon. As for tomorrow . . ." He hadn't meant to tell Tom anything *until* tomorrow; no point in destroying his sleep and peace of mind. But from the look on his young valet's face, it was much too late for any such kindly procrastinations.

"Sit down," Grey said. "Or, rather, get another cup and then sit down."

By the time he had finished explaining matters to Tom, nothing remained of his meal save crumbs.

"And Captain Stubbs means to make these slaves come into Havana and . . . do what?" Tom looked both horrified and curious.

"That, fortunately, is Captain Stubbs's concern. Did my mother say anything about the state of Olivia and her daughter? How ill they might actually be?"

Tom shook his head.

"No, me lord. But from the look on her face—Her Grace's face, I mean—the news must've been pretty bad. I'm sorry to say. She even left her story behind." Tom's face was grave in the flickering shadows. He'd lighted half a dozen thick candles, and despite muslin covering the windows, clouds of tiny insects had filtered into the room like dust, their minuscule shadows frantic on the dim white walls.

The sight made Grey itch. He'd been ignoring insects all day and sported more than a dozen mosquito bites on neck and arms. A high, mocking *zeeeee!* sang past his ear, and he slapped at it in futile reflex. The gesture made Tom brighten.

"Oh!" he said. "Wait a bit, me lord, I've got summat for you."

He returned almost at once with a stoppered vial of blue glass, looking pleased with himself.

"Try that, me lord," he said, handing it to his employer. Grey pulled the stopper, and a delicious, rich scent floated out.

"Coconut oil," Tom said proudly. "The cook uses it, and she gave me some. I mixed the mint into it, for good measure, but she says the mosquitoes don't like the oil. Flies do," he added judiciously, "but most of them don't bite."

"Thank you, Tom." Grey had shucked his coat to eat; he rolled up his shirtsleeves and anointed himself, rubbing it into every inch of exposed skin. Something occurred to him.

"What did you mean, Tom? About my mother leaving her story behind—a book of some sort?"

"Well, I don't know as whether it *might* be a book," Tom said dubiously. "It's not one yet, but the servants say she writes some of it every day, so sooner or later . . ."

"She's *writing* a book?"

"So Dolores said, me lord. It's in there." He turned and lifted his chin toward the secretaire that Grey had seen his mother use—Christ, had it been only this morning?

Consumed by curiosity, Grey got up and opened the secretaire. Sure enough, there was a small stack of written pages, neatly bound with blue tape. The page on top was a title page—evidently she *did* mean it to be a book. It said, simply, *My Life*.

"A memoir?"

Tom shrugged.

"Dunno, me lord. None of the servants can read English, so they don't know."

Grey was torn between amusement, curiosity, and a certain unease. To the best of his knowledge, his mother had led a rather adventurous life—and he was well aware that his knowledge of that life was limited, by unspoken mutual consent. There were a lot of things he didn't want her to know about his own life; he could respect her secrets. Though, if she was writing them down . . .

He touched the manuscript lightly, then closed the lid of the secretaire. Food, beer, and the living, candlelit silence of the Casa Hechevarria had quieted both his body and his mind. He could think of a thousand possibilities, but in fact, there was only one thing he could *do:* ride to the Valdez plantation as fast as he could and assess the situation when he got there.

Two weeks—about—before the British fleet arrived. Two weeks minus one. God willing, that would be enough time for him to sort things out.

"What did you say, Tom?"

Tom was piling up the empty dishes on the table but stopped to answer him.

"I said, that word you said—*huevón?*"

"Oh. Yes, I heard it from a young lady I met on the road from Cojimar. Do you know what it means?"

"Well, I know what Juanito *says* it means," Tom replied, striving for accuracy. "He says it means a chap what's lazy because his balls are too big to stir himself." Tom gave Grey a sidelong glance. "A lady said that to you, me lord?"

"She was speaking to the mule—or at least I hope she was speaking to the mule." Grey stretched himself, feeling the joints of his shoulders and arms pop, inviting the caress of sleep. "Go to bed, Tom. It will be a long day tomorrow, I'm afraid."

He paused on his way out, to look at the painting of the things with wings. They were angels, rendered crudely but with a simplicity that made them oddly moving. Four of them hovered protectively over an infant Christ, lying in his manger of straw, asleep. And where was Stubbs sleeping tonight? In a cold spring field, a dim tobacco shed?

"God bless you, Malcolm," he whispered, and went to seek his bed.

A MODEST COUGH woke him, well after dawn, to find Tom Byrd beside his bed, holding a tray containing breakfast, a steaming cup of the local equivalent of tea, and a note from his mother.

"Her Grace met Rodrigo and Azeel late last night," Tom informed him. "Them being on the way back posthaste to fetch her, and happen as how she stopped at the same inn where they were stopping to water their horses."

"She—my mother—isn't traveling by herself, surely?" At this stage of her life, he wouldn't put it past her, but . . .

"Oh, no, me lord," Tom assured him, with a slightly reproachful look. "She took Eleana and Fatima and three good lads by way of escort. Her Grace ain't afraid of things, but she's no ways reckless, as you might say."

Grey detected a certain emphasis on "she's" that he might have taken personally but chose to ignore in favor of reading his mother's message.

> *Dear John,*
>
> *I trust Tom Byrd has told you that Olivia sent Word asking me to come to her at Hacienda Valdez. I met your two Servants at a Hovel somewhere on the Road, they being on their Way back with a similar but more detailed Message, this one written by the local Priest.*
> *Padre Cespedes says that nearly everyone in the House is affected by the Illness, which he—having seen many Occurrences of Fever during his Years serving God near the Zapata Swamp—is sure is not a relapsing Fever, like the tertian Ague, but is almost certainly the Yellow Jack.*

A small shock ran through him. "Fever" was a vague word, which might mean anything from a touch of the sun to malaria. Even "ague" might be a passing ill, easily shaken off. But "yellow jack" was stark and definite as a knife in the chest. Most of his army career had involved postings in northern climes; the closest he had come to the dread disease was the sight of ships—now and then—in Kingston Harbor, flying the yellow quarantine flag. But he'd seen the corpses being carried off those ships, too.

His hands had gone cold, and he wrapped one around the hot pottery cup while he read the rest.

> *Don't come here, unless I write to say so. There is one thing to be said for the Yellow Jack, which is that it is fearfully quick. All will likely be resolved—one Way or the Other—within a Week. That may leave enough Time in which to execute your original Intent. If not . . . not.*
> *I think I will see you again, but should God will otherwise, tell Paul and Edgar, Hal and his family, that I love them, tell George— well, tell him that he knows my Heart and what I would say were we together. And for you, John . . . you are my dearest Son and I carry my Thought of you through all that lies before us.*
>
> *Your Most Affectionate Mother*

John swallowed several times before he could pick up the cup and drink from it. If she had ridden through the night, which seemed likely, she might be arriving at the plantation now. To meet . . .

Grey said something very obscene in German, under his breath. He put the cup back and swung out of bed, thrusting the letter at Tom; he couldn't speak coherently enough to transmit the contents.

He had to piss, and did so. This elemental act gave him some semblance of control, and he shoved the utensil back under the bed and straightened up.

"Tom, go and ask where the nearest doctor is to be found. I'll dress myself."

Tom gave him a look, but not the look of profound doubt that might have been expected in response to his last statement. This was a very patient look, and one much older than Tom's years.

"Me lord . . ." he said, very gently, and set the letter on the chest of drawers. "If Her Grace wanted you to send a doctor, she'd've said so, don't you think?"

"My mother has very little faith in doctors." Neither did Grey, but, dammit, what *else* was he to do? "That doesn't mean one might not . . . help."

Tom looked at him for a long moment, then nodded soberly and went.

John could indeed dress himself, though his hands shook so much that he decided to forgo shaving. Malcolm's ghastly wig lay on the chest of drawers beside his mother's letter, looking like a dead animal. Ought he wear it?

Why? he wondered. He couldn't hide his Englishness from the doctor. He probably should send Jacinto to talk to the doctor, in any case. But he couldn't bloody stand to stay in the house, doing nothing. He picked up the now-lukewarm cup and drained the bitter contents. Christ, what *was* this stuff?

He rubbed more of Tom's coconut-oil concoction into his exposed skin, brushed his hair and bound it simply with a ribbon, then strode out to see what Tom had found out from the other servants.

They were on the patio, which seemed the center of the house. The usual cheerful racket was much subdued, though, and Ana-Maria crossed herself and bobbed a curtsy when she saw him.

"Lo siento mucho, señor," she said. *"Su madre . . . su prima y los ninos—"* She waved a graceful hand outward, encompassing his mother, Olivia, and the children, then again inward, this time indicating all the servants around her, and laid the hand on her heart, looking at him with a great compassion in her softly lined face. *"Tenemos dolor, señor."*

He took her meaning clearly, if not every word, and bowed low to her, nodding to the other servants as he straightened.

"Muchas gracias . . ." Señora? Señorita? Was she married? He didn't know, so he just repeated, *"Muchas gracias,"* with more emphasis.

Tom wasn't among the servants; he'd likely gone to talk to Jacinto about doctors. John bowed again to the servants generally and turned toward the house.

There were voices toward the front of the house, speaking very rapid Spanish, with an occasional baffled word from Tom edging its way into the conversation. Curious, John made his way past the *sala* and into the small vestibule, where he found Jacinto and Tom blocking the front door and heard a woman's voice outside, raised in agitation, saying his name.

"Necessito hablar con el Señor Grey! Ahorita!"

"What's going on?" He spoke sharply, and the two men turned toward him, allowing him a view of a yellow bandanna and the desperate face of Inocencia.

She seized the moment and pushed her way between the butler and Tom, snatched a crumpled note from her bosom, and thrust it into Grey's hand. Then she fell to her knees, clutching the hem of his coat.

"Por favor, señor!"

The note was limp with the sweat of her body, and the ink had blurred a little but was still clearly readable. There was neither salutation nor signature, and it was very short:

I'm nabbed, old cock. Your ball.

"WHAT DOES THIS MEAN, *señor?*" Jacinto had been reading the note over his shoulder, without the slightest attempt to pretend he wasn't. "This is . . . not English, is it?"

"It is," he assured the butler, carefully folding the note and putting it in his pocket. He felt as though someone had punched him in the chest, very hard, and he had trouble catching his breath.

It was English, all right—but English that no one but an Englishman would understand. And not even an Englishman like Tom—who was frowning at Inocencia in puzzlement—would know the meaning of that last, paralyzing sentence.

Your ball.

Grey swallowed, tasting the last bitterness of the breakfast drink, and made himself breathe deep. Then he stooped and raised Inocencia to her feet. She was gasping for breath, too, he saw, and there were tracks of dried tears on her cheeks.

"The consul has been arrested?" he asked. She looked helplessly from him to Jacinto, who coughed and translated what Grey had said. She nodded violently, biting her lower lip.

"Está en El Morro," she managed, gulping, and added something else that Grey couldn't follow. A quick back and forth, and Jacinto turned to Grey, his long old face very grave.

"This woman says that your friend was arrested at the city wall last night and has been taken to El Morro. That is where the *gobierno*—the government, excuse me—where they keep prisoners. This . . . lady"—he inclined his head, giving Inocencia the benefit of the doubt—"she saw

Señor Stubbs being taken to the governor's office soon after dawn, and so she waited nearby and followed when they took him down to—" He broke off to ask Inocencia a sharp question. She shook her head and said something in reply.

"He is not in the dungeon," Jacinto reported. "But he is locked in a room where they put gentlemen when it is necessary to contain them. She was able to come and talk to him through the door, once the guards had left, and he wrote this note and told her to hurry and bring it to you at once, before you left the city." Jacinto shot Grey a glance but then coughed and looked away. "He said you would know what to do."

Grey felt a black dizziness come over him and a prickle of rising hair on the back of his neck. His lips felt stiff.

"Did he, indeed."

"YOU CAN'T, ME LORD!" Tom stared at him, aghast.

"I'm very much afraid you're right, Tom," he said, striving for calm. "But I don't see that I have any choice but to try."

He thought Tom was going to be sick; the young valet's face was pale as the morning mist that blanketed the tiny garden where they'd gone for a bit of privacy. Grey was himself just as pleased that he hadn't had a chance to eat breakfast; he recalled Jamie Fraser telling him once, in inimitable Scottish fashion, that his "wame was clenched like a fist," a phrase that described his own present sensation to a T.

He'd have given a lot to have Fraser beside him on this occasion.

He'd have given almost as much to have Tom.

As it was, he was apparently going into battle supported by a stuttering ex-zombie, an African woman of unpredictable temper and known homicidal tendencies, and Malcolm Stubbs's concubine.

"It will be fine," he told Tom firmly. "Inocencia will provide an introduction to the ringleaders and establish my *bona fides*." And if she failed to convince these men that Grey had any such qualifications, all of them would likely be for the chop within seconds: He'd seen machetes wielded with casually murderous ease yesterday—God, was it only yesterday?—by field hands on his way to Cojimar.

"And Rodrigo and Azeel will be there to help me speak to them," he added, with a little more confidence. To his surprise, when he had put the situation before them, the Sanchezes had shared a long marital look, then nodded soberly and said they would go.

"Rodrigo's a good 'un," Tom admitted reluctantly. "But he won't be no good to you in a fight, me lord." His own fists had been clenched throughout the conversation, and it was clear that he had a higher opinion of his own abilities in that regard.

Actually, Grey thought, he might be right. Used as he was to Tom's constant presence, he hadn't taken conscious notice, but his valet was no longer the pie-faced seventeen-year-old who had bluffed his way into Grey's service. Tom had grown a few inches, and while not in Malcolm Stubbs's class in the matter of bulk, he'd definitely filled out. His shoulders were square and his freckled forearms nicely muscled. However . . .

"If it comes to that sort of fight, it wouldn't matter if I had an entire company of infantry with me," he said. He smiled at his valet with true affection. "And besides, Tom:—I cannot depend on anyone but you to see to things here. You must go with Jacinto to find a doctor—cost is no consideration; I'm leaving you with all of our English money, and there's enough gold there to buy half of Havana—and then take the man to the Valdez plantation, along with any medicines he thinks useful. I've written a note to my mother—" He reached into his bosom and withdrew a small folded square, sealed with smoky candle wax and stamped with his smiling half-moon signet. "See that she gets that."

"Yes, me lord." Tom glumly accepted the note and tucked it away.

"And then find someplace nearby to stay. Don't stay in the house; I don't want you to be exposed to the fever. But keep an eye on things: Visit twice a day, make sure the doctor does what he can, give Her Grace any assistance she'll let you give, and send back reports every day as to the state of things. I don't know when I'll get them"—*or if*— "but send them anyway."

Tom sighed but nodded.

Grey stopped, unable to think of anything else. The *casa* was well awake by now, and there was a muted sense of bustle in the distant patio, a rising scent of boiling beans and the sweetness of fried plantains. He hadn't told the house servants anything of his own unspeakable mission—they couldn't help, and to know anything at all of it would put both himself and them in danger. But they knew about the situation at Hacienda Valdez, and he'd heard the murmur of prayers and the clicking of rosary beads when he'd passed by the patio a few minutes ago. It was oddly comforting.

He reached out and clasped Tom's hand, squeezing.

"I trust you, Tom," he said softly.

Tom's Adam's apple bobbed in his throat. His deft, sturdy fingers turned and squeezed back.

"I know, me lord," he said. "You can."

FOUR DAYS LATER—it had taken more time than anticipated to find what was needed—Lord John Grey stood naked in the middle of a grove of mangoes, on a hill overlooking the hacienda of the Mendez family.

He'd seen the big house as they rode into the plantation, a sprawling establishment of rooms added over the years, odd wings sprouting from unexpected places, outbuildings scattered near it in an untidy constellation. *One of the complicated constellations,* he thought, looking down on it. *Cassiopeia, maybe, or Aquarius. One of the ones where you just take the ancient astronomer's word for what you're looking at.*

The windows in the main house had been lighted, with servants passing to and fro like shadows in the dusk, but he had been too far away to hear any of the noises of the place, and he was left with a queer sensation of having seen something ghostly that might suddenly be swallowed by the night.

In fact, it had been, in the sense that the hacienda was invisible from his present situation—and a good thing, too. His traveling clothes lay puddled on the leaf mold in which his bare feet were sunk, and small insects were treating his private parts with an unseemly familiarity. This caused him to rummage his pack first for the bottle of coconut–mint elixir and apply this lavishly before getting dressed.

Not for the first time—nor, he was sure, the last—he deeply regretted the absence of Tom Byrd. He *was* actually capable of dressing himself, though both he and Tom acted on the tacit assumption that he wasn't. But what he missed most at the moment was the sense of solemn ceremony that attended Tom's dressing him in full uniform. It was as though he assumed a different persona with scarlet coat and gold lace, Tom's respect giving him belief in his own authority, as though he put on not only uniform but armor and office.

He could bloody use that belief just now. He swore softly under his breath as he struggled into the moleskin breeches and brushed bits of leaf off each foot before pulling on his silk stockings and boots. It was a gamble, but he felt that the chances of these men taking him seriously, listening to him, and—above all—trusting him would be increased if he appeared not just as a stand-in for Malcolm Stubbs but as the incarnation of England, as it were: a true representative of the king. They had to trust that he could do what he said he would do for them, or it was all up. For the *hacendados*—and for him.

"Wouldn't do the bloody navy any good, either," he muttered, tying his neckcloth by feel.

Done at last, his traveling clothes bundled into the pack, he heaved a sigh of relief and stood still for a minute to gather himself, settle into the uniform.

He'd had no idea mango trees grew to such a size; this was an old grove, the trees each more than a hundred feet in height, the leaves rising and falling gently on the evening breeze, making a sound like the sea overhead. Something slithered heavily in the fallen leaves near him and he froze. But the serpent—if that's what it was—continued on its way, untroubled by his presence.

Rodrigo, Azeel, and Inocencia were where he had left them, no more than a hundred yards away, but he felt entirely alone. His mind had gone blank, and he welcomed that respite. Windfalls of unripe fruit knocked down by a storm lay all around like pale-green cricket balls in the leaves, but the fruit still on the trees had gone yellow—he'd seen it in the twilight as they came up into the grove—and had begun to blush crimson. Now it was dark, and he only sensed the mangoes when he brushed a low-lying branch and felt the heavy swing of the fruit.

He was walking, not having made up his mind to do so nor remembering the taking of the first step, but walking, propelled into motion by a sense that it was time.

He came down through the grove and found Rodrigo and the girls on their feet, in murmured conversation with a tall, spare young woman—Inocencia's cousin, Alejandra, who would take them to the tobacco shed.

All of them turned to see him, and Alejandra's eyes widened, gleaming in the moonlight.

"Hijo," she said in admiration.

"Thank you, madam," he said, and bowed to her. "Shall we go?"

HE'D IMAGINED IT vividly, from Malcolm's account. The bulk of the big tobacco barn, the dark, the whispering of the drying leaves overhead, the sense of waiting men . . . What Malcolm hadn't mentioned was the overpowering scent that lay in a cloud over the shed, a thick incense that reached out to grab him by the throat from thirty feet away. It wasn't unpleasant, by any means, but it was strong enough to make him breathe shallowly for a moment—and he needed all the breath he could get.

Cano. That was the name of the man he must convince. Cano was headman of the slaves of the Mendez plantation. There was a headman from Saavedra, too, named Hamid, but Alejandra said that it was Cano's opinion that counted most heavily among the slaves

"If he says yes, they all will do it," she had assured Grey.

There was a great deal more to the barn's atmosphere than the heavy scent of tobacco. He could smell the reek of constant sweat the instant he stepped inside—and the sharp, dark stink of angry men.

There was a single lantern burning, hung from a nail in one of the uprights supporting the high roof. It made a small pool of light, but the glow of it diffused much farther, showing him the men massed in the shadows. No more than the curve of a skull, a shoulder, the gleam of light on black skin, the whites of staring eyes. Below the lantern stood two men, turned to meet him.

There was no question which was Cano. A tall black man, wearing only short, ragged breeches, though his companion (and most of the men in the shadows, as a sidelong glimpse confirmed) was dressed in both breeches and shirt and wore a spotted bandanna tied around his head.

No question why, either. Gray scars mottled Cano's back and arms like barnacle scars on an old whale—the marks of whips and knives. The man watched Grey approach and smiled.

Smiled to show that his front teeth were gone, but the canines remained, sharp and stained brown with tobacco.

"Mucho gusto, señor," he said. His voice was light and mocking. Grey bowed, very correctly. Alejandra had come in behind him, and she made the introductions in soft, rapid Spanish. She was nervous; her hands were twisted in her apron and Grey could see sweat shining in the hollows under her eyes. Which was her lover? he wondered, this man or Hamid?

"Mucho gusto," Grey said politely, when she had finished, and bowed to her. "Madam—will you be so good as to tell these gentlemen that I have brought with me two interpreters, so that we can be assured of understanding one another?"

At this cue, Rodrigo came in, Azeel a pace or two behind him. She looked as though she were wading into a pool filled with crocodiles, but Rodrigo's manner was cool and dignified. He wore his best black suit, with immaculate white linen that shone like a beacon in the grubby brown light of the barn.

There was a palpable ripple of interest—and a just-as-palpable hostility at sight of him. Grey felt it like a jab in the stomach. Christ, was he going to get Rodrigo killed, as well as himself?

And they don't even know what he is yet, he thought. He'd been told—often enough to believe it—that the fear of zombies was so great that sometimes even the rumor of it was enough that a crowd would fall upon the suspected person and beat them to death.

Well, best get on with it. He wasn't armed, save for the regimental dirk at his belt. Nothing was going to get them through this but words, so best start talking.

This he did, presenting his compliments (that got the breath of a laugh—encouraging . . .) and stating that he came as the friend and representative of Malcolm Stubbs, whom they knew. Nods of wary approval. He came (he said) also as the representative of the King of England, who intended to overthrow the Spaniards in Cuba and take the island.

This was pretty bold, and Azeel stammered a little as she said it for him, but it went over quite well; it appeared that the crowd was quite united with the king in this desire.

"My friend, Señor Stubbs, has asked your help in this endeavor," Grey said, looking deliberately from one side of the barn to the other, speaking to all of them. "I have come to counsel with you and to decide how best to accomplish our desires, so that—"

"*Dónde está el Señor Malcolm?*" Cano interrupted him. "*Por qué él no está aquí?*"

That didn't need interpretation, but for the sake of protocol, he let Azeel translate it before replying that, alas, Señor Malcolm had been arrested and was imprisoned in Morro Castle. Hence he, John Grey, had come to carry out Señor Malcolm's plan.

A small rumble of doubt, a shuffling of bare feet in the dust.

"For your assistance in this matter, Señor Malcolm promised you your freedom. I promise this, too." He spoke as simply as he could, hoping that this would carry sincerity.

Exhalations, quiet murmurs. They were worried—and were more than right to be, he thought. The barn was hot, packed with so many men, and damp with their sweat and the exudations of the drying tobacco leaves. Sweat was seeping through his linen.

Suddenly the other man—Hamid, it must be—said something abrupt and jerked his chin at Grey. The man was bearded, and it occurred to Grey that perhaps he was a Mussulman.

"This gentleman wants to know how you will accomplish the things you speak of," Azeel said, glancing at Grey. "You are only one man. Do you have soldiers, weapons?"

Grey wondered what the views of the Prophet were with regard to zombies . . . because it was clear that he was going to have to use Rodrigo.

Rodrigo himself stood close beside his wife, his face calm and unmoving, despite the weight of eyes upon him, but Grey saw him straighten a little and take a deep breath.

"Tell Señor Hamid"—and Grey bowed to the bearded man—"that I am indeed one man . . . but I am an Englishman. And I am a man of my word. To show that this is true, I have brought my servant, Rodrigo Sanchez, who will tell them why they may believe me and trust what I say."

Heart thumping audibly in his ears, Grey stepped back and inclined his head toward Rodrigo. He saw Rodrigo squeeze Azeel's hand lightly, and drop it, before he moved forward.

Unhurried, composed, civilized in a way that these men had never known, Rodrigo picked up a wooden bucket standing near the wall, carried this to a central spot in the light of the lantern, turned it upside down, set it on the floor, and sat down. Very slowly, Azeel moved to stand behind him, her eyes fixed on the men in the shadows.

Rodrigo began to speak, his voice deep, soft but carrying. There was an audible intake of massed breath from the audience, and a ripple of horror moved through the barn. Azeel turned to Grey.

"My husband, he says . . ." Azeel's voice trembled, and she stopped to clear her throat. Then she straightened and, putting her hand on her husband's shoulder, spoke clearly.

"He says this: *'I have been dead. I died in the hands of a* houngan, *and I woke in my grave, smelling the rot of my own body. I could not move—how should I move? I was dead. And then, years later, I felt the air on my face and a hand on my arm. The* houngan *pulled me from my grave and told me that I was indeed dead. But that now I was a zombie.'"*

Grey felt the ripple of horror that moved through the room, and heard the intake of massed breath, the shocked murmur that had broken out at this. But Azeel put both hands on Rodrigo's shoulders and glared over his head, turning her eyes from one side of the room to the other.

"I tell you—listen!" she said violently. *"Escuchen!"*

Grey saw Cano jerk back a little, whether from affront or shock, he couldn't tell. But the man gave an explosive snort and over the murmuring in the shed said loudly, *"Háblanos!"* The murmurs stopped abruptly, and Azeel turned her head to look at Cano, the light of the lantern gleaming on her skin, in her eyes.

"Háblame," she said softly to Rodrigo. *"Sólo a mí. Háblame."* Speak to me. Only to me.

Rodrigo's hand rose slowly and rested on hers. He raised his chin and went on, Azeel translating softly for Grey as he spoke:

"I was dead, and a zombie, in the power of an evil man, in the power of hell. But this man—" He moved his head a little, indicating Grey. "This man, he came for me. He came alone, into the high mountains, and he walked into the cavern of Damballa, the great serpent—"

At this, exclamations and agitations broke out in such a confusion of noise that Rodrigo was obliged to stop speaking. This he did and went on sitting there, unmoved as a statue.

God, he's beautiful. The thought sparked for a moment in Grey's mind and then vanished as Rodrigo raised a slow hand, palm out. He waited, and the noise died away in a smother of shushings.

"In the cavern of serpents, this man walked—alone—through the dark and through demons. He turned the *houngan*'s magic back upon himself, and then he came out of the cave and he took me back. By his own power, he raised me from death."

There was a moment's silence, as Azeel's soft words vanished among the hidden leaves and the dark bodies. Then Rodrigo nodded, once, and said simply, *"Es verdad."*

It's true.

Utter silence for a long moment, and then a murmur, another. Wonder. Doubt. Amazement. Grey thought the language had changed; they weren't all speaking Spanish but some other language—or perhaps languages. African tongues. He caught the word *"houngan,"* and Cano was looking sharply at him, eyes narrowed.

Then the bearded man spoke gruffly to Grey in English, jerking his chin at Rodrigo.

"Tell your zombie to go outside."

Grey exchanged a quick look with Rodrigo, who nodded very slightly and stood up.

"If you will oblige me, Señor Sanchez?" Grey bowed, gesturing toward the door. Rodrigo returned the bow, moving very slowly, and walked with equal slowness to the big open door. Grey thought he might be exaggerating the stiffness of his gait, but perhaps he was imagining that.

Had it worked? *"Your zombie,"* the man had said. Did they believe that he had rescued Rodrigo from the *houngan,* from death, or did they think that he was himself some sort of English *houngan* who controlled Rodrigo and had compelled him to make that speech? Because if so . . .

Rodrigo's black form merged with the night and disappeared. There was a noticeable relaxation of the atmosphere, as though every man there had released a sigh of relief.

Cano and the bearded man exchanged a long look, and after a moment, Hamid nodded reluctantly.

Cano turned to Grey and said something in Spanish. Azeel, who had gone nearly as stiff as her husband as he walked away, pulled her eyes away from the open door and translated Cano's question.

"So, then. How shall we do this thing?"

Grey let out a long, long breath.

Simple as the concept was, it took no little time to explain. Some of the slaves had seen a cannon—all of them had heard one fire, though only in the far distance, when the cannons of the two fortresses were fired on holidays or to salute a ship coming in—but almost none of them had any notion of the operation of a gun.

A space on the floor was swept free of tracks and trampled tobacco leaves and another lantern was brought. The men gathered close. Grey drew the outline of a gun in the reddish dirt with a stick, talking slowly and simply as he explained the loading and firing of a cannon, and repeatedly pointed out the touchhole.

"Here is where they put fire. The powder"—he prodded the barrel—"explodes"—a murmur of confusion, explanations from those who had seen this thing—"and BOOM!" Everyone looked stunned for an instant, then broke into laughter. When the repetitions of "BOOM!" had died down, he pointed again at the touchhole.

"Fire," he said, and waited expectantly.

"Fire!" several voices said happily.

"*Exactamente,*" he said, and, smiling at them, reached into his pocket. "Look."

"*Miren,*" Azeel said, but it was unnecessary. Every eye was fixed on the six-inch metal spike in Grey's hand. He had a large bag of them in his pack, of different sizes, as he'd had to take whatever he could find from the various ironmongers and ship chandlers of Havana, but from what Inocencia and Azeel had been able to tell him of the guns in Morro Castle, he thought they would suffice.

He squatted above his drawing and mimed pushing the spike into the touchhole. Then he pulled a small hammer from his other pocket and pounded the spike vigorously into the dirt.

"No fire," he said, looking up.

"*Bueno!*" said several voices, and there was much murmuring and nudging.

He took a deep breath of the thick, intoxicant air. So far, so good. His heart was thumping audibly in his ears and seemed to be going much faster than usual.

It took much longer to explain the map. Only a few had seen a map or chart before, and it was very difficult for some of them to make the mental connection between lines on a piece of paper and the positions of corridors, doors, rooms, cannon batteries, and powder stores in El Castillo de los Tres Reyes Magos del Morro. They *had* all seen the fortress itself, at least: when they were taken from ships onto the dock, on their way to the slave markets in the city.

Sweat was running down Grey's back under his uniform coat, his body throbbing with the effects of moist heat and mental tension, and he took the coat off, to avoid fainting.

Finally, a consensus of sorts was achieved. Inocencia very bravely said that she would go into the fortress with the men and help to show them where the guns were. This was met with a moment's silence, and then Hamid nodded at her and raised a brow at Cano, who, after a moment's hesitation, also nodded, and a murmur of approval rustled through the men.

Nearly done. He resisted the urge to give in to relief, though. The last item on his agenda might spike his personal guns—or get him killed. He rolled up the crude maps that Inocencia had drawn and handed them ceremoniously to Cano. Then he withdrew from his pack another rolled paper—this one blank—a capped inkwell, and a quill.

His head was not so much spinning as it was floating, and he had some difficulty in fixing his eyes on things. He made an effort, though, and spoke firmly to Cano.

"I will write here that you are performing a great service for the King of England and that I say you should receive your freedom for doing this thing. I am a . . . *God, let me get this right . . . un hombre de gracia,* and I will sign my name." *Hombre de gracia* was as close as Azeel could come to the notion of "nobleman."

He waited, watching their faces, while Azeel translated this. Wary, curious, some—the younger ones—with a touch of hope that stabbed at his heart.

"You must then put down your names. If you do not . . . have letters . . . you can tell me your name, I will write it, and you can make a mark to say it is yours."

Instant alarm, much looking to and fro, the shine and flicker of eyes in the dark, agitation, a gabble of voices. He raised a hand and waited patiently. It took several minutes, but at last they calmed enough for him to speak again.

"I will go with you into the castle, too," he pointed out. "What if I am killed? Then I will not be there to tell the king you should have your freedom. But this will tell him." He tapped a finger on the blank sheet.

"What if some of you become lost in the city after we leave the castle? If you go later to the chief of the English sailors and say to him that you have done this great thing and now you must be free, how will he believe you?" He tapped again.

"This will speak for you. You will tell the English chief your name, and he will see it on this paper and know what you say is true."

". . . *es verdad.*" Azeel looked as though she, too, was about to faint from the strain, the heat, and—no doubt—the fear of the situation, but her voice was loud and firm.

Cano and Hamid had drawn together, were engaged in a low-voiced debate. Sweat was dripping from the tail of Grey's hair; he could feel it hitting the small of his back through his shirt with the regularity of grains of sand—slow grains of sand, he thought wryly, very slow—in an hourglass.

At last they settled things between them, though, and Cano took several steps forward, to face Grey himself. He spoke, looking intently into Grey's face from a distance of no more than a foot; Grey could smell the man's breath, hot with tobacco and with a hint of rot from his teeth.

"He says," Azeel said, and stopped to work a little saliva into her mouth, "he says that they will do it. But you must make three papers—one for you, one for him, and one for Hamid, because if you are killed and have the only paper, what good is it?"

"Very reasonable," Grey said gravely. "Yes, I will do that."

The sense of relief ran through his limbs like warm water. But he wasn't quite done yet.

"One thing," Grey said, and took a breath. Too deep a breath; it made him dizzy, and he took another, shallower.

Cano inclined his head, listening.

"The people in the haciendas—the Mendez family, the Saavedras—I know what your intention was, and we will say no more of that. But you must assure me that these people will not be harmed, will not be killed."

". . . *Ellos no serán asesinados.*" Azeel's voice was soft now, remote, as though she was reading the terms of a contract. Which, Grey reflected, it was, in all justice.

Cano's nostrils flared at that, and there was a low sound—not quite a growl—from the men in the shadows. The sound of it made Grey's scalp contract.

The man nodded, as though to himself, then turned to look into the shadows, first to one side and then the other, deliberate, as a barrister might look to see the temper of a jury. Then he turned back to Grey and nodded again.

"*No los mataremos,*" he said.

"We will not kill them," Azeel whispered.

Grey's heart had stopped thumping and now seemed to be beating with unusual slowness. The thought of fresh, clean air steadied his mind.

Without thinking about it, he spat into his palm, as soldiers and farmers did, and held out his hand. Cano's face went quite blank for an instant but then he nodded, made a small "huh" under his breath, spat in his hand, and clasped Grey's.

He had an army.

TOO LATE. That was his first thought when he heard the firing of artillery in the distance as they approached the city. The British fleet had arrived, and the siege of Havana was begun. A moment's heavy breathing, though, and the panic passed. It didn't matter, he realized, and a wave of relief went over him.

Ever since Malcolm had first sprung this plan on him, the matter of timing had been in his mind: the notion that the slaves' raid must happen just before the arrival of the fleet. But Malcolm's reference had been with respect to his original plan, having the slaves sabotage the boom chain, to allow the fleet into the harbor.

That truly wouldn't have worked, unless the fleet was in sight when the chain was sunk; any delay and the Spaniards would have it raised again. But the spiking of the fortress's guns . . . that would be helpful at any time.

Granted, he thought, tilting his head to try to gauge the direction of the firing, it would certainly be more dangerous to carry out such a mission with the fortress's gun crews in place. On the other hand, said gun crews would be focused entirely on their business. It was very likely that the gun crews would be taken completely unaware. For the first few moments.

It was going to be a bloody business, on both sides. He didn't like the thought but didn't shy away from it. It was war, and he was—once again—a soldier.

Still, his mind was uneasy. He had no doubt of the slaves' ferocity or their will, but to pit completely untrained, lightly armed men against practiced soldiers in close combat . . .

Wait. Perhaps a night attack—could that be managed? He reined his mule in to a walk, the better to think it out.

With the British Navy on their doorstep, the guns of El Morro would never sleep—but neither would they necessarily be manned at full strength during the night watches. He'd seen enough, during his brief excursion to Cojimar, to convince him that the small harbor there was the only possible base for an attack on Morro Castle. What were the distances?

General Stanley had referred repeatedly to an intended siege of Havana. Clearly the navy knew about the boom chain, and, just as clearly, an effective siege must be mounted from the ground, not from ships. So—

"*Señor!*" A shout from the line of wagons broke his train of thought, but he tucked the notion safely away for further analysis. He didn't want the slaves to be butchered, if it could be helped; still less did he want to suffer the same fate.

THEY WERE WELL in sight of the city wall of Havana now. In one way, the fleet's arrival was fortuitous: A city under siege needed food, above all things. Faced with the problem of getting a hundred slaves past the city guard, Hamid had suggested loading the plantation wagons with anything that came to hand and letting each wagon be accompanied by a half dozen men, there presumably to do the unloading and delivery. Between the two plantations, they could muster ten wagons—with driver and assistant, that was eighty men. The rest could easily slip in by ones and twos.

A decent plan, but what, Grey had asked, about the plantations' owners, their servants? It would take time to load wagons, and their departure couldn't be easily concealed. An alarm would be raised, surely?

No, no, he was assured. The wagons were kept in barns near the fields. The loading would happen by night; they would be gone before daylight. And, Cano added, through Azeel, the female slaves who worked in the house could be relied upon to create distractions, as necessary. The thought made him grin his empty black grin, wolf teeth flashing yellow in the lantern light.

It had worked, insofar as no one had come shouting out of the hacienda, demanding to know what was going on as the wagons rumbled out by moonlight. Now, what might happen when the owners and overseers discovered that a hundred able-bodied slaves were missing . . .

But whatever distractions the women had devised had evidently been effective. No one had pursued them.

He stopped the wagons just out of sight of the city gate, had a hasty check-round with the various teams, reassuring the men and making sure everyone knew where and when they were to meet—and that all the machetes were carefully concealed. Even though he had packed away his uniform and was once more in mufti—complete with Malcolm's wig—he thought it better not to come into Havana with the wagons. He would go back to the Casa Hechevarria with Rodrigo and Azeel and find out from Jacinto what the news of the invasion was; Inocencia would try to speak with Malcolm in Morro Castle and, in the process, discover anything in the present situation that might be of strategic value.

"*Muchas gracias,* my dear," he told her, and bowed low over her hand. "Azeel, please tell her that we could not even contemplate this venture without her courage and help. The entire British Navy is in her debt."

Inocencia's lips made a smile, and she bobbed her head in response, but Grey could see that she was trembling with exhaustion, and her brilliant eyes were sunk in her face. Tears quivered on her lashes.

"It will be all right," he said, taking her hand. "We will succeed—and we will rescue Señor Stubbs. I promise you."

She swallowed and nodded, wiping her face on the edge of her filthy apron. Her mouth twitched, as though she meant to say something, but she changed her mind and, pulling her hand free, dropped him a curtsy, turned, and hurried away, lost at once in the crowd of women in the market, all pushing and shouting in an effort to procure food.

"She is afraid," Azeel said quietly, behind him.

She's not the only one . . . He'd felt a coldness at the bone ever since he walked into the tobacco shed, and it hadn't gone away, though the day was bright and sunny. There was a small flame of excitement at the prospect of action, though, and it was normal for the nerves to be raw—

There was a sharp report from the direction of El Morro, echoed at once by another, and he was suddenly on the Plains of Abraham in Quebec, the cannon firing from the walls, and the army waiting, waiting there on the open ground, waiting in the agony of delay . . .

He shook himself like a dog and felt better.

"It will be all right," he said again, firmly, and turned in to the Calle Yoenis.

HE COULD TELL at once that something had happened. There was no singing, no chatter from the patio, no one working in the garden. He did hear muted voices, and food was being cooked—but there was no spice in the air. Only the slightly soapy smell of long-boiled beans and scorched eggs.

He walked rapidly through the empty front rooms, and his heart stopped as he heard a baby's high-pitched squall.

"Olivia?" he called. The muted voices paused, though the baby's mewling continued.

"John?" His mother stepped out of the *sala*, peering into the murk of the unlighted corridor. She was disheveled, her hair in a half-unraveled plait, and she had a tiny baby in her arms.

"Mother." He hurried to her, his heart suddenly feeling as though it had come loose in his chest. She took a step toward him that brought her face into the bar of sunlight from a window, and one look told him.

"Jesus," he said under his breath, and reached out to embrace her, draw her close, as though he could fix her in space, prevent her talking, put off knowing for one minute more. She was shaking.

"Olivia?" he said quietly into her hair, and felt her nod. The baby had stopped fussing but was moving between them, odd, small, tentative proddings.

"Yes," his mother said, and drew a long, quivering breath. He let go of her and she stepped back in order to look him in the face. "Yes, and poor little Ch-Charlotte, too." She bit her lip briefly and straightened herself.

"The yellow fever has two stages," she said, and lifted the child to her shoulder. It had a head like a small cantaloupe, and Grey was reminded shockingly of its father. "If you survive the first stage—it lasts several days—then sometimes you recover. If not, there's a lull in the fever—a day or two when the—the person seems to be improving, but then . . . it comes back."

She closed her eyes for a moment, and he wondered when she had last slept. She looked at once a thousand years old and ageless, like a stone.

"Olivia," she said, and opened her eyes, patting the child's tiny back, "recovered, or seemed to. Then she went into labor, and—" She lifted the baby slightly in illustration. "But the next day . . . it came back. She was dead in—in hours. It took Charlotte a day later . . . she was . . . so small. So fragile."

"I am so sorry," Grey said softly. He had been fond of his cousin, but his mother had raised Olivia from the age of ten, when his cousin had lost her own parents. A thought came to him.

"Cromwell?" he asked, afraid to hear but needing to know. He'd delivered Olivia's son, very much by accident, but as a result had always felt close to the boy.

His mother gave him a watery smile.

"He's fine. The fever never touched him, thank God. Nor this little one." She cupped a hand behind the infant's fuzzy skull. "Her name is Seraphina. Olivia had time . . . to hold her, at least, and give her a name. We christened her at once, in case . . ."

"Give her to me, Mother," he said, and took the child from her arms. "You need to go and sit down, and you need something to eat."

"I'm not—" she began automatically, and he interrupted her.

"I don't care. Go sit down. I'll go and blow up the cook."

She tried to give him a smile, and the twitch of her lips reminded him with a jolt of Inocencia. And everything else. His own mourning would have to wait.

IF YOU *HAD* TO attack a fortress at night, on foot and lightly armed, doing it with black men was distinctly an advantage, Grey thought. The barely risen moon was a crescent, a thread of light against the dark sky. Cano's men had removed their shirts and, dressed only in rough canvas breeches, they were no more than shadows, flowing barefoot and silent through the empty marketplace.

Cano himself materialized suddenly behind Grey's shoulder, announced by a waft of foul breath.

"Ahorita?" he whispered. Now?

Grey shook his head. Malcolm's wig was wadded up in his pocket and he had assumed instead an infantryman's cap—a contrivance of steel plates, punctured and laced together, to be worn under a uniform hat— this covered with a black knitted cap. He felt as though his head were melting, but it would turn the blade of a sword—or a machete.

"Inocencia," he murmured, and Cano grunted in reply and faded back into the night. The girl wasn't yet late; the church bells had only just rung midnight.

Like any self-respecting fortress, El Castillo de los Tres Reyes Magos del Morro—the Castle of the Three Magi of the Hump, as Azeel had kindly translated its full name for him—the hump being the big black rock at the opening of the harbor—had only one way in and one way out. It also had steeply sloping walls on all sides, to deter both climbers and cannonballs.

True, there were small penetrations on the water side, used for the disposal of garbage or inconvenient bodies, or for the arrival of provisions or the secret deliverance of a guest or prisoner held incognito. Those were of no use in the present venture, though, as the only possible approach was by boat.

One bell bonged the quarter hour. Two for the half hour. Grey had just pulled his head covering off in order to avoid fainting when there was a stir in the darkness nearby.

"*Señor?*" said a soft, low voice by his elbow. "*Es listo. Venga!*"

"*Bueno,*" he whispered back. "*Señor Cano?*"

"*Aquí.*" Cano *was aquí,* so quickly that Grey realized the man must have been standing no more than a few feet away.

"*Venga,* then." Grey moved his head toward the fortress, then paused to put on his two caps. By the time he had managed this, they were all there, a breathing mass like a herd of cattle, eyes shining now and then in an errant gleam of light.

He took Inocencia by the arm, to prevent her being lost or trampled, and they walked quietly into the small stone guardhouse that shielded the castle's entrance, for all the world like a bride and groom walking sedately into church, followed by a horde of machete-wielding wedding guests.

This absurd fancy disappeared directly as they stepped into the torchlit room. There were four guards, one slumped over a table, the others on the floor. Inocencia shuddered under his hand, and, glancing at her in the flickering light, he saw that her dark dress was torn at the shoulder, and her lip was bleeding. She had drugged the guards' wine, but evidently it hadn't acted fast enough.

"*Bueno,*" he whispered to her, and squeezed her arm. She didn't smile but nodded, swallowed hard, and gestured toward the door on the other side of the guards' room.

This was the entrance to the fortress proper, portcullis and all, and his heart began to beat in his ears as they passed beneath its teeth with no sound but the shuffle of feet and the occasional clink from the bags of metal spikes.

He had gone over and over the maps of the floors, knew where the batteries were—though not which ones were manned at the moment. Inocencia led them into a broad corridor half-lit by torches, with doors on either side. She jerked her chin upward—a stairway at the end.

Up. He could hear the panting of the men behind him—even barefoot they made a lot of noise; surely they would be heard.

They were. A surprised-looking guard stood at the head of the stair, his musket still on his shoulder. Grey rushed him and knocked him down; the men behind him knocked *him* down and trampled him in their eagerness. There was a gurgle and the smell of blood, and something wet soaked through the knee of his breeches.

Up again, no longer in the lead, following the rush of men. He had lost Inocencia but saw her up ahead, being pulled along by Hamid and another of the Mussulman slaves, heads covered with dark bandannas. Another stair, pushing and shoving, grunting bodies hot for a fight.

The next guard had his musket out and fired on them. Shouts from the guard, though he was quickly borne down. Shouts from beyond him and a draft of cold air—the first battery, on the rooftop.

"Primero!" Grey bellowed, and a gang of slaves rushed the first cannon. He didn't wait to see how they fared; he was already plunging down a stairwell at the far end of the roof, shouting, *"Segundo!"* at the top of his voice, then pawing and shoving through a clot of slaves and cannon crew that had poured after him and collided, struggling in the narrow space at the foot of the stair.

He shouted, *"Tres! Tres!"* but he couldn't be heard. The air was thick with shrieks and curses and the reek of blood and sweat and fury.

He pushed out of the scrum and pressed himself against a wall, panting for breath. They were gone now, out of anyone's control. He heard the dull *bong* of hammer on iron, though—at least one man had remembered their purpose . . . then the ring and clash of others, striking through the riot. Yes!

Suddenly the Mussulman who had accompanied Hamid burst out of the crowd, Inocencia clutched by the arm. He hurled her at Grey like a bag of wheat and he caught her in much the same way, grunting at the impact.

"Jesús, Maria, Jesús, Maria," she was gasping, over and over. She was splattered with blood, blotches showing wet on the black of her dress, and her eyes showed white all around.

"Are you hurt? Er . . . *dolor?*" he shouted in her ear. She stared at him, dazed.

He must get her out. She'd done all she promised.

"Venga!" he shouted in her ear, and jerked her after him, back toward the stair.

"No!" she panted, setting her heels. *"Allí!"* He didn't know that word, but she was dragging him toward the far end of the corridor. This meant leapfrogging squirming bodies on the floor, but he followed her without demur, throwing his body between her and a cannoneer armed with a ramrod. It hit him in the shoulder, numbing his arm, but didn't knock him down. Someone had dropped a bag of spikes, spilling them on the floor, and he nearly fell as these rolled under his feet, clinking on the stones.

They had almost reached the momentary sanctuary of the stairhead when something hit him on the head and he collapsed to his knees. His vision had gone black and his ears were ringing, but through it he could hear Inocencia shrieking at the top of her voice, calling his name.

He struggled blindly, trying to reach the wall so he could get up, but another blow came in from the right. It was a machete—he heard the blade rip the air an instant before the dull *thunk* of metal rang through his head.

Shock and nausea rocked him back against the wall, but he had a hand on the dagger at his waist. He scrabbled it free and, crouching as low as he could, flung himself round on his knees, slashing. He hit someone. The impact jarred the knife from his hand, but his vision was coming back and he found the dagger again, through flashing black and white lights.

Another scream from Inocencia, this one pure terror. He stumbled to his feet, dagger in hand. A scarred back just before him . . . Cano brought down his machete with murderous force and Inocencia dropped to the floor, blood spraying from her head. Without a second's hesitation, Grey thrust the dagger up beneath the man's ribs, as hard as he could.

Cano stiffened, dropped his machete, clattering. He swayed, and fell, but Grey was already by Inocencia's side, scooping her into his arms.

"Fucking bloody hell, oh, bloody hell, please, God . . ." He staggered with her into the stairwell and leaned against the wall for a moment, fighting for breath. She stirred, saying something he couldn't hear for the ringing in his ears.

"No . . ." He shook his head, meaning that he didn't understand, and she flung out a hand, pointing down, emphatically, down, *down!*

"All right." He took a tighter hold and caromed down the narrow stair, slipping and crashing into the stones, then finding his footing once again. He could hear the battle still raging above—but also heard through the fading buzz in his ears the clash of steel and hammers.

He tried to exit at the next landing, but she was having none of it and urged him down, still down. The spots were thickening at the corners of his eyes again, and he smelled damp and seaweed, the brackish scent of low tide.

"Jesus Christ, where are we?" he gasped. He had to set her down but tried to support her with one arm.

"Malcolm," she gasped. "Malcolm," and pointed to a crooked passageway that curved away to the right.

It was like the sort of nightmare that involves endless repetition of something insane, he thought. The last such nightmare hadn't smelled like a dead octopus, though . . .

"¡Aquí!" She squirmed suddenly and he lost his grip on her. She staggered and crashed into a door that looked as though it had been left outdoors for a century or two. *Still pretty solid,* he thought dimly.

"God, do you mean I have to break it *down?*"

She ignored him, swaying as she fumbled in her skirts. Her face, her hair, and her shoulder were drenched with blood, and her hands shook so hard that she dropped the keys as soon as she found them. They landed in a clash of metal, drops of blood blooming on the stones around them.

John fumbled in his sleeve for a handkerchief, in some hope of stopping the bleeding, and there ensued an awkward struggle, him trying to tie the cloth around her head, she bending and snatching vainly at the keys, falling every time she bent over.

Grey finally said something in German and grabbed the keys himself. He thrust the handkerchief into Inocencia's twitching fingers and stabbed at the door.

"Quién es?" said Malcolm's voice, quite loudly, near his ear.

"Es mi, querida!" Inocencia collapsed against the door, palms plastered to the wood, and left streaks of blood as she slid slowly down it. Grey dropped the keys, fell to his knees, and grabbed his handkerchief out of her limp hand. He found Malcolm's wig in his pocket, wadded it, and bound it as tightly to her head as he could. There was a long slash through her scalp, and her left ear was hanging by a thread, but he thought dimly that it wasn't that bad—if she didn't bleed to death.

She was gray as a storm cloud and gasping heavily, but her eyes were open, fixed on the door.

Malcolm had been shouting for the last few minutes, pounding on the door 'til it shook. Grey stood up and kicked it several times. The pounding and shouting stopped for a moment.

"Malcolm?" Grey said, bending to look for the keys. "Bloody get dressed. We're leaving as soon as I get this damn door open."

BY THE TIME they reached the main level of the fortress, most of the noise above had ceased. Grey could still hear shouts and the sounds of an occasional scuffle;—there was a lot of muffled Spanish that had an official tone—the officers of the fortress marshaling men, assessing damage, starting the clearing up.

He'd told the slaves: *"Spike the guns, and run. Don't wait about for your companions or for anything else. Make your way into the city and hide. When you think it's safe, go to Cojimar, where the British ships are. Ask for General Stanley or the admiral. Tell them my name."*

He'd given a letter of explanation, and the document signed by the slaves, to Tom Byrd, with instructions to find General Stanley. He hoped Tom had made it to the siege lines without being shot—but he'd sent Tom because of his face. No one could doubt he was an Englishman, at whatever distance.

The night outside was quiet. He breathed the clean sea air and felt the touch of it soft on his face. Then he touched Malcolm's arm—Malcolm was carrying the girl—and pointed toward Calle Yoenis.

"We'll go to my mother's house," he said. "I'll tell you everything when we get there."

SOME LITTLE TIME later, too restless to sit, he limped from the *sala* into the garden and leaned against a flowering quince tree. His ears still rang with the sounds of steel, and he closed his eyes, seeking silence.

Maricela had assured him that Inocencia would live. She herself had stitched the ear back on and applied a *pulpa* of several herbs whose names Grey didn't recognize. Malcolm was still with her. Grey hadn't had the strength to tell Malcolm that he was now a widower rather than an adulterer. The night would vanish, all too soon, but for the moment, time had no meaning. Nothing need be done.

He couldn't know the extent of the slaves' success—but they *had* been successful. Even in the brief frantic interstices of the fighting, he'd seen a dozen guns spiked, and heard the ring of hammers above as he'd half-fallen down the stairs with Inocencia. As he and Malcolm had made their way out of the fortress with her, he'd heard Spanish shouting from the rooftop, furious and thick with curses.

He stood among the fragrant bushes for what seemed a long time, feeling his heart beat, content simply to be breathing. He stirred, though, at the sounds of the garden gate opening and low voices.

"Tom?" he came out from under his sheltering quince, to find both Tom and Rodrigo—both of whom were amazingly, if flatteringly, delighted to see him.

"We thought you was done for, sure, me lord," Tom said for the third or fourth time, following Grey into the kitchen. "You sure you're all right, are you?"

The tone of accusing doubt in this question was so familiar that Grey felt tears come to his eyes. He blinked them away, though, assured Tom that he was somewhat banged about but essentially undamaged.

"*Gracias a Dios,*" Rodrigo said, with such heartfelt sincerity that Grey looked at him in surprise. He said something else in Spanish that Grey didn't understand; John shook his head, then stopped abruptly, wincing.

Tom looked at Rodrigo, who made a small helpless gesture at his inability to be understood and nodded at Tom, who took a deep breath and looked at his employer searchingly.

"What?" Grey said, somewhat disturbed by their solemn attitudes.

"Well, me lord," Tom squared his shoulders, "it's just what Rodrigo told me this afternoon—after you left." He glanced at Rodrigo, who nodded again.

"See, he's been a-wanting to tell you, ever since you come back from the plantations, but he didn't want his wife or Inocencia to hear it. But he got Jacinto to come translate for him, so he could tell me."

"Tell you what?" Grey was discovering the stirrings of hunger and was rummaging through the larder, pulling out sausages and cheese and a jar of some kind of fruit preserve.

"Well, he told me about what happened when you talked to the slaves in the tobacco shed and when the one man told him to leave because he's a zombie." Tom looked protectively at Rodrigo; he'd quite lost any sense of fear about it.

"So he didn't want to stay too near—he says sometimes people gets very upset about him—and he walked down toward the plantation house."

Approaching the house, Rodrigo had come upon the woman Alejandra—Inocencia's cousin, the one who had revealed the slave revolt, in hopes that Inocencia's English lover might be able to do something before anything dreadful could happen.

"She was worried, you could see, Rodrigo says, and talked a lot about her lover—that's Hamid, what he says you met—and how she didn't want him or the others to die, and they would if . . . well, anyway, they got summat close to the big hacienda, and she stopped sudden."

Alejandra had stood there in the darkness, her white dress seeming to float in the air beside Rodrigo like a ghost. He stood with her, quiet, waiting to see what she would say next. But she hadn't spoken, only stood frozen for what seemed a long time but probably wasn't, the night wind rising and stirring her skirts.

"Then she took his arm and said they should go back, and they did. But . . ." Tom coughed, his round face troubled, and looked at Rodrigo again.

"Rodrigo said Azeel told him on the way back to Havana what happened in the shed. What you said to that man, Cano, and what he said to you—about the people what owned the plantation."

"Yes?" Grey paused in the act of buttering a chunk of bread.

Rodrigo said something quiet, and Tom nodded.

"He said something didn't seem right while they were looking at the house. There were servants going in and out, but it just didn't feel right to him. And when he heard what this Cano said to you—"

"*No los mataremos,*" Grey said, suddenly uneasy. "'We will not kill them'?"

Rodrigo nodded, and Tom cleared his throat.

"You can't kill somebody what's already dead, can you, me lord?"

"Already . . . no. No, you can't mean that the slaves had already . . . No." But a worm of doubt was taking up residence in his stomach, and he put the bread down.

"The . . . wind," Rodrigo said, with his usual agonizing pause to find an English word. *"Muerto."*

He lifted his hand, a beautiful, slender hand, and drew his knuckles gently beneath his nose.

"I . . . know . . . the smell . . . of death."

COULD IT BE TRUE? Grey was too exhausted to feel more than a distant sense of cold horror at the notion, but he couldn't dismiss it. Cano had not struck him as a patient man. He could easily imagine that the slave had grown frustrated when Malcolm didn't appear soon enough and had decided to carry out his original plan. But then when Grey *did* come— Christ, he must have arrived on the heels of the . . . the massacre . . .

He remembered his sight of the hacienda: lights burning inside but so quiet. No sense of movement within; only the silent passage of the house-slaves outside. And the stink of anger in the tobacco shed. He shuddered.

He took his leave of Tom and Rodrigo but, too tired and shocked to sleep, then sought refuge in the *sala,* which seemed always to have light. One of the kitchen maids, undoubtedly roused by Tom, came in with a pitcher of wine and a plate of cheese; she smiled sleepily at him, murmured, *"Buenas noches, señor,"* and stumbled back toward her bed.

He couldn't eat, or even sit down, and after a moment's hesitation went out again, into the deserted patio. He stood there for some time, looking up into the black velvet sky. What time was it? The moon had set and surely dawn could not be far off, but there was no trace of light save the distant stars.

What should he do? Was there anything he *could* do? He thought not. There was no way of telling whether Rodrigo was right—and even if he was (a small, cold feeling at the back of Grey's neck was inclined to believe it) . . . there was nothing to be done, no one to tell who could investigate, let alone try to find the murderers, if murderers they were.

The city lay suspended between the Spanish and the British invaders; there was no telling when the siege would be successful—though he thought it would. The spiking of El Morro's guns would help, but the navy must be informed, so as to take advantage of it.

Come dawn, he would try to leave the city with his mother and the children and his servants. He thought it could be managed easily enough; he had brought as much gold from Jamaica as he could, and there was more than enough left to bribe their way past the guard at the city gate.

What then? Exhausted as he was, he wasn't even thinking, just watching dimly as the future unrolled in small, disjointed pictures: a carriage for his mother and the children and Azeel, himself on the stubborn white mule, two more animals for Tom and Rodrigo.

The slaves' contract . . . if any of them had survived . . . freedom . . . the general could see to that . . .

Malcolm and the girl . . . he wondered dimly for a moment about Inocencia; why had Cano tried to kill her . . . ?

Because she saw him try to kill you, fathead, some dim, dispassionate watcher in his skull observed. *And he had to kill you, for fear you'd find out what they'd done at Hacienda Mendez . . .*

Freedom . . . even if they'd? . . . but Cano was dead, and Grey would never know who was guilty of what.

"Not my place . . ." he murmured and shut his eyes.

His hand touched the breast of his shirt and found it stiff with dried blood. He'd left his uniform coat in the kitchen . . . perhaps one of the women could clean it. He'd need to wear it again, to approach the British lines in Cojimar . . . Cojimar . . . a brief vision of white graveled sand, sunlight, fishing boats . . . the tiny white stone fort, like a doll's house . . . find General Stanley.

Thought of the general drew his fragmented thoughts together, a magnet in a scatter of loose iron filings. Someone to depend on . . . a man to share the burden . . . he wanted that, above all things.

"Oh, God," he whispered, and moths touched his face, gentle in the dark.

HE WAS GROWING COLD. He went back inside to the *sala* and found his mother sitting there. She had taken the manuscript from the secretaire; it sat on the small table beside her, her hand resting on it and a distant look in her eyes. He didn't think she'd noticed him come in.

"Your . . . manuscript," John said awkwardly. His mother came back abruptly from wherever she had been, her eyes alert but calm.

"Oh," she said. "You read it?"

"No, no," he said, embarrassed. "I . . . I only wondered . . . why are you writing your memoirs? I mean, that *is* what it is, isn't it?"

"Yes, it is," she said, looking faintly amused. "It would have been quite all right if you'd read it—you may read it whenever you like, in fact, though perhaps it would be better to wait until I've finished. If I do."

He felt a small sense of relaxation at this. His mother was both honest and blunt by nature, and the older she got the less she cared for anyone's opinion save her own—but she did have a very deep degree of emotional perception. She was reasonably sure that whatever she'd written wouldn't embarrass him seriously.

"Ah," he said. "I wondered whether perhaps you meant it for publication. Many"—he choked off the words "old people" just in time, replacing them with—"people who've led interesting lives choose to, er, share their adventures in print."

That made her laugh. It was no more than a low, soft laugh, but nonetheless it brought tears to her eyes, and he thought it was because he'd inadvertently cracked the shell she'd built over the course of the last weeks and let her own feelings bubble back to the surface. The thought made him happy, but he looked down to hide it, pulled a clean handkerchief from his sleeve, and handed it to her without comment.

"Thank you, dear," she said, and, having dabbed her eyes, shook her head.

"Persons who have truly interesting lives *never* write about them, John—or not with an eye to publication, at least. The ability to keep their own counsel is one of the things that makes them interesting and is also what causes other truly interesting people to confide in them."

"I assure you, Mother," he said dryly, "you are undoubtedly the most interesting woman I've ever met."

She snorted briefly and gave him a direct look.

"I suppose that's why you haven't yet married, is it?"

"I didn't think a wife needed to be interesting," he replied, with some honesty. "Most of the ones I know certainly aren't."

"How true," she said briefly. "Is there any wine in the house, John? I've got rather fond of Spanish wine since I've been here."

"*Sangria* do you? One of the maids brought me a pitcher of it, but I hadn't drunk any yet." He got up and fetched the pitcher—a beautiful smooth stoneware thing the color of mulberries—and brought it with a pair of glasses to the table between their chairs.

"That will be perfect," she said, and leaned forward with a sigh, massaging her temples. "Oh, God. I go about all day, feeling that none of it is real, that everything is just as I left it, and then suddenly—" She broke off and dropped her hands, her features drawn with pain and tiredness. "Suddenly it's real again."

She glanced at the secretaire as she said this, and John caught a hint of something in her voice. He poured the wine carefully, not to let the sliced lemons and oranges floating in it fall out into the glasses, and didn't speak until he'd put the pitcher down and taken his seat again.

"When you write it down . . ." he said. "Does that make it—whatever it is—real again? Or does the act of putting it into words make it unreal? You know, something . . . separate from yourself." What had happened at El Morro had taken place mere hours before, and yet it seemed like years.

But the scent of blood and guns hung about him like a shroud, and his muscles still twitched with the memory of desperate exertion.

His own words brought back to him the letters he had written now and then. The phantoms, as he thought of them: letters he'd written to Jamie Fraser—honest, conversational, heartfelt, and very real. No less real because he'd burned them all.

His mother looked at him in surprise, then took a meditative sip of the cool spiced wine.

"Both," she said at last. "It's completely real to me as I write it—and should I go back to read it again later, it's real again." She paused for a moment, thinking. "I can live in it," she said softly. She finished her wine—the glasses were small, the sort of cup called a shot glass because the heavy base made it possible to slam it on the table with a loud report at the conclusion of a toast—and carefully poured more.

"But when it's done, and I leave it . . ." She sipped again, the scent of red wine and oranges softening the smells of travel and sickness in her clothes. "It . . . seems somehow to separate itself from me. I can set it—whatever it was, whatever it is—aside in my mind then, just as I set aside the page."

"How very useful," John murmured, half to himself, thinking that he must try that. The wine was dissolving his own sense of sorrow and exhaustion—if only temporarily. The room grew peaceful around them, candlelight warm on the plastered walls, the wings of angels.

"But as to why—" His mother refilled his glass, and hers again.

"It's a duty. The book—should it be a book—I'll have it printed and bound, but privately. It's for you and the other boys, for the children—for Cromwell and Seraphina," she added softly, and her lips quivered for an instant.

"Mother," he said quietly, and laid his hand on hers. She bent her head and put her free hand on his, and he saw how the tendrils of her hair, still thick, once blond like his own but mostly silver now, escaped from their plait and curled on her neck.

"A duty," she said, holding his hand between her own. "The duty of a survivor. Not everyone lives to be old, but if you do, I think you owe it to those who didn't. To tell the stories of those who shared your journey . . . for as long as they could."

She closed her eyes and two tears ran down her cheeks.

He put his arm around her and drew her head down on his shoulder, and they sat silently together, waiting for the light to come back.

AUTHOR'S NOTE

Whale Oil

WHALE OIL VERSUS SPERMACETI. NOW, SEE, I ACTU-
ally read the entirety of the infamous "list of whales" chapter of
Moby-Dick and thought it was hilarious. But I admit that I was (at
one point in a highly checkered career) a marine biologist, so I may
have been slightly more aligned with Melville's frame of reference
than is the casual modern reader, who might be inclined to think of
whale oil as being the same thing as spermaceti (assuming the CMR
to be sufficiently widely read as to have encountered "spermaceti" in
print at all).

In fact, though, these are two completely different (though equally
combustible) substances. Whale oil is rendered from the flensed
blubber of slaughtered whales. In other words, it's the liquefied body
fat of something that feeds mostly on small crustaceans. Body chem-
istry being what it is, an organism that stores energy in body fat also
tends to store iffy chemicals it encounters in the same depository.

Your own body, for instance, stores excess hormones in your body
fat, as well as various toxic or otherwise dubious compounds like
PBCs, strontium, and insecticides.

The point here is that dead crustaceans are rather pungent. Think
of the last time you left a package of thawed frozen shrimp in your
refrigerator for a week. These aromatic compounds are stored in the
body fat of things that eat the organism that makes them.

I first encountered this phenomenon when I had a postdoctoral
appointment in which my principal job was dissecting gannets. These
are big diving seabirds (related to boobies) that feed largely on squid.
Their body fat smells like rotting squid, especially when you put it in
a drying oven in order to desiccate it. So if you're burning whale oil
in your lamps (it was cheap, as Tom Byrd notes), your establishment
is probably going to smell like week-old krill. And, being fat, it makes
smoke when you burn it.

Spermaceti, by contrast, is not body fat as such—though it is oily and very burnable. It's an oil that is secreted and stored in the head case (basically, a storage compartment for this oil) of a sperm whale. The appearance of this liquid—white, thickish, slippery—is why they're called sperm whales; that's what the old whalers thought the gunk was, though plainly occurring in the wrong place. . . . However, the point here is that spermaceti was also very popular as lamp fuel and general lubricant—because it didn't stink. It's very clean-burning and almost odorless. But it's much more limited in availability, as only sperm whales make it, and thus much more expensive than whale oil.

So, what's the sperm whale using this substance for? Nobody knows, though speculation is that it's part of the whale's sensory system, perhaps acting as an echolocation device, assisting the whale to locate things like giant squid (a major component of its diet, and I'm profoundly grateful that I will likely never be called upon to dissect and analyze the body tissues of a sperm whale) in the black abyssal depths.

Ambassadors, Consuls, and British Diplomats

An ambassador is an appointed office in the British diplomatic service, and very formal. An ambassador may receive official tenders from the foreign power to which he is appointed—declarations of war, statements of intent, official notices of concern, etc.—and by and large acts as the delegated (nonmilitary) authority of the British government within his own territory (they didn't have female ambassadors in the eighteenth century; it was always "his").

A consul is a much less formal office, though also appointed by the government. A consul's duties are to look after the welfare of British citizens in the country to which he's appointed. He would assist with things like permits to do business, small trade agreements, the relief of British citizens who have run into trouble in the foreign country, and so on. He does not have full diplomatic powers but is generally regarded as part of the diplomatic service.

Now, Britain didn't have a real ambassador to Cuba until sometime in the late 1800s. They did have consuls appointed for some time prior to the appointment of a real ambassador, though, and Malcolm Stubbs would have been one of these.

The Siege of Havana

The thing about a siege is that it's usually rather a long-drawn-out affair. The 1762 siege of Havana (there was more than one, so we need to specify the date) took several weeks, beginning with the arrival of the Duke of Albemarle's fleet (under the command of Admiral George Pocock—a real person, and, no, I have No Idea whether he might have anything to do with anyone else we've met recently . . .) on June 6 and ending on August 14, when the British entered the conquered city.

It was a fairly traditional siege, in that the British were obliged to throw up breastworks from which to fire. That's the traditional way of referring to the act of erecting or digging barriers to shelter the besieging forces—and in some instances, it *is* pretty rapid. Others, not so much.

At Havana, the rock of the promontory on which the fortress of El Morro sat was impervious to digging and prevented a head-on advance. The British (or, rather, the American volunteers from Connecticut and New Hampshire—though, mark me, these men *were* still Englishmen at the time) had to blast trenches through the hard coral rock to approach from the sides and erect wooden breastworks above the trenches to cover the advance. This was naturally a tedious business, made worse by mosquitoes and yellow fever (which killed an enormous number of both besiegers and inhabitants of the city).

If you want an account of the actual siege, there are plenty of them available online, some with considerable detail. However . . . this particular story is not really *about* the siege (let alone how many ships of the line and how many men took part—21 ships of the line, 24 lesser warships, and 168 other vessels, mainly transports, carrying 14,000 seamen and marines, 3,000 hired sailors, and 12,862 regulars, if you *do* care) but about Lord John and his personal sense of honor and responsibility.

That being so, I've chosen to shorten the duration of the siege considerably rather than find a way for Lord John to spend an extra six weeks doing nothing.

Now, I will note that while the slave revolt at the Mendez and Saavedra plantations is a fictional one, there *were* several slave revolts on Cuba during the second half of the eighteenth century, and such an event would not be improbable in the least.

Likewise, while I found no account of the guns of El Morro being spiked, it *is* true that the siege was finally ended by a naval bombardment of the fortress—taking advantage of the sudden silence of most of the guns of the castle's battery.

And there is a historical note that ninety slaves were given their freedom after the battle, *in return for their services during the siege.*

ACKNOWLEDGMENTS

I'd like to acknowledge . . .

The invaluable suggestions regarding the French bits of dialogue contributed by Bev LaFrance (France), Gilbert Sureau (French Canada), and a number of other nice people whose names I unfortunately didn't write down at the time . . .

The assistance of Maria Syzbek in the delicate matter of Polish vulgarities (any errors in grammar, spelling, or accent marks are entirely mine) and of Douglas Watkins in the technical descriptions of small-plane maneuvers (also the valuable suggestion of the malfunction that brought Jerry's Spitfire down) . . .

The help of several people in researching aspects of Jewish history, law, and custom for "Virgins": Elle Druskin (author of *To Catch a Cop*), Sarah Meyer (registered midwife), Carol Krenz, Celia K. and her Reb mom, and especially Darlene Marshall (author of *Castaway Dreams*). I'm indebted also to Rabbi Joseph Telushkin's very helpful book *Jewish Literacy*. Any errors are mine . . .

Eve Ackermann and Elle Druskin for helpful notes and references regarding Sephardic wedding traditions and rituals . . .

Catherine MacGregor and her Francophone associates, especially Madame Claire Fluet, for unblushing help with the lascivious French bits . . .

Selina Walker and Cass DiBello for kind assistance with eighteenth-century London geography . . .

Simcha Meijer, for help with the Dutch language bits, and to a number of helpful Dutch readers on Facebook, for suggestions as to appropriate powdered sugar pastries for a pregnant lady . . .

And a number of kind Cuban Facebook readers, for helpful observations and suggestions on the color of Cuban dirt, the appearance of Cuban bread, traditional Cuban food, and the correct spelling of "inocencia" . . .

And the wonderful Penguin Random House team who have, as usual, killed themselves to produce a wonderful book: My editor, Jennifer Hershey, for insight and helpful suggestions, Anne Speyer, who did most of the heavy lifting on this one, Erin Kane for useful Spanish suggestions, our heroically prompt and always astute copy editor, Kathy Lord, and—as always—Virginia Norey, for the beautiful design of the book.

PHOTO: © DOUG WATKINS

DIANA GABALDON is the #1 *New York Times* bestselling author of the wildly popular Outlander novels—*Outlander, Dragonfly in Amber, Voyager, Drums of Autumn, The Fiery Cross, A Breath of Snow and Ashes* (for which she won a Quill Award and the Corine International Book Prize), *An Echo in the Bone,* and *Written in My Own Heart's Blood*—as well as the related Lord John Grey books *Lord John and the Private Matter, Lord John and the Brotherhood of the Blade, Lord John and the Hand of Devils,* and *The Scottish Prisoner;* two works of nonfiction, *The Outlandish Companion, Volumes 1* and *2;* the Outlander graphic novel *The Exile;* and *The Official Outlander Coloring Book.* She lives in Scottsdale, Arizona, with her husband.

dianagabaldon.com
Facebook.com/AuthorDianaGabaldon
Twitter: @Writer_DG

To inquire about booking Diana Gabaldon for a speaking engagement, please contact the Penguin Random House Speakers Bureau at speakers@penguinrandomhouse.com.

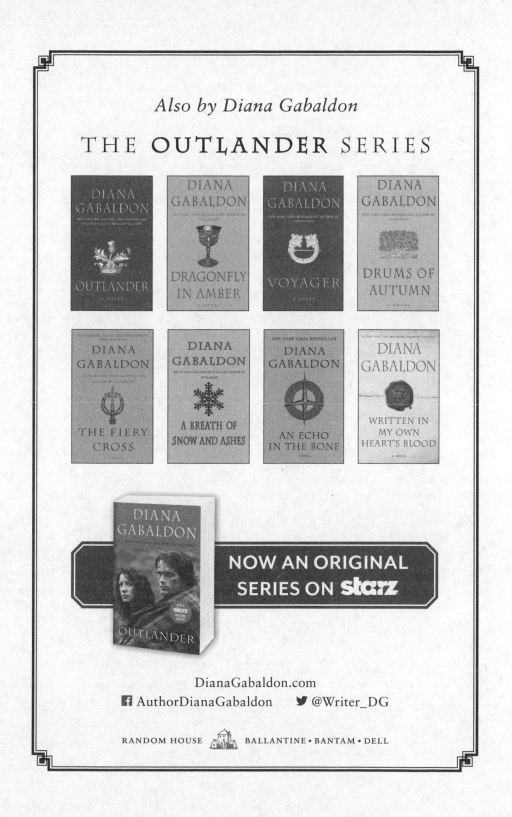

Also by DIANA GABALDON

The Companion Volumes

The Outlander
Graphic Novel

Seven Stones to
Stand or Fall

THE
LORD JOHN
SERIES

Lord John and the Private Matter
Lord John and the Brotherhood of the Blade
Lord John and the Hand of Devils
The Scottish Prisoner

Continue the saga with original eNovellas,
engrossing tales to complement the Outlander series.

A Plague
of Zombies

The Custom
of the Army

A Leaf on the Wind
of All Hallows

The Space
Between

Virgins

 DIANAGABALDON.COM

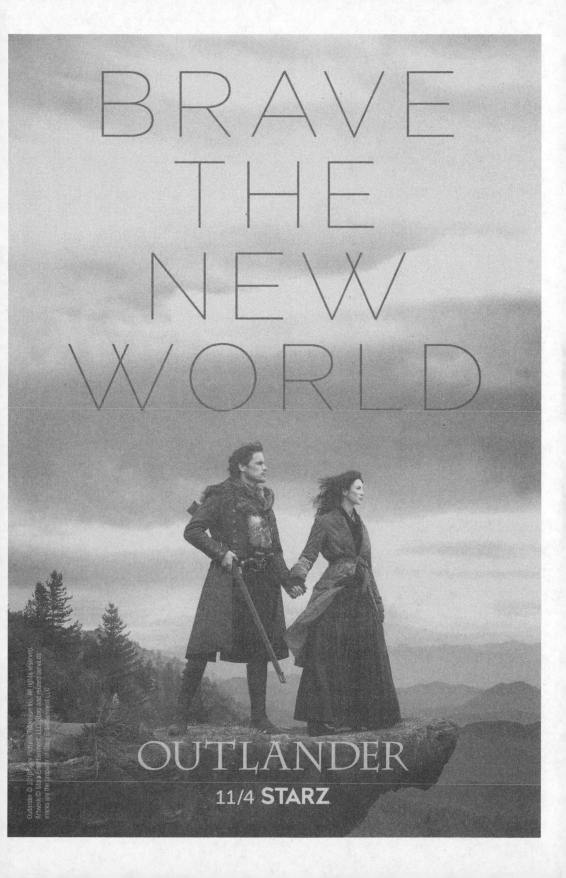

BRAVE
THE
NEW
WORLD

OUTLANDER
11/4 STARZ